THE DUMAS CLUB

Arturo Pérez-Reverte was born in Cartagena in 1951. He has been a journalist and television reporter specialising in covering the world's trouble-spots. Since the publication of his first novel, *The Fencing Master*, Pérez-Reverte has become one of Spain's best-selling authors. *The Flanders Panel* was awarded the Grand Prix Annuel de Littérature Policière. *The Dumas Club* has been made into a film entitled *The Ninth Gate*, directed by Roman Polanski and starring Johnny Depp.

Sonia Soto is half Spanish and was educated at the French Lycée in London and at the University of Cambridge. She is a translator from Spanish, French and Russian and is the translator of *The Ages of Lulu* by Almudena Grandes.

Arturo Pérez-Reverte

THE DUMAS CLUB

TRANSLATED FROM THE SPANISH BY
Sonia Soto

V

VINTAGE

Published by Vintage 2003

2 4 6 8 10 9 7 5 3

First published with the title *El club Dumas* by
Alfaguara S.A., Madrid, 1993

First published in Great Britain in 1996 by
The Harvill Press

Vintage
Random House, 20 Vauxhall Bridge Road,
London SW1V 2SA

The Random House Group Limited Reg. No. 954009
www.randomhouse.co.uk

A CIP catalogue record for this book
is available from the British Library

ISBN 0 09 944859 9

Papers used by Random House are natural, recyclable
products made from wood grown in sustainable forests. The
manufacturing processes conform to the environmental
regulations of the country of origin

Printed and bound in Great Britain by
Bookmarque Ltd, Croydon, Surrey

To Cala, who set me on the right track

Contents

The flash projected the outline of the hanged man onto the wall. He hung motionless from a light fitting in the centre of the room, and as the photographer moved around him, taking photos, the flash threw the silhouette onto a succession of pictures, glass cabinets full of porcelain, shelves of books, open curtains framing great windows, beyond which the rain was falling.

The examining magistrate was a young man. His thinning hair was untidy and still damp, as was the raincoat he wore while he dictated the formalities to a clerk who sat on the sofa as he typed, his typewriter on a chair. His tapping punctuated the monotonous voice of the magistrate and the whispered comments of the policemen who were moving about the room:

". . . wearing pyjamas and a robe. The cord of this garment was the cause of death by hanging. The deceased has his hands bound in front of him with a tie. On his left foot he is still wearing one of his slippers, the other foot is bare . . ."

The magistrate touched the slippered foot of the dead man and the body turned slightly, slowly, on the end of the taut silk cord which ran from his neck to the light fitting on the ceiling. It moved from left to right, and then back again until it came gradually to a stop in its original position, like the needle of a compass reverting to North. As he moved away, the magistrate turned sideways to avoid a uniformed policeman who was searching for fingerprints beneath the corpse. There was a broken vase on the floor and a book open at a page covered in red pencil marks. The book was an old copy of Bragelonne, The Vicomte de Bragelonne, a cheap edition bound in cloth. Leaning over the policeman's shoulder, the magistrate glanced at the underlined sentences:

"They have betrayed me," he murmured, "All is known!"
"All is known at last," answered Porthos, who knew nothing.

He made the clerk note this down, ordering that the book should be included in the report. Then he went to join a tall man who was standing smoking by one of the open windows.

"What do you think?" he asked.

The tall man wore his police badge fastened to a pocket of his leather jacket. Before answering he took time to finish his cigarette, and then threw it over his shoulder and out of the window without looking.

"If it's white and in a bottle, it tends to be milk," he answered cryptically, at last, but not so cryptically that the magistrate didn't smile slightly.

Unlike the policeman he was looking out into the street where it was still raining hard. Somebody opened a door on the other side of the room and a blast of air splashed drops of water against his face.

"Shut the door," he ordered without turning round. Then he spoke to the policeman. "Sometimes homicide disguises itself as suicide."

"And vice versa," the other man pointed out calmly.

"What do you think of the hands and tie?"

"Sometimes they're scared they'll change their minds at the last minute . . . Otherwise he'd have had them tied behind him."

"It makes no difference," objected the magistrate. "It's a strong, thin cord. Once he'd lost his footing he wouldn't have had a chance, even with his hands free."

"Anything's possible. The autopsy will tell us more."

The magistrate glanced once more at the corpse. The policeman searching for fingerprints stood up with the book.

"Strange, that business of the page."

The tall policeman shrugged his shoulders.

"I don't read much," he said, "but Porthos, wasn't he one of those . . . Athos, Porthos, Aramis and d'Artagnan." He was counting with his thumb on the fingers of one hand and when he'd finished he stopped, looking thoughtful. "Funny. I've always wondered why they were called the three musketeers when really there were four of them."

2

I
The Anjou Wine

The reader must be prepared to witness the most sinister scenes.
E. Sue: *The Mysteries of Paris*

My name is Boris Balkan and I once translated *The Charterhouse of Parma*. Apart from that, I've edited a few books on the nineteenth-century popular novel, my reviews and articles appear in supplements and journals throughout Europe and I organize courses on contemporary writers at summer schools. Nothing spectacular, I'm afraid. Particularly these days when suicide disguises itself as homicide, novels are written by Roger Ackroyd's doctor, and far too many people insist on publishing two hundred pages on the fascinating emotions they experience when they look in the mirror.

But let's stick to the story.

I first met Lucas Corso when he came to see me carrying 'The Anjou Wine' under his arm. Corso was a mercenary of the book world, hunting down books for other people. That meant talking fast and getting his hands dirty. He needed good reflexes, patience and a lot of luck – and a prodigious memory to recall the exact dusty corner of an old man's shop where a book now worth a fortune lay forgotten. His clientèle was small and select: a couple of dozen bookdealers in Milan, Paris, London, Barcelona or Lausanne, the kind that sells through catalogues, only makes safe investments, and never handles more than fifty or so titles at any one time. High-class dealers in early printed books for whom thousands of dollars depend on whether something is parchment or vellum, or three centimetres wider in the margin. Jackals on the scent of the Gutenberg Bible, antique fair sharks, auction room leeches, they would sell their grandmothers for a first edition. But they receive their clients in rooms with leather sofas, views of the Duomo or Lake Constance, and they never get their hands – or their consciences – dirty. That's what men like Corso are for.

He took his canvas bag off his shoulder and put it on the floor, down by his scuffed Oxfords. He stared at the framed portrait of Rafael Sabatini that stands on my desk, next to the fountain pen I use for correcting articles and proofs. I was pleased because most visitors paid him little attention, taking him for an aged relative. I waited for his reaction. He was half-smiling as he sat down – a youthful expression, like a cartoon rabbit in a dead-end street. The kind of look that wins over the audience straight away. In time I found out he could also smile like a cruel, hungry wolf, and that he would choose a smile to suit the circumstances. But that was much later. Now he seemed convincing, so I decided to risk a password:

"He was born with the gift of laughter," I quoted, pointing at the portrait, "and with a feeling that the world was mad . . ."

He nodded slowly and deliberately. I felt a friendly complicity with him which, in spite of all that happened later, I still feel. From a hidden packet he brought out an unfiltered cigarette that was as crumpled as his old overcoat and corduroy trousers. He turned it over in his fingers, watching me through steel-rimmed glasses, set crookedly on his nose under his untidy fringe of slightly greying hair. As if holding a hidden gun, he kept his other hand in one of his pockets, huge and deformed by books, catalogues, papers and, as I also found out later, a hip flask full of Bols gin.

". . . and this was his entire inheritance." He completed the quotation effortlessly, before settling himself in the armchair and smiling again. "But if I must be honest, I prefer *Captain Blood*."

With a stern expression I lifted my fountain pen.

"You're mistaken. *Scaramouche* is to Sabatini what *The Three Musketeers* is to Dumas." I bowed briefly to the portrait. "'He was born with the gift of laughter . . .' In the entire history of the adventure serial no two opening lines can compare."

"That may be true," he conceded after a moment's reflection. Then he laid the manuscript on the table, in a protective folder with plastic pockets, one for each page. "It's a coincidence you should mention Dumas."

He pushed the folder towards me, turning it round so I could read its contents. The text was in French, written on one side of the page only. There were two types of paper, both discoloured by age: one white, and the other pale blue with light squares. The handwriting on each was different – on the white pages it was smaller and more spiky. The handwriting on the blue paper, in black ink, also appeared on the white pages but as annotations. There were fifteen pages in all, eleven of them blue.

"Interesting." I looked up at Corso. He was watching me, his calm gaze moving from the folder to me, then back again. "Where did you find it?"

He scratched his eyebrow, no doubt calculating whether he needed to provide such details in exchange for the information he wanted. The result was a third facial expression, this time an innocent rabbit. Corso was a professional.

"Around. Through a client of a client."

"I see."

He paused briefly, cautious. Caution is a sign of prudence and reserve, but also of shrewdness. And we both knew it.

"Of course," he added, "I'll give you names if you request them."

I answered that it wouldn't be necessary, which seemed to reassure him. He adjusted his glasses before asking my opinion of the manuscript. Not answering immediately, I turned the pages until I came to the first. The title was written in capital letters, in thicker strokes: *LE VIN D'ANJOU*.

I read out the first few lines:

Après de nouvelles presque désespérées du roi, le bruit de sa convalescence commençait a se répandre dans le camp . . .

I couldn't help smiling. Corso indicated his approval, inviting me to comment.

"Without the slightest doubt," I said, "this is by Alexandre Dumas père. 'The Anjou Wine': chapter forty-something, I seem to remember, of *The Three Musketeers*."

"Forty-two," confirmed Corso. "Chapter forty-two."

"Is it authentic? Dumas's original manuscript?"

"That's why I'm here. I want you to tell me."

I shrugged slightly, reluctant to assume such a responsibility.

"Why me?"

It was a stupid question, the kind that only serves to gain time. It must have seemed like false modesty, because he suppressed a look of impatience.

"You're an expert," he retorted, somewhat dryly. "As well as being Spain's most influential literary critic, you know all there is to know about the nineteenth-century popular novel."

"You're forgetting Stendhal."

"Not at all. I read your translation of *The Charterhouse of Parma*."

"Indeed. I am honoured."

"Don't be. I preferred Consuelo Berges's version."

We both smiled. I continued to find him likeable, and I was beginning to form an idea of his style.

"Do you know any of my books?" I asked.

"Some. *Lupin, Raffles, Rocambole, Holmes*, for instance. And your studies of Valle-Inclán, Baroja and Galdós. Also *Dumas: the Shadow of a Giant*. And your essay on *The Count of Monte Cristo*."

"Have you read all those?"

"No. I work with books but that doesn't mean I have to read them."

He was lying. Or at least exaggerating. The man was conscientious: before coming to see me he'd looked at everything about me he could lay his hands on. He was one of those compulsive readers who've devoured anything in print since a most tender age – although it was highly unlikely that Corso's childhood had ever merited the term "tender".

"I understand," I answered, just to say something.

He frowned for a moment, wondering whether he'd forgotten anything. He took off his glasses, breathed on the lenses and set about cleaning them with a very crumpled handkerchief which he pulled out from one of the bottomless pockets of his coat. However fragile the over-sized coat made him appear, with his rodent-like incisors and calm expression Corso was as solid as a concrete block. His features were sharp and precise, full of angles. They framed alert eyes always ready to express an innocence which was dangerous for anyone who was taken in by it. At times, particularly when still, he seemed slower and more clumsy than he really was. He looked vulnerable and defenceless: barmen gave him an extra drink on the house, men offered him cigarettes, and women wanted to adopt him on the spot. Later, when you realized what had happened, it was too late to catch him. He was disappearing into the distance, having notched up another victory.

He gestured with his glasses towards the manuscript. "Going back to Dumas. Surely anyone who's written five hundred pages about him ought to sense something familiar when faced with one of his original manuscripts?"

With the reverence of a priest handling holy vestments I laid a hand on the pages protected by the plastic folders.

"I fear I'm going to disappoint you, but I don't feel anything."

We both laughed, Corso in a peculiar way, almost under his breath, like someone who is not sure whether he and his companion are laughing at the same thing. An oblique, distant laugh, with a hint of insolence, the kind that lingers in the air even after it has faded. Even when its owner has been gone for some time.

"Let's take this a step at a time," I went on. "Does the manuscript belong to you?"

"I've already told you that it doesn't. A client of mine has just acquired it, and he finds it strange that no one should have heard of this complete, original chapter of *The Three Musketeers* until now . . . He wants it authenticated by an expert, so that's what I'm working on."

"I'm surprised at you dealing with such a minor matter." This was true. I'd heard of Corso before this meeting. "I mean, after all, nowadays Dumas . . ."

I left the sentence hanging and smiled with the appropriate expression of bitter complicity. But Corso didn't take up my invitation and stayed on the defensive:

"The client's a friend of mine," he said evenly. "It's a personal favour."

"I see, but I'm not sure that I can be any help to you. I have seen some of the original manuscripts, and this one could be authentic. However, certifying it would be another matter. For that you'd need a good graphologist . . . I know an excellent one in Paris, Achille Replinger. He owns a shop which specializes in autographs and historical documents, near Saint-Germain-des-Prés . . . He's an expert on nineteenth-century French writers, a charming man and a good friend of mine." I pointed to one of the frames on the wall. "He sold me that Balzac letter many years ago. For a very high price."

I took out my diary to copy down the address for Corso and gave him a card. He put it in an old worn wallet full of notes and papers. Then he brought out a notepad and pencil from one of his coat pockets. The pencil had a rubber at one end, chewed like a schoolboy's.

"Could I ask you a few questions?"

"Yes, of course."

"Did you know of any complete handwritten chapter of *The Three Musketeers*?"

I shook my head and replaced the cap on my Mont Blanc.

"No. The novel came out in instalments in *Le Siècle* between March and July 1844 . . . Once the text had been typeset by a compositor the original manuscript was thrown away. A few fragments remained, however. You can have a look at them in an appendix to the 1968 Garnier edition."

"Four months isn't very long," Corso was chewing the end of his pencil thoughtfully. "Dumas wrote quickly."

"They all did in those days. Stendhal wrote *The Charterhouse of Parma* in seven weeks. And in any case Dumas used collaborators, ghost writers. The one for *The Three Musketeers* was called Auguste Maquet . . . They worked together on the sequel, *Twenty Years After*, and *The Vicomte de Bragelonne* which completes the cycle. And on *The Count of Monte Cristo* and a few other novels. You will have read those I suppose."

"Of course. Everybody has."

"Everybody had in the old days, you mean." I leafed respectfully through the manuscript. "The times are long gone when Dumas's name increased print runs and made publishers rich. Almost all his novels came out like that – in instalments ending in 'To be continued . . .' The readers would be on tenterhooks until the next episode. But of course you know about all that."

"Don't worry. Go on."

"What more can I tell you? In the classic serial, the recipe for success is simple: the hero, or heroine, has qualities or features that make the reader identify with him or her . . . If it happens nowadays in TV soaps, imagine the effect in those days when there was no television or radio, on a middle class hungry for surprise and entertainment, and undiscriminating when it came to formal quality or taste . . . Dumas was a genius and he understood all this. Like an alchemist in his laboratory he added a dash of this, another dash of that, and, with his talent, combined it all to create a drug which had many addicts." I tapped my chest, not without pride. "Which has them still."

Corso was taking notes. Precise, unscrupulous and deadly as a black mamba, was how one of his acquaintances described him later when his name came up in conversation. He had a singular way of facing people, peering through his crooked glasses and slowly nodding in agreement with a reasonable, well-meaning but doubtful expression, like a whore tolerantly listening to a romantic sonnet. As if he was giving you a chance to correct yourself before it was too late.

After a moment he stopped and looked up.

"But your work doesn't only deal with the popular novel. You're a well-known literary critic of other more –" he hesitated, searching for a word – "more serious works. And Dumas himself described his novels as easy literature . . . Sounds rather patronizing towards his readers."

This device was typical of him. It was one of his trademarks, like Rocambole leaving a playing card instead of a calling card. He'd put something forward casually, as if he himself had no opinion on the matter, slyly goading you into a reaction. Somebody who is annoyed will put forward arguments and justifications, giving out more inform-ation to his opponent. I wasn't a fool and I knew what Corso was doing, but even so, or maybe because of it, I felt annoyed.

"Don't talk in clichés," I said irritably. "The serial genre produced a lot of disposable stuff, but Dumas was way above all that . . . In literature, time is like a shipwreck in which God looks after his own. I challenge you to name any fictional heroes who have survived in as good health as d'Artagnan and his friends, with the possible exception of Sherlock Holmes . . . *The Three Musketeers* was undoubt-edly a swashbuckling novel full of melodrama with all the sins typical of the genre. But it's also a distinguished example of the serial, and of a standard well above the norm. A tale of friendship and adventure that has stayed fresh even though tastes have changed and that there is now an idiotic tendency to despise action in novels. It would seem that since Joyce we have had to make do with Molly Bloom and give up Nausicaa on the beach after the shipwreck . . . Have you read my essay, 'Friday, or the Ship's Compass?' Give me Homer's *Ulysses* any day."

I raised my tone at that point, waiting for Corso's reaction. He smiled slightly and remained silent but I remembered his expression when I had quoted Scaramouche so I felt sure I was on the right track.

"I know what you're referring to," he said at last. "Your views are well known and controversial, Mr Balkan."

"My views are well known because I've made sure of it. And as for patronizing his readers, as you claimed a moment ago, perhaps you didn't know that the author of *The Three Musketeers* fought in the streets during the revolutions of 1830 and 1848. And he supplied arms, paid for out of his own pocket, to Garibaldi . . . Don't forget that

Dumas's father was a famous republican general . . . The man was full of love for the people and liberty."

"Although his respect for the truth was only relative."

"That's not important. Do you know how he answered those who accused him of raping History? 'True, I have raped History, but it has produced some beautiful offspring.'"

I put my pen down and went to the glass cabinets full of books covering the walls of my study. I opened one and took out a volume bound in dark leather.

"Like all great writers of fables," I went on, "Dumas was a liar . . . Countess Dash, who knew him well, says in her memoirs that all he had to do was tell some apocryphal anecdote and it would be taken as the historical truth . . . Take Cardinal Richelieu: he was the greatest man of his time but once the treacherous Dumas had finished with him, the distorted image we've been left with is that of a sinister villain . . ." I turned to Corso, holding the book. "Do you know this? It was written by Gatien de Courtilz de Sandras, a musketeer who lived in the late seventeenth century. They're the memoirs of the real d'Artagnan, Charles de Batz-Castelmore, Comte d'Artagnan. He was a Gascon, born in 1615, and was indeed a musketeer. Although he didn't live in Richelieu's time, but Mazarin's. He died in 1673 during the siege of Maastricht when, like his fictional namesake, he was about to be awarded the marshal's staff . . . So you see, Dumas's raping did indeed breed beautiful offspring . . . An obscure flesh and blood Gascon, forgotten by History, transformed into a legendary giant by the novelist's genius."

Corso sat there and listened. I handed him the book and he leafed through it carefully, with great interest. He turned the pages slowly, barely brushing them with his fingertips, only touching the very edge. From time to time he would pause over a name, or a chapter. Behind his spectacles his eyes worked sure and fast. He stopped once to note the details in his pad: '*Mémoires de M. d'Artagnan*, G. de Courtilz, 1704, P. Rouge, 4 volumes in 12mo, 4th edition'. Then he shut the notebook and looked up at me.

"You said it: he was a trickster."

"Yes," I agreed, sitting down again. "But a genius. While some would simply have plagiarized others' material, he created a fictional world which still endures today . . . 'Man does not steal, he conquers,' he often said. 'Every province he seizes becomes an annexe of his empire: he imposes laws, and fills it with themes and characters, casting his shadow over it . . .' What else is literary creation? For him, the history of France was a rich source of material. His was an extraordinary trick: he'd leave the frame alone but alter the picture, mercilessly plundering the treasure that was offered to him . . . Dumas turned central characters into minor ones, humble secondary characters became protagonists, and he wrote pages about events that only took up two lines in the historical chronicles. The pact of friendship between d'Artagnan and his companions never existed, one of the reasons being that half of them didn't even know each other . . . Nor was there a Comte de la Fère. Or rather there were several of them, though none called Athos. But Athos did exist. He was called Armand de Sillègue, Lord of Athos, and he was killed in a duel before d'Artagnan had even joined the King's musketeers . . . Aramis was Henri d'Aramitz, a squire and lay priest in the seneschalship of Oloron, who enrolled in the musketeers under his uncle's command in 1640. He ended his days on his estate, with a wife and four children. As for Porthos . . ."

"Don't tell me there was a Porthos too."

"Yes. His name was Isaac de Portau and he must have known Aramis because he joined the musketeers just three years after him, in 1643. According to the chronicles he died prematurely, either from a disease, at war, or in a duel like Athos."

Corso drummed his fingers on d'Artagnan's *Mémoires* and shook his head. He was smiling.

"Any minute now you're going to tell me there was a Milady . . ."

"Correct. But her name wasn't Anne de Breuil, and she wasn't the Duchesse de Winter. Nor did she have a fleur-de-lis tattooed on her shoulder. But she was one of Richelieu's secret agents. Her name was the Countess of Carlisle and she stole two diamond tags from the Duke of Buckingham . . . Don't look at me like that. It's all in La Rochefoucauld's memoirs. And La Rochefoucauld was a very reliable man."

Corso was staring at me intently. He didn't seem the type to be easily surprised, particularly when it came to books, but he looked impressed. Later, when I came to know him better, I wondered whether his admiration was sincere, or just another of his professional wiles. Now that it's all over, I think I know: I was one more source of information, and Corso was trying to get as much out of me as possible.

"This is all very interesting," he said.

"If you go to Paris, Replinger can tell you much more than I can." I looked at the manuscript on the table. "Though I'm not sure it's worth the price of a trip . . . What would this chapter fetch on the market?"

He started chewing his pencil again and looked doubtful.

"Not much. I'm really after something else."

I gave a sad conspiratorial smile. Amongst my few possessions I have an Ibarra edition of *Don Quixote* and a Volkswagen. Of course the car cost more than the book.

"I know what you mean," I said warmly.

Corso made a resigned gesture. He bared his rodent-like teeth in a bitter smile:

"Unless the Japanese get fed up with Van Gogh and Picasso," he suggested, "and start investing in rare books."

I recoiled in horror.

"God help us if that ever happens."

"Speak for yourself." He looked at me sardonically through his crooked glasses. "I plan to make a fortune."

He put his notebook away and stood up, hanging his canvas bag on his shoulder. I couldn't help reflecting on his falsely placid appearance, with his steel-rimmed glasses sitting unsteadily on his nose. I found out later that he lived alone, surrounded by books, both his own and other people's, and that as well as being a hired hunter of books he was an expert on Napoleon's battles. He could set out on a board, from memory, the exact order of battle on the eve of Waterloo. A family-related story, slightly strange, and I only found out all about it much later. I have to admit, described like that, Corso doesn't sound very attractive. And yet, if I keep to the strict accuracy with which I am narrating this story, I must add that his awkward appearance, the very clumsiness which seemed – and I don't know how he managed it – at once caustic and vulnerable, ingenuous and aggressive, made him both attractive to women and sympathetic to men. But the positive feeling suddenly evaporated, as when you feel in your pocket and realize that you've just had your wallet stolen.

Corso picked up his manuscript and I saw him to the door. He shook my hand in the hallway, where portraits of Stendhal, Conrad and Valle-Inclán looked out severely at an atrocious print that the block's residents' association had decided to hang on the landing a few months earlier, much against my wishes.

Only then did I dare ask him:

"I confess I'm intrigued as to where you found it."

He hesitated before answering, weighing up the pros and cons. I had received him in a friendly manner so he was in my debt. Also he might need my help again, so he really had no choice.

"Maybe you know him," he answered at last. "My client bought the manuscript from a certain Taillefer."

I allowed myself a look of moderate surprise.

"Enrique Taillefer? The publisher?"

He was gazing absently around the hallway. At last he nodded.

"The very same."

We both fell silent. Corso shrugged, and I very well knew why. The cause could be read about in the pages of any newspaper: Enrique Taillefer had been dead a week. He had been found hanged in his house, the cord of his silk robe around his neck and his feet dangling in empty space, over an open book and a porcelain vase smashed into pieces.

Some time later, when it was all over, Corso agreed to tell me the rest of the story. So I can now give a fairly accurate picture of a chain of events that I didn't witness, leading to the fatal dénouement and the solution to the mystery surrounding the Dumas Club. Thanks to what Corso told me I can now, like Dr Watson, tell you that the following scene took place in Makarova's bar an hour after our meeting. Flavio La Ponte came in shaking off the rain, leant on the bar next to Corso and ordered a beer while he caught his breath. Then he looked back at the street, aggressive but triumphant, as if he had just come through sniper fire. It was raining with biblical force.

"The firm of Armengol & Sons, Antiquarian Books and Bibliographical Curiosities, intends to sue you," he said. He had a ring of froth on his curly blond beard, round his mouth. "Their solicitor has just telephoned."

"What are they accusing me of?" asked Corso.

"Cheating a little old lady and plundering her library. They swear the deal was theirs."

"Well, they should have got up early like I did."

"That's what I said but they're still furious. When they went to pick up the books, the *Persiles* and the *Royal Charter of Castille* had disappeared. And you gave a valuation for the rest which was way over the odds. So now the owner won't sell. She wants double what they're prepared to pay . . ." He drank some beer and winked conspiratorially. "That neat manoeuvre is known as nailing a library."

"I know what it's called." Corso smiled malevolently. "And Armengol & Sons know it too."

"You're being unnecessarily cruel," said La Ponte impartially. "But what they're most sore about is the *Royal Charter*. They say that your taking it was a low blow."

"How could I leave it there? Latin glossary by Díaz de Montalvo, no typographical details but printed in Sevilla by Alonso Del Puerto, possibly 1482 . . ." He adjusted his glasses and looked at his friend. "What do you think?"

"Sounds good to me. But they're a bit jumpy."

"They should take a Valium."

It was early evening. There was very little room at the bar and they were pressed shoulder to shoulder, surrounded by cigarette smoke and the murmur of conversation, trying not to dunk their elbows in the puddles of beer on the counter.

"Apparently," added La Ponte, "the *Persiles* is a first edition. The binding's signed by Trautz-Bauzonnet."

Corso shook his head.

"By Hardy. Morocco leather."

"Even better. Anyway I swore I'd had nothing to do with it. You know I have an aversion to lawsuits."

"But not to your thirty per cent."

La Ponte raised his hand with dignity.

"Stop right there. Don't confuse business with pleasure, Corso. One thing is our beautiful friendship. Food for my children is quite another."

"You don't have any children."

La Ponte looked at him mischievously.

"Give me time. I'm still young."

He was short, good-looking, neat and something of a dandy. His hair was thinning on top. He smoothed it down with his hand, checking to see how it looked in the bar's mirror. Then he cast a practised eye around the room, checking out the ladies. He was always on the look-out, just as he always liked to use short sentences in conversation. His father, a very cultured bookseller, had taught him to write by dictating texts by Azorín to him. Hardly anyone reads Azorín any more but La Ponte still constructed his sentences like him. With lots of full stops. It gave him a certain aplomb when it came to seducing female customers in the back room of his bookshop in the Calle Mayor where he kept his erotic classics.

"Anyway," he added, "I've got some business outstanding with Armengol & Sons. Rather delicate, but I could make a quick profit."

"You've got business with me too," said Corso over his beer. "You're the only poor bookseller I work with. And you're going to be the one to sell those books."

"All right, all right," said La Ponte equably. "You know I'm a practical man. A despicable pragmatist."

"Yes."

"Imagine this was a Western. As your friend, I'd take a bullet for you, but only in the shoulder."

"At the very most," said Corso.

"Anyway, it doesn't matter." La Ponte was looking round distractedly. "I've already got a buyer for the *Persiles*."

"Then get me another beer. An advance on your commission."

They were old friends. They both loved frothy beer and Bols gin in its glazed earthenware bottle. But above all they loved antiquarian books and the auctions held in old Madrid auction rooms. They had met many years earlier when Corso was rooting around in bookshops specializing in Spanish authors. A client of his was looking for a bogus copy of *Celestina* which was supposed to pre-date the known 1499 edition. La Ponte didn't have the book and hadn't even heard of it. But he did have an edition of the *Dictionary of Rare and Improbable Books* by Julio Ollero in which it was mentioned. They chatted about books and realized they had a lot in common. La Ponte shut his shop and they sealed their friendship by drinking all there was to drink in Makarova's bar, while swapping anecdotes about Melville. La Ponte had been brought up on tales of the *Pequod* and the escapades of Azorín. "Call me Ishmael," he said as he drained his third Bols straight down. And Corso called him Ishmael, quoting from memory and in his honour, the episode of the forging of Ahab's harpoon:

Three punctures were made in the heathen flesh, and the White Whale's barbs were then tempered.

They duly drank a toast. By then La Ponte was no longer watching the girls coming in and out of the bar. He swore eternal friendship to

Corso. Despite his militant cynicism and his occupation as a rapacious seller of old books, underneath he was a naive man. So he was unaware that his new friend with the crooked glasses was discreetly outflanking him: Corso had glanced over his shelves and spotted a few books he planned to make an offer for. In fact, La Ponte, with his pale, curly beard, the gentle look of seaman Billy Budd with daydreams of a frustrated whale hunter, had awakened Corso's sympathy. He could even recite the names of all the crew of the *Pequod*: Ahab, Stubb, Starbuck, Flask, Perth, Parsee, Queequeg, Tasthego, Daggoo . . . Or the names of all the ships mentioned in *Moby Dick*: the *Goney*, the *Town-Ho*, the *Jeroboam*, the *Jungfrau*, the *Rose Bud*, the *Bachelor*, the *Delight*, the *Rachel* . . . And, proof of proof, he even knew what ambergris was. They had talked of books and whales. And so that night the Brotherhood of Nantucket Harpooneers was founded, with Flavio La Ponte as chairman, Lucas Corso as treasurer. They were the only two members and had Makarova's tolerant patronage. She'd given them their last round on the house and ended up sharing another bottle of gin with them.

"I'm going to Paris," said Corso, watching the reflection of a fat woman putting coin after coin in a fruit machine. It seemed as if the silly little tune and the colours, fruits and bells would keep her there for all eternity, hypnotized and motionless but for her hand pushing the buttons. "To see about your 'Anjou Wine'."

His friend wrinkled his nose and gave him a sideways glance. Paris meant more expense, complications. La Ponte was a stingy, small-time bookseller.

"You know I can't afford it."

Corso slowly emptied his glass.

"Yes, you can." He took out a few coins and paid his round. "I'm going about something else."

"Oh yes?" said La Ponte, intrigued.

Makarova put two more beers on the counter. She was large, blonde, in her forties, and had short hair and a ring in one ear, a souvenir of her time on a Russian trawler. She wore narrow trousers and a shirt with the sleeves rolled up to her shoulders. Her over-developed biceps weren't the only masculine thing about her. She always had a lighted cigarette smouldering in the corner of her mouth. With her Baltic look and her way of moving, she looked like a fitter from a ball-bearing factory in Leningrad.

"I read that book," she told Corso accentuating her r's. As she spoke, ash from her cigarette dropped onto her damp shirt. "That tart Bovary. Poor little fool."

"I'm so glad you grasped the nub of the matter."

Makarova wiped down the counter with a cloth. At the other end of the bar Zizi was watching as she worked the till. She was the complete opposite of Makarova: much younger, slight and terribly jealous. Sometimes, just before closing time, they would quarrel drunkenly and come to blows, with the last few regulars watching. Once, with a black eye after one of these rows, Zizi upped and left, furious and vindictive. Makarova wept copiously into the beer until she returned three days later. That night they closed early and left with their arms around each other's waists, kissing in doorways like two teenagers in love.

"He's off to Paris." La Ponte nodded in Corso's direction. "To see what he can pull out of the hat."

Makarova collected the empty glasses and looked at Corso through the smoke of her cigarette.

"He's always up to something," she said in her flat, guttural tone. Then she put the glasses in the sink and went to serve some other customers, swinging her broad shoulders. Corso was the only member of the opposite sex who escaped her contempt, and she would proclaim this when she didn't charge him for a drink. Even Zizi looked upon him with a certain neutrality. Once when Makarova was arrested for punching a policeman in the face during a gay rights march, Zizi had waited all night on a bench in the police station. Corso called all his contacts in the police, stayed with her and supplied sandwiches and a bottle of gin. It all made La Ponte absurdly jealous.

"Why Paris?" he asked, though his mind was on other things. His left elbow had just prodded something deliciously soft. He was delighted to find that his neighbour at the bar was a young blonde with enormous breasts.

Corso took another gulp of beer.

"I'm also going to Sintra in Portugal." He was still watching the fat woman at the fruit machine. She'd run out of coins and was now getting change from Zizi. "On some business for Varo Borja."

His friend made a whistling sound. Varo Borja, Spain's leading bookdealer. His catalogue was small and select. He was also well known as a booklover to whom money was no object. Impressed,

17

La Ponte asked for more beer and more information, with the greedy look that automatically clicked on when he heard the word *book*. Although he admitted to being a miser and a coward, he wasn't an envious man, except when it came to pretty, harpoonable women. In professional matters, he was always glad to get hold of good pieces with little risk, but he also had real respect for his friend's work and clientèle.

"Have you ever heard of *The Nine Doors*?"

The bookseller was searching slowly through his pockets, hoping that Corso would pay for that round too. He was also just about to turn round and take a closer look at his voluptuous neighbour, but Corso's words caused him to forget her instantly. He was open-mouthed.

"Don't tell me Varo Borja's after that book . . ."

Corso put his last few coins on the counter. Makarova brought another two beers.

"He's had it for some time. He paid a fortune for it."

"I'll bet he did. There are only three or four known copies."

"Three," specified Corso. "One in Sintra, in the Fargas collection. Another at the Ungern Foundation in Paris. And the third, from the sale of the Terral-Coy library in Madrid, was bought by Varo Borja."

Fascinated, La Ponte stroked his curly beard. Of course he had heard of Fargas, the Portuguese bookcollector. As for Baroness Ungern, she was a potty old woman who'd become a millionairess from writing books about demonology and the occult. Her recent book, *Naked Isis*, was a runaway bestseller in all the stores.

"What I don't understand," concluded La Ponte, "is what you've got to do with any of it."

"Do you know the book's history?"

"Vaguely," said La Ponte.

Corso dipped a finger in his beer and began to draw pictures on the marble counter.

"Period: mid seventeenth century. Scene: Venice. Central character: a printer by the name of Aristide Torchia, who had the idea of publishing the so-called *Book of the Nine Doors of the Kingdom of Shadows*, a kind of manual for summoning the Devil . . . It wasn't a good time for that sort of thing: the Holy Office managed, without much trouble, to have Torchia handed over to them. He was charged with practising satanic arts and all that goes with them, aggravated by the fact, they said, that he'd reproduced nine prints from the famous *Delomelanicon*, the occult classic which, tradition has it, was written by Lucifer himself . . ."

Makarova had moved closer on the other side of the bar and she was listening with interest, wiping her hands on her shirt. La Ponte, about to take another gulp of beer, stopped and instinctively looking like a greedy bookseller, asked:

"What happened to the book?"

"You can imagine: it all went onto a big bonfire." Corso frowned evilly. He seemed sorry to have missed it. "They also say that as it burned you could hear the Devil screaming."

Her elbows on Corso's beer diagrams, Makarova grunted sceptically amongst the beer handles. With her blonde, manly looks and her cool, Nordic temperament she didn't go in for these murky southern superstitions. La Ponte was more impressionable. Suddenly thirsty, he gulped down his beer.

"It must have been the printer they heard screaming."

"Imagine."

La Ponte shivered at the thought.

Corso went on: "Tortured with the thoroughness the Inquisition reserved for dealing with the Evil Arts, the printer finally confessed, between screams, that there still remained one book, hidden somewhere. Then he shut his mouth and didn't open it again until they burnt him alive. And even then it was only to say *Aagh.*"

Makarova smiled contemptuously at the memory of Torchia the printer, or maybe at the executioners who hadn't been able to make him confess. La Ponte was frowning.

"You say that only one of the books was saved," he objected. But before, you said there were three known copies."

Corso had taken off his glasses and was looking at them against the light to check how clean they were.

"And that's the problem," he said. "The books have appeared and then disappeared through wars, thefts and fires. It's not known which is the authentic one."

"Maybe they're all forgeries," Makarova suggested sensibly.

"Maybe. So I've got to find out whether Varo Borja has been taken for a ride. That's why I'm going to Sintra and Paris." He adjusted his glasses and looked at La Ponte. "While I'm there I'll see about your manuscript as well."

The bookseller agreed thoughtfully, eyeing the girl with the big breasts in the mirror.

"Compared to that, it seems ridiculous to make you waste your time on *The Three Musketeers* . . ."

"What are you talking about?" said Makarova, no longer neutral. She was really offended. "It's the best book I've ever read!"

She slammed her hands down on the bar for emphasis, making the muscles on her bare forearms bulge. Boris Balkan would be happy to hear that, thought Corso. As well as the Dumas novel, Makarova's list of top ten books, for which he was literary adviser, included amongst others *War and Peace, Watership Down,* and *Carol* by Patricia Highsmith.

"Don't worry," he told La Ponte, "I'll charge the expenses to Varo Borja. But I'd say your 'Anjou Wine' is authentic . . . Who would forge something like that?"

"People do all sorts of things," Makarova pointed out sagely.

La Ponte agreed with Corso – forging such a document would be absurd. The late Taillefer had guaranteed its authenticity to him. It was in Dumas's own hand. And Taillefer could be trusted.

"I used to take him old newspaper serials. He'd buy them all." He took a sip and then laughed to himself. "Good excuse to go and get a look at his wife's legs. She's a pretty spectacular blonde. Anyway, one day he opened a drawer and put 'The Anjou Wine' on the table. 'It's yours,' he said straight out, 'as long as you get an expert opinion on it and put it on sale immediately.'"

A customer called Makarova and ordered a tonic water. She told him to go to hell. She stayed where she was, her cigarette burning down in her mouth and her eyes half-closed because of the smoke. Waiting for the rest of the story.

"Is that all?" asked Corso.

La Ponte gestured vaguely.

"Almost. I tried to dissuade him because I knew he was crazy about that sort of thing. He'd have sold his soul for a rare book. But he'd made up his mind. 'If you don't do it I'll give it to someone else,' he said. That touched a nerve, of course. My professional nerve, I mean."

"You don't need to explain," said Corso. "What other kind do you have?"

La Ponte turned to Makarova for support. But one glance at her slate grey eyes and he gave up. They were about as warm as a Scandinavian fjord at three in the morning.

"It's nice to feel loved," he said at last, bitterly.

The man after a tonic water must really have been thirsty, Corso thought, because he was getting insistent. Makarova, looking at him out of the corner of her eye and without moving a muscle, suggested he find another bar before she gave him a black eye. The man thought it over. He seemed to get the message and left.

"Enrique Taillefer was a strange man." La Ponte ran his hand over his thinning hair again, still eyeing the voluptuous blonde in the mirror. "He wanted me to sell the manuscript and get publicity for the whole business." He lowered his voice so as not to worry the blonde. "'Somebody's going to get a surprise,' he told me mysteriously. He winked at me as if he was going to play a joke on someone. Four days later he was dead."

"Dead," repeated Makarova in her guttural way, savouring the word. She was more and more interested.

"Suicide," explained Corso.

But she shrugged, as if to say there wasn't much difference between suicide and murder. There was one doubtful manuscript and a definite corpse: quite enough for a conspiracy theory.

On hearing the word suicide La Ponte nodded lugubriously.

"So they say."

"You don't seem too sure."

"No, I'm not. It's all a bit odd." He frowned again, suddenly looking sombre and forgetting the blonde in the mirror. "Smells very fishy to me."

"Did Taillefer never tell you how he got hold of the manuscript?"

"At the beginning I didn't ask. Then it was too late."

"Did you speak to his widow?"

La Ponte suddenly looked brighter. He grinned from ear to ear.

"I'll save that story for another time." He sounded like someone who has just remembered he has a brilliant trick up his sleeve. "That'll be your payment. I can't afford even a tenth of what you'll get out of Varo Borja for his *Book of the Nine Lies*."

"I'll do the same for you when you find an *Audubon* and become a millionaire. I'll just collect my money later."

La Ponte again looked hurt. For such a cynic, Corso thought, he seemed rather sensitive.

"I thought you were helping me as a friend," protested La Ponte. "You know. The Club of Nantucket Harpooneers. 'There she blows' and all that."

"Friendship," said Corso, looking round as if waiting for someone to explain the word to him. "Bars and cemeteries are full of good friends."

"Whose side are you on, damn it?"

"On his own side," sighed Makarova. "Corso's always on his own side."

La Ponte was disappointed to see the girl with the big breasts leave with a smart young man who looked like a model. Corso was still watching the fat woman at the fruit machine, who'd run out of coins. She was standing next to the machine with a disconcerted, blank look, her hands by her sides. Her place at the machine had been taken by a tall, dark man. He had a thick, black moustache and a scar on his face. For a fleeting moment Corso thought he looked familiar, but the impression vanished before he could grasp it. To the fat woman's despair the machine was now spewing out a noisy stream of coins.

Makarova offered Corso one last beer on the house. La Ponte had to pay for his own this time.

II

The Dead Man's Hand

Milady smiled, and d'Artagnan felt that he would go to hell and back for that smile.

A. Dumas: *The Three Musketeers*

There are inconsolable widows, and then there are widows to whom any adult male would be delighted to provide the appropriate consolation. Liana Taillefer was undoubtedly the second kind. Tall and blonde, with pale skin, she moved languorously. The type of woman who takes an age to light a cigarette, and looks straight into a man's eyes as she does so. She had the cool composure that was a result of knowing she looked a little like Kim Novak with a full, almost over-generous figure and, being the sole beneficiary of the late Enrique Taillefer, Publisher, Ltd., of having a bank account for which the term *solvent* was a pale euphemism. It's amazing how much dough you can make, if you'll excuse the feeble pun, from publishing cookery books, such as *The Thousand Best Desserts of La Mancha*, or all fifteen bestselling editions of a classic, *The Secrets of the Barbecue*.

The Taillefers lived in part of what had once been the palace of the Marques de Los Alumbres, now converted into luxury apartments. In matters of décor, the owners seemed to have more money than taste. This could be the only excuse for placing a vulgar Lladro porcelain figure – a little girl with a duck, noted Lucas Corso dispassionately – in the same glass cabinet as a group of little Meissen shepherds for which the late Enrique Taillefer, or his wife, must have paid some sharp antique dealer a handsome sum. There was a Biedermeier desk, of course, and a Steinway piano standing on a luxurious, oriental rug. And a comfortable-looking, white leather sofa on which Liana Taillefer was sitting at that moment, crossing her extraordinarily shapely legs. She was dressed, as befits a widow, in a black skirt. It came to just above the knee when she was sitting, but hinted at the voluptuous curves higher up hidden in mystery and shadow, as Lucas Corso later put it. I would add that Corso's comment should not be ignored. He looked like one of those dubious men one can easily imagine living with an elderly mother who knits and brings him cocoa in bed on a Sunday morning; the kind of son one sees in films, a solitary figure with reddened eyes walking behind the coffin in the rain, and moaning *Mama* inconsolably, like a helpless orphan. But Corso had never been helpless in his life. And when one got to know him slightly better, one wondered if he had ever had a mother.

"I'm sorry to bother you at a time like this," said Corso.

He was sitting facing the widow, still in his coat, his canvas bag on his knees. He held himself straight on the edge of the seat. Liana Taillefer's large ice-blue eyes studied him from top to toe, determined to pigeonhole him in some known category of the male species. He was sure she'd find it difficult. He submitted to her scrutiny, trying not to create any particular impression. He was familiar with the procedure, and he knew that at that moment he didn't rate very highly in the estimation of Enrique Taillefer's widow. This limited the operation to a kind of contemptuous curiosity. She'd kept him waiting for ten minutes, after he'd had a skirmish with a maid who'd taken him for a salesman and was about to slam the door in his face. But now the widow was glancing at the plastic folder that Corso had taken out of his bag, and the situation had changed. As for him, he tried to hold Liana Taillefer's gaze through his crooked glasses, avoiding the thundering reefs – to the South, her legs, and to the North her bust (exuberant was the word, he told himself, having pondered the matter for some time) moulded to devastating effect by her black angora sweater.

"It would be a great help," he added at last, "if you could tell me whether you knew about this document."

He handed her the folder, and as he did so accidentally brushed her hand with its long blood-red fingernails. Or maybe it was her hand that brushed his. Whichever, this slight contact showed that Corso's prospects were looking more favourable. So he adopted a suitably embarrassed expression, just enough to show her that bothering beautiful widows wasn't his speciality. Her ice-blue eyes weren't on the folder now, they were watching Corso with a flicker of interest.

"Why would I know about it?" asked the widow. Her voice was deep, slightly husky. The echo of a heavy night. She hadn't looked inside the folder yet and was still watching Corso, as if she expected something else before examining the document and satisfying her curiosity. He adjusted his glasses on the bridge of his nose and adopted a suitably serious expression. This was the formal stage, so he kept his efficient "honest rabbit" smile for later.

"Until recently it belonged to your husband." He paused a moment. "May his soul rest in peace."

She nodded slowly, as if that explained it, and opened the folder. Corso was looking over her shoulder at the wall. There, between an adequate painting by Tapies and another with a signature he couldn't make out, was a framed piece of child's needlepoint depicting little coloured flowers, signed and dated: *Liana Lasauca, school year 1970–71*. Corso would have found it touching if flowers, embroidered birds and little girls in short socks and blonde pigtails had been the sort of thing that made his heart melt. But they weren't. So he turned to another, smaller picture in a silver frame. It showed the late Enrique Taillefer, Publisher, with a gold wine sampling ladle round his neck, wearing a leather apron that made him look rather like a Mason. He was smiling at the camera and preparing to cut into a roast sucking-pig. He held a plate in one hand and one of his publishing successes in the other. He appeared placid, chubby and paunchy, happy at the sight of the little animal laid out before him on the dish. Corso reflected how Taillefer's premature demise meant that at least he wouldn't have to worry about high cholesterol and gout. He also wondered, with cold technical curiosity, how Liana Taillefer had managed, while her husband was alive, when she needed an orgasm. With that thought he cast another quick glance at the widow's bust and legs, before deciding he'd been right. She was too much of a woman to be satisfied with the sucking-pig.

"This is that Dumas thing," she said, and Corso sat up slightly, alert and clear-headed. Liana Taillefer was tapping one of her red nails on the plastic folders protecting the pages. "The famous chapter. Of course I know about it." As she leaned her head forward, her hair fell over her face. Behind the blonde curtain she observed her visitor suspiciously. "Why have you got it?"

"Your husband sold it. I'm trying to find out if it's authentic."

The widow shrugged her shoulders.

"As far as I know it's not a forgery." She gave a long sigh and handed back the folder. "You say he sold it? That's strange." She thought a moment. "These papers meant a lot to Enrique."

"Perhaps you can recall where he might have bought them."

"I couldn't say. I think somebody gave them to him."

"Did he collect original manuscripts?"

"As far as I know this was the only one he ever had."

"Did he ever mention he was intending to sell it?"

"No. This is the first I've heard about it. Who bought it?"

"A bookseller who's a client of mine. He's going to put it on the market once I give him a report on it."

Liana Taillefer decided to grant him a little more attention. Corso's prospects took another little leap. He took off his glasses and cleaned them with his crumpled handkerchief. Without them he looked more vulnerable, and he knew it. Everybody felt they just had to help him cross the road when he squinted like a short-sighted rabbit.

"Is this your job?" she asked. "Authenticating manuscripts?"

He nodded vaguely. The widow looked slightly blurred and, strangely, closer.

"Sometimes. I also look for rare books, prints, things like that. I get paid for it."

"How much?"

"It depends." He put his glasses back on and her image was sharp again. "Sometimes a lot, others not so much. The market has its ups and downs."

"You're a kind of detective, aren't you?" she said, amused. "A book detective."

This was the moment to smile. He did so, showing his incisors, with a modesty calculated to the millimetre. Adopt me, said his smile.

"Yes. I suppose you could call it that."

"And your client asked you to come and see me . . ."

"That's right." He could now allow himself to look more confident, so he tapped the manuscript with his knuckles. "After all, this came from here. From your house."

She nodded slowly, looking at the folder. She seemed to be thinking something over.

"It's strange," she said. "I can't imagine Enrique selling this Dumas manuscript. Although he was acting strangely those last few days . . . What did you say the name of the bookseller was? The new owner."

"I didn't."

She looked him up and down, with calm surprise. It seemed she was unused to waiting for more than three seconds for any man to do as she said.

"Well, tell me then."

Corso waited a moment, just long enough for Liana Taillefer to start tapping her nails impatiently on the arm of the sofa.

"His name's La Ponte," he said at last. This was another of his tricks: he made only trivial concessions but allowed others to feel they'd won. "Do you know him?"

"Of course I know him. He supplied my husband with books." She frowned. "He'd come round every so often to bring him those stupid serials. I suppose he has a receipt . . . I'd like a copy of it if he doesn't mind."

Corso nodded vaguely and leant towards her slightly.

"Was your husband a great fan of Alexandre Dumas?"

"Of Dumas?" Liana Taillefer smiled. She had shaken back her hair and now her eyes shone, mocking. "Come with me."

She stood up, taking her time, and smoothed down her skirt, glancing round as if she had suddenly forgotten why she had got up. She was much taller than Corso, even though she was only wearing low heels. She led him into the adjoining study. As he followed her he noticed her broad back, like a swimmer's, and her cinched-in waist. He guessed she must be about thirty. She would probably become one of those Nordic matrons, on whose hips the sun never sets, made to give birth effortlessly to blond Eriks and Siegfrieds.

"I wish it had only been Dumas," she said, gesturing towards the contents of the study. "Look at this."

Corso looked. The walls were covered with shelves bowing under the weight of thick, bound volumes. Professional instinct made his mouth water. He took a few steps towards the shelves, adjusting his glasses. *The Countess de Charny*, A. Dumas, eight volumes, the Illustrated Novel collection, editor Vicente Blasco Ibáñez. *The Two Dianas*, A. Dumas, three volumes. *The Musketeers*, A. Dumas, Miguel Guijarro publisher, engravings by Ortega, four volumes. *The Count of Monte Cristo*, A. Dumas, four volumes in the Juan Ros edition, engravings by A. Gil . . . Also forty volumes of *Rocambole*, by Ponson du Terrail. The complete edition of the *Pardellanes* by Zevaco. More Dumas, together with nine volumes of Victor Hugo and the same number by Paul Féval, with an edition of *The Hunchback* luxuriously bound in red morocco and edged with gold. And Dickens's *Pickwick Papers*, translated into Spanish by Benito Pérez Galdós, alongside several volumes by Barbey d'Aurevilly and *The Mysteries of Paris* by

27

Eugène Sue. And yet more Dumas – *The Forty-Five, The Queen's Necklace, The Companions of Jehu* – and *Corsican Revenge* by Mérimée. Fifteen volumes of Sabatini, several by Ortega y Frías, Conan Doyle, Manuel Fernández y González, Mayne Reid, Patricio de la Escosura . . .

"Very impressive," commented Corso. "How many books are there here?"

"I don't know. Around two thousand. Almost all of them first editions of serials, as they were bound after being published in instalments . . . Some of them are illustrated editions. My husband was an avid collector, he'd pay whatever the asking price."

"A true enthusiast, from what I can see."

"Enthusiast?" Liana Taillefer gave an indefinable smile. "It was a real passion."

"I thought gastronomy . . ."

"The cookery books were just a way of making money. Enrique had the Midas touch: in his hands, any cheap recipe book turned into a bestseller. But this was what he really loved. He liked to shut himself in here and leaf through these old serials. They were often printed on poor quality paper, and he was obsessed with preserving them. Do you see that thermometer and humidity gauge? He could recite whole pages from his favourite books. He'd sometimes even say 'gadzooks', 'ye gods', things like that. He spent his last months writing."

"A historical novel?"

"A serial. Keeping to all the clichés of the genre, of course." She went to a shelf and took down a heavy manuscript with hand-stitched pages. The handwriting was large and round. "What do you think of the title?"

"*The Dead Man's Hand, or Anne of Austria's Page,*" read Corso. "Well, it's certainly – " He ran a finger over his eyebrow, searching for the right word – "suggestive."

"And dull," she added, putting the manuscript back. "And full of anachronisms. And completely idiotic, I can assure you. Believe me, I know what I'm talking about. At the end of each writing session he'd read it to me page by page, from beginning to end." She tapped bitterly on the title, handwritten in capitals. "My God. I really hated that stupid queen and her page."

"Was he intending to publish it?"

"Yes, of course. Under a pseudonym. I assume he would have chosen something like Tristan de Longueville, or Paulo Florentini. It would have been so typical of him."

"What about hanging himself? Was that typical of him?"

Liana Taillefer stared intently at the book-lined walls and said nothing. An uncomfortable silence, Corso thought, even a little forced. She seemed absorbed in her thoughts, like an actress pausing before going on with her speech in a convincing manner.

"I'll never know what happened," she answered at last, her composure once again perfect. "During his last week he was hostile and depressed. He hardly left this study. Then, one afternoon, he went out and slammed the door. He came back in the early hours. I was in bed and I heard the door close. In the morning I was woken by the maid screaming. Enrique had hanged himself from the light fitting."

Now she was looking at Corso, to see the effect of her words. She didn't seem too upset, Corso thought, and remembered the photo with the apron and the sucking-pig. He even saw her blink once, as if to hold back a tear, but her eyes stayed perfectly dry. Of course that didn't mean anything. Centuries of make-up that can be smudged by emotion have taught women to control their feelings. And Liana Taillefer's make-up – light shadow accentuating her eyes – was perfect.

"Did he leave a note?" asked Corso. "People who commit suicide often do."

"He decided to save himself the effort. No explanation, not even a few words. Nothing. Because of his selfishness I've had to answer a lot of questions from an examining magistrate and several policemen. Very unpleasant, believe me."

"I understand."

"Yes. I'm sure you do."

Liana Taillefer made it obvious that their meeting was now at an end. She saw him to the door and held out her hand to him. With the folder under his arm and his bag on his shoulder, Corso held out his hand and felt her firm grip. Inwardly he gave her a good mark for her perform-ance. Not the happy widow, or devastated by grief; not a cold "I'm glad that idiot's gone," or "Alone at last," or "You can come out of the wardrobe now, darling." There probably was someone in the ward-robe, but it was none of Corso's business. Nor was Enrique Taillefer's suicide, however strange – and it was mighty strange, gadzooks, with all that business of the queen's page and the disappearing manuscript.

But neither this nor the beautiful widow were any concern of his. For now.

He looked at Liana Taillefer. I'd love to know who's having you, he thought with cool technical curiosity. He drew a mental picture: handsome, mature, cultured, wealthy. He was almost a hundred per cent sure he must be a friend of her deceased husband. He wondered if the publisher's suicide had anything to do with it, but then stopped himself in disgust. Professional quirk or not, he sometimes had the absurd habit of thinking like a policeman. He shivered in horror at the thought. Who knows what depths of depravity, or stupidity, lie hidden in our souls.

"I must thank you for taking the time to see me," he said, choosing the most touching smile from his repertoire. He resembled a friendly rabbit.

He was met with a blank. She was looking at the Dumas manuscript.

"You don't have to thank me. I'm just naturally interested to know how all this will end."

"I'll let you know how it's going . . . Oh, and there's something else. Do you intend to keep your husband's collection, or are you thinking of selling it?"

She looked at him, disconcerted. Corso knew from experience that when a bookcollector died, the books often followed the body out through the front door twenty-four hours later. He was surprised in fact that none of his predatory colleagues had yet dropped by. After all, as she had admitted herself, Liana Taillefer didn't share her husband's literary tastes.

"The truth is, I haven't had time to think about it . . . Do you mean you'd be interested in those old serials?"

"I could be."

She hesitated a moment. Perhaps a few seconds longer than necessary.

"It's all too recent," she said at last, with a suitable sigh. "Maybe in a few days' time."

Corso put his hand on the banister and started down the stairs. He dragged his feet, taking the first few steps slowly. He felt uneasy, as if he'd left something behind but couldn't remember what. But he was certain he hadn't forgotten anything. When he reached the first landing he looked up and saw that Liana Taillefer was still at the door, watching him. She appeared both worried and curious. Corso carried on down the stairs, and, like a slow film shot, his frame of vision slid down

Liana Taillefer's body. He could no longer see the inquiring look in her ice-blue eyes but instead her bust, hips, and finally her firm, pale legs set slightly apart, strong and suggestive as temple columns.

Corso was still reeling as he crossed the hall and went into the street. He could think of at least five unanswered questions and he needed to put them in order of importance. He stopped at the kerb, opposite the railings of the park of El Retiro, and looked casually to his left, waiting for a taxi. An enormous Jaguar was parked a few metres away. The chauffeur, in a dark grey, almost black, uniform, was leaning on the bonnet reading a newspaper. At that instant, he looked up and his eyes met Corso's. It only lasted for a second and then he went back to reading his paper. He was dark, with a moustache, and his cheek was scored from top to bottom by a pale scar. Corso thought he looked familiar: he definitely reminded him of somebody. It could have been, he remembered, the tall man playing the fruit machine in Makarova's bar. But there was something else. His face stirred some vague, distant memory. But before he could give it any more thought an empty taxi appeared. A man in a Loden coat carrying an executive briefcase hailed it from the other side of the street. But the taxi-driver was looking in Corso's direction. Corso made the most of it and stepped quickly off the kerb to snatch the taxi from under the other man's nose.

He asked the taxi-driver to turn down the radio and then settled himself in the back seat, looking out at the surrounding traffic but not taking it in. He always enjoyed the sense of peace he got inside a taxi. It was the closest he ever came to a truce with the outside world: everything beyond the window was suspended for the duration of the journey. He leant his head on the back of the seat and savoured the prospect.

It was time to think of serious matters. Such as *The Book of the Nine Doors*, and his trip to Portugal, the first step in this job. But Corso couldn't concentrate. His meeting with Enrique Taillefer's widow had raised too many questions and left him strangely uneasy. There was something he couldn't quite put his finger on, like watching a landscape from the wrong angle. And there was something else: it took him several stops at traffic lights to realize that the chauffeur of the Jaguar kept reappearing in his mind's eye. This bothered him. He was sure that he'd never seen him before the time at Makarova's bar. But an irrational memory recurred. I know you, he thought. I'm sure I do.

Once, a long time ago, I bumped into a man like you. And I know you're out there somewhere. On the dark side of my memory.

Grouchy was nowhere to be seen, but it no longer mattered. Bulow's Prussians were retreating from the heights of Chapelle St Lambert, with Sumont and Subervie's light cavalry at their heels. There was no problem on the left flank: the red formations of the Scottish infantry had been overtaken and devastated by the charge of the French cuirassiers. In the centre, the Jérôme division had at last taken Hougoumont. And to the north of Mont St Jean the blue formations of the good Old Guard were gathering slowly but implacably, with Wellington withdrawing in delicious disorder to the little village of Waterloo. It only remained to deal the coup de grâce.

Lucas Corso observed the field. The solution was Ney, of course. The bravest of the brave. He placed him at the front, with Erlon and the Jérôme division, or what remained of it, and made them advance at a charge along the Brussels road. When they made contact with the British troops, Corso leant back slightly in his chair and held his breath, sure of the implications of his action: in a few seconds he had just sealed the fate of 22,000 men. Savouring the feeling, he looked lovingly over the compact blue and red ranks, the pale green of the forest of Soignes, the dun-coloured hills. God, it was a beautiful battle.

The blow struck them hard, poor devils. Erlon's corps was blown to pieces like the three little pigs' hut, but the lines formed by Ney and Jérôme's men held. The Old Guard was advancing, crushing everything in its path. The English formations disappeared one by one from the map. Wellington had no choice but to withdraw, and Corso used the French cavalry's reserves to block his path to Brussels. Then, slowly and deliberately, he dealt the final blow. Holding Ney between his thumb and forefinger, he made him advance three hexagons. He compared forces, consulting his tables: the British were outnumbered by eight to three. Wellington was finished. But there was still one small opening left to chance. He consulted his conversion table and saw that all he needed was a three. He felt one more stab of anxiety as he threw the dice to decide what the small factor of chance would be. Even with the battle won, losing Ney in the final minute was only for real enthusiasts. In the end he got a factor of five. He smiled broadly as he gave an affectionate little tap to the blue counter representing Napoleon. I know how you feel, friend. Wellington and his remaining five thousand wretches were all either dead or taken prisoner, and the Emperor had just won the Battle of Waterloo. *Allons, enfants de la Patrie!* The history books could go to hell.

He yawned. On the table, next to the board which represented the battlefield on a scale of 1:5,000, amongst reference books, charts, a cup of coffee and an ashtray full of cigarette ends, his wristwatch showed it was three in the morning. To one side, on the drinks cabinet, from his red label the colour of a hunting jacket, Johnnie Walker looked mischievous as he took a step. Rosy-cheeked little so-and-so, thought Corso. He didn't give a damn that several thousand of his fellow countrymen had just bitten the dust in Flanders.

He turned his back on the Englishman and addressed an unopened bottle of Bols on a shelf between the *Memoirs of Saint-Helena* in two volumes, and a French edition of *Scarlet and Black* which he laid before him on the table. He tore the seal off the bottle and leafed casually through the book as he poured himself a glass of gin:

> . . . Rousseau's *Confessions* was the only book through which his imagination pictured the world. The collection of Grande Armée reports and the *Memoirs of Saint-Helena* completed his Bible. He would have died for those three books. He never believed in any others.

He stood there sipping his gin and stretching his stiff limbs. He gave a last glance to the battlefield, where the sounds of the fighting were dying down after the slaughter. He emptied his glass, feeling like a drunken god playing with real lives as if they were little tin soldiers. He pictured Lord Arthur Wellesley, Duke of Wellington, handing over his sword to Ney. Dead young soldiers lay in the mud, horses cantered by without riders, and an officer of the Scots Greys lay dying beneath a shattered cannon, holding a gold locket with the portrait of a woman and a lock of blonde hair in his bloody fingers. On the other side of the shadows into which he was sinking he could hear the beat of the last waltz. And the little dancer watched him from her shelf, with the sequin on her forehead reflecting the flames in the fireplace, ready to fall into the hands of the spirit of the tobacco pouch. Or the shopkeeper on the corner.

Waterloo. The bones of his great-great-grandfather, the old Grenadier, could rest in peace. He pictured him in any one of the blue formations on the board along the brown line of the Brussels road. His face blackened, his moustache singed by the explosions of gunpowder, he advanced, hoarse and feverish from three days of fighting with his bayonet. He had the same absent expression that Corso had a thousand times imagined that all men in all wars had had. Exhausted, he and his comrades raised their bearskin caps, riddled with holes, on the end of their rifles. Long live the Emperor! Bonaparte's solitary, squat, cancerous ghost was avenged. May he rest in peace. Hip, hip, hurray.

He poured himself another glass of Bols and, facing the sabre hanging on the wall, drank a toast to the faithful ghost of Grenadier Jean-Pax Corso, 1770–1851, Legion of Honour, knight of the Order of Saint Helena, staunch Bonapartist to the end of his days, and French consul in the Mediterranean town where his great-great-grandson was born a century later. With the taste of gin still lingering in his mouth he recited under his breath the only inheritance left him by his great-great-grandfather, transmitted down the century by the line of Corsos that would die with him:

> . . . And the Emperor, at the head of
> his impatient army
> will ride amidst the clamour.
> And armed I will leave this land,
> and once more I will follow
> the Emperor to war.

He was laughing to himself as he picked up the phone and dialled La Ponte's number. In the quiet of the room you could hear the record spinning on the turntable. There were books on the walls, rain-soaked roofs through the dark window. The view wasn't great, except on winter afternoons when the sunset filtered through the blasts of centrally-heated air and pollution from the street, and the sky turned red and ochre, like a thick curtain catching fire. His desk, his computer and the board with the battle of Waterloo sat facing the view, in front of the window against which the rain was falling that night. There were no mementoes, pictures or photos on the wall. Only the sabre of the Old Guard in its brass and leather sheath. Visitors were surprised to find no signs there of his personal life, none of the ties with their memories and their past that people instinctively preserve, only his books and the sabre. Just as there were objects lacking from his house, Lucas Corso came from a world that was long since dead and gone. None of the grave faces which sometimes stood out in his memory would have recognized him had they come back to life. And maybe it was better that way. It was as if he had never owned anything, or left anything behind. As if he had always been completely self-contained, needing nothing but the clothes he stood up in, an erudite, urban itinerant carrying all his worldly possessions in his pockets. And yet, the few people he had allowed to see him on one of those crimson evenings, sitting at his window, dazzled by the sunset, his eyes bleary with gin, say that his expression – that of a clumsy, helpless rabbit – seemed sincere.

La Ponte's sleepy voice answered.

"I've just crushed Wellington," announced Corso.

After a stunned silence, La Ponte said that he was very happy for him. Perfidious Albion – steak and kidney pie and gas meters in dingy hotel rooms. Kipling. Balaclava, Trafalgar, the Falklands and all that. And he'd like to remind Corso – the line went silent while La Ponte fumbled for his watch – that it was three in the morning. Then he mumbled something incoherent, the only intelligible words being "damn you" and "bastard", in that order.

Corso was still laughing to himself as he hung up. Once he had made a reverse-charge call to La Ponte from an auction in Buenos Aires, just to tell him a joke, about a whore who was so ugly she died a virgin. Ha, ha, very funny. And I'll make you swallow the phone bill when you get back, you bloody idiot. And then there was the time, years earlier, when he'd woken up in Nikon's arms. The first thing he'd done was phone La Ponte and tell him he'd met a beautiful woman and it was very much like being in love. Any time he wanted to, Corso could shut his eyes and see Nikon waking slowly, her hair flowing all over the pillow. He had described her to La Ponte over the phone, feeling a strange emotion, an inexplicable, unfamiliar tenderness while he spoke, and she listened, watching him silently. And he knew that at the other end of the line – I'm happy for you Corso, it was about time, I'm really happy for you, my friend – La Ponte was sincerely happy to share in his awakening, his triumph, his happiness. That morning he had loved La Ponte as much as he loved her. Or maybe it was the other way round.

But that was all a long time ago. Corso turned out the light. Outside it was still raining. In his bedroom he lit one last cigarette. He sat motionless on the edge of the bed in the dark, listening for an echo of her absent breathing. Then he put out his hand to stroke her hair, no longer spilling over the pillow. Nikon was his only regret. The rain was coming down harder now, and the droplets on the window broke the faint light outside up into minute reflections, sprinkling the sheets with moving dots, black trails, tiny shadows plunging in no particular direction, like the shreds of a life.

"Lucas."

He said his own name out loud like she used to. She was the only one who'd always called him that. That name was a symbol of the common homeland, now destroyed, that they had once wanted to share. Corso focused his attention on the tip of his cigarette glowing red in the darkness. Once he'd thought he really loved Nikon. When he found her beautiful and intelligent, infallible as a papal encyclical, and passionate, like her black-and-white photos: wide-eyed children, old people, dogs with faithful expressions. When he watched her defending the freedom of peoples and signing petitions for the release of imprisoned intellectuals, oppressed ethnic minorities, things like that. And seals. Once she'd even managed to get him to sign something about seals.

He got up slowly from the bed so as not to wake the ghost sleeping by his side, listening out for the sound of her breathing. Sometimes he believed he could hear it. "You're as dead as your books, Corso. You've never loved anyone." That was the first and last time she'd ever called him by his surname. The first and last time she'd refused him her body, before leaving him for good. In search of the child he'd never wanted.

He opened the window and felt the cold damp night as rain splashed against his face. He took one last puff of his cigarette and then dropped it into the shadows, a red dot fading into the darkness, the curve of its fall broken, or hidden.

That night it was raining on other landscapes too. On the footprints Nikon left behind. On the fields of Waterloo, great-great-grandfather Corso and his comrades. On the scarlet and black tomb of Julien Sorel, guillotined for believing that, with Bonaparte's death, the bronze statues lay dying on old forgotten paths. A stupid mistake. Lucas Corso knew better than anyone that an itinerant, clear-headed soldier could still choose his battlefield and get his pay, standing guard alongside ghosts of paper and leather, amidst the hangover from a thousand failures.

III

Men of Words and Men of Action

"The dead do not speak."
"They speak if God wishes it," retorted Lagardère.
P. Féval: *The Hunchback*

The secretary's heels clicked loudly on the polished wood floor. Lucas Corso followed her down the long corridor – pale cream walls, hidden lighting, ambient music – until they came to a heavy oak door. He obeyed her sign to wait there a moment. Then, when she moved aside with a perfunctory smile, he went into the office. Varo Borja was sitting in a black leather reclining chair, between half a ton of mahogany and a window with a magnificent panoramic view of Toledo: ancient ochre rooftops, the gothic spire of the cathedral silhouetted against a clean blue sky, and in the background the large grey mass of the Alcázar palace.

"Do sit down, Corso. How are you?"

"Fine."

"You've had to wait."

It wasn't an apology but a statement of fact. Corso frowned.

"Don't worry. Only forty-five minutes this time."

Varo Borja didn't even bother to smile as Corso sat down in the armchair reserved for visitors. The desk was completely clear except for a complicated, high-tech telephone and intercom system. The book-dealer's face was reflected in the desk surface together with the view from the window as a backdrop. Varo Borja was about fifty. He was bald, with a tan acquired on a sunbed, and he looked respectable, which was very far from being the truth. He had sharp, darting little eyes. He hid his excessive girth beneath tight-fitting, exuberantly patterned waistcoats and bespoke jackets. He was some sort of marquis and his stormy past as a rake included a police record, a scandal over fraud and four prudent years of self-imposed exile in Brazil and Paraguay.

"I have something to show you."

He had a deliberately abrupt manner, bordering on rudeness, which he cultivated carefully. Corso watched him walk over to a small glass cabinet. He opened it with a tiny key on a gold chain pulled from his pocket. He had no public premises, apart from a stand reserved at the major international fairs. Varo Borja's catalogue never included more than a few dozen select titles. He would follow the trail of rare books to any corner of the world, fight hard and dirty to get hold of them, and then speculate on the vagaries of the market. On his payroll at any one time he had collectors, curators, engravers, printers and suppliers, like Lucas Corso.

"What do you think?"

Corso took the book as carefully as if he were being handed a newborn baby. It was an old volume bound in brown leather, decorated in gold and in excellent condition.

"*La Hypnerotomachia di Poliphilo* by Colonna," he said. "You managed to get hold of it at last."

"Three days ago. Venice, 1545. *In casa di figlivoli di Aldo*. One hundred and seventy woodcuts. Do you think that Swiss you mentioned would still be interested?"

"I suppose so. Is the book complete?"

"Of course. All but four of the woodcuts in this edition are reprints from the 1499 edition."

"My client really wanted a first edition, but I'll try to convince him a second edition is good enough . . . Five years ago a copy just slipped through his fingers at the Monaco auction."

"Well, you have the option on this one."

"Give me a couple of weeks to get in touch with him."

"I'd prefer to deal directly." Varo Borja smiled like a shark after a swimmer. "Of course you'd still get your commission, at the usual rate."

"No way. The Swiss is *my* client."

Varo Borja smiled sarcastically.

"You don't trust anyone, do you? I can picture you as a baby, testing your mother's milk before you'd breastfeed."

"And you'd sell your mother's milk, wouldn't you?"

Varo Borja stared pointedly at Corso, who at that instant didn't look in the least bit like a friendly rabbit. More like a wolf baring his fangs.

"You know what I like about you, Corso? The easy way you fall into the part of a mercenary, with all the demagogues and charlatans out there . . . You're like one of those thin, dangerous men Julius Caesar was so afraid of . . . Do you sleep well at night?"

"Like a log."

"I'm sure you don't. I'd wager a couple of Gothic manuscripts that you're the type who spends a long time staring into the darkness . . . Can I tell you something? I instinctively distrust thin men who are willing and enthusiastic. I only use well-paid mercenaries, rootless, straightforward types. I'm suspicious of anyone who's tied to a homeland, family or cause."

The bookdealer put the *Poliphilo* back in the cabinet and gave a dry, humourless laugh:

"Sometimes I wonder if someone like you can have friends. Do you have any, Corso?"

"Go to hell."

He had said it with an impeccably cold tone. Varo Borja smiled slowly and deliberately. He didn't seem offended.

"You're right. Your friendship doesn't interest me in the least. I buy your loyalty instead. It's more solid and lasting. Isn't that right? The professional pride of a man meeting his contract even though the king who employed him has fled, the battle is lost and there is no hope of salvation . . ."

His expression was teasing, provocative, as he waited for Corso's reaction. But Corso just gestured impatiently, tapping his watch.

"You can write down the rest and send it to me," he said. "I don't get paid to laugh at your little jokes."

Varo Borja seemed to think this over. Then he agreed, though still mocking.

"Once again, you're right, Corso. Let's get back to business . . ." He looked round before getting to the point. "Do you remember the *Treatise on the Art of Fencing* by Astarloa?"

"Yes. A very rare 1870 edition. I got hold of a copy for you a couple of months ago."

"I've now been asked for *Académie de l'épée* by the same client. Maybe one you're acquainted with?"

"I'm not sure if you mean the client or the book . . . You're so convoluted, sometimes I get in a muddle."

Judging by his hostile look, Varo Borja had been stung by this remark.

"We don't all possess your clear, concise prose, Corso. I was referring to the book."

"It's a seventeenth-century Elzevir. Large format, with engravings. Considered the most beautiful treatise on fencing. And the most valuable."

"The buyer is prepared to pay any price."

"Then I'll have to find it."

Varo Borja sat down again in his armchair in front of the window with the panoramic view of the ancient city. He crossed his legs, looking pleased with himself, his thumbs hooked in his waistcoat pockets. Business was obviously going well. Only very few of his most high-powered European colleagues could afford such a view from their desks. But Corso wasn't impressed. Men like that depended on men like him, and they both knew it.

He adjusted his crooked glasses and stared at the bookdealer.

"What shall we do about the *Poliphilo*, then?"

Varo Borja hesitated between antagonism and curiosity. He glanced at the cabinet and then at Corso.

"All right," he said half-heartedly, "you make the deal with the Swiss."

Corso nodded without showing any satisfaction at his small victory. The Swiss didn't exist, but that was his business. It wouldn't be hard to find a buyer for a book like that.

"Let's talk about *The Nine Doors*," he said. The dealer's face grew more animated.

"Yes. Will you take the job?"

Corso was biting a hangnail on his thumb. He gently spat it out onto the spotless table.

"Let's suppose for a moment that your copy is a forgery. And that either of the others is the authentic one. Or none of them is."

Varo Borja, irritated, seemed to be looking to see where Corso's tiny hangnail had landed. At last he gave up.

"In that case," he said, "you'll take good note and follow my instructions."

"Which are?"

"All in good time."

"No. I think you should give me your instructions now." He saw the bookdealer hesitate for a second. In a corner of his brain, where his hunter's instinct lay, something didn't feel quite right. An almost imperceptible jarring sound like a badly tuned machine.

"We'll decide things," said Varo Borja, "as we go along."

"What's there to decide?" Corso was beginning to feel irritated. "One of the books is in a private collection and the other is in a public foundation. Neither is for sale. That's as far as things can go. My part in this and your ambitions end there. As I said: one or other is a forgery, or isn't. Either way, once I've done my job you pay me and that's it."

Much too simple, said the bookdealer's half-smile.

"That depends."

"That's what worries me . . . You've got something up your sleeve, haven't you?"

Varo Borja raised his hand slightly, contemplating its reflection in the polished surface of his desk. Then he slowly lowered it, until the hand came down to meet its reflection. Corso watched the wide, hairy hand, with a huge gold signet ring on the little finger. He was all too familiar with it. He'd seen it sign cheques on non-existent accounts, add emphasis to complete lies, shake the hands of people he would soon be betraying. He could still hear the jarring sound, warning him. Suddenly he felt strangely tired. He was no longer sure if he wanted the job.

"I'm not sure I want this job," he said aloud.

Varo Borja must have realized he meant it because his manner changed. He sat motionless, his chin resting on his hands, the light from the window burnishing his perfectly tanned bald head. He seemed to be weighing things up as he stared intently at Corso.

"Have I ever told you why I became a bookdealer?"

"No. And I really don't give a damn."

Borja laughed theatrically to show he was prepared to be magnanimous and take Corso's rudeness. Corso could safely vent his bad temper, for the moment.

"I pay you to listen to whatever I want to tell you."

"You haven't paid me yet, this time."

Borja took a cheque-book from one of the drawers and put it on the desk, while Corso looked round, resigned and defenceless. This was the moment to say, "So long," or stay put and wait. It was also the moment to be offered a drink, but Borja wasn't that kind of host. So Corso shrugged, feeling the flask of gin in his pocket. It was absurd. He knew perfectly well he wouldn't leave, whether or not he liked what Borja was about to propose. And Borja knew it. He wrote out a figure, signed and tore out the cheque, then pushed it towards Corso.

Without touching it, Corso glanced at it.

"You've convinced me," he sighed. "I'm listening."

The bookdealer didn't even allow himself a look of triumph. Just a brief nod, cold and confident, as if he had just made some insignificant deal.

"I got into this business by chance," he began. "One day I found myself penniless, with my great-uncle's library as my only inheritance . . . About two thousand books. Only about a hundred were of any value. But amongst them there was a first edition *Don Quixote*, a couple of eighteenth-century Psalters and one of the only four known copies of *Champfleuri* by Geoffroy Tory . . . What do you think?"

"You were too lucky."

"You can say that again," agreed Varo Borja in an even, confident tone. He didn't have the smugness of so many successful people when they talk about themselves. "In those days I knew nothing about collectors of rare books, but I grasped the essential fact: they're willing to pay a lot of money for scarce products . . . I learnt terms I'd never heard of before, like colophon, dented chisel, golden mean or fanfare binding. And while I was becoming interested in the business I discovered something else: some books are for selling and others are for keeping. Becoming a bookcollector is like joining a religion: it's for life."

"Very moving. So now tell me what I and your *Nine Doors* have got to do with your taking vows."

"You asked me what I'd do if you discovered my copy was a forgery . . . Well, let me make this clear: it is a forgery."

"How do you know?"

"I am absolutely certain of it."

Corso grimaced, showing what he thought of absolute certainty in matters of rare books.

"Well, in Mateu's *Universal Bibliography* and in the Terral-Coy catalogue it's listed as authentic . . ."

"Yes," said Varo Borja. "Though there's a small error in Mateu: it states that there are eight illustrations when there are nine of them . . . But its *formal* authenticity means very little. According to the bibliographies, the Fargas and Ungern copies are also authentic."

"Maybe all three of them are."

Borja shook his head.

"That's not possible. The records of Torchia's trial leave no doubt: only one copy was saved." He smiled mysteriously. "I have other proof."

"Such as?"

"It doesn't concern you."

"Then why do you need me?"

Varo Borja pushed back his chair and stood up.

"Come with me."

"I've already told you – " Corso was shaking his head – "I'm not remotely interested in all of this."

"You're lying. You're burning with curiosity. You'd do the job for free."

He took the cheque and put it in his waistcoat pocket. Then he led Corso up a spiral staircase to the floor above. Borja's office was at the back of his house. It was a huge, medieval building in the old part of the city, and he'd paid a fortune for it. He took Corso along a corridor leading to the hall and main entrance, up to a door which opened with a modern security keypad. It was a large room, with a black marble floor, a beamed ceiling and ancient iron bars at the windows. There was a desk, leather armchairs and a large stone fireplace. All the walls were covered with glass cabinets full of books, and prints in beautiful frames. Some of them by Holbein and Dürer, Corso noted.

"Nice room," he said. He'd never been in there before. "But I thought you kept your books in the storeroom in the basement . . ."

Varo Borja stopped at his side.

"These are mine. They're not for sale. Some people collect chivalric or romantic novels. Some search for *Don Quixotes* or uncut volumes . . . All those you see here have the same central character: the Devil."

"Can I take a look?"

"That's why I brought you here."

Corso took a few steps forward. The books all had ancient bindings from the leather-covered boards of the incunabula to the morocco leather decorated with plaques and rosettes. His scuffed shoes squeaked on the marble floor as he stopped in front of one of the cabinets and leaned over to examine the contents: *De spectris et apparitionibus* by Juan Rivio. *Summa diabolica* by Benedicto Casiano. *La haine de Satan* by Pierre Crespet. The *Steganography* by Abbot Tritemius. *De Consummatione sæculi* by St Pontius . . . They were all extremely rare and valuable books, most of which Corso knew only from bibliographical references.

"Have you ever seen anything more beautiful?" said Varo Borja, watching Corso closely. "There's nothing like that sheen, the gold on leather, behind glass . . . Not to mention the treasures they contain: centuries of study, of wisdom. Answers to the secrets of the universe and the heart of man." He raised his arms slightly and let them drop, giving up his attempt to express in words his pride at owning them all. "I know people who would kill for a collection like this."

Corso nodded without taking his eyes off the books.

"You, for instance," he said. "Although you wouldn't do it yourself. You'd get somebody else to do the killing for you."

Varo Borja laughed contemptuously.

"That's one of the advantages of having money – you can hire henchmen to do your dirty work. And remain pure yourself."

Corso looked at the bookdealer.

"That's a matter of opinion," he said after a few moments' thought. He seemed to ponder the matter. "I despise people who don't get their hands dirty. The pure ones."

"I don't care what you despise, so let's get down to serious matters."

Varo Borja took a few steps past the cabinets, each containing about a hundred volumes.

"*Ars Diavoli . . .*" He opened the one nearest to him and ran his finger over the spines of the books, almost in a caress. "You'll never see such a collection anywhere else. These are the rarest, most choice books. It took me years to build up this collection, but I was still lacking the prize piece."

He took out one of the books, a folio bound in black leather in the Venetian style, with no title on the outside but with five raised bands on the spine and a golden pentacle on the front cover. Corso took it and opened it carefully. The first printed page, the original title page, was in Latin: *De umbrarum regni novem portis*: the book of the nine doors of the kingdom of shadows. Then came the printer's mark, place, name and date: '*Venetiæ, apud Aristidem Torchiam. M.DC.LX.VI. Cum superiorum privilegio veniaque.*' With the privilege and permission of the superiors.

Varo Borja was watching to see his reaction.

"One can always tell a booklover," he said, "by the way he handles a book."

"I'm not a booklover."

"True. But sometimes you make one forgive that you have the manners of a mercenary. When it comes to books, certain gestures can be reassuring. The way some people touch them is criminal."

Corso turned more pages. All the text was in Latin, printed in a handsome type on thick, good quality paper which had withstood the passage of time. There were nine splendid full-page engravings, showing scenes of a medieval appearance. He paused over one of them, at random. It was numbered with a Latin V, together with one Hebrew and one Greek letter or numeral. At the foot, one word which was incomplete or in code: "*FR.ST.A*". A man who looked like a merchant was counting out a sack of gold in front of a closed door, unaware of the skeleton behind him holding an hourglass in one hand and a pitchfork in the other.

"What do you think?" asked Borja.

"You told me it was a forgery, but this doesn't look like one. Have you examined it thoroughly?"

"I've gone over the whole thing, down to the last comma, with a magnifying glass. I've had plenty of time. I bought it six months ago, when the heirs of Gualterio Terral decided to sell his collection."

The bookhunter turned more pages. The engravings were beautiful, of a simple, mysterious elegance. In another one, a young girl was about to be beheaded by an executioner in armour with his sword raised.

"I doubt if the heirs would have put a forgery on sale," said Corso when he'd finished examining it. "They've got too much money, and they don't give a damn about books. The catalogue for the collection even had to be drawn up by Claymore's auctioneers . . . And I knew old Terral. He would never have accepted a book that had been tampered with or forged."

"I agree," said Borja. "And Terral inherited *The Nine Doors* from his father-in-law, Don Lisardo Coy, a bookcollector with impeccable credentials."

"And he," said Corso as he put the book down on the desk and pulled out his notebook from his coat pocket, "bought it from an Italian, Domenico Chiara, whose family, according to the Weiss catalogue, had owned it since 1817 . . ."

Borja nodded, obviously pleased.

"I see you've gone into the matter in some depth."

"Of course I have." Corso looked at him as if he'd just said something very stupid. "It's my job."

Varo Borja made a placatory gesture.

"I don't doubt Terral and his heirs' good faith," he clarified. "Nor did I say that the book wasn't old."

"You said it was a forgery."

"Maybe forgery isn't the right word."

"Well, what is it then? It all belongs to the right era." Corso picked up the book again, then with his thumb against the edge of the pages he flicked them, listening to the sound they made. "Even the paper sounds right."

"There's something in it that doesn't sound right. And I don't mean the paper."

"Maybe the prints." ·

"What's the matter with them?"

"They're not quite right. I would have expected copperplates. By 1666 nobody used woodcuts any more."

"Don't forget this was an unusual edition. The engravings are reproductions of other older ones, supposedly discovered or seen by the printer."

"The *Delomelanicon* . . . Do you really believe it?"

"You don't care what I believe. But the book's nine original engravings aren't attributed to just anybody . . . Legend has it that Lucifer, after being defeated and thrown out of Heaven, drew up the magic formula to be used by his followers: the authoritative handbook of the shadows. A terrible book kept in secret, burnt many times, sold for huge sums by the few privileged to own it . . . These illustrations are really satanic hieroglyphs. Interpreted with the aid of the text and the appropriate knowledge, they can be used to summon the prince of darkness."

Corso nodded with exaggerated gravity.

"I can think of better ways to sell one's soul."

"Please don't joke, it's more serious than it seems . . . Do you know what *Delomelanicon* means?"

"I think so. It comes from the Greek: *Delo*, meaning to summon. And *Melas*: black, dark."

Varo Borja's high-pitched laugh rang out. He said in a tone of approval:

"I was forgetting that you're an educated mercenary. You're right: to summon the shadows, or illuminate them . . . The prophet Daniel, Hippocrates, Flavius Josephus, Albertus Magnus and Leo III all mention this wonderful book. Men have only been writing for the last six thousand years, but the *Delomelanicon* is reputed to be three times as old . . . The first direct mention of it is in the Turis papyrus, written thirty-three centuries ago. Then, between 1 BC and the second year of our era, it is quoted several times in the *Corpus Hermeticum*. According to the *Asclemandres*, the book enables one to 'face the Light' . . . And in an incomplete inventory of the library at Alexandria, before it was destroyed for the third and last time in the year 646, there is a specific reference to the nine magic enigmas it contains . . . We don't know if there was only one copy or several, or if any survived the burning of the library . . . Since then its trail has disappeared and reappeared throughout history, through fires, wars and disasters."

Corso looked doubtful.

"That's always the case. All magic books have the same legend: from Thoth to Nicholas Flamel . . . Once a client of mine who was fascinated by alchemy asked me to find him the bibliography quoted by Fulcanelli and his followers. I couldn't convince him that half the books didn't exist."

"Well, this one did exist. It must have done for the Holy Office to list it in its Index. Don't you think?"

"It doesn't matter what I think. Some lawyers don't believe their clients are innocent and they still get them acquitted."

"That's the case here. I'm not hiring you because you believe in it but because you're good at your job."

Corso turned more pages of the book. Another engraving, number I, showed a walled city on a hill. A strange unarmed horseman was riding towards it, his finger to his lips requesting complicity or silence. The caption to the engraving read: "*Nem. perv.t qui n.n leg. cert.rit.*"

"It's in an abbreviated but decipherable code," explained Varo Borja watching him. '*Nemo pervenit qui non legitime certaverit.*'"

"'Only he who has fought according to the rules will succeed'?"

"That's about it. For the moment it's the only one of the nine captions that we can decipher with any certainty. An almost identical one appears in the works of Roger Bacon, a specialist in demonology, cryptography and magic . . . Bacon claimed to own a *Delomelanicon* which had belonged to King Solomon, containing the key to terrible mysteries. The book was made of rolls of parchment with illustrations. It was burned in 1350 by personal order of Pope Innocent VI who declared: 'It contains a method to summon devils.' In Venice, three centuries later, Aristide Torchia decided to print it with the original illustrations."

"They're too perfect," objected Corso. "They can't be the originals: they'd be in an older style."

"I agree. Torchia must have updated them."

Another engraving, number III, showed a bridge with gate towers spanning a river. Corso looked up and saw that Varo Borja was smiling mysteriously, like an alchemist confident of what's cooking in his crucible.

"There's one last connection," said the bookdealer. "Giordano Bruno, martyr of rationalism, mathematician and champion of the theory that the Earth rotates round the sun . . ." He waved his hand contemptuously, as if all this was trivial. "But that was only part of his work. He wrote sixty-one books, and magic played an important part in them. And how about this: Bruno makes specific reference to the *Delomelanicon*, even using the Greek words *Delo* and *Melas*, and he adds: 'On the path of men who want to know, there are nine secret doors.' He then goes on to describe the methods for making the Light shine once more . . . '*Sic luceat Lux*,' he writes, which is actually the same motto – " he showed Corso the printer's mark: a tree split by lightning, a snake and a motto – "that Aristide Torchia used on the frontispiece of *The Nine Doors* . . . What do you think of that?"

"It's all well and good. But it all comes to the same. You can make a text mean anything, especially if it's old and full of ambiguities."

"Or precautions. Although Giordano Bruno forgot the golden rule for survival: '*Scire, tacere*.' To know and keep silent. Apparently he knew the right things but he talked too much. And there are more coincidences: Giordano Bruno was arrested in Venice, declared an obdurate heretic and burned alive in Rome at Campo dei Fiori in February 1600. The same journey, the same places and the same dates that marked Aristide Torchia's path to execution sixty-seven years later: he was arrested in Venice, tortured in Rome and burned at Campo dei Fiori in February 1667. By then very few people were still being burned at the stake and yet he was."

"I'm impressed," said Corso, who wasn't in the least.

Varo Borja tutted reprovingly.

"Sometimes I wonder if you believe in anything."

Corso seemed to think about it for a moment, then shrugged.

"A long time ago I did believe in something. But I was young and cruel then. Now I'm forty-five: I'm old and cruel."

"I am too. But there are things I still believe in. Things that make my heart beat faster."

"Like money?"

"Don't make fun of me. Money is the key that opens the door to man's dark secrets. And it pays for your services. And grants me the only thing in the world I respect: these books." He took a few steps along the cabinets full of books. "They're mirrors in the image of those who wrote them. They reflect their concerns, questions, desires, life, death . . . They're living beings: you have to know how to feed them, protect them . . ."

"And use them."

"Sometimes."

"But this one doesn't work."

"No."

"You've tried it."

It was a statement, not a question. Varo Borja looked at Corso with hostility.

"Don't be absurd. Let's just say I'm certain that it's a forgery, and leave it at that. That's why I need to compare it to the other copies."

"I still say it doesn't have to be a forgery. Books often differ, even if they're part of the same edition. No two books are the same really. From birth they all have distinguishing details. And each book lives a different life: it can lose pages, or have them added or replaced, or have a new binding . . . Over the years two books printed on the same press can end up looking entirely different. That's what might have happened to this one."

"Well, find out. Investigate *The Nine Doors* as if were a crime. Follow trails, check each page, each engraving, the paper, the binding . . . Work your way backwards and find out where my copy comes from. Then do the same with the other two, in Sintra and in Paris."

"It would help me if I knew how you found out yours was a forgery."

"I can't tell you. Trust my intuition."

"Your intuition is going to cost you a lot of money."

"All you have to do is spend it."

He pulled the cheque out of his pocket and gave it to Corso, who turned it over in his fingers, undecided.

"Why are you paying me in advance? You've never done that before."

"You'll have a lot of expenses to cover. This is so you can start getting on with things." He handed him a thick bound file. "Everything I know about the book is in there. You may find it useful."

Corso was still looking at the cheque.

"This is too much for an advance."

"You may encounter certain complications . . ."

"You don't say."

As he said this he heard Borja clear his throat. They were getting to the crux of the matter at last.

"If you find out that the three copies are forgeries or are incomplete," Borja said, "then you'll have done your job and we'll settle up . . ." He paused briefly and ran his hand over his tanned head. He smiled awkwardly at Corso. "But one of the books may turn out to be authentic, so then you'll have more money at your disposal. Because if that's the case I want it by whatever means, and without regard to expense."

"You're joking, aren't you?"

"Do I look as if I'm joking, Corso?"

"It's against the law."

"You've done illegal things before."

"Not this kind of thing."

"Nobody's ever paid you what I'll pay you."

"How can I be sure of that?"

"I'm letting you take the book with you. You'll need the original for your work. Isn't that enough of a guarantee?"

The jarring sound again, warning him. Corso was still holding *The Nine Doors*. He put the cheque in between the pages like a bookmark and blew some imaginary dust off the book before returning it to Varo Borja.

"A moment ago you said that you can buy anything with money, so now you can test that out yourself. Go and see the owners of the books and do the dirty work yourself."

He turned and walked towards the door, wondering how many steps he'd take before the bookdealer said anything. Three.

"This isn't a matter for men of words," said Varo Borja. "It's a matter for men of action."

His tone had changed. Gone was the arrogant composure and the disdain for the mercenary he was hiring. On the wall, an engraving of an angel by Dürer gently beat its wings behind the glass of a picture frame, while Corso's shoes turned on the black marble floor. Next to his cabinets full of books and the barred window with the cathedral in the background, next to everything that his money could buy, Varo Borja stood blinking, disconcerted. His expression was still arrogant.

He was even tapping on the book cover with mechanical disdain. But even before that glorious moment, Lucas Corso had learnt to recognize defeat in a man's eyes. And fear.

His heart was beating with calm satisfaction as, without a word, he retraced his steps. As he came up to Varo Borja he took the cheque poking out from between the pages of *The Nine Doors*. He folded it carefully and put it in his pocket. Then he took the file and the book.

"I'll be in touch," he said.

He realized he'd thrown the dice. That he'd moved on to the first square in a dangerous game of Snakes and Ladders and it was too late to turn back. But he felt like playing. He went down the stairs followed by the echo of his own dry laughter. Varo Borja was wrong. There were certain things money couldn't buy.

The stairs from the main entrance led to an interior courtyard, with a well and two Venetian marble lions, fenced off from the street by railings. An unpleasant dankness rose from the Tagus and Corso stopped beneath the Moorish arch at the entrance to turn up his collar. He walked along the silent, narrow, cobbled streets with uneven paving, until he came to a small square. There was a bar with metal tables, and chestnut trees with bare branches beneath the bell tower of a church. He sat down in a patch of tepid sun on the terrace and tried to warm his stiff limbs. Two glasses of neat gin helped things along. Only then did he open the file on *The Nine Doors* and look through it properly for the first time.

There was a forty-two-page typed report giving the book's historical background, both for the supposed original version, the *Delomelanicon* or *Invocation of Darkness*, and for Torchia's version, *The Nine Doors of the Kingdom of Shadows*, printed in Venice in 1666. There were various appendices providing a bibliography, photocopies of citations in classical texts and information on the other two known copies – their owners, any restoration work, purchase dates, present locations. There was also a transcription of the records of Aristide Torchia's trial, with the account of an eyewitness, one Gennaro Galeazzo, describing the unfortunate printer's last moments:

* * *

. . . He mounted the scaffold without agreeing to be reconciled with God and maintained an obstinate silence. When the fire was lit smoke began to suffocate him. He opened his eyes wide and uttered a terrible cry, commending himself to the Father. Many of those present crossed themselves, for in death he requested God's mercy. Others say that he shouted at the ground, in other words towards the depths of the earth . . .

A car drove past on the other side of the square and turned down one of the corner streets leading to the cathedral. The engine paused for a moment beyond the corner, as if the driver had stopped before driving on down the street. Corso paid little attention, engrossed as he was in the book. The first page was the title page and the second was blank. The third, which began with a handsome capital N, was the first real page of text and began with a cryptic introduction:

Nos p.tens L.f.r, juv.te Stn. Blz.b, Lvtn, Elm, atq Ast.rot. ali.q, h.die ha.ems ace.t pct fo.de.is c.m t. qui no.st; et h.ic pol.icem am.rem mul. flo.em virg.num de.us mon. hon v.lup et op. for.icab tr.d.o,.os.ta int. nos ma.et eb.iet i.li c.ra er. No.is of.ret se.el in ano sag. sig. s.b ped. cocul.ab sa Ecl.e et no.s r.gat i.sius er.t; p.ct v.v.t an v.q fe.ix in t.a hom. et ven D:
    Fa.t in inf int co.s daem.
    Satanas. Belzebub, Lcfr, Elimi, Leviathan, Astaroth
    Siq pos mag. diab. et daem. pri.cp dom.

After the introduction, whose supposed authorship was obvious, came the text. Corso read the first lines:

D.mine mag.que L.fr, te D.um m. et.pr ag.sco. et pol.c.or t ser.ire. a.ob.re quam.d p. vvre; et rn.io al.rum d. et js.ch.st. et a.s sn.ts tq.e s.ctas e. ec.les. apstl. et rom. et om. i sc.am. et o.nia ips. s.cramen. et o.nes.atio et r.g. q.ib fid. pos.nt int.rcd. p.o me; et

t.bi po.lceor q. fac. qu.tqu.t m.lum pot., et atra. ad mala p. omn.
Et ab.rncio chrsm. et b.ptm et omn . . .

He looked up at the church portico. The arches were carved with images of the Final Judgement worn down by the elements. Beneath them, dividing the door in two, a niche sheltered an angry-looking Pantocrator. His raised right hand suggested punishment rather than mercy. In his left hand he held an open book, and Corso could not help drawing parallels. He looked round at the church tower and the surrounding buildings. The façades still wore bishops' coats of arms, and he reflected that this square too had once watched the bonfires of the Inquisition burn. After all, this was Toledo. A crucible for underground cults, initiation mysteries, false converts. And heretics.

He drank some gin before going back to the book. The text, in an abbreviated Latin code, took up another hundred and fifty-seven pages, the final one being blank. The other nine contained the famous engravings inspired, according to legend, by Lucifer himself. Each print had a Latin, Hebrew and Greek numeral at the top, including a Latin phrase in the same abbreviated code as the rest. Corso ordered a third gin and went over them. They looked like the figures of the Tarot, or old medieval engravings: the king and the beggar, the hermit, the hangman, death, the executioner. In the last engraving a beautiful woman was riding a dragon. Too beautiful, he thought, for the religious morality of the time.

He found an identical illustration on a photocopy of a page in Mateu's *Universal Bibliography*. But it wasn't the same. Corso was holding the Terral-Coy copy, whereas the engraving reproduced came, as recorded by the scholarly Mateu in 1929, from another one of the books:

Torchia (Aristide). *De Umbrarum Regni Novem Portis. Venetiæ, apud Aristidem Torchiam. MDCLXVI*. Folio. 160 pages incl. title page. 9 full-page woodcuts. Of exceptional rarity. Only 3 known copies. Fargas Library, Sintra, Port. (see illustration). Coy Library, Madrid, Sp. (engraving 9 missing). Morel Library, Paris, Fr.

por ti solo ser causada
siente agora el gran dolor
que me das en tu partida
agradesce el gran amor
que te puse con fauor
reparando tu venida.

S. l. ni a. *(hácia* 1525*)*. 4.° let.
gót. 4 *hojas sin foliacion con la sign.* a.

HOMERO. La Vlyxea de Ho-
mero. Repartida en XIII. Libros.
Tradvzida de Griego en Romance
castellano por el Señor Gonçalo Perez. Venetia, en casa de Gabriel Gio-
lito de Ferrariis, y svs hermanos,
MDLIII. 12.° let. curs. 209 *hojas fo-
liadas, inclusos los prels.* y una al
*fin, en cuyo reverso se repiten las se-
ñas de la impresion.*

He visto la primera edicion, con el si-
guiente título: *De la Ulyxea de Homero.
XIII. libros, traduzidos de Griego en Romance Castellano por Gonçalo Perez. Anuers, en
casa de Iuan Stelsio,* 1550. 8.° let. cursiva. 4
hojas prels. y 295 fols.
Nic. Antonio menciona otra tambien de
Anuers, 1553. 12.°

Poema en ciento treinta y cinco octavas.
Hal al fin una disertacion en prosa, intitula-
da: *Prueba, que huuo Gigantes, y que oy los
ay,* y por cierto mi solo prueba que el
autor era sumamente cándido ó tenia mui
grandes tragaderas: sea esto dicho con per-
don de los varios testos bíblicos y de Santos
Padres que aduce en confirmacion de sus
ideas gigantescas.

OVIDIO NASON. Metamor-
phoseos del excelente poeta Ouidio
Nasson. Traduzidos en verso suelto y
octaua rima: con sus allegorias al fin
de cada libro. Por el Doctor Antonio
Perez Sigler. Nueuamente agora en-
mēdados, y añadido por el mismo autor
vn Diccionario Poetico copiosissimo.
Bvrgos, Iuan Baptista Varesio, 1609.
12.° let. curs. 21 *hojas prels.* y 584 *fols.*

Este tomito por ser tan grueso suele ha-
llarse dividido en dos volumenes. No estoi
cierto si mi ejemplar está perfectamente
completo con las 21 hojas de preliminares.

VIIII

N.NC SCO TEN.BR. LVX

Sedano, en el tom. VII. del *Autores* llama
á esta primera edicion; sin embargo me
pone en duda el ver lleva la Aprobacion, la
Censura, el Privilegio, la Fe de erratas y la
Tasa fechadas en 1666. Por otra parte tambien puede ser cierto lo sentado por dicho
Sedano, pues D. José Pellicer, al principio
de su introduccion biográfico-literaria, ob-
serva que *salen ya á luz publica, despues de*

He found an identical illustration in
Mateu's *Universal Bibliography* . . .

Engraving 9 missing. Corso checked and saw this was wrong. Engraving number nine was there in the copy he was holding, originally from the Coy, later the Terral-Coy Library, and now the property of Varo Borja. It must have been a printing error, or a mistake by Mateu himself. In 1929, when the *Universal Bibliography* was published, printing techniques and distribution methods weren't as efficient. Many scholars mentioned books that they only knew of through third parties. Maybe the engraving was missing from one of the other copies. Corso made a note in the margin. He needed to check it.

A clock somewhere struck three and pigeons flew up off the tower and roofs. Corso shuddered gently, as if slowly coming to. He felt in his pocket and took out some money. He left it on the table and then stood up. The gin made him feel pleasantly detached, blurring external sounds and images. He put the book and file in his canvas bag, slung it over his shoulder and then stood for a few seconds looking at the angry Pantocrator in the portico. He wasn't in a hurry and he wanted to clear his head so he decided to walk to the railway station.

When he reached the cathedral he took a short cut through the cloisters. He passed the closed souvenir kiosk, and stood for a moment looking at the empty scaffolding over the murals undergoing restoration. The place was deserted, and his steps echoed beneath the vault. For a moment he thought he heard something behind him. A priest late to confession.

He came out through an iron gate into a dark, narrow street, where passing cars had taken chunks out of the walls. As he turned to the right he heard a car coming from somewhere to the left. There was a traffic sign, a triangle warning that the street narrowed, and when he came to it the car accelerated unexpectedly. He could hear it behind him moving closer. Too fast, he thought as he turned to look round. But he only had time to half-turn, just enough to see a dark shape bearing down on him. His reflexes were dulled by the gin, but by chance his attention was still on the traffic sign. Instinct pushed him towards it, seeking the narrow area of protection between the metal post and the wall. He slid into the small gap like a bullfighter hiding from the bull behind the barrier. The car only managed to strike his hand as it passed him. The blow was sharp and the pain made his knees buckle. He fell onto the uneven cobbles, and saw the car disappear down the street with a screeching of tyres.

Corso walked on to the station, rubbing his bruised hand. But now he turned every so often to look behind him, and his bag, with *The Nine Doors* inside, was burning his shoulder. For three seconds he'd caught a fleeting glimpse, but it had been enough: this time he was driving a black Mercedes, not a Jaguar, but the man who'd nearly run him down was dark, with a moustache and a scar on his face. The man from Makarova's bar. The same man he'd seen in a chauffeur's uniform, reading a newspaper outside Liana Taillefer's house.

IV

The Man with the Scar

I know not where he comes from. But I know where he is going: he is going to Hell.

A. Dumas: *The Count of Monte Cristo*

Night was falling when Corso got home. Inside his coat pocket his bruised hand was throbbing painfully. He went to the bathroom, picked up his crumpled pyjamas and a towel from the floor, and held the hand under a stream of cold water for five minutes. Then he opened a couple of tins and ate them standing up in the kitchen.

It had been a strange and dangerous day. As he thought about it, he felt confused, though he was less worried than curious. For some time, he had treated the unexpected with the detached fatalism of one who waits for life to make the next move. His detachment, his neutrality, meant that he could never be the prime mover. Until that morning in the narrow street in Toledo, his role had been merely to carry out orders. Other people were the victims. Every time he lied or made a deal with someone, he remained objective. He formed no relationships with the persons or things involved – they were simply tools of the trade. Lucas Corso remained on the edge, a mercenary with no cause other than financial gain. The indifferent third man. Perhaps this attitude had always made him feel safe, just as, when he took off his glasses, people and distant objects became blurred, indistinct; he could ignore them by removing their sharp outline. Now, though, the pain from his injured hand, the sense of imminent danger, of violence aimed directly at him alone, implied frightening changes in his world. Lucas Corso, who had acted as executioner so many times, wasn't used to being a victim. And he found it highly disconcerting.

In addition to the pain in his hand, he felt that his muscles were rigid with tension and his mouth was dry. So he opened a bottle of Bols and searched for aspirin in his canvas bag. He always carried a good supply, together with books, pencils, pens, half-filled notepads, a many-bladed Swiss Army knife, passport, money, a bulging address book, and books belonging to him and to others. He could, at any time, disappear without a trace like a snail with its shell. With his bag he could make himself at home wherever chance, or his clients, might lead him – airports, railway stations, dusty European libraries, hotel rooms which merged in his memory into a single room with fluid dimensions, where he would wake with a start, disorientated and confused in the darkness, searching for the light switch only to stumble upon the phone. Blank moments torn from his life and his consciousness. He was never very sure of himself, or anything, for the first thirty seconds after he opened his eyes, when his body woke up more quickly than his mind or his memory.

He sat at his computer and put his notepads and several reference books on his desk to his left. On his right he put *The Nine Doors* and Varo Borja's file. Then he leaned back in his chair, letting his cigarette burn down in his hand for five minutes, only rarely bringing it to his lips. During that time all he did was sip the rest of his gin and stare at the blank computer screen and the pentacle on the book's cover. At last he seemed to wake up. He stubbed out the cigarette in the ashtray and, adjusting his crooked glasses, set to work. Varo Borja's file agreed with Crozet's *Encyclopedia of Printers and Rare and Curious Books*:

TORCHIA, Aristide. Venetian printer, engraver and bookbinder. (1620–67). Printer's mark: a snake and a tree split by lightning. Trained as an apprentice in Leyden (Holland), at the workshop of the Elzevirs. On his return to Venice he completed a series of works on philosophical and esoteric themes in small formats (12mo, 16mo), which were highly esteemed. Among these stand out *The Secrets of Wisdom* by Nicholas Tamisso (3 vols, 12mo, Venice 1650) and a strange *Key to Captive Thoughts* (1 vol, 132 x 75 mm, Venice 1653). *The Three Books of the Art* by Paolo d'Este (6 vols, 8vo, Venice 1658), *Curious Explanation of Mysteries and Hieroglyphs* (1 vol, 8vo, Venice 1659), a reprint of *The Lost Word* by Bernardo Trevisano (1 vol, 8vo, Venice 1661) and *The Nine Doors of the Kingdom of Shadows* (1 vol, folio, Venice 1666). Owing to the printing of the latter he fell into the hands of the Inquisition. His workshop was destroyed, together with all the printed matter and texts yet to be printed that it contained. Torchia suffered the same fate. Condemned for magic and witchcraft, he was burned at the stake on 17 February 1667.

Corso looked away from the computer and examined the first page of the book that had cost the Venetian printer his life. The title was *De Umbrarum Regni Novem Portis*. Beneath it came the printer's mark, the stamp acting as the printer's signature which might be anything from a simple monogram to an elaborate illustration. In Aristide Torchia's case, as mentioned in Crozet, the mark was a tree with one branch snapped off by lightning and a snake coiled round the trunk, devouring its own tail. The picture was accompanied by the motto *Sic luceat Lux*: 'Thus shines the light'. At the foot of the page, there was the location, name and date: '*Venetiæ, apud Aristidem Torchiam*'. Printed in Venice, at the establishment of Aristide Torchia. Underneath, separated by a decoration: '*MDCLXVI. Cum superiorum privilegio veniaque.*' By authority and permission of the superiors.

Corso typed in:

Copy has no bookplates or handwritten notes. Complete according to catalogue for Terral-Coy collection auction (Claymore, Madrid). Error in Mateu (states 8, not 9, engravings in this copy). Folio. 299 x 215 mm. 2 blank flyleaves, 160 pages and 9 full-page prints, numbered I to VIIII. Pages: 1 title page with printer's mark. 157 pages of text. Last one blank, no colophon. Full-page engravings on right-hand page. Reverse blank.

DE VMBRARVM REGNI
NOVEM PORTIS

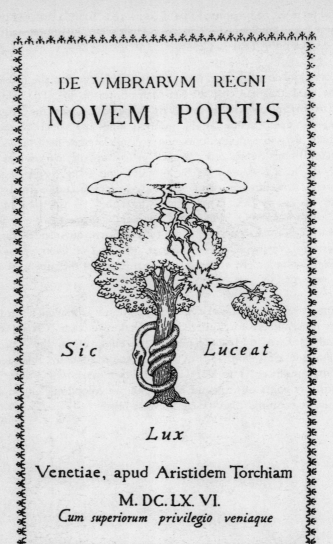

Sic   *Luceat*

Lux

Venetiae, apud Aristidem Torchiam

M. DC. LX. VI.

Cum superiorum privilegio veniaque

NEM. PERV.T QVI N.N LEG. CERT.RIT

CLAVS. PAT.T

VERB. D.SVM C.S.T ARCAN.

FOR. N.N OMN. A.QVE

FR.ST.A

DIT.SCO M.R.

DIS.S P.TI.R M.

VIC. I.T VIR.

N. NC SC.O TEN. BR. LVX

He examined the illustrations one by one. According to Varo Borja, legend attributed the original drawings to the hand of Lucifer himself. Each print was accompanied by a Roman ordinal, its Hebrew and Greek equivalent, and a Latin phrase in abbreviated code. He started writing again:

I NEM. PERV.T QUI N.N LEG. CERT.RIT: A horseman rides towards a walled city. He has a finger to his lips advising caution or silence.

II CLAUS. PAT.T: A hermit in front of a locked door holding 2 keys. A lantern on the ground. He is accompanied by a dog. At his side a sign resembling the Hebrew letter Teth.

III VERB. D.SUM C.S.T ARCAN.: A vagabond, or pilgrim, heads towards a bridge over a river. At both ends of the bridge, gate towers with closed doors bar the way. An archer on a cloud aims at the path leading to the bridge.

IIII (The Latin numeral appears in this form, not the more usual IV). FOR. N.N OMN. A.QUE: A jester stands in front of a stone labyrinth. The entrance is also closed. Three dice on the ground all showing the numbers 1, 2 and 3.

V FR.ST.A. A miser, or merchant, is counting out a sack of gold pieces. Behind him, Death holds an hourglass in one hand and a pitchfork in the other.

VI DIT.SCO M.R.: A hanged man, like the one in the Tarot, hands tied behind his back, is hanging by his foot from the battlements of a castle, next to a closed postern. A hand in a gauntlet is sticking out of a slot window holding a flaming sword.

VII DIS.S P.TI.R M.: A king and a beggar are playing chess on a board with only white squares. The Moon can be seen through the window. Beneath the window next to a closed door two dogs are fighting.

VIII VIC. I.T VIR.: Next to the wall of a city a woman is kneeling on the ground offering up her bare neck to the executioner.

In the background there is a wheel of fortune with three human figures: one at the top, one going up and one going down.

VIIII (Also in this form, not the usual numeral IX). N.NC SC.O TEN.BR. LUX: A naked woman riding a seven-headed dragon. She is holding an open book, and a half-moon hides her sex. On a hill in the background there is a castle in flames. The door is closed as in the other engravings.

He stopped typing, stretched his stiffened limbs, and yawned. The room was in darkness beyond the cone of light from his work lamp and his computer screen. Through the window there was the pale glow of street lights. He went up to it and looked out, not quite knowing what he hoped to see. A car waiting at the kerb perhaps, its headlights off and a dark figure inside. But nothing attracted his attention except, for a moment, the siren of an ambulance fading amongst the dark masses of buildings. He looked at the clock on the nearby church tower: it was five minutes past midnight.

He sat down again at the computer and the book. He examined the first illustration – the printer's mark on the title page, the snake with its tail in its mouth which Aristide Torchia had chosen as the symbol of his work. '*Sic luceat Lux*'. Snakes and devils, invocations and hidden meanings. He lifted his glass to drink a sarcastic toast to Torchia's memory. He must have been very brave, or very stupid. You paid a high price for that kind of thing in seventeenth-century Italy, even if it was printed '*cum superiorum privilegio veniaque*'.

But then Corso stopped and cursed out loud, looking into the dark corners of the room, for not having noticed before. 'With the privilege and licence of the superiors.' That wasn't possible.

Without taking his eyes from the page, he sat back in his chair and lit another of his crushed cigarettes. Spirals of smoke rose in the lamp light, a translucent grey curtain behind which the lines of print rippled.

'*Cum superiorum privilegio veniaque*' didn't make sense. Or else it was brilliantly subtle. The reference to the *imprimatur* couldn't possibly apply to a conventional authorization. The Catholic Church would never have allowed such a book in 1666 because its direct predecessor, the *Delomelanicon,* had been listed in the index of forbidden books for the previous hundred and fifty years. So Aristide Torchia wasn't referring to the permission to print granted by the

Church censors. Nor to a civil authority, the government of the republic of Venice. He must have had other superiors.

The telephone interrupted his thought. It was Flavio La Ponte. He wanted to tell Corso how he'd found, in with some books (he'd had to buy the whole lot, that was the deal), a collection of European tram tickets, 5,775 of them to be exact. All of them palindromic numbers, sorted by country in shoe boxes. He wasn't joking. The collector had just died and the family wanted to get rid of them. Maybe Corso knew someone who'd be interested. Naturally. La Ponte knew that apart from the tireless, and pathological, activity of collecting 5,775 palindromic tickets, it was completely pointless. Who would buy such a stupid collection? Yes, perhaps it was a good idea: the Transport Museum in London. The English and their perversions . . . Would Corso deal with the matter?

La Ponte was also worried about the Dumas chapter. He'd received two telephone calls, from a man and a woman who didn't identify themselves, asking about 'The Anjou Wine'. And it was strange because he hadn't mentioned the chapter to anyone and wasn't intending to until he had Corso's report. Corso told him of his conversation with Liana Taillefer, to whom he had revealed the identity of the new owner.

"She knew you because you used to go and see her late husband. Oh, and by the way," he remembered, "she wants a copy of the receipt."

La Ponte laughed at the other end of the line. There was no bloody receipt. Taillefer had sold it to him, and that was that. But if the lovely widow wanted to discuss the matter, he added laughing lewdly, he'd be delighted. Corso mentioned the possibility that before he died Taillefer might have told someone about the manuscript. But La Ponte didn't think so. Taillefer had been very insistent that the matter should be kept secret until he himself gave a sign. In the end he never gave any sign, unless hanging himself from the light fitting could be seen as one.

"It's as good a sign as any," said Corso.

La Ponte agreed, chuckling cynically. Then he asked about Corso's visit to Liana Taillefer. After a couple more lecherous comments La Ponte said goodbye. Corso hadn't mentioned the skirmish in Toledo. They agreed to meet the following day.

After he hung up, Corso went back to *The Nine Doors*. But his mind was on other things. He was drawn back to the Dumas manuscript.

Finally he went and got the file with the white and blue pages. He rubbed his painful hand and typed in the name of the DUMAS files. The computer screen began to flicker. He stopped at a file called BIO:

DUMAS DAVY DE LA PAILLETERIE, Alexandre. Born 24.7.1802. Died 5.12.1870. Son of Thomas Alexandre Dumas, general of the Republic. Author of 257 volumes of novels, memoirs and other stories. 25 volumes of plays. Mulatto on his father's side. His black blood gave him certain exotic features. Appearance: tall, powerful neck, curly hair, fleshy lips, long legs, physically strong. Character: bon viveur, fickle, overpowering, liar, unreliable, popular. He had 27 known mistresses, 2 legitimate children and 4 illegitimate. He earned several fortunes and squandered them on parties, travel, expensive wines and bunches of flowers. As he earned money from his writing he lost it all through his extravagant spending on his mistresses, friends and hangers-on who besieged his castle home on Montecristo. When he was forced to flee Paris it was to escape his creditors, not for political reasons like his friend Victor Hugo. Friends: Hugo, Lamartine, Michelet, Gérard de Nerval, Nodier, George Sand, Berlioz, Théophile Gautier, Alfred de Vigny and others. Enemies: Balzac, Badère and others.

None of this really got him anywhere. He felt he was stumbling around in the dark, surrounded by countless false, or useless clues. And yet, there had to be a link somewhere. With his good hand he typed DUMAS.NOV:

Novels by Alexandre Dumas that appeared in instalments:
1831: *Historical Scenes* (*Revue des Deux Mondes*). 1834: *Jacques I et Jacques II* (*Journal des Enfants*). 1835: *Elizabeth of Bavaria* (*Dumont*). 1836: *Murat* (*La Presse*). 1837: *Pascal Bruno* (*La Presse*). Story of a Tenor (*Gazette Musicale*). 1838: *Count Horatio* (*La Presse*). *Nero's Night* (*La Presse*). *The Arms Hall* (*Dumont*). *Captain Paul* (*Le Siècle*). 1839: *Jacques Ortis* (*Dumont*). *The Life and Adventures of John Davys* (*Revue de Paris*). *Captain Panphile* (*Dumont*). 1840: *The Fencing Master* (*Revue de Paris*). 1841: *Le Chevalier d'Harmental* (*Le Siècle*). 1843: *Sylvandire* (*La Presse*). *The Wedding Dress* (*La Mode*). *Albine* (*Revue de Paris*). *Ascanio* (*Le Siècle*). *Fernande* (*Revue de Paris*). *Amaury* (*La Presse*). 1844:

The Three Musketeers (*Le Siècle*). *Gabriel Lambert* (*La Chronique*). *The Regent's Daughter* (*Le Commerce*). *The Corsican Brothers* (*Démocratie Pacifique*). *The Count of Monte Cristo* (*Journal des Débats*). *Countess Bertha* (*Hetzel*). *Story of a Nutcracker* (*Hetzel*). *Queen Margot* (*La Presse*). 1845: *Nanon* (*La Patrie*). *Twenty Years After* (*Le Siècle*). *Le Chevalier de la Maison Rouge* (*Démocratie Pacifique*). *The Lady of Monsoreau* (*Le Constitutionnel*). *Madame de Condé* (*La Patrie*). 1846: *The Viscountess of Cambes* (*La Patrie*). *The Half-Brothers* (*Le Commerce*). *Joseph Balsam* (*La Presse*). *Pessac Abbey* (*La Patrie*). 1847: *The Forty-Five* (*Le Constitutionnel*). *Le Vicomte de Bragelonne* (*Le Siècle*). 1848: *The Queen's Necklace* (*La Presse*). 1849: *The Weddings of Father Olifus* (*Le Constitutionnel*). 1850: *God's Will* (*Evènement*). *The Black Tulip* (*Le Siècle*). *The Dove* (*Le Siècle*). *Angel Pitou* (*La Presse*). 1851: *Olympe de Clèves* (*Le Siècle*). 1852: *God and the Devil* (*Le Pays*). *The Comtesse de Charny* (*Cadot*). *Isaac Laquedem* (*Le Constitutionnel*). 1853: *The Shepherd of Ashbourn* (*Le Pays*). *Catherine Blum* (*Le Pays*). 1854: *The Life and Adventures of Catherine-Charlotte* (*Le Mousquetaire*). *The Brigand* (*Le Mousquetaire*). *The Mohicans of Paris* (*Le Mousquetaire*). *Captain Richard* (*Le Siècle*). *The Page of the Duke of Savoy* (*Le Constitutionnel*). 1856: *The Companions of Jehu* (*Journal pour Tous*). 1857: *The Last Saxon King* (*Le Monte-Cristo*). *The Wolf Leader* (*Le Siècle*). *The Wild Duck Shooter* (*Cadot*). *Black* (*Le Constitutionnel*). 1858: *The She-Wolves of Machecoul* (*Journal pour Tous*). *Memoirs of a Policeman* (*Le Siècle*). *The Palace of Ice* (*Le Monte-Cristo*). 1859: *The Frigate* (*Le Monte-Cristo*). *Ammalat-Beg* (*Moniteur Universel*). *Story of a Dungeon and a Little House* (*Revue Européenne*). *A Love Story* (*Le Monte-Cristo*). 1860: *Memoirs of Horatio* (*Le Siècle*). *Father La Ruine* (*Le Siècle*). *The Marchioness of Escoman* (*Le Constitutionnel*). *The Doctor of Java* (*Le Siècle*). *Jane* (*Le Siècle*). 1861: *A Night in Florence* (*Lévy-Hetzel*). 1862: *The Volunteer of '92* (*Le Monte-Cristo*). 1863: *The Saint Félice* (*La Presse*). 1864: *The Two Dianas* (*Lévy*). *Ivanhoe* (*Pub. du Siècle*). 1865: *Memoirs of a Favourite* (*Avenir National*). *The Count of Moret* (*Les Nouvelles*). 1866: *A Case of Conscience* (*Le Soleil*). *Parisians and Provincials* (*La Presse*). *The Count of Mazarra* (*Le Mousquetaire*). 1867: *The Whites and the Blues* (*Le Mousquetaire*). *The Prussian Terror* (*La Situation*). 1869: *Hector de Sainte-Hermine* (*Moniteur Universel*).

The Mysterious Physician (Le Siècle). The Marquis's Daughter (Le Siècle).

He smiled, wondering how much the late Enrique Taillefer would have paid to obtain all those titles. His glasses were misted, so he took them off and carefully cleaned the lenses. The lines on the computer were now blurred, as were other strange images he couldn't identify. With his glasses back on, the words on the screen became sharp again, but the images were still floating around, indistinct, in his mind, and without a key to give them any meaning. And yet Corso felt he was on the right path. The screen began to flicker again:

BAUDRY, editor of *Le Siècle*. Publishes *The Three Musketeers* between 14 March and 11 July 1844.

He took a look at the other files. According to his information, Dumas had had, at different periods of his literary life, fifty-two collaborators. Relations with a large number of them had ended stormily. But Corso was only interested in one of the names:

MAQUET, AUGUSTE-JULES. 1813–86. Collaborated with Alexandre Dumas on several plays and on 19 novels, including the most famous ones (*The Count of Monte Cristo, Le Chevalier de la Maison Rouge, The Black Tulip, The Queen's Necklace*) and, in particular, the cycle of *The Musketeers*. His collaboration with Dumas made him famous and wealthy. While Dumas died penniless, Maquet died a rich man at his castle in Saint-Mesme. None of his own works written without Dumas survives.

He looked at his biographical notes. There were some paragraphs taken from Dumas's *Memoirs*:

"We were the inventors, Hugo, Balzac, Soulie, De Musset and myself, of popular literature. We managed, for better or worse, to make a reputation for ourselves with that kind of writing, even though it was popular . . ."

". . . My imagination, confronted with reality, resembles a man who, visiting the ruins of an old building, must walk over the rubble, follow the passageways, bend down to go through doorways so as to reconstruct an approximate picture of the original building when it was full of life, when joy filled it with laughter and song, or when it echoed with sobs of sorrow."

Exasperated, Corso looked away from the screen. He was losing the feeling, it was disappearing into the corners of his memory before he could identify it. He stood up and paced the darkened room. Then he angled his lamp at a pile of books on the floor against the wall. He picked up two thick volumes: a modern edition of the *Memoirs* of Alexandre Dumas père. He went back to his desk and began to leaf through them until three photos caught his eye. In one of them, his African blood clearly visible in his curly hair and mulatto looks, Dumas was sitting smiling at Isabelle Constant who, Corso gathered from the caption, was fifteen when she became the novelist's mistress. The second photo showed an older Dumas, posing with his daughter Marie. Here, at the height of his fame, the father of the adventure serial sat, good-natured and placid, before the photographer. The third photo, Corso decided, was definitely the most amusing and significant. Dumas aged sixty-five, grey-haired but still tall and strong, his frock coat open to reveal a contented paunch, was embracing Adah Menken, one of his last mistresses. According to the text, "after the seances and sessions of black magic of which she was such a devotee, she liked to be photographed, scantily clad, with the great men in her life." In the photograph La Menken's legs, arms and neck were all bare which was scandalous for the time. The young woman, paying more attention to the camera than to the object of her embrace, was leaning her head on the old man's powerful right shoulder. As for him, his face showed the signs of a long life of dissipation, pleasure and parties. His smile, between the bloated cheeks of a bon viveur, was contented, ironic. And his expression for the photographer was teasing, crafty, seeking complicity. The fat old man with the shameless, passionate young girl who showed him off like a rare trophy: he, whose characters and stories had made so many women dream. It was as if old Dumas was asking for understanding, having given in to the girl's capricious wish to be photographed. After all, she was young and pretty, her skin soft and her mouth passionate, this girl that life had kept for him on the last lap of his journey, only three years before his death. The old devil.

Corso shut the book and yawned. His watch, an old chronometer that he often forgot to wind up, had stopped at a quarter past midnight. He went and opened the window and breathed in the cold night air. The street was still deserted.

It was all very strange, he thought, as he went back to his desk and turned off the computer. His eyes came to rest on the folder with

Dumas embraced by Adah Menken, one of his last lovers

the manuscript. He opened it mechanically and took another look at the fifteen pages covered in two different types of handwriting, eleven of them blue, four of them white. "*Après de nouvelles presque désespérées du roi* . . ." Upon almost desperate news from the king . . . In the pile of books he found a huge red tome, a facsimile edition – J. C. Lattès 1988 – containing the entire cycle of *The Musketeers* and *Monte Cristo* in the Le Vasseur edition with engravings, published shortly after Dumas's death. He found the chapter called 'The Anjou Wine' on page 144 and started to read, comparing it to the original manuscript. Except for a small error here or there, both texts were identical. In the book, the chapter was illustrated with two drawings by Maurice Leloir, engraved by Huyot. King Louis XIII arriving at the siege of La Rochelle with ten thousand men, with four horsemen at the head of his escort, holding their muskets, wearing the wide-brimmed hat and jacket of de Treville's company. Three of them are without doubt Athos, Porthos and Aramis. A moment later they will be meeting their friend d'Artagnan, still a simple cadet in Monsieur des Essarts's company of guards. The Gascon still doesn't know that the bottles of Anjou wine, a gift from his mortal enemy Milady, Richelieu's agent, are poisoned. She wants to avenge the insult done to her by d'Artagnan. He has passed himself off as the Comte de Wardes, slipped into her bed, and enjoyed a night of love that should have been the Count's. To make matters worse, d'Artagnan has by chance discovered Milady's terrible secret, the fleur-de-lis on her shoulder, the shameful mark branded on her by the executioner's iron. With such preliminaries, and given Milady's disposition, the contents of the second illustration are easy to guess: as d'Artagnan and his companions watch in astonishment, the manservant Fourreau expires in terrible agony after drinking the wine intended for his master. Sensitive to the magic of a text he hadn't read in twenty years, Corso came to the passage where the Musketeers and d'Artagnan are speaking about Milady:

" . . . Well," said d'Artagnan to Athos. "So you see, dear friend. It is a fight to the death."

Athos nodded.

"Yes, yes," he said. "I know. But do you think it's really her?"

"I am sure of it."

"Nevertheless, I confess I still have doubts."

"And the fleur-de-lis on her shoulder?"

"She is an Englishwoman who must have committed some crime in France, and who has been marked for her crime."

"Athos, that woman is your wife, I tell you," repeated d'Artagnan. "Do you not recall that both marks are identical?"

"Nevertheless, I would have sworn that the woman was dead, I hanged her very well."

This time it was d'Artagnan who shook his head.

"Well? What are we to do?" said the young man.

"We certainly can't go on like this, with a sword hanging eternally over our heads," said Athos. "We must find a way out of this situation."

"But how?"

"Listen, try to have a meeting with her and explain everything. Tell her: 'Peace or war! My word as a gentleman that I will never say or do anything against you. For your part, give me your solemn word to do nothing against me. Otherwise I will go to the Chancellor, the King, the executioner, I will incite the Court against you, I will denounce you as a marked woman, I will have you put on trial, and should you be acquitted, then upon my word as a gentleman, I will kill you myself, in any corner, as I would a rabid dog.'"

"I am delighted with this plan," said d'Artagnan.

Memories bring other memories in their wake. Corso tried to hold a fleeting, familiar image that had suddenly crossed his mind. He managed to capture it just before it faded, and once again it was the man in the black suit, the chauffeur of the Jaguar outside Liana Taillefer's house, at the wheel of the Mercedes in Toledo . . . The man with the scar. And it was Milady who had stirred his memory.

He thought it over, disconcerted. And suddenly the image became perfectly sharp. Milady, of course. Milady de Winter as d'Artagnan first sees her at the window of her carriage in the opening chapter of the novel, outside the inn at Meung. Milady in conversation with a stranger . . . Corso quickly turned the pages, searching for the passage. He found it easily:

. . . A man around forty to forty-five years of age, with black, piercing eyes, a pale complexion, a strongly pronounced nose, and a perfectly trimmed, black moustache . . .

Rochefort. The Cardinal's sinister agent and d'Artagnan's enemy, who has him beaten in the first chapter, steals the letter of recommendation to Monsieur de Treville and is indirectly responsible for the Gascon almost fighting duels with Athos, Porthos and Aramis . . . Following this somersault of his memory, Corso scratched his head, disconcerted by the unusual association of ideas and characters. What link was there between Milady's companion and the driver who tried to run him down in Toledo? And then there was the scar. The paragraph didn't mention a scar but he remembered clearly that Rochefort had always had a mark on his face. He turned more pages until he found the confirmation of this in chapter three, where d'Artagnan is recounting his adventure to Treville:

"Tell me," he replied, "did this gentleman have a faint scar on his temple?"

"Yes, the sort of mark that might have been made by a bullet grazing it . . ."

A faint scar on his temple. There was his confirmation, but as Corso remembered it the scar was *bigger*, and not on his temple, but on his cheek, like that of the chauffeur dressed in black. He went over it all until at last he let out a laugh. The picture was now complete, and in full colour: Lana Turner in *The Three Musketeers*, at her carriage window, beside a suitably sinister Rochefort, not pale as in Dumas's novel, but dark, with a plumed hat and a long scar – it was definite this time – cutting his right cheek from top to bottom. He remembered it as a film not a novel, and his exasperation at this both amused and irritated him. Bloody Hollywood.

Film scenes apart, he had at last managed to find some order to all of it, a common, if secret, thread, a tune composed of disparate, mysterious notes. Through the vague uneasiness that Corso had experienced since his visit to Taillefer's widow, he could now glimpse outlines, faces, an atmosphere and characters, half way between reality and fiction, and all linked in strange, as yet unclear manner. Dumas and a seventeenth-century book. The Devil and *The Three Musketeers*. Milady and the bonfires of the Inquisition . . . Although it was all more absurd than definite, more like a novel than real life.

He turned out the light and went to bed. But it took him some time to fall asleep because one image wouldn't leave his mind. It floated in the darkness before his open eyes. A distant landscape, that of his reading as a boy, filled with shadows which reappeared now twenty years later, materialized as ghosts that were so close he could almost feel them. The scar. Rochefort. The man from Meung. His Eminence's mercenary.

V

Remember

He was sitting just as he had left him, in front of the fireplace.

A. Christie. *The Murder of Roger Ackroyd*

This is the point at which I enter the stage for the second time. Corso came to me again, and he did so, I seem to remember, a few days before leaving for Portugal. As he told me later, by then he already suspected that the Dumas manuscript and Varo Borja's *Nine Doors* were only the tip of the iceberg. To understand it all he first needed to find out the other stories, all knotted together like the cord Enrique Taillefer used to hang himself. It wouldn't be easy, I told him, because in literature there are never any clear boundaries. Everything is dependent on everything else and one thing is superimposed on top of another. It all ends up as a complicated intertextual game, like a hall of mirrors or those Russian dolls. Establishing a specific fact or the precise source involves risks that only some of my very stupid or very confident colleagues would dare take. It would be like saying that you can see the influence of *Quo Vadis*, but not Suetonius or Apollonius of Rhodes, on Robert Graves. As for me, all I know is that I know nothing. And when I want to know something, I look it up in books – their memory never fails.

"Count Rochefort is one of the most important secondary characters in *The Three Musketeers*," I explained to Corso when he came to see me for the second time. "He is the Cardinal's agent and a friend of Milady's, and the first enemy that d'Artagnan makes. And I can pinpoint the exact date: the first Monday of April 1625, in Meung-sur-Loire . . . I refer to the fictional Rochefort, of course, although a similar character did exist. Gatien de Courtilz described him, in the supposed *Memoirs* of the real d'Artagnan, with the name of

Rosnas . . . But the Rochefort with the scar didn't exist in real life. Dumas took the character from another book, the *Mémoires de MLCDR (Monsieur le Comte de Rochefort)*, possibly apocryphal and also attributed to Courtilz . . . Some say that they could refer to Henri Louis d'Aloigny, Marquis de Rochefort, born around 1625, but that would be stretching things."

I looked out at the lights of the evening traffic in the avenues beyond the window of the café where I meet up with my literary friends. A few of them were sitting with us round a table covered in newspapers, cups and smoking ashtrays – a couple of writers, a painter down on his luck, a lady journalist on the up, a stage actor and four or five students, the kind who sit in a corner and don't open their mouths, watching you as if you were God. Corso was sitting amongst them, still in his coat. He leant against the window, drank gin and occasionally took notes.

"To be sure," I added, "the reader who goes through the sixty-seven chapters of *The Three Musketeers* waiting for a duel between Rochefort and d'Artagnan, is in for a disappointment. Dumas settles the matter in three lines, and is rather underhand about it. Because when we next meet the character in *Twenty Years After*, he and d'Artagnan have fought three times, and Rochefort bears as many scars as a result. Nevertheless, there no longer remains any hatred between them. Instead they have the twisted respect for each other that is only possible between two old enemies. Once again fate has decreed that they fight on different sides, but now friendly, complicit; two gentlemen who have known each other for twenty years. Rochefort falls out of favour with Mazarin, breaks out of the Bastille and helps the Duke of Beaufort to escape. He conspires in the Fronde rebellion and dies in the arms of d'Artagnan, who has stabbed him with his sword, failing to recognize him in all the confusion . . . 'You were my fate,' he more or less says to the Gascon. 'I recovered from three of your sword wounds, but I will not recover from the fourth.' And he dies. 'I have just killed an old friend,' d'Artagnan later tells Porthos . . . This is the only epitaph Richelieu's former agent is given."

My words provoked a lively discussion with several factions. The actor hadn't taken his eyes off the lady journalist all afternoon. He was an old heart-throb who'd played Monte Cristo in a television series and, encouraged by the painter and the two writers, he launched into a brilliant account of his recollections of the characters. In this way we moved from Dumas to Zevaco and Paul Féval, and ended by once again confirming Sabatini's indisputable influence on Salgari. I seem to recall that somebody timidly mentioned Jules Verne, but was shouted down by all those present. Verne's cold, soulless heroes had no place in a discussion of passionate tales of cloak and dagger.

As for the journalist, one of those fashionable young ladies with a column in a leading Sunday newspaper, her literary memory began with Milan Kundera. So she remained in a state of cautious expectation and agreed with relief whenever a title, anecdote or character (the Black Swan, Yañez, Nevers's sword wound) stirred some memory of a film glimpsed on TV. Meanwhile, Corso, with a hunter's calm patience, looked steadily at me over his glass of gin, waiting for a chance to return the conversation to the original subject. And he succeeded, making the most of an awkward silence that fell when the journalist said that, anyway, she found these adventure stories rather lightweight, I mean kind of superficial, don't you think?

Corso chewed the end of his pencil.

"And how do you see Rochefort's role in history, Mr Balkan?" he asked.

They all looked at me, in particular the students, two of them girls. I don't know why, but in certain circles I'm considered a high priest of letters and every time I open my mouth people expect to hear principles of faith. An article of mine, in the appropriate literary reviews, can make or break a writer who's starting out. Absurd, certainly, but that's life. Think of the last Nobel Prize-winner, the author of *I, Onan. In Search of Myself* and the ultra-successful *Oui, c'est moi*. It was I who made him a household name fifteen years ago, with a page and a half in *Le Monde* on April Fools Day. I'll never forgive myself, but that's how things work.

"At first, Rochefort is the enemy," I said. "He symbolizes the hidden forces, darkness . . . He is the agent of the satanic conspiracy surrounding d'Artagnan and his friends, the Cardinal's plot growing in the shadows, threatening their lives . . ."

I saw one of the students smile, but I couldn't tell if her absorbed, slightly mocking expression, was a result of my comments or of private thoughts which had nothing to do with the discussion. I was surprised because, as I've said, students tend to listen to me with the awe of an editor of the *Osservatore Romano* getting the exclusive rights to one of the Pope's encyclicals. So it made me look at her with interest. Although she'd already caught my eye at the beginning, when she joined us, because of her unsettling green eyes. She was wearing a blue duffle coat and carried a pile of books under her arm. Her chestnut hair was cut very short like a boy's. Now she sat at a slight distance, not quite part of the group. There are always a few young people at our table, literature students that I invite for a coffee. But this girl had never attended before. It was impossible to forget her eyes. In contrast to her tanned face their colour was so light it was almost transparent. A slender, supple girl, one could tell she spent a lot of time outdoors. Under her jeans her long legs were no doubt also tanned. And I retained one other thing about her: she wore neither rings, watch nor earrings. Her ears weren't pierced.

" . . . Rochefort is also the man glimpsed, never caught," I went on, getting back to the subject. "A mysterious mask with a scar. He stands for paradox and d'Artagnan's powerlessness. D'Artagnan is always in pursuit but he never quite catches up with him. He tries to kill him but only manages to do so by mistake twenty years later. By then he is no longer an adversary but a friend."

"Your d'Artagnan's a bit jinxed," said one of my circle, the older of the two writers. He'd only sold five hundred copies of his last novel, but he earned a fortune writing crime stories under the perverse pseudonym of Emilia Forster. I looked at him gratefully, pleased by his opportune remark.

"Absolutely. The love of his life gets poisoned. Despite all his exploits and services to the crown of France, he spends twenty years as an obscure lieutenant in the musketeers. And in the last lines of *The Vicomte de Bragelonne*, when he is finally awarded the marshal's baton, which has taken him four volumes and four hundred and twenty-five chapters to achieve, he is killed by a Dutch bullet."

"Like the real d'Artagnan," said the actor, who had managed to place his hand on the fashionable lady columnist's thigh.

I took a sip of coffee before agreeing. Corso was staring at me intently.

"There are three d'Artagnans," I explained. "Of the first, Charles de Batz Castlemore, we know that he died on 23 June 1673, from a shot in the throat during the siege of Maastricht, as reported in the *Gazette de France* at the time. Half his men fell with him . . . Apart from this posthumous detail, in life he was only slightly more fortunate than his fictional namesake."

"Was he a Gascon too?"

"Yes, from Lupiac. The village still exists, and he is commemorated by a stone plaque there: 'D'Artagnan, whose real name was Charles de Batz, was born here around 1615. He died in the siege of Maastricht in 1673.'"

"It doesn't quite fit historically," said Corso, looking at his notes. "According to Dumas, d'Artagnan was eighteen at the start of the novel, around 1625. But at that time the real d'Artagnan would only have been ten years old." He smiled like a clever, sceptical little rabbit. "Too young to handle a sword."

I agreed. "Yes. Dumas altered things so d'Artagnan could take part in the adventure of the diamond tags under Richelieu and Louis XIII. Charles de Batz must have arrived in Paris very young: he was listed amongst the guards of Monsieur des Essarts's company in documents on the siege of Arras in 1640, and two years later in the Roussillon campaign. But he never served as a musketeer under Richelieu because he only joined the elite regiment after Louis XIII's death. His real protector was Cardinal Jules Mazarin. There is indeed a jump of ten or fifteen years between the two d'Artagnans. But following the success of *The Three Musketeers*, Dumas extended the action to cover almost forty years of France's history. In later volumes he adjusted his story to coincide better with real events."

"Which events have been verified? I mean historical events in which the real d'Artagnan was involved?"

"Quite a few. His name appears in Mazarin's letters and in the correspondence of the Ministry of War. Like the fictional hero, he was the Cardinal's agent during the Fronde rebellion, with important responsibilities at the court of Louis XIV. He was even entrusted with the delicate matter of detaining and escorting the finance minister Fouquet. All these events were confirmed in the letters of Madame de Sévigné. And he could even have met the painter Velázquez on the Isle of Pheasants when he accompanied Louis XIV on his journey to meet his bride-to-be, Maria Theresa of Austria . . ."

"He was quite a man of the Court, then. Very different from Dumas's swashbuckling d'Artagnan."

I raised my hand, in defence of Dumas's respect for the facts.

"Don't be fooled. Charles de Batz, or d'Artagnan, went on fighting to the end of his life. He served under Turenne in Flanders, and in 1657 was appointed lieutenant in the grey musketeers, which was equivalent to commander. Ten years later he became a captain in the musketeers and fought in Flanders, a post equivalent to cavalry general . . ."

Corso was squinting behind his glasses.

"Excuse me." He leant across the table towards me, pencil in hand. He'd been writing down a name or date. "In which year did this happen?"

"His promotion to general? 1667. Why did that draw your attention?"

He was showing his incisors as he bit his lower lip. But only for an instant.

"No reason." As he spoke his face regained its impassivity. "That same year a certain person was burned at the stake in Rome. A strange coincidence . . ." Now he was staring at me blankly. "Does the name Aristide Torchia mean anything to you?"

I tried to remember. I had no idea.

"Not a thing," I answered. "Does he have anything to do with Dumas?"

He hesitated.

"No," he said at last, although he didn't seem very convinced. "I don't think so. But please go on. You were talking about the real d'Artagnan in Flanders."

"He died at Maastricht, as I've said, at the head of his men. A heroic death. The English and the French were besieging the town. They needed to cross a dangerous pass and d'Artagnan offered to go first out of courtesy to his allies . . . A musket bullet tore through his jugular."

"He never got to be marshal, then."

"No. Alexandre Dumas deserves exclusive credit for giving the fictional d'Artagnan what a miserly Louis XIV refused his flesh and blood predecessor . . . There are a couple of interesting books on the subject. You can take down the titles if you want. One is by Charles Samaran, *D'Artagnan, capitaine des mousquetaires du roi, histoire véridique d'un héros de roman*, published in 1912. The other one is *Le vrai d'Artagnan*, written by the Duke of Montesquieu-Fezensac, a direct descendant of the real d'Artagnan. Published in 1963, I think."

None of this information was obviously related to the Dumas manuscript, but Corso noted it down as if his life depended on it. Occasionally he looked up from his notepad and glanced at me inquisitively through his crooked glasses. Or he put his head to one side as if he were no longer listening and was absorbed in his own thoughts. At that time, I myself knew all the details regarding 'The Anjou Wine', even certain keys to the mystery of which Corso was unaware. But

I had no idea of the complex implications that *The Nine Doors* would have for this story. Despite his logical turn of mind, Corso was already beginning to glimpse sinister links between the facts at his disposal, and – how shall I put it – the literary source of those facts. It may all appear rather confused, but we must remember that this was how it seemed to Corso at the time. And although I am narrating this story after the resolution of the momentous events to come, the very nature of the loop – think of Escher's paintings, or the work of that old joker, Bach – forces us to return continually to the beginning and limit ourselves to the narrow confines of Corso's knowledge. The rule is to know and keep silent. Even if there is foul play, without rules there is no game.

"OK," said Corso once he'd written down the recommended titles. "That's the first d'Artagnan, the real one. And Dumas's fictional character is the third one. I'm assuming the link between them is the book by Gatien de Courtilz you showed me the other day, the *Mémoires de M. d'Artagnan*."

"Correct. We can call him the missing link, the least famous of the three. A Gascon who is an intermediary, a literary and a real character all at the same time. The very same one that Dumas used to create his character . . . The writer Gatien de Courtilz de Sandras was a contemporary of d'Artagnan's. He recognized the novelesque potential of the character and set to work. A century and a half later, Dumas found out about the book during a trip to Marseilles. His landlord had a brother who ran the municipal library. Apparently the brother showed him the book, edited in Cologne in 1700. Dumas saw that he could make use of the story and asked to borrow the book. He never returned it."

"What do we know about this predecessor of Dumas, Gatien de Courtilz?"

"Quite a lot. Partly because he had a sizeable police file. He was born in 1644 or 1647 and was a musketeer, a bugler in the Royal-Etranger, which was a type of foreign legion of the time, and captain of the cavalry regiment of Beaupré-Choiseul. At the end of the war against Holland, in which d'Artagnan was killed, Courtilz remained in Holland and traded his sword for a pen. He wrote biographies, historical monographs, more or less apocryphal memoirs, shocking tales of gossip and intrigue at the French Court . . . This got him into trouble. The *Mémoires de M. d'Artagnan* was astonishingly successful: five editions in ten years. But they displeased Louis XIV. He disliked the irreverent tone used to recount certain details regarding the royal family and its entourage. As a result Courtilz was arrested on his return to France and held in the Bastille at His Majesty's pleasure until shortly before his death."

The actor made the most of my pause to slip in, quite irrelevantly, a quotation from "The sun has set in Flanders" by Marquina: "Our captain," he recited, "/gravely wounded led us/ sparing no effort though in his final agony./Sirs, what a captain/he was indeed that day . . ." Or something like that. It was a shameless attempt to shine in front of the lady journalist, whose thigh he now held with a proprietorial air. The others, in particular the novelist who wrote under the pseudonym of Emilia Forster, were looking at him with envy or barely concealed resentment.

After a polite silence, Corso decided to hand control of the situation back to me.

"How much does Dumas's d'Artagnan owe to Courtilz?"

"A great deal. Although in *Twenty Years After* and in *Bragelonne* he used other sources, the basic story of *The Three Musketeers* is to be found in Courtilz. Dumas applied his genius to it and gave it breadth, but it contained a rough outline of all the elements of the story: d'Artagnan's father granting his blessing, the letter to Treville, the challenge to the musketeers, who incidentally were brothers in the first draft . . . Milady also appears. And the two d'Artagnans were like two peas in a pod. Courtilz's character was rather more cynical, more miserly and less trustworthy. But they're one and the same."

Corso leaned forward slightly.

"Earlier you said that Rochefort stands for the evil plot surrounding d'Artagnan and his friends . . . But Rochefort is just a henchman."

"Indeed. In the pay of His Eminence Armand Jean du Plessis, Cardinal Richelieu . . ."

"The evil one," said Corso.

"The spirit of evil," commented the actor, determined to butt in. Impressed by our foray into the subject of serials that afternoon, the students were taking notes or listening open-mouthed. Only the girl with the green eyes remained impassive, slightly apart, as if she had only dropped in by chance.

"For Dumas," I went on, returning to the subject, "at least in the first part of *The Musketeers* cycle, Richelieu provided the character essential to all romantic adventure and mystery stories: the powerful enemy lurking in the shadows, the embodiment of Evil. For the history of France, Richelieu was a great man. But in *The Musketeers* he is only rehabilitated twenty years later. Shrewd Dumas fitted in with reality without diminishing the novel's interest. He'd already found another villain: Mazarin. This correction, even as voiced by d'Artagnan and his companions when they praise the nobility of their former enemy, is morally questionable. For Dumas it was a convenient act of contrition . . . Nevertheless, in the first volume of the cycle, whether plotting Buckingham's murder, Anne of Austria's downfall, or giving carte blanche to the sinister Milady, Cardinal Richelieu is the embodiment of the perfect villain. His Eminence is to d'Artagnan what Prince Gonzaga was to Lagardère, or Professor Moriarty to Sherlock Holmes. A mysterious, demonic presence . . ."

Corso seemed about to interrupt me, which I thought odd. I was getting to know him and typically he wouldn't interrupt until the other person had given up all his information, when every last detail had been squeezed out.

"You've used the word *demonic* twice," he said looking over his notes. "And both times referring to Richelieu . . . Was the Cardinal a devotee of the occult?"

His words had a strange effect. The young girl had turned to look curiously at Corso. He was looking at me, and I was watching the girl. He was waiting for my answer, unaware of this strange triangle.

"Richelieu was keenly interested in many things," I explained. "In addition to turning France into a great power, he had time to collect pictures, carpets, porcelain and statues. He was also an important bookcollector. He bound his books in calf skin and red morocco leather . . ."

" . . . And had weapons of silver and three red angles on his coat of arms." Corso gestured impatiently. All this information was trivial and he didn't need me to tell him about it. "There's a very well-known Richelieu catalogue."

"The catalogue is incomplete because the collection was broken up. Parts of it are now kept in the national library of France, the Mazarin library and the Sorbonne, while other books are in private hands. He owned Hebrew and Syrian manuscripts, notable works on mathematics, medicine, theology, law and history . . . And you were right. Scholars were most surprised to find many ancient texts on the occult, from the Cabbala to black magic."

Corso swallowed without taking his eyes off mine. He seemed tense – a bowstring about to snap.

"Any book in particular?"

I shook my head before I answered. His insistence intrigued me. The girl was listening attentively, but it was apparent that she was no longer directing her attention at me.

I excused myself. "My information on Richelieu as a character in a serial doesn't go that far."

"What about Dumas? Was he interested in the occult too?"

Here I was emphatic:

"No. Dumas was a bon viveur who did everything out in the open, to the great enjoyment and shock of all those around him. He was also somewhat superstitious. He believed in the evil eye, he wore an amulet on his watch chain and he'd have his fortune told by Madame Desbarolles. But I don't see him practising black magic in the back room. He wasn't even a Mason, as he confesses in *The Century of Louis XV* . . . He had debts and he was hounded by his publishers and his creditors – he was too busy to go round wasting his time on such things. Perhaps at one time, when researching one of his characters, he studied the subject, but never in much depth. I believe he drew all the Masonic practices described in *Joseph Balsam* and in *The Mohicans of Paris* directly from Clavel's *Picturesque History of Freemasonry.*"

"What about Adah Menken?"

I looked at Corso with genuine respect. This was a real expert's question.

"That was different. Adah-Isaacs Menken, his last lover, was an American actress. During the Exhibition of 1867, while attending a performance of *The Pirates of the Savannah*, Dumas noticed a pretty young woman on stage who had to grab hold of a galloping horse. The girl embraced the novelist as he left the theatre and told him bluntly that she had read all his books and was prepared to go to bed with him straight away. Old Dumas needed a great deal less than that to become infatuated with a woman, so he accepted her tribute. She claimed to have been the wife of a millionaire, a king's lover, the general of a republic . . . Really she was a Portuguese Jew born in America and the mistress of a strange man, a mixture of pimp and boxer. Her relationship with Dumas caused a great deal of scandal because Menken liked to be photographed scantily clad and she frequented number 107 Rue Malesherbes, Dumas's last house in Paris. She died from peritonitis after falling from a horse, aged thirty-one."

"Was she keen on black magic?"

"So they say. She liked strange ceremonies where she'd dress up in a tunic, burn incense and make offerings to the Prince of Darkness . . . Sometimes she'd claim to be possessed by Satan, with various connotations that today we might describe as pornographic. I'm sure old Dumas never believed a word of it, but he must have enjoyed the whole performance. It seems that when Menken was possessed by the Devil she was very hot in bed."

There was laughter round the table. I even allowed myself a slight smile, but the girl and Corso remained serious. She seemed to be thinking, her light-coloured eyes intent on Corso while he nodded slowly, though he now looked distracted and distant. He was looking through the window at the streets and he seemed to be searching in the night, in the silent flow of car lights reflected in his glasses, for the lost word, the key to uniting all these different stories which floated like dead leaves on the dark waters of time.

I must now once more move into the background, as the near-omniscient narrator of Lucas Corso's adventures. In this way, with the information Corso later confided to me, the subsequent tragic events can be put into some sort of order. So we now come to the moment when, returning home, he sees that the concierge has just swept the hallway and is about to leave. He passes him as he is bringing the dustbins up from the basement.

"They came to fix your TV this afternoon, Mr Corso."

Corso had read enough books and seen enough films to know what that meant. So he couldn't help laughing, much to the concierge's astonishment.

"I haven't had a television for ages."

The concierge let out a stream of confused apologies but Corso barely paid attention. It was all beginning to seem wonderfully predictable. Since this was a question of books, he had to approach the problem as a lucid, critical reader not as the hero of a cheap novelette, which was what somebody was trying to make of him. Nor did he have another option. And, after all, he was naturally cool and sceptical. He wasn't likely to break out into a sweat and moan, "Woe is me!"

"I hope I haven't done anything wrong, Mr Corso."

"Not at all. The repair man was dark, wasn't he? With a moustache and a scar on his face?"

"Exactly."

"Don't worry. He's a friend of mine. A bit of a joker."

The concierge sighed with relief.

"That's a weight off my mind, Mr Corso."

Corso wasn't worried about *The Nine Doors* or the Dumas manuscript. When he wasn't carrying them with him in his canvas bag he left them for safekeeping at Makarova's bar. This was the safest place for any of his things. So he climbed the stairs calmly, trying to picture the coming scene. By now he had become what some refer to as a second-level reader, and he would have been disappointed had he been met by too stereotypical a scene. He was relieved when he opened the door. There were no papers strewn on the floor, no turned-out drawers. Not even any armchairs slashed with knives. It was all tidy, just as he'd left it in the early afternoon.

He went to his desk. The boxes of floppy disks were in their place, the papers and documents in their trays just as he remembered them. The man with the scar, Rochefort or whoever the hell he was, was certainly efficient. But there are limits to everything. When he switched on the computer Corso smiled triumphantly.

```
DAGMAR PC 555 K (S1) ELECTRONIC PLC
LAST USED AT 19.35/THU/21/3
A>ECHO OFF
A>
```

Last used at 19.35 that day, the screen stated. But he hadn't touched the computer in the last twenty-four hours. At 19.35 he was with us round the table at the café, while the man with the scar was lying his way into Corso's flat.

He found something else, which he hadn't noticed at first, by the telephone. It hadn't been left there by chance, or due to carelessness on the part of the mysterious visitor. In the ashtray, amongst the butts left by Corso himself, he found a fresh one which wasn't his. It was a Havana cigar almost completely burnt down, but the band was intact. He held it up by the tip. He couldn't believe it. Then, gradually, as he understood its meaning, he laughed, showing his eye-teeth like a malicious, angry wolf.

The brand was Montecristo. Naturally.

Flavio La Ponte had had a visitor too. The plumber in his case.

"It's not bloody funny," he said by way of a greeting. He waited for Makarova to serve the gin and then emptied the contents of a small Cellophane packet on to the counter. The cigar end was identical, and the band was also intact.

"Edmundo Dantés strikes again," said Corso.

La Ponte couldn't get into the spirit of the thing.

"Well, he smokes expensive cigars, the bastard." His hand was trembling and he spilt some gin down his curly blond beard. "I found it on my bedside table."

Corso teased him.

"You should take things more calmly, Flavio. You've got to be hard." He patted him on the shoulder. "Remember the Nantucket Harpooneers' Club."

La Ponte shook his hand, frowning.

"I was hard, until I was exactly eight years old. Then I came to understand the benefits of survival. After that I got a bit softer."

Between gulps of gin Corso quoted Shakespeare. A coward dies a thousand deaths but the brave man and so on . . . But La Ponte wasn't about to be reassured by quotations. At least not by that type.

"I'm not scared really," he said thoughtfully, looking down. "What worries me is losing things . . . like money. Or my incredible sexual powers. Or my life."

These were weighty arguments and Corso had to admit that any possible developments might turn out to be slightly uncomfortable. La Ponte added that there had been other clues: strange clients wanting to purchase the Dumas manuscript at any price, mysterious phone calls during the night . . .

Corso sat up, interested.

"You're getting calls in the middle of the night?"

"Yes, but they don't say anything. They just stay quiet for a bit and then hang up."

While La Ponte was recounting his misfortunes, Corso felt the canvas bag he had retrieved moments earlier. Makarova had kept it there all day, under the counter, between boxes of bottles and barrels of beer.

"I don't know what to do," ended La Ponte tragically.

"Why don't you sell the manuscript and have done with it? Things are getting out of hand."

La Ponte shook his head and ordered another gin. A double.

"I promised Enrique Taillefer that the manuscript would go on public sale."

"Taillefer's dead. And anyway you've never kept a promise in your life."

La Ponte agreed gloomily, as if he didn't want to be reminded. But then he suddenly brightened. A slightly dazed expression showed through his beard. If one really tried one could take it for a smile.

"By the way, guess who called."

"Milady."

"Almost. Liana Taillefer."

Corso looked at his friend wearily. Then he picked up his glass of gin and emptied it in one long gulp.

"You know what, Flavio?" he said at last, wiping his mouth with the back of his hand. "Sometimes it seems that I've read this book before."

La Ponte was frowning again.

"She wants 'The Anjou Wine' back," he explained. "Just as it is, without authentication or anything . . ." He took a drink and then smiled uncertainly at Corso. "Strange, isn't it, this sudden interest?"

"What did you tell her?"

La Ponte raised his eyebrows.

"That it wasn't in my control. You have the manuscript and I've signed a contract with you."

"That's a lie. We haven't signed anything."

"Of course it's a lie. But this way I lumber you with everything if things get nasty. And it doesn't mean I can't consider any offers. I'm going to have dinner with the lovely widow one evening. To discuss business. I'm the daring harpooneer."

"You're not a harpooneer. You're a dirty, lying bastard."

"Yes. England made me, as that pious old goody-goody Graham Greene would have said. At school my nickname was *Wasn't-me* . . . Haven't I ever told you how I passed maths?" He raised his eyebrows again, tenderly nostalgic at the memory. "I'm a born liar."

"Well, be careful with Liana Taillefer."

"Why?" La Ponte was admiring himself in the bar mirror. He smiled lewdly. "I've had the hots for that woman ever since I started taking serials over to her husband. She's got a lot of class."

"Yes," admitted Corso, "a lot of middle class."

"What have you got against her?"

"There's something funny going on."

"That's fine by me, if it involves a beautiful blonde."

Corso was tapping his finger against the knot of his tie.

"Listen, idiot. In mystery stories the friend always dies. Don't you see? This is a mystery story and you're my friend." He winked at him for emphasis. "So you're going to get it."

Obstinately clinging to his dreams of the widow, La Ponte wouldn't be intimidated.

"Oh come on. I've never hit the jackpot before. Anyway I told you where I intend to take the bullet: in the shoulder."

"I'm serious. Taillefer's dead."

"He committed suicide."

"Who knows? More people could die."

"Well, you go and die, you bastard, ruining my fun."

The rest of the evening consisted of variations on the same theme. They left after five or six more drinks and agreed to speak on the phone once Corso got to Portugal. La Ponte, rather unsteady on his feet, left without paying, but he did give Corso Rochefort's cigar butt. Now you've got a pair, he told him.

VI
Of Apocrypha and Interpolations

Chance? Permit me to laugh, by God. That is an explanation that would only satisfy an imbecile.

M. Zevaco: *Los Pardellanes*

CENIZA BROS.
BOOKBINDING
AND RESTORATION

The wooden sign hung in a window thick with dust. It was cracked and faded with age and damp. The Ceniza brothers' workshop was on the mezzanine floor of an old four-storey building, shored up at the back, in a shady street in the old quarter of Madrid.

Lucas Corso rang the bell twice, but nobody answered. He looked at his watch, and leant against the wall, preparing himself for a wait. He knew the habits of Pedro and Pablo Ceniza well. At that hour they would be a few streets away, at the marble counter of the bar La Taurina, draining half a litre of wine for their breakfast and discussing books and bullfighting. Both grumpy bachelors and fond of their drink, they were inseparable.

They arrived ten minutes later, side by side, their grey overalls floating like shrouds on their skinny frames. Stooping from a lifetime spent hunched over their press and stamping tools, stitching pages together and gilding leather. They were both under fifty, but one could easily have believed they were ten years older. Their cheeks were sunken, their hands and eyes were worn out by their painstaking craft, and their skin was faded, as if the parchment they worked with had transmitted its pale, cold quality to them. The resemblance between the two brothers was extraordinary. They had the same large nose, identical ears stuck to their skulls and sparse hair combed straight back. The only noticeable differences between them were that Pablo, the younger of the two, was taller and quieter. His brother Pedro was frequently racked by the

97

hoarse rattling cough of a heavy smoker and his hands shook as he lit one cigarette after another.

"It's been a long time, Mr Corso. How nice to see you."

They led him up stairs that were worn with use, to a door that creaked as it opened, and switched on the light to reveal their motley workshop. An ancient printing press presided. Next to this a zinc-topped table was covered with tools, half-stitched or already backed gatherings, guillotines, dyed skins, bottles of glue, tooled designs and other equipment. There were books everywhere: large piles of them, bound in morocco, shagreen or vellum, packets of them ready for dispatch or only half-prepared, books without boards or with limp covers. Ancient tomes damaged by worms or damp sat waiting to be restored on benches and shelves. It smelt of paper, glue and new leather. Corso breathed it in with pleasure. Then he took the book out of his bag and laid it on the table.

"I'd like your opinion on this."

This wasn't the first time. Slowly, even cautiously, Pedro and Pablo Ceniza moved closer. As usual, the older of the two brothers spoke first.

"*The Nine Doors . . .*" He touched the book without moving it. His bony, nicotine-stained fingers seemed to be stroking living skin. "Beautiful. A very valuable book."

His eyes were grey, like a mouse. Grey overalls, grey hair, grey eyes, just like his surname.* He looked at it greedily.

"Have you ever seen it before?"

"Yes. Less than a year ago when Claymore asked us to clean twenty books from the library of Mr Gualterio Terral."

"What condition was it in when you got it?"

"Excellent. Mr Terral knew how to look after his books. Almost all of them came to us in good condition, except for a Teixeira which we had to do quite a bit of work on. The rest, including this one, only needed some cleaning."

"It's a forgery," said Corso bluntly. "Or so I'm told."

The two brothers looked at each other.

"Forgeries . . ." muttered the older of the two grumpily. "People speak too lightly of forged books."

"Much too lightly," echoed his brother.

"Even you, Mr Corso. And that comes as a surprise. It isn't

*In Spanish *ceniza* means 'ash'.

98

worth forging a book, it's too much effort to be profitable: I mean a high-quality forgery, not a facsimile for fooling gullible ignoramuses."

Corso made a gesture as if pleading for clemency.

"I didn't say that the *entire* book was a forgery, only part of it. Pages from complete copies can be interpolated into books that have one or several pages missing."

"Of course, that's a basic trick of the trade. But adding a photocopy or facsimile doesn't give the same results as completing a book with missing pages following . . ." He half-turned towards his brother, but still looked at Corso. "Tell him, Pablo."

"Following all the rules of our art," added the younger Ceniza.

Corso gave them a conspiratorial look. A rabbit sharing half a carrot.

"That could be the case with this book."

"Who says so?"

"The owner. Who isn't a gullible ignoramus, by the way."

Pedro Ceniza shrugged his narrow shoulders and lit a cigarette with the previous one. As he took his first drag he was shaken by a dry cough. But he carried on smoking, unperturbed.

"Have you had access to an authentic copy, to compare them?"

"No, but I soon will. That's why I want your opinion first."

"It's a valuable book, and ours is not an exact science." He turned again towards his brother. "Isn't that so, Pablo?"

"It's an art," insisted his brother.

"Yes. We wouldn't want to disappoint you, Mr Corso."

"I'm sure you won't. You know what you're talking about. After all, you were able to forge a *Speculum Vitæ* from the only known copy, and have it listed as an original in one of the best catalogues in Europe."

They both smiled sourly at exactly the same time. Si and Am, thought Corso, a cunning pair of cats who've just been stroked.

"It was never proved to be our work," said Pedro Ceniza at last. He was rubbing his hands, looking at the book out of the corner of his eye.

"No, never," repeated his brother sadly. They seemed sorry not to have gone to prison in return for public recognition.

"True," admitted Corso. "Nor was there any proof in the case of the Chaucer, allegedly bound by Marius Michel, listed in the catalogue for the Manoukian collection. Or for that copy of Baron Bielke's *Polyglot Bible* with three missing pages you replaced so perfectly that even today experts don't dispute its authenticity . . ."

Pedro Ceniza lifted his yellowed hand, with its long nails.

"I'd like to deal with a couple of points in greater detail, Mr Corso. It's one thing to forge books for profit, and quite another to do it out of love for one's art, creating something for the satisfaction provided by that very act of creation, or, as in most cases, of re-creation . . ." The bookbinder blinked a few times and then smiled mischievously. His small, mouse-like eyes shone as he looked at *The Nine Doors* again. "Although I don't recall having had a hand in the works you've just described as admirable, and I'm sure my brother doesn't either."

"I called them perfect."

"Did you? Well, never mind." He put his cigarette in his mouth and sucked in his cheeks as he took a long drag. "But whoever the person, or persons, responsible, you can be sure that he, or they, obtained a great deal of enjoyment out of it, a degree of personal satisfaction that money can't buy . . ."

"*Sine pecunia*," added his brother.

Pedro Ceniza blew cigarette smoke through his nose and half-open mouth and recalled:

"Let's take the *Speculum*, for instance, which the Sorbonne bought in the belief that it was authentic. The paper, typography, printing and binding alone must have cost those you call forgers five times more than any profit they might have made. People just don't understand . . . What would be more satisfying to a painter with as much talent as Velázquez and the skill to imitate his works: making money or seeing one of his own paintings hanging in the Prado, between *Las Meninas* and *Vulcan's Forge*?"

Corso agreed. For eight years, the Ceniza brothers' *Speculum* had been one of the most valuable books owned by the University of Paris. It was discovered to be a forgery not by experts, but due to a chance indiscretion by a go-between.

"Do the police still bother you?"

"Rarely. You must remember that the business of the Sorbonne erupted in France between the buyer and the intermediaries. True, our name was linked to the affair but nothing was ever proved." Pedro Ceniza smiled his crooked smile again, and sounded sorry that there had been no proof. "We have a good relationship with the police. They even come to see us sometimes when they need to identify a stolen book." He waved his cigarette in his brother's direction. "There's no one as good as Pablo when it comes to erasing traces of library stamps, or removing bookplates and marks of origin. But sometimes they want him to work his way backwards through the process. You know how it is: live and let live."

"What do you think of *The Nine Doors*?"

The older Ceniza looked at his brother, then at the book. He shook his head.

"Nothing drew our attention while we were working on it. The paper and ink are as they should be. Even at first glance, you notice that sort of thing."

"We notice them," specified his brother.

"What's your opinion now?"

Pedro Ceniza took a last puff of his cigarette, now reduced to a tiny stub between his fingers. Then he dropped it on the floor, between his feet, where it burnt itself out. The linoleum was covered in similar burns.

"Seventeenth-century Venetian binding, in good condition . . ." The brothers leant over the book, but only the elder of the two touched the pages with his pale, cold hands. They looked like a pair of taxidermists working out the best way to stuff a corpse with straw. "The leather is black morocco, with gold rosettes imitating flowers . . ."

"Somewhat sober for Venice," added Pablo Ceniza.

His elder brother agreed with another coughing fit.

"The artist kept it restrained. No doubt the subject matter . . ." He looked at Corso. "Have you tested the core of the binding? Sixteenth- or seventeenth-century books bound in leather or hide sometimes contain surprises. The board inside was made of separate sheets, assembled with paste and pressed. Sometimes they used proofs of the same book, or earlier editions . . . Some discoveries are now more valuable than the copies they bind." He pointed to some papers on the table. "There's an example there. Tell him about it, Pablo."

"Papal bulls of the Holy Crusade, dated 1483." The brother was smiling equivocally. He might have been talking about pornographic material rather than a pile of old papers. "Bound using the boards of some sixteenth-century memorials of no value."

Pedro Ceniza was still examining *The Nine Doors*.

"The binding seems to be in order," he said. "It all fits. Odd book, isn't it? The five raised bands on the spine, no title, and this strange pentacle on the cover. Torchia, Venice 1666. He might have bound it himself. A beautiful piece of work."

"What about the paper?"

"That's just like you, Mr Corso. A good question." The bookbinder licked his lips as if he was trying to warm them. Then he listened carefully to the sound of the pages as he flicked them, just as Corso had done at Varo Borja's. "Excellent paper. Nothing like the cellulose they use nowadays. Do you know the average lifespan of a book printed today? Tell him, Pablo."

"Sixty years," said the brother bitterly as if it were Corso's fault. "Sixty miserable years."

His elder brother was searching amongst the tools on the table. At last he found a special high magnification lens and held it up to the book.

"In a century's time," he murmured as he lifted a page and examined it against the light, closing one eye, "almost all the contents of today's libraries will have disappeared. But these books, printed two hundred or even five hundred years ago will remain intact . . . We have the books, and the world, that we deserve . . . Isn't that so, Pablo?"

"Lousy books printed on lousy paper."

Pedro Ceniza nodded in agreement. He was still examining the book through the lens.

"That's right. Cellulose paper turns yellow and brittle as a wafer, and cracks irreparably. It just ages and dies."

"Not the case here," said Corso, pointing at the book.

The bookbinder was still examining the pages against the light.

"Rag content paper, which is as it should be. Good paper handmade from rags, it'll withstand the passage of time, and human stupidity . . . No, I tell a lie. It's linen. Authentic linen paper." He put down the lens and looked at his brother. "How strange, it's not Venetian paper. It's thick, spongy, fibrous . . . Could it be Spanish?"

"From Valencia," said his brother. "Jativa linen."

"That's right. One of the best in Europe at the time. The printer could have got hold of an imported batch . . . He really set out to do things properly."

"He was very conscientious," said Corso, "and it cost him his life."

"Risks of the trade." Pedro Ceniza accepted the crushed cigarette Corso offered him. He lit it immediately, coughing indifferently. "As you know yourself, it's difficult to fool anyone about the paper. The ream used would have had to be blank, from the same time, and even then there would be differences: the sheets go brown, the inks fade and change over time . . . Of course, added pages can be stained, or washed in tea to darken them . . . Any restoration work, or addition of missing pages, should leave the book all of a piece. It's these small details that count. Don't they, Pablo? Always the damned details."

"What's your diagnosis?"

"So far, considering only the impossible, the probable, and the convincing, we have established that the binding could be seventeenth-century . . . That doesn't mean that the pages match this binding and not another. But let's assume they do. As for the paper, it seems similar to other batches whose origin has been authenticated. And it does seem to be of the time."

"Right. The binding and paper are authentic. Let's look at the text and illustrations."

"Now that's more complicated. We can approach the typography from two different angles. One: we can assume that the book is authentic. The owner, however, denies this, and according to you he has powerful motives for knowing. So it's possible but not very probable. Let's consider the other theory, that it's a forgery, and work out the possibilities. On the one hand the entire text might be a forgery, a fabrication, printed on paper dating from the time and bound using earlier boards. This might be the case, but it's unlikely. Or, to be more precise, not very convincing. The cost of the book would be disproportionately high . . . There's a second reasonable alternative: the forgery might have been made very soon after the first edition of the book. I mean that it was reprinted with alterations, disguised to resemble the first edition, some ten or twenty years after this date of 1666 which appears in the frontispiece. But to what end?"

"It was a banned book," pointed out Pablo Ceniza.

"It's possible," agreed Corso. "Somebody who had access to the equipment – the plates and types – used by Aristide Torchia might have been able to print it again . . ."

The elder of the two brothers had picked up a pencil and was scribbling on the back of a printed sheet.

"That would be one explanation. But the other alternatives, or theories, seem more plausible . . . Imagine, for instance, that most of the book's pages are authentic, but that some were missing, either torn out or lost . . . And that somebody has replaced those missing pages using paper dating from the time, good printing techniques and a lot of patience. In that case there are two further possibilities: one is that the added pages are reproductions of those from another complete copy . . . Another is that, in the absence of the original to reproduce or

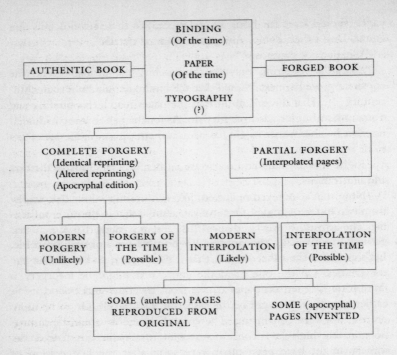

copy, the contents of the pages were invented." The bookbinder then showed Corso what he had been writing. "It would be a true case of forgery, as illustrated by this diagram."

While Corso and the younger of the two brothers were looking at the paper, Pedro Ceniza again leafed through *The Nine Doors*.

"I am inclined to think," he added after a moment, once he had their attention again, "that if some pages were interpolated it was either done around the time of the original edition, or now, in our time. We can discount the time between the two because such a perfect reproduction of an ancient work has only very recently been possible."

Corso handed back the diagram.

"Imagine you were faced with a book that had pages missing. And you wanted to complete it using modern techniques. How would you go about it?"

The Ceniza brothers sighed deeply in unison, professionally relishing the prospect. They were now both staring intently at *The Nine Doors*.

"Let us suppose," the elder one said, "that this 168-page book has page 100 missing . . . Page 100 and page 99, since it's one sheet, with two sides or pages. And we want to complete it. The trick is to locate a twin."

"A twin?"

"As we say in the trade," said Pablo Ceniza. "Another complete copy."

"Or at least, one in which the two pages we need to copy are intact. If possible, it would also be advisable to compare the twin with our incomplete copy, to see if the pressures are different or if the types are more worn in one or the other . . . As you know yourself, at that time types were movable and could easily wear out or alter. So with manual printing, the first and last copy of a same print run could vary greatly. They might have crooked or broken letters, differing ink shades, things like that. Examining such variations means that on the interpolated page imperfections can later be added or removed so that it matches the rest of the book. We would then proceed with photomechanical reproduction and produce a plastic photolith. And from that we would obtain a polymer or a zinc."

"A plate in relief," said Corso, "made of resin or metal."

"Exactly. However perfect the reproduction technique, we would never get the relief, the mark on paper typical of ancient printing techniques using inked wood or metal. So the entire page has to be reproduced using a mouldable material – resin or metal. These create very similar effects to printing with movable lead types as would have been the case in 1666. Then we put the plate on the press and print the page manually as it would have been done four centuries ago. Using paper dating from the same time, of course, treated both before and after with artificial ageing methods . . . The composition of the ink has to be thoroughly researched. It has to be treated with chemical agents so that it matches the other pages. And there you are, the crime is carried out."

"But suppose the original sheet doesn't exist. That there's no model from which to copy the two missing pages."

The Ceniza brothers both smiled confidently.

"That," said the older of the two, "makes it even more interesting."

"Research and imagination," added his brother.

"And daring, of course, Mr Corso. Suppose Pablo and I have that copy of *The Nine Doors* with pages missing. The remaining 166 pages would then provide us with a catalogue of all the letters and symbols used by the printer. So we would take samples until we had obtained an entire alphabet. We'd reproduce the alphabet on photographic paper, which is easier to handle, and then multiply each letter by the number of times needed to compose the entire page . . . The ideal, the artistic flourish, would be to reproduce the types in molten lead as ancient printers used to do . . . Unfortunately this is too complicated and expensive. So we'd make do with modern techniques. We'd divide up the letters with a blade into loose types, and Pablo, who has a steadier hand for the job, would compose the two pages on a template, line by line, just as a compositor would have done in the seventeenth century. From that we would produce another proof on paper and eliminate any joins or imperfections in the letters, or add faults similar to those found in other letters, lines or pages of the original text . . . After that all we would have to do is make a negative. From that you get a reproduction in relief and there you have your printing plate."

"What if the missing pages are illustrations?"

"It makes no difference. If we had access to the original engraving, the technique for making a copy would be even easier. In this case, the fact that the engravings are all woodcuts, which have lighter lines than copperplate or dry point, means that we can produce an almost perfect piece of work."

"Suppose the original engraving no longer exists."

"That's not a problem either. If we know of it from references, we can imitate it. If not, we can invent it. After studying the technique used for the other known engravings, of course. Any good draughtsman could do it."

"What about printing it?"

"As you know, a woodcut is an engraving in relief. A cube of wood is cut with the grain and covered with a white background. The picture is drawn on top. Then it has to be carved, and the ink applied on the crests, or ridges, so that it can be transferred onto paper. When reproducing woodcuts there are two options. One is to make a copy of the drawing, in this case preferably in resin. But the alternative, if you have a good engraver, is to make another real woodcut, with the same techniques used to produce the original engravings, and to print directly from that. In my case, as I have a good engraver in my brother, I would hand-print it from a woodcut. Wherever possible, art should imitate art."

"You get better results," added Pablo.

Corso looked at him conspiratorially.

"As was the case of the Sorbonne's *Speculum*."

"Maybe. The creator, or creators, of that piece of work may have thought like us . . . Don't you think, Pablo?"

"They must have been romantics," agreed his brother, not quite managing a smile.

"Yes, they must." Corso pointed at the book. "So, what's your verdict?"

"I would say that it's original," answered Pedro Ceniza without hesitation. "Even we wouldn't be able to produce such perfect results. Look, the quality of the paper, stains on the pages, identical tones and variations in the ink, and typography . . . It's possible that some forged pages may have been inserted, but I think it improbable. If it is a forgery, the only explanation is that it must have been done around the same time. How many known copies are there? Three? I assume you have considered the possibility that all three are forgeries."

"Yes, I have. What about the woodcuts?"

"They're definitely very strange. With all those symbols . . . But they do date from the time. The degree of pressure on the plates is identical. The ink, the shades of the paper . . . Maybe the key lies not in how and when they were printed, but in their contents. We're sorry we haven't got any further."

"You're wrong." Corso prepared to close the book. "In fact we've come a long way."

Pedro Ceniza stopped him.

"There's one more thing . . . I'm sure you've noticed them yourself. The printer's marks."

Corso looked at him, confused.

"I don't know what you mean."

"The microscopic signatures at the foot of each illustration. Show him, Pablo."

The younger of the two brothers made as if to wipe his hands on his overall, as if to dry off imaginary sweat. Then, moving closer to *The Nine Doors,* he showed Corso some of the pages through a magnifying glass.

"Each engraving," he explained, "has the usual abbreviations: *Inv.* for *invenit,* with the signature of the original artist, and *Sculp.* for *sculpsit,* the engraver . . . Look. In seven of the nine woodcuts the abbreviation A.TORCH appears as both the *sculp.* and the *inv.* Obviously the printer himself drew and engraved seven of the illustrations. But in the other two he is only named as the *sculp.* That means that he only engraved them. And that someone else created the original drawings, someone else was the *inv*. Somebody with the initials L.F."

Pedro Ceniza, who had briefly nodded in approval during his brother's explanation, lit his umpteenth cigarette.

"Not bad, eh?" He started to cough amidst the smoke. He watched for Corso's reaction, a malicious little glint in his astute mouse-like eyes. "He might have been the one burnt at the stake, but that printer wasn't the only one involved."

"No," agreed his brother, "somebody helped him to light the fire at his feet."

That same afternoon, Corso had a visit from Liana Taillefer. The widow arrived unannounced, at that hour which is neither one thing nor the other when Corso, dressed in a faded cotton shirt and old corduroys, was standing by the west-facing window, watching the sunset turn the city rooftops red and ochre. Maybe it wasn't a good moment, and much of what happened later might have been avoided had she turned up at a different time of day. But we'll never know. What we do know is that Corso was looking out of the window, his eyes growing mistier as he emptied his glass of gin. The doorbell rang and Liana Taillefer – blonde, impressively tall, in an English raincoat, tailored suit and black stockings – appeared on the doorstep. Her hair was gathered into a bun beneath a tobacco-coloured, wide-brimmed hat elegantly tilted to one side that suited her very well. She was a beautiful woman. She knew it and she expected everyone to notice.

"To what do I owe the honour?" asked Corso. It was a stupid question, but at that hour and having drunk all that Bols he couldn't be expected to shine in conversation. Liana Taillefer had already stepped into the room. She was standing at the desk where the folder with the Dumas manuscript was lying, next to his computer and box of diskettes.

"Are you still working on this?"

"Of course."

She lifted her gaze from 'The Anjou Wine' and glanced round calmly at the books covering the walls and piled up all over the room. Corso knew she was looking for photographs, mementoes, clues to the personality of the occupant. Arrogantly, she arched an eyebrow, irritated at not finding any. At last she saw the sabre of the Old Guard.

"Do you collect swords?"

This was a logical inference. Of an inductive nature. At least, Corso thought with relief, Liana Taillefer's ability to smooth over embarrassing situations didn't match her appearance. Unless she was teasing him. He smiled warily, feeling cornered.

"I collect that one. It's called a sabre."

She nodded, expressionless. Impossible to tell if she was simple, or a good actress.

"A family heirloom?"

"An acquisition," lied Corso. "I thought it would look nice on the wall. Books on their own can get a bit boring."

"How come you don't have any pictures or photos?"

"There's no one I particularly want to remember." He thought of the photo in the silver frame, the late Taillefer in an apron carving the sucking-pig. "In your case it's different, of course."

She looked at him intently, possibly trying to weigh up how rude his comment had been. There was a glint of steel in her blue eyes, so icy they made one feel chilled. She paced around the room, stopping to look at some of his books, at the view from the window, and then back at the desk. She slid a finger with its blood-red nail over the folder with the Dumas manuscript. Maybe she was expecting Corso to say something but he remained silent. He just waited patiently. If she was after something – and it was pretty obvious she was – he'd let her do all the work. He wasn't going to make it easier for her.

"May I sit down?"

The slightly husky voice. The echo of a heavy night, thought Corso again. He stood in the middle of the room, his hands in his pockets, waiting. Liana Taillefer took off her hat and raincoat. She looked around with one of her interminably slow gestures and chose an old sofa. She went over to it and sat down slowly, her skirt riding up very high. She crossed her legs with an effect that anyone, even Corso with half a gin less in him, would have found devastating.

"I've come on business."

That was obvious. She must be after something, to put on such a display. Corso had as much self-esteem as the next person, but he was no fool.

"Fine," he said. "Have you had dinner with Flavio La Ponte yet?"

No reaction. For a few seconds she carried on looking at him unperturbed, with the same air of contemptuous confidence.

"Not yet," she answered at last, without anger. "I wanted to see you first."

"Well, here I am."

Liana Taillefer leant back slightly farther into the sofa. One hand was resting on a split in the shabby leather upholstery where the horsehair stuffing was poking through.

"You work for money," she said.

"I do."

"You sell yourself to the highest bidder."

"Sometimes." Corso showed one of his eye teeth. He was on his own territory so he could allow himself his friendly rabbit expression. "Generally what I do is hire myself out. Like Humphrey Bogart in the movies. Or like a whore."

For a widow who'd spent her schooldays doing needlework, Liana Taillefer didn't seem shocked by his language.

"I want to offer you a job."

"How nice. Everybody's offering me jobs these days."

"I'll pay you very well."

"Wonderful. They all want to pay me lots of money too."

She pulled at some of the horsehair poking out of the sofa arm and twisted it absent-mindedly round her index finger.

"What are you charging your friend La Ponte?"

"Flavio? Nothing. You couldn't get a penny out of him."

"Why are you working for him, then?"

"As you put it yourself, he's my friend."

She repeated the word thoughtfully.

"It sounds strange to hear you say that word," she then said. She was smiling almost imperceptibly, with curious disdain. "Do you have girlfriends as well?"

Corso looked at her legs unhurriedly, from her ankles to her thighs. Shamelessly.

"I have memories of some. The memory of you might be useful tonight."

She took his crudeness stoically. Or maybe, Corso wondered, she hadn't caught his subtle reference.

"Name a price," she said coldly. "I want my husband's manuscript."

Things were looking good. Corso went and sat in an armchair opposite Liana Taillefer. From there he could get a better view of her legs. She had taken off her shoes and was resting her bare feet on the rug.

"You didn't seem very interested last time."

"I've thought it over. That manuscript has . . ."

"Sentimental value?" mocked Corso.

"Something like that." Her voice now sounded defiant. "But not in the sense you'd suppose."

"What would you be prepared to do to get it?"

"I've told you. Pay you."

Corso smiled leeringly.

"You offend me. I'm a professional."

"You're a professional mercenary, Mr Corso. And mercenaries change sides. I've read books too, you know."

"I've got as much money as I need."

"I'm not talking of money now."

She was lying right back on the sofa, and with one of her bare feet she was stroking the instep of the other. Corso pictured her toenails painted red under the black stockings. As she moved, her skirt rode up giving a glimpse of white flesh above her black garters where all mysteries are reduced to a single one, as old as Time itself. Corso looked up with difficulty. Her ice-blue eyes were still fixed intently on him.

He took off his glasses before standing up and moving towards the sofa. Liana Taillefer followed him impassively with her eyes, even when he was right in front of her, so close that their knees were touching. Then she lifted her hand and placed her fingers with their red lacquered nails precisely on the zipper of Corso's corduroy trousers. She was smiling again almost imperceptibly, contemptuous and self-assured, when at last Corso leant over her and lifted her skirt up to her waist.

It was a mutual assault, rather than an exchange. A settling of scores there on the sofa. A crude, hard struggle between adults, with the appropriate moans at the right moment, a few muttered curses and the woman's nails digging mercilessly into Corso's back. And it happened in barely any space, without them taking their clothes off. Her skirt was up over her strong, wide hips which he gripped as the studs on her suspender belt pressed into his groin. He never even saw her breasts, although he did manage to touch them a couple of times, dense, warm, abundant flesh beneath the bra, silk shirt and jacket. In the heat of the fray, Liana Taillefer hadn't had time to remove them. And now there they were, the two of them, still tangled up in each other, amongst a mess of crumpled clothes, and breathless, like two exhausted wrestlers. Corso was wondering how to extricate himself from this mess.

"Who's Rochefort?" he asked, prepared to precipitate the crisis.

Liana Taillefer looked at him from a few inches away. The setting sun threw reddish glints onto her face. The hairpins had fallen out of her bun, and her blonde hair was spread untidily over the leather sofa. She looked relaxed for the first time.

"It doesn't matter," she answered, "now that I'm getting the manuscript back."

Corso kissed her disordered cleavage, bidding farewell to its contents. He had a feeling it would be some time before he kissed it again.

"What manuscript?" he said, for the sake of it, and he saw her expression harden instantly. Her body went rigid under his.

"'The Anjou Wine'." For the first time there was a hint of anxiety in her voice. "You're going to return it to me, aren't you, Mr Corso?"

Corso didn't like the sound of the return to a formal mode of address. He vaguely remembered having been on first name terms during the skirmish.

"I never said that."

"I thought . . ."

"You thought wrong."

Her steely blue eyes flashed with anger. She sat up, furious, pushing him away abruptly with her hips.

"Bastard!"

Corso, who was about to laugh the whole thing off with a couple of cynical jokes, felt himself pushed back violently. He fell to his knees. As he struggled to his feet, fastening his belt, he saw Liana Taillefer stand up, pale and terrifying, unconcerned by her dishevelled clothes, her magnificent thighs still exposed. She slapped him so hard his left ear vibrated like a drum.

"Pig!"

Corso staggered from the blow. Stunned, he looked round like a boxer searching for a fixed point to stop him falling into the ropes. Liana Taillefer crossed his field of vision but he didn't pay her too much attention because of the agonizing pain in his ear. He was staring stupidly at the sabre from Waterloo when he heard the sound of breaking glass. He saw her again against the reddish light from the window. She had pulled her skirt down. In one hand she was holding the manuscript, and in the other the neck of a broken bottle. Its edge was pointed at Corso's throat.

. . . Keeping her at bay with the tip of his sword

Instinctively he raised his arm and stepped back. The danger had brought him back to his senses and made the adrenaline pump. He pushed aside the hand with the bottle and punched her in the neck. It left her winded, stopping her dead. The following scene was somewhat calmer. Corso picked the manuscript and broken bottle off the floor. Liana Taillefer was once again sitting on the sofa, her tousled hair hanging over her face. She was holding a hand to her aching neck, breathing with difficulty between sobs of fury.

"They'll kill you for this, Corso," she said at last. The sun had now set beyond the city, and the corners of the room were filling with shadow. Ashamed, he switched on the light and held out her coat and hat before ringing for a taxi. He avoided her eyes. Then, as he listened to her steps receding down the stairs, he stood for a moment by the window, watching the dark roofs against the brightness of the rising moon.

"They'll kill you for this, Corso."

He poured himself a large glass of gin. He couldn't rid himself of Liana Taillefer's expression once she realized she'd been tricked. Eyes as deadly as a dagger, a rictus of vengeful fury. And she meant it, she really had wanted to kill him. Once again the memories stirred, gradually filling his mind. This time, though, he needed no effort to relive them. The image was sharp and he knew exactly where it came from. The facsimile edition of *The Three Musketeers* was on his desk. He opened it and searched for the scene. Page 129. There, amongst overturned furniture, leaping from the bed, dagger in hand like a furious demon, Milady throws herself at d'Artagnan who retreats, terrified, in his shirt, keeping her at bay with the tip of his sword.

VII

Book Number One and Book Number Two

*The truth is that the Devil is very cunning. The truth is
that he is not always as ugly as they say.*

J. Cazotte: *The Devil in Love*

With only a few minutes to go before the departure of the express train
to Lisbon, he saw the girl. Corso was on the platform, about to mount
the steps to his carriage – *Companhia Internacional de Carruagems-
Camas* – when he bumped into her in a group of other passengers, heading
towards the first-class carriages. She was carrying a small rucksack and
wearing the same blue duffle coat, but he didn't recognize her at first.
He only felt there was something familiar about her green eyes, so light
they seemed transparent, and her very short hair. He continued to watch
her for a moment, until she disappeared two carriages further down.
The whistle blew. As he climbed aboard the train and the guard shut the
door behind him, Corso remembered the scene: the girl sitting at one end
of the table at the gathering of Boris Balkan and his circle in the café.

He walked along the corridor to his compartment. The station lights
streamed past increasingly quickly beyond the windows and the train
clattered rhythmically. Moving around the cramped compartment with
difficulty, he hung up his coat and jacket before sitting down on the
bunk, his canvas bag beside him. In it, together with *The Nine Doors*
and the folder with the Dumas manuscript, was a book by Las Cases,
the *Memorial of Saint-Helena*:

Friday 14 July 1816. The Emperor has been unwell all night . . .

He lit a cigarette. Occasionally, when lights from the window
strobed across his face, Corso would glance out before returning to the
tale of Napoleon's slow agony and the wiliness of his English gaoler,
Sir Hudson Lowe. He frowned as he read and adjusted his glasses on

the bridge of his nose. From time to time he stopped and stared for a moment at his own reflection in the window, and pulled a funny face. Even now, he still felt indignant at the victors condemning the fallen titan to a miserable end, clinging to a rock in the middle of the Atlantic. Strange, going over the historical events and his earlier feelings about them from his present clear-headed perspective. How far away he seemed, that other Lucas Corso who reverently admired the Waterloo veteran's sabre; the boy absorbing the family myths with aggressive enthusiasm, the precocious bonapartist and avid reader of books with engravings of the glorious campaigns, names that echoed like drumrolls for a charge: Wagram, Jena, Smolensk, Marengo . . . The boy wide-eyed with wonder who had long since ceased to exist; a hazy ghost sometimes appearing in his memory, between the pages of a book, in a smell or a sound, or through a dark window with the rain from Another Country beating against it, outside in the night.

The guard passed the door ringing his bell. Half an hour till the restaurant car closed. Corso shut the book. He put on his jacket, slung the canvas bag over his shoulder and left the compartment. At the end of the corridor, beyond the door, a cold draught blew through the passageway leading to the next sleeper. He felt the thundering beneath his feet as he crossed into the section of first-class carriages. He let a couple of passengers pass and then looked into the nearest compartment, which was only half-full. The girl was there, by the door, wearing a jumper and jeans, her bare feet resting on the seat opposite. As Corso passed she looked up from her book and their eyes met. He was about to nod briefly in her direction, but when she showed no sign of recognition, he stopped himself. She must have sensed something because she looked up at him with curiosity. But by then Corso had already moved on down the corridor.

He ate his dinner, rocked by the swaying of the train, and had time for a coffee and a gin before they closed for the evening. The moon, in shades of raw silk, was rising in the night. Telephone poles rushed past in the darkened plain, fleeting frames for a sequence of stills from a badly-adjusted movie projector.

He was on his way back to his compartment when he saw the girl in the corridor of the first-class carriage. She had opened the window and the cold night air was blowing against her face. As he came up to her, Corso turned sideways so he could get past. Then she turned towards him.

"I know you," she said.

Close up, her green eyes seemed even lighter, like liquid crystal, and luminous against her suntanned skin. It was only March, and with her hair parted like a boy's, her tan made her look unusual, sporty, pleasantly ambiguous. She was tall, slim and supple. And very young.

"Yes," said Corso, pausing a moment. "A few days ago, at the café."

She smiled. Another contrast, this time of white teeth against brown skin. Her mouth was big and well defined. A pretty girl, Flavio La Ponte would have said, stroking his curly beard.

"You were the one asking about d'Artagnan."

The cold air from the window was blowing her hair. She was still barefoot. Her white plimsolls were on the floor by her empty seat. He instinctively glanced at the book lying there: *The Adventures of Sherlock Holmes*. A cheap paperback, he noticed. The Mexican edition from the publishers Porrua.

"You'll catch cold," he said.

Still smiling, the girl shook her head, but she turned the handle and shut the window. Corso, about to go on his way, paused to find a cigarette. He did it as he always did, taking one directly from his pocket and putting it in his mouth, when he realized she was watching him.

"Do you smoke?" he asked hesitantly, stopping his hand halfway.

"Sometimes."

He put the cigarette in his mouth and took out another one. It was dark tobacco, without a filter, and as crushed as all the packets he usually carried with him. The girl took it. She looked to see the make. Then she leant over for Corso to light it, after his own, with the last match in the box.

"It's strong," she said, breathing out her first mouthful of smoke, but then made none of the fuss he expected. She held the cigarette in an unusual way, between forefinger and thumb, with the ember outward. "Are you in this carriage?"

"No, in the next one."

"You're lucky to have a sleeper." She tapped her jeans pocket, indicating a non-existent wallet. "I wish I could. Luckily the compartment's half-empty."

"Are you a student?"

"Sort of."

The train thundered into a tunnel. The girl turned then as if the darkness outside drew her attention. Tense and alert, she leant against her own reflection in the window. She seemed to be expecting something in the noisy rush of air. Then, when the train came out into the open and small lights again punctuated the night like brush strokes as the train passed, she smiled, distant.

"I like trains," she said.

"Me too."

The girl was still facing the window, touching it with the fingertips of one hand.

"Imagine," she said. She was smiling nostalgically, obviously remembering something. "Leaving Paris in the evening to wake up on the lagoon in Venice, en route to Istanbul . . ."

Corso made a face. How old could she be? Eighteen, maybe twenty at most.

"Playing poker," he suggested, "between Calais and Brindisi."

She looked at him more attentively.

"Not bad." She thought a moment. "How about a champagne breakfast between Vienna and Nice?"

"Interesting. Like spying on Basil Zaharoff."

"Or getting drunk with Nijinsky."

"Stealing Coco Chanel's pearls."

"Flirting with Paul Morand . . . Or Mr Barnabooth."

They both laughed, Corso under his breath. She laughed openly, leaning her forehead against the cold window. Her laugh was loud, frank and boyish, matching her hair and her luminous green eyes.

"Trains aren't like that any more," he said.

"I know."

The lights of a signal post passed like a flash of lightning. Then a dimly-lit, deserted platform, with a sign made illegible by their speed. The moon was rising and now and then clarified the confused outline of trees and roofs. It seemed to be flying alongside the train in a mad, purposeless race.

"What's your name?"

"Corso. And yours?"

"Irene Adler."

He looked at her intently and she held his gaze, calmly.

"That's not a proper name."

"Neither is Corso."

"You're wrong. I am Corso. The man who courses after things."

"You don't look like a man who runs anywhere. You seem like the calm type."

He bowed his head slightly, looking at the girl's bare feet on the floor of the corridor. He could tell she was staring at him, examining him. Unusually, it made him feel slightly uncomfortable. She was too young, he told himself. And too attractive. He automatically adjusted his crooked glasses and was about to go on his way.

"Have a good journey."

"Thanks."

He took a few steps, knowing that she was watching him.

"Maybe we'll see each other around," she said, behind him.

"Maybe."

Impossible. That was another Corso returning home, uneasy, the Grande Armée about to melt in the snow. The fire of Moscow was crackling in his wake. He couldn't leave like that, so he stopped and turned round. As he did so he was smiling like a hungry wolf.

"Irene Adler," he repeated, as if trying to remember. "*A Study in Scarlet*?"

"No," she answered calmly. "*A Scandal in Bohemia*." Now she was smiling too and her gaze shone emerald green in the dimly-lit corridor. "*The Woman*, my dear Watson."

Corso gave himself a slap on the forehead as if he'd just remembered.

"Elementary," he said. And he was sure they'd meet again.

Corso spent just under fifty minutes in Lisbon. Just enough time to get from Santa Apolonia Station to Rossio Station. An hour and a half later he stepped onto the platform in Sintra, beneath a sky full of low clouds blurring the tops of the melancholy grey towers of the castle of Da Pena further up the hill. There was no taxi in sight so he walked to the small hotel opposite the National Palace with its two large chimneys. It was ten o'clock on a Wednesday morning and the esplanade was empty of tourists and coaches. He had no trouble getting a room. It looked out onto the uneven landscape, where the roofs and towers of old houses peered above the thick greenery, their ruined gardens suffocating in ivy.

After a shower and a coffee he asked for the Quinta da Soledade, and the hotel receptionist told him the way, up the road. There weren't any taxis on the esplanade either, although there were a couple of horse-drawn carriages. Corso negotiated a price and a few minutes later he was passing under the lacy baroque stonework of the Regaleira Tower.

The sound of the horse's hooves echoed against the dark walls, the drains and fountains running with water, the ivy-covered walls, railings and tree trunks, the stone steps carpeted with moss and the ancient tiles on the abandoned manor houses.

The Quinta da Soledade was a rectangular, eighteenth-century house, with four chimneys and an ochre plaster façade covered in trails and stains. Corso got out of the carriage and stood looking at the place for a moment before opening the iron gate. Two mossy, grey-green stone statues on granite columns stood at either end of the wall. One was a bust of a woman. The other seemed to be identical but the features were hidden by the ivy climbing up it, about to take over the sculpted face beneath and merge with it.

As he walked towards the house the dead leaves crackled beneath his steps. The path was lined with marble statues, almost all of them lying broken next to their empty pedestals. The garden was completely wild. Vegetation had taken over, climbing up benches and into alcoves. The wrought iron left rusty trails on the moss-covered stone. To his left, in a pond full of aquatic plants, a fountain with cracked tiles sheltered a chubby angel with empty eyes and mutilated hands. It slept with its head resting on a book, and a thread of water trickled from its mouth. Everything seemed suffused with infinite sadness and Corso couldn't help being affected. Quinta da Soledade, he repeated. House of Solitude. The name suited it.

He climbed the stone steps leading to the door and looked up. Beneath the grey sky no time was indicated on the Roman numerals of the ancient sundial on the wall. Above it ran the legend: '*Omnes vulnerant, postuma necat.*'

They all wound, he read. The last one kills.

"You've arrived just in time," said Fargas, "for the ceremony."

Corso held out his hand, slightly disconcerted. Victor Fargas was as tall and thin as an El Greco figure. He seemed to move around inside his loose, thick woollen jumper and baggy trousers like a tortoise in its shell. His moustache was trimmed with geometrical precision, and his old-fashioned, worn-out shoes gleamed. Corso noticed this much at first glance, before his attention was drawn to the huge, empty house, with its bare walls, and the paintings on the ceilings falling into mildewed shreds, eaten by damp.

Fargas examined his visitor closely.

"I assume you'll accept a brandy," he said at last after some thought. He set off down the corridor, limping slightly, without bothering to check whether Corso was following or not. They passed other rooms, which were empty or contained the remains of broken furniture thrown in a corner. Bare light fittings and dusty light bulbs hung from the ceilings.

The only rooms that seemed to be in use were two interconnecting reception rooms. There was a sliding door between them with coats of arms etched into the glass. It was open, revealing more bare walls, with their ancient wallpaper marked by long-gone pictures and furniture, rusty nails, and fittings for non-existent lamps. Above this gloomy scene hung a ceiling painted to resemble a vault of clouds with the sacrifice of Abraham in the centre. The cracked figure of the old patriarch was holding a dagger, about to strike a blond young man. His hand was held back by an angel with huge wings. Beneath the trompe l'œil sky, dusty French windows, some of the panes replaced with cardboard, led to the terrace and, beyond that, to the garden.

"Home sweet home," said Fargas.

His irony was unconvincing. He seemed to have made the remark too often and was no longer sure of its effect. He spoke Spanish with a heavy, distinguished Portuguese accent. And he moved very slowly, perhaps because of his bad leg, like someone who has all the time in the world.

"Brandy," he said again, as if he didn't quite remember how they'd reached that point.

Corso nodded vaguely but Fargas didn't notice. At one end of the vast room was an enormous fireplace with logs piled up in it. There was a pair of unmatched armchairs, a table and a sideboard, an oil lamp, two big candlesticks, a violin in its case, and little else. But on the floor, lined up perfectly neatly on old, faded, threadbare rugs, as far away as possible from the windows and the leaden light coming through them, there were a great many books; five hundred or more, Corso calculated, maybe even a thousand. Many codices and incunables amongst them. Wonderful old books bound in leather or parchment. Ancient tomes with studs in the covers, folios, Elzevirs, their bindings decorated with gophering, bosses, rosettes, locks, their spines and fore-edges covered in gilding and calligraphy done by medieval monks in the scriptoria of their monasteries. He also noticed a dozen or so rusty mousetraps in various corners.

Fargas, who had been searching through the sideboard, turned round holding a glass and a bottle of Rémy Martin. He held it up to the light to look at the contents.

"Nectar of the gods," he said triumphantly. "Or the Devil." He smiled only with his mouth, twisting his moustache like an old-fashioned movie star. His eyes remained fixed and expressionless, with bags beneath them as if from chronic insomnia. Corso noticed his delicate hands – a sign of good breeding – as he took the glass of brandy. The glass vibrated gently as he raised it to his lips.

"Nice glass," he said to make conversation.

Fargas agreed, and made a gesture halfway between resignation and self-mockery, suggesting a different reading of it all: the glass, the tiny amount of brandy in the bottle, the bare house, his own presence. An elegant, pale, worn ghost.

"I only have one more left," he confided in a calm, neutral tone. "That's why I take care of them."

Corso nodded. He glanced at the bare walls and then again at the books.

"This must have been a beautiful house," he said.

Fargas shrugged.

"Yes, it was. But old families are like civilizations. One day they just wither and die." He looked around without seeing. All the missing objects seemed to be reflected in his eyes. "At first one resorts to the barbarians to guard the *limes* of the Danube but it makes them rich and they end up as one's creditors . . . Then one day they rebel and invade, looting everything." He suddenly peered at his visitor suspiciously. "I hope you understand what I mean."

Corso nodded. By now he was smiling his best conspiratorial smile.

"Perfectly," he said. "Hobnail boots crushing Meissen porcelain. Isn't that it? Skivvies in evening dress. Working-class parvenus who wipe their arses on illuminated manuscripts."

Fargas nodded approvingly. He was smiling. Then he limped over to the sideboard in search of the other glass.

"I think I'll have a brandy too," he said.

They drank a toast in silence, looking at each other like two members of a secret fraternity who have just agreed the signs of recognition. Then, moving closer to the books, Fargas gestured towards them with the hand holding the glass, as if Corso had just passed his initiation test and he were inviting him to go through an invisible barrier.

"There they are. Eight hundred and thirty-four volumes. Less than half of them are worth anything." He drank some more and then ran his finger over his damp moustache, looking around. "It's a shame that you didn't know them in better days, lined up on their cedarwood shelves . . . I managed to collect five thousand of them. These are the survivors."

Corso put his canvas bag down on the floor and went over to the books. His fingers were itching instinctively. It was a magnificent sight. He adjusted his glasses and immediately saw a 1588 first edition Vasari in quarto, and a sixteenth-century *Tractatus* by Berengario de Carpi bound in parchment.

"I would never have dreamt that the Fargas collection listed in all the bibliographies was kept like this. Piled up on the floor against the wall, in an empty house . . ."

"That's life, my friend. But I have to say, in my defence, that they are all in immaculate condition. I clean them and make sure they're aired. I check that insects or rodents don't get at them, and that they're protected against light, heat and damp. In fact I do nothing else all day."

"What happened to the rest?"

Fargas looked towards the window, asking himself the same question. He was frowning.

"You can imagine," he answered, and he looked a very unhappy man when he turned back to look at Corso. "Apart from the house, a few pieces of furniture and my father's library, I inherited nothing but debts. Whenever I got any money I invested it in books. And when my income dwindled I got rid of what was left – pictures, furniture and china. I think you understand what it is to be a passionate collector of books. But I'm pathologically obsessed. I suffered atrociously just thinking about breaking up my collection."

"I've known people like that."

"Really?" Fargas looked at him interested. "I still doubt you can really imagine what it's like. I used to get up at night and wander about like a lost soul looking at my books. I'd talk to them, and stroke their spines, swearing I'd always take care of them . . . But none of it was any use. One day I took my decision: to sacrifice most of the books, and keep only the most cherished, valuable ones. Neither you nor anyone can ever understand how that felt, letting the vultures pick over my collection."

"I can imagine," said Corso, who wouldn't have minded in the least joining in the feast.

"Can you? I don't think so. Not in a million years. Separating the ones from the others took me two months. Sixty-one days of agony, and an attack of fever that almost killed me. At last, they took them away, and I thought I would go mad . . . I remember it as if it were yesterday, although it was twelve years ago."

"And now?"

Fargas held up the empty glass, as if it were symbolic.

"For some time now I've had to resort to selling my books again. Not that I need very much. Once a week someone comes in to clean, and I get my food brought from the village . . . Almost all the money goes in tax paid to the State for keeping on the house."

He pronounced the word *State* as if he'd said vermin. Corso looked sympathetic, glancing again at the bare walls.

"You could sell it."

"Yes," Fargas agreed indifferently. "There are things you can't understand."

Corso bent down to pick up a folio bound in parchment and leafed through it with interest. *De Symmetria* by Dürer, Paris 1557, reprinting of the first Nuremberg edition in Latin. In good condition, with wide margins. Flavio La Ponte would have gone wild over it. Anybody would have gone wild over it.

"How often do you have to sell books?"

"Two or three a year is enough. After going over and over it, I choose one book to sell. That's the ceremony I was referring to when I answered the door. I have a buyer, a compatriot of yours. He comes here a couple of times a year."

"Do I know him?" asked Corso.

"I've no idea," answered Fargas, without supplying a name. "In fact, I'm expecting him any day now. When you arrived I was getting ready to choose a victim . . ." He made a guillotine movement with one of his slender hands, still smiling wearily. "The one that has to die in order for the others to stay together."

Corso looked up at the ceiling, drawing the inevitable parallel. Abraham, a deep crack across his face, was making visible efforts to free the hand in which he held the dagger. The angel was holding on to it firmly with one hand and severely reprimanding the patriarch with the other. Beneath the blade, his head resting on a stone, Isaac waited, resigned to his fate. He was blond with pink cheeks, like an ancient Greek youth who never said no. Beyond him a sheep was tangled up in brambles, and Corso mentally voted for the sheep to be spared.

"I suppose you have no other choice," he said, looking at Fargas.

"If there was one I would have found it . . ." Fargas smiled bitterly. "But the lion demands his share, the sharks smell the bait. Unfortunately there aren't any people left like the Comte d'Artois, who was king of France. Do you know the story? The old Marquis de Paulmy, who owned sixty thousand books, went bankrupt. To escape his creditors he sold his collection to the Comte d'Artois. But the Count stipulated that the old man should keep them until his death. In that way Paulmy used the money to buy more books and extend the collection even though it was no longer his . . ."

He had put his hands in his pockets and was limping up and down alongside the books examining each one, like a shabby, gaunt Montgomery inspecting his troops at El Alamein.

"Sometimes I don't even touch them or open them." He stopped and leant over to straighten up a book in its row, on the old rug. "All I do is dust them and stare at them for hours. I know what lies inside each binding down to the last detail . . . Look at this one: *De revolutionis celestium*, Nicholas Copernicus. Second edition, Basle, 1566. A mere trifle, don't you think? Like the *Vulgata Clementina* to your right, between the six volumes of the *Polyglot* by your compatriot Cisneros, and the Nuremberg *Cronicarum*. And look at the strange folio over there: *Praxis criminis persequendi* by Simon de Colines, 1541. Or that monastic binding with four raised bands and bosses that you see there. Do you know what's inside? *The Golden Legend* by Jacopo de Voragine, Basle 1493, printed by Nicholas Kesler."

Corso leafed through the book. It was a magnificent edition, also with very wide margins. He put it back carefully. Then he stood up, wiping his glasses with his handkerchief. It would have made the coolest of men break out in a sweat.

"You must be crazy. If you sold all this you wouldn't have any money problems."

"I know." Fargas was leaning over to adjust the position of the book imperceptibly. "But if I sold them all I'd have no reason to go on living. So I wouldn't care if I had problems or not."

Corso pointed at a row of books in very bad condition. There were several incunables and manuscripts. Judging from the bindings, none dated from later than the seventeenth-century.

"You've got a great many ancient editions of chivalric novels . . ."

"Yes. Inherited from my father. His obsession was acquiring the ninety-five books of Don Quixote's collection, in particular those mentioned in the priest's expurgation . . . He also left me that strange *Quixote* that you see there, next to the first edition of *Os Lusiadas*. It's a 1789 Ibarra in four volumes. In addition to the corresponding illustrations, it is enriched with others printed in England in the first half of the eighteenth century, six wash drawings and a facsimile of Cervantes' birth certificate printed on vellum. To each his own obsessions. My father's, a diplomat who lived for many years in Spain, was Cervantes. In some people it's a mania. They won't accept restoration work, even if it's invisible, or won't buy a book numbered over fifty . . . My passion, as you must have noticed, was uncut books. I scoured auctions and bookshops, ruler in hand, and I went weak at the knees if I found one that was intact or hadn't been ploughed. Have you read Nodier's burlesque tale about the bookcollector? The same happened to me. I'd have happily shot any bookbinder who'd been too free with the guillotine. I was in ecstasy if I discovered an edition with margins two millimetres wider than those described in the canonical bibliographies."

"Me too."

"Congratulations, then. Welcome to the brotherhood."

"Not so fast. My interest is financial rather than aesthetic in nature."

"Never mind. I like you. I believe that when it comes to books, conventional morality doesn't exist." He was at the other end of the room but leaned slightly towards Corso, confidingly. "Do you know something? You Spaniards have a story about a bookseller in Barcelona who committed murder. Well, I'd be capable of killing for a book too."

"I wouldn't recommend it. That's how it all starts. It doesn't seem like a big deal but then you end up lying, voting in elections, things like that."

"Even selling one's own books."

"Even that."

Fargas was shaking his head sadly. Then he stood still a moment, frowning. When he came to, he studied Corso closely for some time.

"Which brings us," he said at last, "to the business I was engaged in when you rang at the door . . . Every time I have to address the problem I feel like a priest renouncing his beliefs. Are you surprised that I should think of this as a sacrilege?"

"Not at all. I suppose that's exactly what it is."

Fargas wrung his hands tormentedly. He looked round at the bare room and the books on the floor, and then back at Corso. His smile seemed false, painted on.

"Yes. Sacrilege can only be justified in faith . . . Only a believer can sense the terrible enormity of the action. We'd feel no horror at profaning a religion to which we were indifferent. It would be like an atheist blaspheming. Absurd."

Corso agreed.

"I know what you mean. It's Julian the Apostate crying, 'You have defeated me, Galileo.'"

"I'm not familiar with that quotation."

"It may be apocryphal. One of the Marist brothers used to quote it when I was at school. He was warning us not to go off at a tangent. Julian ends up shot through with arrows on the battlefield, spitting blood at a heaven without God."

Fargas assented, as if it were all terribly close to him. There was something disturbing in the strange rictus contracting his mouth, in the obsessive intensity of his eyes.

"That's how I feel now," he said. "I get up because I can't sleep and stand here, resolved to commit another desecration." He had moved so close to Corso as he spoke that Corso wanted to take a step back. "To sin against myself and against them . . . I touch one book, then change my mind, choose another one but end up putting it back in its place . . . I must sacrifice one so that the others can stay together, snap off a branch to continue enjoying the rest . . ." He held up his right hand. "I would rather cut off one of my fingers."

As he made the gesture his hand trembled. Corso nodded. He knew how to listen. It was part of the job. He could even understand. But he wasn't prepared to join in. It was none of his business. As Varo Borja would have said, he was a mercenary, and he was paying a visit. What Fargas needed was a confessor, or a psychiatrist.

"Nobody would pay a penny for an old bookcollector's finger," Corso said lightly.

The joke became lost in the immense void filling Fargas's eyes. He was looking through Corso. In his dilated pupils and absent eyes there were only books.

"So which should I choose?" Fargas went on. Corso had taken a cigarette from his coat pocket and was now offering it to the old man, but he didn't notice Corso's gesture. Absorbed, obsessed, he was listening only to himself. He was aware of nothing but the hallucinations of his tortured mind. "After much thought I have chosen two candidates." He took two books from the floor and put them on the table. "Tell me what you think."

Corso leaned over the books. He opened one of them at a page with an engraving, a woodcut of three men and a woman working in a mine. It was a second edition of *De re metallica* by Georgius Agricola, in Latin, printed by Froben and Episcopius in Basle only five years after its first edition in 1556. He gave a grunt of approval as he lit his cigarette.

"As you can see, making a choice isn't easy." Fargas was following Corso's movements intently. Anxiously he watched him turn the pages, just brushing them with his fingertips. "I have to sell one book each time. And not just any one. The sacrifice has to ensure that the rest are safe for another six months . . . It's my tribute to the Minotaur." He tapped his temple. "We all have one at the centre of the labyrinth . . . Our reason creates him, and he imposes his own horror."

"Why don't you sell several less valuable books at one time? Then you'd raise the money you need and still keep the rarer ones. Or your favourites."

"And reject some for the benefit of the others?" Fargas shuddered. "I simply couldn't do it. They all have the same immortal soul. To me they all have the same rights. I do have my favourites, of course. How could I not? But I never distinguish between them by a gesture, a word which might raise them above their less favoured companions. Rather the opposite. Remember that God designated his own son to be sacrificed. For the redemption of mankind. And Abraham . . ." He seemed to be referring to the painting on the ceiling because he looked up and smiled sadly at the empty space, leaving the sentence unfinished.

Corso had opened the second book, a folio with an Italian parchment binding from the seventeen hundreds. Inside was a magnificent Virgil. Giunta's Venetian edition, printed in 1544. This revived Fargas.

"Beautiful, isn't it?" He stepped in front of Corso and snatched it from him impatiently. "Look at the title page, at the architectural border . . . One hundred and thirteen woodcuts, all perfect except for page 345, which has a small, ancient restoration, almost imperceptible, in one of the bottom corners. As it happens, this is my favourite. Look: Aeneas in Hell, next to the Sibyl. Have you ever seen anything like it? Look at these flames behind the triple wall, the cauldron of the damned, the bird devouring their entrails . . ." The old bookcollector's pulse was almost visible, throbbing in his wrists and temples. His voice became deeper as he held the book up to his eyes so he could read more clearly. His expression was radiant. "*Mœnia amnlata videt, triplici circundata muro, quae rapidus flamnis ambit torrentibus amnis . . .*" He paused, ecstatic. "The engraver had a beautiful, violent, medieval view of Virgil's Hades."

"A magnificent book," confirmed Corso, dragging on his cigarette.

"It's more than that. Feel the paper. '*Esemplare buono e genuino con le figure assai ben impresse,*' assure the old catalogues . . ." After this feverish outburst, Fargas once more gazed into empty space, absorbed, engrossed in the dark corners of his nightmare. "I think I'll sell this one."

Corso exhaled impatiently.

"I don't understand. This is obviously one of your favourites. So is the Agricola. Your hands tremble as you touch them."

"My hands? What you mean is my soul burns in the torments of hell. I thought I'd explained . . . The book to be sacrificed can never be one to which I am indifferent. What meaning would this painful act have otherwise? A sordid transaction determined by market forces, several cheap ones instead of a single expensive one . . ." Scornful, he shook his head violently. He looked round grimly, searching for someone on whom to vent his anger. "These are the ones I love most. They shine above the rest for their beauty, for the love they have inspired. These are the ones I walk hand in hand with to the very brink of the abyss . . . Life may strip me of all I have. But it won't turn me into a miserable wretch."

He paced aimlessly about the room. The sad scene, his bad leg, his shabby clothes, all added to his weary, fragile appearance.

"That's why I remain in this house," he went on. "The ghosts of my lost books roam within its walls." He had stopped in front of the fireplace and was looking at the wretched pile of logs in the hearth. "Sometimes I feel they come back to demand that I make amends . . . So, to placate them, I take up the violin that you see there and I play for hours, wandering through the house in darkness, like one of the damned . . ." He had turned round to look at Corso and was silhouetted against the dirty window. "The wandering bookcollector."

He walked slowly to the table and laid a hand on each book, as if he had delayed making his decision until that moment. Now he was smiling, inquiringly.

"Which one would you choose, if you were in my place?"

Corso fidgeted uneasily.

"Please, leave me out of this. I'm lucky enough not to be in your place."

"That's right. Very lucky. How clever of you to realize. A stupid man would envy me I suppose. All this treasure in my house . . . But you haven't told me which one to sell. Which son to sacrifice." His face suddenly became distorted with anguish, as if both his mind and body were in pain. "May his blood taint me and mine," he added in a very low, intense voice, "down to the seventh generation."

He returned the Agricola to its place on the rug and stroked the parchment of the Virgil, muttering "his blood". His eyes were moist and his hands were shaking uncontrollably.

"I think I'll sell this one," he insisted.

Fargas might not be out of his mind yet, but he soon would be. Corso looked at the bare walls, the marks left by pictures on the damp-stained wallpaper. The highly unlikely seventh generation didn't give a damn about any of it. Like Lucas Corso's own, the Fargas line would end here. And find peace at last. Corso's cigarette smoke rose up to the decrepit paintings on the ceiling, straight upwards like the smoke from a sacrifice in the calm of dawn. He looked out of the window, at the garden overrun with weeds, searching for a way out like the sheep tangled in the brambles. But there was nothing but books. The angel let go of the hand holding up the knife and went away, weeping. And left Abraham alone, the poor fool.

Corso finished his cigarette and threw it into the fireplace. He was tired and cold. He had heard too many words within those bare walls. He was glad there were no mirrors for him to see the expression on his face. He looked at his watch, without noticing the time. With a fortune sitting there on the old rugs and carpets, Victor Fargas had more than paid their price in suffering. For Corso it was now time to talk about business.

"What about *The Nine Doors*?"

"What about it?"

"That's what brought me here. I assume you got my letter."

"Your letter? Yes, of course. I remember. It's just that with all of this . . . Forgive me. *The Nine Doors*. Of course."

He looked round, bewildered, like a sleepwalker who had just been jolted awake. He suddenly seemed infinitely tired, after a long ordeal.

He lifted a finger, requesting a minute to think, then limped over to a corner of the room. Some fifty or so books were lined up there on the floor on a faded French rug. Corso could just make out that it depicted Alexander's victory over Darius.

"Did you know," asked Fargas, pointing at the scene on the Gobelin, "that Alexander used his rival's treasure chest to store Homer's books?" He nodded, pleased, looking at the Macedonian's threadbare profile. "He was a fellow bookcollector. A good man."

Corso didn't give a damn about Alexander the Great's literary tastes. He had knelt down and was reading the titles printed on some of the spines and fore-edges. They were all ancient treatises on magic, alchemy and demonology. *Les trois livres de l'Art, Destructor omnium rerum, Dissertazioni sopra le apparizioni de' spiriti e diavoli, De origine, moribus et rebus gestis Satanæ* . . .

"What do you think?" asked Fargas.

"Not bad."

The bookcollector laughed wearily. He knelt down on the rug next to Corso and went over the books mechanically, making sure that none of them had moved by a millimetre since he last checked them.

"Not bad at all. You're right. At least ten of them are extremely rare . . . I inherited all this part of the collection from my grandfather. He was a devotee of the hermetic arts and astrology, and he was a Mason. Look. This is a classic, the *Infernal Dictionary* by Collin de Plancy, a first edition dating from 1842. And this is the 1571 printing of the *Compendi dei secreti*, by Leonardo Fioravanti . . . That strange duodecimo there is the second edition of the *Book of Wonders*." He opened another book and showed Corso an engraving. "Look at Isis . . . And do you know what this is?"

"Yes, of course. The *Œdipus Ægiptiacus* by Atanasius Kircher."

"Correct. The 1652 Rome edition." Fargas put the book back and picked up another one. Corso recognized the Venetian binding: the black leather with five raised bands, and a pentacle but no title on the cover. "Here's the one you're looking for, *De umbrarum regni novem portis* . . . The nine doors of the kingdom of shadows."

Corso shivered in spite of himself. On the outside at least the book was identical to the one he had in his canvas bag. Fargas handed him the book and Corso stood up as he leafed through it. They looked absolutely identical, or almost. The leather on the back of Fargas's copy was slightly worn, and there was an old mark left by a label that had been added and then removed. The rest was in the same immaculate condition as Varo Borja's copy, even engraving number VIIII which was intact.

"It's complete and in good condition," said Fargas, correctly interpreting the look on Corso's face. "It's been out in the world for three centuries and a half, but when you open it, it looks as fresh as the day it came off the press . . . As if the printer made a pact with the Devil."

"Maybe he did," said Corso.

"I wouldn't mind knowing the magic formula. My soul in exchange for keeping all this." The bookcollector made a sweeping gesture which took in the desolate room, the rows of books on the floor.

"You could try it," said Corso, pointing at *The Nine Doors*. "They say the formula is in there."

"I never believed all that nonsense. Although maybe now would be a good time to start. Don't you think? You have a saying in Spain: If all is lost we may as well jump in the river."*

"Is the book in order? Have you noticed anything strange about it?"

"Nothing whatsoever. There are no pages missing. And the engravings are all there, nine of them, plus the title page. Just as it was when my grandfather bought it at the turn of the century. It matches the description in the catalogues and it's identical to the other two copies, the Ungern in Paris, and the Terral-Coy."

"It's no longer Terral-Coy. Now it's in the Varo Borja collection in Toledo."

Corso saw that Fargas's expression had become suspicious, alert.

"Varo Borja, you say?" He'd been about to add something, but changed his mind at the last moment. "His collection is remarkable. And very well known." He paced around aimlessly and then looked at the books lined up on the rug again. "Varo Borja . . ." he repeated thoughtfully. "He's a specialist in demonology, isn't he? A very rich bookcollector. He's been after that *Nine Doors* you've got there for years. He's always been prepared to pay any price . . . I didn't know that he'd managed to find a copy. And you work for him."

"Occasionally," admitted Corso.

Fargas nodded a couple of times, looking puzzled, and then turned his attention to the books on the floor again.

"Strange that he should send you. After all . . ."

---

*equivalent to "In for a penny, in for a pound".

He broke off and let his sentence hang in mid-air. He was looking at Corso's bag.

"Have you brought the book with you? Could I see it?"

They went up to the table and Corso laid his copy next to Fargas's. As he did so he could hear the old man's agitated breathing. His face looked ecstatic again.

"Look at them closely," he whispered as if he was afraid of waking something sleeping between their pages. "They're perfect, beautiful. And identical . . . Two of the only three copies which escaped the flames, brought together for the first time since they were parted three hundred and fifty years ago . . ." His hands were trembling again. He rubbed his wrists to slow down the blood coursing violently through them. "Look at the errata on page 72. The split *s* here, in the fourth line of page 87 . . . The same paper, identical printing . . . Isn't it a wonder?"

"Yes." Corso cleared his throat. "I'd like to stay for a while. Have a thorough look at them."

Fargas gave him a piercing look. He seemed to hesitate.

"As you wish," he said at last. "But if you have the Terral-Coy copy, there's no doubt as to its authenticity." He looked at Corso with curiosity, trying to read his mind. "Varo Borja must know that."

"I suppose he must." Corso gave his best neutral smile. "But I'm getting paid to make sure." He kept smiling. They were getting to the difficult part. "By the way, talking of money, I've been told to make you an offer."

The bookcollector's curiosity turned to suspicion.

"What kind of offer?"

"Financial. And substantial." Corso laid his hand on the second copy. "You could solve your money problems for some time."

"Would it be Varo Borja paying?"

"It could be."

Fargas stroked his chin.

"He already has one of the books," he concluded. "Does he want all three of them?"

The man might have been slightly insane but he was no fool. Corso gestured vaguely, not wanting to commit himself. Perhaps. One of those things collectors get into their heads. But if he sold it Fargas would then be able to keep the Virgil.

"You don't understand," said Fargas. But Corso understood only too well. He wasn't going to get anywhere with the old man.

"Forget it," he said. "It was just a thought."

"I don't sell at random. I choose the books. I thought I'd made that clear."

The veins on the back of his tensed hands were knotted. He was beginning to get irritated, so Corso spent the next few minutes in placatory mode. The offer was a secondary matter, a mere formality. What he really wanted, he concluded, was to make a comparative study of both books. At last, to his relief, Fargas nodded in agreement.

"I don't see any problem with that," he said. His mistrust was receding slightly. It was obvious he liked Corso or things would have gone quite differently. "Although I can't offer you many creature comforts here . . ."

He led him down a bare passage to another, smaller room which had a dilapidated piano in one corner. There was a table with an old bronze candelabrum covered in wax drips and a couple of rickety chairs.

"At least it's quiet here," said Fargas. "And all the window-panes are intact."

He clicked his fingers as if he'd forgotten something. He disappeared for a moment and returned holding the rest of the bottle of brandy.

"So Varo Borja finally managed to get hold of it . . ." he repeated. He smiled to himself, as if at some thought that obviously caused him great satisfaction. Then he put the bottle and glass on the floor, at a safe distance from the two copies of *The Nine Doors*. Like an attentive host, he looked round to make sure that everything was in order, and then made a final, ironic comment before leaving.

"Make yourself at home."

Corso poured the rest of the brandy into the glass. Then he took out his notes and set to work. He had drawn three boxes on a sheet of paper. Each one contained a number and name:

COPY ONE (Varo Borja) Toledo
COPY TWO (Fargas) Sintra
COPY THREE (Von Ungern) Paris

Page after page he noted down any difference between Book Number One and Number Two, however slight: a stain on the paper, the ink slightly darker in one copy or another. When he came to the first engraving – 'NEM. PERV.T QUI N.N LEG. CERT.RIT', the horseman advising the reader to keep silent – he took out a magnifying glass with a magnification of seven from his bag and examined both woodcuts, line by line. They were identical. He noticed that even the pressure of the engravings on the paper, like that of the typography, was the same. The lines and characters looked worn, broken or crooked in exactly the same places in both copies. This meant that Number One and Number Two had been printed one after the other, or almost, and on the same press. As the Ceniza brothers would have put it, Corso was looking at a pair of twins.

He went on making notes. An imperfection in line six of page nineteen in Book Number Two made him stop a moment, but then he realized it was just an ink stain. He turned more pages. Both books had the same structure: two flyleaves and one hundred and sixty pages stitched into twenty signatures of eight. All nine illustrations in both books occupied a full page. They had been printed separately on the same type of paper, blank on the reverse, and inserted into the book during the binding process. They were positioned identically in both books:

NEM. PERV.T QVI N.N LEG. CERT.RIT

CLAVS. PAT.T

VERB. D.SVM C.S.T ARCAN.

FOR. N.N OMN. A.QVE

FR. ST. A

DIT.SCO M.R.

DIS.S P.TI.R M.

VIC. I.T VIR.

N.NC SC.O TEN.BR. LVX

Either Varo Borja was raving, or this was a very strange job he'd been sent on. There was no way that they were forgeries. At the most they might have both come from an apocryphal edition, but which still dated from the seventeenth century. Number One and Number Two were the embodiment of honesty on printed paper.

He drank the rest of the brandy and then examined illustration II with his magnifying glass. "*CLAUS. PAT.T.*", the bearded hermit holding two keys, the closed door, a lantern on the ground. He had the illustrations side by side and he suddenly felt rather silly. It was like playing "spot the difference". He grimaced. Life as a game. And books as a reflection of life.

Then he saw it. It happened suddenly, just as from the correct angle something that has previously seemed meaningless all at once appears ordered and precise. Corso breathed out as if he were about to laugh, astounded. But all that emerged was a dry sound, like a laugh of disbelief but without the humour. It wasn't possible. One didn't joke with that kind of thing. He shook his head, confused. This wasn't a cheap book of puzzles bought at a railway station. These books were three and a half centuries old. Their printer had lost his life over them. They had been included amongst the books banned by the Inquisition. And they were listed in all the serious bibliographies. "Illustration II. Caption in Latin. Old man with two keys and a lantern, standing in front of a closed door". . . But nobody had compared two of the three known copies until then. It wasn't easy bringing them together. Or necessary. Old man with two keys. That was enough.

Corso got up and went to the window. He stood there for a while, looking through the panes misted by his own breath. Varo Borja was right after all. Aristide Torchia must have been laughing to himself on his pyre at Campo dei Fiori, before the flames took away his sense of humour forever. As a posthumous joke it was brilliant.

VIII

Postuma necat

"Is anybody there?"
"No."
"Too bad. He must be dead."

M. Leblanc: *Arsène Lupin*

Lucas Corso knew better than anyone one of the main problems of his profession: bibliographies are drawn up by scholars who have never actually seen the books they're citing, relying instead on second-hand accounts and information recorded by others. An error or incomplete description might circulate for generations without being noticed. Then, by chance it comes to light. This was the case with *The Nine Doors*. Apart from its obligatory mention in the canonical bibliographies, even the most precise references had only ever included summary descriptions of the nine engravings, without minor details. In the case of the book's second illustration, all the known texts referred to an old man who looked like a sage or a hermit, standing before a door with two keys in his hand. But nobody had ever bothered to specify in which hand he was holding the keys. Now Corso had the answer: in the *left* in the engraving in Book Number One, and in the *right* in Number Two.

He still had to find out what Number Three was like. But this wasn't possible yet. Corso stayed at the Quinta da Soledade until dark. He worked solidly in the light of the candelabra, taking copious notes, checking both books over and over again. He examined each engraving until he had confirmed his theory. More proof emerged. At last he sat looking at his booty in the form of notes on a sheet of paper, tables and diagrams with strange links with each other. Five of the engravings were not identical in both books. In addition to the old man in engraving II holding the keys in different hands, the labyrinth in IIII had an exit in one of the books but not in the other. In illustration V of Book One, Death was brandishing an hourglass with the sand in the lower half, while in Book Two the sand was in the upper half. As for the chessboard in number VII, in Varo Borja's copy the squares were all white while in Fargas's copy they were black. And in engraving number VIII, the executioner poised to behead the young girl in one of the books became an avenging angel in the other through the addition of an aureole above his head.

And there were yet more differences. Close examination through the magnifying glass yielded unexpected results. The printer's marks hidden in the woodcuts contained another subtle clue. *A.T.* – Aristide Torchia – was named as the *sculptor* in the engraving of the old man, but as the *inventor* only in the same engraving in Book Number Two. As the Ceniza brothers had pointed out, the signature in Book One was *L.F.* The same occurred in four more of the illustrations. This could mean that all the woodcuts were carved by the printer himself, but that the original drawings from which he copied some of his engravings were created by somebody else. So this wasn't a matter of a forgery dating from the same era as the books, nor of apocryphal reprintings. It was the printer, Torchia himself, "by authority and permission of the superiors," who had altered his own work in accordance with a pre-established plan. He had signed the engravings he had changed so as to make sure it was clear that L.F. had created the others. Only one copy remains, he told his executioners. Whereas in actual fact he had left three copies behind, and a key which might possibly turn them into a single one. The rest of his secret he took with him to the grave.

He resorted to an ancient collating system: the comparative tables used by Umberto Eco in his study of the Hanau. Having set out in order on paper the illustrations which contained differences, he obtained the following table:

	I	II	III	IIII	V	VI	VII	VIII	VIIII
ONE	–	left hand	–	no exit	sand down	–	white board	no aureole	–
TWO	–	right hand	–	exit	sand up	–	black board	aureole	–

As for the engraver's marks, the variations in the signatures *A.T.* (the printer, Torchia) and *L.F.* (unknown? Lucifer?) corresponding to the *sculptor* and the *inventor,* they were set out as follows:

	I	II	III	IIII	V	VI	VII	VIII	VIIII
ONE	AT(s) AT(i)	AT(s) LF(i)	AT(s) AT(i)	AT(s) AT(i)	AT(s) LF(i)	AT(s) AT(i)	AT(s) AT(i)	AT(s) AT(i)	AT(s) AT(i)
TWO	AT(s) AT(i)	AT(s) AT(i)	AT(s) AT(i)	AT(s) LF(i)	AT(s) AT(i)	AT(s) AT(i)	AT(s) LF(i)	AT(s) LF(i)	AT(s) AT(i)

Strange code. But Corso at last had something definite. He now knew there was a key of some sort. He stood up slowly, as if he were afraid that all the links would vanish before his eyes. But he was calm, like a hunter who is sure that he will catch his prey at the end of the trail, however confusing.

Hand. Exit. Sand. Board. Aureole.

He glanced out of the window. Beyond the dirty panes, a remnant of reddish light silhouetting a branch refused to disappear into the night.

Books One and Two. Differences in numbers 2, 4, 5, 7 and 8.

He had to go to Paris. Book Number Three was there, together with the possible solution to the mystery. But he was now preoccupied with another matter, something he had to deal with urgently. Varo Borja had been categorical. Now that Corso was sure he wouldn't be able to obtain Book Number Two by conventional methods, he had to devise a plan to acquire it by more unorthodox means. With the minimum chance of risk to Fargas, and to Corso himself, of course. Something gentle and discreet. He took out his diary from his coat pocket and searched for the phone number he needed. It was the perfect job for Amilcar Pinto.

One of the candles had burnt right down and went out with a small spiral of smoke. Corso could hear the violin being played somewhere in the house. He laughed drily again as the flames of the candelabra made shadows dance on his face when he leant over to light a cigarette. Then he straightened up and listened. The music sounded like a lament floating through the dark empty rooms with their remains of dusty, worm-eaten furniture, painted ceilings, stained walls covered in spiders' webs and shadows; echoes of footsteps, voices extinguished long ago. And outside, above the rusty railings, the two statues, one with its eyes open in the darkness, the other covered by a mask of ivy, listened motionless, as time stood still, to the music that Victor Fargas played on his violin to summon the ghosts of his lost books.

He returned to the village on foot, his hands in his coat pockets and his collar turned up. It took him twenty minutes on the deserted road. There was no moon and Corso walked into large patches of darkness beneath the black canopy of trees. There was almost total silence, broken only by the sound of his shoes crunching on the gravel at the side of the road, and channels of water coursing down the hill between rockrose and ivy, invisible in the darkness.

A car came from behind and overtook him. Corso saw his own shadow, with its enlarged, ghostly outline, glide undulating across the nearby tree-trunks and dense woods. Only once he was again enveloped in shadow did he breathe out and feel his tense muscles relax. He wasn't one who saw ghosts around every corner. Instead he viewed things, however extraordinary, with the southern fatalism of an old soldier, no doubt inherited from this great-great-grandfather Corso. However much one spurred one's horse in the opposite direction, the inevitable was always lurking at the gate of the nearest Samarkand, picking its nails with a Venetian dagger, or a Scottish bayonet. Even so, since the incident in the street in Toledo, Corso felt understandably apprehensive every time he heard a car behind him.

Maybe because of this, when the lights of another car pulled up beside him, Corso turned round sharply and changed his canvas bag over to his other shoulder. He found his bunch of keys inside his coat pocket. It was a weapon of fortune but with it he could poke the eye out of anybody who got too close. But now there seemed no reason to worry. He saw a large, dark shape, like that of an old berlin, and inside, lit by the faint glow from the dashboard, the profile of a man. His voice was friendly, well-educated.

"Good evening . . ." The accent was indefinable, neither Portuguese nor Spanish. "Do you have a match?"

The request could be genuine, or just a pretext, he couldn't be sure. But he didn't need to run away or brandish his sharpest key just because he'd been asked for a light. So Corso let go of his keyring. He took out his matches and lit one, shielding the flame with his hand.

"Thanks."

There was the scar, of course. It was an old one, long and vertical, from his temple to halfway down his left cheek. He was able to see it closely as the man leant forward to light his Montecristo cigar. Corso held up the light long enough to glimpse the thick, black moustache and dark eyes watching him intently from the gloom. Then the match went out and it seemed as if a black mask had covered the stranger's face. He had become a shadow again, his outline only just distinguishable in the faint light from the dashboard.

"Who the bloody hell are you?"

His tone wasn't calm. Nor was it a particularly brilliant question. Anyway it was too late. The question was drowned out by the sound of the engine accelerating. The twin red points of the car's rear lights were already heading off into the distance, leaving a fleeting trail against the dark ribbon of road. It shone more intensely for an instant as the car turned the first corner, and then disappeared as if it had never been there.

The bookhunter stood motionless by the side of the road, trying to piece the picture together. Madrid, outside Liana Taillefer's house. Toledo, his visit to Varo Borja. And Sintra, after an afternoon at Victor Fargas's house. There were also Dumas's serials, a publisher hanged in his study, a printer burnt at the stake with his strange manual . . . And among all of this, shadowing Corso: Rochefort, a fictional, seventeenth-century swordsman reincarnated as a uniformed chauffeur of luxury cars. Responsible for an attempted hit-and-run incident, and breaking and entering. A smoker of Montecristo cigars. A smoker without a lighter.

He swore gently under his breath. He'd have given a rare incunabulum – in good condition – to punch the face of whoever was writing this ridiculous script.

As soon as he got back to the hotel he made several telephone calls. The first was to the Lisbon number in his diary. He was lucky, Amilcar Pinto was at home. He ascertained as much in a conversation with his bad-tempered wife, the sound of a television blaring in the background, the high-pitched crying of children and adult voices arguing violently coming through the black Bakelite earpiece. Finally Pinto came to the phone. They agreed to meet an hour and a half later, the time it would take the Portuguese to travel the fifty kilometres to

Sintra. Having arranged this, Corso looked at his watch and dialled Varo Borja's number. But the bookdealer wasn't at his house in Toledo. He left a message on the answerphone and dialled Flavio La Ponte's number in Madrid. He wasn't at home either, so Corso hid his canvas bag on top of the wardrobe and went out for a drink.

The first thing he saw as he pushed open the door of the small hotel lounge was the girl. It couldn't be anyone else: her cropped hair giving her a boyish look, her skin as tanned as if it were August. She was sitting in an armchair reading in the cone of light from a lamp, her legs stretched out and crossed on the seat opposite. She was barefoot, in jeans and a white cotton T-shirt, her sweater around her shoulders. Corso stopped, his hand on the door handle, an absurd feeling hammering at his brain. Coincidence or deliberate occurrence, this was too much.

At last, still incredulous, he went up to the girl. He was almost by her side when she looked up from her book and fixed her green eyes on him with their deep, liquid clarity which he remembered so well from their meeting on the train. He stopped, not knowing what to say. He had the strange feeling he was going to fall into her eyes.

"You didn't tell me you were coming to Sintra," he said.

"Nor did you."

She smiled calmly as she said it, looking neither surprised nor embarrassed. She seemed sincerely pleased to see him.

"What are you doing here?" asked Corso.

She took her feet down from the armchair and gestured for him to sit down. But the bookhunter remained standing.

"Travelling," said the girl, and she showed him her book. It wasn't the same one as on the train. *Melmoth the Wanderer* by Charles Maturin. "Reading. And bumping into people unexpectedly."

"Unexpectedly," repeated Corso like an echo.

He'd bumped into too many people for one evening, whether unexpectedly or not. He found himself trying to find a link between her presence at the hotel and Rochefort's appearance on the road. From a certain angle all these things must have fitted together, but he was nowhere near finding it. He didn't even know where to start.

"Won't you sit down?"

He did so, vaguely anxious. The girl had shut her book and was looking at him curiously.

"You don't look like a tourist," she said.

"I'm not."

"Are you working?"

"Yes."

"Any job in Sintra must be interesting."

That's all I need, thought Corso, adjusting his glasses. Being interrogated after all I've been through, even if it was by an extremely young, beautiful girl. Maybe that was the problem. She was too young to be a threat. Or maybe that was where the danger lay. He picked up the girl's book from the table and flicked through it. It was a modern, English edition, some of the paragraphs underlined in pencil. He read one:

His eyes remained fixed in the diminishing light and growing darkness. That preternatural blackness which seems to be saying to God's most luminous and sublime creation: "Give me space. Stop shining."

"Do you enjoy Gothic novels?"

"I enjoy reading." She had bowed her head slightly and the light made a foreshortened outline of her bare neck. "And touching books. I always carry several in my rucksack when I travel."

"Do you travel a lot?"

"Yes. I've been travelling for ages."

Corso winced when he heard her answer. She had said it very seriously, frowning slightly like a little girl talking about serious matters.

"I thought you were a student."

"I am sometimes."

Corso put the *Melmoth* back on the table.

"You're a strange young lady. How old are you? Eighteen? Nineteen? Sometimes your expression changes, as if you were much older."

"Maybe I am. One's gestures are influenced by what one has experienced and read. Look at you."

"What's the matter with me?"

"Have you ever seen yourself smile? You look like an old soldier."

He shifted slightly in his seat, embarrassed.

"I don't know how an old soldier smiles."

"Well, I do." The girl's eyes darkened. She was searching in her memory. "Once I knew ten thousand men who were looking for the sea."

Corso lifted an eyebrow in mock-interest.

"Really. Is that something you read or experienced?"

"Guess." She stopped and looked at him intently before adding, "You seem like a clever man, Mr Corso."

She stood up, taking the book from the table and her white tennis shoes off the floor. Her eyes brightened, and Corso recognized the reflections in them. He glimpsed something familiar in her gaze.

"Maybe we'll see each other around," she said as she left.

Corso had no doubt that they would. He wasn't very sure whether he wanted to or not. One way or another, the thought only lasted an instant. As she left, the girl passed Amilcar Pinto at the door.

He was a short, greasy little man. His skin was dark and shiny, as if it had just been varnished, and he had a thick, wiry moustache, roughly trimmed. He would have been an honest policeman, even a good policeman, if he hadn't had to feed five children, a wife and a retired father who secretly stole his cigarettes. His wife was a mulatto and had been very beautiful twenty years ago. He brought her back from Mozambique at the time of Independence, when Maputo was called Lourenço Marques and he himself was a decorated sergeant in the paratroops, a slight, brave man. During the course of some of the deals they did from time to time he had caught sight of Pinto's wife, eyes ringed with fatigue, large, flaccid breasts, in old slippers and her hair tied with a red scarf, in the hallway to their house which smelt of dirty kids and boiled vegetables.

The policeman came straight into the lounge, looking at the girl out of the corner of his eye as he passed her, and sank into the armchair opposite Corso. He was out of breath, as if he'd just walked all the way from Lisbon.

"Who was the girl?"

"Nobody important," answered Corso. "She's Spanish. A tourist."

Pinto nodded, having caught his breath. He wiped his sweaty palms on his trouser legs. It was something he often did. He sweated abundantly, and his shirt collars always had a dark ring where they touched his skin.

"I've got a bit of a problem," said Corso.

Pinto's grin widened. No problem is insoluble, his expression seemed to say. Not as long as you and I still get along.

"I'm sure we'll be able to solve it together," he answered.

Now it was Corso's turn to smile. He'd met Amilcar Pinto four years before. Some stolen books had appeared on stands at the Ladra Book Fair – a bad business. Corso came to Lisbon to identify them, Pinto made a couple of arrests, and en route back to their owner a few very valuable books disappeared forever. To celebrate the beginning of a fruitful friendship, they got drunk together in the fados bars of the Barrio Alto. The ex-paratroop sergeant reminisced about his time in the colonies with tales of how he'd nearly had his balls blown off at the battle of Gorongosa. They ended up singing '*Grandola vila morena*' at the tops of their voices up on Santa Luzia. Illuminated by the moon, the district of Alfama lay at their feet with the Tagus beyond it, wide and gleaming like a sheet of silver. The dark shapes of boats, moving very slowly, headed out towards the Belém tower and the Atlantic.

A waiter brought Pinto the coffee he had ordered. Corso waited for him to leave before continuing.

"It's about a book."

The policeman leant over the little low table and put sugar in his coffee.

"It's always about a book," he said gravely.

"This one's special."

"Which one isn't?"

Corso smiled again. A sharp, metallic smile.

"The owner doesn't want to sell."

"That's bad." Pinto drank some coffee, savouring it. "Trade's a good thing. Things moving, coming and going. It generates wealth, makes money for the go-betweens . . ." He put the cup down and wiped his hands on his trousers. "Products have to circulate. It's the law of the market, of life. Not selling should be banned: it's almost a crime."

"I agree," said Corso. "You should do something about it."

Pinto leaned back in his chair. Calm and confident, he looked at Corso expectantly. Once, after an ambush in the *mato* in Mozambique, he had fled, carrying a dying officer for ten kilometres through the jungle. At dawn he felt the lieutenant die, but didn't want to leave him behind. So he went on, with the corpse over his shoulders, until he reached the base. The officer was very young, and Pinto thought that his mother would like to have him buried back in Portugal. They gave him a medal for it. Now Pinto's children played about the house with his old tarnished medals.

"Maybe you know the man: Victor Fargas."

The policeman nodded.

"The Fargases are a very old, very respectable family," he said. "In the past they had a lot of influence, but not any more."

Corso handed him a sealed envelope.

"This is all the information you need: owner, book and location."

"I know the house." Pinto licked his upper lip, wetting his moustache. "Very unwise, keeping valuable books there. Any unscrupulous individual might get in." He looked at Corso sadly, as if he really thought Victor Fargas was being irresponsible. "I can think of one, a petty thief from Chiado who owes me a favour."

Corso shook some invisible dust from his clothes. It had nothing to do with him. Not in the operational phase anyway.

"I don't want to be in the area when it happens."

"Don't worry. You'll get your book and Mr Fargas will be disturbed as little as possible. A broken window-pane at the most. It'll be a clean job. About payment . . ."

Corso pointed at the envelope that Pinto was holding, still unopened.

"That's an advance of a quarter of the total. The rest on delivery."

"That's fine. When are you leaving?"

"First thing tomorrow morning. I'll get in touch with you from Paris." Pinto was about to get up, but Corso stopped him. "There's something else. I need an identification. Tall man, about six feet, with a moustache and a scar on his face. Black hair, dark eyes. Slim. He's not Spanish or Portuguese. And he was lurking around here tonight."

"Is he dangerous?"

"I don't know. He's followed me from Madrid."

Pinto was taking notes on the back of the envelope.

"Does this have anything to do with our business?"

"I'm assuming it does. But I don't have any more information."

"I'll do what I can. I've got friends at the police station here in Sintra. And I'll take a look at the files at central headquarters in Lisbon."

He stood up and put the envelope in the inside pocket of his jacket. Corso caught a fleeting glimpse of a revolver in the holster under his left arm.

"Why don't you stay for a drink?"

Pinto sighed and shook his head.

"I'd like to, but three of the kids have got measles. They catch it off each other, the little swine."

He said this with a tired smile. All the heroes in Corso's world were tired.

They went to the hotel entrance where Pinto had parked his old Citroën 2CV. As they shook hands, Corso mentioned Victor Fargas again.

"Make sure that Fargas is disturbed as little as possible. This is just a burglary."

Pinto switched on the engine and turned on the lights. He looked at Corso reproachfully through the open window. He looked offended.

"Please. You don't need to tell me again. I know what I'm doing."

After Pinto had left, Corso went up to his room to sort out his notes. He worked on late into the night, his bed covered in papers and *The Nine Doors* open on his pillow. He felt extremely tired and thought a hot shower might help him relax. He was on his way to the bathroom when the phone rang. It was Varo Borja, wanting to know how he had got on with Fargas. He gave him a general idea of how things were going, including the discrepancies he had found in five of the nine engravings.

"By the way," he added, "our friend Fargas won't sell."

There was a silence at the other end of the line. Borja seemed to be thinking, although there was no way of telling whether it was about the engravings or Fargas's refusal to sell. When he spoke again his tone was extremely cautious.

"That seemed likely," he said. Corso still couldn't tell exactly what he was referring to. "Is there any way of getting round the problem?"

"There might be."

Borja was silent again. Corso counted five seconds by his watch.

"I'll leave it in your hands."

They didn't say much else after that. Corso didn't mention his conversation with Pinto, and Borja didn't enquire how Corso was going to solve the "problem", as he had euphemistically put it. He only asked if Corso needed more money, and Corso said no. They agreed to talk again when Corso reached Paris.

Corso then dialled La Ponte's number, but there was still no answer. The blue pages of the Dumas manuscript remained in their folder. He gathered up his notes and the black leather-bound book with the pentacle on the cover. He put them back in his canvas bag and slipped it under the bed, tying the strap to one of the legs. In that way, if anybody got into the room and tried to take it, they'd have to wake him however soundly he was sleeping. Rather an awkward piece of luggage to carry around, he thought as he went to the bathroom to turn on the shower. And, for some reason, dangerous too.

He brushed his teeth. Then he undressed and dropped his clothes on the floor. The mirror was almost completely steamed over but he could see his reflection, thin and hard like an emaciated wolf. Once again he felt a burst of anxiety from the distant past, swamping his mind in a painful wave. Like a string vibrating in his flesh and his memory. Nikon. He remembered her every time he undid his belt. She'd always insisted on undoing it for him as if it were a strange ritual. He shut his eyes and saw her in front of him, sitting on the edge of the bed, slipping his trousers and then his underpants down very slowly, savouring the moment with a conspiratorial, tender smile. Relax, Lucas Corso. Once she had taken a photo of him secretly, while he was sleeping. He was face down with a vertical crease on his brow and his cheek was darkened by stubble. It made his face look thinner and emphasized the tense, bitter lines at the corners of his half-open mouth. He looked like an exhausted wolf, suspicious and tormented in the deserted snow plain of the pillow. He didn't like the photo. He found it by chance, in the fixing tray in the bathroom that Nikon used as a dark room. He'd torn it, and the negative, into little pieces. She'd never mentioned it.

When he stepped into the shower the hot water scalded him. He let it run over his face, burning his eyelids. He put up with the pain, his jaw clenched and his muscles tensed, suppressing the urge to howl with loneliness in the suffocating steam. For four years, one month and twelve days, Nikon always got into the shower with him after they had made love and soaped his back slowly, interminably. And often she put her arms round him, like a little girl in the rain. One day I'll leave without ever really knowing you. You'll remember my big, dark eyes. The reproachful silences. The moans of anxiety as I slept. The nightmares you couldn't save me from. You'll remember all this once I'm gone.

He leant his head against the dripping white tiles, in a damp steaming desert which seemed like a kind of hell. Nobody had ever soaped his back before or since Nikon. Nobody. Ever.

After his shower he got into bed with the *Memoirs of Saint-Helena* but only managed to read a couple of lines:

Returning to the subject of war, the Emperor continued: "The Spaniards en masse acted as a man of honour."

He frowned at Napoleon's praise, two centuries old. He remembered words he'd heard as a child, perhaps from one of his grandparents, or his father. "There's one thing we Spaniards do better than anyone else: appear in Goya's pictures." Men of honour, Bonaparte had said. Corso thought of Varo Borja and his cheque-book. Of Flavio La Ponte and widows' libraries plundered for a pittance. Of Nikon's ghost wandering in a lonely, white desert. Of himself, a hunter who worked for the highest bidder. These were different times.

He was still smiling, desperate and bitter, when he fell asleep.

When he woke the first thing he saw was the grey light of dawn through the window. Too early. Confused, he tried to find his watch on the bedside table when he realized that the phone was ringing. He dropped the receiver twice before managing to lodge it between his ear and the pillow.

"Hello?"

"This is your friend from last night. Remember? Irene Adler. I'm in the lobby. We have to talk. Now."

"What the hell . . ."

But she'd already hung up. Cursing, Corso searched for his glasses. He threw back the sheets and put on his trousers, drowsy and disconcerted. With sudden panic, he looked under the bed. The bag was still there, intact. With an effort he managed to focus on the things around him. Everything in the room was in order. It was outside that things were happening. He had time to go to the bathroom and splash water on his face before she knocked at the door.

"Do you know what the bloody time is?"

The girl was standing there in her blue duffle coat with her rucksack on her back. Her eyes were even more green than Corso remembered.

"It's half past six in the morning," she announced calmly. "And you've got to get dressed right now."

"Have you gone crazy?"

"No." She came into the room without being asked and looked round critically. "We've got very little time."

"We?"

"You and I. Things have got rather complicated."

Corso snorted, irritated.

"It's too early for jokes."

"Don't be stupid." She wrinkled her nose with an expression of concentration. Despite her youth and boyishness, she looked different, older and more self-assured. "I'm serious."

She put her rucksack on the unmade bed. Corso gave it back to her and showed her the door.

"Go to hell."

She didn't move, just looked at him intently.

"Listen." Her light eyes were very near, like liquid ice, so luminous against her tanned skin. "Do you know who Victor Fargas is?"

Corso caught sight of his own face in the mirror above the chest of drawers, beyond the girl's shoulder. He was open-mouthed, like a complete idiot.

"Of course I do."

He'd taken several seconds to react and was still blinking, confused. She waited, not entirely satisfied with his reaction to her words. It was obvious her mind was on other things.

"He's dead," she said.

She said it neutrally as if she'd just told him Fargas had coffee for breakfast, or had gone to the dentist. Corso took a deep breath, trying to take in what she'd just said.

"That's not possible. I was with him last night. He was fine."

"Well, now he's not. He's not fine at all."

"How do you know?"

"I just do."

Corso shook his head, suspicious, before going to get a cigarette. En route he saw the flask of Bols, so he took a swig. The gin hitting his empty stomach made his hair stand on end. Then he waited, forcing himself not to look at the girl until he'd inhaled his first puff of smoke. He wasn't at all happy with the part he was being forced to play this morning. He needed time to think.

"The café in Madrid, the train, last night and now this morning here in Sintra . . ." He counted on the fingers of his left hand, with his cigarette in his mouth, his eyes half-closed because of the smoke. "That's a lot of coincidences, don't you think?"

She shook her head impatiently.

"I thought you were smarter than that. Who said anything about coincidences?"

"Why are you following me?"

"I like you."

Corso didn't feel like laughing. He just twisted his mouth slightly.

"That's ridiculous."

She looked at him for a time, thoughtfully.

"I suppose it is," she said at last. "You don't exactly look breathtaking, always in that old coat and those glasses."

"What is it, then?"

"Find another answer. Anything would do. But now get dressed, will you? We've got to go to Victor Fargas's house."

"We?"

"You and I. Before the police get there."

The dead leaves crackled beneath their feet as they pushed the iron gate and walked up the path lined with broken statues and empty pedestals. The grey morning light cast no shadows and above the stone staircase the sundial still showed no time. '*Postuma necat.*' The last one kills, Corso read again. The girl had followed his gaze.

"Absolutely true," she said coldly and pushed the door. It was locked.

"Let's try the back," suggested Corso.

They went round the house, past the tiled fountain with the chubby stone angel, eyes empty and hands cut off, water still trickling from its mouth into the pond. Surprisingly composed, the girl – Irene Adler or whatever her name was – went ahead of Corso in her blue duffle coat with the small rucksack on her back. She walked, her long supple legs in jeans, her stubborn head leaning forward with the determined air of someone who knew exactly where she was going. Unlike Corso. He had overcome his doubt and let the girl lead him. He was leaving the questions till later. Clear-headed after a quick shower, carrying all he was most concerned about in his canvas bag, he could think of nothing else now but Victor Fargas's *Nine Doors*, Book Number Two.

They got in without difficulty through the French window leading from the garden into the drawing-room. On the ceiling, dagger aloft, Abraham was still watching over the books lined up on the floor. The house seemed deserted.

"Where's Fargas?" asked Corso.

The girl shrugged.

"I've no idea."

"You said he was dead."

"He is." After glancing at her surroundings, at the bare walls and the books, she picked up the violin from the sideboard and looked at it curiously. "What I don't know is where he is."

"You're pulling my leg."

She placed the violin under her chin and plucked at the strings before putting it back in its case, unhappy with the sound. Then she looked at Corso.

"Oh ye of little faith."

She was smiling again, absently. To Corso her composure seemed both deep and frivolous, incongruously mature. This young lady behaved according to a strange code of conduct, determined by thoughts that were more complex than her age and appearance let one suppose.

Suddenly, these thoughts – the girl, the strange events, even the supposed corpse of Victor Fargas – all left Corso's mind. On the threadbare rug depicting the battle of Arbelas, between books on satanic arts and the occult, there was a gap. *The Nine Doors* was no longer there.

"Shit," he said.

He muttered it again as he leant over the row of books and knelt beside them. His expert glance, accustomed to finding a book instantly, wandered from one side to another without success. Black morocco, five raised bands, no title on the exterior, a pentacle on the cover. *Umbrarum regni*, etc. He wasn't mistaken. A third of the mystery, exactly 33.33 recurring per cent, had vanished.

"Damn."

It couldn't have been Pinto, he wouldn't have had time to organize anything. The girl was watching him as if waiting for him to do something interesting. Corso stood up.

"Who are you?"

It was the second time in less than twelve hours that he'd asked the question, but of two different people. Things were getting complicated far too quickly. For her part, the girl didn't react to the question and held his gaze. After a time she looked away from Corso into empty space. Or possibly at the books lined up on the floor.

"It doesn't matter," she answered at last. "You'd be better off wondering where the book has gone."

"What book?"

She looked at him again but didn't answer. He felt incredibly stupid.

"You know too much," he said to the girl. "Even more than me."

Again she shrugged. She was looking at Corso's watch.

"You don't have much time."

"I don't give a damn how much time I've got."

"That's up to you. But there's a flight from Lisbon to Paris in five hours' time, from Portela airport. We have just enough time to get there."

God. Corso shivered under his coat, horrified. She sounded like an efficient secretary, diary in hand, listing her boss's appointments for the day. He opened his mouth to complain. And so young with those disturbing eyes. Damned little witch.

"Why should I leave now?"

"Because the police might arrive."

"I don't have anything to hide."

The girl smiled indefinably, as if she had just heard a funny but very old joke. Then she put her rucksack on her back and waved goodbye.

"I'll bring you cigarettes in prison. Though they don't sell your brand here in Portugal."

She went out into the garden without a backward glance at the room. Corso was about to go after her and stop her. But then he saw something on the mantelpiece.

After an initial moment of disbelief he went over to it. Very slowly, so that things might return to normal. But when he reached the fireplace and leant on the mantelpiece he saw that the situation was irreversible. In the brief time lapse between the previous night and this morning, a minute period of time compared to their centuries-old contents, the antiquarian bibliographies had just gone out of date. There now remained not three known copies of *The Nine Doors*, but only two. The third, or what was left of it, was still smouldering among the embers.

He knelt, taking care not to touch anything. The binding, no doubt because of the leather covering, was less damaged than the pages inside. Two of the five raised bands on the spine were intact, and the pentacle was only half-burnt. But the pages had been almost entirely consumed by the flames. There only remained a few charred edges, with fragments of writing. Corso held his hand over the still warm remains.

He took out a cigarette and put it in his mouth, but didn't light it. He remembered how the logs had been piled up in the fireplace the night before. Judging by the ashes – the burnt logs were underneath those of the book, nobody had raked over the embers – the fire had burnt until it had gone out with the book on top. He remembered seeing enough logs piled there to last about four or five hours. And the still warm ashes indicated that the fire had gone out about the same number of hours ago. This added up to a total of eight to ten hours. Somebody must have lit it between ten o'clock and midnight, and then put the book into the fire. And whoever had done so hadn't hung around afterwards to rake over the embers.

Corso wrapped any remains that he could save from the fireplace in some old newspaper. The page fragments were stiff and brittle, so it took him some time. As he did so he noticed that the pages and cover had burnt separately. Whoever had thrown them into the fire had torn them apart so they should burn more efficiently.

Once he had retrieved all the pieces, he paused to glance round the room. The Virgil and the Agricola were where Fargas had put them. The *De re metalica* lined up with the others on the rug, and the Virgil on the table, just as Fargas had left it when, with the tone of a priest performing a ritual sacrifice, he had uttered the words, "I think I'll sell this one" . . .There was a sheet of paper between its pages. Corso opened the book. It was a handwritten receipt, unfinished.

Victor Coutinho Fargas, Identity Card No. 3554712, address: Quinta da Soledade, Carretera de Colares, km.4, Sintra.
Received with thanks the sum of 800,000 escudos for the work in my possession, "Virgil. Opera nunc recens accuratissime castigata . . . Venezia, Giunta, 1544". (Essling 61. Sander 7671). Folio, 10.587, 1c, 113 woodcuts. Complete and in good condition. The buyer . . .

There was no name or signature. The receipt had never been completed. Corso put the paper back and shut the book. Then he went to the room where he'd spent the previous afternoon, to make sure he'd left no trace, papers with his handwriting or anything like that. He also removed his cigarette butts from the ashtray, and put them in his pocket wrapped in another piece of newspaper. He looked around for a little while longer. His steps echoed through the empty house. No sign of the owner.

As he again passed the books lined up on the floor, he stopped, tempted. It was too easy – a couple of conveniently small Elzevirs attracted his attention. But Corso was a sensible man. It would only complicate matters if things became nasty. So, with a sigh, he bade farewell to the Fargas collection.

He went out through the French window into the garden to look for the girl, dragging his feet on the leaves on the ground. He found her sitting on a short flight of steps leading to the pond. He could hear the water trickling from the chubby angel's mouth onto the greenish surface, covered in floating plants. She was staring engrossed, at the pond. Only the sound of his steps interrupted her contemplation and made her turn her head.

Corso put his canvas bag on the bottom step and sat down next to her. Then he lit the cigarette he'd had in his mouth for some time. He inhaled, his head to one side, and threw away the match. Then he turned to the girl.

"Now tell me everything."

Still staring at the pond, she gently shook her head. Not abruptly, or unpleasantly. On the contrary, the movement of her head, her chin and the corners of her mouth was sweet and thoughtful, as if Corso's presence, the sad, neglected garden, the sound of the water, were all peculiarly moving. With her duffle coat and her rucksack still on her back she looked incredibly young. Almost defenceless. And very tired.

"We have to go," she said so low that Corso scarcely heard her. "To Paris."

"First tell me what's your link with Fargas. With all of this."

She shook her head again, in silence. Corso blew out some smoke. The air was so damp that it floated in front of him for a moment and condensed, before gradually disappearing. He looked at the girl.

"Do you know Rochefort?"

"Rochefort?"

"Or whatever his name is. He's dark, with a scar. He was lurking round here last night." As he spoke, Corso was aware of how silly it all was. He ended with an incredulous grimace, doubting his own memories. "I even spoke to him."

The girl again shook her head, still staring at the pond.

"I don't know him."

"What are you doing here, then?"

"I'm looking after you."

Corso stared at the tips of his shoes, rubbing his numb hands. The tinkle of the water in the pond was beginning to get on his nerves. He took a last drag on his cigarette. It was about to burn his lips and tasted bitter.

"You're mad, girl."

He threw away the cigarette end, staring at the smoke fading before his eyes.

"Completely mad," he added.

She still said nothing. After a moment, Corso brought out his flask of gin and took a long swig, without offering her any. Then he looked at her again.

"Where's Fargas?"

She took a moment to answer, still absorbed, lost. At last she indicated with her chin.

"Over there."

Corso followed the direction of her gaze. In the pond, beneath the thread of water from the mouth of the mutilated angel with empty eyes, he saw the vague outline of a man floating face down among the water lilies and dead leaves.

IX

The Bookseller in the Rue Bonaparte

"My friend," Athos said gravely, "remember that the dead are the only ones whom one does not risk meeting again on this earth."

A. Dumas: *The Three Musketeers*

Lucas Corso ordered a second gin and leant back comfortably in the wicker chair. It was pleasant in the sun. He was sitting on the terrace of the Café Atlas in the Rue de Buci, in the rectangle of light framing the tables. It was one of the cold luminous mornings when the left bank of the Seine crawls with people: disorientated Japanese, Anglo-Saxons in trainers with metro tickets marking their place in a Hemingway novel, ladies with baskets full of lettuces and baguettes, and slender gallery owners who've had their noses fixed, heading for a café during their lunch break. A very attractive young woman was looking in the window of a luxury charcuterie, on the arm of a mature, well-dressed man who might have been an antique dealer, or a scoundrel, or both. There was also a Harley Davidson with all its shiny chrome, a bad-tempered fox terrier tied up at the door of an expensive wine shop, a young man with plaits playing the flute outside a boutique. And at the table next to Corso's, a couple of very elegant Africans kissing on the mouth in a leisurely way, as if they had all the time in the world and the arms race, AIDS, the hole in the ozone layer were all trivial anecdotes on that sunny Parisian morning.

He saw her at the end of the Rue Mazarin, turning the corner towards the café where he waited. With her boyish looks, her duffle coat open over her jeans, her eyes like two points of light against her suntan, visible from a distance in the crowd, in the street overflowing with dazzling sunlight. Devilishly pretty, Flavio La Ponte would no doubt have said, clearing his throat and turning his best side – where his beard was slightly thicker and more curly – towards her. But Corso wasn't La Ponte, so he didn't say or think anything. He just gave a hostile glance at the waiter who was putting a glass of gin on his table – "*Pas d'Bols, m'sieu*" – and handed him the exact amount on the bill – "*Service compris*, young man" – before looking back at the girl approaching. As far as that stuff went, Nikon had left him a hole in the stomach the size of a clipful of bullets. That was enough. Nor was Corso very sure whether he had, now or ever, a better profile than anyone else. And he was damned if he cared anyway.

He took off his glasses and cleaned them with his handkerchief. The street became a series of vague outlines, of shapes with blurred faces. One stood out, and became clearer as it got nearer, although it never grew completely sharp: short hair, long legs, white tennis shoes acquired definition as he focused on her with difficulty and partial success when she reached him and sat down in the empty chair.

"I've found the shop. It's a couple of blocks away."

He put his glasses back on and looked at her without answering. They had travelled together from Lisbon. They left Sintra for the airport posthaste, as old Dumas would have described it. Twenty minutes before the plane's departure Corso phoned Amilcar Pinto to tell him that Victor Fargas's torment as a bookcollector was over and that the plan was cancelled. Pinto would still be paid the sum agreed, on account of his trouble. Apart from being surprised – the call had woken him – Pinto reacted fairly well. All he answered was, "I don't know what you're on about, Corso, you and I never saw each other last night in Sintra." Nevertheless, he promised he'd make some discreet enquiries into Victor Fargas's death. But only once he'd heard about it officially. For the time being he knew nothing about it, nor did he want to, and as for the autopsy, Corso could only hope that the forensic report would give the cause of death as suicide. Just in case, Pinto would pass the description of the individual with the scar on to the relevant departments as a possible suspect. He'd keep in touch by phone and he strongly urged Corso not to come back to Portugal for some time. "Oh, and one last thing," added Pinto as the departure of the Paris flight was being announced. Next time, before he thought of involving a friend in possible murders, Corso could go to hell. Corso hurriedly protested his innocence as the phone swallowed his last escudo. "Yeah, yeah," said Pinto, "that's what they all say."

The girl was waiting in the departure lounge. Corso, who was still dazed and not up to tying all the loose ends appearing all over the place, was surprised to see she had been extremely efficient and managed to get them two plane tickets without any difficulty. "I've just inherited some money," was her answer when, on seeing her pay for both tickets, he made some snide remarks about the limited funds he'd assumed her to have up till then. Afterwards, during the two-hour flight from Lisbon to Paris, she refused to answer any of his questions. All in good time, was all she would say, looking at Corso out of the corner of her eye, almost sneaking a glance at him, before she became absorbed in the trails of condensation left by the plane in the cold air. Then she fell asleep, or rather pretended to, resting her head on his shoulder. Corso could tell from her breathing that she was still awake. Feigning sleep was merely a convenient way of avoiding questions that she wasn't prepared, or allowed, to answer.

Anyone else in his situation would have insisted on answers, shaking her abruptly out of her pretence. But he was a well-trained, patient wolf, with the instincts and reflexes of a hunter. After all, the girl was his only real link in this unreal, novelesque, unjustifiable situation. In addition, by that stage in the script he had fully assumed the part of qualified reader and protagonist that someone, whoever was tying the knots on the back of the rug, on the underside of the plot, seemed to be offering him with a wink that could either be contemptuous, or conspiratorial, he couldn't tell which.

"Somebody's setting me up," Corso said out loud, nine thousand metres above the Bay of Biscay. Then he glanced at the girl out of the corner of his eye, waiting for a reaction, but she didn't move. Her breathing was slow, and either she really was asleep or she hadn't heard. Annoyed by her silence, he moved his shoulder away. Her head lolled for a moment. Then she sighed and made herself comfortable again, this time leaning against the window.

"Of course they are," she said at last sleepily and scornfully, her eyes still closed. "Any idiot could see that."

"What happened to Fargas?"

She didn't answer immediately. Out of the corner of his eye he could see her blinking, looking intently at the seat in front of her.

"You saw yourself," she said after a moment. "He drowned."

"Who did it?"

She turned her head slowly, from one side to the other, and ended up looking out. She slid her hand, slender and tanned with short unvarnished nails, slowly across the armrest. She stopped at the edge as if her fingers had come up against some invisible object.

"It doesn't matter."

Corso grimaced. He looked as if he were about to laugh, but didn't. He just showed his teeth.

"It does to me. It matters a lot."

The girl shrugged. They weren't concerned about the same things, she seemed to imply. Or at least didn't have the same priorities.

Corso persisted.

"What's your part in all this?"

"I've already told you. To take care of you."

She turned towards him and looked at him as firmly as she had been evasive a moment ago. She slid her hand over the armrest again, as if trying to bridge the distance between her and Corso. She was altogether too near, so Corso moved away instinctively, embarrassed and slightly disconcerted. In the pit of his stomach, in Nikon's wake, obscure, disturbing emotions were stirring. With the emptiness the pain was gently returning. In the girl's eyes, silent and without memory, Corso could see the reflection of ghosts from the past and he could feel them brush his skin.

"Who sent you?"

She lowered her eyelashes over her luminous irises, and it was as if she had turned a page. There was nothing there any more, just emptiness. The girl wrinkled her nose, irritated.

"You're boring me, Corso."

She turned to the window and looked at the view. The great expanse of blue flecked with tiny white threads seemed to be split in the distance by a yellow and ochre line. Land ahoy. France. Next stop, Paris. Or next chapter. To be continued in next week's issue. Ending, sword aloft, a cliffhanger typical of all romantic serials. He thought of the Quinta da Soledade, the water trickling from the fountain, Fargas's body among the water lilies and dead leaves in the pond. He flushed and shifted uncomfortably in his seat. With good reason, he felt like a man on the run. Absurd. Rather than fleeing by choice he was being forced to.

He looked at the girl and then tried to see his own situation with the necessary objectivity. Maybe he wasn't running away but towards something instead. Or maybe the mystery he was trying to escape was hidden in his own suitcase. 'The Anjou Wine'. *The Nine Doors*. Irene Adler. The stewardess, with a trained, fatuous smile, said something as she passed. Corso looked at her without seeing her, absorbed in his own thoughts. If only he knew whether the end of the story was already written, or whether he himself was writing it as he went along, chapter by chapter.

He didn't say another word to the girl that day. When they arrived at Orly he ignored her, although he was aware of her walking behind him along the airport corridors. At passport control, after showing his identity card, he turned round to see what kind of document she had, but he couldn't see clearly. All he saw was a passport bound in black leather without any markings. It must be European because she had gone through the gate for EC citizens. Outside, while Corso was climbing into a taxi, giving his usual address, the Louvre Concorde, she slipped into the seat next to him. They drove to the hotel in silence. There she got out of the taxi first and let him pay the fare. The taxi-driver didn't have any change so Corso was slightly delayed. By the time he at last crossed the lobby she had already checked in and was walking away behind a porter carrying her rucksack. She waved at him before she entered the elevator.

"It's a very nice shop. Replinger, Booksellers, it says. Autographs and historical documents. And it's open."

She indicated a sign to the waiter that she didn't want to order and leant slightly towards Corso across the table, in the café on the Rue de Buci. Like a mirror, the liquid transparency of her eyes reflected the street scenes which were themselves reflections in the café window.

"We could go there now."

They had met again at breakfast, as Corso was reading the papers at one of the windows overlooking the Place du Palais Royal. She said good morning and sat down at the table. She devoured toast and croissants with a healthy appetite. Then she looked at Corso. She had a rim of milky coffee on her upper lip, like a little girl.

"Where do we start?"

So now there they were, two blocks from Achille Replinger's bookshop. The girl had offered to go and find it while Corso drank his first gin of the day. He had a feeling it wouldn't be the last.

"We could go there now," she said again.

Corso still hesitated. He'd seen her tanned skin in his dreams. He was holding her hand, crossing a deserted plain in the shadow of dusk. Columns of smoke rose on the horizon, volcanoes about to erupt.

Occasionally they passed a soldier with a grave face, his armour covered in dust, who stared at them in silence, distant and cold like the sullen Trojans of Hades. The plain was darkening on the horizon and the columns of smoke grew thicker. The impassive, ghostly faces of the dead warriors contained a warning. Corso wanted to get away. He pulled the girl along by the hand anxious not to leave her behind, but the air was becoming thick and hot, stifling, dark. Their flight ended in an interminable fall, an agony in slow motion. The darkness burnt like an oven. The only link with the outside was Corso's hand, holding on to hers in an effort to go on. The last thing he felt was her hand, its grip fading, finally turn to ash. And in front of him, in the darkness closing in on the burning plain and on his mind, white marks, traces as fleeting as lightning, picked out the ghostly contour of a skull. It wasn't pleasant to recall. To try to remove the taste of ash from his mouth and erase these horrors, Corso finished his glass of gin and looked at the girl. She was watching him, a disciplined collaborator waiting calmly for instructions. Serene, she simply accepted her strange part in the story. Her loyal expression was inexplicable and disconcerting.

She stood up at the same time as Corso. He put the canvas bag over his shoulder and they made their way slowly towards the river. The girl walked along the inside of the pavement and occasionally stopped in front of a shop window, calling his attention to a picture, an engraving, a book. She looked at everything with wide eyes and intense curiosity, seeming slightly nostalgic as she smiled thoughtfully. She seemed to be searching for traces of herself in those old things. As if, in some corner of her memory, she shared a common past with the few survivors washed up by the tide after each of history's inexorable shipwrecks.

There were two bookshops facing each other on either side of the street. Achille Replinger's had a very old, elegant shopfront, of varnished wood, with a sign saying "*Livres anciens, autographes et documents historiques*". Corso told the girl to wait outside and she didn't object. As he headed towards the door he looked in the window and saw her reflection over his shoulder. She was standing on the other side of the road, watching him.

A bell rang as he pushed the door. There was an oak table, shelves full of old books, stands with folders of prints and a dozen old wooden filing cabinets. These had letters in alphabetical order, carefully written in brass slots. On the wall there was a framed autograph with the caption, "Fragment of *Tartuffe*. Molière". Also three good prints, Victor Hugo and Flaubert, and Dumas in the centre.

Achille Replinger was standing by the table. He was thick-set with a reddish complexion. Porthos with a bushy grey moustache and thick double chin overlapping the collar of his shirt worn with a knitted tie. He was expensively but carelessly dressed. His jacket was straining to contain his girth and his flannel trousers were creased and sagging.

"Corso . . . Lucas Corso," he said holding Boris Balkan's letter of introduction in his thick, strong fingers and frowning. "Yes, he called me the other day. Something about Dumas."

Corso put his bag on the table and took out the folder with the fifteen manuscript pages of 'The Anjou Wine'. The bookseller spread them out in front of him, arching his brow.

"Interesting," he said quietly. "Very interesting."

He wheezed as he spoke, breathing with difficulty like an asthmatic. He took his glasses from one of his jacket pockets and put them on after a brief glance at his visitor. Then he leant over the pages. When he looked up he was smiling ecstatically.

"Extraordinary," he said, "I'll buy it from you here and now."

"It's not for sale."

Replinger seemed surprised. He pursed his lips, nearly pouting.

"I thought . . ."

"I just need an expert opinion. You'll be paid for your time, of course."

Achille Replinger shook his head. He didn't care about the money. He looked confused and a couple of times he stopped to look at Corso mistrustfully over his glasses. Then he leant over the manuscript again.

"A pity," he said at last, and cast a curious glance at Corso. He looked as if he was wondering how on earth it had fallen into his hands. "How did you get hold of it?"

"I inherited it from an old aunt. Have you ever seen it before?"

Still suspicious, Replinger looked over Corso's shoulder, through the window at the street, as if someone out there might be able to give him some information about his visitor. Or maybe he was considering how to answer Corso's question. He pulled at his moustache, as if it were false and he was checking it was still in place, and smiled evasively.

"Here in the *quartier* you can never be sure if you've seen something before . . . This has always been a good area for people dealing in books and prints. People come here to buy and sell, and everything has passed several times through the same hands." He paused to catch his breath and then looked at Corso uneasily. "I don't think so . . . No, I've never seen this manuscript before," he said. He looked out at the street again, flushed. "I'd be sure if I had."

"Do I take it that it's authentic?" asked Corso.

"Well . . . In fact, yes." Replinger wheezed as he stroked the blue pages. He seemed to be trying to stop himself touching them. Finally he held one up between his thumb and forefinger. "Semi-rounded, medium weight handwriting, no annotations or erasures . . . Almost no punctuation marks, and unexpected capital letters. This is definitely Dumas at his peak, towards the middle of his life, when he wrote *The Musketeers* . . ." He'd become more animated as he spoke. Now he suddenly fell silent and lifted a finger. Corso could see him smiling beneath his moustache. He seemed to have reached a decision. "Wait just one moment."

He went over to one of the filing cabinets marked "D" and took out some buff-coloured folders.

"All of this is by Alexandre Dumas père. The handwriting is identical."

There were about a dozen documents, some unsigned or else initialled A.D. Some had the full signature. Most of them were short notes to publishers, letters to friends, or invitations.

"This is one of his American autographs," explained Replinger. "Lincoln requested one, and Dumas sent him ten dollars and a hundred autographs. They were sold in Pittsburgh for charity . . ." He showed Corso all the documents with a restrained but obvious professional pride. "Look at this one. An invitation to dine with him on Montecristo, at the house he had built in Port-Marly. Sometimes he only signed his initials, at others he used pseudonyms. But not all the autographs that are in circulation are authentic. At the newspaper *The Musketeer*, which he owned, there was a man called Viellot who could imitate his handwriting and signature. And during the last three years of his life, Dumas's hands trembled so much he had to dictate his work."

"Why blue paper?"

"He would have it sent from Lille. It was made for him specially by a printer who was a great admirer. He almost always used this colour, especially for the novels. Occasionally he used pale pink for his articles, or yellow for poetry. He used several different pens, according to what kind of thing he was writing. And he couldn't stand blue ink."

Corso pointed to the four white pages of the manuscript, with notes and corrections.

"What about these?"

Replinger frowned.

"Maquet. His collaborator Auguste Maquet. These are corrections made by Dumas to the original text." He stroked his moustache. Then he leant over and read aloud in a theatrical voice. "'Horrifying! Horrifying!' murmured Athos, as Porthos shattered the bottles and Aramis gave somewhat belated orders to send for a confessor . . .'" Replinger broke off with a sigh. He nodded, satisfied, and then showed Corso the page. "Look: all Maquet wrote was: 'And he expired before d'Artagnan's terrified companions.' Dumas crossed out that line and added others above it, fleshing out the passage with more dialogue."

"What can you tell me about Maquet?"

Replinger shrugged his powerful shoulders, hesitating.

"Not a great deal." Once again he sounded evasive. "He was ten years younger than Dumas. A mutual friend, Gérard de Nerval, recommended him. He wrote historical novels without success. He showed Dumas the original version of one, *Buvat the Good, or the Conspiracy of Cellamare*. Dumas turned the story into *The Chevalier d'Harmental* and had it published under his name. In return Maquet was paid 1,200 francs."

"Can you tell from the handwriting and the style of writing when 'The Anjou Wine' was written?"

"Of course I can. It's similar to other documents from 1844, the year of *The Three Musketeers* . . . These white and blue pages fit in with his way of working. Dumas and his associate would piece the story together. From Courtilz's *D'Artagnan* they took the names of their heroes, the journey to Paris, the intrigue with Milady, and the character of the innkeeper's wife – Dumas created Madame Bonacieux, giving her the features of his mistress, Belle Krebsamer. Constance's kidnap came from the *Memoirs* of De la Porte, a man in the confidence of Anne of Austria. And they obtained the famous story of the diamond tags from La Rochefoucauld and from a book by Roederer, *Political and Romantic Intrigues from the Court of France*. At that time, in addition to *The Three Musketeers*, they were also writing *Queen Margot* and *The Chevalier de la Maison Rouge*."

Replinger paused again for breath. He was becoming more and more flushed and animated as he spoke. He mentioned the last few titles in a rush, stumbling slightly over the words. He was afraid of boring Corso but, at the same time, he wanted to give him all the information he could.

"There's an amusing anecdote about *The Chevalier de la Maison Rouge*," he went on once he'd caught his breath. "When the serial was announced with its original title, *The Knight of Rougeville*, Dumas received a letter of complaint from a marquis of the same name. This made him change the title, but soon afterwards he received another letter. 'My dear Sir," wrote the marquis, "Please give your novel whatever title you wish. I am the last of my family and am going to blow my brains out in an hour." And the Marquis de Rougeville did indeed commit suicide, over some woman."

He gasped for air again. Large and pink-cheeked, he smiled almost apologetically. He leant one of his strong hands on the table next to the blue pages. He looked like an exhausted giant, thought Corso. Porthos in the cave at Locmaria.

"Boris Balkan didn't do you justice. You're an expert on Dumas. I'm not surprised you're friends."

"We respect each other. But I'm only doing my job." Replinger looked down, slightly embarrassed. "I'm a conscientious Frenchman who works with annotated books and documents and handwritten dedications. Always by nineteenth-century French authors. I couldn't give a valuation of the things that come to me if I wasn't sure who they were written by, and how. Do you understand?"

"Perfectly," answered Corso. "It's the difference between a professional, and a vulgar salesman."

Replinger looked at him with gratitude.

"You're in the profession. It's very obvious."

"Yes," Corso grimaced. "The oldest profession."

Replinger's laugh ended in another asthmatic wheeze. Corso made the most of the pause to direct the conversation towards Maquet again.

"Tell me how they did it," he said.

"Their technique was complicated." Replinger gestured towards the chairs and table, as if the scene had taken place there. "Dumas drew up a plan for each novel and discussed it with his collaborator, who then did the research and made an outline of the story, or a first draft. These were the white pages. Then Dumas would rewrite it on the blue paper. He worked in his shirt sleeves, and only in the morning or at night, almost never in the afternoon. He didn't drink coffee or spirits, only seltzer water. Also he hardly smoked. He wrote page after page under pressure from his publishers who always demanded more. Maquet sent him the material in bulk by post, and Dumas would complain about the delays." He took a sheet from the folder and put it on the table in front of Corso. "Here's proof, in one of the notes they exchanged during the writing of *Queen Margot*. As you can see, Dumas was complaining slightly. 'All is going perfectly, despite the six or seven pages of politics we'll have to endure so as to revive interest . . . If we're not going faster, dear friend, it is your fault. I've been hard at work since nine o'clock yesterday.'" He paused to take a breath and pointed at 'The Anjou Wine'. "These four pages in Maquet's handwriting with annotations by Dumas were probably only received by Dumas moments before *Le Siècle* went to press. So he had to make do with rewriting a few of them and hurriedly correcting some of the other pages on the original itself."

He put the papers back in their folders and returned them to the filing cabinet, under "D". Corso had time to cast a final glance at Dumas's note demanding more pages from his collaborator. In addition to the handwriting, which was similar in every way, the paper was identical – blue with faint squaring – to that of the *Anjou Wine* manuscript. One folio cut in two – the bottom part was more uneven than the others. Maybe all the pages had been part of the same ream lying on the novelist's desk.

"Who really wrote *The Three Musketeers*?"

Replinger, busy shutting the filing cabinet, took some time to answer.

"I can't give you a definite answer. Maquet was a resourceful man, he was well-versed in history, he had read a lot . . . But he didn't have the master's touch."

"They fell out with each other in the end, didn't they?"

"Yes. A pity. Did you know they travelled to Spain together at the time of Isabel II's wedding? Dumas even published a serial, *From Madrid to Cadiz*, in the form of letters. As for Maquet, he later went to court to demand that he should be declared the author of eighteen of Dumas's novels, but the judges ruled that his work had only been preparatory. Today he is considered a mediocre writer, who made the most of Dumas's fame to make money. Although there are some who believe he was exploited – the great man's ghost writer . . ."

"What do you think?"

Replinger glanced furtively at Dumas's portrait above the door.

"I've already told you that I'm not an expert like my friend Mr Balkan . . . Just a trader, a bookseller." He seemed to reflect, weighing up where his professional opinion ended and his personal taste began. "But I'd like to draw your attention to something. In France between 1870 and 1894 three million books and eight million serials were sold with the name of Alexandre Dumas on the title page. Novels written before, during and after his collaboration with Maquet. I think that has some significance."

"Fame in his lifetime, at least," said Corso.

"Definitely. For half a century he was the voice of Europe. Boats were sent over from the Americas for the sole purpose of bringing back consignments of his novels. They were read just as much in Cairo, Moscow, Istanbul or Chandernagore. Dumas lived life to the full, enjoying all his pleasures and his fame. He lived and enjoyed himself, stood on the barricades, fought in duels, was taken to court, chartered boats, paid pensions out of his own pocket, loved, ate, drank, earned ten million and squandered twenty, and died gently in his sleep like a child . . ." Replinger pointed at the corrections to Maquet's pages. "It could be called many things: talent, genius . . . But whatever it was, he didn't improvise, or steal from others." He thumped his chest like Porthos. "It's something you have in here. No other writer has ever known such glory in his lifetime. Dumas rose from nothing to have it all. As if he'd made a pact with God."

"Yes," said Corso. "Or with the Devil."

He crossed the road to the other bookshop. Outside, under an awning, stacks of books were piled up on trestle tables. The girl was still there, rummaging about amongst the books and bunches of old pictures and postcards. She was standing against the light. The sun was on her shoulders, turning the hair on the back of her head and her temples golden. She didn't stop what she was doing when he arrived.

"Which one would you choose?" she asked. She was hesitating between a sepia postcard of Tristan and Isolde embracing, and another of Daumier's *The Picture Hunter*. Undecided, she held them both out in front of her.

"Take both of them," suggested Corso. Out of the corner of his eye he caught sight of a man who had stopped at the stall and was about to pick up a thick bundle of cards held together by a rubber band. Corso shot out his arm with the reflex of a hunter, almost grabbing the packet from the man's hand. The man left, muttering. Corso looked through the cards and chose several with a Napoleonic theme: Empress Marie-Louise, the Bonaparte family, the death of the Emperor, and his final victory: a Polish lancer and two hussars on horseback in front of Reims cathedral, during the French campaign of 1814, waving flags snatched from the enemy. After hesitating a moment he added one of Marshal Ney in dress uniform and another of an elderly Wellington posing for posterity. Lucky old devil.

The girl's long tanned hands moved deftly amongst the cards and yellowed printed paper. She chose a few more postcards: Robespierre and Saint-Just, and an elegant portrait of Richelieu in his cardinal's habit and wearing the insignia of the Order of the Holy Spirit.

"How appropriate," remarked Corso acidly.

She didn't answer. She headed towards a pile of books and the sun slid across her shoulders, enveloping Corso in a golden haze. Dazzled, he closed his eyes. When he opened them again the girl was showing him a thick volume in quarto that was over to one side.

"What do you think?"

He glanced at it: *The Three Musketeers*, with the original illustrations by Leloir, bound in cloth and leather, in good condition. When he looked at her again he saw that she had a lopsided smile and was waiting, looking at him intently.

"Nice edition," was all he said. "Are you intending to read it?"

"Of course. Don't tell me the ending."

Corso laughed quietly, half-heartedly.

"As if I could tell you the ending," he said, sorting the bundles of cards.

"I've got a present for you," said the girl.

They were walking along the Left Bank, past the stalls of the *bouquinistes* with their prints hanging up in plastic and Cellophane covers and second-hand books lined up along the parapet. A *bateau-mouche* was heading slowly up-river, straining under the weight of what Corso estimated must have been about five thousand Japanese, and as many Sony camcorders. Across the street, behind exclusive shop windows covered in Visa and American Express stickers, snooty antique dealers scanned the horizon for a Kuwaiti, a black marketeer or an African minister of state to whom they might sell Eugénie Grandet's Sèvres porcelain bidet. Their sales patter delivered in the most proper accent, of course.

"I don't like presents," muttered Corso sullenly. "Some guys once accepted a wooden horse. Handcrafted by the Achaeans, it said on the label. The fools."

"Weren't there any dissenters?"

"One, with his sons. But some beasts came out of the sea, and made a lovely sculpture out of them. Hellenistic, I seem to remember. Rhodes school. In those days the gods were too biased."

"They always have been." The girl was staring at the muddy river as if it were sweeping away her memories. Corso saw her smile, thoughtfully, absently. "I never knew an impartial god. Or devil." She turned to him suddenly – her earlier thoughts seemed to have been washed downstream. "Do you believe in the Devil, Corso?"

He looked at her intently, but the river had also swept away the images that had filled her eyes seconds before. All he could see there now was liquid green, and light.

"I believe in stupidity and ignorance." He smiled wearily at the girl. "And I think that the best cut of all is the one you get here. See?" He pointed at his groin. "In the femoral artery. While you're in somebody's arms."

"What are you so afraid of, Corso? That I'll put my arms around you? That the sky'll fall in on you?"

"I'm scared of wooden horses, cheap gin and pretty girls. Especially when they give me presents. And when they go by the name of the woman who defeated Sherlock Holmes."

They had continued walking and were now on the wooden boards of the Pont des Arts. The girl stopped and leaned on the metal rail, by a street artist selling tiny watercolours.

"I like this bridge," she said. "No cars. Only lovers, and old ladies in hats. People with nothing to do. This bridge has absolutely no common sense."

Corso said nothing. He was watching the barges, masts down, pass between the pillars supporting the iron structure. Nikon's steps had once echoed alongside his on that bridge. He remembered that she too stopped at a stall selling watercolours. Maybe it was the same one. She wrinkled up her nose because her light meter couldn't deal with the dazzling sunshine slanting across the spire and towers of Notre-Dame. They bought *foie gras* and a bottle of Burgundy. Later they ate it for dinner in their hotel room, sitting on their bed watching one of those wordy discussions on TV with huge studio audiences that the French like so much. Earlier, on the bridge, Nikon had taken a photo of him without him knowing. She confessed this, her mouth full of bread and *foie gras*, her lips moistened with Burgundy, as she stroked his side with her bare foot. I know you hate it, Lucas Corso, you'll just have to put up with it. I got you in profile on the bridge watching the barges pass underneath, you almost look handsome this time, you bastard. Nikon was Ashkenazi, with large eyes. Her father had been number 77,843 in Treblinka, saved by the bell in the last round. If Israeli soldiers ever appeared on TV, invading places in huge tanks, she jumped off the bed, naked, and kissed the screen, her eyes wet with tears, whispering "Shalom, Shalom" in a caressing tone. The same tone she used when she called Corso by his first name, until the day she stopped. Nikon. He never got to see the photo of him leaning on the Pont des Arts, watching the barges pass under the arches. In profile, almost looking handsome, you bastard.

When he looked up Nikon had gone. Another girl was by his side. Tall, with tanned skin, short boyish haircut and eyes the colour of freshly washed grapes, almost colourless. For a second, he blinked, confused, until everything fell back into place. The present cut a line cleanly like a scalpel. Corso, in profile, in black and white (Nikon always worked in black and white) fluttered down into the river and was swept downstream with the dead leaves and the rubbish discharged by the barges and the drains. Now, the girl who wasn't Nikon was holding a small, leather-bound book. She was holding it out to him.

"I hope you like it."

The Devil in Love by Jacques Cazotte, the 1878 edition. When he opened it, Corso recognized the prints from the first edition in a facsimile appendix: Alvaro in the magic circle before the Devil, who asks, "*Che vuoi?*"; Biondetta untangling her hair with her fingers; the handsome pageboy sitting at the harpsichord . . . He chose a page at random:

. . . man emerged from a handful of earth and water. Why should a woman not be made of dew, earthly vapours and rays of light, of the condensed residues of a rainbow? Where does the possible lie? And where the impossible?

He closed the book and looked up. His eyes met the smiling eyes of the girl. Below, in the water, the sun sparkled in the wake of a boat, and lights moved over her skin like the reflections from the facets of a diamond.

"'Residues of a rainbow,'" quoted Corso. "What do you know of any of that?"

The girl ran her hand through her hair and turned her face to the sun, closing her eyes against the glare. Everything about her was light: the reflection of the river, the brightness of the morning, the two green slits between her dark eyelashes.

"I know what I was told a long time ago. The rainbow is the bridge between heaven and earth. It will shatter at the end of the world, once the Devil has crossed it on horseback."

"Not bad. Did your grandmother tell you that?"

She shook her head. She looked at Corso again, absorbed and serious.

"I heard it told to a friend, Bileto." As she said his name she stopped a moment and frowned tenderly, like a little girl revealing a secret. "He likes horses and wine, and he's the most optimistic person I know. He's still hoping to get back to Heaven."

They crossed to the other side of the bridge. Strangely, Corso felt that the gargoyles of Notre-Dame were watching him from a distance. They were forgeries, of course, like so many other things. They, and their infernal grimaces, horns and goatee beards, hadn't been there when honest master builders had looked up, sweaty and proud, and drunk a glass of *eau de vie*. Or when Quasimodo brooded in the bell towers over his unrequited love for the gypsy Esmeralda. But since Charles Laughton, as the hideous hunchback who resembled them, and Gina Lollobrigida in the remake – Technicolor, as Nikon would have specified – was executed in their shadow, it was impossible to think of Notre-Dame without the sinister neo-medieval sentinels. Corso imagined the bird's eye view: the Pont Neuf, and beyond it, narrow and dark in the luminous morning, the Pont des Arts over the grey-green band of river, with two tiny figures moving imperceptibly towards the Right Bank. Bridges and rainbows with black Caronte barges gliding slowly beneath the pillars and vaults of stone. The world is full of banks, and rivers running between them, of men and women crossing bridges and fords, unaware of the consequences, not looking back or beneath their feet, and with no loose change for the boatman.

They emerged opposite the Louvre and stopped at traffic lights before crossing. Corso shifted the strap of his canvas bag on his shoulder and glanced absently to right and left. The traffic was heavy, and he happened to notice one of the passing cars. He froze, turned to stone like one of the gargoyles on the cathedral.

"What's the matter?" asked the girl when the lights turned green and she saw that Corso wasn't moving. "You look like you've seen a ghost!"

He had. Not just one but two. They were in the back of a taxi already moving off in the distance, engaged in animated conversation, and they didn't notice Corso. The woman was blonde and very attractive. He recognized her immediately despite her hat and the veil covering her eyes. Liana Taillefer. Next to her, his arm round her shoulders, showing his best side and stroking his curly beard vainly, was Flavio La Ponte.

X

Number Three

They suspected that he had no heart.
                   R. Sabatini: *Scaramouche*

Corso had a rare knack: he could make a loyal ally of a stranger instantly, in return for a tip or even a smile. As we've seen, there was something about him – the half-calculated clumsiness, his customary, friendly rabbit expression, his air of absent-minded helplessness which was nothing of the sort – that won people over. This had happened to some of us. And it had happened to Gruber, the concierge of the Louvre Concorde, with whom Corso had had dealings for fifteen years. Gruber was dry and imperturbable, with a crew-cut and a permanent poker player's expression round the corners of his mouth. During the retreat of 1944, when he was sixteen years old, a Croat volunteer in the *Horst Wessel* 18th Panzergrenadier division, a Russian bullet had hit him in the spine. It left him with an Iron Cross second class and three fused vertebrae for life. This was why he was so stiff and upright behind the reception desk, as if he was wearing a steel corset.

"I need a favour, Gruber."

"Yes, sir."

He almost clicked his heels as he stood to attention. His impeccable burgundy jacket with the gold keys on the lapels gave the old exile a military air, very much to the taste of the Central Europeans who stayed at the hotel. After the fall of communism and the fragmenting of the Slav hordes, they arrived in Paris to glance at the Champs-Elysées out of the corners of their eyes and dream of a Fourth Reich.

"La Ponte, Flavio. Spanish nationality. Also Herrero, Liana, though she may be going by the name of Taillefer or De Taillefer. I want to know if they're at a hotel in the city."

He wrote the names down on a card and handed it to Gruber,

together with five hundred francs. Corso always gave tips or bribes with a shrug of the shoulders, as if to say, "I'll do the same for you sometime." It made it a friendly, almost conspiratorial, exchange and it was difficult to tell who was doing who a favour. Gruber, who murmured a polite "*Merci, m'sieu*" to Spaniards on package tours, Italians in loud ties and Americans with airline bags and baseball caps for a miserable ten-franc tip, took Corso's banknote without a word or even a nod. He just slipped it in his pocket with an elegant, semi-circular movement of his hand and a croupier's impassive gravity, reserved for the few, like Corso, who still knew how to play the game. Gruber had learnt the job in the days when a guest just had to raise an eyebrow for hotel employees to come running. The dear old Europe of international hotels was now reduced to a few cognoscenti.

"Are the lady and gentleman staying together?"

"I don't know." Corso frowned. He pictured La Ponte emerging from the bathroom in an embroidered dressing-gown and Taillefer's widow lying on the bed in a silk nightdress. "I'd like to know that too."

Gruber bowed imperceptibly.

"It'll take a few hours, Mr Corso."

"I know." He glanced down the corridor leading from the lobby to the dining-room. The girl was there, her duffle coat under her arm and her hands in her pockets, staring at a display of perfumes and silk scarves. "What about her?"

The concierge took a card from under the desk.

"Irene Adler," he read. "British passport, issued two months ago. Nineteen years old. Address: 223b Baker Street, London."

"Don't joke with me, Gruber."

"I'd never take such a liberty, Mr Corso. That's what it says here."

There was the hint, the faintest suggestion of a smile on the face of the old SS Waffen. Corso had only seen him smile once: the day the Berlin Wall came down. He observed Gruber's white crew-cut, stiff neck, hands arranged symmetrically, his wrists resting exactly on the edge of the desk. Old Europe, or what was left of it. He was too old to go back home and risk finding that nothing was as he remembered; neither the bell tower in Zagreb, nor the warm, blonde peasant girls smelling of fresh bread, nor the green plains with rivers and bridges that he had seen blown up twice: once in his youth, in the retreat from Tito's guerrillas, and then on TV, autumn '91, in the faces of the Serbian *Chetniks*. Corso could picture him in his room standing in front of a dusty portrait of the Emperor Franz Joseph, taking off the maroon jacket with little golden keys on the lapels as if it were his Austro-Hungarian army jacket. He probably played the Radetsky March on the record-player, drank a toast with a glass of Montenegrin liqueur and masturbated to videos of the Empress Sissy.

The girl was no longer staring at the display but was now looking at Corso. 223b Baker Street, he repeated to himself and he felt the urge to laugh uncontrollably. He wouldn't have been in the least surprised had a bellboy appeared with an invitation from Milady de Winter to take tea at If Castle or at the palace in Ruritania with Richelieu, Professor Moriarty and Rupert of Hentzau. Since this was a literary matter, it would have seemed the most natural thing in the world.

He asked for a phone book and looked up Baroness Ungern's number. Then, ignoring the girl's stare, he went to the phone booth in the lobby and made an appointment for the following day. He also rang Varo Borja's number in Toledo but there was no answer.

He was watching the television with the sound down: a film with Gregory Peck surrounded by seals, a fight in a hotel ballroom, two schooners side by side, with the waves crashing against the bow, heading north in full sail, towards true freedom which only begins ten miles away from the nearest coast. On Corso's side of the TV screen, a bottle of Bols with the level below the Plimsoll line stood guard on the bedside table, like the old, alcoholic grenadier on the eve of battle, between *The Nine Doors* and the folder with the Dumas manuscript.

Lucas Corso took off his glasses and rubbed his eyes, red from cigarette smoke and gin. On the bed, with the precision of an archaeologist, he had laid out the fragments of Book Number Two rescued from the fireplace in Victor Fargas's house. There wasn't much left: the boards, protected by the covering of leather, were less damaged than the rest, of which there remained no more than the charred margins and a few barely legible paragraphs. He picked up one of the pieces, made yellow and brittle by the fire. '. . . *si non obig.nem me. ips.s fecere, f.r q.qe die, tib. do vitam m.m sicut t.m* . . .'. This came from one of the bottom corners. He examined it for a few moments and then searched for the same page in Book Number One. It was page 89, and the two paragraphs were identical. He did the same with as many paragraphs as he could and managed to identify sixteen. It was impossible to tell where another twenty-two of the fragments came from as they were too small or too damaged. Eleven more fragments were blank and he managed to identify only one, thanks to a crooked "7" which was the third and only legible digit in the page number, page 107.

The cigarette had burnt right down and was burning his lips. He stubbed it out in the ashtray. Then he grabbed the Bols and took a swig directly from the bottle. He was wearing an old cotton khaki shirt with big pockets, sleeves rolled up, and a crumpled tie. On the TV the man from Boston standing by the helm was embracing a Russian princess. They were both moving their lips soundlessly, happy and in love under a Technicolor sky. The only noise in the room was the gentle rattling of the window-panes caused by the traffic rumbling by, two floors below, heading for the Louvre.

Nikon loved that kind of thing. Corso remembered how she would be moved, like a sentimental little girl, by a couple kissing against a cloudy sky, to the sound of violins and "The End" across the screen. Sometimes, munching on crisps at the cinema or in front of the TV, she'd lean on Corso's shoulder and cry quietly, gently for a long time, her eyes fixed on the screen. It might be Paul Henreid singing the Marseillaise in Rick's café; Rutger Hauer dying, head bowed, in the final shots of *Blade Runner*; John Wayne and Maureen O'Hara in front of the fireplace in Innisfree; Custer and Arthur Kennedy on the eve of Little Big Horn; O'Toole as Jim deceived by gentleman Brown; Henry Fonda on his way to the OK Corral; or Marcello Mastroianni up to his waist in a pond at a spa retrieving a woman's hat, waving to right and left, elegant, imperturbable, and in love with a pair of black eyes. Nikon was happy crying over it all and she was proud of her tears. It's because I'm alive, she'd say afterwards, laughing, her eyes still wet. Because I'm part of the rest of the world and I'm glad I am. Films are for everyone, collective, generous, with children cheering when the Cavalry arrives. They're even better on TV: two of you can watch and comment. But your books are selfish. Solitary. Some of them can't even be read, they fall to bits if you open them. Somebody who's only interested in books doesn't need anyone else, and that frightens me. Nikon was eating the last crisp and watching him intently, her lips parted, searching his face for signs of an illness that would soon manifest itself. Sometimes you frighten me.

Happy endings. Corso pressed a button on the remote control and the image disappeared from the screen. Now he was in Paris and Nikon was photographing children with tragic eyes somewhere in Africa, or in the Balkans. Once, in a bar, he thought he caught sight of her on the news, in the chaotic shots of a bombardment. She was surrounded by terrified fleeing refugees, her hair in a plait, cameras round her neck and one at her eye, backed by smoke and flames. Nikon. Of all the universal lies she accepted unquestioningly, the happy ending was the most absurd. They lived happily ever after, and the ending seemed indisputable, definitive. No questions asked about how long does love, or happiness, last, in that "forever" that could be divided into lifetimes, years, months. Even days. Until the very end, their inevitable end, Nikon refused to accept that the hero might have drowned two weeks later when his boat struck a reef in the Southern Hebrides. Or that the heroine was run over by a car three months later. Or that maybe everything turned out differently, in a thousand different ways: one of them had an affair, one of them became bitter or bored, one of them wanted to back out. Maybe nights full of tears, silence, loneliness followed that screen kiss. Maybe cancer killed him before he was forty. Maybe she lived on and died in an old people's home aged ninety. Maybe the handsome officer turned into a pathetic ruin, his wounds become hideous scars and his glorious battles forgotten by all. And maybe, old and defenceless, they suffered ordeals without the strength to fight or defend themselves, tossed this way and that by the storms of life, by stupidity, by cruelty, by the miserable human condition.

Sometimes you frighten me, Lucas Corso.

Five minutes before eleven that night he solved the mystery of the fire at Victor Fargas's house. Although it still didn't make things any clearer. He looked at his watch as he stretched and yawned. Then, after glancing again at the fragments spread out on the bedcover, he caught sight of his reflection in the mirror next to the old postcard of the hussars outside Reims Cathedral stuck into the wooden frame. He was dishevelled, unshaven, and his glasses sat crookedly on his nose. He started to laugh quietly. One of his slightly bad-tempered, wolf-like, twisted laughs reserved for special occasions. And this was one. All the fragments of *The Nine Doors* that he had managed to identify came from pages with text. No trace remained of the nine engravings and the frontispiece on the title page. There were two possibilities: either they had burnt in the fire, or, the more likely option hinted at by the torn-off cover, somebody had taken them before throwing the rest of the book into the flames. Whoever it was must have thought himself, or herself, very clever. Or themselves. Maybe, after the unexpected sighting of La Ponte and Liana Taillefer at the traffic lights, he should get used to the third person plural. The question was knowing whether the clues Corso was following were his opponent's mistakes, or tricks. At any rate they were very elaborate.

Talking of tricks. The door bell rang and Corso opened it to find the girl standing there. He had just had enough time to hide Book Number One and the Dumas manuscript carefully under the cover. She was barefoot and wearing her usual jeans and white T-shirt.

"Hello, Corso. I hope you're not intending to go out tonight."

She didn't come in but stood at the door with her thumbs in her pockets. She was frowning, as if expecting bad news.

"You can relax your guard," he reassured her. She smiled, relieved.

"I'm exhausted."

Corso turned his back on her and went to the bedside table. The bottle of gin was empty so he started searching the drinks cabinet until he stood up triumphantly holding a miniature bottle of gin. He emptied it in to a glass and took a sip. The girl was still at the door.

"They took the engravings. All nine of them." Corso waved his glass at the fragments of Book Number Two. "They burnt the rest so that it wouldn't show. That's why not all of it was burnt. They made sure some pieces were left intact . . . Like that, the book would be recorded as officially destroyed."

She leant her head to one side, looking at him intently.

"You're clever."

"Of course I am. That's why they got me involved."

The girl took a few steps around the room. Corso looked at her bare feet on the carpet, next to the bed. She was looking closely at the charred bits of paper.

"Fargas didn't burn the book," he added. "He wasn't capable of something like that . . . What did they do to him? Was it suicide, like Enrique Taillefer?"

She didn't answer straight away. She picked up a piece of paper and examined the words.

"Find your own answers," she said, not looking at him. "That's why they got you involved."

"What about you?"

She was reading silently, moving her lips as if she knew the words. When she put the fragment down on the bedcover, her smile was nostalgic, unsuited to her young face.

"You already know why I'm here: I've got to look after you. You need me."

"What I need is more gin."

He cursed to himself and finished his drink, trying to hide his impatience, or his confusion. Damn everything. Emerald green, luminous white – her eyes and her smile against her tanned skin, her bare, straight neck, warm and alive. Can you believe it, Corso? Even now, with all you've got to deal with, and you're thinking about her tanned arms, fine wrists, long fingers. Thinking about things like that. He noticed that her breasts, under her tight-fitting T-shirt, were magnificent. He hadn't been able to get a good look at them before. He imagined them tanned and heavy under the white cotton, flesh of clarity and shadow. Once again he was struck by her height. She was as tall as he was. Maybe taller.

"Who are you?"

"The Devil," she said. "The Devil in love."

And she laughed. The book by Cazotte was on the sideboard, next to the *Memoirs of Saint-Helena* and some papers. The girl looked at it but didn't touch it. Then she laid one finger on it and looked at Corso.

"Do you believe in the Devil?"

"I'm paid to believe in him. On this job anyway."

She nodded slowly, as if she already knew what he was going to say. She stared at Corso with curiosity, her lips parted, waiting for a sign or gesture which only she would understand.

"Do you know why I like this book, Corso?"

"No. Tell me."

"Because the protagonist is sincere. His love isn't just a trick to damn a soul. Biondetta is tender and faithful. She admires in Alvaro the same things the Devil loves in mankind: his courage, his independence . . ." Her eyelashes came down over her light irises for a moment. "His desire for knowledge and his lucidity."

"You seem very well informed. What do you know of all this?"

"Much more than you imagine."

"I don't imagine anything. Everything I know about the Devil and his loves and hates comes from literature: *Paradise Lost, The Divine Comedy*, passing through *Faust* and *The Brothers Karamazov* . . ."

He made a vague, evasive gesture. "I only know Lucifer second-hand."

Now she was looking at him mockingly.

"And which Devil do you prefer? Dante's?"

"No way. Much too terrifying. Excessively medieval for my taste."

"Mephistopheles?"

"No, not him either. He's too pleased with himself. Too much of a trickster, like a crooked lawyer . . . And anyway I never trust people who smile too much."

"What about the one in *The Karamazovs*?"

Corso made a face.

"Petty. A vulgar civil servant with dirty nails." He paused. "I suppose the one I prefer is Milton's fallen angel." He looked at her with interest. "That's what you were hoping I would say."

She smiled enigmatically. She still had her thumbs in her pockets. He'd never seen anyone wear jeans like that. It needed her long legs, of course. The legs of a young girl hitchhiking at the roadside, her rucksack at her feet and all the light in the world in those damned green eyes.

"How do you see Lucifer?" asked the girl.

"No idea." Corso thought a moment and then grimaced, indifferent. "Taciturn and silent, I suppose. Boring." His expression became acid. "On the throne in a deserted hall. At the centre of a cold, desolate, monotonous kingdom where nothing ever happens."

She looked at him in silence.

"You surprise me, Corso," she said at last.

"I don't know why. Anyone can read Milton. Even me."

She moved slowly round the bed, in a semi-circle, keeping the same distance, until she was standing between him and the lamp. Whether casual or premeditated, it meant that her shadow fell over the fragments of *The Nine Doors* spread out on the bedcover.

"You've just mentioned the price to be paid." Her face was now in darkness, against the light. "Pride, freedom . . . Knowledge. Whether at the beginning or at the end you've got to pay for everything. Even courage, don't you think? Don't you think you need a lot of courage to face God?"

Her words were a soft murmur in the silence filling the room, slipping under the door and through the gaps around the window. Even the noise of the traffic outside in the street seemed to fade. Corso looked at one silhouette, then the other. First the shadow, stylized against the bedcover and the fragments of the book. Then the body standing against the light. At that moment he wondered which was the more real.

"With all those archangels," she, or her shadow, added. There was bitterness in her words, even a contemptuous breath, a sigh of defeat. "Beautiful and perfect. As disciplined as Nazis."

At that instant she didn't seem so young. She seemed to be carrying the weariness of the ages: an obscure inheritance, the guilt of others which he, in his confusion and surprise, couldn't identify. After all, he thought, maybe neither the shadow across the bed nor the outline against the light was real.

"There's a painting in the Prado. Do you remember it, Corso? Men with knives facing horsemen with their swords. I've always been certain: the fallen angel looked like that as he rebelled. With the same lost expression as those poor bastards with the knives. The courage of desperation."

She moved slightly as she spoke, only a few inches, but as she did so her shadow moved nearer to Corso's, as if it had a will of its own.

"What do you know about any of that?" he asked.

"More than I want to."

Her shadow was lying across all the fragments of the book and almost touching Corso's. He moved back instinctively, leaving a section of light between them, on the bed.

"Imagine him," she said in the same absorbed tone. "The most beautiful of the fallen angels plotting, alone in his empty palace . . . He clings desperately to a routine he despises, but which at least allows him to hide his grief. His failure." The girl laughed gently, joylessly, as if from a great distance. "He misses Heaven."

The shadows had now come together and almost merged amongst the fragments snatched from the fireplace at the Quinta da Soledade. The girl and Corso, on the bed, with the nine doors of the kingdom of other shadows, or maybe the same ones. Singed paper, incomplete clues, a mystery shrouded in several veils, by the printer, by time and by fire. Enrique Taillefer swinging, his feet dangling in empty space, on the end of a silk cord; Victor Fargas floating face down in the murky waters of the pond. Aristide Torchia burning at Campo dei Fiori, shouting the name of the father, not looking at Heaven but down at the ground beneath his feet. And old Dumas writing, sitting at the top of the world, while there in Paris, very near where Corso was at that very moment, another shadow, of a cardinal whose library contained too many books on the Devil, held all the threads of the plot.

The girl, or her outline against the light, moved towards Corso. Only slightly, a single step. Enough for his shadow to disappear under hers.

"It was worse for those who followed him." Corso took a moment to understand who she meant. "Those he dragged down with him: soldiers, messengers, servants by trade and by calling. Some mercenaries, like you . . . Many didn't even realize that they were choosing between submission and freedom, between God and mankind. Out of habit, with the absurd loyalty of faithful soldiers, they followed their leader in rebellion and defeat."

"Like Xenophon's Ten Thousand," teased Corso.

She was silent a moment, surprised by his accuracy.

"Maybe," she said at last. "Out in the world alone, they still hope that their leader will one day take them home."

Corso bent down to look for a cigarette, and as he did so his shadow reappeared. Then he switched on the other lamp, on the bedside table, and the dark outline of the girl disappeared as her face was lit up. Her light eyes were fixed on him. She seemed very young again.

"Very moving," said Corso. "All those old soldiers searching for the sea."

She blinked as if now, with her face illuminated, she didn't understand what he was saying. There was no longer a shadow on the bed. The fragments of the book were merely pieces of charred paper. All he had to do was open the window and a gust of air would blow them all over the room.

She smiled. Irene Adler, 223b Baker Street. The café in Madrid, the train, that morning in Sintra . . . The battle lost, the retreat of the defeated legions: she was very young to remember such things. She smiled like a little girl both mischievous and innocent, and there were faint traces of tiredness under her eyes. She was sleepy and warm.

Corso swallowed. A part of him went up to her and pulled her T-shirt up over her tanned skin, undid her jeans and laid her on the bed, among the remains of the book that could summon the forces of darkness. And sank into her warm flesh, settling scores with God and Lucifer, with the inexorable flow of time, with his own ghosts, with life and death. But he just lit a cigarette and breathed out smoke in silence. She stared at him for a long time, waiting for something, a gesture, a word. Then she said good night and went to the door. But in the doorway she turned and slowly raised her hand, palm inwards, index and middle fingers joined and pointing upwards. And her smile was both tender and conspiratorial, ingenuous and knowing. Like a lost angel pointing nostalgically up to Heaven.

Baroness Frieda Ungern had two sweet little dimples when she smiled. She looked as if she had smiled continuously for the past seventy years and it had left a permanently benevolent expression around her eyes and mouth. Corso, a precocious reader, had known since childhood that there are many different types of witch: wicked stepmothers, bad fairies, beautiful, evil queens, and even nasty old witches with warts on their noses. But despite all he'd heard about the septuagenarian baroness, he didn't know to which category she belonged. She might have been one of those elderly ladies who live, as if cushioned by a dream, outside real life where no unpleasantness ever intrudes upon their existence, had it not been for the depth of her quick, intelligent, suspicious eyes cancelling that first impression. And if the right-hand sleeve of her cardigan hadn't hung empty, her arm amputated above the elbow. Otherwise she was small and plump, and looked like a French teacher at a boarding school for young ladies. In the days when "young ladies" still existed, that is. Or so Corso thought as he looked at her grey hair tied into a bun at the nape of her neck, and her rather masculine shoes worn with white ankle socks.

"Mr Corso. Pleased to meet you."

She held out her only hand – small like the rest of her – with unusual energy, and showed her dimples. She had a slight accent which was German rather than French. A certain von Ungern, Corso remembered reading somewhere, had become notorious in Manchuria, or Mongolia, in the early twenties. A warlord of sorts, he had made a last stand against the Red Army at the head of a ragged army of White Russians, Cossacks, Chinese, deserters and bandits. With armoured trains, looting, killing, that sort of thing, concluding with the epilogue at dawn before a firing squad. Maybe he was a relation.

"He was my husband's great-uncle. His family was Russian and emigrated to France with a fair amount of money before the Revolution." There was neither nostalgia nor pride in her tone. It had all happened in the past, to other people, to another family, she seemed to imply. Strangers who disappeared before she even existed. "I was born in Germany. My family lost everything under the Nazis.

I was married here in France after the war." She carefully removed a dead leaf from a plant by the window and smiled slightly. "I never could stand my in-laws' obsession with the past: their nostalgia for St Petersburg, the Tsar's birthday. It was like a wake."

Corso looked at the desk covered in books, the packed shelves. He calculated there must be a thousand volumes in that room alone. The most rare and valuable ones seemed to be there, from modern editions to more ancient, leather-bound tomes.

"And what about all this?"

"That's different. It's material for research, not worship. I use it for my work."

Times are bad, thought Corso, when witches, or whatever they are, talk about their in-laws and exchange their cauldron for a library, filing cabinets and a place in the bestseller list. Through the open door he could see more books in the other rooms and in the corridor. Books and plants. There were pots of them all over the place: on the window-sills, on the floor, on the wooden shelves. It was a large, expensive apartment with views of the river and, in another time, the bonfires of the Inquisition. There were several reading tables occupied by young people who looked like students, and all the walls were covered in books. Ancient, gilded bindings shone from between the plants. The Ungern Foundation contained the largest collection of books on the occult in Europe. Corso glanced at the books closest to him. *Dæmonolatriæ Libri* by Nicholas Rémy. *Compendium Maleficarum* by Francesco Maria Guazzo. *De Dæmonialitate et Incubus et Succubus* by Ludovico Sinistrari . . . In addition to one of the best catalogues of demonology, and the foundation named after her late husband, the baron, Baroness Ungern had a solid reputation as a writer of books on magic and witchcraft. Her last book, *Isis, the Naked Virgin*, had been on the bestseller list for three years. The Vatican had boosted sales by publicly condemning the work which drew worrying parallels between the pagan deity and the mother of Christ. There had been eight editions in France, twelve in Spain, and seventeen in Catholic Italy.

"What are you working on at the moment?"

"It's called *The Devil, History and Legend*. An irreverent biography. It'll be ready by the beginning of next year."

Corso stopped by a row of books. His attention had been drawn by the *Disquisitionum Magicarum* by Martin del Rio, the three volumes of the Lovaina first edition, 1599–1600: a classic on demonic magic.

"Where did you get hold of this?"

Frieda Ungern must have been considering how much information to provide, because she took a moment to answer.

"At an auction in Madrid in '89. I had a great deal of trouble preventing your compatriot, Varo Borja, getting hold of it." She sighed as if still recovering from the effort. "And money. I would never have managed it without help from Paco Montegrifo. Do you know him? A delightful man."

Corso smiled crookedly. Not only did he know Montegrifo, the head of the Spanish branch of Claymore's Auctioneers, but he had worked with him on several unorthodox and highly profitable deals. Such as the sale, to a certain Swiss collector, of a *Cosmography* by Ptolemy, a gothic manuscript dating from 1456, which had mysteriously disappeared from the University of Salamanca not long before. Montegrifo had found himself in possession of the book and used Corso as an intermediary. The entire operation had been clean and discreet, and had included a visit to the Ceniza brothers' workshop where a compromising stamp had been removed. Corso had delivered the book himself to Lausanne. All inclusive for a thirty per cent commission.

"Yes, I know him." He stroked the spines of the several volumes of the *Disquisitionum Magicarum* and wondered how much Montegrifo must have charged the Baroness for rigging the auction in her favour. "As for the Martin del Rio, I've only seen a copy once before, in the collection of the Jesuits in Bilbao . . . Bound in a single piece of leather. But it's the same edition."

As he spoke he moved his hand along the row of books, touching some. There were many interesting volumes, with good-quality bindings in vellum, shagreen, parchment. Many others were only mediocre, or in poor condition, and looked much-used. Nearly all of them had page-markers, strips of white card covered in a small, spiky hand, written in pencil. Material for her research. He stopped in front of a book which looked very familiar: black, no title, five raised bands on the spine. Book Number Three.

"How long have you had this?"

Now, Corso was a steady character. Especially at this stage in the story. But he'd spent the night sorting through the ashes of Number Two, and he couldn't prevent the Baroness from noticing something peculiar in his tone of voice. He saw that she was looking at him suspiciously despite the friendly dimples in her youthful old face.

"*The Nine Doors*? I'm not sure. A long time." Her only hand moved quickly and deftly. She took the book from the shelf effortlessly and, supporting the spine in her palm, she opened it at the first page, decorated with several bookplates, some very old. The last one was an arabesque design with the name von Ungern, and the date written in ink. As she saw it she nodded nostalgically. "A present from my husband. I married very young. He was twice my age. He bought the book in 1949."

That was the problem with modern-day witches, thought Corso: they didn't have any secrets. Everything was out in the open, you could read all about them in any *Who's Who* or gossip column. Baronesses or not, they'd become predictable. Vulgar. Torquemada would have been bored to death by it all.

"Did your husband share your interest in this sort of thing?"

"Not in the slightest. He never read a single book. He just made all my wishes come true like the genie of the lamp." Her amputated arm seemed to shudder for a moment in the empty sleeve of her cardigan. "An expensive book or a perfect pearl necklace, it was all the same to him." She paused and smiled with gentle melancholy. "But he was an amusing man, capable of seducing his best friends' wives. And he made excellent champagne cocktails."

She was silent for a moment and looked round as if her husband had left a glass behind.

"I collected all this myself," she added, waving at her library, "One by one, down to the last book. I even chose *The Nine Doors*, after discovering it in the catalogue of a bankrupt, former Pétain supporter. All my husband did was sign the cheque."

"Why are you so interested in the Devil?"

"I saw him once. I was fifteen and I saw him as clearly as I'm seeing you. He had a hard collar, a hat and a walking stick. He was very handsome. He looked like John Barrymore as Baron Gaigern in *Grand Hotel*. So, like a fool, I fell in love." She became thoughtful again, her only hand in her cardigan pocket, as if remembering something distant, familiar. "I suppose that's why I was never really troubled by my husband's infidelities."

Corso looked around as if there might be someone else in the room and then leaned over confidentially.

"Only three centuries ago you would have burnt at the stake for telling me this."

She made a guttural sound of amusement, stifling her laughter, and almost stood on tiptoes to whisper in the same tone:

"Three centuries ago I wouldn't have mentioned it to anyone. But I know a lot of people who would gladly burn me at the stake." She smiled again, showing her dimples. She was always smiling, Corso decided. But her bright, intelligent eyes remained alert, studying him. "Even now, in this day and age."

She handed him *The Nine Doors* and watched him as he leafed through the book slowly, although he could barely contain his impatience to check if there were any differences in the nine engravings. Sighing with relief to himself, he found them intact. In fact, Mateu's *Bibliography* was wrong: none of the three books had the final engraving missing. Book Number Three was in worse condition than Varo Borja's, and Victor Fargas's before it was thrown into the fire. The lower half had been exposed to damp and almost all the pages were stained. The binding also needed a thorough clean, but the book seemed complete.

"Would you like a drink?" asked the Baroness. "I've got tea or coffee."

No potions or magic herbs, Corso thought with disappointment. Not even a tisane.

"Coffee."

It was a sunny day and the sky over the nearby towers of Notre Dame was blue. Corso went over to a window and parted the net curtains so he could see the book in better light. Two floors down, between the bare trees on the banks of the Seine, the girl was sitting on a stone bench in her duffle coat, reading a book. He knew it was *The Three Musketeers* because he'd seen it on the table when they met at breakfast. Afterwards Corso walked along the Rue de Rivoli knowing that the girl was following fifteen or twenty paces behind. He deliberately ignored her, and she kept her distance. Now he saw her look up. She must have seen him clearly from down there, but she made no sign of recognition. Expressionless and still, she continued to watch him until he moved away from the window. When he looked out again she had gone back to her book, her head bowed.

There was a secretary, a middle-aged woman with thick glasses, moving amongst the tables and books, but Frieda Ungern brought the coffee herself, two cups on a silver tray which she carried with ease. One glance from her told him not to offer help, and they sat down at the desk, the tray amongst all the books, plant pots, papers and note cards.

"What gave you the idea of setting up this foundation?"

"I can claim against tax. Also it means that people come here, I can find collaborators . . ." She smiled melancholically. "I'm the last of the witches and I felt lonely."

"You don't look anything like a witch." Corso made the appropriate face, like an ingenuous, friendly rabbit. "I read your *Isis*."

She was holding her coffee cup in her one hand and slightly raised the stump of her other arm, at the same time tilting her head as if to rearrange her hair. Although incomplete, it was an unconsciously coquettish gesture, as old as the world itself and yet ageless.

"Did you like it?"

He looked her in the eyes, as he raised his cup to his mouth.

"Very much."

"Not everyone did. Do you know what *L'Osservatore Romano* said? It regretted the demise of the Index of the Holy Office. And you're right." She indicated *The Nine Doors* that Corso had put by her on the table. "In the past I would have been burnt at the stake, like the poor wretch who wrote the gospel according to Satan."

"Do you really believe in the Devil, Baroness?"

"Don't call me Baroness. It's ridiculous."

"What would you like me to call you?"

"I don't know. Mrs Ungern. Or Frieda."

"Do you believe in the Devil, Mrs Ungern?"

"Sufficiently to dedicate my life, my collection, this foundation, many years of work and the five hundred pages of my new book all to him . . ." She looked at him with interest. Corso had taken off his glasses to clean them. His helpless smile completed the effect. "What about you?"

"Everybody's asking me that lately."

"Of course. You've been going round asking questions about a book that has to be read with a certain kind of faith."

"My faith is limited," Corso said, risking a hint of sincerity. This kind of frankness often proved profitable. "Really I work for money."

The dimples appeared again. She must have been very pretty about half a century ago, thought Corso. With both arms intact, casting spells, or whatever they were, slender and mischievous. She still had something of that.

"Pity," remarked Frieda Ungern. "Others, who worked for nothing, had blind faith in the book's protagonist . . . Albertus Magnus,

Raymund Lully, Roger Bacon, none of them ever disputed the Devil's existence, only his nature."

Corso adjusted his glasses, and gave a hint of a sceptical smile.

"Things were different a long time ago."

"You don't have to go that far back. 'The Devil does exist, not only as a symbol of evil, but as a physical reality.' How do you like that? Well, it was written by a pope, Paul VI. In 1974."

"He was a professional," said Corso equably. "He must have had his reasons."

"In fact all he was doing was confirming a point of doctrine: the existence of the Devil was established by the fourth Lateran Council. I mean in 1215 . . ." She paused and looked at him doubtfully. "Are you interested in erudite facts? I can be unbearably scholarly if I try . . ." The dimples appeared. "I always wanted to be top of the class. The smart aleck."

"I'm sure you were. Did you win all the prizes?"

"Of course. And the other girls hated me."

They both laughed. Corso sensed that Frieda Ungern was now on his side. So he took two cigarettes from his coat pocket and offered her one. She refused, glancing at him slightly apprehensively. Corso ignored this and lit his cigarette.

"Two centuries later," continued the Baroness as Corso craned over the lighted match, "Innocent VIII's papal bull *Sumnis Desiderantes Affectibus* confirmed that Western Europe was plagued by demons and witches. So two Dominican monks, Kramer and Sprenger, drew up the *Malleus Malleficarum*, a manual for inquisitors . . ."

Corso raised his index finger.

"Lyon, 1519. An octavo in the Gothic style, with no author's name. At least, not the copy I know."

"Not bad." She looked at him, surprised. "Mine is a later one." She pointed at a shelf. "It's over there. Published in 1668, also in Lyon. But the very first edition dated from 1486 . . ." She shuddered, half-closing her eyes. "Kramer and Sprenger were fanatical and stupid. Their *Malleus* was a load of nonsense. It might even seem funny, if thousands of poor wretches hadn't been tortured and burnt in its name."

"Like Aristide Torchia."

"Yes, like him. Although he wasn't remotely innocent."

"What do you know about him?"

199

The Baroness shook her head, drank the last of her coffee and then shook her head again.

"The Torchias were a Venetian family of well-to-do merchants who imported vat paper from Spain and France . . . As a young man he travelled to Holland and was an apprentice of the Elzevirs, who had corresponded with his father. He stayed there for a time and then went to Prague."

"I didn't know that."

"Well, there you are. Prague was Europe's capital of magic and the occult, just as Toledo had been four centuries earlier . . . Can you see the links? Torchia chose to live in Saint Mary of the Snows, the district of magic, near Jungmannove Square where there is a statue of Jan Hus . . . Do you remember Hus at the stake?"

"'From my ashes a swan will rise that you will not be able to burn . . .'"

"Exactly. You're easy to talk to. I expect you already know that. It must help you in your work." The Baroness involuntarily inhaled some of Corso's cigarette smoke. She looked slightly reproachful but he remained unperturbed. "Now, where were we? Ah yes. Prague, act two. Torchia moves to a house in the Jewish quarter nearby, next to the synagogue. A district where the windows are lit up every night and the Cabbalists are searching for the magic formula of the Golem. After a while he moves again, this time to the district of Mala Strana . . ." She smiled at him conspiratorially. "What does all this sound like to you?"

"Like a pilgrimage. Or a study trip, as we'd say nowadays."

"That's what I think," the Baroness agreed with satisfaction. Corso, now well and truly adopted, was moving quickly to the top of the class. "It must be more than coincidence that Aristide Torchia went to the three districts in which all the esoteric knowledge of the time was concentrated. And in a Prague whose streets still echoed with the steps of Agrippa and Paracelsus, where the last manuscripts of Chaldean magic and the Pythagorean keys lost or dispersed after the murder of Metapontius were to be found . . ." She leaned over towards him and lowered her voice. Miss Marple about to confide in her best friend that she's found cyanide in the teacakes. "In that Prague, Mr Corso, in those dark studies, there were men who practised the *carmina*, the art of magic words, and necromancy, or the art of communicating with the dead." She paused, holding her breath, before whispering, "And goety . . ."

"The art of communicating with the Devil."

"Yes." The Baroness leaned back in her armchair, deliciously shocked by it all. She was in her element. Her eyes shone and she was speaking quickly as if she had much to say and too little time. "At that time, Torchia lived in the place where the pages and engravings that had survived wars, fires and persecution were hidden . . . The remains of the magic book which opens the doors to knowledge and power: the *Delomelanicon,* the word that summons the darkness."

She said it in a conspiratorial, almost theatrical tone, but she was also smiling, as if she didn't quite take it seriously herself, or was suggesting that Corso maintain a healthy distance.

"Once he had completed his apprenticeship, Torchia returned to Venice," she went on. "Take note of this because it's important: in spite of the risks he would run in Italy, the printer left the relative safety of Prague to return to his home town. There he published a series of compromising books which led to his being burnt at the stake. Isn't that strange?"

"Seems as if he had a mission to accomplish."

"Yes. But entrusted by whom?" The Baroness opened *The Nine Doors* at the title page. "'By authority and permission of the superiors.' Makes one think, doesn't it? It's very likely that Torchia became a member of a secret brotherhood in Prague that entrusted him with spreading a message. A kind of preaching."

"You said it yourself earlier: the gospel according to Satan."

"Maybe. The fact is that Torchia published *The Nine Doors* at the worst time. Between 1550 and 1666, humanist neo-platonism and the hermetic and Cabbalist movements were losing the battle amid rumours of demonism . . . Men like Giordano Bruno and John Dee were burnt at the stake, or died persecuted and destitute. With the triumph of the Counter-Reformation, the Inquisition grew unhindered. Created to fight heresy, it specialized in witches, wizards and sorcery to justify its shadowy existence. And here they were offered a printer who had dealings with the Devil . . . Torchia made things easy for them, it must be said. Listen." She turned several pages of the book at random. "'*Pot. m.vere im.go . . .*'" She looked at Corso. "I've translated numerous passages. The code is quite simple. 'I will bring wax images to life,' it says. 'And unhinge the moon, and put flesh back on dead bodies . . .' What do you think of that?"

"Rather childish. It seems stupid to die for that."

"Maybe. One never knows . . . Do you like Shakespeare?"

"Sometimes."

"'There are more things in heaven and earth, Horatio,/ Than are dreamt of in your philosophy.'"

"Hamlet. A very insecure man."

"Not everyone is able, or deserves, to gain access to these occult things, Mr Corso. As the old saying goes, one must know and keep silent."

"But Torchia didn't."

"As you know, according to the Cabbala, God has a terrible and secret name . . ."

"The Tetragrammaton."

"That's right. The harmony and balance of the Universe rests upon its four letters . . . As the Archangel Gabriel warned Mohammed: 'God is hidden by seventy thousand veils of light and darkness. And were those veils to be lifted, even I would be annihilated . . .' But God isn't the only one to have such a name. The Devil has one too. A terrible, evil combination of letters which summons him when spoken . . . And unleashes terrifying consequences."

"That's nothing new. It had a name long before Christianity and Judaism: Pandora's box."

She looked at him with satisfaction, as if awarding top marks.

"Very good, Mr Corso. In fact, down the centuries, we've always talked about the same things, but with different names. Isis and the Virgin Mary, Mithras and Jesus Christ, the 25th of December as Christmas or the festival of the winter solstice, the anniversary of the unconquered sun . . . Think of St Gregory. Even in the seventh century he was recommending that missionaries use the pagan festivals and adapt them to Christianity."

"Sound business sense. In essence it was a marketing operation: they were trying to attract somebody else's customers . . . Could you tell me what you know about Pandora's boxes and such like? Including pacts with the Devil."

"The art of locking devils inside bottles or books is very ancient . . . Gervase of Tilbury and Gerson both mentioned it in the thirteenth and fourteenth centuries. As for pacts with the Devil, the tradition goes back even further: from the Book of Enoch to St Jeronimus, through the Cabbala and the Fathers of the Church. Not forgetting Bishop Theophilus, who was actually a 'lover of knowledge', the historical Faust and Roger Bacon . . . Or Pope Sylvester II, of whom it was said that he robbed the Saracens of a book which 'contained all one needs to know'."

"So it was a question of obtaining knowledge."

"Of course. Nobody would take so much trouble, wandering to the very edge of the abyss just to pass the time. Scholarly demonology identifies Lucifer with knowledge. In *Genesis*, the Devil in the form of a serpent succeeds in getting man to stop being a stupid simpleton and gain awareness, free will, lucidity, knowledge, with all the pain and uncertainty that they entail."

The evening conversation was too fresh so, inevitably, Corso thought of the girl. He picked up *The Nine Doors* and with the excuse of looking at it in better light again, he went to the window. But she was no longer there. Surprised, he looked up and down the street, along the embankment and the stone benches under the trees, but couldn't see her. He was intrigued but didn't have time to think about it. Frieda Ungern was speaking again.

"Do you like guessing games? Puzzles with hidden keys? In a way the book you're holding is exactly that. Like any intelligent being, the Devil likes games, riddles. Obstacle races where the weak and incapable fall by the wayside and only superior spirits – the initiates – win." Corso moved closer to the desk and put down the book, open at the frontispiece. The serpent with the tail in its mouth wound round the tree. "He who sees nothing but a serpent in the figure devouring its tail, deserves to go no further."

"What is this book for?" asked Corso.

The Baroness put a finger to her lips like the knight in the first engraving. She was smiling.

"St John of Patmos says that in the reign of the Second Beast, before the final, decisive battle of Armageddon, 'only he who has the mark, the name of the Beast or the number of his name will be able to buy and sell' . . . Waiting for the hour to come, Luke (iv, 13) tells us at the end of his story of the Temptation that the Devil, repudiated three times, 'withdrew until another time'. But he left several paths for the impatient, including the way to reach him, to make a pact with him."

"To sell him one's soul."

Frieda Ungern giggled confidentially. Miss Marple with her cronies, engaged in gossip about the Devil. You'll never guess the latest about Satan. This, that and the other. I don't know where to start, Peggy my dear.

"The Devil learnt his lesson," she said. "He was young and naïve, and he made mistakes. Souls escaped at the last minute through the false door, saving themselves for the sake of love, God's mercy and other specious promises. So he ended up including a non-negotiable clause for the handing over of body and soul once the deadline had expired 'without reserve of any right to redemption, or future recourse to God's mercy . . .' The clause is in fact to be found in this book."

"What a lousy world," said Corso. "Even Lucifer has to resort to the small print."

"You must understand. Nowadays people will swindle you out of anything. Even their soul. His clients slip away and don't comply with their contractual obligations. The Devil's fed up and he has every reason to be."

"What else is in the book? What do the nine engravings mean?"

"In principle they're puzzles that have to be solved. Used in conjunction with the text they confer power. And provide the formula for constructing the magic name to make Satan appear."

"Does it work?"

"No. It's a forgery."

"Have you tried it yourself?"

Frieda Ungern looked shocked.

"Can you see me at my age, standing in a magic circle, invoking Beelzebub? Please! However much he looked like John Barrymore fifty years ago, heart throb too. Can you imagine the disappointment at my age? I prefer to be faithful to the memories of my youth."

Corso looked at her in mock surprise.

"But surely you and the Devil . . . Your readers take you for a committed witch."

"Well, they're mistaken. What I look for in the Devil is money, not emotion." She looked round, towards the window. "I spent my husband's fortune building up this collection, so I have to live off my royalties."

"Which are considerable, I'm sure. You're the queen of the bookshops . . ."

"But life is expensive, Mr Corso. Very expensive, especially when one has to make deals with people like our friend Mr Montegrifo to get the rare books one wants . . . Satan serves as a good source of income nowadays, but that's all. I'm seventy years old. I don't have time for gratuitous, silly fantasies, spinsters' dreams . . . Do you understand?"

It was Corso's turn to smile.

"Perfectly."

"When I say that this book is a forgery," continued the Baroness, "it's because I've studied it in depth . . . There's something in it that doesn't work. There are gaps in it, blanks. I mean this figuratively, because my copy is in fact complete. It belonged to Madame de Montespan, Louis XIV's mistress. She was a high priestess of Satanism and she managed to have the ritual of the Black Mass included in the palace routine. There is a letter from Madame de Montespan to Madame de Peyrolles, her friend and confidante, in which she complains of the inefficacy of a book which, she states 'has all that which the sages specify and yet, there is something incorrect in it, a play on words which never falls into the correct sequence'."

"Who else owned it?"

"The Count of Saint-Germain, who sold it to Cazotte."

"Jacques Cazotte?"

"Yes. The author of *The Devil in Love*, who was guillotined in 1792. Do you know the book?"

Corso nodded cautiously. The links were so obvious that they were impossible.

"I read it once."

Somewhere in the apartment a phone rang, and the secretary's steps could be heard along the corridor. The ringing stopped.

"As for *The Nine Doors*," the Baroness continued, "the trail went cold here in Paris, at the time of the Terror after the Revolution. There are a couple of subsequent references but they're very vague. Gérard de Nerval mentions it in passing in one of his articles, assuring us that he's seen it at a friend's house."

Corso blinked imperceptibly behind his glasses.

"Dumas was a friend of his," he said, alert.

"Yes. But Nerval doesn't say at whose house. The fact is nobody saw the book again until the Pétain collaborator's collection was auctioned, which is when I got hold of it . . ."

Corso was no longer listening. According to the legend, Gérard de Nerval hanged himself with the cord from a bodice, Madame de Montespan's. Or was it Madame de Maintenon's? Whoever it belonged to, he couldn't help drawing worrying parallels with the cord from Enrique Taillefer's dressing-gown.

The secretary came to the door, interrupting his thoughts. Somebody wanted Corso on the telephone. He excused himself and walked past the tables of readers out into the corridor, full of yet more books and plants. On a walnut corner table there was an antique metal phone with the earpiece off the hook.

"Hello."

"Corso? It's Irene Adler."

"So I gather." He looked behind him down the empty corridor. The secretary had disappeared. "I was surprised you weren't still keeping a lookout. Where are you calling from?"

"The bar on the corner. There's a man watching the house. That's why I came here."

For a moment Corso just breathed slowly. Then he bit off a hangnail with his teeth. It was bound to happen sooner or later, he thought with twisted resignation. He was part of the landscape, or the furniture. Then, although he knew it was pointless, he said:

"Describe him."

"Dark, with a moustache and a big scar on his face." The girl's voice was calm, without a trace of emotion or awareness of danger. "He's sitting in a grey BMW across the street."

"Has he seen you?"

"I don't know. But I can see him. He's been there an hour. He's got out of the car twice: first to look at the names at the door, and then to buy a newspaper."

Corso spat the hangnail out of his mouth and sucked his thumb. It smarted.

"Listen. I don't know what the man's up to. I don't even know if the two of you are part of the same set-up. But I don't like him being near you. Not at all. So go back to the hotel."

"Don't be an idiot, Corso. I'll go where I have to."

Then she added, "Regards to Treville," and hung up. Corso made a gesture halfway between exasperation and sarcasm because he was thinking the same thing and he didn't like the coincidence. So he stood for a moment looking at the earpiece before hanging up. Of course, she was reading *The Three Musketeers*. She'd even had the book open when he saw her from the window. In chapter three, having just arrived in Paris, and during an audience with Monsieur de Treville, commander of the King's musketeers, d'Artagnan sees Rochefort from the window. He runs after him, bumps into Athos's shoulder, Porthos's

206

shoulder-belt and Aramis's handkerchief. Regards to Treville. It was a clever joke, if it was spontaneous. But Corso didn't find it at all funny.

After he'd hung up he stood thinking for a moment in the darkness of the corridor. Maybe that's exactly what they were expecting him to do: rush downstairs after Rochefort, sword in hand, taking the bait. The girl's call might even have been part of the plan. Or maybe – and this was really getting convoluted – it had been a warning about the plan, if there was one. That's if she was playing fair – Corso was too experienced to put his hand in the fire for anybody.

Bad times, he said to himself again. Absurd times. After so many books, films and TV shows, after reading on so many different possible levels, it was difficult to tell if one was seeing the original or a copy; to know when one was seeing a real image, an inverted image, or both, in a hall of mirrors. And what were the authors' intentions. It was as easy to fall short of the truth as to go over the top with one's interpretations. Here was one more reason to feel envious of his great-great-grandfather with his grenadier's moustache, the smell of gunpowder floating over the muddy fields of Flanders. In those days a flag was still a flag, the Emperor was the Emperor, a rose was a rose was a rose. But now at least, here in Paris, something was clear to Corso: even as a second-level reader he was only prepared to play the game up to a certain point. And he no longer had the youth, the innocence or the desire to go and fight at a place chosen by his opponents, three duels arranged in ten minutes, in the grounds of the Carmelite convent or wherever the hell it might be. When the time came to say hello, he'd make sure he approached Rochefort with everything in his favour, if possible from behind, with a steel bar in his hand. He owed it to him since that narrow street in Toledo, not forgetting the interest accrued in Sintra. Corso would settle his debts calmly. Biding his time.

XI

The Banks of the Seine

This mystery is considered insoluble for the very same reasons that should lead one to consider it solvable.
E. A. Poe: *The Murders in the Rue Morgue*

"The code is simple," said Frieda Ungern, "consisting of abbreviations similar to those used in ancient Latin manuscripts. This may be because Aristide Torchia took the major part of the text word for word from another manuscript, possibly the legendary *Delomelanicon*. In the first engraving, the meaning is obvious to anyone slightly familiar with esoteric language: '*Nem. perv.t qui n.n leg. cert.rit*' is obviously '*Nemo pervenit qui non legitime certaverit.*'"

"'Only he who has fought according to the rules will succeed.'"

They were on their third cup of coffee, and it was obvious, at least on a formal level, that Corso had been adopted. He saw the Baroness nod, gratified.

"Very good. Can you interpret any part of this engraving?"

"No," Corso lied calmly. He had just noticed that in the Baroness's copy there were only three, instead of four towers to the walled city with the horseman riding towards it. "Except for the character's gesture, which seems eloquent."

"And so it is: he is turned towards any follower with a finger to his lips, advising silence . . . It's the *tacere* of the philosophers of the Occult. In the background the city walls surround the towers, the secret. Notice that the door is closed. It has to be opened."

Tense and very alert, Corso turned more pages until he came to the second engraving, the hermit in front of another door, holding the keys in his *right* hand. The legend read "*Claus. pat.t.*"

"'*Clausæ patent,*'" the Baroness deciphered. "'They open that which is closed,' the closed doors . . . The hermit symbolizes knowledge, study, wisdom. And look, at his side there's the same black dog that, according to legend, accompanied Agrippa. The faithful dog . . . From Plutarch to Bram Stoker and his *Dracula*, not forgetting Goethe's *Faust*, the black dog is one of the animals the Devil most often chose to embody him. As for the lantern, it belongs to the philosopher Diogenes who so despised worldly powers. All he requested of powerful Alexander was that he should not overshadow him, that he move because he was standing in front of the sun, the light."

"And this letter Teth?"

"I'm not sure." She tapped the engraving lightly. "The Hermit in the Tarot, very similar to this one, is sometimes accompanied by a serpent, or by the stick which symbolizes it. In occult philosophy, the serpent and the dragon are the guardians of the wonderful enclosure, garden or Fleece, and they sleep with their eyes open. They are the Mirror of the Art."

"'*Ars diavoli*,'" said Corso casually, and the Baroness half smiled, nodding mysteriously. But he knew, from Fulcanelli and other ancient texts, that the term 'Mirror of the Art' didn't come from demonology, but from alchemy. He wondered how much charlatanism lay beneath the Baroness's display of erudition. He sighed to himself. He felt like a gold prospector standing up to his waist in the river, sieve in hand. After all, he thought, she had to find something to fill her five-hundred-page bestsellers.

But Frieda Ungern had already moved on to the third engraving.

"The motto is '*Verb. d.sum c.s.t. arcan.*' This stands for '*Verbum dimissum custodiat arcanum.*' It can be translated as 'The lost word keeps the secret.' And the engraving is significant: a bridge, the union between the light and the dark banks. From classical mythology to Snakes and Ladders, its meaning is clear. Like the rainbow, it links earth with heaven or hell . . . To cross this one, of course, one has to open the fortified gates."

"What about the archer hiding in the clouds?"

This time his voice shook as he asked the question. In Books One and Two, the quiver hanging from the archer's shoulder was empty. But in Book Three it contained an arrow. Frieda Ungern was resting her finger on it.

"The bow is the weapon of Apollo and Diana, the light of the supreme power. The wrath of the god, or God. It's the enemy lying in wait for anyone crossing the bridge." She leaned forward and said quietly and confidentially, "Here it represents a terrible warning. It's not advisable to trifle with this sort of thing."

Corso nodded and moved on to the fourth engraving. He could sense the fog lifting in his mind. Doors opening with a sinister creak. Now he was looking at the joker and his stone labyrinth, with the caption: "*For. n.n omn. a.que.*" Frieda Ungern translated it as "*fortuna non omnibus æque*": "Fate is not the same for all."

"The character is similar to the madman in the Tarot," she explained. "God's madman in Islam. And, of course, he's also holding a stick or symbolic serpent . . . He's the medieval fool, the Joker in a pack of cards, the jester. He symbolizes Destiny, chance, the end of everything, the expected or unexpected conclusion. Look at the dice. In the Middle Ages, jesters were privileged beings. They were permitted to do things forbidden to others. Their purpose was to remind their masters that they were mortal, that their end was as inevitable as other men's . . ."

"Here he's stating the opposite," objected Corso. "'Fate is not the same for all.'"

"Of course. He who rebels, exercises his freedom and takes the risk, can earn a different fate. That's what this book is about, hence the joker, paradigm of freedom. The only truly free man, and also the most wise. In occult philosophy the joker is identified with the mercury of the alchemists. Emissary of the gods, he guides souls through the kingdom of shadows . . ."

"The labyrinth."

"Yes. There it is." She pointed at the engraving. "And as you can see, the entry door is closed."

So is the exit, thought Corso with an involuntary shudder. Then he turned more pages to the next engraving.

"This legend is simpler," he said. "'*Fr.st.a.*' It's the only one I dare take a guess at. I'd say there's a 'u' and an 'r' missing: '*Frustra.*' Which means 'In vain.'"

"Very good. That's exactly what it says, and the picture matches the caption. The miser is counting his gold pieces, unaware of Death who is holding two clear symbols: an hourglass and a pitchfork."

"Why a pitchfork and not a scythe?"

"Because Death reaps, but the Devil harvests."

They stopped at the sixth engraving, the man hanging from the battlements by his foot. Frieda Ungern pretended to yawn with boredom, as if it were too obvious.

"'*Dit.sco m.r*' stands for '*Ditesco mori*': 'I am enriched by death,' a sentence the Devil can utter with his head held high. Don't you think?"

"I suppose so. It's his trade, after all." Corso ran a finger over the engraving. "What does the hanged man symbolize?"

"Firstly, arcanum number twelve in the Tarot. But there are other possible interpretations. I believe it symbolizes change through sacrifice . . . Are you familiar with the saga of Odin?

"'Wounded, I hung from a scaffold
swept by the winds,
for nine long nights . . .'

"You can make the following associations," continued the Baroness. "Lucifer, champion of freedom, suffers from love of mankind. And he provides him with knowledge through sacrifice, thus damning himself."

"What can you tell me about the seventh engraving?"

"'*Dis.s p.ti.r m.*' doesn't seem very clear at first. But I would infer that it's a traditional saying, much liked by occult philosophers: '*Discipulus potior magistro.*'"

"'The disciple surpasses the master'?"

"More or less. The king and the beggar play chess on a strange board where all the squares are the same colour, while the black dog and the white dog, Good and Evil, viciously tear each other to pieces. The moon, representing both darkness and the mother, can be seen through the window. Think of the mythical belief that, after death, souls take refuge on the Moon. You read my *Isis*, didn't you? Black is the symbolic colour of darkness and Cimmerian shadows, sable in heraldry, earth, night, death . . . The black of Isis corresponds with the colour of the Virgin, who is robed in blue and dwells on the Moon. When we die we return to her, to the darkness from which we came. That darkness is ambiguous as it is both protective and threatening . . . The dogs and the Moon can also be interpreted another way. The goddess of hunting, Artemis, the Roman Diana, was known to take revenge on those who fell in love with her or tried to take advantage of her femininity . . . I assume you know the story."

Corso, who was thinking about Irene Adler, nodded slowly.

"Yes. She would let her dogs loose on gawkers after turning them into stags." He swallowed, in spite of himself. The two dogs in the engraving, locked in mortal combat, now seemed ominous. Himself and Rochefort? "So they'd be torn to pieces."

The Baroness glanced at him, expressionless. It was Corso who was providing the context, not her.

"The basic meaning of the eighth engraving," she continued, "is not difficult to grasp. '*Vic. i.t Vir.*' stands for a rather nice motto, '*Victa iacet Virtus.*' Which means: 'Virtue lies defeated.' The damsel about to have her throat slit by the handsome young man in armour carrying a sword, represents Virtue. Meanwhile, the wheel of Fortune or Fate, turns inexorably in the background, moving slowly but always making a complete turn. The three figures on it symbolize the three stages which, in the Middle Ages, were referred to as '*regno*' (I reign), '*regnavi*' (I have reigned) and '*regnabo*' (I shall reign)."

"There's one more engraving."

"Yes. The last one, and also the most the significant picture. '*N.nc sc.o ten.br. lux*' stands without doubt for '*Nunc scio tenebris lux*': 'Now I know that from darkness comes light'. . . What we have here is in fact a scene from the Revelation of St John. The final seal has been broken, the secret city is in flames. The time of the Whore of Babylon has come and, having pronounced the terrible name or the number of the Beast, she rides, triumphant, on the dragon with seven heads . . ."

"Doesn't seem very profitable," said Corso, "taking all that trouble only to find this horror."

"That's not what it's about. All the allegories are kinds of compositions in code, rebuses . . . Just as on a puzzle page the word 'in' followed by the pictures of a fan and a tree make up the word 'infantry', these engravings and their captions combined, together with the book's text, enable one to determine a sequence, a ritual. The formula which provides the magic word. The '*verbum dimissum*' or whatever it might be."

"And then the Devil will put in an appearance."

"In theory."

"What language is this spell in? Latin, Hebrew or Greek?"

"I don't know."

"And where's the fault Madame de Montespan mentions?"

"As I said, I don't know that either. All I've been able to establish is that the celebrant must construct a magic territory in which to place the words obtained, having arranged them in sequence. I don't know the order of that sequence, but the text on pages 158 and 159 of *The Nine Doors* may give an indication. Look."

She showed him the text in abbreviated Latin. There was a card covered in the Baroness's small, spiky handwriting marking the page.

"Have you managed to work out what it says?" asked Corso.

"Yes. At least, I think so." She handed him the card. "There you are."

Corso read:

> It is the animal with the tail in its mouth that encircles the
>   labyrinth
> where you will go through eight doors before the dragon
> which comes to the enigma of the word.
> Each door has two keys:
> one is air and the other matter,
> but both are the same thing.
> You will place matter on the serpent's skin
> in the direction of the rising sun,
> and on its belly the seal of Saturn.
> You will break the seal nine times,
> and when the reflection in the mirror shows the way
> you will find the lost word
> which brings light from the darkness.

"What do you think?" asked the Baroness.

"It's disturbing, I suppose. But I don't understand a word. Do you?"

"As I said, not much." She turned the pages of the book, preoccupied. "It provides a method, a formula. But there's something in it which isn't as it should be. And I ought to know what that is."

Corso lit another cigarette but said nothing. He already knew the answer to the question: the hermits' keys, the hourglass, the exit from the labyrinth, the board, the aureole . . . And other things. While Frieda Ungern was explaining the meaning of the pictures, he had discovered more differences, confirming his theory: each book differed from the other two. The game of errors continued, and he needed to set to work urgently. But not like that, not with the Baroness breathing down his neck.

"I'd like to take a good, long look at all of this," he said.

"Of course. I've got plenty of time. I'd like to see how you work."

Corso cleared his throat, embarrassed. They'd reached the point he'd worried about: the unpleasantness.

"I work better on my own."

It sounded false. Frieda Ungern frowned.

"I'm afraid I don't understand." She glanced at Corso's canvas bag suspiciously. "Are you hinting that you want me to leave you alone?"

"If you wouldn't mind." Corso swallowed, trying to hold her gaze as long as possible. "What I'm doing is confidential."

The Baroness blinked lightly. Her frown became more threatening and Corso knew that everything could go out of the window at any moment.

"You're free to do as you like, of course." Frieda Ungern's tone could have frozen all the plants in the room. "But this is my book and my house."

At that point anyone else would have apologized and beat a retreat, but not Corso. He remained seated, smoking, his eyes fixed on the Baroness. At last, he smiled cautiously, like a rabbit playing blackjack about to ask for another card.

"I don't think I've explained myself fully." He smiled slightly as he took a well-wrapped object from his canvas bag. "I just need to spend some time here with the book and my notes." He gently tapped the bag as he held out the package with his other hand. "As you can see, I've brought all I need."

The Baroness undid the wrapping and looked at its contents in silence. It was a book in German – Berlin, September 1943 – a thick brochure entitled *Iden*, a monthly publication from the Idus group, a circle of devotees of magic and astrology which was very close to the leaders of Nazi Germany. Corso had put in a marker at a page with a photograph. It showed a young and very pretty Frieda Ungern smiling at the photographer. She had a man on each arm (for she still had them both). One of the men was in civilian clothes and the caption named him as the Fürher's personal astrologer. She was mentioned as his assistant, the distinguished Miss Frieda Wender. The man on the left was wearing steel-rimmed glasses and had a timid expression. He was wearing a black SS uniform. One didn't need to read the caption to recognize the *Reichsführer* Heinrich Himmler.

When Frieda Ungern, née Wender, looked up and her eyes met Corso's, she no longer seemed like a sweet little old lady. But it only lasted a moment. Then she nodded slowly and carefully tore out the page with the photo, ripping it into tiny pieces. And Corso reflected that witches and baronesses and little old ladies working surrounded by books and pot plants, had their price, just like anyone else. '*Victa iacet Virtus.*' And he didn't see why it should be any other way.

* * *

Once he was alone he took the folder from his bag and set to work. He sat at a table by the window, with *The Nine Doors* open at the frontispiece. Before starting he parted the net curtains and glanced out. A grey BMW was parked across the street. The tenacious Rochefort was at his post. Corso couldn't see the girl at the bar on the corner.

He turned his attention to the book: the type of paper, the pressure of the engravings, any flaws or misprints. Now he knew that the three copies were only outwardly identical: the same black leather binding with no lettering on the outside, five raised bands, a pentacle on the cover, the same number of pages and location of the engravings . . . With great patience, page by page, he gradually completed the comparative tables he'd begun with Book Number One. On page 81, at the blank page on the reverse side of engraving V, he found another of the Baroness's cards. It was the translation of a paragraph on the page.

You will accept the pact of alliance that I offer you, surrendering myself to you. And you will promise me the love of women and the flower of the maidens, the honour of nuns, the rank, pleasures and riches of the powerful, princes and ecclesiastics. I will fornicate every three days and the intoxication will be pleasing to me. Once a year I will pay homage to you in confirmation of this contract signed with my blood. I will tread upon the sacraments of the Church and I will address prayers to you. I will fear neither rope, nor sword, nor poison. I will pass amongst the plague-ridden and the lepers without sullying my flesh. But above all I will possess the Knowledge, for which my first parents renounced Paradise. By virtue of this pact you will erase me from the book of life and enter me in the black book of death. And from now I will live for twenty happy years on man's earth. But then I will go with you to your kingdom and curse God.

There was another note on the back of the card, relating to a paragraph deciphered on another page:

I will recognize your servants, my brothers, by the sign impressed on some part of their body, here or there, a scar or your mark . . .

Corso cursed emphatically under his breath, as if he were muttering a prayer. Then he looked round at the books on the walls, at their dark, worn spines, and he seemed to hear a strange, distant murmur coming from them. Each one of the closed books was a door and behind it stirred shadows, voices, sounds, heading towards him from a deep, dark place.

He came out in goose bumps. Just like a vulgar fan.

It was night by the time he left. He paused in the doorway a moment and glanced to left and right, but saw nothing to worry him. The grey BMW had disappeared. A low mist was rising from the river, flowing over the stone parapet and sliding along the damp paving stones. The yellowish glow of the street lamps, illuminating successive stretches of the embankment, was reflected on the ground, lighting up the empty bench were the girl had been sitting.

He went to the bar. He searched for her face amongst the people standing at the bar or sitting at the narrow tables at the back but couldn't find her. He sensed that a piece of the jigsaw was out of place, something that had been setting off alarm signals intermittently in his brain ever since her call to warn him of Rochefort's reappearance. Corso, whose instincts had become a great deal sharper recently, could smell danger in the deserted street, in the damp vapour rising from the river and trailing to the door of the bar where he was standing. He shook his shoulders to try to rid himself of the feeling. He bought a packet of Gauloises and gulped down two gins one after the other. They made his nostrils dilate, and everything fell slowly into place, like a picture coming into focus. The alarms faded in the distance, and echoes from the outside world were now comfortably softened. Holding a third gin he went to sit down at an empty table by the slightly misted window. He looked out at the street, the quayside and the mist sliding over the parapet and across the paving stones, swirling up as the wheels of a car cut through it. He sat there for a quarter of an hour looking out for any unusual signs, his canvas bag on the floor by his feet. In it were most of the answers to the mystery posed by Varo Borja. The bookdealer wasn't wasting his money.

In the first place, Corso had now solved the problem of the differences between eight of the nine engravings. Book Number Three differed from the other two copies in engravings I, III and VI. In engraving I, the walled city with the horseman riding towards it had only three towers instead of four. In engraving III there was an arrow in the archer's quiver, while in the Toledo and Sintra copies the quiver was empty. And in engraving VI, the hanged man was hanging by his right foot, but the figures in Books One and Two were hanging by their left. He could now fill in the comparative table he'd started in Sintra.

	I	II	III	IIII	V	VI	VII	VIII	VIIII
ONE	Four towers	Left hand	No arrow	No exit	Sand down	Left foot	White board	No aureole	No dif.
TWO	Four towers	Right hand	No arrow	Exit	Sand up	Left foot	Black board	Aureole	No dif
THREE	Three towers	Right hand	Arrow	No exit	Sand up	Right foot	White board	No aureole	No dif.

NEM. PERV.T QVI N.N LEG. CERT. RIT

CLAVS. PAT.T

VERB. D.SVM C.S.T ARCAN.

FOR. N.N OMN. A.QVE

FR. ST. A

DIT.SCO M.R.

DIS.S P.TI.R M.

VIC. I.T VIR.

N.NC SC.O TEN.BR. LVX

As a conclusion, this meant that although the engravings appeared identical, one of the three was always different, with the exception of engraving number VIIII. And the differences were distributed over the three books. But the apparently arbitrary distribution acquired some meaning on examining these differences alongside those between the printer's marks for the signatures of the *inventor* (the original creator of the pictures) and of the *sculptor* (the artist who made the engravings), *A.T.* and *L.F.*

	I	II	III	IIII	V	VI	VII	VIII	VIIII
ONE	AT(s) AT(i)	AT(s) LF(i)	AT(s) AT(i)	AT(s) AT(i)	AT(s) LF(i)	AT(s) AT(i)	AT(s) AT(i)	AT(s) AT(i)	AT(s) AT(i)
TWO	AT(s) AT(i)	AT(s) AT(i)	AT(s) AT(i)	AT(s) LF(i)	AT(s) AT(i)	AT(s) AT(i)	AT(s) LF(i)	AT(s) LF(i)	AT(s) AT(i)
THREE	AT(s) LF(i)	AT(s) AT(s)	AT(s) LF(i)	AT(s) AT(i)	AT(s) AT(i)	AT(s) LF(i)	AT(s) AT(s)	AT(s) AT(s)	AT(s) AT(s)

If he superimposed the two tables he found a coincidence: in each of the engravings which differed from the other, supposedly identical, two, the initials of the *inventor* were also different. This meant that Aristide Torchia, as the *sculptor,* had made all the woodcuts for the prints in the book. But he was only identified as the *inventor* of the original drawing or works in nineteen of the twenty-seven engravings contained in total in the three books. The other eight, distributed over the three copies – two engravings in Book One, three in Book Two and the same number in Book Three – had been created by somebody else, somebody with the initials *L.F.* Phonetically very close to the name Lucifer.

Towers. Hand. Arrow. Exit from the labyrinth. Sand. Hanged man's foot. Board. Aureole. This was where the errors lay. Eight differences, eight correct engravings, no doubt copied from the original, the obscure *Delomelanicon,* and nineteen altered, unusable engravings, distributed over the pages of the three copies, only identical in text and outward appearance. This meant that none of the three books was a forgery, but it wasn't entirely authentic either. Aristide Torchia had confessed the truth to his executioners, but not the entire truth. There did indeed only remain one book. Hidden and as safe from the flames as it was forbidden to the unworthy. And the engravings were the key. There remained a single book, hidden within the three copies. For the disciple to surpass the master he had to reconstruct the book using the codes, the rules of the Art.

	I	II	III	IIII	V	VI	VII	VIII	VIIII
ONE	Four towers	Left hand	No arrow	No exit	Sand down	Left foot	White board	No aureole	No dif.
TWO	Four towers	Right hand	No arrow	Exit	Sand up	Left foot	Black board	Aureole	No dif.
THREE	Three towers	Right hand	Arrow	No exit	Sand up	Right foot	White board	No aureole	No dif.

	I	II	III	IIII	V	VI	VII	VIII	VIIII
ONE	AT(s) AT(i)	AT(s) LF(i)	AT(s) AT(i)	AT(s) AT(i)	AT(s) LF(i)	AT(s) AT(i)	AT(s) AT(i)	AT(s) AT(i)	AT(s) AT(i)
TWO	AT(s) AT(i)	AT(s) AT(i)	AT(s) AT(i)	AT(s) LF(i)	AT(s) AT(i)	AT(s) AT(i)	AT(s) LF(i)	AT(s) LF(i)	AT(s) AT(i)
THREE	AT(s) LF(i)	AT(s) AT(s)	AT(s) LF(i)	AT(s) AT(i)	AT(s) AT(i)	AT(s) LF(i)	AT(s) AT(s)	AT(s) AT(s)	AT(s) AT(s)

He sipped his gin and looked out at the darkness over the Seine, beyond the street lights that lit up part of the quayside and threw deep shadows beneath the bare trees. But he didn't feel euphoric at his victory, nor even simply satisfied at finishing a difficult job. He knew the mood well: the cold, lucid calm when he finally got hold of a book he'd been chasing for a long time. When he managed to cut in front of a competitor, nail a book after a delicate negotiation, or dig up a gem in a pile of old papers and rubbish. He remembered Nikon in another time and place sticking labels on video tapes, sitting on the floor by the television, rocking gently in time to the music – Audrey Hepburn in love with a journalist in Rome – keeping her big dark eyes that constantly expressed her wonder at life fixed on Corso. By then, they already hinted at the hardness and reproach, premonitions of the loneliness closing in on them like an inexorable, fixed-term debt. The hunter with his prey, Nikon had whispered, amazed at her discovery, because maybe seeing him like that for the first time. Corso recovering his breath, like a hostile wolf rejecting his catch after a long chase. A predator feeling no hunger or passion, no horror at the sight of blood or flesh. With no aim other than the hunt itself. You're as dead as your prey, Lucas Corso. Like the dry, brittle paper that has become your flag.

Dusty corpses that you don't love either, that don't even belong to you, and that you don't give a damn about.

For a moment he wondered what Nikon would think of him, the tingling in his groin, the dryness of his mouth despite the gin, as he sat at the narrow table in the bar, watching the street and unable to leave because there, in the warmth and light, surrounded by cigarette smoke and the murmur of conversation, he felt temporarily safe from the dark premonition, from the danger without name or shape that he sensed approaching him through the deadening thickness of the gin in his blood, with the sinister low mist rising from the river. As on that English moor, in black and white. Nikon would have understood. Basil Rathbone, alert, listening to the hound of the Baskervilles howling in the distance.

At last he made up his mind. He finished his gin and left some coins on the table. Then he put the canvas bag over his shoulder and went out into the street, turning up his coat collar. As he crossed he looked in both directions and, when he reached the stone bench where the girl had been reading, he turned and walked along the parapet on the left bank. The yellow lights of a barge on the river lit him from below as he passed a bridge, surrounding him with a halo of dirty mist.

The street and the riverside seemed deserted, with few cars passing. By the narrow passageway of the Rue Mazarin he hailed a taxi, but it didn't stop. He walked on to the Rue Guénégaud, intending to cross the Pont Neuf to the Louvre. The mist and dark buildings gave the scene a sombre, timeless appearance. Like a wolf sensing danger, sniffing the air to left and right, Corso felt unusually anxious. He moved the bag to his other shoulder so as to free his right hand and stopped to look round, perplexed. In that precise spot – Chapter XI: The plot thickens, d'Artagnan saw Constance Bonacieux emerge from the Rue Dauphine, also on her way towards the Louvre and the same bridge. She was accompanied by a gentleman who turned out to be the Duke of Buckingham, whose nocturnal adventure almost earned him a thrust of d'Artagnan's sword through his body:

I loved her, Milord, and I was jealous . . .

Maybe the feeling of danger was false, the perverse effect of reading too many novels and the strange atmosphere. But the girl's telephone call and the grey BMW at the door hadn't been figments of his imagination. A clock struck the hour in the distance and Corso breathed out. This was all absurd.

Then Rochefort jumped him. He seemed to emerge from the river, materializing from the shadows. In fact he had followed him along the riverside below the parapet, and then climbed a flight of stone steps to reach him. Corso found out about the steps when he found himself rolling down them. He'd never fallen down steps before and he thought it would go on for longer, one step at a time or something, like in films. But it was all over very quickly. A very professional first punch behind the ear and the night became a blur. The outside world seemed very distant, as if he'd drunk a whole bottle of gin. Thanks to this he didn't feel much pain as he rolled down the steps, hitting the stone edges. He reached the bottom bruised but conscious. Possibly a little surprised not to hear the "splash" – a Conradian onomatopeia, he thought incongruously – of his body hitting the water. From the ground, his head on damp paving stones and his legs on the bottom steps, he looked up, confused, and saw Rochefort's black outline descending the steps three by three and jump on top of him.

You're buggered, Corso. This was all he had time to think. Then he did two things. First he tried to kick as Rochefort jumped over him. But his weak attempt hit only air. So all he had left was the old, familiar reflex of forming a square and letting the gunfire fade away into the dusk. What with the damp from the river and his own private darkness – he'd lost his glasses in the scuffle – he winced. The Guard dies but falls down the stairs too. So he formed a square, curled into a ball to protect the bag, still hanging, or rather tangled round his shoulder. Maybe his great-great-grandfather Corso from the other shore of Lethe would have appreciated his move. It was difficult to tell what Rochefort thought of it. Like Wellington, he rose to the occasion with traditional British efficiency: Corso heard a distant cry of pain, which he suspected came from his own mouth, as Rochefort dealt him a clean, precise kick in the back.

Nothing good was going to come of this, so he closed his eyes and waited, resigned, for someone to turn the page. He could feel Rochefort's breathing very near, leaning over him, searching inside the bag. Then Rochefort yanked violently at the strap. This made Corso open his eyes again, just enough to make out the flight of steps in his field of vision. But as his face was pressed down against the paving stones, it appeared horizontal, crooked and slightly out of focus. So at first he didn't really understand whether the girl was going up or down. He just saw her move incredibly fast, from right to left, her long legs jumping from one step to another. Her duffle coat which she had just taken off, spread out in the air, or rather moved towards a corner of the screen surrounded by swirls of mist, like the cape of the Phantom of the Opera.

He blinked with interest, in an attempt to focus, and moved his head slightly to keep the scene in the frame. Out of the corner of his eye he saw Rochefort, his image inverted, give a start as the girl jumped down the last few steps. She fell on top of him with a brief, sharp cry, harder and more piercing than broken glass. He heard a thick sound – a thump – and Rochefort disappeared from Corso's field of vision as suddenly as if he'd been on springs. Now all Corso could see was the empty flight of steps. So, with difficulty, he turned his head towards the river and laid his other cheek on the paving stones. The image was still crooked: the ground on one side, the black sky on the other, the bridge below and the river above. But now at least it contained Rochefort and the girl. For a split second Corso saw her silhouetted against the hazy lights of the bridge. She was standing, her legs apart and her hands out in front of her, as if asking for a moment of calm to listen to some distant tune. Rochefort was facing her, with a knee and a hand on the ground, like a boxer who can't quite get up while the referee counts to ten. His scar was visible in the light from the bridge. Corso just had time to see his look of amazement before the girl again gave a piercing cry. She balanced on one leg and, raising the other in a semi-circular movement that seemed quite effortless, she kicked Rochefort sharply in the face.

XII

Buckingham and Milady

The crime was committed with the help of a woman.
E. de Queiroz: *The Mystery of the Sintra Road*

Corso sat on the bottom step attempting to light a cigarette. He was still too stunned to have recovered his spatial awareness so he couldn't get the match in the same plane as the tip of the cigarette. Also one of the lenses in his glasses was cracked and he had to squint with one eye to see with the other. Once the flame reached his fingers he dropped the match between his feet and kept the cigarette in his mouth. The girl, who had been collecting the contents of the bag strewn over the ground, came and handed it to him.

"Are you all right?"

Her tone was neutral, without concern or worry. She was probably annoyed at the stupid way that Corso had been taken by surprise in spite of her warning on the phone. He nodded, humiliated and confused. But he was comforted when he remembered the look on Rochefort's face just before he got kicked. The girl had struck him precisely and cruelly but she didn't follow up as he lay sprawled on his back. He turned over in pain, but didn't challenge her or try to retaliate. He dragged himself away, while she lost interest in him and went to pick up the bag. If it had been up to Corso he would have gone after him and, without a second thought, wrung his neck until he'd extracted everything from him. But he wasn't sure whether the girl would have let him, and anyway he was too weak even to stand. Now she'd dealt with Rochefort all she was concerned with was Corso and the bag.

"Why did you let him go?"

They could make him out in the distance, a staggering figure just disappearing into the darkness round a bend of the riverbank, among moored barges that looked like ghost ships in the low mist. Corso pictured Rochefort retreating, humiliated, his face smashed to a pulp, wondering how on earth the girl could have done so much damage. Corso felt jubilant at his revenge.

"We should have questioned the bastard," he complained.

She'd gone to find her duffle coat. She came back and sat next to him, but didn't answer immediately. She seemed tired.

"He'll come after us again," she said. She glanced at Corso before looking out at the river. "Make sure you're more careful next time."

He took the damp cigarette from his mouth and started turning it over in his fingers, which made it fall apart.

"I thought that . . ."

"All men think that. Until they get their faces smashed in."

Then he saw that the girl was wounded. It wasn't much: blood was trickling from her nose to her lip, and then down her chin.

"Your nose is bleeding," he said stupidly.

"I know," she answered calmly. She touched her face and then looked at the blood on her fingers.

"How did he do that to you?"

"It was my fault really." She wiped her fingers on her jeans. "I fell on top of him at the beginning. We collided."

"Where did you learn to do that kind of thing?"

"What kind of thing?"

"I saw you, down by the water." Corso moved his hands in a clumsy imitation of her movement. "Giving him what he deserved."

She smiled gently and stood up, brushing the back of her jeans.

"I once fought with an archangel. He won, but it taught me a thing or two."

With the blood running from her nose she looked impossibly young. She put the bag over her shoulder and held out her hand to help him. He was surprised by her firm grip. When he stood up all his bones ached.

"I thought archangels fought with lances and swords."

She was sniffing and holding her head back to stop the blood running from her nose. She looked at him sideways, annoyed.

"You've looked at too many Dürer engravings, Corso. And see where that's got you."

They returned to the hotel via the Pont Neuf and the passageway alongside the Louvre, without any more incidents. By the light of a street lamp he saw that the girl was still bleeding. He took his handkerchief from his pocket but when he tried to help her she took it from him and held it to her nose herself. She walked along absorbed in her own thoughts. Corso glanced at her sideways: her long, bare neck and perfect profile, her matt skin in the hazy light from the lamps of the Louvre. He couldn't tell what she was thinking. She walked with the bag on her shoulder, and leaned her head slightly forward, which made her look determined, stubborn. Occasionally, when they turned a dark corner her eyes darted to right and left, and she put the hand holding the handkerchief to her nose down by her side, tense and alert. Then under the archways of the Rue de Rivoli where there was more light she seemed to relax. Her nose was no longer bleeding and she returned his handkerchief stained with dry blood. Even her mood improved. She didn't seem to find it so reprehensible that Corso let himself be caught like a fool. She put her hand on his shoulder a couple of times, as if they were two old friends returning from a walk. It was a spontaneous, natural gesture. But maybe she was also tired and needed support. Corso, his head clearing with the walk, found it pleasant at first. Then it began to trouble him slightly. The feel of her hand on his shoulder awakened a strange feeling in him, not entirely disagreeable but unexpected. He felt tender, like the soft centre of a sweet.

Gruber was on duty that evening. He allowed himself a brief, inquisitive glance at the pair – Corso in his damp, dirty coat, his glasses cracked, the girl with her face stained with blood – but otherwise remained expressionless. He raised an eyebrow courteously and nodded, indicating that he was at Corso's disposal but Corso gestured that he didn't need anything. Gruber handed him a sealed envelope with the two room keys. They stepped into the lift and he was about to open the envelope when he saw that the girl's nose was bleeding again. He put the message in his pocket and gave her his handkerchief again. The lift stopped at her floor. Corso said she should call a doctor, but the girl shook her head and got out of the lift. After hesitating for a moment he went after her. She had dripped some blood on the carpet. Once in the room he made her sit on the bed. Then he went to the bathroom and soaked a towel in water.

"Put it against the nape of your neck and lean your head back."

She obeyed without a word. All the energy she'd shown down by the river seemed to have evaporated. Maybe because of the nosebleed. He took off her coat and shoes and laid her on the bed, folding the pillow behind her back. Like an exhausted little girl, she let him. Before turning off all the lights except for the one in the bathroom, Corso glanced round. Other than a toothbrush, toothpaste and shampoo above the washbasin, the only belongings he could see were her duffle coat, the rucksack open on the sofa, the postcards bought the day before together with *The Three Musketeers*, a grey sweater, a couple of cotton T-shirts and some white panties drying on the radiator. He looked at the girl, embarrassed. He wasn't sure whether he ought to sit on the edge of the bed or elsewhere. His feeling in the Rue de Rivoli was still there in his stomach, or wherever. But he couldn't leave. Not until she felt better. In the end he decided to remain standing. He had his hands in his coat pockets, and with one of them he could feel the empty flask of gin. He glanced greedily at the drinks cabinet, which still had the unopened seal of the hotel. He was dying for a drink.

"You were great down there by the river," he said for the sake of it. "I haven't thanked you."

She smiled sleepily. But her eyes, with pupils dilated in the darkness, followed Corso's every move.

"What's going on?" he asked.

She looked back at him slightly ironically, implying that his question was absurd.

"They obviously want something you've got."

"The Dumas manuscript? Or *The Nine Doors*?"

The girl sighed gently. Maybe none of this is terribly important, she seemed to be saying.

"You're clever, Corso," she said at last. "You ought to have a theory."

"I've got too many. What I don't have is any proof."

"You don't always need proof."

"That's only in crime novels. All Sherlock Holmes or Poirot have to do is imagine who the murderer is and how he committed the crime. They invent the rest and tell it as if they knew it was a fact. Then Watson or Hastings congratulate them admiringly and say, "Well done, sir, that's exactly how it happened." And the murderer confesses. The idiot."

"I'd congratulate you."

This time there was no irony in her voice. She was watching him intently, waiting for him to say or do something.

He shifted uneasily.

"I know," he said. The girl still held his gaze, as if she truly had nothing to hide. "But I wonder why."

He was about to add, "This is real life, not a crime novel," but didn't. At this stage in the story, the line between fantasy and reality appeared rather blurred. The flesh and blood Corso, identity-card holder with a known place of residence, with – following the episode on the stone steps – a physical presence of which his aching bones were proof, was increasingly tempted to see himself as a real character in an imaginary world. But that wasn't much good. It was only a small step away from believing he was an imaginary character who sees himself as real in an imaginary world. Only a small step away from going nuts. And he wondered whether someone, some twisted novelist or drunken writer of cheap screenplays, at that very moment saw him as an *imaginary* character who considered himself *imaginary* in an *imaginary* world. That really would be too much.

These thoughts had made his mouth quite dry. He stood in front of the girl, his hands in his pockets, his tongue feeling like sandpaper. If I was imaginary, he thought with relief, my hair would stand on end, I'd exclaim "Woe is me!" and my face would be beaded with sweat. But I wouldn't be this thirsty. I drink, therefore I am. So he lunged at the drinks cabinet, broke the seal and gulped down a miniature bottle of gin in one go, neat. He was almost smiling when he stood up, shutting the cabinet like someone closing a reliquary. Things gradually assumed their proper place.

The room was fairly dark. The dim light from the bathroom slanted across the bed where the girl was still lying. He looked at her bare feet, her legs, the T-shirt spattered with dry blood. Then his gaze lingered over her long, tanned, bare neck. The half-open mouth showing the tips of her white teeth in the gloom. Her eyes still watching him intently. He touched the key to his room inside his coat pocket and swallowed. He ought to leave.

"Are you feeling better?"

She nodded. Corso looked at his watch, although he didn't really care about the time. He didn't remember having switched on the radio as they came into the room, but there was music playing somewhere. A melancholy song, in French. A waitress in a bar, in a port, in love with a sailor.

"Right. I've got to go."

The woman on the radio went on singing. The sailor, predictably, had gone for good, and the girl in the bar gazed at his empty chair and the wet ring left by his glass on the table. Corso went to the bedside table to get his handkerchief and used the cleanest part to wipe his undamaged lens. Then he saw that the girl's nose had once more started to bleed.

"It's started again."

Blood was running down to her mouth again. She put her hand to her face and smiled stoically, looking at her bloodstained fingers.

"It doesn't matter."

"You ought to see a doctor."

She half-closed her eyes and shook her head, gently. She looked helpless in the dim light of the room, dark spots of blood staining the pillow. Still holding his glasses, he sat down on the edge of the bed and leant over to hold the handkerchief to her nose. As he did so, his shadow, outlined on the wall by the slanting light from the bathroom, seemed to hesitate a moment between light and darkness before disappearing into the corner.

Then the girl did something strange, unexpected. She ignored the handkerchief he was offering her and stretched out her bloody hand towards Corso. She touched his face and drew four red lines with her fingers, from his forehead to his chin. Instead of moving her hand away after this singular caress she kept it there, damp and warm, while he felt the drops of blood running down the four lines on his face. Her luminous irises reflected the light from the half-open door, and Corso shuddered as in each he saw the image of his lost shadow.

Another song was playing on the radio but neither of them was listening. The girl smelt of heat and fever, a gentle pulse throbbing under the skin of her bare neck. The room was light and dark, and things became lost in the deep shadows. She whispered something unintelligible, very low, and light glinted in her eyes as she slipped her hand round Corso's neck, spreading the trail of warm blood. With the taste of blood on his tongue he leant towards her, towards her soft, half-open mouth. She gave a gentle moan which seemed to come from far away, slow and monotonous, centuries-old. For a brief moment, in the pulse of her flesh all Lucas Corso's previous deaths came to life, as if brought by the current of a dark, slow river whose waters were as thick as varnish. He regretted that she didn't have a name that he could carve in his memory with that moment.

It only lasted a second. Then, recovering his clear-headedness, Corso saw his other self sitting on the edge of the bed, still in his coat, mesmerized as she moved back slightly and undid her jeans, arching her back like a beautiful young animal. He watched her with a kind of internal, benevolent wink, with a familiar indulgence both weary and sceptical. With more curiosity than desire. As she slid her zipper down the girl uncovered a dark triangle of skin contrasting with her white cotton panties that came down with her jeans. Her long, tanned legs, stretched out on the bed, took Corso's – both the Corsos' – breath away, just as they had kicked in Rochefort's teeth. Then she lifted up her arms and took off her T-shirt. She did it completely naturally, neither flirtatious nor indifferent. She kept her calm, sweet eyes on him until her T-shirt covered her face. Then the contrast was even greater – more white cotton, this time sliding upwards over her tanned skin, her firm, warm flesh, her slender waist, her heavy, perfect breasts, outlined against the light in the darkness, her neck, her half-open mouth and once again her eyes, with all the light robbed from the sky in them. With Corso's shadow in them, like a soul locked in the bottom of a double crystal ball or emerald.

From that moment on, he knew with absolute certainty that he wouldn't be able to do it. He sensed it with the lugubrious intuition that precedes certain events and marks them, even before they have taken place, with intimations of inevitable disaster. To be prosaic, Corso realized, as he threw the rest of his clothes on top of his coat at the foot of the bed, that the initial erection caused by the circumstances was now in visible retreat. Cut down in his prime. Or as his Bonapartist great-great-grandfather would have said, "*La Garde recule.*" Totally. It made him suddenly anxious, although he hoped that, as he was standing against the light, his unfortunate flaccid state wouldn't be noticed. Very carefully he lay face down next to her tanned, warm body waiting in the dark, and used what the Emperor, out on the muddy fields of Flanders, would have called an indirect approach tactic – sizing up the terrain from the middle distance and making no contact in the critical zone. From a prudent distance he tried to play for time in case Grouchy arrived with reinforcements, caressing the girl and kissing her unhurriedly on the mouth and neck. But no luck. Grouchy was nowhere to be seen. The old fool was chasing Prussians miles from the battlefield. Corso's anxiety turned to panic as the girl moved nearer to him and slipped her firm, warm thigh between his. She must have become aware of the scale of the disaster. He saw her smile, slightly dis-concerted. An encouraging smile which said something like, "I know you can do it!" Then she kissed him with extreme tenderness and put out her hand, ready to help things along. And just when he felt her hand at the very epicentre of the drama, Corso went down completely. Like the *Titanic*. Straight to the bottom, no half measures. The orchestra playing on deck, women and children first. The next twenty minutes were agony, atonement for all his sins. Heroic attacks meeting the immovable barrier of the Scottish fusiliers. The infantry on the attack glimpsing only the slightest chance of victory. Improvised incursions by the light infantry, in the vain hope of taking the enemy by surprise. Skirmishes of hussars and heavy charges by cuirassiers. But all attempts met with the same results – Wellington was messing around in a remote Belgian village, while his pipers were playing the march of the Scots Greys in Corso's face. The Old Guard, or what remained of it, was glancing desperately to left and right, teeth clenched and face against the sheets, twenty minutes by the watch which, for his sins, he hadn't removed. Drops of sweat the size of fists ran from the roots of his hair down his neck. He looked round with wide staring eyes over the girl's shoulder, desperately wishing for a gun to shoot himself.

She was asleep. He stretched out an arm, carefully so as not to wake her, and searched for a cigarette inside his coat. Once it was lit he raised himself up on his elbow and stared at her. She was on her back, naked, her head tilted back on the pillow spotted with dry blood, breathing gently through her half-open mouth. She still smelt of fever and warm flesh. In the glow from the bathroom which traced her outline in light and shadow, Corso admired her perfect body. This, he told himself, is a masterpiece of genetic engineering. And he wondered what mixture of blood, or mysteries, saliva, skin, flesh, semen and chance had commingled to create her. All women, all females produced by the human species were there, summed up in her eighteen- or twenty-year-old body. He saw the pulse at her neck, the almost imperceptible beat of her heart, the gentle curve from her back to her waist, widening out at the hips. He put out his hand and stroked the small curly triangle down where the skin was slightly lighter, between her thighs where he'd been unable to bivouac in the classic manner. The girl had taken the situation with perfect good humour. She'd made light of it and they'd drifted into a light-hearted, friendly game once she understood that on Corso's part and in that particular bout, there wasn't going to be any more action. This eased the tension. And, lacking a gun – they shoot horses, don't they – at least it stopped him dashing his head against the corner of the bedside table in an attempt to crack his skull. He'd considered it in his blind rage but discounted it, and ended up discreetly punching the wall, almost breaking his hand. Surprised by his abrupt move and the sudden tensing of his body, she looked at him, startled. Corso's effort not to shout out in pain slightly calmed him. He even managed to smile rather tensely and tell the girl it tended only to happen to him the first thirty times or so. She laughed, her arms around him, and kissed his eyes and mouth, amused and tender. You idiot, Corso. I don't mind at all. Even so, he did the only thing he could at that point – a meticulous play of fingers in the right place, with results that were, if not glorious, at least satisfactory. As she caught her breath, the girl stared at him for a long time in silence before kissing him slowly, conscientiously, until the pressure of her lips diminished and she fell asleep.

The burning tip of his cigarette lit up Corso's fingers in the darkness. He kept the smoke in his lungs as long as he could and then exhaled it in one go, watching the patterns it made in the segment of light above the bed. He felt the girl's breathing falter for a moment and he looked at her sharply. She was frowning and moaning quietly, like a little girl having a nightmare. Then, still asleep, she half-turned towards him, her arm under her bare breasts and her hand under her face. Who the bloody hell are you, he asked her soundlessly once again, bad-temperedly, although he then leaned over to kiss her. He stroked her short hair, the curve of her waist and hips now sharply silhouetted against the light. There was more beauty in that gentle line than in a melody, a sculpture, a poem or a picture. He moved closer and smelt her warm neck, and at that instant his own pulse started to hammer more strongly, awakening his flesh. Keep calm now, he said to himself. Keep cool and don't panic this time. Let's continue. He didn't know how long he could keep it up, so he hurriedly stubbed out his cigarette and pressed himself against the girl. His body seemed to respond in a satisfactory manner. Then he parted her legs and at last, bewildered, entered a moist, welcoming paradise, of warm cream and honey. He felt the girl shift, sleepily, and put her arms round him although she wasn't quite awake. He kissed her on the neck and mouth. She was moaning gently, and he realized that she was moving her hips in time with him. And when he sank right to the root of the flesh and himself, making his way easily to a place lost in his memory, she opened her eyes and looked at him, surprised and happy, green reflections through her long damp eyelashes. I love you, Corso. IloveyouIloveyouIloveyouIloveyou. I love you. Later he had to bite his tongue so as not to say something equally stupid. Amazed and incredulous, he watched from a distance and barely recognized himself. He was attentive to her, watching her beats, movements, anticipating her desires and discovering her secret springs, the intimate key to the soft yet tense body wound firmly round his own. They went on like that for about an hour. Afterwards Corso asked the girl if there was any risk of pregnancy, and she told him not to worry, that she had everything under control. Then he put it all away deep inside him, next to his heart.

He woke at daybreak. The girl was sleeping pressed against him. For some time Corso didn't move in order not to wake her. He stopped himself thinking about what had happened or might be about to happen. He closed his eyes and drifted, enjoying the peace of the moment. He could feel her breath on his skin. Irene Adler, 223b Baker Street. The Devil in love. The outline in the mist, facing Rochefort. The blue duffle coat falling slowly, unfolding, on to the quayside. And Corso's shadow in her eyes. She slept, relaxed and tranquil, aware of nothing. He couldn't link the images in his mind logically. At that moment logic had no appeal. He felt lazy and content. He put his hand between the girl's warm thighs and kept it there, very still. Her naked body, at least, was real.

Later he got out of bed carefully and went to the bathroom. In the mirror he saw that he still had traces of dried blood on his face, and also, as the result of his encounter with Rochefort and the stone steps, a bluish bruise on his left shoulder, and another across a couple of ribs which hurt when he pressed it. He had a quick wash and then went to look for a cigarette. As he was searching in his coat he found the note Gruber had handed him.

He cursed under his breath for having forgotten it, but there was nothing he could do about that now. So he opened the envelope and went back to the light in the bathroom to read the note inside. It was brief and its contents – two names, a number and an address – made him smile malevolently. He glanced at himself again in the mirror. His hair was matted and he needed a shave. He put on his glasses as if arming himself, a mean wolf off to hunt. He picked up his clothes and canvas bag quietly, and gave the sleeping girl a last glance. Maybe it was going to be a beautiful day after all. Buckingham and Milady were about to choke on their breakfast.

The Hotel Crillon was too expensive for Flavio La Ponte. Enrique Taillefer's widow must have been paying the bill. Corso reflected on this as he paid his taxi on the Place de la Concorde and crossed the marble lobby towards the stairs and Room 206. There was a "Do not disturb" sign on the door and no sound when he rapped loudly on it three times.

Three punctures were made in the heathen flesh, and the White Whale's barbs were then tempered.

The Brotherhood of Nantucket Harpooneers was about to be dissolved. Corso didn't know if he was sorry or not. He and La Ponte had once imagined an alternative version of *Moby Dick*. Ishmael writes the story, places the manuscript in the caulked coffin and drowns with the rest of the crew of the *Pequod*. Queequeg is the only survivor, the wild harpooneer with no intellectual pretensions. In time he learns to read. One day he reads his friend's novel and discovers that Ishmael's version and his own memories of what happened are completely different. So he writes his own version of the story. "Call me Queequeg" the story begins, and he calls it *A Whale*. From the harpooneer's professional point of view Ishmael was a pedantic scholar who blew things out of all proportion. Moby Dick wasn't to blame, he was just a whale like any other. It was all a matter of an incompetent captain wanting to settle a personal score instead of filling barrels with oil. "What does it matter who tore his leg off?" writes Queequeg. Corso could remember the scene around the table in Makarova's bar. Makarova, with her masculine, Nordic reserve, listening carefully to La Ponte explaining the use of the caulking on the carpenter's coffin while Zizi looked on jealously from the other side of the bar. In those days, if Corso dialled his own number, Nikon – he always pictured her emerging from the darkroom, hands wet with fixative – would answer. That's what happened the night they rewrote *Moby Dick*. They all ended up at Corso's place, emptied more bottles and watched a John Huston movie on the video. They drank a toast to old Melville when the *Rachel*, searching the seas for her lost sons, at last finds another orphan.

That's how it was. But now, standing outside Room 206, Corso couldn't feel the anger of one about to confront another with his treachery. Maybe because, deep down, he believed that in politics, business and sex, betrayal was only a question of timing. Politics aside, he didn't know whether his friend was in Paris because of business or sex. Maybe it was both, because even Corso, in his cynicism, couldn't imagine La Ponte getting into trouble for money alone. He remembered Liana Taillefer during their brief skirmish at his flat, beautiful and sensual, wide hips, smooth pale skin, a wholesome Kim Novak playing the femme fatale. He arched an eyebrow – friendship consisted of that kind of detail – he could well understand La Ponte's motives. Maybe this was why, when he opened the door, La Ponte found no hostility in Corso's expression. He was barefoot and in pyjamas. He just had time to open his mouth before Corso gave him a punch that sent him staggering across the room.

In other circumstances Corso might have relished the scene. A luxury suite, with a view of the obelisk in the Place de la Concorde, thick pile carpet and a huge bathroom. La Ponte on the floor, rubbing his jaw, trying to focus after the punch. A huge bed, with two breakfast trays. And Liana Taillefer sitting on it, blonde and stunned, holding a half-eaten piece of toast, and one voluminous white breast peeping out of the plunging neckline of her silk nightdress. With a nipple two inches wide, noted Corso dispassionately as he shut the door behind him. Better late than never.

"Good morning," he said.

Then he walked to the bed. Liana Taillefer, motionless, still holding her toast, stared as he sat next to her. Having put the canvas bag down on the floor and glanced at the breakfast tray, he poured himself a cup of coffee. For nearly half a minute nobody said a word. At last, Corso took a sip and smiled at Liana Taillefer.

"I seem to remember that the last time we met I was somewhat abrupt . . ." The stubble on his chin seemed to emphasize his features. His smile was as sharp as a razor blade.

She didn't answer. She had put the toast on the tray and hidden her generous figure inside her nightdress. She stared at Corso inscrutably. There was neither fear nor arrogance nor rancour in it. She looked almost indifferent. After the scene at his flat, Corso would have expected to see hatred in her eyes. "They'll kill you for this," etc. . . . And they'd almost succeeded. But Liana Taillefer's steely blue eyes had the same expression as a puddle of icy water, and this worried Corso more than an explosion of fury. He pictured her staring impassively at her husband's corpse hanging from the light fitting in his room. He remembered the photo of the poor bastard in his leather apron holding a plate, about to dismember a roast sucking-pig. This was some serial they'd all written him.

"Bastard," muttered La Ponte from the floor. He seemed to have managed to focus on Corso at last. He started to get up, still dazed, hanging on to the furniture. Corso watched him with interest.

"You don't look very pleased to see me, Flavio."

"Pleased?" La Ponte was rubbing his beard and looking at the palm of his hand from time to time as if he was worried he was going to find a tooth there. "You've gone nuts. Completely bloody nuts."

"Not yet. But you've nearly managed it. You and your henchmen." He pointed at Liana Taillefer. "Including the grieving widow there."

La Ponte moved slightly closer, but kept at a cautious distance.

"Would you mind explaining what on earth you're talking about?"

Corso raised his hand and began counting.

"I'm talking about the Dumas manuscript and *The Nine Doors*. About Victor Fargas drowned in Sintra. About Rochefort, who's like my shadow. He attacked me a week ago in Toledo, and last night here in Paris." He pointed at Liana Taillefer again. "And about Milady. And about you, whatever your part is in all this."

La Ponte had watched as Corso counted, and blinked five times in a row, once for each finger. When Corso finished, he rubbed his beard again, but this time not from pain but confusion. He started to say something but thought better of it. When at last he made up his mind to speak, he addressed Liana Taillefer.

"What have we got to do with all this?"

She shrugged contemptuously. She wasn't interested in possible explanations and she wasn't prepared to co-operate. She was still reclining against the pillows with the breakfast tray beside her. Her red polished nails were tearing apart one of the pieces of toast. Her only other noticeable movement was her breathing, which made her ample bosom move up and down inside her plunging nightdress. Otherwise she just stared at Corso like someone waiting for the other to show their hand at cards, as unmoved by it all as a sirloin steak.

La Ponte scratched his bald spot. He didn't look too dignified, standing in the middle of the room in crumpled stripey pyjamas, his cheek swollen from the punch. He gazed disconcertedly at Corso, then at Liana Taillefer, and back again.

"I demand an explanation," he said.

"That's a coincidence. That's exactly what I came here to get from you."

La Ponte again glanced anxiously at Liana Taillefer. He looked humiliated, and with good reason. He glanced down at his pyjamas and then at his bare feet. To be dealing with a crisis in such an outfit really was laughable. At last he gestured towards the bathroom.

"Let's go in there." He was trying to sound dignified but his swollen cheek made his speech unintelligible. "You and me."

Liana Taillefer remained inscrutable, motionless, calm. She looked at them with the bored expression of someone watching a quiz on TV. Corso thought to himself that he'd have to do something about her, but for the time being he couldn't think what. After a brief moment's hesitation he picked up his canvas bag from the floor and went into the bathroom. La Ponte followed and shut the door behind him.

"Can you tell me why you hit me?"

He spoke quietly, worried the widow would hear them. Corso put his bag on the bidet, noticed the whiteness of the towels and rummaged around on the bathroom shelf before turning back calmly to La Ponte.

"Because you're a liar and a traitor," he answered. "You didn't tell me you were mixed up in all this. You've let them trick me, follow me and beat me up."

"I'm not mixed up in anything. And I'm the only one who's been beaten up here." La Ponte was examining his face in the mirror. "God! Look what you've done to me! I'm disfigured."

"I'll disfigure you even more if you don't tell what this is all about."

"What all what is about?" La Ponte was prodding his swollen cheek, looking at Corso sideways as if he'd gone completely nuts. "It's no secret. Liana and I have . . ." He broke off, searching for the appropriate words. "Hm. We've . . . Well, you saw yourself."

"You've become intimate."

"That's right."

"When?"

"The day you left for Portugal."

"Who approached who?"

"I did. Virtually."

"What do you mean, virtually?"

"More or less. I went to see her."

"What for?"

"To make an offer for her husband's collection."

"The idea just suddenly popped into your head, did it?"

"Well, no. She phoned me first. I told you about it at the time."

"That's true."

"She wanted the manuscript her late husband sold me."

"Did she give any explanation?"

"Sentimental reasons."

"And you believed her."

"Yes."

"Or rather, it was all the same to you."

"Really . . ."

"Yeah, I know. What you really wanted was to screw her."

"That too."

"And she fell into your arms."

"Like a stone."

"Of course. And you came to Paris on your honeymoon."

"Not exactly. She had things to do here."

"And she asked you to come with her."

"That's right."

"Quite casually? All expenses paid, so you could continue the romance."

"Something like that."

Corso frowned.

"Love is a beautiful thing, Flavio. When you really are in love."

"Don't be such a cynic. She's extraordinary. You can't imagine . . ."

"Yes, I can."

"No, you can't."

"I said I can."

"I'd bet you'd like to. She's quite a woman."

"We're going off the subject, Flavio. We were here, in Paris."

"Yes."

"What were you planning to do with me?"

"We weren't planning anything. We were thinking of finding you today or tomorrow. To get the manuscript back."

"Just like that."

"Of course. How else?"

"You didn't think I might refuse?"

"Liana had her doubts."

"What about you?"

"I didn't."

"You didn't what?"

"I didn't think it would be a problem. We're friends, after all. And 'The Anjou Wine' is mine."

"I see. You were her second choice."

"I don't know what you mean. Liana's wonderful. And she adores me."

"Yes. She seems very much in love."

"Do you think so?"

"You're a fool, Flavio. They've pulled the wool over your eyes as well as mine."

He'd had a sudden intuition as piercing as a fire alarm. Corso pushed La Ponte abruptly aside and ran into the bedroom to find Liana Taillefer out of bed, half-dressed and packing a suitcase. For a second he saw her icy eyes – the eyes of Milady de Winter – fixed on him, and he realized that all the while he was shooting his mouth off like an idiot, she'd been waiting for something, a sound or a signal. Like a spider in its web.

"Goodbye, Mr Corso."

He heard the words. He could well remember her deep, slightly husky voice. But he didn't know what she meant, other than that she was about to leave. He took another step towards her, not knowing what he would do when he reached her, before realizing there was someone else in the room. A shadow behind him to his left by the door. He went to turn round, to face the danger. He knew he'd made another mistake but it was too late. He heard Liana Taillefer laughing, like the wicked blonde vamp in a film. And he felt the blow – his second in less than twelve hours – in the same spot as before, behind the ear. And he just had time to see Rochefort fading before his blurry eyes.

He was out cold before he hit the floor.

XIII
The Plot Thickens

*At this moment you're trembling because of the situation
and the prospect of the hunt. Where would the tremor be
if I were as precise as a railway timetable?*
A. Conan Doyle: *The Valley of Fear*

First he heard a voice in the distance, an unintelligible murmur. He made an effort, sensing he was being spoken to. Something about his appearance. Corso had no idea what he looked like at that moment and couldn't have cared less. He was comfortable there, wherever he was, lying on his back. He didn't want to open his eyes and make his head hurt even more.

Somebody was gently slapping his face so he reluctantly opened one eye. Flavio La Ponte was leaning over him, looking worried. He was still wearing pyjamas.

"Get your hands off me," Corso said grumpily.

La Ponte sighed with relief.

"I thought you were dead," he said.

Corso opened the other eye and started to sit up. He immediately felt his brain moving around inside his skull like jelly on a plate.

"They really gave it to you," La Ponte informed him unnecessarily as he helped him up. Corso leant on his shoulder and glanced round the room. Liana Taillefer and Rochefort had disappeared.

"Did you see who hit me?"

"Of course I did. A tall, dark guy with a scar on his face."

"Have you ever seen him before?"

"No." La Ponte frowned indignantly. "Seemed like she knew him well, though . . . She must have let him in while we were arguing in the bathroom . . . By the way, he had a split lip, it was all swollen. He'd had a couple of stitches." He prodded his own cheek. The swelling was going down. He gave a spiteful little laugh. "Seems like everyone round here's got what they deserve."

248

Corso, searching unsuccessfully for his glasses, glanced at him resentfully.

"What I don't understand," he said, "is why they didn't clobber you too."

"They intended to. But I told them it wasn't necessary. They could just go about their business. I was an accidental tourist."

"You could have done something."

"Me? You must be joking. That punch you gave me was quite enough. I held up my hands like this . . . Peace signs. I just sat on the toilet seat nice and quiet until they left."

"My hero."

"I'd rather be safe than sorry. Hey, look at this." He handed him a folded piece of paper. "They left this behind, under an ashtray with a Montecristo cigar end in it."

Corso had trouble focusing on the handwriting. The note was written in ink, in an attractive copperplate hand with complicated flourishes on the capitals:

It is by my order and for the benefit of the State that the bearer of this note has done what he has done.
3 December 1627
Richelieu

Despite the situation, he almost burst out laughing. It was the safe-conduct granted at the siege of La Rochelle when Milady demanded d'Artagnan's head, later stolen at gunpoint by Athos ('Bite if you can, viper') and used to justify the woman's execution to Richelieu at the end of the novel . . . In short, too much for a single chapter. Corso staggered to the bathroom, turned on the tap and held his head under the stream of cold water. Then he looked at himself: puffy eyes, unshaven, and dripping with water. Not a pretty sight. And his head was buzzing like a wasps' nest. What a way to start the day.

La Ponte appeared in the mirror, beside him, handing him a towel and his glasses.

"By the way," he said, "they took your bag."

"Son of a bitch."

"Hey, I don't know why you're taking it out on me. All I did was get laid."

* * *

Anxious, Corso crossed the hotel lobby, trying to think quickly. But with every passing minute it became more unlikely that he would catch the fugitives. All was lost except for a single link in the chain, Book Number Three. They still had to get hold of it, and that offered, at least, the possibility of getting to them, as long as he moved quickly. While La Ponte paid for the room he went to the phone and dialled Frieda Ungern's number. But the line was engaged. He hesitated a moment and then rang the Louvre Concorde. He asked for Irene Adler's room. He wasn't sure how things stood on that front, but he calmed down slightly when he heard the girl's voice. He let her know the situation in a few words and asked her to meet him at the Ungern Foundation. He hung up as La Ponte was coming towards him, very depressed, putting his credit card back in his wallet.

"The bitch. She left without paying the bill."

"Serves you right."

"I'll kill her, with my own hands, I swear."

The hotel was extremely expensive and La Ponte was outraged at her treachery. He had a clearer idea of what was going on, but he was now gloomy as Ahab bent on revenge. They climbed into a taxi and Corso gave the driver Baroness Ungern's address. En route he told La Ponte the rest of the story – the train, the girl, Sintra, Paris, the three copies of *The Nine Doors*, Fargas's death, the incident beside the river . . . La Ponte listened and nodded, incredulous at first and then stunned.

"I've been living with a viper," he moaned, shuddering.

Corso was in a bad mood. He remarked that vipers very rarely bit cretins. La Ponte thought about it. He didn't seem offended.

"She's a determined woman," he said. "And what a body!"

In spite of his resentment at the recent dent in his finances, his eyes shone lecherously as he stroked his beard.

"What a body!" he repeated with a silly little smile.

Corso was staring out the window.

"That's exactly what the Duke of Buckingham said."

"Who's the Duke of Buckingham?"

"In *The Three Musketeers*. After the episode with the diamond tags, Richelieu entrusts Milady with the Duke's murder. But the Duke imprisons her when she returns to London. There she seduces her gaoler, Felton, an idiot like you but in a more puritanical, fanatical guise. She persuades him to help her escape, and while they're at it, to murder the Duke."

"I don't remember that episode. So what happened to Felton?"

"He stabs the Duke. He's later executed. I don't know whether for the murder or just for being stupid."

"At least he didn't have to pay the hotel bill."

They were driving along the Quai de Conti, near where Corso had had his last-but-one encounter with Rochefort. Just then La Ponte remembered something.

"Doesn't Milady have a mark on her shoulder?"

Corso nodded. They were passing the stone steps he'd fallen down the night before.

"Yes," he answered. "Branded by the executioner with a red-hot iron. The mark of criminals. She already has it when she's married to Athos . . . D'Artagnan discovers it when he sleeps with her, and it almost gets him killed."

"It's odd. Liana has a mark too, you know."

"On her shoulder?"

"No. On her hip. A small tattoo. Very pretty, in the shape of a fleur-de-lis."

"I don't believe it."

"I swear."

Corso didn't remember seeing a tattoo. He'd hardly had time to notice that kind of thing during the brief encounter with Liana Taillefer at his flat. It seemed like years ago. One way or another, things were getting out of control. This was more than a matter of quaint coincidences. It was a premeditated plan, too complex and dangerous for the performances of Liana Taillefer and her henchman to be dismissed as mere parody. Here was a plot with all the classic ingredients of the genre, and somebody – aptly, an *Eminence Grise* – must be pulling the strings. He felt Richelieu's note in his pocket. It was too much. And yet, the key to the mystery must lie in its very strangeness and novelesque nature. He remembered something he'd read once, in Edgar Allan Poe or Conan Doyle. "This mystery seems insoluble for the very same reasons that make it solvable: the excessive, *outré* nature of the circumstances."

"I'm still not sure whether this is one big hoax, or an elaborate plot," he said aloud.

La Ponte had found a hole in the plastic seat and was nervously tugging at it.

"Whatever it is, I don't like it." He whispered even though there was a pane of safety glass between them and the driver. "I hope you know what you're doing."

"That's the problem. I'm not sure."

"Why don't we go to the police?"

"And say what? That Milady and Rochefort, Cardinal Richelieu's agents, have stolen from us a chapter of *The Three Musketeers* and a book for summoning Lucifer? That the Devil has fallen in love with me and been incarnated as a twenty-year-old girl who now acts as my bodyguard? What would you do if you were Inspector Maigret and I came and told you all that?"

"I'd assume you were drunk."

"There you are."

"What about Varo Borja?"

"That's another thing." Corso moaned anxiously. "I don't even want to think about it, when he finds out I've lost his book . . ."

The taxi was making its way slowly through the morning traffic. Corso looked at his watch impatiently. At last they reached the bar where he'd sat the night before. There were people hanging around on the pavement and "No entry" signs on the corner. As he got out of the taxi, Corso saw a police van and a fire engine. He clenched his teeth and swore loudly, making La Ponte start. Book Number Three had got away too.

The girl came towards them through the crowd, the small rucksack on her back and her hands in her coat pockets. There were still faint traces of smoke coming from the roofs.

"The fire started at three a.m.," she said, taking no notice of La Ponte, as if he didn't exist. "The firemen are still inside."

"What about Baroness Ungern?" She made a vague gesture, not exactly indifferent, but resigned, fatalistic. As if it had been pre-ordained. "Her charred remains were found in the study. That's where the fire started. The neighbours say it must have been an accident. A cigarette not properly stubbed out."

"The Baroness didn't smoke," said Corso.

"She did last night."

Corso glanced over the heads of the crowd gathered in front of the police cordon. He couldn't see much – the top of a ladder leaning against the building, intermittent flashing from the ambulance at the door, and the tops of lots of policemen's and firemen's helmets. The air smelt of burnt wood and plastic. Amongst the onlookers, a couple of

American tourists were photographing each other posing next to the policemen by the cordon. Somewhere a siren sounded and suddenly stopped. Somebody in the crowd said they were bringing out the corpse, but it was impossible to see anything. Not that there would be much to see anyway, thought Corso.

He met the girl's gaze fixed on him. There was no sign of the night before. Her expression was attentive, practical, that of a soldier approaching the battlefield.

"What's happened?" she asked.

"I was hoping you'd tell me."

"I don't mean this." She seemed to notice La Ponte for the first time. "Who's he?"

Corso told her. Then after a moment's hesitation, wondering whether La Ponte would catch on, he said, "The girl I told you about. Irene Adler."

La Ponte didn't catch on at all. He just gave them a slightly disconcerted look, first the girl, then his friend, and finally put out his hand. She didn't notice, or pretended not to. She was looking at Corso.

"You haven't got your bag," she said.

"No. Rochefort got it at last. He went off with Liana Taillefer."

"Who's Liana Taillefer?"

Corso gave her a hard look, but she looked back at him calmly.

"Don't you know the grieving widow?"

"No."

Unruffled, she met his look without anxiety or surprise. In spite of himself, Corso almost believed her.

"It doesn't matter," he said at last. "The fact is, they've gone."

"Where?"

"I've no idea." He grimaced with desperation and suspicion, showing his teeth. "I thought you'd know something."

"I don't know anything about Rochefort. Or that woman." She sounded indifferent, implying it was none of her business. This confused Corso even more. He'd expected some emotion from her. Amongst other things, she had set herself up as his protector. He thought she'd at least reproach him, something like, Serves you right for thinking you're so clever. But she said nothing. She looked around as if searching for a familiar face in the crowd. He had no idea whether she was thinking about what had just happened, or whether her mind was far away on other things.

"What can we do?" he asked no one in particular. He was bewildered. Attacks aside, he'd seen the three copies of *The Nine Doors* and the Dumas manuscript disappear one after the other. He had three corpses in his wake, if he counted Enrique Taillefer, and he'd spent a huge amount of money that wasn't his but Varo Borja's . . . Varus, Varus, give me back my legions. Damn his luck! At that instant he would have liked to be thirty-five years younger so he could sit down on the kerb and burst into tears.

"We could go and have a coffee," suggested La Ponte.

He said it jokily, as if to imply "Come on, guys, things aren't that bad," and Corso realized that the poor sod had no idea of the enormous mess they were in. Still, it didn't seem such a bad idea. In the circumstances he couldn't think of anything better.

"Let's see if I've understood." Coffee ran down La Ponte's beard as he dunked his croissant in his cup. "In 1666 Aristide Torchia hid a special book. A kind of safety copy distributed over three copies. Is that it? With differences in eight of the nine engravings. And the three original copies have to be brought together for the spell to work." He took a bite of croissant and wiped his mouth on his serviette. "How am I doing?"

The three of them were sitting on a terrace opposite Saint-Germain-des-Prés. He was making up for his interrupted breakfast at the Crillon. The girl, still slightly aloof, was sipping an orangeade through a straw and listening in silence. She had *The Three Musketeers* open in front of her on the table and was reading distractedly, turning a page from time to time, and then looking up and listening again. As for Corso, events had knotted his stomach, he couldn't swallow a thing.

"Pretty good," he told La Ponte. He was leaning back in his chair, hands in his coat pockets and staring blankly at the church tower. "Although it's possible that the complete work, the one burnt by the Holy Office, also consisted of three books with illustrations altered so that only those who were truly expert on the subject, the initiated, would be able to combine the three copies correctly . . ." He arched his eyebrows, frowning wearily. "But now we'll never know."

"Who says there were only three? Maybe he printed four, or nine different versions."

"In that case all this would be pointless. There are only three known copies."

"Whatever the case, somebody wants to piece together the original book. And is getting hold of the authentic engravings . . ." La Ponte spoke with his mouth full. He continued to eat his breakfast with a hearty appetite. "But he couldn't give a damn about the market value. Once he has the correct engravings he destroys the rest. And murders the owner. Victor Fargas in Sintra. Baroness Ungern here in Paris. And Varo Borja in Toledo . . ." He broke off and looked at Corso with disappointment. "This theory doesn't work. Varo Borja's still alive."

"I've got his copy. And they've certainly tried to set me up, first last night and then this morning."

La Ponte didn't look too convinced.

"If they set you up, why didn't Rochefort kill you?"

"I don't know." He shrugged. He'd asked himself the same question. "He had the chance twice but didn't do it . . . As for Varo Borja still being alive, I wouldn't know what to say. He hasn't answered my calls."

"That makes him another potential corpse. Or suspect."

"Varo Borja is a suspect by definition, and he's got the means to have organized the whole thing." He pointed at the girl. She was still reading and appeared not to be following the conversation. "I'm sure she could shed some light on it all, if she wanted to."

"And she doesn't?"

"No."

"So, turn her in. When people are getting murdered, there's a name for it: accomplice."

"How can I turn her in? I'm up to my neck in this, Flavio. And so are you."

The girl had stopped reading and held both their gazes placidly. She said nothing, just sipped her drink. Her eyes went from one to the other, reflecting them each in turn. Finally they rested on Corso.

"Do you really trust her?" asked La Ponte.

"Depends what for. Last night she fought off Rochefort and made a pretty good job of it."

La Ponte frowned, perplexed, and stared at the girl. He must be trying to imagine her as a bodyguard. He must also have been wondering how far things had gone between Corso and her. Corso saw him stroke his beard and cast an expert eye over the parts of her body visible beneath the duffle coat. Even if he did suspect her, there was no doubt how far La Ponte himself would take things if the girl gave him the chance. Even at times like these, the ex-chairman of the Brotherhood of Nantucket Harpooneers always wanted to return to the womb. To any womb.

"She's too pretty." La Ponte shook his head. "And too young. Too young for you that is."

Corso smiled.

"You'd be surprised how old she sometimes seems."

La Ponte tutted dubiously.

"Gifts like this don't just fall from Heaven."

The girl had followed the conversation in silence. Now, they saw her smile for the first time that day, as if she'd just heard a funny joke.

"You talk too much, Flavio Whatever-your-name-is," she said to La Ponte, who blinked nervously. She grinned, like a naughty little child. "Anyway, whatever there is between me and Corso is none of your business."

It was the first time she'd said anything to La Ponte. He was disconcerted for a moment and then, embarrassed, turned in vain to his friend for support. But Corso just smiled again.

"I think I'm in the way here." La Ponte made as if to stand up but he hesitated and didn't quite make his move. He stayed like that until Corso tapped him on the arm. A dry, friendly little tap.

"Don't be stupid. She's on our side."

La Ponte relaxed slightly, but he still didn't look entirely convinced.

"Well, let her prove it. She can tell us what she knows."

Corso turned to the girl and looked at her half-open mouth, her warm, comfortable neck. He wondered if she still smelt of heat and fever, and became lost in the memory for an instant. Her limpid green eyes, full of the morning light, as always met his gaze, unflinching, lazy and calm. Her smile, full of contempt for La Ponte a second before, now changed. Once again it was like an imperceptible breath, a silent conspiratorial word.

"We were talking about Varo Borja," said Corso. "Do you know him?"

She stopped smiling and again looked like a tired, indifferent soldier. But just before, for a split second, Corso thought he saw a glint of contempt in her expression. Corso leant his hand on the marble-topped table.

"He may have been using me," he added. "And put you on my trail." It seemed absurd all of a sudden. He couldn't picture the millionaire bookdealer resorting to a young girl to set him a trap. "Or maybe Rochefort and Milady are working for him."

She went back to reading *The Three Musketeers* and didn't answer. But the mention of Milady had reminded La Ponte of his wounded pride. He finished his coffee and raised a finger.

"That's the part I don't understand," he said. "The link with Dumas . . . What's my 'Anjou Wine' got to do with any of this?"

" 'The Anjou Wine' is only yours by accident." Corso had taken off his glasses and was peering at them against the light, wondering if the cracked lens would hold up with all the goings-on. "It's what I find most puzzling. But there are several intriguing coincidences. Cardinal Richelieu, the wicked character in *The Three Musketeers*, was interested in books on the occult. Pacts with the Devil give power, and Richelieu was the most powerful man in France. And to complete the cast, it turns out that in Dumas's novel, the Cardinal has two faithful agents who carry out his orders – the Count of Rochefort and Milady de Winter. She is blonde, evil, and has been branded by the executioner with a fleur-de-lis. He's dark and has a scar on his face . . . Do you see what I'm saying. They both have some sort of mark. And if we're going to look for links, according to Revelations, the servants of the Devil can be recognized by the mark of the Beast."

The girl took another sip of her orangeade but didn't look up from her book. La Ponte shuddered as if a ghost had just walked over his grave. He clearly felt it was one thing getting involved with a statuesque blonde and quite another for his groin to take part in a witches' sabbath. He fidgeted.

"Shit. I hope it's not contagious."

Corso looked at him unsympathetically.

"There are too many coincidences, aren't there? Well, there's more." He breathed on his lenses and wiped them on a napkin. "In *The Three Musketeers* it turns out that Milady has been married to Athos, d'Artagnan's friend. When Athos discovers that his wife bears the executioner's mark, he decides to carry out the sentence himself. He hangs her and leaves her for dead, but she survives, etc." He put his glasses back on. "Somebody must be having a lot of fun with all this."

"I can sympathize with Athos hanging his wife," said La Ponte frowning, no doubt remembering the hotel bill. "I'd like to get hold of her and do the same myself."

"Or like Liana Taillefer did to her husband. I'm sorry to hurt your pride, Flavio, but she was never interested in you in the slightest. She just wanted to get the manuscript her late husband sold you."

"The bitch," muttered La Ponte bitterly. "I bet she did him in. Helped by our friend with the moustache and the scar on his face."

"What I still don't understand," Corso went on, "is the link between *The Three Musketeers* and *The Nine Doors*. All I can think is that Alexandre Dumas was on top of the world. He had success and the kind of power he wanted – fame, wealth and women. Everything went swimmingly for him, as if he was privileged or had made some special pact. And when he died, his son, the other Dumas, wrote a strange epitaph for him: 'He died as he lived – unaware.'"

La Ponte looked sceptical.

"Are you insinuating that Alexandre Dumas sold his soul to the Devil?"

"I'm not insinuating anything. I'm just trying to work out the serial that somebody's writing at my expense. It obviously all started when Enrique Taillefer decided to sell the Dumas manuscript. The mystery began there. His presumed suicide, my visit to his widow, my first encounter with Rochefort . . . And the job Varo Borja gave me."

"What's so special about the manuscript? Why is it important and to whom?"

"I've no idea." Corso glanced at the girl. "Unless she can explain any of it."

She shrugged indifferently and didn't look up from her book.

"This is your story, Corso," she said. "I understand you're getting paid for it."

"You're involved too."

"Up to a certain point." She made a vague, non-committal gesture and turned the page. "Only up to a certain point."

Annoyed, La Ponte leaned over towards Corso.

"Have you tried giving her a couple of slaps?"

"Shut up, Flavio."

"Yes, shut up," echoed the girl.

"This is ridiculous," complained La Ponte. "Who does she think she is, talking like that? And instead of giving her the third degree you just leave her alone. This isn't like you, Corso. However cute this little girl is I don't think . . ." He spluttered searching for the words. "How did she get so cheeky?"

"She once fought an archangel," explained Corso. "And last night I saw her kick Rochefort's teeth in, remember? The same guy who clobbered me this morning while you sat safely out of the way on the bidet."

"On the toilet."

"Makes no difference. You, in your pyjamas, looking like Prince Danilo in *Imperial Violets*. I didn't know you wore pyjamas when you slept with your conquests."

"What do you care?" La Ponte glanced at the girl, embarrassed, and backed off, annoyed. "I get cold at night, if you must know. Anyway," he said, changing the subject, "we were talking about 'The Anjou Wine' . How's the report going?"

"We know that it's authentic, and in two different hands – Dumas's and his collaborator's, Auguste Maquet."

"What have you found out about him?"

"Maquet? There's not much to find out. He ended up on bad terms with Dumas with all sorts of lawsuits and claims for money. There is one strange thing – Dumas spent everything during his lifetime, he died without a penny. But Maquet was wealthy in his old age and even owned a castle. Each in his own way, things went well for them."

"What about the half-written chapter?"

"Maquet wrote the original story, a simple first draft, and Dumas added to it, giving it style and quality. You're familiar with the subject – Milady trying to poison d'Artagnan."

La Ponte peered anxiously into his empty coffee cup.

"To conclude . . ."

"Well, I'd say someone who believes he's Richelieu's reincarnation has managed to collect all the original engravings from the *Delomelanicon*. Also the Dumas chapter. For some unknown reason, they seem to hold the key to what's going on. This person may be trying to summon Lucifer as we speak. Meanwhile, you no longer have your manuscript and Varo Borja doesn't have his book. I've really screwed up."

He took Richelieu's note out of his pocket and read it again. La Ponte seemed to agree with him.

"The loss of the manuscript isn't serious," he said. "I paid Taillefer for it. But not that much." He gave a cunning little laugh. "At least with Liana I got paid in kind. But you really are in a mess."

Corso looked at the girl, who was still reading in silence.

"Maybe she could tell us what kind of mess I'm in."

He frowned and then banged the table with his knuckles like a resigned player throwing in the towel. But she didn't answer this time either. La Ponte grunted reprovingly.

"I still don't understand why you trust her."

"He's already told you," the girl answered at last, reluctantly. She put the straw from her drink in between the pages of her book as a marker. "I look after him."

Corso nodded, looking amused, although there wasn't much in his situation to be amused about.

"You heard her. She's my guardian angel."

"Really? Well, she should take better care of you. Where was she when Rochefort stole your bag?"

"You were there."

"That's different. I'm just a cowardly bookseller. Peace-loving. The exact opposite to a man of action. If I entered a coward competition, I'm sure I'd be disqualified, for being too cowardly."

Corso wasn't listening because he'd just made a discovery. The shadow of the church tower was being thrown on the ground near them. The wide, dark shape had been gradually moving in the opposite direction to the sun. He noticed that the cross on the top was at the girl's feet, very near but never actually touching her. The shadow of the cross maintained a prudent distance.

He phoned Lisbon from a post office to find out how the investigation into Victor Fargas's death was going. The news wasn't encouraging. Pinto had seen the forensic report: death by forced immersion in the pond. The police in Sintra had accepted that the robbery was the motive. Perpetrator or perpetrators unknown. The good news was that, for the time being, nobody had linked Corso with the murder. Pinto added that he had put out the description of the man with the scar, just in case. Corso told him to forget about Rochefort, the bird had flown.

It didn't seem that the situation could get any worse. But at midday it became even more complicated. As soon as he entered the hotel lobby with La Ponte and the girl, he knew something was wrong. Gruber was at the reception desk and beneath his usual imperturbable expression there was a warning. As they approached, Corso saw that the concierge turned to look round casually at the pigeonhole with his room key and then gave his lapel a slight tug, in a gesture recognized throughout the world.

"Keep going," Corso told the others.

He almost had to drag the disconcerted La Ponte away. The girl walked ahead of them down the narrow corridor that led to the restaurant-bar looking out onto the Place du Palais Royal. Corso looked back at Gruber and saw him place his hand on the telephone.

They were back out in the street, La Ponte glancing nervously behind him.

"What's the matter?"

"Police," explained Corso. "In my room."

"How do you know?"

The girl didn't ask any questions. She just looked at Corso, waiting for instructions. He took out the envelope that Gruber had handed him the night before, removed the note informing him of La Ponte's and Liana Taillefer's whereabouts, and put a five-hundred franc bill inside instead. He did it slowly, trying to remain calm and make sure the others didn't notice that his hands were trembling. He sealed the envelope, crossed out his own name and wrote Gruber's on it, and then handed it to the girl.

"Give this to one of the waiters in the restaurant." The palms of his hands were sweating. He wiped them on the insides of his pockets, and then pointed at a phone booth across the square. "Meet me over there."

"What about me?" asked La Ponte.

In spite of the seriousness of the situation Corso almost laughed in La Ponte's face. He just looked at him mockingly instead.

"You can do what you like. Although I think you might have just gone underground, Flavio."

He crossed the square through the traffic, heading towards the phone booth without waiting to see whether La Ponte was following. When he closed the door and inserted the card in the slot Corso saw him a few metres away, gazing round anxious and defenceless.

He dialled the hotel number and asked for Reception.

"What's going on, Gruber?"

"Two policemen came, Mr Corso." The former SS officer had lowered his tone but he sounded calm and in control. "They're still up in your room."

"Did they give any explanation?"

"No. They wanted to know the date you checked in and asked whether we knew what your movements had been up till two a.m. I said I didn't and passed them on to my colleague who was on night duty. They also wanted a description because they don't know what you look like. We left it that I would get in touch with them when you got back. I'm about to do so now."

"What are you going to tell them?"

"The truth, of course. That you came into the lobby for a moment and went straight out again accompanied by an unknown bearded man. As for the young lady, they didn't ask about her, so I see no reason to mention her."

"Thanks, Gruber." He paused and added with a smile, "I'm innocent."

"Of course you are, Mr Corso. All our guests at this hotel are." There was a sound of paper being torn. "Ah. I've just been handed your envelope."

"Be seeing you, Gruber. Keep my room for a couple of days. I'm hoping to come back for my things. If there's any problem charge it to my credit card. And thanks again."

"At your service."

Corso hung up. The girl was back, standing next to La Ponte. Corso came out of the cabin.

"The police have got my name. That means somebody must have given it to them."

"Don't look at me," said La Ponte. "This whole thing has been beyond me for some time."

Corso thought bitterly that it was beyond him too. Everything had got out of control, the boat tossed about with no one at the helm.

"Can you think of anything?" he asked the girl. She was the last strand of the mystery still in his hands. His final hope.

She looked over Corso's shoulder at the traffic and the nearby railings of the Palais Royal. She had taken off her rucksack and put it down by her feet. She was frowning slightly, silent as usual, absorbed in her own thoughts. She looked obstinate, like a little boy refusing to do what he's told. Corso smiled like a tired wolf.

"I don't know what to do," he said.

He saw her nod slowly, possibly as a conclusion to her secret reflections. Or maybe she was just agreeing that, indeed, he didn't know what to do.

"You're your own worst enemy," she said at last, distantly. She looked tired now too, as she had the night before when they returned to the hotel. "Your imagination." She tapped her forehead. "You can't see the wood for the trees."

La Ponte grunted. "Let's leave the botany for later, shall we?" He was becoming increasingly worried, glancing round anxiously in case the *gendarmes* pounced. "We should get out of here. I can hire a car. If we hurry we can be over the border by tomorrow. Which is April 1st by the way."

"Shut up, Flavio." Corso was looking into the girl's eyes, searching for an answer. All he saw were reflections – the light of the square, the passing traffic, his own image, misshapen and grotesque. The defeated soldier. But defeat was no longer heroic. It hadn't been for a long time.

The girl's expression had changed. She stared at La Ponte now as if he was worth it for the first time.

"Say that again," she ordered.

La Ponte stuttered, surprised.

"The bit about hiring a car?" He looked at them open-mouthed. "It's obvious. On planes they've got passenger lists. And they can look at your passport on the train . . ."

"I didn't mean that. Tell us what date it is tomorrow."

"The first of April. Monday." La Ponte fiddled with his tie, confused. "My birthday."

But the girl was no longer paying attention. She'd leant over her rucksack and was searching for something inside it. When she straightened up she was holding *The Three Musketeers*.

"You haven't paid enough attention to your reading," she said to Corso, handing it to him. "Chapter One, first line."

Corso, who hadn't been expecting this, took the book and glanced at it. 'The Three Gifts of Monsieur d'Artagnan the Elder'. As soon as he read the first line he knew where they had to go to find Milady.

XIV

The Cellars of Meung

It was a dismal night.
P. du Terrail: *Rocambole*

It was a dismal night. The Loire was flowing turbulently and rising, threatening to flood the old dykes in the small town of Meung. The storm had been raging since late afternoon. Occasionally a flash of lightning lit up the black mass of the castle, and bright zigzags cracked like whips on the deserted wet pavements of the medieval town. Across the river, in the distance, amidst the wind, the rain and the leaves torn from the trees, as if the gale drew a line between the recent past and a distant present, the headlights of cars could be seen moving silently along the motorway from Tours to Orleans.

At the Auberge Saint-Jacques, the only hotel in Meung, a window was lit. It gave onto a small terrace which could be reached from the street. Inside the room, a tall, attractive blonde, her hair tied back, was dressing in front of the mirror. She had just zipped up her skirt, covering the small tattoo of a fleur-de-lis on her hip. She stood up straight, her hands behind her back to fasten the bra supporting her pale, voluminous bust which shook gently as she moved. Then she put on a silk blouse. As she buttoned it she smiled slightly to herself in the mirror, no doubt finding herself beautiful. She must have been thinking about a date, because nobody gets dressed at eleven at night unless they're going to meet someone. Although maybe the smile, with its hint of cruelty, was due to the new leather folder lying on the bed containing the pages of the manuscript of 'The Anjou Wine' by Alexandre Dumas, père.

A flash of lightning lit up the small terrace outside. There, under the dripping eaves, Lucas Corso finished his damp cigarette and threw it on the ground. He turned up his collar against the wind and rain. During the next bolt of lightning, as intense as a giant camera flash, he saw Flavio La Ponte's deathly-pale face, drawn in light and dark, his hair and beard dripping wet. He resembled a tormented monk, or maybe Athos, taciturn as desperation, sombre as punishment. There were no more flashes for a time, but Corso could distinguish, in the third shadow, crouching beside them beneath the eaves, the slender shape of Irene Adler wrapped up in her duffle coat. And when at last another flash of lightning tore diagonally across the night sky, and thunder rolled amidst the slate roofs, her bright green eyes were suddenly lit up beneath the hood of her coat.

The journey to Meung had been quick and tense. A single stint in appalling visibility, in a car hired by La Ponte: motorway from Paris to Orleans, then 16 kilometres on towards Tours. La Ponte sat in the passenger seat and, by the flame of a cigarette lighter, studied the Michelin map they'd bought at a petrol station. La Ponte was in a mess. Not far to go now, I think we're on the right road. Yes, I'm sure we are. The girl was in the back, silent. She stared at Corso intently and he met her eyes in the mirror every time they were passed by the dazzling lights of an oncoming car. La Ponte got it wrong, of course. They missed the turn and headed off in the direction of Blois. When they realized their mistake they had to drive back up the motorway in the wrong direction to get off it. Corso gripped the steering-wheel, praying that the storm was keeping all the *gendarmes* indoors. Beaugency. La Ponte insisted they should cross the river and turn left but luckily they ignored him. They retraced their steps, this time on the Nationale 152 – the same route d'Artagnan took in Chapter One – amidst gusts of wind and rain, the black, roaring expanse of the Loire running to their right, the windscreen wipers working furiously and hundreds of little black dots, the shadows of raindrops, dancing in front of Corso's eyes as they passed other cars. At last they were driving through deserted streets, an old district of medieval rooftops, façades with thick beams in the shape of crosses: Meung-sur-Loire. Journey's end.

"She's about to leave," whispered La Ponte. He was soaked through and his voice trembled from the cold. "Why don't we go in now?"

Corso leaned over to take another look. Liana Taillefer had put on a tight-fitting sweater over her blouse, emphasizing her spectacular figure, and, from the wardrobe, she took a long, dark cape fit for a masked ball. She hesitated a moment and looked round. Then she put the cape over her shoulders and picked up the folder with the manuscript from the bed. At that instant she noticed the open window and went to close it.

Corso put out his hand to stop her. There was a flash of lightning almost above his head and his dripping face was lit up. He was framed in the window, his hand held out as if accusingly at the woman standing paralysed with surprise. Milady screamed wildly in unprecedented terror, as if she had just seen the Devil.

Corso jumped over the ledge and hit her so hard with the back of his hand that she stopped screaming and fell on the bed, scattering the pages of 'The Anjou Wine'. The change in temperature misted Corso's glasses, so he took them off quickly, threw them on the bedside table and then flung himself at Liana Taillefer who was trying to get up and head for the door. He grabbed her first by her leg and then pinned her down to the bed by the waist, while she struggled and kicked. She was strong, and he wondered where the hell La Ponte and the girl could be. While he waited for them to help he tried to hold her down by her wrists, keeping his face away from her nails as she tried to scratch him. Entwined, they rolled on the bedcover and Corso ended up with his leg between hers, his face buried in her large, firm breasts. Up so close, through her fine wool sweater, he thought again how incredibly springy they were. He felt an unmistakable erection and cursed in exasperation, while he struggled with this Milady with the physique of a champion swimmer. Where are you when I need you, he thought bitterly. Then La Ponte arrived, shaking himself like a wet dog, seeking revenge for his wounded pride, and, above all, for the hotel bill burning a hole in his wallet. It was beginning to resemble a lynching.

"I presume you're not going to rape her," said the girl.

She was sitting on the window ledge, still wearing her hood, watching the scene. Liana Taillefer had stopped struggling and was now motionless. Corso was on top of her and La Ponte was holding her down by one arm and one leg.

"Pigs," she said loudly and clearly.

"Whore," grunted La Ponte, out of breath from the struggle.

After this brief exchange they all calmed down slightly. Certain that she could not escape, they let her sit up. She was still beside herself with fury and flashed venomous looks at both Corso and La Ponte as she rubbed her wrists. Corso stood between her and the door. The girl was still at the window, now closed. She had lowered her hood and was staring at Liana Taillefer with blatant curiosity. La Ponte, after drying his hair and beard on the bedcover, started to gather the pages of the manuscript spread around the room.

"We need to have a little talk," said Corso. "Like reasonable people."

Liana Taillefer gave him a searing look.

"We don't have anything to talk about."

"That's where you're wrong, beautiful lady. Now that we've got you I don't mind going to the police. Either you talk to us or you'll have to explain things to a *gendarme*. Your choice."

She frowned. She looked round like a hounded animal searching for any way out of a trap.

"Careful," said La Ponte. "She's up to something."

Her eyes shot glances as sharp as steel needles. Corso twisted his mouth theatrically.

"Liana Taillefer," he said. "Or maybe we should call you Anne de Breuil, Comtesse de la Fère. You also go by the names of Charlotte Backson, Baroness Sheffield, and Lady de Winter. And betray your husbands and your lovers. A murderess and poisoner, as well as Richelieu's agent. Better known by your alias –" he paused dramatically: "Milady."

He stopped because he'd just tripped on the strap of his bag which was protruding from under the bed. He pulled it out, not taking his eyes off Liana Taillefer or the door. She obviously intended to escape at the slightest opportunity. He checked the contents of the bag and his sigh of relief made all of them, including Liana Taillefer, look at him in surprise. Varo Borja's copy of *The Nine Doors* was there, intact.

"Bingo," he said, showing it to the others. La Ponte looked triumphant, as if Queequeg had just harpooned the whale. But the girl didn't move or show any emotion, an indifferent spectator.

Corso returned the book to the bag. The wind whistled at the window where the girl was still standing. At intervals she was silhouetted by a flash of lightning, followed by a rumble of thunder, dull and muffled, which made the rain-spattered glass vibrate.

"Fitting weather," said Corso, and looked at the woman. "As you can see, Milady, we didn't want to miss our appointment. We've come prepared to do justice."

"As a group and at night, like cowards," she answered, spitting out the words contemptuously. "Just as they did to the other Milady. The only one missing is the executioner of Lille."

"All in good time," said La Ponte.

The woman was gradually recovering her confidence. Her own mention of the executioner didn't seem to have cowed her. She stared back at La Ponte defiantly.

"I see that you've all got into your respective parts," she added.

"You shouldn't be surprised," answered Corso. "You and your accomplices have made sure of that." His face twisted into a cruel wolf-like smile, without humour or pity. "We've all had such fun."

The woman tensed her lips. She slid one of her blood-red nails across the bedcover. Corso followed it with his eyes, fascinated, as if it were a blade and he shuddered when he thought how close it had come to his face during their struggle.

"You have no right to do this," she said at last. "You're intruders."

"You're wrong. We're part of the game, just as you are."

"But you don't know the rules."

"Wrong again, Milady. The proof is, we're here." Corso looked round for his glasses and saw them on the bedside table. He put them on and pushed them up with his finger. "That's precisely what was tricky about it – accepting the nature of the game. To accept the fiction by entering the story and following the logic required by the text, not that of the outside world . . . After that it's easy. In the real world many things happen by chance but in fiction nearly everything is logical."

Liana Taillefer's red fingernail stopped moving.

"In novels?"

"Especially in novels. If the protagonist follows the internal logic of the criminal, he'll obviously arrive at the same point. That's why the hero and the villain, the detective and the murderer always meet in the end." He smiled, pleased with his reasoning. "What do you think?"

"Brilliant," said Liana Taillefer sarcastically. La Ponte was staring at Corso open-mouthed, but in his case the admiration was sincere. "Brother William Baskerville, I presume."

"Don't be superficial, Milady. You're forgetting Conan Doyle and Edgar Allan Poe. And Dumas himself . . . I thought you were better read."

The woman stared intently at Corso.

"As you can see, you're wasting your talent on me," she said contemptuously. "I'm not the right audience."

"I know. That's exactly why I've come here – for you to take us to him." He looked at his watch. "In a little over an hour it'll be the first Monday in April."

"I'd like to know how you guessed that, too."

"I didn't guess." He turned to the girl who was still by the window. "She put the book under my nose. And in an investigation a book is more helpful than the outside world. It's self-contained, with no annoying interruptions. Like Sherlock Holmes's laboratory."

"Stop showing off, Corso," said the girl, annoyed. "You've impressed her quite enough."

The woman arched one eyebrow and looked at the girl as if she were seeing her for the first time.

"Who's she?"

"Don't tell me you don't know. Haven't you ever seen her before?"

"No. They mentioned a young girl, but not where she came from."

"Who mentioned her?"

"A friend."

"Tall, dark, with a moustache and a scar on his face? And a split lip? Our good friend Rochefort! I'd really like to know where he is. Not far away, I assume. The two of you chose worthy characters, didn't you?"

For some reason, at this Liana Taillefer lost her cool. She dug her blood-red nail into the bedcover as if it were Corso's flesh and her eyes glinted with fury.

"Are any of the other characters in the novel any better?" There was disdain and an insulting arrogance in the way Milady threw back her head and stared at them one after another. "Athos, a drunk. Porthos, an idiot. Aramis, a hypocritical conspirator . . ."

"That's one way of looking at it," said Corso.

"Shut up. What do you know?" Liana Taillefer paused, jutting out her chin, her eyes fixed on Corso as if it were now his turn. "And as for d'Artagnan, he's the worst of all of them. A swordsman? He only has four duels in *The Three Musketeers*. He only wins because in one, Jussac is getting to his feet, and in another Bernajoux, in a blind attack, impales himself on d'Artagnan's sword. In the attack on the Englishmen all he does is disarm the Baron. And it takes three sword thrusts to bring down the Comte de Wardes . . . As far as generosity goes –" she jerked her chin contemptuously in La Ponte's direction – "d'Artagnan is even more of a miser than your friend here. He pays for a round for his friends for the first time in England, after the Monk affair. Thirty years later."

"I see you're an expert, although I should have guessed you would be. All those serials you claimed to hate so much . . . Congratulations.

You played the part of the widow sick of her husband's extravagances perfectly."

"I wasn't pretending in the slightest. Most of it was mediocre – useless old paper. Like Enrique himself. My husband was a fool. He never knew how to read between the lines, or appreciate quality. He was one of those idiots who go round collecting postcards of monuments and just don't have a clue."

"Unlike you."

"Of course. Do you know which were the first two books I ever read? *Little Women* and *The Three Musketeers*. Each one, in a different way, made a deep impression."

"How moving."

"Don't be stupid. You asked questions and I'm giving you some answers. There are unsophisticated readers, like poor Enrique, and readers who go into things in more depth, looking beyond stereotypes: the brave d'Artagnan, chivalrous Athos, kind-hearted Porthos, faithful Aramis . . . It makes me laugh!" And her laughter did actually ring out, as dramatic and sinister as Milady's. "Nobody has any idea. Do you know what my most enduring image is, the one I've always admired most? The woman fighting alone, faithful to an idea of herself and to the man she's chosen as her master, relying only on herself, ignominiously murdered by four heroes who are no more than cardboard cut-outs . . . And what about her long-lost son, an orphan, who appears twenty years later!" She bowed her head, sombre, and there was so much hatred in her eyes that Corso almost took a step back. "I can picture the engraving as if I had it in front of me now – the river at night, the four scoundrels kneeling, but without mercy. And on the other side, the executioner raising his sword above the woman's bare neck . . ."

A flash of lightning suddenly cast its brutal light across her distorted face – the delicate white flesh of her neck, her eyes full of the tragic scenes she described as vividly as if she had experienced them herself. Then the window-panes shook as the thunder rumbled.

"Bastards," she whispered, absorbed, and Corso didn't know whether she meant him and his companions, or d'Artagnan and his friends.

Still at the window, the girl rummaged in her rucksack and pulled out *The Three Musketeers*. Like a neutral spectator, she searched calmly for a page. When she found it she threw the book on the bed without a word. It was the engraving described by Liana Taillefer.

. . . And on the other side, the executioner raising his sword

"'*Victa iacet Virtus*,'" murmured Corso, shivering at the similarity of the scene with the eighth illustration in *The Nine Doors*.

The woman had calmed down again on seeing the engraving. She arched an eyebrow, cold and imperious once again. Sarcastic.

"It's true," she admitted. "You can't tell me d'Artagnan symbolizes virtue. He's just an opportunist. And don't mention his skills as a seducer. In the entire novel he only conquers three women, two of them through deceit. His great love is a little *bourgeoise* with big feet, lady-in-waiting to the Queen. The other is an English maid of whom he ignominiously takes advantage." Liana Taillefer's laughter rang out like an insult. "And what about his love-life in *Twenty Years After*? Living with the landlady of a guesthouse to save himself the rent . . . Very fine affairs he went in for! Maids, landladies and servants!"

"But d'Artagnan does seduce Milady," Corso pointed out mischievously.

A flash of anger once again cracked the ice in Liana Taillefer's eyes. If looks could kill, Corso would have died at her feet that instant.

"He doesn't get her," answered the woman. "The bastard gets into her bed through deceit, passing himself off as another man." Her manner was cold again, her ice-blue eyes piercing Corso like daggers. "You and he would have made a famous pair."

La Ponte was listening attentively. One could almost hear his brain working. Then he frowned.

"You don't mean to say that you two . . ."

He turned to the girl for support. He was always the last to find out what was going on. But she remained impassive, watching them as if they had nothing to do with her.

"I'm an idiot," concluded La Ponte. Then he went up to the window-frame and started to bang his head against it.

Liana Taillefer looked at him contemptuously and then said to Corso:

"Did you have to bring him?"

La Ponte was repeating, "I'm an idiot," banging his head hard.

"He thinks he's Athos," explained Corso.

"Or rather Aramis. Fatuous and conceited. Do you know he admires his shadow on the wall while he's making love?"

"I don't believe it."

"I can assure you he does."

La Ponte decided to forget about the window.

"We've gone off the subject," he said, embarrassed.

"True," said Corso. "We were talking about virtue, Milady. You were giving us lessons on the subject with regard to d'Artagnan and his friends."

"And why not? Why should a bunch of show-offs who use women, accept money from them, and only think of getting ahead and making their fortune, be more virtuous than Milady who is intelligent and courageous, who chooses to work for Richelieu and serve him faithfully, and risk her life for him?"

"And commit murder for him."

"You said it yourself a moment ago – the internal logic of the narrative."

"Internal? It depends on your point of view. Your husband's murder happened *outside* the novel, not in it. His death was real."

"You're mad, Corso. Nobody murdered Enrique. He hanged himself."

"I suppose Victor Fargas drowned himself? And last night Baroness Ungern got carried away with the microwave, did she?"

Liana Taillefer turned towards La Ponte and then to the girl, waiting for someone to confirm what she'd just heard. She looked disconcerted for the first time since they'd got in through the window.

"What are you talking about?"

"The nine correct engravings," said Corso. "From *The Nine Doors of the Kingdom of Shadows*."

A striking clock could be heard out in the wind and rain beyond the closed window. Almost simultaneously a clock inside the building, downstairs, struck eleven times.

"I see there are more madmen in this affair," said Liana Taillefer. She was still watching the door. There had been a noise behind it as the final chime struck, and a glint of triumph flashed across the woman's eyes.

"Careful," whispered La Ponte with a start. Corso knew what was going to happen. Out of the corner of his eye he saw the girl stand up straight, tense and alert, and he felt a sudden rush of adrenaline through his veins.

They all looked at the door handle. It was turning very slowly, like in the movies.

"Good evening," said Rochefort.

He was wearing a raincoat buttoned to the neck, shiny with rain. His dark eyes shone intensely beneath his felt hat. The pale zigzag of the scar stood out against his dark face. The bushy black moustache accentuated his southern looks. He stood motionless at the door for some fifteen seconds, his hands in his coat pockets, a puddle forming around his wet shoes. Nobody said a word.

"I'm glad you're here," said Liana Taillefer at last. Rochefort nodded briefly, but didn't answer. Still sitting on the bed, the woman pointed at Corso. "They were getting rather impertinent."

"Not too much, I hope," said Rochefort. His voice was pleasant, educated, with no definite accent, as Corso remembered it from the Sintra road. He didn't move from the doorway, his eyes fixed on Corso, as if La Ponte and the girl didn't exist. His lower lip still looked swollen, with traces of mercurochrome, two stitches holding the recent wound together. Souvenir from the banks of the Seine, thought Corso malevolently. Then he looked with interest to see the girl's reaction. But after her initial surprise, she had resumed the role of a detached spectator.

Without taking his eyes off Corso, Rochefort spoke to Milady.

"How did they get here?"

The woman gestured vaguely.

"They're pretty smart." She quickly looked over La Ponte and then stopped at Corso. "One of them anyway."

Rochefort nodded again. His eyes half-closed, he seemed to be analyzing the situation.

"It complicates things," he said at last. He took off his hat and threw it on the bed. "Really complicates things."

Liana Taillefer agreed. She smoothed down her skirt and stood up with a deep sigh. This made Corso turn slightly towards her, tense and hesitant. Then Rochefort took his hand out of his coat pocket and Corso worked out he must be left-handed. The discovery didn't do him much good – it was his left hand and in it he was holding a short-barrelled revolver, small and dark-blue, almost black. Meanwhile, Liana Taillefer went over to La Ponte and took the Dumas manuscript from his hands.

"Now try calling me a whore again." She was so close and staring at him with such contempt that she almost spat in his face. "If you've got the guts."

La Ponte hadn't. He was a born survivor. His "intrepid harpooneer" act was reserved for moments of alcohol-induced euphoria. So he made sure he said nothing at all.

"I was just passing," he said placatingly, hoping to wash his hands of the whole business.

"What would I do without you, Flavio?" said Corso, resigned.

La Ponte looked apologetic.

"You're being unfair," he said, looking offended. He went and stood nearer to the girl. It must have seemed the safest place in the room. "From a certain point of view, this is your adventure, Corso. And what's death to a guy like you? Nothing. A formality. Anyway you're getting paid a fortune. And life is basically unpleasant." He ended up looking down the barrel of Rochefort's revolver. Then he put his arm round the girl's shoulder and gave a melancholy sigh. "I hope nothing happens to you. But if it does, it'll be hardest for us: we'll have to go on living."

"Bastard. Traitor."

La Ponte looked saddened.

"My friend, I'll ignore that last remark. You're very tense."

"Of course I'm tense, you sewer rat."

"I'll ignore that too."

"Son of a bitch."

"I get the message, old buddy. Friendship is made up of little touches like that."

"Nice to see you've kept your team spirit," said Milady caustically.

Corso was thinking fast, even though there was nothing he could do. No amount of thinking could get the gun out of Rochefort's hand, although he wasn't pointing it at anyone in particular. He seemed rather half-hearted, as if he just needed to show it to get the desired effect. On the other hand, however intense his desire to settle a few outstanding scores with the man with the scar, Corso didn't possess the necessary technical skill to do so. With La Ponte not in the running, the girl was his only hope of shifting the balance of power. But unless she was an extremely accomplished actress he saw at first glance that he couldn't hope for anything on that flank. The supposed Irene Adler had shaken herself free of La Ponte's arm and had sat down on the window-ledge, from where she observed them with inexplicable detachment. She seemed absurdly determined to stay on the sidelines.

Liana Taillefer went over to Rochefort holding the Dumas manuscript, delighted to have retrieved it so quickly. Corso found it strange that she showed no similar interest in *The Nine Doors* which was still inside the canvas bag at the foot of the bed.

"What do we do now?" he heard her whisper to Rochefort.

To Corso's surprise Rochefort looked unsure. He was moving the revolver from one side to the other as if he didn't quite know where to point it. Then, exchanging a long and meaningful look with Milady, he took his right hand out of his pocket and passed it over his face, hesitant.

"We can't leave them here," he said at last.

"But we can't take them with us either," she said.

He nodded slowly. Judging by his renewed grip on the revolver, his indecision vanished. Corso felt his abdominal muscles tense as Rochefort pointed the gun at him. At the same time he tried to make some sort of syntactically coherent protest. All he managed was an indistinct, guttural sound.

"You're not going to kill him, are you?" asked La Ponte, trying to deflect attention from himself.

"Flavio," Corso managed to say in spite of the dryness in his mouth, "if I get out of this I swear I'll smash your face in. Right in."

"I was just trying to help."

"Better help your mother get off the streets."

"OK, OK, I'll shut up."

"Yeah, shut it," interrupted Rochefort menacingly. He'd exchanged a final glance with Liana Taillefer and seemed to have reached a decision. He locked the door behind him, still pointing the revolver at Corso, and put the key in his raincoat pocket. What have I got to lose, thought Corso, his pulse throbbing at his temples and wrists. The drums of Waterloo rolled somewhere in his memory when, in the final moment of clarity before desperation set in, he found himself working out the distance between him and the gun, and how long it would take him to cross it. He wondered when the first shot would ring out and in what position he'd be when it hit him. The chances of getting out of there unscathed were minimal, but maybe if he left it five seconds longer he would have no chance at all. So the bugle sounded. The last charge with Ney at the head, the bravest of the brave, before the Emperor's weary eyes. With Rochefort instead of the Scots Guards, but a bullet was still a bullet. This is ridiculous, he told himself just before he went into action. And he wondered if, in this context, the death blow about to strike him in the chest was going to be real or imaginary, and if he'd find himself floating in the void or in the Valhalla for fictional heroes. If only the luminous eyes he felt staring intently at his back – the Emperor? The Devil in love? – were waiting for him in the darkness to guide him to the other side.

Then Rochefort did something very odd. He raised his free hand, as if to say, "Give me time", rather an absurd gesture at this stage, and went to put the revolver back in his pocket. His movement only lasted a moment and he pointed it at Corso once again, but without too much conviction. And Corso, his pulse racing, his muscles taut, about to leap blindly forward, held back, bewildered, realizing it wasn't his time to die.

Still stunned, he watched Rochefort cross the room, press the number for an outside line and then dial a longer number. From where he was he could hear the sound of the phone ringing on the line and then a click.

"I've got Corso here," said Rochefort, and then he was quiet, waiting, as if there was a silence at the other end of the line. He was still lazily pointing the gun at a vague point in space. The man with the scar said "yes" twice. Then he listened, motionless, and muttered "OK" before finally hanging up.

"He wants to see him," he said to Milady. They both turned to look at Corso. Milady looked annoyed, Rochefort looked anxious.

"This is ridiculous," she complained.

"He wants to see him," Rochefort said again.

Milady shrugged. She took a few steps and angrily turned a few pages of 'The Anjou Wine'.

"As for us . . . ." La Ponte started to say.

"You're staying here," said Rochefort, pointing the gun at him. Then he felt the wound on his lip. "The girl too."

In spite of his split lip he didn't seem to bear the girl much of a grudge. Corso even thought he saw a hint of curiosity as he looked at her. Then he turned to Liana Taillefer and handed her the revolver.

"Make sure they don't get out."

"Why don't you stay here?"

"He wants me to take him. It's safer."

Milady nodded sullenly. She'd obviously imagined herself playing a different part that evening. But like her fictional namesake she was a disciplined hired assassin. In exchange for the weapon she handed Rochefort the Dumas manuscript. Then she scrutinized Corso anxiously.

"I hope he won't give you any trouble."

Rochefort smiled calmly and confidently. He took a large switchblade from his pocket and stared at it thoughtfully, as if he'd only just remembered it was there. His white teeth looked bright against his dark, scarred face.

"I don't think he will," he answered, putting back the knife unopened, and gesturing to Corso in a way that was both friendly and sinister. Then he took his hat from the bed, turned the key in the lock and motioned towards the corridor with an exaggerated bow as if he was holding a large plumed hat.

"His Eminence awaits, sir," he said. And then he gave a short, dry laugh, perfectly befitting a skilled henchman.

Before leaving the room Corso looked at the girl. Milady was pointing the gun at her and La Ponte, but she had turned her back and was taking no notice of what was going on. She leant against the window and looked out, watching the wind and the rain, silhouetted against the night sky illuminated by flashes of lightning.

They went out into the storm. Rochefort was holding the folder with the Dumas manuscript under his raincoat to protect it from the rain. He led Corso through the narrow streets to the old part of the town. Blasts of rain shook the branches of the trees and splashed noisily in the puddles and on the paving stones. Large drops poured through Corso's hair and down his face. He turned up his collar. The town was in darkness and there was not a soul to be seen. Only the brightness of the storm lit up the streets intermittently, showing the medieval roofs, Rochefort's dark profile beneath his dripping hat, the shadows of the two men on the wet ground. The electrical discharges, like thunder from Hell, struck the turbulent current of the river Loire with a sound like the cracking of whips.

"Wonderful evening," said Rochefort turning towards Corso to make himself heard above the roar.

He seemed to know his way. He walked along confidently, turning occasionally to make sure his companion was still there. He didn't need to, because at that moment Corso would have followed him to the very gates of Hell. And he didn't discount the possibility that this might be their ultimate destination. With each flash of lightning he saw first a medieval archway, then a bridge over an ancient moat, a sign saying *Boulangerie-Patisserie*, a deserted square, a conical tower and finally, an iron gate with the sign: *Château de Meung-sur-Loire. XIIème-XIIIème siècle.*

A window was lit up in the distance, beyond the gate, but Rochefort turned right and Corso followed. They walked along a stretch of ivy-clad wall until they reached a half-hidden door in the wall. Rochefort took out a huge, ancient iron key and put it in the lock.

"Joan of Arc came through this door," he told Corso as he turned the key. One final flash of lightning revealed steps descending into darkness. In the momentary brightness Corso also saw Rochefort's smile, his dark eyes shining beneath the hat, the livid scar on his cheek. At least he was a worthy opponent, he thought. Nobody could have any complaints about the impeccable staging. In spite of himself he was beginning to feel a kind of twisted sympathy for the man – whoever he was – capable of playing the part of such a villain so conscientiously. Alexandre Dumas would have enjoyed it all hugely.

Rochefort was holding a small torch, lighting up the long, narrow staircase disappearing down to the cellar.

"You go in front," he said.

Their steps echoed round the turns of the passageway. After a moment, Corso shivered inside his damp coat. Cold, musty air, smelling of the damp of centuries, rose towards them. The torch beam lit worn steps, water stains on the vaulted ceiling. The staircase ended in a narrow corridor with rusty railings. Rochefort shone the torch for a moment on a circular pit to their left.

"These are the ancient dungeons of Bishop Thibault D'Aussigny," he told Corso. "From there they threw the corpses into the Loire. François Villon was a prisoner here."

And he muttered the following line melodramatically:

"Ayez pitié, ayez pitié de moi . . ."

Definitely a well-educated villain. Self-assured and with a hint of didacticism. Corso couldn't decide whether this made the situation better or worse. But he had an idea that had been going round in his head since they entered the passageway. If all is lost we may as well jump in the river, he thought. But he didn't find his joke funny.

The underground passageway was now rising beneath the dripping arches. The bright eyes of a rat shone for a moment at the end of the gallery and then disappeared with a cry. The torch lit up the passageway which widened into a circular room. Its ceiling, supported by pointed ribs, rested on a thick central column.

"The crypt," said Rochefort, moving the torch beam around. He was becoming more and more talkative. "Twelfth century. The women and children hid here when the castle was attacked."

Very interesting. But Corso wasn't in the mood to appreciate the information provided by his outlandish guide. He was tense and alert, waiting for the right moment. They were now climbing a spiral staircase, light from the storm still booming beyond the castle walls filtered through the slot windows.

"Only a few metres more and we're there," said Rochefort from behind, slightly lower down. He sounded quite conciliatory. The light from his torch shone between Corso's legs. "Now all this business is nearly over," he added, "I must tell you something. In spite of everything, you did very well. The proof is that you got this far . . . I hope you don't bear me too much of a grudge over the business by the Seine and at the Hotel Crillon. Occupational hazards."

He didn't say which occupation, but it didn't matter. Corso had already turned casually and stopped, as if to answer or ask him a question. It didn't look in the least suspicious, so in all fairness Rochefort couldn't object in any way. Maybe this was why he didn't react when, as a continuation of the same move, Corso fell on top of him, his arms and legs stretched out towards the wall so he wouldn't be dragged down the stairs. Rochefort's position was different – the steps were narrow, the wall smooth and without handholds, and in addition he wasn't expecting the attack. The torch, miraculously intact, illuminated the scene for several moments as it rolled down the staircase: Rochefort with his eyes wide open and a stunned look on his face; Rochefort flailing wildly, trying desperately to grab hold of something, disappearing down the spiral staircase, his hat rolling down until it came to a halt on one of the steps . . . And then, six or seven metres further down, a muffled sound, something like "thump", or maybe "splat". Corso, who was still gripping the walls with his arms and legs outstretched so as not to accompany his opponent on his uncomfortable journey, suddenly sprang into action. His heart was pounding uncontrollably as he leapt down the stairs three by three. He leant down for a moment to pick up the torch and then reached the bottom of the stairs where Rochefort, rolled into a ball, was moving weakly, in pain and in a bad way.

"Occupational hazard," said Corso, shining the torch on his face so that, from the floor, Rochefort could see his friendly smile. Then he kicked him in the head and heard it slam hard against the bottom step. He raised his foot to kick him again, just to make sure, but one look told him he didn't need to – Rochefort was lying with his mouth open and blood was trickling from his ear. He leant over to see if he was breathing and saw that he was. Then he opened his raincoat and rifled through his pockets. He took the switchblade, a wallet full of money, a French identity card and the folder with the Dumas manuscript, which he put under his coat, between his belt and his shirt. Then he pointed the torch beam at the spiral staircase and climbed right to the top this time. He reached a landing with a door with thick iron hinges and hexagonal nails. A crack of light filtered from beneath it. He stood motionless for some thirty seconds, trying to catch his breath and calm the beating of his heart. The solution to the mystery lay on the other side and he prepared to face it with his teeth clenched, the torch in one hand and Rochefort's knife, which opened with a menacing click, in the other.

And that's how, knife in hand, his hair soaked and dishevelled, and his eyes shining with homicidal determination, I saw Corso enter the library.

XV
Corso and Richelieu

And I, who had created a short novel around him, had been completely mistaken.

Souvestre et Allain: *Fantomas*

The time has come to identify the viewpoint of the narrator. Faithful to the tradition that the reader of mystery novels must have the same information as the protagonist, I have tried to present the facts only from Lucas Corso's perspective, except on two occasions: chapters one and five of this story, when I had no choice but to appear myself. In both these cases, and as now for the third and final time, I used the first person for the sake of coherence. It would have been absurd to refer to myself as "he", a publicity stunt that may have yielded dividends for Julius Caesar in his campaign in Gaul but would, in my case, have been judged, entirely reasonably, as unpardonable pedantry. There is another, fairly perverse reason: telling the story as if I were Dr Sheppard addressing Poirot struck me as, if not ingenious (everybody does that sort of thing now), then an amusing device. After all, people write for amusement, or excitement, or out of self-love, or to have others love them. I write for some of the same reasons. To quote Eugène Sue, villains who are all of a piece, if you'll permit me the expression, are very rare phenomena. Assuming – and it may be too much to assume – that I really am a villain.

The fact is that I the undersigned, Boris Balkan, was there in the library, awaiting our guest. Corso entered suddenly, knife in hand and a dangerous avenging gleam in his eye. I noticed that he had no escort, which worried me slightly, although I tried to retain my mask of imperturbability. Otherwise I had planned the effect well: the library in darkness, candelabra burning on the desk before me, a copy of *The Three Musketeers* in my hands . . . I was even wearing a red velvet jacket – which must have seemed like pure coincidence to Corso, but was in fact nothing of the sort – strongly reminiscent of cardinal's purple.

My big advantage was that I was expecting Corso, with or without escort, but he wasn't expecting me. So I decided to make the most of his surprise. I found the knife he was holding, together with the menacing look in his eyes, worrying. I opted to speak to forestall any move from him.

"Congratulations," I said, closing the book as if his arrival had interrupted my reading. "You've managed to play the game right to the end."

He stood staring at me from the other side of the room, and I have to say that I found his look of disbelief highly amusing.

"Game?" he managed to say hoarsely.

"Yes, game. Tension, uncertainty, a high level of skill . . . The possibility of acting freely, but according to obligatory rules, as an end in itself. Together with a sense of tension and pleasure at the difference from ordinary life . . ." These were not my own words, but Corso wasn't to know that. "Do you think that's an adequate definition? As the Second Book of Samuel says: 'Let the young men now arise, and play before us . . .' Children are the perfect players and readers: they do everything with the utmost seriousness. In essence, games are the only universally serious activity. They leave no room for scepticism, wouldn't you agree? However incredulous or doubting one might be, if one wants to play one has no choice but to follow the rules. Only the person who respects the rules, or at least knows and applies them, can win . . . Reading a book is the same: one has to accept the plot and the characters to enjoy the story." I paused, assuming that my flow of words would have had a sufficiently calming effect. "By the way, you didn't get here on your own. Where is he?"

"Rochefort?" Corso was grimacing in a very unpleasant way. "He had an accident."

"You call him Rochefort, do you? How amusing and appropriate. I see you've obviously followed the rules. I don't know why it should surprise me."

Corso treated me to a rather unnerving smile.

"He certainly looked surprised the last time I saw him."

"That sounds rather alarming." I smiled coolly, although I actually was alarmed. "I hope nothing serious has happened."

"He fell down the stairs."

"What?"

"You heard me. But don't worry. Your henchman was still breathing when I left him."

"Thank God." I managed to smile again and hide my unease. This went way beyond what I'd planned. "So you've done a touch of cheating, have you? Well," I said, spreading my hands magnanimously, "no need to worry about it."

"I'm not. You're the one who should be worried."

I pretended not to hear this.

"The important thing is you've arrived," I went on, although I'd lost the thread momentarily. "As far as cheating goes, you have illustrious predecessors . . . Theseus escaped from the labyrinth thanks to Ariadne's thread, Jason stole the Golden Fleece with Medea's help . . . The Kaurabas used subterfuge to win at dice in the Mahabharata, and the Achæans checkmated the Trojans by moving a wooden horse . . . Your conscience is clear."

"Thanks. But my conscience is my business."

From his pocket he took Milady's letter, folded in four, and threw it down on the table. I immediately recognized my own handwriting, with the slightly affected capitals. It is by my order and for the benefit of the State that the bearer of this note, etc.

"I hope, at least, that the game was enjoyable," I said holding the paper in the candle flame.

"At times."

"I'm glad." I dropped the letter in the ashtray and we both watched it burn. "In matters of literature, the intelligent reader may even enjoy the strategy used to turn him into the victim. I believe that enjoyment is an excellent reason for playing. Or reading a story, or writing one."

I stood up, holding *The Three Musketeers*, and paced around the room, glancing discreetly at the clock on the wall. There were still twenty long minutes to go before twelve. The gilding gleamed on the spines of the ancient books lined up on their shelves. I looked at them a moment, having seemingly forgotten Corso, and then turned towards him.

"There they are." I made a sweeping gesture to include the whole library. "They look still and silent but they talk amongst themselves, even though they seem to ignore each other. They communicate through their authors, just as the egg uses the hen to produce another egg."

I put *The Three Musketeers* back on its shelf. Dumas was in good company: between *Los Pardellanes* by Zevaco and *The Knight with the*

Yellow Doublet by Lucus de René. As there was time to spare, I opened it at the first page and began to read aloud:

"As Saint Germain l'Auxerrois struck twelve, three horsemen descended the Rue des Astruces each wrapped in a cape, seemingly as sure as the stride of their horses . . .

"The first lines," I said. "Always those extraordinary first lines. Do you remember our conversation about Scaramouche? 'He was born with the gift of laughter . . .'. Some opening sentences leave their mark a whole lifetime, don't you agree? 'I sing of arms and the man.' Have you never played this game with someone you trust? 'A modest young man headed in midsummer . . .', or that other one, 'For a long time I used to go to bed early . . .'. And of course, 'On the 15th of May 1796 General Bonaparte entered Milan.'"

Corso frowned.

"You're forgetting the one which brought me here: 'On the first Monday of April 1625, the market town of Meung, the birthplace of the author of the *Roman de la Rose*, was in a state of commotion.'"

"Indeed, Chapter One," I said. "You have done very well."

"That's what Rochefort said before he fell down the stairs."

There was silence, broken only by the clock striking a quarter to twelve. Corso pointed at the clockface.

"Fifteen minutes to go, Balkan."

"Yes," I said. The man was devilishly intuitive. "Fifteen minutes till the first Monday in April."

I put *The Knight with the Yellow Doublet* back on the shelf and paced around the room. Corso stood watching me, still holding the knife.

"You could put that away," I ventured.

He hesitated a moment before shutting the blade and putting it away in his pocket, still watching me. I smiled approvingly and again indicated the library.

"One is never alone with a book nearby, don't you agree?" I said to be conversational. "Every page reminds one of a day that has passed and makes one relive the emotions that filled it. Happy hours underlined in chalk, dark ones in pencil . . . Where was I then? What prince called me his friend, what beggar called me his brother?" I hesitated a moment, searching for more phrases with which to round off my speech.

"What son of a bitch called you his buddy?" suggested Corso.

I looked at him reprovingly. The wet blanket insisted on bringing down the tone.

"No need to be unpleasant."

"I'll do what I please. Your Eminence."

"I detect a hint of sarcasm," I said, truly offended. "From that I deduce that you have given in to prejudice, Mr Corso. It was Dumas who made Richelieu a villain when he wasn't one, and falsified reality for the sake of literary expediency. I thought I'd explained that during our last meeting at the café in Madrid."

"A dirty trick," said Corso, not specifying whether he was referring to Dumas or to me.

I raised a finger, ready to state my case vigorously.

"A legitimate device," I objected, "inspired by the shrewdness and genius of the greatest novelist who ever lived. And yet . . ." at this point I smiled bitterly – "Sainte-Beuve respected him but didn't accept him as a man of letters. His friend, Victor Hugo, merely praised Dumas's capacity for dramatic action, but nothing more. Prolific, long-winded, they said. With little style. They accused him of not delving into the anxieties of human beings, of lacking subtlety . . . Lacking subtlety!" I touched the volumes of *The Three Musketeers* lined up on the shelf. "I agree with our good father Stevenson – there is no pæan to friendship as long, eventful or beautiful. In *Twenty Years After*, when the protagonists reappear they are distanced at first. They are now men of mature years, selfish, with all the pettiness that life imposes. They're even fighting in opposing camps . . . Aramis and d'Artagnan lie and dissemble, Porthos fears being asked for money . . . When they agree to meet in the Place Royale they come armed and almost fight. And in England, when Athos's imprudence puts them all in danger, d'Artagnan refuses to shake his hand . . . In *The Vicomte de Bragelonne*, with the mystery of the iron mask, Aramis and Porthos stand against their old comrades. This happens because they're alive, because they're human, full of contradictions. But always, at the moment of truth, friendship wins out. A great thing, friendship! Do you have friends, Corso?"

"That's a good question."

"For me, Porthos in the cave at Locmaria has always embodied friendship: the giant struggling beneath a rock to save his friends . . . Do you remember his last words?"

"It's too heavy?"

"Exactly!"

I confess I felt almost moved. Like the young man in a cloud of pipe smoke described by Captain Marlow, Corso was one of us. But he was also a bitter, stubborn man determined not to feel.

"You're Liana Taillefer's lover," he said.

"Yes," I admitted, reluctantly leaving thoughts of good Porthos aside. "Isn't she a splendid woman? With her own particular obsessions . . . Beautiful and loyal, like Milady in the novel. It's strange. There are fictional characters in literature who have a life of their own, familiar to millions of people who haven't even read the books in which they feature. In English literature there are three: Sherlock Holmes, Romeo, and Robinson Crusoe. In Spanish, two: Don Quixote and Don Juan. And in French literature, there is one: d'Artagnan. But you see I . . ."

"Let's not go off at a tangent again, Balkan."

"I'm not. I was about to add the name of Milady to d'Artagnan's. An extraordinary woman. Like Liana, in her own way. Her husband never measured up to her."

"Do you mean Athos?"

"No, I mean poor old Enrique Taillefer."

"Was that why you murdered him?"

My amazement must have looked sincere. It *was* sincere.

"Enrique murdered? Don't be ridiculous. He hanged himself. He committed suicide. I should imagine that, with his way of looking at the world, he thought it a heroic gesture. Very regrettable."

"I don't believe you."

"Please yourself. But his death was the starting point for this entire story and, indirectly, the reason you're here."

"Explain it to me then. Nice and slowly."

He had certainly earned it. As I said earlier, Corso was one of us, although he didn't know it. And anyway – I looked at the clock – it was almost twelve.

"Do you have 'The Anjou Wine' with you?"

He looked at me alertly, trying to guess my intentions. Then I saw him give in. Reluctantly, he took the folder from under his coat, then hid it again.

"Excellent," I said. "And now follow me."

* * *

He must have been expecting a secret passage leading from the library, some sort of diabolical trap. I saw him put his hand in his pocket in search of the knife.

"You won't be needing that," I assured him.

He didn't look too convinced, but he said nothing. I held one of the candelabra up high and we walked down the Louis XIII-style corridor. A magnificent tapestry hung on one of the walls: Ulysses, bow in hand, recently returned to Ithaca, Penelope and the dog rejoicing, the suitors drinking wine in the background, unaware of what awaits them.

"This is a very ancient castle, full of history," I said. "It has been plundered by the English, by the Huguenots, by revolutionaries . . . Even the Germans set up a command post here during the war. It was very dilapidated when the present owner – a British millionaire, a charming man and a gentleman – acquired it. He restored and furnished it with extraordinary good taste. He even agreed to open it to the public."

"So what are you doing here out of visiting hours?"

As I passed a leaded window I glanced out. The storm was dying down at last, the glow of lightning fading beyond the Loire, to the north.

"An exception is made once a year," I explained. "After all, Meung is a special place. A novel like *The Three Musketeers* doesn't open just anywhere."

The wooden floors creaked beneath our feet. A suit of armour – genuine sixteenth-century – stood in a bend in the corridor. The light from the candelabra was reflected in the smooth, polished surfaces of the cuirass. Corso glanced at it as he walked past, as if there might be someone hidden inside.

"I'm going to tell you a long story which began ten years ago," I said, "at an auction in Paris of a lot of uncatalogued documents . . . I was writing a book on the nineteenth-century popular novel in France, and the dusty packages fell into my hands quite by chance. When I went through them I saw they were from the old archives of *Le Siècle*. Almost all consisted of printing proofs of little value, but one package of blue and white sheets attracted my attention. It was the original text, handwritten by Dumas and Maquet, of *The Three Musketeers*. All sixty-seven chapters, just as they were sent to the printers. Someone, possibly Baudry, the editor of the newspaper, had kept them after composing the galley proofs, and then forgotten all about them . . ."

I slowed down and stopped in the middle of the corridor. Corso was very still and the light from the candelabra I was holding lit up his face from below, making shadows dance in his eye sockets. He seemed to be listening intently to my story, unaware of anything else. Solving the mystery that had brought him there was the only thing that mattered to him. But he still kept his hand on the knife in his pocket.

"My discovery," I went on, pretending not to notice this, "was of extraordinary importance. We knew of a few fragments of the original draft from Dumas's and Maquet's notes and papers, but we were unaware of the existence of the complete manuscript. At first I thought I would make my finding public, in the form of an annotated facsimile edition. But then I came across a serious moral obstacle."

The light and shadow on Corso's face moved and a dark line crossed his mouth. He was smiling.

"I don't believe it. A moral obstacle, after all this."

I moved the candelabra to remove the sceptical smile from his face, unsuccessfully.

"I'm quite serious," I protested as we moved on. "On examining the manuscript I concluded that the real creator of the story was Auguste Maquet . . . He had done all the research and outlined the story in broad strokes. Dumas, with his enormous talent, his genius, had then brought the raw material to life and turned it into a masterpiece. Although obvious to me, it might not have been quite so evident to detractors of the author and his work." I gestured with my free hand as if to sweep them all aside. "But I had no intention of throwing stones at my hero. Even less so now, in these times of mediocrity and lack of imagination . . . Times in which people no longer admire marvels, as theatre audiences and the readers of serials used to. They hissed at the villains and cheered on the heroes with no inhibitions." I shook my head sadly. "Applause which unfortunately can no longer be heard. It's become the exclusive domain of innocents and children."

Corso was listening with an insolent, mocking expression. I don't know whether he agreed with me, but he was the grudge-bearing type and refused to accept that my explanation granted me any sort of moral alibi.

"To sum up," he said, "you decided to destroy the manuscript."

I smiled smugly. He was trying to be too clever.

"Don't be ridiculous. I decided to do something better: to make a dream come true."

We had stopped in front of the closed door to the reception room. Through it the muffled sound of music and voices could be heard. I put the candelabra down on a console table while Corso watched me, again suspicious. He was probably wondering what new trick was hidden there. I realized he didn't understand that we really had reached the solution to the mystery.

"Please allow me to introduce you," I said, opening the door, "to the members of the Dumas Club."

Almost everyone was there. Through the French windows opening onto the castle terrace, late arrivals entered the room full of people, cigarette smoke and the murmur of conversation above a background of gentle music. On the central table, covered with a white linen table-cloth, there was a cold buffet: bottles of Anjou wine, sausages and hams from Amiens, oysters from La Rochelle, boxes of Montecristo cigars. Groups of guests, around fifty men and women, were drinking, and conversing in several languages. Many of them were well-known faces from the press, cinema and television. I saw Corso check he had his glasses on.

"Surprised?" I asked, looking to see his reaction.

He nodded, surly and disconcerted. Several guests came to greet me, so I shook hands, exchanged pleasantries and jokes. The atmosphere was agreeably cordial. Corso looked like someone about to fall out of bed and wake up. I was highly amused. I introduced him to some of the guests and watched with perverse satisfaction as he greeted them, confused and unsure of the terrain he was crossing. His customary composure was in shreds, and this was my small revenge. After all, it was he who had first come to me with 'The Anjou Wine' under his arm, determined to complicate things.

"Please allow me to introduce Mr Corso . . . Bruno Lostia, an antique dealer from Milan. Permit me. Yes, indeed. Thomas Harvey, of Harvey's, Jewellers: New York–London–Paris–Rome . . . And Count von Schlossberg, owner of the most famous collection of paintings in Europe. As you can see, we have something of everything here: a Venezuelan Nobel prize winner, an Argentine ex-President, the Crown Prince of Morocco . . . Do you know, his father is an avid reader of Alexandre Dumas? Look who's arrived. You know him, don't you? Professor of Semiotics in Bologna . . . The blonde lady talking to him is Petra Neustadt, the most influential literary critic in Central Europe. In that group, next to the Duchess of Alba, there's the financier Rudolf Villefoz and the English writer Harold Burgess. Amaya Euskal, of the Alpha Press group, with the most powerful publisher in the USA, Johan Cross, of O&O Papers, New York . . . And I assume you remember Achille Replinger, the bookdealer, from Paris."

This was the last straw. I savoured Corso's shaken expression, almost pitying him. Replinger was holding an empty glass and smiling pleasantly beneath his musketeer's moustache, just as he had when identifying the Dumas manuscript at his shop on the Rue Bonaparte. He greeted me with a huge bear hug and then warmly patted Corso on the back before going off in search of another drink, puffing away like a jovial, rosy-cheeked Porthos.

"Damn this," muttered Corso, drawing me aside. "What's going on here?"

"I already told you, it's a long story."

"Well, finish telling it, will you?"

We had moved close to the table. I poured us a couple of glasses of wine, but he refused with a shake of his head.

"Gin," he muttered. "Haven't you got any gin?"

I indicated the drinks cabinet at the other end of the room. We walked over to it, stopping three or four times on the way to exchange more greetings: a well-known film director, a Lebanese millionaire, a Spanish Minister of the Interior . . . Corso grabbed a bottle of Beefeater gin and filled a glass to the brim, swallowing half of it in a single gulp. He shuddered slightly and his eyes shone behind his glasses (one lens was broken, the other was intact). He held the bottle to his chest as if afraid to lose it.

"You were going to tell me something," he said.

I suggested we go out on to the terrace beyond the French windows, where we could talk without interruption. Corso filled his glass up again before following me. The storm had died down. Stars shone above us.

"I'm all ears," he announced after another large gulp.

I leaned on the balustrade, still damp from the rain, and took a sip from my glass of Anjou wine.

"Owning the manuscript of *The Three Musketeers* gave me the idea," I said. "Why not form a literary society, a sort of club for devoted admirers of the novels of Alexandre Dumas and the classic adventure serial? Through my work I already had contact with several ideal candidates . . ." I gestured towards the brightly-lit salon. Through the tall French windows the guests could be seen coming and going, chatting animatedly. It was proof of my success and I didn't conceal my authorial pride. "A society dedicated to studying novels of that kind, rediscovering writers and forgotten works, promoting their re-publication and sale under an imprint with which you may be familiar: Dumas & Co."

"I know it," confirmed Corso. "They're based in Paris and have just published the entire works of Ponson du Terrail. Last year it was *Fantomas* . . . I didn't know you had a part in it."

I smiled.

"That's the rule: no names, no starring roles . . . As you can see, the matter is scholarly and slightly childish at the same time. A nostalgic literary game which rediscovers long-lost novels and returns us to our innocence, to how we used to be. As one matures, one becomes a fan of Flaubert or Stendhal, favours Faulkner, Lampedusa, García Marquez, Durrell and Kafka . . . We become different from each other, opponents even. But we all share a conspiratorial wink when we talk about certain magical authors and books. Those that made us discover literature without weighing us down with dogma or teaching us bad rules. This is our true common heritage: stories faithful not to what people see, but to what they dream."

I left the words hanging and paused, awaiting their effect. But Corso just raised his glass to look at it against the light. His homeland was in there.

"That was before," he answered. "Now, neither children nor young people nor anyone else has a spiritual home. They just watch bloody TV."

I shook my head confidently. I had written something on that very subject for the literary supplement of the *Abc* newspaper a couple of weeks before.

"I don't agree. Even then they're treading, unknowingly, in old footsteps. Films on television, for instance, maintain the link. Those old movies. Even Indiana Jones is the direct descendant of all that."

Corso grimaced in the direction of the brightly-lit French windows.

"It's possible. But you were telling me about these people. I'd like to know how you . . . recruited them."

"It's no secret," I answered. "I've been running this select society, the Dumas Club, for ten years now. It holds its annual meeting here in

Meung. As you can see, the members arrive punctually from all corners of the globe. Every last one of them is a first-class reader . . ."

"Of serials? Don't make me laugh."

"I don't have the slightest intention of making you laugh, Corso. Why are you looking at me like that? You know yourself that a novel, or a film made for pure consumption, can turn into an exquisite work, from *The Pickwick Papers* to *Casablanca* and *Goldfinger* . . . Audiences turn to these stories full of archetypes to enjoy, whether consciously or unconsciously, the device of repeated story lines with small variations. *Dispositio* rather than *elocutio* . . . That's why the serial, even the most trite television serial, can become a cult both for a naïve audience and for a more demanding one. There are people who look for excitement in Sherlock Holmes risking his life, and others go for the pipe, the magnifying glass and the "Elementary, my dear Watson" which, by the way, Conan Doyle never actually wrote. The plot devices, the variations and repetition, are so old that they're mentioned in Aristotle's *Poetics*. And what is a television serial if not an updated version of a classic tragedy, a great romantic drama or the Dumas novel? That's why an intelligent reader can obtain a lot of enjoyment from all this, by way of exception. For there are exceptions based on rules."

I thought Corso was interested in what I was saying, but then he shook his head. A gladiator refusing to accept the dangerous terrain offered by his opponent.

"Stop the literature lecture and get back to your Dumas Club, will you?" he said impatiently. "To that loose chapter that was floating around . . . Where's the rest?"

"In there," I answered, looking at the salon. "I based the organization of the society on the sixty-seven chapters of the manuscript – a maximum of sixty-seven members, each having a chapter as a registered share. Allocation is strictly based on a list of applicants, and changes in holding require the approval of the executive board, which I chair . . . Each applicant is discussed in depth before his admission is approved."

"How are shares transferred?"

"On no account are the shares to be transferred. If a club member dies, or wishes to leave the society, their chapter must be returned. The board then allocates it to another applicant. A member may never freely dispose of it."

"Is that what Enrique Taillefer tried to do?"

"In a way. In theory he was an ideal applicant. He was a model member of the Dumas Club until he broke the rules."

Corso finished his gin. He put the glass down on the mossy balustrade and said nothing for a moment, staring intently at the lights of the reception room. Then he shook his head.

"That's not a reason for murdering someone," he said quietly, as if talking to himself. "I can't believe that all these people . . ." He looked at me stubbornly. "They're all well-known and respectable, in theory. They'd never get mixed up in something like this."

I suppressed another impatient gesture.

"I think you're blowing things up out of all proportion . . . Enrique and I were friends for some time. We shared a fascination for this kind of fiction, although his taste in literature wasn't on a level with his enthusiasm . . . The fact is his success as a publisher of bestselling cookery books meant he could spend time and money on his hobby. And to be fair, if anybody deserved to be a member of the club it was Enrique. That's why I recommended his admission. As I said, we shared, if not the same tastes, at least the enthusiasm."

"You shared more than that, I seem to remember."

Corso's sarcastic smile had returned and I found it highly irritating.

"I could tell you that it's none of your business," I retorted uneasily. "But I want to explain everything . . . Liana has always been very special, as well as very beautiful. She was a precocious reader. Do you know that at sixteen she had a fleur-de-lis tattooed on her hip? She didn't have it done on the shoulder, like her idol, Milady de Winter, so that her family and the nuns at her boarding-school shouldn't find out . . . What about that?"

"Very moving."

"You don't seem very moved. But I assure you she's an admirable person . . . The fact is that, well . . . we became intimate. You'll recall that earlier I mentioned the homeland that is the lost paradise of childhood. Well Liana's homeland is *The Three Musketeers*. She was fascinated by the world depicted in its pages. She decided to marry Enrique after meeting him by chance at a party where they spent the evening exchanging quotes from the novel. He was already a very wealthy publisher."

"So it was love at first sight," said Corso.

"I don't know why you say it like that. They married for the most sincere reasons. The thing is that, in the long run, even for someone as good-natured as his wife, Enrique could be tiresome . . . We were good friends and I often visited them. Liana . . ." I put my glass on the balustrade next to his empty one. "Anyway. You can imagine the rest."

"Yes, I can. Very clearly."

"I wasn't talking about that. She became an excellent collaborator. So much so that, four years ago, I sponsored her entry to the society. She owns Chapter Thirty-Seven, *Milady's Secret*. She chose it herself."

"Why did you put her on my trail?"

"Let's take this one bit at a time. Lately Enrique had become a problem. Instead of limiting himself to the very profitable business of cookery books he was determined to write a serial. But the fact was the novel was awful. Absolutely dreadful, believe me. He had brazenly plagiarized all the plots of the genre. It was called . . ."

"*The Dead Man's Hand.*"

"Exactly. Even the title wasn't his. And what's worse, unbelievably, he wanted Dumas & Co. to publish it. I refused, of course. His monstrous creation would never have been approved by the board. Anyway, Enrique had more than enough money to publish it himself, and I told him so."

"I assume he took it badly. I saw his library."

"Badly? That is something of an understatement. The argument took place in his study. I can still picture him, small and chubby, standing very straight, on tiptoes, staring at me with wild eyes. He looked as if he might burst a blood vessel. All very unpleasant. He said he'd decided to devote his whole life to it. And who was I to judge his writing. That was up to posterity. I was a biased critic and an insufferable pedant. And on top of everything I was involved with his wife . . . This left me absolutely stunned – I didn't realize he knew. But it seems that Liana talks in her sleep, and between cursing d'Artagnan and his friends (who, by the way, she hates as if she had known them personally) she'd been broadcasting the whole affair to her husband . . . You can imagine my predicament."

"Very difficult for you."

"Extremely. Although the worst was yet to come. Enrique was in full flow. He said that if he himself was mediocre, Dumas wasn't much of a writer either. Where would he have been without Auguste Maquet, whom he wretchedly exploited? The proof lay in the white and blue pages of 'The Anjou Wine', which he kept in his safe . . . The argument became more heated. He called me an adulterer – rather an old-fashioned insult – and I called him a moron, adding a few snide comments about his latest cookery book successes. I ended up comparing him to the baker in *Cyrano* . . . 'I'll get my revenge,' he said, sounding rather like the Count of Monte Cristo. 'I'm going to publicize the fact that your beloved Dumas was a big cheat who appropriated other people's work. I'll make the manuscript public, and everyone will see how the old fraud produced his serials. I don't give a damn about the rules of the society. That chapter's mine and I'll sell it to whoever I like. So go to hell.'"

"He got pretty nasty."

"You don't know how spiteful a spurned author can get. My objections were to no avail. He threw me out. Later I found out through Liana that he'd called that bookseller, La Ponte, to offer him the manuscript. He must have thought himself very clever and devious, like Edmundo Dantés. He wanted to create a scandal without being directly implicated and keep his reputation intact. That's how you became involved. You can understand my surprise when you came to see me with 'The Anjou Wine'."

"You certainly didn't show it."

"I had my reasons. With Enrique dead, Liana and I had assumed the manuscript was lost."

I saw Corso search his coat for one of his crumpled cigarettes. He put it in his mouth but didn't light it. He paced around the terrace.

"Your story's ridiculous," he said at last. "No Edmundo Dantés would commit suicide before savouring his revenge."

I nodded, although he had his back to me and couldn't see my gesture.

"Well, other things happened," I said. "The day after our conversation Enrique came to my house in a final attempt to convince me. I'd had enough. And I won't put up with blackmail. So, not quite realizing what I was doing, I dealt him the death blow. His serial, in spite of being very bad, felt very familiar. So, when Enrique made a scene for the second time, I went to my library, searched for an ancient edition of *The Popular Illustrated Novel*, a little-known late nineteenth-century publication, and opened it at the first page of a story signed by a certain Amaury de Verona entitled: *Angeline de Gravaillac, or Unsullied Virtue*. Well, you can imagine the sort of thing. As I read out the first paragraph Enrique went pale, as if the ghost of Angeline had risen from the grave. Which is more or less what happened. He'd assumed nobody would remember the story and had plagiarized it. He copied it almost word for word, all except for a chapter he took whole from Fernandez y Gonzalez, in fact the best part of the story . . . I was sorry I didn't have my camera to take a picture of him. He put his hand on his forehead as if to exclaim, 'Damnation!' but he couldn't actually get the word out. He just made a kind of gurgling sound, as if he was about to suffocate. Then he turned, went home and hanged himself from the light fitting."

Corso turned towards me. He still had his forgotten cigarette in his mouth, unlit.

"Then things became more complicated," I went on, sure that he was now starting to believe me. "You already had the manuscript and your friend La Ponte wasn't willing, at first, to part with it. I couldn't go round playing Arsène Lupin, I've got a reputation to protect. That's why I gave Liana the task of retrieving the chapter. The date of the annual meeting was approaching and we had to find a new member to replace Enrique. I admit, Liana did make a few mistakes. Firstly, she went to see you . . ." I cleared my throat, embarrassed. I didn't want to go into any detail. "Then she tried to get La Ponte on her side, for him to get 'The Anjou Wine' back. But I didn't know how tenacious you could be . . . The problem is she had always dreamt of an adventure similar to her heroine's, full of deception, love affairs and persecution. And this episode, based on the stuff of her dreams, gave her a great opportunity. So she set off on your trail enthusiastically. 'I'll bring you the manuscript bound in the skin of that Corso,' she promised. I told her not to get carried away. But now I recognize that the mistake was mine: I encouraged her in her fantasy, releasing the Milady that had been inside her ever since she first read *The Three Musketeers*."

"Well, I wish she'd read something else. Like *Gone with the Wind*. She could have identified with Scarlett O'Hara and gone around pestering Clark Gable and not me."

"I do admit she went slightly over the top. It's a pity you should have taken it so seriously."

Corso rubbed the spot behind his ear. I could imagine what he was thinking: the one who must really have taken it seriously was the man with the scar.

"Who's Rochefort?"

"His name is Laszlo Nicolavic. He's an actor who specializes in supporting roles. He played Rochefort in the series Andreas Frey made for British television a couple of years ago. He's actually played almost all the well-known villains: Gonzaga in *Lagardère,* Levasseur in *Captain Blood*, La Tour d'Azyr in *Scaramouche,* Rupert of Hentzau in *The Prisoner of Zenda* . . . He's fascinated by the genre, and has applied to join the Dumas Club. Liana was quite taken with him, and insisted he should work with her on this matter."

"Well, old Laszlo certainly took his part seriously . . ."

"I'm afraid he did. I suspect he's trying to gain points so his admission is approved quickly. I also suspect that he serves as her occasional lover." I smiled like a man of the world, hoping that I'd be convincing. "Liana is young, beautiful and passionate. Let's say I encourage her intellectual side with calm romantic ardour, and Laszlo Nicolavic presumably takes care of the more down-to-earth side of her impetuous nature."

"What else?"

"That's almost all. Nicolavic, or Rochefort, took charge of getting the Dumas manuscript from you. That's why he followed you from Madrid to Toledo and Sintra, while Liana headed for Paris, taking La Ponte with her as a back-up in case their original plan failed and you didn't see reason. You know the rest: you didn't let them snatch the manuscript from you, Milady and Rochefort got slightly carried away, and that brought you here." I reflected on the events. "Do you know something? I wonder whether instead of Laszlo Nicolavic I shouldn't propose you as a member of the club."

He didn't even ask whether I was being sarcastic or really meant it. He removed his battered glasses and cleaned them mechanically, absorbed in his thoughts.

"Is that all?" he said at last.

"Of course." I pointed to the reception room. "There's your proof."

He put his glasses on and took a deep breath. I didn't like the look on his face at all.

"What about the *Delomelanicon*? And Richelieu's connection with *The Nine Doors of the Kingdom of Shadows*?" He came closer, tapping me on the chest until I had to take a step back. "Do you take me for a fool? You're not going to tell me that you knew nothing about the link between Dumas and that book, his pact with the Devil and all the rest of it – Victor Fargas's murder in Sintra, and the fire at Baroness Ungern's flat in Paris. Did you give my name to the police yourself? And what about the book hidden in the three copies? Or the nine prints engraved by Lucifer, reprinted by Aristide Torchia on his return from Prague 'by authority and permission of the superiors', and the whole damn business . . ."

He said it all in a fast torrent, sticking out his chin aggressively, his eyes piercing into me. I took another step back and stood looking at him open-mouthed.

"You've gone mad!" I protested indignantly. "Can you tell me what you're talking about?"

He took out a box of matches and lit his cigarette, cupping a hand round the flame. Through the glare reflected in his glasses he kept his eyes fixed on me. Then he told me his version of events.

When he finished we both fell silent. We were leaning on the damp balustrade, next to each other, watching the lights of the reception room. Corso's story had lasted for the duration of the cigarette and he now stubbed it out on the ground.

"I suppose," I said, "I should now confess and say, 'Yes, it's true,' and then hold out my hands for you to handcuff them. Is that really what you're expecting?"

He took a moment to answer. Having recounted the story aloud didn't seem to have made him confident of his conclusions.

"But there is a link," he muttered.

I looked at his narrow shadow on the terrace floor, dark against the rectangles of light from the reception room cast on the marble flagstones and stretched beyond the steps into the darkness of the garden.

"I fear," I concluded, "that your imagination has played tricks on you."

He shook his head slowly.

"I didn't imagine that Victor Fargas was drowned in the pond, or that Baroness Ungern was burnt with her books. Those things happened. They were real. The two stories are mixed up."

"You've just said it yourself – there are two stories. Maybe all that links them is your own intertextual reading."

"Please leave out the technical jargon. The Dumas chapter triggered everything." He looked at me resentfully. "Your bloody club and all your little games."

"Don't lay all the blame on me. Games are perfectly valid. If this was a work of fiction and not a real story, as the reader you would be principally responsible."

"Don't be absurd."

"I'm not. From what you've just told me I deduce that, playing with the facts and your own personal literary references, you constructed a theory and drew erroneous conclusions. But the facts are objective and you can't overlay them with your personal errors. The story of 'The Anjou Wine' and the one about this mysterious book, *The Nine Doors*, are completely unrelated."

"You all led me to believe . . ."

"We, and by that I mean Liana Taillefer, Laszlo Nicolavic and myself, did nothing of the sort. It was you who filled in the blanks on your own, as if it was a novel based on trickery and Lucas Corso a reader being too clever for his own good. Nobody ever told you that events were actually happening as you thought. So the responsibility is entirely yours, my friend. The real culprit is your excessive intertextual reading and linking of literary references."

"What else could I do? In order to take action I needed some sort of strategy, and I couldn't just sit there waiting. In any strategy you build up a picture of your opponent and this influences your next move . . . Wellington did such-and-such, thinking that Napoleon was thinking of doing such-and-such. And Napoleon . . ."

"Napoleon made the mistake of confusing Blücher with Grouchy. Military strategy is as risky as literary strategy. Listen, Corso, there are no innocent readers any more. Each overlays the text with his own perverse view. A reader is all that he's read before, in addition to all the films and TV that he's seen. To the information supplied by the author, he'll always add his own. And that's where the danger lies: an excess of references may have caused you to create the wrong opponent, or an imaginary opponent."

"The information was false."

"Don't insist. The information a book provides tends to be objective. It may be set out by a malevolent author who wishes to mislead, but it is never false. It's you who makes a false reading."

He seemed to be thinking carefully. He had moved slightly and was again leaning on the balustrade, facing the garden in darkness.

"Then there must be another author," he said very quietly.

He stood motionless. After a time he took the folder with 'The Anjou Wine' from under his coat and put it to one side, on the moss-covered stone.

"This story has two authors," he insisted.

"That's possible," I said and took the Dumas manuscript. "And maybe one is more malevolent than the other. My story was the serial. You'll have to look for the crime novel elsewhere."

XVI
A Device Worthy of a Gothic Novel

> *"Here is the vexing part of the matter," said Porthos. "In the old days one didn't have to explain anything. One just fought because one fought."*
>
> A. Dumas: *The Vicomte de Bragelonne*

Leaning his head against the driver's seat, Lucas Corso looked at the view. He had parked the car in a small lay-by on the final bend of the road before it dipped down into the town. Surrounded by ancient walls, the old quarter floated in mist from the river, suspended in the air like a ghostly blue island. It was a hazy world without light or shadow. A cold, hesitant dawn over Castille, with the first glimmer of light showing roofs, chimneys and bell towers to the east.

He wanted to look at the time, but his watch had let in water during the storm in Meung. The glass was misted and the dial was illegible. Corso caught sight of his exhausted eyes in the rear-view mirror. Meung-sur-Loire, on the eve of the first Monday in April. They were now very far away, and it was Tuesday. It had been a long return journey and they all seemed to fade into the distance: Balkan, the Dumas Club, Rochefort, Milady, La Ponte. The echoes of a story concluded with the turning of a page. The author striking the final key – Qwerty keyboard, bottom row, second from the right – or the final blow. So with one arbitrary action it became no more than pages of type, strange, inert paper. Lives suddenly alien.

On that dawn so similar to the awakening from a dream, Corso sat, dirty and unshaven, with reddened eyes. All that remained was his old canvas bag containing the remaining copy of *The Nine Doors*. And the girl. That was all that was left on the shore after the tide had gone out. She moaned gently at his side and he turned to look at her. She was sleeping in the seat next to him, under her duffle coat, her head resting on Corso's right shoulder. She was breathing gently, her lips parted, occasionally shaken by small shivers which made her start. Then she'd moan again very quietly. A small vertical crease between her eyebrows made her look like an upset little girl. One hand protruded from under her coat. It was turned palm up, her fingers half-open as if she had just let something slip from them, or as if she were waiting.

Corso thought again about Meung, and about the journey. And Boris Balkan two nights earlier, standing next to him on the terrace which was still damp from the rain. Holding the pages of 'The Anjou Wine', Richelieu had smiled like an old opponent, both admiring and sympathetic. "You're very special, my friend." He had offered these final words as consolation, or as a farewell; they were the only ones with any meaning. The rest – an invitation to join the other guests – was uttered with little conviction. Not that Balkan wanted to get rid of him – he had in fact seemed disappointed when Corso left – but because he knew that Corso would refuse to come inside and would stay on the terrace, which he did. He stood for some time alone, leaning on the balustrade, listening to the echo of his own defeat. He slowly came to and looked round, remembering where he was. Then he walked away from the brightly-lit windows and returned unhurriedly to the hotel, wandering through the dark streets. He didn't come across Rochefort again, and at the Auberge Saint-Jacques he was told that Milady too had left. They both departed from his life and returned to the nebulous regions from which they had come, fictional characters once more, as unaccountable as chess pieces. He found La Ponte and the girl without difficulty. He hadn't worried about La Ponte, but he was reassured when he saw that she was still there. He'd thought – feared – that he would lose her along with the other characters in the story. He took her quickly by the hand before she too vanished in the dust of the library of the castle of Meung. He led her to the car, as La Ponte watched, disconcerted. Corso saw him receding in the rear-view mirror, looking lost, calling on their long, much-abused friendship. He didn't understand what was going on or even dare ask. Like a discredited, useless harpooneer, not to be trusted, abandoned with some bread and three days' supply of water, left to drift: "Try to reach Batavia, Mr Bligh." But then, at the end of the street, Corso stopped the car and sat with his hands on the wheel, looking at the road ahead, the girl staring, curious, at his profile. La Ponte wasn't a real character either. With a sigh, Corso reversed the car and went back to collect him. For the rest of the following day and night, until they left him at some traffic lights in a Madrid street, La Ponte said not one word. He didn't even protest when Corso told him he'd have to say goodbye to the Dumas manuscript. There wasn't much he could say.

He glanced at the canvas bag by the sleeping girl's feet. The sense of defeat was painful, of course, like a knife wound in his memory. He knew he'd played according to the rules – '*legitime certaverit*' – but had gone in the wrong direction. At the very moment of victory, even if only a partial and incomplete one, any pleasure at winning had been snatched from him. It had been imaginary. It was like defeating imaginary ghosts, or punching into the wind, or shouting at silence. Maybe that's why Corso had been staring suspiciously for some time at the city suspended in the mist, waiting to make sure that its foundations were firmly rooted in the ground before entering it.

He could hear the girl's gentle, rhythmic breathing, at his shoulder. He stared at her bare neck between the folds of the duffle coat. Then he moved his hand closer until he could feel the heat of her warm flesh throbbing in his fingers. As always, her skin smelt of youth and fever. In his imagination and in his memory he could easily follow the long, curving lines of her slender body, down to her bare feet by her plimsolls and the bag. Irene Adler. He still didn't know what to call her. But he could remember her naked body in the shadows, the curve of her hips traced by the light, her parted lips. Impossibly beautiful and silent, absorbed in her own youth and at the same time as serene as tranquil waters, with the wisdom of ages. And in the luminous eyes watching him intently from the shadows, the reflection, the dark image of Corso himself amongst all the light snatched from the sky.

She was watching him now, her emerald green eyes framed by long lashes. She had woken and was moving sleepily, rubbing against his shoulder. Then she sat up, alert. She looked round and then at him.

"Hello, Corso." Her duffle coat slid to her feet. Her white T-shirt clung to her perfect torso, as supple as a beautiful young animal's. "What are we doing here?"

"Waiting." He gestured towards the town which seemed to be floating in the mist from the river. "For it to become real."

She looked, not understanding at first. Then she smiled slowly.

"Maybe it never will," she said.

"Then we'll stay here. It's not such a bad place . . . Up here, with the strange unreal world at our feet." He turned towards the girl and waited before going on. "'I'll give you everything, if you prostrate yourself and adore me . . .' Isn't that the kind of offer you're going to make me?"

The girl's smile was full of tenderness. She bowed her head, thoughtful, and then looked up and held Corso's gaze.

"No, I'm poor."

"Yes, I know." It was true. Corso knew it, he didn't have to read it in the clarity of her eyes. "Your luggage, and the train compartment . . . It's strange. I always thought you all had unlimited wealth, out there, at the end of the rainbow." His smile was as sharp as the knife he still had in his pocket. "Peter Schlehmil's bag of gold and all that."

"Well, you're wrong." Now she was pursing her lips obstinately. "I'm all I have."

This was true too, and Corso had known it from the start. She had never lied. Both innocent and wise, she was faithful and in love, chasing after a shadow.

"I see." He made a gesture in the air, as if wielding an imaginary pen. "Aren't you going to give me a document to sign?"

"A document?"

"Yes. It used to be called a pact. Now it would be a contract with lots of small print, wouldn't it? 'In the event of litigation, the parties are to submit to the jurisdiction of the courts of . . .' That's a funny thing. I wonder which court covers all of this."

"Don't be silly."

"Why did you choose me?"

"I'm free," she sighed sadly, as if she'd paid the price for her right to say it. "I can choose. Anyone can."

Corso searched in his coat for his crumpled packet of cigarettes. There was only one left. He took it out and stared, undecided as to whether to put it in his mouth or not, before finally putting it back in the packet. Maybe he'd need a smoke later. He was sure he would.

"You knew everything right from the beginning," he said. "That there were two completely unrelated stories. That's why you never cared about the Dumas strand . . . Milady, Rochefort, Richelieu – they were nothing but film extras to you. Now I understand why you were so disconcertingly passive. You must have been horribly bored. You just flicked the pages of your *Musketeers*, watching me make all the wrong moves . . ."

She was staring through the windscreen at the town veiled in blue mist. She started to raise her hand to add emphasis to her answer, but then just let it drop, as if what she was about to say was pointless.

"All I could do was go with you," she answered at last. "Everyone has to walk certain paths alone. Haven't you heard of free will?" She smiled sadly. "Some of us have paid a very high price for it."

"But you didn't always stay on the sidelines. That night, by the Seine . . . Why did you help me against Rochefort?"

She touched the canvas bag with her bare foot.

"He was after the Dumas manuscript. But *The Nine Doors* was in there too. I just wanted to avoid any stupid interferences." She shrugged. "And I didn't want him to hit you."

"What about Sintra? You warned me about the Fargas business."

"Of course. The book was tied up with it."

"And then the key to the meeting in Meung . . ."

"I didn't know about it. I just worked it out from the novel."

Corso made a face.

"I thought all of you were omniscient."

"Well, you were wrong." Now she was looking at him, annoyed. "And I don't know why you keep talking to me as if I was one of many. I've been alone for a long time."

Centuries, Corso was sure. Centuries of solitude. He couldn't deceive himself about that. He had embraced her naked body, drowned in the clarity of her eyes. He had been inside her, tasted her skin, felt the gentle throbbing of her neck against his lips. He'd heard her moan quietly, like a frightened child, or a lonely fallen angel in search of warmth. He'd watched her sleep with her fists clenched, tormented by nightmares of gleaming, blond archangels, implacable in their armour, as dogmatic as the God who made them march in time.

Now, thanks to her, although too late, he understood Nikon and her ghosts and the desperate way she clung to life. Her fear, her black-and-white photographs, her vain attempt to exorcise memories transmitted through genes that survived Auschwitz, the number tattooed on her father's skin, the Black Order which had never been anything new but as old as the spirit and the curse of man. Because God and the Devil could be one and the same thing, and everybody understood it in their own way.

But just as with Nikon, Corso was still cruel. It was too heavy a burden for him and he didn't have Porthos's noble heart.

"Was that your mission?" he asked the girl. "Protecting *The Nine Doors*? I don't think you'll get a medal for it."

"That's unfair, Corso."

Almost the same words. Once again, Nikon left to drift, small and fragile. Who did she cling to now, to escape her nightmares?

He looked at the girl. Maybe Nikon's memory was his penance. But he was no longer prepared to accept it with resignation. He glimpsed his face in the rear-view mirror: it was contracted into a lost, bitter expression.

"Is it? We've lost two out of the three books. And what about the pointless deaths of Fargas and the Baroness?" They mattered little to him but he continued to look bitter. "You could have prevented them."

She shook her head, very serious, her eyes fixed on his.

"Some things can't be avoided, Corso. Some castles have to burn and some men must hang. There are dogs destined to tear each other to pieces, virtuous people to be beheaded, doors to be opened for others to enter . . ." She frowned and bowed her head. "My mission, as you call it, was to make sure you reached the end of the journey safely."

"Well, it's been a long journey, only to end up at the starting-point." Corso indicated the town suspended in the mist. "And now I've got to go down there."

"You don't *have* to. Nobody's forcing you. You could just forget about it and leave."

"Without finding out the answer?"

"Without undergoing the test. You have the answer within you."

"That's a pretty sentence. Put it on my headstone when I'm burning in Hell."

She gave him a gentle, almost friendly tap on the knee.

"Don't be an idiot, Corso. Things are as one wants them to be more often than people think. Even the Devil can adopt different guises. Or essences."

"Remorse, for instance."

"Yes. But also knowledge and beauty." She again looked anxiously at the town. "Or power and wealth."

"But the end result is the same: damnation." He repeated his gesture of signing an imaginary contract. "You have to pay with the innocence of your soul."

She sighed again.

"You paid long ago, Corso. You're still paying. It's a strange habit, postponing it all till the end. Like the final act of a tragedy . . .

Everyone drags their own damnation with them from the beginning. As for the Devil, he is no more than God's pain; the wrath of a dictator caught in his own trap. The story told by the winners."

"When did it happen?"

"A longer time ago than you can conceive. It was very hard. I fought for a hundred days and a hundred nights without hope or refuge." A gentle, almost imperceptible smile appeared on her lips. "That's the only thing I'm proud of – having fought to the end. I retreated but didn't turn my back, surrounded by others also falling from on high. I was hoarse from shouting out my fury, my fear and exhaustion . . . After the battle I walked across a desolate plateau, as lonely as eternity is cold . . . I still sometimes come across a trace of the battle, or an old comrade who passes by without daring to look up."

"Why me, then? Why didn't you look for someone on the side of the winners? I only win battles on a scale of 1:5,000."

The girl turned to look into the distance. The sun was rising, and the first horizontal ray of light cut the morning air with a fine, reddish line that directly intersected her gaze. When she looked back at Corso he felt vertigo as he peered into all the light reflected in her green eyes.

"Because lucidity never wins. And seducing an idiot has never been worth the trouble."

Then she leant over and kissed him very slowly, with infinite tenderness. As if she had had to wait an eternity to do so.

The mist slowly began to clear. It was as if the town, suspended in mid-air, had decided to sink its foundations in the earth. The dawn shone on the grey and ochre mass of the Alcázar palace, the cathedral bell tower, and the stone bridge with its pillars in the dark waters of the river, resembling a sinister hand stretched between the two banks.

Corso started the engine. He let the car slide gently down the deserted road. As they descended, the light of the rising sun was left behind, held above them. The town gradually moved closer and they slowly entered the world of cold tones and immense solitude which persisted in the remnants of blue mist.

He hesitated before crossing the bridge, stopping the car beneath the stone arch which led onto it; his hands on the steering-wheel, head slightly bowed and his chin jutting out: the profile of a tense, alert hunter. He took off his glasses and cleaned them though they didn't need it. He took his time, staring intently at the bridge which had now become a vague path with disturbingly imprecise outlines. He didn't look at the girl but he knew that she was watching his every move. He put on his glasses, adjusting them on the bridge of his nose, and the landscape recovered its sharp lines, but became no more reassuring. The other bank looked dark and distant. The current flowing between the pillars resembled the black waters of time and of Lethe. In the remnants of the night which refused to die, his sense of danger was tangible, acute, like a steel needle. Corso could feel the pulse beating in his wrist when he grasped the gear lever. You can still turn back, he told himself. In that way, none of what has happened had ever happened, and none of what was to take place would ever take place. As to the practical value of '*Nunc scio*': 'Now I know', coined by God or by the Devil, it was highly dubious. He frowned. Anyway, they were nothing but words. He knew that a few minutes later he would be on the other side of the bridge and river. '*Verbum dimissum custodiat arcanum.*' He gazed up at the sky, looking for an archer with or without arrows in his quiver, before putting the car into gear and gently moving off.

It was cold outside the car so he turned up his collar. He could feel the girl's intent gaze upon him as he crossed the street without looking back, holding *The Nine Doors* under his arm. She hadn't offered to go with him, and for some obscure reason he knew that it was better that way. As for the house, it occupied almost an entire block and its grey stone bulk presided over a narrow square, amongst medieval buildings whose closed windows and doors made them look like motionless film extras, blind and mute. The façade was of grey stone with four gargoyles on the eaves: a billy goat, a crocodile, a gorgon and a serpent. There was a star of David on the Moorish arch above the wrought-iron gate that lead to the interior courtyard with two Venetian marble lions and a well. It was all familiar to Corso but he had never been so apprehensive upon entering the house. He remembered an old quotation: 'Perhaps men who have been caressed by many women cross the valley of shadows with less remorse, or less fear . . ." It went something like that. Maybe he hadn't been caressed enough because his mouth was dry and he would have sold his soul for half a bottle of Bols. And *The Nine Doors* felt as if it contained nine lead plates instead of prints.

He pushed open the gate but the silence remained unbroken. Not even his shoes caused the slightest echo as he crossed the courtyard, its paving stones worn down by ancient footsteps and centuries of rain. An archway led to the steep, narrow staircase. At the top he could see the dark, heavy door decorated with thick nails. It was closed: the last door. For an instant, Corso winked privately, sarcastically at empty space, baring his teeth. He was both involuntary author and victim of his own joke or his own error. An error, carefully planned by an unscrupulous hand, and full of serpentine, illusory invitations to participate that had led him to certain conclusions, only for them to be refuted. But in the end he'd had them confirmed by the text itself as if it had been a damned novel, which it wasn't. Or what if it was? The fact is, the last thing he saw in the polished metal plate nailed to the door was his own, very real face. A distorted image that contained the name on the plate, as well as his own shape against the light behind him in the archway over the stairs, leading down to the courtyard and the street. The last stop on a strange journey to the other side of the shadows.

He rang. Once, twice, three times. No answer. The brass bellpush lay dead, and there had been no sound inside when he pressed it. In his pocket he felt the crumpled packet containing his last cigarette. Again he decided against lighting it. He rang the bell a fourth time. And a fifth. He clenched his fist and knocked hard, twice. Then the door opened. Not with a sinister creak, but smoothly, on greased hinges. And without any dramatic effects, quite casually, Varo Borja stood in the doorway.

"Hello, Corso."

Varo Borja didn't seem surprised to see him. There were beads of sweat all over his head and he was unshaven. His shirtsleeves were rolled up and his waistcoat undone. He looked tired, with dark rings under his eyes from a sleepless night. But his eyes shone feverishly. He didn't ask what Corso was doing there at such an hour, and he seemed barely to notice the book under his arm. He stood there without moving for a moment, as if he had just been interrupted during some meticulous job, or dream, and just wanted to get back to it.

Here was the man responsible, Corso knew it, seeing his own stupidity materialize before him. Of course. Varo Borja – millionaire, international bookdealer, famous collector and methodical murderer.

With an almost scientific curiosity, Corso scrutinized the face before him. He tried now to isolate the features, the clues that should have alerted him so much earlier. Signs overlooked, angles of madness, horror or shadow in the familiar, vulgar features. But he couldn't see anything. Just a feverish, distant expression, devoid of curiosity or passion, lost in images far removed from the man now ringing at the door. But Corso was holding his copy of the cursed book. It had been he, Varo Borja, in the shadow of that same book, following Corso's footsteps like an evil snake, who had killed Victor Fargas and Baroness Ungern. Not only to reunite the twenty-seven engravings and combine the nine correct ones, but also to cover any trails and make sure that nobody else should resolve the riddle set by Torchia, the printer. For the entire plot, Corso had been a tool for confirming a theory which proved correct – that the real book was distributed over three copies. He was also the victim of any repercussions involving the police. Now, paying twisted homage to his own instincts, he remembered how he felt looking up at the paintings on the ceiling of the Quinta da Soledade. Abraham's sacrifice with no alternative victim: he was the scapegoat. And Varo Borja, of course, was the dealer who went to see Victor Fargas to purchase one of his treasures every six months. That day, while Corso was visiting Fargas, Borja was in Sintra, finalizing the details of his plan, waiting for confirmation of his theory that all three copies were needed to resolve Torchia's riddle. Fargas's half-written receipt was intended for him. That's why Corso hadn't been able to get hold of Borja when he phoned his house in Toledo. Then later that same evening, before going to his final appointment with Fargas, he had called Corso at the hotel pretending he was making an international call. Corso had not only confirmed Borja's suspicions about the book, but also the very key to the mystery, thus condemning Fargas and the Baroness. With bitter certainty Corso could see the pieces of the puzzle falling into place. Apart from the false clues by chance linking the Dumas Club, Varo Borja was the key to all the inexplicable events of that other, diabolic, strand of the plot. It was enough to make one laugh out loud. If the whole damn business had been at all funny that is.

"I've brought the book," he said showing him *The Nine Doors*.

Varo Borja nodded vaguely and took the book, barely glancing at it. He had his head slightly turned to the side, as if listening out for a sound behind him, inside the house. After a moment he noticed Corso again and blinked, surprised that he was still there.

"You've given me the book. What else do you want?"

"To be paid for the job."

Varo Borja stood staring at him uncomprehendingly. It was obvious that his thoughts were miles away. At last, he shrugged, as if to say it had nothing to do with him. Then he went into the house, leaving it up to Corso whether he shut the door, stayed where he was or turned back the way he'd come.

Corso followed him through a safety door into the room leading off the corridor and the vestibule. The shutters were closed so no light could enter, and the furniture had been pushed to the far end, leaving the black marble floor empty. Some of the glass bookcases were open. The room was lit by dozens of candles that had almost burnt down. The wax was dripping everywhere: on the mantelpiece above the empty fireplace, on to the floor, the furniture and objects in the room. They gave off a tremulous, reddish light which danced about with any draught or movement. It smelt like a church, or a crypt.

Still taking no notice of Corso, Varo Borja stopped in the middle of the room. There, at his feet, a circle of approximately three feet in diameter was marked out in chalk, with a square divided into nine boxes. It was surrounded by Roman numerals and strange objects: a piece of string, a waterclock, a rusty knife, a dragon-shaped silver bracelet, a gold ring, a small metal brazier full of burning charcoal, a glass vial, a small pile of earth, a stone. But Corso winced when he saw the other things strewn on the floor. Many of the books he'd admired lined up on shelves a few days earlier were now lying ruined, dirty, with pages torn out, covered with drawings and underlinings, and full of strange marks. Candles burnt on top of several of the books and thick drops of wax were dripping onto their covers or open pages. Some had burnt down and singed the paper. Amongst the wreckage he recognized the engravings from the copies of *The Nine Doors* belonging to Victor Fargas and Baroness Ungern. They were mixed up with the others on the floor and also covered in wax drips and mysterious annotations.

Corso bent down to look more closely at the remains, not quite able to believe the magnitude of the disaster. One engraving from *The Nine Doors*, number VI, the man hanging by his right foot instead of his left, had been half burnt away by the flickering flame of a candle. Two copies of engraving number VII, one with a white chessboard and the other with a black one, lay beside the remains of a 1512 *Theatrum diabolicum* torn from its binding. Another engraving, number I, was protruding from the pages of a *De magna imperfectaque opera* by Valerio Lorena, an extremely rare incunabulum that Borja had shown Corso a few days earlier, barely allowing him to touch it. It now lay on the floor, battered and torn.

"Don't touch anything," he heard Varo Borja say. He was standing before the circle, leafing through his copy of *The Nine Doors*, engrossed. He seemed to see not the pages themselves but something beyond them, inside the square and circle on the floor, or even farther away still: in the depths of the earth.

Motionless, Corso looked at him for a moment as if seeing him for the first time. Then he stood up slowly. As he did so the candle flames around him flickered.

"It makes no difference if I touch anything," he said gesturing towards the books and papers lying scattered over the floor. "After what you've done."

"You don't know anything, Corso. You think you do, but you don't. You're ignorant and very stupid. The kind who believes chaos is random and ignores the existence of a hidden order."

"Don't talk rubbish. You've destroyed everything and you had no right to. Nobody has."

"You're wrong. In the first place they're *my* books. And what's more important their purpose is to be used. They had practical, rather than artistic or aesthetic value. As one travels along the path one must ensure that no one else can follow. These books have now served their purpose."

"You bloody madman. You deceived me right from the start."

Varo Borja didn't seem to be listening. He stood motionless, holding the remaining copy of *The Nine Doors*, scrutinizing engraving number I.

"Deceived?" He kept his eyes fixed on the book as he spoke, which underlined his contempt for Corso. "You do yourself too much honour. I hired you without telling you my reasons or my intentions. A servant has no reason to participate in the decisions of whoever is paying him. You were to steal the items I wanted to collect, and at the same time incur the technical consequences of certain unavoidable actions. I should imagine that as we speak the police in both Portugal and France are on your tail."

"What about you?"

"I'm very far removed from all that, and quite safe. In a little while nothing will matter."

Then, to Corso's horror, he tore the page with the engraving from *The Nine Doors.*

"What are you doing?"

Varo Borja was calmly tearing out more pages.

"I'm burning my boats, destroying any bridges behind me. And moving into *terra incognita.*" He'd torn the engravings from the book, one by one, until he had all nine, and was looking at them closely. "It's a pity you can't follow me where I'm going. As the fourth engraving states, fate is not the same for all."

"Where do you believe you're going?"

Borja dropped his mutilated copy on the floor with the other remains. He was looking at the nine engravings and at the circle, checking strange correspondences between them.

"To meet someone," was his enigmatic answer. "To search for the stone that the Great Architect rejected, the philosopher's stone, the basis of the philosophical work. Of power. The Devil likes metamorphoses, Corso. From Faust's black dog, to the false angel of light who tried to break down St Anthony's resistance. But most of all, stupidity bores him and he hates monotony . . . If I had the time and inclination I'd invite you to take a look at some of the books at your feet. Several of them mention an ancient tradition: the advent of the Antichrist will occur in the Iberian peninsula, in a city with three superimposed cultures, on the banks of a river as deep as an axe cut, the Tagus."

"Is that what you're trying to do?"

"It's what I'm about to achieve. Brother Torchia showed me the way: '*Tenebris Lux.*'"

He was bending over the circle on the floor, laying some of the engravings round it and removing others, which he threw away from him, crumpled or torn. The candles illuminated his face from below, making him look ghostly, with deep shadows for eyes.

"I hope it all fits together," he muttered after a moment. His mouth was a line of shadow. "The ancient masters of the black art who taught the printer Torchia the most terrible and valuable mysteries, knew the path leading to the kingdom of night. 'It is the animal with its tail in its mouth that encircles the place.' Do you understand? The *ourobouros* of the Greek alchemists: the serpent on the frontispiece, the magic circle, the source of wisdom. The circle in which everything is written."

"I want my money."

Varo Borja didn't seem to have heard Corso.

"Have you never been curious about these things?" he went on, peering out from shadowed eyes. "To investigate, for instance, the Devil-serpent-dragon constant which has reappeared suspiciously in all the texts on the subject since Antiquity?"

He had picked up a glass object next to the circle, a goblet with handles in the shape of two linked serpents, and he raised it to his mouth and took a few sips. It held some dark liquid, Corso noticed, almost black, like very strong tea.

"'*Serpens aut draco qui caudam devoravit.*'" Varo Borja smiled into empty space, wiping his mouth. He left a dark smear on the back of his hand and his left cheek. "They guard the treasures: the tree of knowledge in the Garden of Eden, the Hesperides' apples, the Golden Fleece . . ." As he talked he looked absent, insane, as if describing a dream from the inside. "They're the serpents or dragons that the ancient Egyptians painted in a circle, with their tail in their mouth to indicate that they came from a single thing, and were self-sufficient . . . Sleepless guardians, proud and wise. Hermetic dragons that kill the unworthy and only allow themselves to be seduced by one who has fought according to the rules. Guardians of the lost word: the magic formula which opens eyes and makes one the equal of God."

Corso stuck out his jaw. He was standing, still and thin in his coat, with the shadows of the candles dancing between his half-closed eyelids, making his unshaven cheeks look sunken. He had his hands in his pockets, one touching the packet with its remaining cigarette, the other round the closed switchblade, next to his flask of gin.

"I said give me my money. I want to get out of here."

There was a slight threat in his voice, but Corso couldn't tell if Varo Borja had noticed it. He saw him come to unwillingly, slowly.

"Money?" He was looking at him with renewed contempt. "What are you talking about, Corso? Don't you understand what's about to happen? You have before you the mystery that men throughout the centuries have dreamt of . . . Do you know how many have been burnt, tortured and torn to pieces just for a glimpse of what you are about to witness? You can't come with me, of course. You will just stay still and watch. But even the most vile mercenary can share in his master's triumph."

"Pay me once and for all. Then you can go to the Devil."

Varo Borja didn't even look at him. He was moving round the circle and touching some of the objects laid next to the numbers.

"How appropriate that you should send me to the Devil. So typical of your down-to-earth style. I'd even honour you with a smile if I wasn't so busy. Although your remark was ignorant and imprecise: it will be the Devil who comes to me." He paused and turned his head as if he could already hear distant footsteps. "And I feel him coming."

He muttered, his speech interspersed with strange guttural exclamations, or words that sometimes seemed addressed to Corso and at others to a third dark presence near them, in the shadows:

"'You will go through eight doors before the dragon . . .' Do you see? Eight doors come before the beast who guards the word, number nine, which possesses the final secret . . . The dragon sleeps with its eye open and it is the Mirror of Knowledge . . . Eight engravings plus one. Or one plus eight. Which coincides with the number that St John of Patmos attributed to the Beast: 666."

Corso saw him kneel and write out numbers in chalk on the marble floor:

$$666$$
$$6 + 6 + 6 = 18$$
$$1\text{-}8$$
$$1 + 8 = 9$$

Then he stood up, triumphant. For a moment the candles lit up his eyes. He must have swallowed some kind of drug with the dark liquid. His pupils were so dilated that almost none of the iris was visible, and the whites had taken on a reddish tinge from the light in the room.

"Nine engravings, or nine doors." Shadow once again covered his face like a mask. "They can't be opened by just anyone . . . 'Each door has two keys.' Each engraving provides a number, a magic element and a key word, if it's all studied in the light of reason, the Cabbala, the occult, the true philosophy . . . Of Latin and its combination with Greek and Hebrew." He showed Corso a piece of paper covered in signs and strange links. "You can take a look, if you like. You'll never understand it:

Aleph	Eis	I	ONMA	Air
Beth	Duo	II	CIS	Earth
Gimel	Treis	III	EM	Water
Daleth	Tessares	IIII	EM	Gold
He	Pente	V	OEXE	String
Vau	Es	VI	CIS	Silver
Zayin	Epta	VII	CIS	Stone
Cheth	Octo	VIII	EM	Iron
Teth	Ennea	VIIII	ODED	Fire

There were beads of sweat on his forehead and round his mouth, as if the flame of the candles were also burning inside his body. He began to walk round the circle slowly and carefully. He stopped a couple of times and bent over to adjust the position of some object: the rusty knife, the silver bracelet.

"'You will place the elements on the serpent's skin . . .'" he recited without looking at Corso. He was following the circle with his finger but not quite touching it. "The nine elements are to be placed around it 'in the direction of the rising sun': from right to left."

Corso took a step towards him.

"Once more. Give me my money."

Varo Borja took no notice. He had his back to him, and was pointing to the square drawn inside the circle.

"'The serpent will swallow the seal of Saturn . . .' The seal of Saturn is the most ancient and simple of the magic squares: the first nine numbers placed inside nine boxes, set out so that each row, whether down, across, or diagonally, adds up to the same number."

He bent down and wrote out nine numbers inside the box in chalk:

4	9	2
3	5	7
8	1	6

Corso took another step. As he did so he trod on a piece of paper covered in numbers:

$$4+9+2=15 \qquad 4+3+8=15 \qquad 4+5+6=15$$
$$3+5+7=15 \qquad 9+5+1=15 \qquad 2+5+8=15$$
$$8+1+6=15 \qquad 2+7+6=15$$

A candle went out with a hiss, having burnt down onto the charred frontispiece of a *De occulta philosophia* by Cornelius Agrippa. Varo Borja's attention was still on the circle and the square. He stared at them intently, his arms folded on his chest and his head bowed. He looked like a player before a strange board, pondering his next move.

"There's one thing," he said, now no longer addressing Corso but talking to himself. It seemed that hearing his own voice helped him to think. "Something that the ancients didn't foresee, at least not expressly . . . Added together in any direction, from up to down, down to up, left to right, or right to left, you get 15. But applying the codes of the Cabbalists it also becomes a 1 and a 5, which, added together, make six . . . And that surrounds each side of the magical square with the serpent, the dragon or the Beast, or whatever you want to call it."

Corso didn't even have to work it out for himself. It was set out on another piece of paper on the floor:

$$
\begin{array}{ccccc}
 & 6 & 6 & 6 & \\
6 & 4 & 9 & 2 & 6 \\
6 & 3 & 5 & 7 & 6 \\
6 & 8 & 1 & 6 & 6 \\
 & 6 & 6 & 6 &
\end{array}
$$

Varo Borja knelt before the circle, his head bowed. The sweat on his face gleamed in the candlelight. He was holding another piece of paper and reading out the strange words written on it.

"'You will open the seal nine times,' says Torchia's text . . . That means the key words obtained must be placed in the box that corresponds to its number. In that way we get the following sequence:

1	2	3	4	5	6	7	8	9
ONMAD	CIS	EM	EM	OEXE	CIS	CIS	EM	ODED

" . . . Written on the serpent, or the dragon." He rubbed out the numbers in the boxes and inserted the corresponding words in their place. "This is how it looks, to God's shame:"

EM	ODED	CIS
EM	OEXE	CIS
EM	ONMAD	CIS

"It has all been carried out," muttered Varo Borja as he wrote out the final letters. His hand was trembling, and one of the drops of sweat slid from his forehead down his nose and onto the chalk-covered floor. "According to Torchia's text, it is sufficient for 'the mirror to reflect the path' to pronounce the lost word which brings the light from the darkness . . . These phrases are in Latin. They mean nothing on their own. But inside they contain the exact essence of the '*Verbum dimissum*', the formula which makes Satan, our forebear, our mirror and our accomplice, appear."

He was kneeling in the centre of the circle, surrounded by all the signs, objects and words written in the square. His hands were shaking so violently that he clasped them together, claw-like, his fingers covered in chalk, ink and wax. Proud and sure of himself, he started to laugh like a madman, under his breath. But Corso was sure he wasn't insane. He looked around, aware that he was running out of time, and he started to cross the distance between him and the bookdealer. But he couldn't make up his mind to cross the line and stand with him inside the circle.

Varo Borja looked at him malevolently, guessing his fears.

"Come on, Corso. Don't you want to read it with me? Are you scared, or have you forgotten your Latin?" Light and shadow alternated with increasing speed on his face, as if the room around him were starting to spin. But the room was still. "Don't you want to know what these words contain? On the back of that engraving poking from between the pages of the Valerio Lorena, you'll find the translation into Spanish. Place them before the mirror, as the masters of the art ordered. At least then you will know what Fargas and Baroness Ungern died for."

Corso looked at the book, an incunabulum with a very old and worn parchment binding. Then he bent over cautiously, as if the pages contained a dangerous trap, and pulled out the engraving poking from between the pages. It was engraving I of Book Number Three, Baroness Ungern's copy, with three towers instead of four. On the reverse Varo Borja had written nine words:

> OGERTNE EM ISA
>
> OREBIL EM ISA
>
> OREDNOC EM ISA

"Courage, Corso," said the bookdealer's sour, disagreeable voice. "You have nothing to lose . . . Hold the words to the mirror."

There was, indeed, a mirror very near on the floor, amongst the melted wax from candles about to burn themselves out. It was silver, old and stained, with a baroque worked handle. It lay face up and Corso's image appeared in it, tiny and distorted, as if at the end of a long tunnel of trembling red light. The image and its double, the hero and his infinite weariness, Bonaparte chained in agony to his rock on Saint Helena. Nothing to lose, Varo Borja had said. A cold, desolate world, where the solitary skeletons of Waterloo grenadiers stood guard along dark, forgotten paths. He saw himself before the final door, holding the key like the hermit in engraving II, the letter Teth coiled round his shoulder like a serpent.

He stepped on the mirror and crushed it with his heel, slowly, without violence. The mirror shattered with a cracking sound. The fragments now multiplied Corso's image in countless tunnels of shadow at the end of which countless replicas of himself stood motionless, too small and indistinct to concern him.

"Black is the school of the night," he heard Varo Borja say. He was still kneeling in the centre of the circle with his back to Corso, leaving him to his fate. Corso leant over one of the candles and held a corner of engraving I, with the nine inverted words on the reverse, to the flame. He watched the castle towers, the horse, the horseman turned towards the viewer advising silence, burn between his fingers. At last he dropped the remaining piece, which turned to ash a second later and floated on the hot air of the candles lit around the room. Then he entered the circle and moved towards Varo Borja.

"I want my money. Now."

Lost ever deeper in darkness, Borja took no notice. Then, anxiously, as if the objects on the floor suddenly appeared incorrectly laid out, he crouched and altered the position of some of them. After a brief hesitation, he began intoning a sinister prayer:

"'Admai, Aday, Eloy, Agla . . .'"

Corso grabbed him by the shoulder and shook him violently. But Varo Borja showed no emotion or fear. Nor did he try to defend himself. He continued to recite as if he were in a trance, a martyr praying unaware of the roar of the lions or the executioner's sword.

"For the last time. Give me my money."

It was no good. All he saw before him were Borja's empty eyes looking through him, wells of darkness, blank, intent on the chasms of the kingdom of shadows.

"'Zatel, Gebel, Elimi . . .'"

He was summoning the devils, Corso realized in disbelief. Standing inside the circle, aware of nothing, neither Corso's presence nor even his threats, the man was invoking devils regardless, by their first names.

"'Gamael, Bilet . . .'"

Borja only stopped when Corso struck him for the first time, a blow with the back of his hand that sent his head over to one side. His eyes rolled and then fixed on a vague point in space.

"'Zaquel, Astarot . . .'"

By the time he received the second blow, blood was already trickling from a corner of his mouth. With revulsion Corso pulled his hand away, stained with red. He'd felt he was striking something damp, viscous. He took a couple of breaths and then counted ten beats of his heart before clenching his teeth, then his fists, and striking again. Blood was now flowing from the bookdealer's twisted mouth. He was still muttering his prayer, a disturbing, delirious smile of absurd joy on his swollen lips. Corso grabbed him by his shirt collar and dragged him brutally outside the circle before hitting him again. Only then did Varo Borja cry out like an animal, in pain and anguish, struggling free with unexpected energy and dragging himself back to the circle. Corso pushed him from it three times, and three times he returned to it, obstinately. By then a trail of blood was smeared over the signs and letters written on the seal of Saturn.

"'*Sic dedo me . . .*'"

Something was wrong. In the trembling candlelight, Corso saw him hesitate, perplexed, and check the arrangement of the objects in the magic circle. But the last few drops were draining from the waterclock. Varo Borja seemed to have little time left. He repeated his last words with greater emphasis, touching three of the nine boxes:

"'*Sic dedo me . . .*'"

An acrid taste in his mouth, Corso looked round hopelessly, wiping his bloodstained hand on his coat. Yet more candles had burnt right down and went out with a hiss. Spirals of smoke rose from their charred wicks in the reddish gloom. Like serpents, he thought with bitter irony. Then he went to the desk that had been pushed into a corner with the rest of the furniture, and searched through the drawers. There was no money. Not even a cheque-book. Nothing.

"'*Sic exeo me . . .*'"

The bookdealer continued to intone his litany. Corso glanced at him, at the magic circle one last time. Kneeling within it, leaning his distorted, fervent face towards the floor, Varo Borja was opening the last of the nine doors with a smile of insane joy; his bleeding mouth, a black, demonic line across his face, like a cut from a knife made of night and shadow.

"Son of a bitch," said Corso. And with that he took his contract to be terminated.

He headed towards the grey light at the foot of the steps, beneath the arch leading to the courtyard. There, by the well and the marble lions, before the gate leading to the street, he stopped and breathed deeply, savouring the fresh, clean morning air. Then he searched in his coat until he found the crumpled packet with one remaining cigarette. He put it in his mouth but didn't light it. He stood there a moment while, red and slanting, the first ray of the sun which he'd left behind on entering the city, reached him. It slipped between the grey stone façades of the square, projecting the shadow of the wrought-iron gate on his face, and making him half-close his sleepless, weary eyes. Then the light grew, spreading slowly to fill the entire patio with the Venetian lions, who bowed their marble manes as if receiving a caress. The same glow, first red, then luminous as a suspension of gold dust, enveloped Corso. And at that instant, at the top of the stairs, beyond the last door of the kingdom of the shadows, where the calm light of dawn would never reach, there was a cry. A piercing, inhuman scream, full of horror and despair, in which he could only just recognize the voice of Varo Borja.

Without turning round, Corso pushed the gate and went out into the street. With each step he seemed to move a great distance away from what he was leaving behind, as if, in only a few seconds, he had retraced his steps on a journey that had taken him too long.

He stopped in the middle of the square, dazzled, enveloped in blinding sunlight. The girl was still in the car, and Corso shivered with deep, selfish delight when he saw that she hadn't disappeared with the remnants of the night. She smiled tenderly, looking impossibly young and beautiful, with her hair cut short like a boy's, her tanned skin, her tranquil eyes fixed on him, waiting. And all the golden, perfect light reflected in the liquid green of her eyes – the light driving back the dark angles of the ancient city, the shadow of the bell towers and the pointed arches of the square – seemed to radiate from her smile as Corso went to meet her. He looked down at the ground as he walked, resigned, ready to bid his own shadow farewell. But there was no shadow at his feet.

Behind him, in the house guarded by four gargoyles beneath the eaves, Varo Borja was no longer screaming. Or perhaps he was doing so from some dark place, too far away to be heard from the street. "*Nunc scio*": now I know. Corso wondered if the Ceniza brothers had used resin or wood to forge the illustration, lost through the whim of a child or the barbarity of a collector, in Book Number One. Although, as he thought of their pale, skilled hands, he inclined to think they had carved it in wood, basing it on Mateu's *Bibliography*. That's why things didn't tally for Varo Borja: in the three copies, the final engraving was a forgery. "*Ceniza sculpsit*." For love of their art.

He was laughing under his breath, like a cruel wolf, as he leant over to light his last cigarette. Books play that kind of trick, he thought. And everyone gets the Devil he deserves.

La Navata. April 1993

Arturo Pérez-Reverte

THE SEVILLE COMMUNION

La Piel
— del Tambor

'A beautifully and intricately written *noir* on which unique
plots and counterplots abound'
San Francisco Examiner

Murderous goings-on in a tiny baroque church draw the
Vatican into the dark heart of Seville.

A hacker gets into the Pope's personal computer to leave a
warning about mysterious deaths in a small church in Seville
that is threatened with demolition. Father Quart, a suave
Vatican trouble-shooter, is sent to investigate. Experience
has taught him to deal with enemies of the Church in all their
guises, but nothing has prepared him for the stubborn faith
of Father Ferro, or the appeal of the lovely Macarena
Bruner, desperate to save the church of her ancestors from
her ex-husband, the ruthless banker Pencho Gavira. As
Quart is drawn into an intrigue as labyrinthine as the streets
of Seville, soon more than his vocation is in danger.

'Recounted with panache and subtlety, *The Seville
Communion* [is] one of those infrequent whodunnits that
transcend the genre'
Time

V

VINTAGE

Arturo Pérez-Reverte

THE FLANDERS PANEL

— La tabla de Flandes

'A sleek and sophisticated mystery about art, life and chess
...madly clever'
New York Times

The clue to a murder in the art world of contemporary
Madrid lies hidden in a medieval painting of a game of chess.

In the 15th-century Flemish painting two noblemen are
playing chess. Yet two years before he could sit for the
portrait, one of them was murdered. Now, in 20th-century
Madrid, Julia, a picture restorer preparing the painting for
auction, uncovers an inscription that points to the crime.
Quis necavit equitem? Who killed the knight? But as she
teams up with a brilliant chess theoretician to retrace the
moves, she discovers the deadly game is not yet over.

'In its intellectual background detail it is reminiscent of
Umberto Eco's novels...hard to stop reading'
Times Literary Supplement

V

BY ARTURO PÉREZ-REVERTE
ALSO AVAILABLE IN VINTAGE

☐ **The Fencing Master**	0099448629	£6.99
☐ **The Flanders Panel**	0099453959	£6.99
☐ **The Seville Communion**	0099453967	£6.99

"**Awesome!** . . . Addresses how we have created a false two-track way of looking at life. . . . You must read it. Do it now."
   —BRIAN GODAWA, screenwriter, author, *Hollywood Worldviews*

"**A rich and readable** book . . . an atlas of the intellectual geography of the culture war . . . uncanny insight . . . a gifted writer and thinker."
   —*First Things*

"**Very well written, spiced with anecdotes.** . . . sufficient philosophical substance to be used in a college level class. . . . It would be wonderful if **every Christian pastor would read this book.**"
   —ANGUS MENUGE, Concordia University, *Philosophia Christi*

"**An outstanding writer.** . . . If you buy only one book this year, this would be the book at the top of the list."
   —CHARLES DUNAHOO, Christian Education and Publications,
      Presbyterian Church in America

"**The most serious undertaking on Christian worldview** to date—from one of the finest writers in America."
   —MIKE ADAMS, columnist, author,
      Welcome to the Ivory Tower of Babel

"**Illuminating.** . . . Pearcey has a gift for making complex issues clear. This is a book that even a worldview novice can enjoy and benefit from."
   —LISA ANN COCKREL, *Faithful Reader*

"**A brilliant intellectual and personal journey** for both the religiously committed and the skeptically wary reader."
   —JUDITH REISMAN, author, *Kinsey, Crimes and Consequences*

"**Skillfully explains difficult concepts** in plain language. . . . Pearcey advances well beyond Schaeffer, both in the maturity of her thought and in her original work with source documents."
   —BILL WICHTERMAN, *Townhall.com*

"**Well-written and thoroughly documented** . . . a **rousing call to action** for Christians to wage the culture war . . . presents **a compelling case** for a Christian worldview."
   —*Human Events*

"**Marked by Nancy Pearcey's** signature clarity, readability, and intellectual depth. It is rare to find a book of such religious and intellectual integrity which is at the same time so **accessible and enjoyable.**"
   —AL WOLTERS, author, *Creation Regained*

"Anybody who has read Nancy Pearcey knows to expect a **careful review** of the literature, a **keen discussion** of the issues, and a **creative analysis** of the way ahead—all expressed in a clear and lively way. *Total Truth* does not disappoint."
    —PAUL MARSHALL, author, *Heaven Is Not My Home*

"Viewed by many as the Francis Schaeffer of her generation, I suspect Nancy Pearcey's book *Total Truth* will become **essential reading for all serious-thinking Christians.**"
    —ADRIAN WARNOCK, *UK Evangelical Blog*

"*Total Truth* may just be a **life-changing** book . . . a **masterpiece** that is intellectually stimulating but still accessible and practical."
    —TIM CHALLIES, *Challies.com*

"Pearcey is emerging today as a **Christian thinker and intellectual advocate** of immense importance."
    —MARK TAPSCOTT, Director of The Heritage Foundation's
      Center for Media and Public Policy

"**Spans intersections of secular thought and Christian orientation** over a wide cultural horizon. . . . Demonstrates how correct Schaeffer was in his analysis."
    —UDO MIDDELMANN, Director, Francis A. Schaeffer Foundation

"Exhibits the **depth of research** and **breadth of coverage** we have come to expect from Nancy Pearcey."
    —J. P. Moreland, Talbot School of Theology, Biola University

"It is rare to find a book like this one, which analyzes its own culture's history . . . with **honesty and humbleness.**"
    —GÖKHAN KAYA, *Holiness in Mind*

"**Lucidly stated** arguments . . . deserves to be read by anyone seeking to integrate his or her worldview."
    —PAUL GIEM, *Origins*

"One of those rare books that combines an easy read with serious content, and historical and philosophical depth with **Christian integrity.** . . . Not to be missed."
    —ARTHUR JONES, *Third Way*

"With **the passion of an advocate** and **the skill of a surgeon,** Nancy Pearcey sets forth the elements of a Christian worldview. . . . Makes a persuasive case for Christian involvement in society."
    —KERBY ANDERSON, National Director, Probe Ministries,
      cohost, Point of View

"Nancy Pearcey picks up where Francis Schaeffer left off in this **riveting and informative** new book."
—*The Discerning Reader*

"Offers **wisdom and hope** to the Christian who wants to have a more significant impact for the cause of Christ . . . thoroughly researched, well written and well argued."
—*CaliforniaRepublic.org*

"**Brilliant analysis** and perspective, designed to strengthen and fill out aspects that can be missing in the Christian life, and to equip evangelicals apologetically."
—CATEZ STEVENS, *Allthings2all*

"**A vitally important** work for the church today. . . . Pearcey explains the secular/sacred dichotomy that has permeated and continues to permeate society."
—SARAH FLASHING, The Foundation for Women of Faith in Culture

"**Too intriguing to put down.** . . . a fervent call to evangelicals to wake up from our cultural captivity to the paradigms of the world."
—STEVE ERICKSON, *Smerickson.com*

"**One of the most important Christian books** of the last decade. . . . A must for every Christian's personal library, you'll go back to it again and again. Don't wait; buy it today."
—DANIEL L. EDELEN, *Practical.org*

"**I highly recommend** *Total Truth* and will be bribing my teenagers to read it."
—RANDY BRANDT, Contend 4 The Faith

"**A terrific book** that is a must-have for Christians. . . . a **thoroughly enjoyable** book on a very difficult subject. . . . Get this book and read it for yourself. You will be thankful that you did."
—TOM PARSONS, www.twoorthree.net

"**A rare gem.** . . . If you've never read a book on worldview or apologetics, then **you are in for a treat.** If you do not read any other book this year, this is the one book you *must* read."
—STACY HARP, Mind & Media

"*Total Truth* is probably **the most significant book** of 2004. I pray its influence and impact will be felt for decades."
—RAY BOHLIN, Probe Ministries

"**A fascinating study!** The perspective is fresh, helpful, moving, and challenging. Simple yet profound, passion-filled without being 'preachy,' broad in scope and centered on fundamental issues."
> —JOHN VANDER STELT, Professor Emeritus of Philosophy,
> Dordt College

"**Personal stories** help to incarnate the issues and make them come alive. . . . Clear, concrete, lively writing style. This message should get a wide hearing."
> —MICHAEL GOHEEN, Professor of Worldview Studies,
> Redeemer University College

"**Lucid, easy to understand.** . . . For all of its intellectual and theological sophistication, *Total Truth* is written in a way that the average layperson will understand and appreciate."
> —*World*

"Easy to read, well-documented, sometimes provocative. . . . A superb worldview lens through which we can see things more clearly. **All who read it will live their lives differently.**"
> —BECKY NORTON DUNLOP, VP for External Relations,
> the Heritage Foundation

"**Conversational, anecdote-rich, yet intellectually meaty.** . . . I heartily recommend *Total Truth* as a powerful antidote to what I have elsewhere called "truth decay." . . . Turn off the television, turn off the video games, set aside the iPod, and **read this book** as soon as possible."
> —DOUGLAS GROOTHUIS, Denver Seminary, *Denver Journal*

"**Remarkable . . . a pleasure to read. . . . clear, stimulating, thoughtful. . . .** The Lord has used Nancy Pearcey to bring encouragement to many believers—helping them to **not be ashamed of the Gospel** in their classrooms, their studies, and their workplaces."
> —JERRAM BARRS, Resident Scholar, Francis Schaeffer Institute,
> *Reformation 21*

"A book of such profound importance that all professing Christians should stop whatever they are doing and **read *Total Truth* from cover to cover** before resuming their regular activities. . . . Pearcey is the **best living evangelical Christian writer,** period."
> —TIMOTHY STANDISH, *Andrews University Seminary Studies*

"**Gifted thinker and writer.** . . . Pearcey reinvigorates the type of work that Francis Schaeffer did in the 1960s, but in a more comprehensive and rigorous way."
> —PAUL SPEARS, *Journal of Church and State*

"**Convincing** . . . Pearcey's style is **sophisticated without being preachy.** . . . an excellent source on worldview, whether for group or personal study."
> —*Church Libraries Journal*

TOTAL TRUTH

*Liberating Christianity
from Its Cultural Captivity*

Study Guide Edition

NANCY R. PEARCEY

FOREWORD BY
Phillip E. Johnson

WHEATON, ILLINOIS

Total Truth: Liberating Christianity from Its Cultural Captivity
(Study Guide Edition)

Copyright © 2004, 2005 by Nancy R. Pearcey

Published by Crossway
        1300 Crescent Street
        Wheaton, Illinois 60187

First edition 2004

Study Guide edition 2005

First trade paper edition 2008

Published in association with Yates & Yates, LLP, Attorneys and Counselors, Orange, California.

Cover photo: "Le Semeur 1" http://www.kmm.nl/index_flash.html#voorpagina

First printing 2008

Printed in the United States of America

Unless otherwise indicated, all Scripture quotations are from the ESV® Bible (*The Holy Bible, English Standard Version*®), copyright © 2001 by Crossway Bibles, a publishing ministry of Good News Publishers. Used by permission. All rights reserved.

The Scripture quotation marked KJV is from the King James Version of the Bible.

All emphases in Scripture quotations have been added by the author.

ISBN-13: 978-1-4335-0220-0
ISBN-10: 1-4335-0220-8
ePub ISBN: 978-1-4335-2235-2
PDF ISBN: 978-1-4335-0087-9
Mobipocket ISBN: 978-1-4335-0724-3

Library of Congress Cataloging-in-Publication Data

Pearcey, Nancy.
   Total truth: liberating Christianity from its cultural captivity / Nancy R. Pearcey ; foreword by Phillip E. Johnson. — Study guide ed.
     p.   cm.
   Includes bibliographical references and index.
   ISBN 13: 978-1-58134-746-3
   ISBN 10: 1-58134-746-4 (hc : alk. paper)
   1. Christianity—Philosophy. 2. Apologetics. 3. Christian life.
4. History—Religious aspects—Christianity. 5. History—Philosophy.
I. Title.
BR100.P37   2005
261—dc22   2005011392

Crossway is a publishing ministry of Good News Publishers.

SH		31	30	29	28	27	26	25	24	23	22	21
25	24	23	22	21	20	19	18	17	16	15	14	13

CONTENTS

FOREWORD

When Nancy Pearcey invited me to write a foreword for her "worldview" book, I hastened to accept the honor. I was honored by the invitation because this is a book of unusual importance by an author of unusual ability.

It has been a treat for me to read and study the manuscript, and I feel that I am doing a great favor to every potential reader whom I can persuade to enjoy these pages as I have done. Nancy Pearcey is an author who is greatly respected by all who know her work. I hope that, with this book, she will receive the acclaim that her thought and writing has so long deserved, and that readers will find in its message of liberation the key to intellectual and spiritual renewal.

It would be an understatement to say that worldview is an important topic. I would rather say that understanding how worldviews are formed, and how they guide or confine thought, is the essential step toward understanding everything else. Understanding worldview is a bit like trying to see the lens of one's own eye. We do not ordinarily see our own worldview, but we see everything else by looking through it. Put simply, our worldview is the window by which we view the world, and decide, often subconsciously, what is real and important, or unreal and unimportant.

It may be that a worldview is commonly a collection of prejudices. If so, the prejudices are necessary, because we can't start from a blank slate and investigate everything from scratch by ourselves. When somebody tells me that he receives guidance from God in prayer, or that science is our only way of knowing anything for sure, or that there is no objective difference between good and evil, I need to have some verifiable frame of reference to tell me at once whether he is merely deluded or is saying something that is sufficiently sensible to merit serious consideration.

Similarly, when I tell my fellow Berkeley professors that I don't believe the theory of evolution, I need to know why they find it so difficult to take me seriously or to believe that my objection to the theory is based on scientific evidence rather than on the book of Genesis. The reason is that evolution with its accompanying philosophy is identified with their worldview at such a deep level that they cannot imagine how the theory could possibly be contrary to the evidence.

Every one of us has a worldview, and our worldview governs our thinking even when—or especially when—we are unaware of it. Thus, it is not uncommon to find well-meaning evildoers, as it were, who are quite sincerely convinced that they are Christians, and attend church faithfully, and may even hold a position of leadership, but who have absorbed a worldview that makes it easy for them to ignore their Christian principles when it comes time to do the practical business of daily living. Their sincerely held Christian principles are in one mental category for them, and practical decision making is in another. Such persons can believe that Jesus is coming again to judge the world and yet live as if the standards of this world are the only thing that needs to be taken into account.

Likewise, Christian education is likely to be an exercise in futility if it does not prepare our young people to confront and survive the worldview challenges that they will surely meet as soon as they leave the security of the Christian home, and probably even while they are still living at home and being educated in a Christian environment, due to the pervasive influence of the media and the Internet. For example, a youngster may be taught very fine Christian principles, but he or she may also grow up understanding that these principles fit into a specialized category called "religious belief."

Sooner or later, that youngster will find out that secular college professors, and sometimes even Christian professors, proceed from an implicit assumption that religious beliefs are the kind of thing one is supposed to set aside when learning how the world really works, and that it is usually praiseworthy to "grow" gradually away from those beliefs as a part of the normal process of maturing.

Why do those professors think that? Of course they are being influenced by the dominant belief system in their academic culture, which is also the culture of the newsroom at most daily newspapers or television stations. But just to say that people are influenced by their cultural environment does not explain how our culture has come to be the way it is, when it used to be very different. To survive in modern or postmodern American culture without being overwhelmed by its concealed prejudices, everyone needs to know how to recognize those prejudices, to understand what kind of thinking brought them into existence, and to be able to explain to ourselves and others what is wrong with the pervasive assumptions that often come labeled only as "the way all rational people think," and that will swamp our faith if we are not alert to them.

A fine education in worldview analysis is as basic an element of a modern Christian's defense system as a shield was in the days when a prudent traveler needed to be prepared to repel an attack by sword-wielding robbers. Today the intellectual brigands rob unwary youths of their faith, and they do it with arguments based on the shifting sand of "what everybody knows" and "the way we think today." Those youths need to find the solid rock, and they need to know both why the rock is solid, and why the world prefers the shifting sand.

Only a very gifted author is capable of writing a book about worldview analysis that will make exciting reading for the ordinary person, but which is also sufficiently informed by scholarship to convey a deep understanding of the subject rather than merely a superficial acquaintance. Everyone is aware that American culture changed enormously during the twentieth century, but very few people understand how the change was brought about by ideas and habits that seemed at first to be eccentric or of only minor importance, but that eventually crept into the popular culture and proved to be almost irresistible. The situation we find ourselves in today has deep roots in the thinking of earlier times. Conduct that not very long ago was regarded as perverse or criminal has become not only tolerated but the new norm. Those who dare to disapprove of that conduct, or just fail to applaud the new norm with sufficient enthusiasm, are themselves likely to feel the full weight of society's disapproval. The change in conduct was brought about by changes in worldview, which caused those who followed the new fashions to think differently.

With that much of an introduction, I invite you to read Nancy Pearcey. You will find not only pleasant reading but all the elements and basic information necessary to produce a Christian mind with a map of reality that really works. When Christian parents, pastors, educators, and other leaders learn to give this subject the importance it deserves, and to practice it even as they teach it thoroughly in the home, from the pulpit, and in every classroom, then Christians will find that they are no longer fearful and timid when they have to address claims of worldly wisdom. So let's get started.

—Phillip E. Johnson
Berkeley, California
January 2004

Christianity is not a series of truths in the plural,
but rather truth spelled with a capital "T."
Truth about total reality, not just about religious things.

Biblical Christianity is Truth concerning total reality —
and the intellectual holding of that total Truth
and then living in the light of that Truth.

FRANCIS SCHAEFFER
Address at the University of Notre Dame
April 1981

INTRODUCTION

"Your earlier book says Christians are called to redeem entire cultures, not just individuals," a schoolteacher commented, joining me for lunch at a conference where I had just spoken. Then he added thoughtfully, "I'd never heard that before."

The teacher was talking about *How Now Shall We Live?*[1] and at his words I looked up from my plate in surprise. Was he really saying he'd never even *heard* the idea of being a redemptive force in every area of culture? He shook his head: "No, I've always thought of salvation strictly in terms of individual souls."

That conversation helped confirm my decision to write a follow-up book dealing with the worldview themes in *How Now Shall We Live?* Just a few years ago, when I began my work on that earlier volume, using the term *worldview* was not on anyone's list of good conversation openers. To tell people that you were writing a book on *worldview* was to risk glazed stares and a quick change in subject. But today as I travel around the country, I sense an eagerness among evangelicals to move beyond a purely privatized faith, applying biblical principles to areas like work, business, and politics. Flip open any number of Christian publications and you're likely to find half a dozen advertisements for *worldview* conferences, *worldview* institutes, and *worldview* programs. Clearly the term itself has strong marketing cachet these days, which signals a deep hunger among Christians for an overarching framework to bring unity to their lives.

This book addresses that hunger and offers new direction for advancing the worldview movement. It will help you identify the secular/sacred divide that keeps your faith locked into the private sphere of "religious truth." It will walk you through practical, workable steps for crafting a Christian worldview in your own life and work. And it will teach you how to apply a worldview grid to cut through the bewildering maze of ideas and ideologies we encounter in a postmodern world. The purpose of worldview studies is nothing less than to liberate Christianity from its cultural captivity, unleashing its power to transform the world.

"The gospel is like a caged lion," said the great Baptist preacher Charles Spurgeon. "It does not need to be defended, it just needs to be let out of its cage." Today the cage is our accommodation to the secular/sacred split that reduces Christianity to a matter of private personal belief. To unlock the cage, we need to become utterly convinced that, as Francis Schaeffer said, Christianity is not merely religious truth, it is total truth—truth about the whole of reality.

POLITICS IS NOT ENOUGH

The reason a worldview message is so compelling today is that we are still emerging from the fundamentalist era of the early twentieth century. Up until that time, evangelicals had enjoyed a position of cultural dominance in America. But after the Scopes trial and the rise of theological modernism, religious conservatives turned in on themselves: They circled the wagons, developed a fortress mentality, and championed "separatism" as a positive strategy. Then, in the 1940s and 50s, a movement began that aimed at breaking out of the fortress. Calling themselves *neo-evangelicals*, this group argued that we are called not to escape the surrounding culture but to engage it. They sought to construct a redemptive vision that would embrace not only individuals but also social structures and institutions.

Yet many evangelicals lacked the conceptual tools needed for the task, which has seriously limited their success. For example, in recent decades many Christians have responded to the moral and social decline in American society by embracing political activism. Believers are running for office in growing numbers; churches are organizing voter registration; public policy groups are proliferating; scores of Christian publications and radio programs offer commentary on public affairs. This heightened activism has yielded good results in many areas of public life, yet the impact remains far less than most had hoped. Why? Because evangelicals often put all their eggs in one basket: They leaped into political activism as the quickest, surest way to make a difference in the public arena—failing to realize that politics tends to reflect culture, not the other way around.

Nothing illustrates evangelicals' infatuation with politics more clearly than a story related by a Christian lawyer. Considering whether to take a job in the nation's capital, he consulted with the leader of a Washington-area ministry, who told him, "You can either stay where you are and keep practicing law, or you can come to Washington and *change the culture.*" The implication was that the only way to effect cultural change was through national politics. Today, battle-weary political warriors have grown more realistic about the limits of that strategy. We have learned that "politics is downstream from culture, not the other way around," says Bill Wichterman, policy advisor to Senate Majority Leader Bill Frist. "Real change has to start with the culture. All we can do on Capitol Hill is try to find ways government can nurture healthy cultural trends."[2]

On a similar note, a member of Congress once told me, "I got involved in politics after the 1973 abortion decision because I thought that was the fastest route to moral reform. Well, we've won some legislative victories, but *we've lost the culture.*" The most effective work, he had come to realize, is done by ordinary Christians fulfilling God's calling to reform culture within their local spheres of influence—their families, churches, schools, neighborhoods, workplaces, professional organizations, and civic institutions. In order to effect lasting change, the congressman concluded, "we need to develop a Christian worldview."

Losing Our Children

Not only have we "lost the culture," but we continue losing even our own children. It's a familiar but tragic story that devout young people, raised in Christian homes, head off to college and abandon their faith. Why is this pattern so common? Largely because young believers have not been taught how to develop a biblical worldview. Instead, Christianity has been restricted to a specialized area of religious belief and personal devotion.

I recently read a striking example. At a Christian high school, a theology teacher strode to the front of the classroom, where he drew a heart on one side of the blackboard and a brain on the other. The two are as divided as the two sides of the blackboard, he told the class: The heart is what we use for religion, while the brain is what we use for science.

An apocryphal story? A caricature of Christian anti-intellectualism? No, the story was told by a young woman who was in the class that day. Worse, out of some two hundred students, she was the only one who objected. The rest apparently found nothing unusual about restricting religion to the domain of the "heart."[3]

As Christian parents, pastors, teachers, and youth group leaders, we constantly see young people pulled down by the undertow of powerful cultural trends. If all we give them is a "heart" religion, it will not be strong enough to counter the lure of attractive but dangerous ideas. Young believers also need a "brain" religion—training in worldview and apologetics—to equip them to analyze and critique the competing worldviews they will encounter when they leave home. If forewarned and forearmed, young people at least have a fighting chance when they find themselves a minority of one among their classmates or work colleagues. Training young people to develop a Christian mind is no longer an option; it is part of their necessary survival equipment.

HEART VERSUS BRAIN

The first step in forming a Christian worldview is to overcome this sharp divide between "heart" and "brain." We have to reject the division of life into a sacred realm, limited to things like worship and personal morality, over against a secular realm that includes science, politics, economics, and the rest of the public arena. This dichotomy in our own minds is the greatest barrier to liberating the power of the gospel across the whole of culture today.

Moreover, it is reinforced by a much broader division rending the entire fabric of modern society—what sociologists call the public/private split. "Modernization brings about a novel dichotomization of social life," writes Peter Berger. "The dichotomy is between the huge and immensely powerful institutions of the public sphere [by this he means the state, academia, large corporations] . . . and the private sphere"—the realm of family, church, and personal relationships.

The large public institutions claim to be "scientific" and "value-free," which means that values are relegated to the private sphere of personal choice. As Berger explains: "The individual is left to his own devices in a wide range of activities that are crucial to the formation of a meaningful identity, from expressing his religious preference to settling on a sexual life style."[4] We might diagram the dichotomy like this:

Modern societies are sharply divided:

PRIVATE SPHERE
Personal Preferences

PUBLIC SPHERE
Scientific Knowledge

In short, the private sphere is awash in moral relativism. Notice Berger's telling phrase "religious preference." Religion is not considered an objective truth to which we *submit*, but only a matter of personal taste which we *choose*. Because of this, the dichotomy is sometimes called the fact/value split.

Values have been reduced to arbitrary, existential decisions:

VALUES
Individual Choice

FACTS
Binding on Everyone

As Schaeffer explains, the concept of truth itself has been divided—a process he illustrates with the imagery of a two-story building: In the lower story are science and reason, which are considered public truth, binding on everyone. Over against it is an upper story of noncognitive experience, which is the locus of personal meaning. This is the realm of private truth, where we hear people say, "That may be true for you but it's not true for me."[5]

The two-realm theory of truth:

UPPER STORY
Nonrational, Noncognitive

LOWER STORY
Rational, Verifiable

When Schaeffer was writing, the term *postmodernism* had not yet been coined, but clearly that is what he was talking about. Today we might say that in the lower story is modernism, which still claims to have universal, objective truth—while in the upper story is postmodernism.

Today's two-story truth:

POSTMODERNISM
Subjective, Relative to Particular Groups

MODERNISM
Objective, Universally Valid

The reason it's so important for us to learn how to recognize this division is that it is the single most potent weapon for delegitimizing the biblical perspective in the public square today. Here's how it works: Most secularists are too politically savvy to attack religion directly or to debunk it as false. So what do they do? They consign religion to the *value* sphere—which takes it out of the realm of true and false altogether. Secularists can then assure us that of course they "respect" religion, while at the same time denying that it has any relevance to the public realm.

As Phillip Johnson puts it, the fact/value split "allows the metaphysical naturalists to mollify the potentially troublesome religious people by assuring them that science does not rule out 'religious *belief*' (so long as it does not pretend to be *knowledge*).[6]" In other words, so long as everyone understands that it is merely a matter of private feelings. The two-story grid functions as a gate-keeper that defines what is to be taken seriously as genuine knowledge, and what can be dismissed as mere wish-fulfillment.

JUST A POWER GRAB?

This same division also explains why Christians have such difficulty communicating in the public arena. It's crucial for us to realize that nonbelievers are constantly filtering what we say through a mental fact/value grid. For example, when we state a position on an issue like abortion or bioethics or homosexuality, *we* intend to assert an objective moral truth important to the health of society—but *they* think we're merely expressing our subjective bias. When we say there's scientific evidence for design in the universe, *we* intend to stake out a testable truth claim—but *they* say, "Uh oh, the Religious Right is making a political power grab." The fact/value grid instantly dissolves away the objective content of anything we say, and we will not be successful in introducing the *content* of our belief into the public discussion unless we first find ways to get past this gatekeeper.

That's why Lesslie Newbigin warned that the divided concept of truth is the primary factor in "the cultural captivity of the gospel." It traps Christianity in the upper story of privatized values, and prevents it from having any effect on public culture.[7] Having worked as a missionary in India for forty years, Newbigin was able to discern what is distinctive about Western thought more clearly than most of us, who have been immersed in it all our lives. On his return to the West, Newbigin was struck by the way Christian truth has been marginalized. He saw that any position labeled *religion* is placed in the upper story of values, where it is no longer regarded as objective knowledge.

To give just one recent example, in the debate over embryonic stem cell research, actor Christopher Reeve told a student group at Yale University, "When matters of public policy are debated, *no religions should have a seat at the table.*"[8]

To recover a place at the table of public debate, then, Christians must find a way to overcome the dichotomy between public and private, fact and value, secular and sacred. We need to liberate the gospel from its cultural captivity, restoring it to the status of public truth. "The barred cage that forms the prison for the gospel in contemporary western culture is [the church's] accommodation . . . to the fact-value dichotomy," says Michael Goheen, a professor of worldview studies.[9] Only by recovering a holistic view of total truth can we set the gospel free to become a redemptive force across all of life.

MENTAL MAPS

To say that Christianity is the truth about total reality means that it is a full-orbed worldview. The term means literally a *view* of the *world,* a biblically informed perspective on all reality. A worldview is like a mental map that tells us how to navigate the world effectively. It is the imprint of God's objective truth on our inner life.

We might say that each of us carries a model of the universe inside our heads that tells us what the world is like and how we should live in it. A classic book on worldviews is titled *The Universe Next Door,* suggesting that we all have a mental or conceptual universe in which we "live"—a network of principles that answer the fundamental questions of life: Who are we? Where did we come from? What is the purpose of life? The author of the book, James Sire, invites readers to examine a variety of worldviews in order to understand the mental universe held by other people—those living "next door."

A worldview is not the same thing as a formal philosophy; otherwise, it would be only for professional philosophers. Even ordinary people have a set of convictions about how reality functions and how they should live. Because we are made in God's image, we all seek to make sense of life. Some convictions are conscious, while others are unconscious, but together they form a more or less consistent picture of reality. Human beings "are incapable of holding purely arbitrary opinions or making entirely unprincipled decisions," writes Al Wolters in a book on worldview. Because we are by nature rational and responsible beings, we sense that "we need some creed to live by, some map by which to chart our course."[10]

The notion that we need such a "map" in the first place grows out of the biblical view of human nature. The Marxist may claim that human behavior is ultimately shaped by economic circumstances; the Freudian attributes everything to repressed sexual instincts; and the behavioral psychologist regards humans as stimulus-response mechanisms. But the Bible teaches that the overriding factor in the choices we make is our ultimate belief or religious commitment. Our lives are shaped by the "god" we worship—whether the God of the Bible or some substitute deity.

The term *worldview* is a translation of the German word *Weltanschauung,* which means a way of looking at the world (*Welt* = world; *schauen* = to look). Philosophical idealism developed the idea that cultures are complex wholes, where a certain outlook on life, or spirit of the age, is expressed across the board—in art, literature, and social institutions as well as in formal philosophy. The best way to understand the products of any culture, then, is to grasp the underlying worldview being expressed. But, of course, cultures change over the course of history, and thus the original use of the term *worldview* conveyed relativism.

The word was later introduced into Christian circles through Dutch neo-Calvinist thinkers such as Abraham Kuyper and Herman Dooyeweerd. They argued that Christians cannot counter the spirit of the age in which they live unless they develop an equally comprehensive biblical worldview—an outlook on life that gives rise to distinctively Christian forms of culture—with the important qualification that it is not merely the relativistic belief of a particular culture but is based on the very Word of God, true for all times and places.[11]

NOT JUST ACADEMIC

As the concept of *worldview* becomes common currency, it can all too easily be misunderstood. Some treat it as merely another academic subject to master—a mental exercise or "how to" strategy. Others handle worldview as if it were a weapon in the culture war, a tool for more effective activism. Still others, alas, treat it as little more than a new buzzword or marketing gimmick to dazzle the public and attract donors.

Genuine worldview thinking is far more than a mental strategy or a new spin on current events. At the core, it is a deepening of our spiritual character and the character of our lives. It begins with the submission of our minds to the Lord of the universe—a willingness to be taught by Him. The driving force in worldview studies should be a commitment to "love the Lord your God with all your heart, soul, strength, and mind" (see Luke 10:27).

That's why the crucial condition for intellectual growth is *spiritual* growth, asking God for the grace to "take every thought captive to obey Christ" (2 Cor. 10:5). God is not just the Savior of souls, He is also the Lord of creation. One way we acknowledge His Lordship is by interpreting every aspect of creation in the light of His truth. God's Word becomes a set of glasses offering a new perspective on all our thoughts and actions.

As with every aspect of sanctification, the renewal of the mind may be painful and difficult. It requires hard work and discipline, inspired by a sacrificial love for Christ and a burning desire to build up His Body, the Church. In order to have the mind of Christ, we must be willing to be crucified with Christ, following wherever He might lead—whatever the cost. "Through many tribulations we must enter the kingdom of God" (Acts 14:22). As we undergo refining in the fires of suffering, our desires are purified and we find ourselves wanting nothing more than to bend every fiber of our being, including our mental powers, to fulfill the Lord's Prayer: "Thy Kingdom come." We yearn to lay all our talents and gifts at His feet in order to advance His purposes in the world. Developing a Christian worldview means submitting our entire self to God, in an act of devotion and service to Him.

WORLDVIEW TRAINING

This book approaches the topic of worldview by weaving together insights from three strands.[12] Part 1 sheds light on the secular/sacred dichotomy that restricts Christianity to the realm of religious truth, creating double minds and fragmented lives. To find personal wholeness, we must be willing to lay bare all aspects of our work and life to God's direction and power. Worldview thinking proves to be a rich avenue to joy and fulfillment—a means of letting the spark of God's truth light up every nook and cranny of our lives.

This section also provides practical, hands-on worldview training. It will walk you through concrete steps for crafting a biblically based worldview in any field using the structural elements of Creation, Fall, and Redemption. It will also give you an opportunity to practice apologetics by analyzing non-Christian worldviews. After all, every philosophy or ideology has to answer the same fundamental questions:

1. CREATION: How did it all begin? Where did we come from?

2. FALL: What went wrong? What is the source of evil and suffering?

3. REDEMPTION: What can we do about it? How can the world be
   set right again?

By applying this simple grid, we can identify nonbiblical worldviews, and then analyze where they go wrong.

Part 2 zeroes in on Creation, the foundational starting point for any worldview. In the West, the reigning creation myth is Darwinian evolution; thus, no matter what our field of work is, we must begin by critiquing Darwinism—both its scientific claims and its worldview implications. In this section, you will discover how the latest findings of science discredit naturalistic theories of evolution, while supporting the concept of Intelligent Design. You may also be surprised to learn how aggressively Darwinism has been extended far beyond the bounds of science, even reconfiguring America's social and legal institutions—with devastating effects.

Part 3 peers into the looking glass of history to ask *why* evangelicals do not have a strong worldview tradition. Why is the secular/sacred dichotomy so pervasive? Here we step back from the present to take a tour of the history and heritage of evangelicalism in America. By rummaging about in the attic of our past, we can diagnose the way inherited patterns of thought continue to shape our own thinking today. We can learn how to identify self-defeating barriers to worldview thinking and how to overcome them.

Part 4 reminds us that the heart of worldview thinking lies in its practical and personal application. The renewal of our minds comes about only through the submission of our whole selves to the Lordship of Christ. We must be willing to sit at the feet of Jesus and be taught by Him, as Mary of Bethany did, realizing that only "one thing is necessary" (Luke 10:42). Given our fallen human nature, we typically do not really *sit* before the Lord until our legs are knocked out from under us by crises—sorrow, loss, or injustice. It is only when stripped of our personal dreams and ambitions that we truly die to our own agendas. Union with Christ in His death and resurrection is the only path to sanctification of both heart and mind—to being conformed to the likeness of Christ.

ACKNOWLEDGMENTS

It is a joyful task to express gratitude to those whose ideas and lives have helped shape this book's message. Foremost is Francis Schaeffer, through whose ministry I returned to the Christian faith I had rejected as a teenager. After my first visit to L'Abri (described in chapter 1), I returned a year later for another round of study, when I also met the young man who became my husband. Later we both earned degrees at Covenant Seminary in St. Louis, where Schaeffer once taught. For further graduate studies we attended the Institute for Christian Studies in Toronto, where we were steeped in the philosophy of Dutch Reformed thinkers like Kuyper and Dooyeweerd, whose ideas were seminal for *How Now Shall We Live?* especially its overall framework of Creation, Fall, Redemption, and Restoration. The same background will be evident to readers of this present book as well, and by making frequent references to the original writings, I hope to inspire readers to discover these rich resources for themselves.

Second, I owe much to Dr. Phillip Johnson, professor emeritus of law at the University of California at Berkeley, who provides strategic leadership for the Intelligent Design movement. I have known Phil since 1990, when I interviewed him for the *Bible-Science Newsletter*,[13] and his original way of framing the argument for design has revolutionized the origins debate. His name likewise appears frequently throughout the text, in order to direct readers to his original works.

In my early years as a young Christian, Denis and Margie Haack (founders of Ransom Fellowship) provided crucial support and stability. At Covenant Seminary, I benefited especially from the fine teaching of Dr. David Jones. At the Institute for Christian Studies, a year-long course on neo-Platonism demonstrated that Dr. Al Wolters has a rare gift for bringing ancient Greek philosophy to life. I also had the privilege of taking the last class on neo-Calvinist philosophy taught by Dr. Bernard Zylstra before his untimely death from cancer.

I am grateful to my uncle Bill Overn, a brilliant physicist, whose recommendation helped open a position for me at the *Bible-Science Newsletter* in 1977, where I worked for thirteen years, writing in-depth monthly articles for a section titled "Worldview" on the relation between science and Christian worldview. These lengthy articles traced the impact of evolutionary concepts on education, psychology, law, Marxism, sexuality, New Age religion, and much more—material that later formed the basis for much of my contribution to *How Now Shall We Live?*[14] as well as the present book.

The material for this book was honed through interaction with various audiences, and I would like to thank the following groups: World Journalism Institute and its director Bob Case; Faith and Law (a fellowship of congressional staffers); the *How Now Shall We Live?* reading groups on Capitol Hill; the Megaviews Forum at Los Alamos National Laboratory and its cofounder, former U.S. Congressman Bill Redmond; Regent University School of Law; L'Abri in Rochester, Minnesota; the Association of Christian Schools International; the Renaissance Group (Christian artists and entertainers); Christian Schools International; Trinity Forum Academy; and several Christian colleges and universities. I have also benefited from the opportunity to address events organized by Christian campus groups at Princeton, Dartmouth, Ohio State University, UC Santa Barbara, the University of Minnesota, and USC. Special thanks to John Mark Reynolds, director of the Torrey Honors Institute at Biola University, who invited me to give seminars on the book when it was still in manuscript form, and to the students who contributed by their feedback and comments.

I wish to thank the Discovery Institute's Center for Science and Culture and its director Steve Meyer for a grant that underwrote the initial research stage of the book. The center's staff and fellows form a highly professional group of scientists and scholars who inspire and inform one another's work in countless ways.

I am grateful to those who read or discussed sections of the manuscript: Ila Anderson, Lael Arrington, Michael Behe, Katie Braden, David Calhoun, Bob and Kathy Case, Nancy Chan, Roy Clouser, Jim DeKorne, Michael Goheen, Os Guinness, Darryl Hart, Dana Hill, David Jones, Ranald Macaulay, George Marsden, Tim McGrew, Steven Meyer, Udo Middelmann, Kathleen

Nielson, J. I. Packer, Dieter Pearcey, Dorothy Randolph, Karl Randolph, Jay Richards, Jim Skillen, John Vander Stelt, Tyrone Walters, Linda McGinn Waterman, Richard Weikart, and Al Wolters.

It is an honor to have as my agent Sealy Yates, a man of enormous integrity and a servant's heart. The publisher of Crossway Books, Lane Dennis, along with his wife, Ebeth, welcomed the book project with prayerful enthusiasm from the beginning. Many thanks to the Crossway staff, especially vice president Marvin Padgett and editor Bill Deckard.

The deepest gratitude is due, as always, to family. Thanks to my parents, who sacrificed greatly to send their children to Lutheran schools. I owe an unspeakable debt to my husband, Rick, whose unflagging support, professional editorial expertise, and background in worldview studies contribute to a fruitful writing partnership. The perspective he developed through years of editorial experience on Capitol Hill keeps me grounded in the real world. Finally, I dedicate the book to my two sons, Dieter and Michael, in the hope that they will craft a Christian worldview in their own fields of work, liberating the gospel's power to transform their lives and their world.

—Nancy Randolph Pearcey
Lake Ridge, Virginia
March 2004

PART ONE

WHAT'S
IN A
WORLDVIEW?

1

BREAKING OUT OF THE GRID

Sundays were Sundays,
with the rest of the week largely detached,
operating by a different set of rules.
Can these two worlds that seem so separate ever merge?
JOHN BECKETT[1]

A fashionably dressed college student stepped into the counselor's office, tossing her head in an attempt at bravado. Sarah recognized the type. The Planned Parenthood clinic where she worked often attracted students from the elite university nearby, and most were wealthy, privileged, and self-confident.

"Please sit down. I have your test result . . . and you are pregnant."

The young woman nodded and grimaced. "I kind of thought so."

"Have you thought about what you want to do?" Sarah asked.

The answer was quick and sure. "I want an abortion."

"Let's go over your options first," Sarah said. "It's important for you to think through all the possibilities before you leave today."

Sometimes the young women sitting in her office would grow impatient, even hostile. They had already convinced themselves that there *were* no other viable options. After years of experience in her profession, however, Sarah knew that women who have abortions are often haunted afterward. She hoped to help the students consider the impact an abortion might have in years to come, so they would make an informed decision. If they balked, she fell back on protocol: "This is my job, I have to do it."

Why did Sarah care? Because she was a practicing Christian, as she explained to me many years later,[2] and she thought that's what being a believer meant—showing compassion to women who were considering abortion. Nor was she alone: The Planned Parenthood clinic where she worked was located in the Bible belt, and virtually all the women on staff were regular church-goers. During breaks they would discuss things like their Bible study groups or their children's Sunday school programs.

Sarah's story illustrates how even sincere believers may find themselves drawn into a secular worldview—while remaining orthodox in their theological beliefs. Sarah had grown up in a solidly evangelical denomination. As a teenager, she had undergone a crisis of faith and had emerged from it with a fresh confidence. "I still have the white Bible my grandmother gave me back then," she told me. "I underlined all the passages on how to be sure you were saved." From then on, she never doubted the basic biblical doctrines.

So how did she end up working at Planned Parenthood and referring women for abortion? Something happened to Sarah when she went off to college. There she was immersed in the liberal relativism taught on most campuses today. In courses on sociology, anthropology, and philosophy, it was simply assumed that truth is culturally relative—that ideas and beliefs emerge historically by cultural forces, and are not true or false in any final sense.

And Christianity? It was treated as irrelevant to the world of scholarship. "In a class on moral philosophy, the professor presented every possible theory, from existentialism to utilitarianism, but never said a word about Christian moral theory—even though it's been the dominant religion all through Western history," Sarah recalled. "It was as though Christianity were so irrational, it didn't even merit being listed alongside the other moral theories."

Yet Sarah had no idea how to respond to these assaults on her faith. Her church had helped her find assurance of salvation, but it had *not* provided her with any intellectual resources to challenge the ideologies taught in her classes. The church's teaching had assumed a sharp divide between the sacred and secular realms, addressing itself solely to Sarah's religious life. As a result, over time she found herself absorbing the secular outlook taught in her classes. Her mental world was split, with religion strictly contained within the boundaries of worship and personal morality, while her views on everything else were run through a grid of naturalism and relativism.

"I may have started out picking up bits and pieces of a secular worldview to sprinkle on top of my Christian beliefs," Sarah explained. "But after I graduated and worked for Planned Parenthood, the pattern was reversed: My Christianity was reduced to a thin veneer over the core of a secular worldview. *It was almost like having a split personality.*" To use the categories described in the Introduction, her mind had absorbed the divided concepts of truth characteristic of Western culture: secular/sacred, fact/value, public/private. Though her faith was sincere, it was reduced to purely private experience, while public knowledge was defined in terms of secular naturalism.

Sarah's story is particularly dramatic, yet it illustrates a pattern that is more common than we might like to think. The fatal weakness in her faith was that she had accepted Christian doctrines strictly as individual items of belief: the deity of Christ, His virgin birth, His miracles, His resurrection from the dead—she could tick them off one by one. But she lacked any sense of how Christianity functions as a unified, overarching system of truth that applies to social issues, history, politics, anthropology, and all the other subject areas. In short, she lacked a Christian worldview. She held to Christianity as a collection of truths, but not as Truth.[3]

Only many years later, after a personal crisis, were Sarah's relativistic views finally challenged. "When Congress held hearings on partial-birth abortion, I was appalled. And I realized that if abortion was wrong at nine months, then it was wrong at eight months, and wrong at seven months, and six months— right back to the beginning." It was a shattering experience, and Sarah found she had to take apart her secular worldview plank by plank, and then begin painstakingly constructing a Christian worldview in its place. It was tough work, yet today she is discovering the joy of breaking out of the trap of the secular/sacred split, and seeing her faith come alive in areas where before she had not even known it applied. She is learning that Christianity is not just religious truth, it is total truth—covering all of reality.

DIVIDED MINDS

Like Sarah, many believers have absorbed the fact/value, public/private dichotomy, restricting their faith to the religious sphere while adopting whatever views are current in their professional or social circles. We probably all know of Christian teachers who uncritically accept the latest secular theories of education; Christian businessmen who run their operations by accepted secular management theories; Christian ministries that mirror the commercial world's marketing techniques; Christian families where the teenagers watch the same movies and listen to the same music as their nonbelieving friends. While sincere in their faith, they have absorbed their views on just about everything else by osmosis from the surrounding culture.

The problem was phrased succinctly by Harry Blamires in his classic book *The Christian Mind*. When I was a new Christian many years ago, Blamires's book was almost a fad item, and everyone walked around intoning its dramatic opening sentence: "There *is* no longer a Christian mind."[4]

What did Blamires mean? He was not saying that Christians are uneducated, backwoods hayseeds, though that remains a common stereotype in the secular world. A few years ago an infamous article in the *Washington Post* described conservative Christians as "poor, uneducated, and easily led."[5] Immediately the *Post* was overwhelmed with calls and faxes from Christians across the country, listing their advanced degrees and bank account balances!

But if that's not what Blamires meant, what *did* he mean? To say there is no Christian mind means that believers may be highly educated in terms of technical proficiency, and yet have no biblical worldview for interpreting the subject matter of their field. "We speak of 'the modern mind' and of 'the scientific mind,' using that word *mind* of a collectively accepted set of notions and attitudes," Blamires explains. But there is no "Christian mind"—no shared, biblically based set of assumptions on subjects like law, education, economics, politics, science, or the arts. As a moral being, the Christian follows the biblical ethic. As a spiritual being, he or she prays and attends worship services. "But as a *thinking* being, the modern Christian has succumbed to secularism," accepting "a frame of reference constructed by the secular mind and a set of criteria reflecting secular evaluations."[6] That is, when we enter the stream of discourse in our field or profession, we participate mentally as non-Christians, using the current concepts and categories, no matter what our private beliefs may be.

Living in the Washington, D.C., area, I have witnessed firsthand the growing numbers of believers working in politics today, which is an encouraging trend. But I can also say from experience that few hold an explicitly Christian political philosophy. As a congressional chief of staff once admitted, "I realize that I hold certain views because I'm politically conservative, *not* because I see how they're rooted in the Bible." He knew he should formulate a biblically based philosophy of government, but he simply didn't know how to proceed.

Similarly, through decades of writing on science and worldview, I have interacted with scientists who are deeply committed believers; yet few have crafted a biblically informed philosophy of science. In Christian ministries, I've met many who take great pains to make sure their *message* is biblical, but who never think to ask whether their *methods* are biblical. A journalism professor recently told me that even the best Christian journalists—sincere believers with outstanding professional skills—typically have no Christian theory of journalism. In popular culture, believers have constructed an entire parallel culture of artists and entertainers; yet even so, as Charlie Peacock laments, few "think Christianly" about art and aesthetics.[7] The phrase is borrowed from Blamires, and when I addressed a group of artists and musicians in Charlie's home, he showed me a shelf with half a dozen copies of Blamires's book—enough to lend out to several friends at once.

"Thinking Christianly" means understanding that Christianity gives the truth about the whole of reality, a perspective for interpreting every subject matter. Genesis tells us that God spoke the entire universe into being with His Word—what John 1:1 calls the *Logos*. The Greek word means not only Word but also reason or rationality, and the ancient Stoics used it to mean the rational structure of the universe. Thus the underlying structure of the entire universe reflects the mind of the Creator. There is no fact/value dichotomy in the scriptural account. Nothing has an autonomous or independent identity, separate from the will of the Creator. As a result, all creation must be interpreted in light of its relationship to God. In any subject area we study, we are discovering the laws or creation ordinances by which God structured the world.

As Scripture puts it, the universe speaks of God—"the heavens declare the glory of God" (Ps. 19:1)—because His character is reflected in the things He has made. This is sometimes referred to as "general" revelation because it speaks to everyone at all times, in contrast to the "special" revelation given in the Bible. As Jonathan Edwards explained, God communicates not only "by his voice to us in the Scriptures" but also in creation and in historical events. Indeed, "the whole creation of God preaches."[8] Yet it is possible for Christians to be deaf and blind to the message of general revelation, and part of learning to have the mind of Christ involves praying for the spiritual sensitivity to "hear" the preaching of creation.

The great historian of religion Martin Marty once said every religion serves two functions: First, it is a message of personal salvation, telling us how to get right with God; and second, it is a lens for interpreting the world. Historically, evangelicals have been good at the first function—at "saving souls." But they have not been nearly as good at helping people to interpret the world around them—at providing a set of interrelated concepts that function as a lens to give a biblical view of areas like science, politics, economics, or bioethics. As Marty puts it, evangelicals have typically "accented personal piety and individual salvation, leaving men to their own devices to interpret the world around them."

In fact, many no longer think it's even the *function* of Christianity to provide an interpretation of the world. Marty calls this the Modern Schism (in a book by that title), and he says we are living in the first time in history where Christianity has been boxed into the private sphere and has largely stopped speaking to the public sphere.[9]

"This internalization or privatization of religion is one of the most momentous changes that has ever taken place in Christendom," writes another historian, Sidney Mead.[10] As a result, our lives are often fractured and fragmented, with our faith firmly locked into the private realm of church and family, where it rarely has a chance to inform our life and work in the public realm. The aura of worship dissipates after Sunday, and we unconsciously absorb secular attitudes the rest of the week. We inhabit two separate "worlds," navigating a sharp divide between our religious life and ordinary life.

BIBLE SCHOOL DROP-OUTS

At the same time, most believers find this highly frustrating. We really *want* to integrate our faith into every aspect of life, including our profession. We want to be whole people—people of integrity (the word comes from the Latin word for "whole"). Not long ago, I met a recent convert who was agonizing over how to apply his newfound faith to his work as an art teacher. "I want my whole life to reflect my relationship with God," he told me. "I don't want my faith to be in one compartment and my art in another."

We would all agree with Dorothy Sayers, who said that if religion does not speak to our work lives, then it has nothing to say about what we do with the vast majority of our time—and no wonder people say religion is irrelevant! "How can anyone remain interested in a religion which seems to have no concern with nine-tenths of his life?"[11]

In the secular/sacred dualism, ordinary work is actually denigrated, while church work is elevated as more valuable. In his book *Roaring Lambs,* Bob Briner describes his student days at a Christian college, where the unspoken assumption was that the only way to *really* serve God was in full-time Christian work. Already knowing that he wanted a career in sports management, Briner writes, "I felt I was a sort of second-class campus citizen. My classmates who were preparing for the pulpit ministry or missionary service were the ones who were treated as if they would be doing the *real* work of the church. The rest of us were the supporting cast."

The underlying message was that people in ordinary professions might contribute their prayers and financial support, but that was about it. "Almost nothing in my church or collegiate experiences presented possibilities for a dynamic, involved Christian life outside the professional ministry," Briner concludes. "You heard about being salt and light, but no one told you how to do it."[12] Lip service was paid to the idea of dedicating your work to God, but all it seemed to mean was, *Do your best, and don't commit any obvious sins.*

The same secular/sacred dualism nearly snuffed out the creative talents of the founders of the whimsically funny Veggie Tales videos. Phil Vischer says he always knew he wanted to make movies, but "the implicit message I received growing up was that full-time ministry was the only valid Christian service. Young Christians were to aspire to be either ministers or missionaries." So he dutifully packed his bags and went off to Bible college to study for the ministry.

Yet the more he saw the powerful influence movies have on kids, the more he thought it was important to produce high-quality films. Finally he made up his mind: "I figured God could use a filmmaker or two, regardless of what anyone else said." Dropping out of Bible college, he and his friend Mike Nawrocki started a video company. As their former classmates turned into pastors and youth ministers, they turned into the voices of Bob the Tomato and Larry the Cucumber.[13] The videos have become immensely popular, with their biblical messages and quirky humor. Yet if these two Bible school drop-outs had not broken free from the secular/sacred mentality and decided that Christians have a valid calling in the field of filmmaking, their talents may well have been lost to the church. Every member of the Body of Christ has been gifted for the benefit of the whole, and when those gifts are suppressed, we all lose out.

The pervasiveness of the secular/sacred split is less surprising when we realize that many pastors and teachers have absorbed it themselves. A school superintendent once told me that most educators define "a Christian teacher" strictly in terms of personal behavior: things like setting a good example and showing concern for students. Almost none define it in terms of conveying a biblical worldview on the subjects they teach, whether literature, science, social studies, or the arts. In other words, they are concerned about being a Christian *in* their work, but they don't think in terms of having a biblical framework *on* the work itself.

In many Christian schools, the typical strategy is to inject a few narrowly defined "religious" elements into the classroom, like prayer and Bible memorization—and then teach exactly the same things as the secular schools. The curriculum merely spreads a layer of spiritual devotion over the subject matter like icing on a cake, while the content itself stays the same.

SUBTLE TEMPTATION

The same pattern holds all the way up to the highest academic levels. "Christians in higher education are strongly, though subtly, tempted to compartmentalize our faith," says a sociology professor after teaching for many years at a Christian college. Religion is considered relevant to special areas like church and campus religious activities, he says. "But when we are teaching and doing our research, we usually center our attention upon the theories, concepts, and other subject matter that are conventional in our respective disciplines."

Here we see the danger of the secular/sacred split: It concedes the "theories, concepts, and other subject matter" in our field to nonbelievers. Christians have essentially accepted a trade-off: So long as we're allowed to hold our Bible studies and prayer meetings, we've turned over the *content* of the academic fields to the secularists.

I encountered a particularly egregious example many years ago when I interviewed a physics professor for an article I was writing. He was a sponsor for a well-known campus ministry at a large secular university, so I asked him to explain a Christian perspective on his field, and especially on the "new physics"—relativity theory and quantum mechanics. Now, claims and counterclaims have been tossed back and forth about the supposedly revolutionary impact of the new physics—that it demolished the Newtonian worldview which had held sway for three hundred years, that it destroyed determinism and made room for free will, that it undercut materialism, and much more. In fact, many popular books on the subject even claim that quantum mechanics confirms Eastern metaphysics (the classic example is *The Tao of Physics*[14]). As a young writer, I was intrigued to learn how a Christian professor would evaluate the wide-ranging philosophical implications being drawn from the new physics.

To my dismay, the professor had nothing to offer. Physics and faith are completely separate domains, he told me. The exact words he used are branded into my memory: "Quantum mechanics is like auto mechanics. It has nothing to do with my faith."

This man was deeply involved in campus ministry, but obviously he kept his faith and his science in separate, parallel tracks—running along side by side like train rails that never touch or intersect. He was a Christian and he was a physicist—but he did not have a Christian worldview that brought the two together.[15]

Clearly, developing a Christian mind involves much more than merely earning an advanced degree. Many Christians with Ph.D.'s have simply absorbed a two-track approach to their subject, treating science or sociology or history as though it consisted of religiously neutral knowledge, where biblical truth has nothing important to say. In these areas, the attitude seems to be that God's Word is not a light to our paths after all, and that we must simply accommodate to whatever the secular experts decree.[16] God's Word is robbed of its power to transform our minds, and we become inwardly divided, deprived of the joy of living whole and integrated lives.

ENLIGHTENMENT IDOL

Secularists reinforce this split mentality by claiming that *their* theory does not reflect any particular philosophy—that it is just "the way all reasonable people think." They thus promote their own views as unbiased and rational, suitable for the public square, while denouncing religious views as biased or prejudiced. This tactic has often cowed Christians into being defensive about our faith, which in turn has taken a steep toll on our effectiveness in the broader culture.

The mistake lies in thinking there *is* such a thing as theories that are unbiased or neutral, unaffected by any religious and philosophical assumptions. We know, of course, that in the *sacred* realm, each group has its own religious views—Christian, Jewish, Muslim, New Age, and so on. But in the *secular* realm, it is often thought that we all have access to neutral knowledge where religious and philosophical values are not supposed to interfere.

The irony is that this ideal is itself a product of a particular philosophical tradition. The notion that it is possible to strip the mind of all prior assumptions and religious commitments in order to get down to the bare, unvarnished truths of "reason" comes from the Enlightenment. It was expressed most forcefully in the seventeenth century by René Descartes, often considered the first modern philosopher. The way to find truth, Descartes said, was to strip the mind of everything that can possibly be doubted until we finally reach a bedrock of truths that cannot possibly be doubted. He believed that he himself had dug deep enough to hit that infallible bedrock in his famous *cogito:* "I think, therefore I am." After all, even when we are doubting everything, we are still thinking, and therefore the surest thing we can know is the existence of the thinking subject.

The idea emerged that by a method of systematic doubt, the human mind—or Reason (often capitalized)—could attain to godlike objectivity and certainty. In one of my college philosophy courses, the professor liked to define objectivity as "the way God sees things." Though not a believer, his point was that true objectivity could be attained only by a Being who transcends this world and knows everything as it truly is. The hubris of the Enlightenment lay in thinking that Reason was just such a transcendent power, providing infallible knowledge. Reason became nothing less than an idol, taking the place of God as the source of absolute Truth.

Ironically, Descartes himself was a devout Catholic; he was so certain that God had revealed to him the irrefutable logic of the *cogito* that he vowed to make a pilgrimage to the shrine of Our Lady of Loreto in Italy—which he did a few years later. Thus he is a tragic example of how one may be a sincere Christian and yet promote a philosophy that is certainly *not* Christian. Descartes helped to establish a form of rationalism that treated Reason not merely as the human ability to think rationally but as an infallible and autonomous source of truth. Reason came to be seen as a storehouse of truths independent of any religion or philosophy.

Two Cities

The Enlightenment project was in sharp contrast to the classic Christian tradition, which suggested a far humbler and more realistic view of knowledge (or epistemology). It recognized that what we count as knowledge is profoundly shaped by our spiritual condition. This insight was best expressed by St. Augustine in his image of two cities: the City of God and the City of Man. Augustine wasn't speaking about the divide between church and state, as some have thought; he was talking about two systems of thought and allegiance. We help to build the City of God when our actions are animated and directed by the love of God, offered up to His service. We build the City of Man whenever our actions are motivated by self-love, serving sinful purposes.

Applied to the life of the mind, the image of two cities means we all come to the table with a spiritual motivation already in place, which affects what we will accept as true. Far from being blank slates, our minds are colored by our spiritual stance—either for God or against Him. As Romans 1 puts it, we either worship and serve the true God or we worship and serve created things (idols). Humans are inherently religious beings, created to be in relationship with God—and if they reject God, they don't stop being religious; they simply find some other ultimate principle upon which to base their lives.

Often that idol is something concrete, like financial security or professional success; in other cases, it may be an ideology or set of beliefs that substitutes for religion. Whatever form the idolatry takes, according to Romans 1:18 those who worship idols *actively suppress* their knowledge of God, while seeking out substitute gods. They are far from religiously neutral.

Of course, Christianity is not deterministic: It teaches that, by God's grace, people may be enlightened by His truth to bow before Him, so that they are moved from one side to the other—transferred from the kingdom of darkness to the kingdom of Christ (see Col. 1:13). That's called conversion. Yet at any particular point in time, we are either on one side or the other. We are interpreting our experience in the light either of divine revelation or of some competing system of thought. Our calling as Christians is to progressively clean out all the "idols" remaining in our thought life, so that we may pursue every aspect of our lives as citizens of the City of God.[17]

In recent decades, this classic Christian view has received support from what may seem a surprising source. Contemporary philosophy of science has rejected the older, positivistic definition of knowledge, which treated scientists in white coats as though they were magically freed from preconceptions and prior beliefs the moment they entered the laboratory. Instead philosophers are much quicker today to acknowledge the human factor in deciding what counts as knowledge—to admit that it is impossible to approach the facts from a purely neutral philosophical stance. We all come to the scientific enterprise as whole persons, bringing into the laboratory a panoply of prior experiences, theoretical assumptions, personal beliefs, ambitions, and socioeconomic interests. These preconceptions color virtually every aspect of the scientific endeavor: what we consider worth studying, what we expect to find, where we look, and how we interpret the results.[18]

"All facts are theory-laden," is a popular slogan in philosophy of science today. A bit of an exaggeration, perhaps, but it makes the point that even what we choose to consider a "fact" is influenced by the theories we bring to the table. We always process data in light of some theoretical framework that we have adopted for understanding the world.

ABSOLUTELY DIVINE

The upshot is that no system of thought is a product purely of Reason—because Reason is not a repository of infallible, religiously autonomous truths, as Descartes and the other rationalists thought. Instead, it is simply a human capacity, the ability to reason from premises. The important question, then, is what a person accepts as ultimate premises, for they shape everything that follows.

If you press any set of ideas back far enough, eventually you reach some starting point. Something has to be taken as self-existent—the ultimate reality and source of everything else. There's no reason for it to exist; it just "is." For the materialist, the ultimate reality is matter, and everything is reduced to material constituents. For the pantheist, the ultimate reality is a spiritual force or substratum, and the goal of meditation is to reconnect with that spiritual oneness. For the doctrinaire Darwinist, biology is ultimate, and everything, even religion and morality, is reduced to a product of Darwinian processes. For the empiricist, all knowledge is traceable ultimately to sense data, and anything not known by sensation is unreal.

And so on. Every system of thought begins with some ultimate principle. If it does not begin with God, it will begin with some dimension of creation—the material, the spiritual, the biological, the empirical, or whatever. Some aspect of created reality will be "absolutized" or put forth as the ground and source of everything else—the uncaused cause, the self-existent. To use religious language, this ultimate principle functions as the divine, if we define that term to mean the one thing upon which all else depends for existence. This starting assumption has to be accepted by faith, not by prior reasoning. (Otherwise it is not really the ultimate starting point for all reasoning—something else is, and we have to dig deeper and start there instead.)

In this sense, we could say that every alternative to Christianity is a religion. It may not involve ritual or worship services, yet it identifies some principle or force in creation as the self-existent cause of everything else. Even nonbelievers hold to some ultimate ground of existence, which functions as an idol or false god. This is why the "Bible writers always address their reader as though they already believe in God or some God surrogate," explains philosopher Roy Clouser.[19] Faith is a universal human function, and if it is not directed toward God it will be directed toward something else.

"The need for religion appears to be hard-wired in the human animal," writes philosopher John Gray (though as an atheist he bemoans the fact). "Certainly the behaviour of secular humanists supports this hypothesis. Atheists are usually just as emotionally engaged as believers. Quite commonly, they are more intellectually rigid."[20] In short, it is not as though Christians have faith, while secularists base their convictions purely on facts and reason. Secularism itself is based on ultimate beliefs, just as much as Christianity is. Some part of creation—usually matter or nature—functions in the role of the divine. So the question is not which view is religious and which is purely rational; the question is which is true and which is false.

This is what Augustine meant by his image of two cities. Ever since the Fall, the human race has been divided into two distinct groups—those who follow God and submit their minds to His truth, and those who set up an idol of some kind and then organize their thinking to rationalize their worship of that idol. Over time, as people's ultimate commitments shape the choices they make, their perspective is inevitably molded to support those choices. A false god leads to the formation of a false worldview.

This is why Christians cannot complacently abandon so-called *secular* subject areas to nonbelievers—just so long as they grant us some restricted *sacred* area where we are free to sing hymns and read the Bible. Instead we must identify and critique the dominant intellectual idols, and then construct biblically based alternatives.

ARISTOTLE'S SCREWDRIVER

This is not to deny that Christians and non-Christians often agree across a wide range of subject matter. Nonbelievers may even be *more* capable at constructing buildings, running banks, performing surgery, or writing computer software. The reason is grounded in the doctrine of creation: We are all made in God's image, in order to live in God's world, and our faculties were designed to give us real knowledge of that world. Thus in many fields there can be a significant range of agreement between believers and nonbelievers.

In addition, the Bible teaches the doctrine of common grace. Whereas *special grace* refers to salvation, *common grace* means God's providential care— the way He actively upholds all of creation. God "sends rain on the just and on the unjust," Scripture says (Matt. 5:45). That is, His gifts are given even to nonbelievers, including the intellectual gifts of knowledge and insight. That's why Jesus could say that even sinners "know how to give good gifts to [their] children" (Matt. 7:11) and can be good parents. He could also chide His opponents for failing to interpret the signs of the times: Since they were able to interpret the signs of impending weather, He expected them to be able to discern the meanings of history as well (Matt. 16:1-4). Thus, the Bible itself teaches that nonbelievers are capable of effective functioning in the world, including cognitive functioning.

Yet as soon as we try to *explain* what we know, then our spiritual and philosophical assumptions come into play. Take, for example, mathematics. You might not think there is a Christian view of mathematics, but there is. Certainly everyone, believer or not, will agree that 5+7=12. But when you ask how to *justify* mathematical knowledge, people split into several competing camps.

The ancient Greeks, standing at the dawn of Western history, are famous for having discovered Euclidean geometry. But they did not believe the material world itself exhibited a precise mathematical order, because they regarded matter as independently existing, recalcitrant stuff that would never completely "obey" mathematical rules. So they kept mathematics locked up in an abstract Platonic "heaven."

By contrast, most of the early modern scientists were Christians; they believed that matter was *not* preexisting but had come from the hand of God. Thus it had no power to resist His will but would "obey" the rules He had laid down—with mathematical precision. Historian R. G. Collingwood writes, "The possibility of an applied mathematics is an expression, in terms of natural science, of the Christian belief that nature is the creation of an omnipotent God."[21]

Since my father is a mathematics professor, I like to remind him of Collingwood's words. "The very *existence* of your field," I tell him, "is a product of the Christian worldview."

Today, however, most philosophers no longer even regard mathematics as a body of truths. The dominant philosophy of mathematics treats it as a social construction, like the game of baseball. "Three strikes and you're out" is an arbitrary rule. It's not true or false; it's just the way we choose to play the game. By the same token, mathematical rules are regarded as just the way we play the game.[22]

Even American schoolchildren are now taught this postmodern view of math. A popular middle school curriculum says students should learn that "mathematics is man-made, that it is arbitrary, and good solutions are arrived at by consensus among those who are considered expert."[23] Man-made?

Arbitrary? Clearly, our public schools have waded deeply into the murky waters of postmodernism.

Moreover, if math is arbitrary, then there are no wrong answers, just different perspectives. In Minnesota, teachers are instructed to be tolerant of "multiple mathematical worldviews."[24] In New Mexico, I met a young man who had recently graduated from high school, where a mathematics teacher had labeled him a "bigot" for thinking it was important to get the right answer. As long as students worked together in a group and achieved consensus, the teacher insisted, the outcome was acceptable.

This means that even the simplest, most universal form of knowledge—mathematics—is subject to sometimes radically differing worldview interpretations. Clearly, the impact of worldview will grow even larger as we move up the scale into more complex fields, like biology, economics, law, or ethics.[25]

The danger is that if Christians do not *consciously* develop a biblical approach to the subject, then we will *un*consciously absorb some other philosophical approach. A set of ideas for interpreting the world is like a philosophical toolbox, stuffed with terms and concepts. If Christians do not develop their own tools of analysis, then when some issue comes up that they want to understand, they'll reach over and borrow *someone else's* tools—whatever concepts are generally accepted in their professional field or in the culture at large. But when Christians do that, Os Guinness writes, they don't realize that "they are borrowing not an isolated tool but a whole philosophical toolbox laden with tools which have their own particular bias to every problem." They may even end up absorbing an entire set of alien principles without even realizing it—like Sarah did in our opening story. Using tools of analysis that have non-Christian assumptions embedded in them is "like wearing someone else's glasses or walking in someone else's shoes. *The tools shape the user.*"[26]

In other words, not only do we fail to be salt and light to a lost culture, but we ourselves may end up being shaped by that culture.

BIBLICAL TOOLBOX

What is the antidote to the secular/sacred divide? How do we make sure our toolbox contains biblically based conceptual tools for every issue we encounter? We must begin by being utterly convinced that there *is* a biblical perspective on everything—not just on spiritual matters. The Old Testament tells us repeatedly that "The fear of the LORD is the beginning of wisdom" (Ps. 111:10; Prov. 1:7; 9:10; 15:33). Similarly, the New Testament teaches that in Christ are "all the treasures of wisdom and knowledge" (Col. 2:3). We often interpret these verses to mean spiritual wisdom only, but the text places no limitation on the term. "Most people have a tendency to read these passages as though they say that the fear of the Lord is the foundation of *religious* knowledge," writes Clouser. "But the fact is that they make a very radical claim— the claim that somehow *all* knowledge depends upon religious truth."[27]

This claim is easier to grasp when we realize that Christianity is not unique in this regard. All belief systems work the same way. As we saw earlier, *whatever* a system puts forth as self-existing is essentially what it regards as divine. And that religious commitment functions as the controlling principle for everything that follows. The fear of some "god" is the beginning of every proposed system of knowledge.

Once we understand how first principles work, then it becomes clear that all truth must begin with God. The only self-existent reality is God, and everything else depends on Him for its origin and continued existence. Nothing exists apart from His will; nothing falls outside the scope of the central turning points in biblical history: Creation, Fall, and Redemption.

Creation

The Christian message does not begin with "accept Christ as your Savior"; it begins with "in the beginning God created the heavens and the earth." The Bible teaches that God is the sole source of the entire created order. No other gods compete with Him; no natural forces exist on their own; nothing receives its nature or existence from another source. Thus His word, or laws, or creation ordinances give the world its order and structure. God's creative word is the source of the laws of *physical* nature, which we study in the natural sciences. It is also the source of the laws of *human* nature—the principles of morality (ethics), of justice (politics), of creative enterprise (economics), of aesthetics (the arts), and even of clear thinking (logic). That's why Psalm 119:91 says, "all things are your servants." There is no philosophically or spiritually neutral subject matter.

Fall

The universality of Creation is matched by the universality of the Fall. The Bible teaches that all parts of creation—including our minds—are caught up in a great rebellion against the Creator. Theologians call this the "noetic" effect of the Fall (the effect on the mind), and it subverts our ability to understand the world apart from God's regenerating grace. Scripture is replete with warnings that idolatry or willful disobedience toward God makes humans "blind" or "deaf." Paul writes, "The god of this world has blinded the minds of the unbelievers, to keep them from seeing the light of the gospel" (2 Cor. 4:4). Sin literally "darkens" the understanding (Eph. 4:18).[28]

Of course, nonbelievers still function in God's world, bear God's image, and are upheld by God's common grace, which means they are capable of uncovering isolated segments of genuine knowledge. And Christians should welcome those insights. All truth is God's truth, as the church fathers used to say; and they urged Christians to "plunder the Egyptians" by appropriating the best of secular scholarship, showing how it actually fits best within a biblical worldview. There may even be occasions when Christians are mistaken on some point while nonbelievers get it right. Nevertheless, the overall *systems* of thought constructed by nonbelievers will be false—for if the system is not built on biblical truth, then it will be built on some other ultimate principle. Even individual truths will be seen through the distorting lens of a false worldview. As a result, a Christian approach to any field needs to be both critical and constructive. We cannot simply borrow from the results of secular scholarship as though that were spiritually neutral territory discovered by people whose minds are completely open and objective—that is, as though the Fall had never happened.

Redemption

Finally, Redemption is as comprehensive as Creation and Fall. God does not save only our souls, while leaving our minds to function on their own. He redeems the whole person. Conversion is meant to give new direction to our thoughts, emotions, will, and habits. Paul urges us to offer up our entire selves to God as "living sacrifices," so that we will not be "conformed to this world" but be "transformed by the renewal of [our] minds" (Rom. 12:1-2). When we are redeemed, *all things* are made new (2 Cor. 5:17). God promises to give us "a new heart, and a new spirit" (Ezek. 36:26), animating our entire character with new life.

This explains why the Bible treats sin primarily as a matter of turning away from God and serving other gods, and only secondarily in terms of lists of specific immoral behaviors. The first commandment is, after all, the *first* commandment—the rest follows only *after* we are straight about whom or what it is that we are worshiping. By the same token, redemption consists primarily in casting out our mental idols and turning back to the true God. And when we do that, we will experience His transforming power renewing every aspect of our lives. To talk about a Christian worldview is simply another way of saying that when we are redeemed, our entire outlook on life is re-centered on God and re-built on His revealed truth.

READ THE DIRECTIONS

How do we go about constructing a Christian worldview? The key passage is the creation account in Genesis, because that's where we are taken back to the beginning to learn what God's original purpose was in creating the human race. With the entrance of sin, humans went off course, lost their way, wandered off the path. But when we accept Christ's salvation, we are put back on the right path and are restored to our original purpose. Redemption is not just about being saved *from* sin, it is also about being saved *to* something—to resume the task for which we were originally created.

And what was that task? In Genesis, God gives what we might call the first job description: "Be fruitful and multiply and fill the earth and subdue it." The first phrase, "be fruitful and multiply," means to develop the *social* world: build families, churches, schools, cities, governments, laws. The second phrase, "subdue the earth," means to harness the *natural* world: plant crops, build bridges, design computers, compose music. This passage is sometimes called the Cultural Mandate because it tells us that our original purpose was to create cultures, build civilizations—nothing less.[29]

This means that our vocation or professional work is not a second-class activity, something we do just to put food on the table. It is the high calling for which we were originally created. The way we serve a Creator God is by being creative with the talents and gifts He has given us. We could even say that we are called to continue God's own creative work. Of course, we do not create from nothing, ex nihilo, as God did; our job is to develop the powers and potentials that God originally built into the creation—using wood to build houses, cotton to make clothes, or silicon to make computer chips. Though modern social and economic institutions are not explicitly referred to in the Garden of Eden, their biblical justification is rooted in the Cultural Mandate.

In the first six days of the Genesis narrative, God forms then fills the physical universe—the sky with the sun and moon, the sea with its swimming creatures, the earth with its land animals. Then the narrative pauses, as though to emphasize that the next step will be the culmination of all that has gone before. This is the only stage in the creative process when God announces His plan ahead of time, when the members of the Trinity consult with one another: Let Us make a creature in Our image, who will represent Us and carry on Our work on earth (see Gen. 1:26). Then God creates the first human couple, to have dominion over the earth and govern it in His name.

It is obvious from the text that humans are not supreme rulers, autonomously free to do whatever they wish. Their dominion is a delegated authority: They are representatives of the Supreme Ruler, called to reflect His holy and loving care for creation. They are to "cultivate" the earth—a word that has the same root as "culture." The way we express the image of God is by being creative and building cultures.

This was God's purpose when He originally created human beings, and it remains His purpose for us today. God's original plan was not abrogated by the Fall. Sin has corrupted every aspect of human nature, but it has not made us less than human. We are not animals. We still reflect, "through a glass, darkly" (1 Cor. 13:12, KJV), our original nature as God's image-bearers. Even nonbelievers carry out the Cultural Mandate: They "multiply and fill the earth"—which is to say, they get married, raise families, start schools, run businesses. And they "cultivate the earth"—they fix cars, write books, study nature, invent new gadgets.

After I spoke at a conference, a young woman said to me, "When you talk about the Cultural Mandate, you're not talking about anything distinctively Christian; these are things everybody does." But that's precisely the point: Genesis is telling us our true nature, the things we can't help doing, the way God created everyone to function. Our purpose is precisely to fulfill our God-given nature.

The Fall did not destroy our original calling, but only made it more difficult. Our work is now marked by sorrow and hard labor. In Genesis 3:16 and 17, the Hebrew uses the same word for the "labor" of childbearing and the "labor" of growing food. The text suggests that the two central tasks of adulthood—raising the next generation and making a living—will be fraught with the pain of living in a fallen and fractured world. All our efforts will be twisted and misdirected by sin and selfishness.

Yet when God redeems us, He releases us from the guilt and power of sin and restores us to our full humanity, so that we can once again carry out the tasks for which we were created. Because of Christ's redemption on the cross, our work takes on a new aspect as well—it becomes a means of sharing in His redemptive purposes. In cultivating creation, we not only recover our original purpose but also bring a redemptive force to reverse the evil and corruption introduced by the Fall. We offer our gifts to God to participate in making His Kingdom come, His will be done. With hearts and minds renewed, our work can now be inspired by love for God and delight in His service.

The lesson of the Cultural Mandate is that our sense of fulfillment depends on engaging in creative, constructive work. The ideal human existence is not eternal leisure or an endless vacation—or even a monastic retreat into prayer and meditation—but creative effort expended for the glory of God and the benefit of others. Our calling is not just to "get to heaven" but also to cultivate the earth, not just to "save souls" but also to serve God through our work. For

God Himself is engaged not only in the work of salvation (special grace) but also in the work of preserving and developing His creation (common grace). When we obey the Cultural Mandate, we participate in the work of God Himself, as agents of His common grace.

This is the rich content that should come to mind when we hear the word *Redemption.* The term does not refer only to a one-time conversion event. It means entering upon a lifelong quest to devote our skills and talents to building things that are beautiful and useful, while fighting the forces of evil and sin that oppress and distort the creation. *How Now Shall We Live?* added a fourth category—Creation, Fall, Redemption, *and Restoration*—to emphasize the theme of ongoing vocation. Some theologians suggest the fourth category should be *Glorification,* to call to mind our final goal of living in the new heavens and new earth, for which our work here is a preparation. Whatever term we use, being a Christian means embarking on a lifelong process of growth in grace, both in our personal lives (sanctification) and in our vocations (cultural renewal). The new heavens and new earth will be a continuation of the creation we know now—purified by fire, but recognizably the same, just as Jesus was recognizable in His resurrection body. As C. S. Lewis puts it at the end of his Narnia tales, we have started a great adventure story that will never end. It is the "Great Story which no one on earth has read: which goes on for ever: in which every chapter is better than the one before."[30]

BORN TO GROW UP

In many churches, the message of justification—how to get right with God—is preached over and over again. But much less is said about sanctification—how to live *after* you're converted. In the Lutheran churches where I grew up, it seemed we were always fighting the Reformation over again: Every sermon came back to justification by faith. Shortly after my conversion, I remarked in frustration to my great-aunt Alice, a devout and intelligent woman, that we really didn't need to hear the basic message of salvation by faith *every* Sunday.

Her eyes sparkled at me behind wire-rimmed glasses, and she replied patiently, "But we always need to be reminded, dear, because grace is so contrary to our human tendencies."

She was right, of course, but it remains true that most churches are strong on teaching about conversion but weak on teaching about how to live after conversion. Think of an analogy: In one sense, our physical birth is the most important event in our lives, because it is the beginning of everything else. Yet in another sense, our birth is the *least* important event, because it is merely the starting point. If someone were to mention every day how great it was to be born, we would find that rather strange. Once we have come into the world, the important task is to grow and mature. By the same token, being born again is the necessary first step in our spiritual lives, yet we should not focus our message constantly on how to be saved.[31] It is crucial for churches to lead people forward into spiritual maturity, equipping the saints to carry out the mission God has given us in the Cultural Mandate.

Each of us has a role to play in cultivating the creation and working out God's norms for a just and humane society. By sheer necessity, of course, a large percentage of our time is devoted to running businesses, teaching schools, publishing newspapers, playing in orchestras, and everything else needed to keep a civilization thriving. Even those who work in "full-time Christian service" still need to clean the house, take care of the kids, and mow the lawn. It is imperative for us to understand that in carrying out these tasks, we are not doing inferior or second-tier work for the Kingdom. Instead we are agents of God's common grace, doing His work in the world.

Martin Luther liked to say that our occupations are God's "masks"—His way of caring for creation in a hidden manner through human means. In our work, we are God's hands, God's eyes, God's feet. There are times, says the Lutheran writer Gene Edward Veith, when God works directly and miraculously, as when He fed the Israelites manna from heaven. But ordinarily He feeds people through the myriad workers in agriculture, transportation, food processing, and retailing. Sometimes God may heal the sick miraculously, as Jesus did in the New Testament. But He works just as surely through the work of doctors, nurses, and health care specialists. At times God may rout an enemy army miraculously, as He did in the book of Judges. But in everyday life, He protects us from evil by the means of police officers, attorneys, and judges— and from outside enemies by the military. He raises children through parents, teachers, pastors, and soccer coaches. Even nonbelievers can be "masks" of God, avenues of His providential love and care.[32]

The metaphor of God's "mask" presses home the fact that our vocation is not something *we* do for God—which would put the burden on us to perform and achieve. Instead, it is a way we participate in *God's* work. For God Himself is engaged not only in the work of salvation but also in the work of preserving and maintaining His creation.

Understanding this profound truth also helps prevent a triumphalistic attitude. I have encountered people who are averse to the concept of Christian worldview because they think it means trying to take over the world and impose our beliefs, top down, on everyone else. This is when we must remind them (and ourselves) that God's means of salvation was, after all, the cross. He came in humility and human weakness, even submitting to death at the hands of sinners. In a fallen world, we too may pay a price for being faithful to God's calling. If we stand up for what is right against injustice, we may not be as successful in our careers, or win public and professional recognition, or earn as much money as we might have. Those who follow Christ may end up sharing in His suffering. Luther emphasized these themes in his "theology of the cross,"[33] which can help us to guard against triumphalism, pride, and self-righteousness.

By God's grace, we *can* make a significant difference within our sphere of influence—but only as we "crucify" our craving for success, power, and public acclaim. "If anyone would come after me," Jesus said, "let him deny himself and take up his cross daily and follow me" (Luke 9:23). If we long to be given the mind of Christ, we must first be willing to submit to the pattern of suffering He modeled for us. We should expect the process of developing a Christian worldview to be a difficult and painful struggle—first inwardly, as we uproot the idols in our own thought life, and then outwardly, as we face the hostility of a fallen and unbelieving world. Our strength for the task must come from spiritual union with Christ, recognizing that suffering is the route to being conformed to Him and remade into His image.

A PERSONAL ODYSSEY

To flesh out the theme of Christian worldview on a personal level, I'd like to tell my own conversion story, and then the stories of others who have applied a Christian perspective—often with revolutionary impact. To some people, *worldview* may be a stuffy academic-sounding term that conjures up images of tweedy professors and dusty lecture halls. When *How Now Shall We Live?* was published, Prison Fellowship kicked off the publicity campaign with a conference where one of the invited speakers was a television producer, who seemed a bit discomfited about speaking at a *worldview* conference. I had suggested that she speak along the lines of "A Christian Framework for Popular Culture"—and throughout her presentation she made dismissive, almost mocking comments about "frameworks" and "worldviews" and "perspectives," with audible scare quotes around the words, as though that were something for nerds with plastic pencil guards in their pockets. Certainly not the thing for an *artiste!*

I was scheduled to give my testimony the next morning, so I stayed up half the night completely recasting my personal story in order to emphasize that *worldview* is not something abstract and academic, but intensely personal. Our worldview is the way we answer the core questions of life that everyone has to struggle with: What are we here for? What is ultimate truth? Is there anything worth living for?

I began asking these questions in a serious way myself as a teenager. Since I had grown up in a Scandinavian Lutheran home and attended Lutheran elementary school, I had a good background in knowing *what* Christianity teaches. But I came to realize I didn't know *why* it was true.

Like many teenagers, I was influenced in part by non-Christian friends, particularly one girl who was Jewish. We both played violin in the school orchestra; we attended music camps together; and over time, I came to realize that *she* was Jewish because of her ethnic background and because she respected her parents . . . and in the same way, *I* was Christian because of *my* family background and because I wanted to please my parents. It struck me that if the same motivation led to contrary results, then obviously it was not an adequate epistemological principle.

I didn't quite think of it in those terms, of course. But I did realize that I had no reason for believing Christianity was true over against the other belief systems I was encountering.

When I began asking questions of my parents and pastors, the typical response, unfortunately, was a patronizing pat on the head. One pastor told me, "Don't worry, we all have doubts sometimes." No one seemed to grasp that I was not merely troubled by psychological "doubts" but had stepped outside the circle of faith and was questioning the truth of the whole system.

Manifesto of Unbelief

Failing to find answers, I eventually took a very significant step: I decided that the most intellectually honest course would be to reject my faith—and then to analyze it objectively alongside all the other major religions and philosophies, in order to decide which one was really true. A pretty ambitious project for a sixteen-year-old! Yet I began visiting the high school library and pulling out books from the philosophy shelf and struggling through them. I didn't have the background to understand much of the material, but I thought this must be the place where people discussed the Big Questions—questions about Truth and the Meaning of Life.

I want to emphasize that this was not merely an academic study, but a very dark and difficult period of my life. People who grow up outside the church may not know what they are missing. But I'd had a genuine faith, even though it was only a child's faith: I knew that God created me, that He loved me, that He had a wonderful purpose for my life. These principles seem very simple—until you reject them. Then suddenly I became acutely aware that I had no answers to the most basic questions: Where did I come from? Was life just a

chance accident of blind forces? Did it have any purpose? Were there any principles so true and so real that I could build my life on them?

Eventually I embraced relativism and subjectivism and several of the other
popular "isms" of modern culture. For I was determined to be ruthlessly honest about the logical consequences of unbelief. If there is no God, then what
can be the basis for objective or universal Truth? I realized that it is impossible to step outside our limited experience—our insignificantly small slot in the
vast scope of the history of the universe—in order to gain access to universal
knowledge, valid for all times and places.

And if there is no God, then what can be the basis for universally valid
moral standards? Once, when a classmate described someone's action as
"wrong," I shook my head and began arguing that we cannot know right or
wrong in any ultimate sense.

Eventually I began to wonder whether I could even be sure about any reality outside my own head. I began doodling little cartoons of the entire world
as nothing more than a thought bubble in my mind. When I graduated from
high school, I wrote a senior paper on the topic of "Why I Am Not a
Christian." Later I would discover that Bertrand Russell had written a famous
essay by that title (which I had not read yet)—but this was my own manifesto
of unbelief.

Like a Swiss Farmer

It was a few years later, when I was attending school in Germany and studying violin at the Heidelberg Conservatory, that I stumbled across L'Abri in
Switzerland, the residential ministry of Francis Schaeffer. I was stunned by this
place. It was the first time I had ever encountered Christians who actually
answered my questions—who gave reasons and arguments for the truth of
Christianity instead of simply urging me to have faith. When I arrived, the most
obvious thing that struck me was that most of the guests were not even
Christian. The place was crowded with hippies sporting long hair, beards, and
bell-bottom jeans. At the time, it was extremely rare to discover Christian ministries capable of crossing the countercultural divide to reach alienated young
people, and my curiosity was sparked. Who *were* these Christians?

Schaeffer himself used to strike people as somewhat odd, with his goatee
and knickers. (Though when you were actually at L'Abri, it didn't seem odd at
all: After all, this was the Alps—and he dressed like a Swiss farmer.) But when
he opened his mouth and began to speak, people were transfixed: Here was a
Christian talking about modern philosophy, quoting the existentialists, analyzing worldview themes in the lyrics of Led Zeppelin, explaining the music of

John Cage and the paintings of Jackson Pollock. You must remember that this was in an era when Christian college students were not even allowed to go to Disney movies—yet here he was, discussing films by Bergman and Fellini.[34]

Seeing Christians who engaged with the intellectual and cultural world was a complete novelty. In fact, it was such a novelty that I was afraid that I might make a decision for Christianity based on emotion instead of genuine conviction, and so, after only one month, I returned to the States. (To be honest, I *fled* back home.) And I thought, "I'm going to test these ideas in my college philosophy classes, and see how well they stand up in a secular university setting."

The most dramatic response came almost immediately. Signing up for my first philosophy course, I discovered it was a huge introductory class, with some three hundred students. Pretty intimidating. For the first major assignment, I took out my copy of Schaeffer's *Escape from Reason* and wove some of its themes into my paper. A week or so later, the professor said, "I have your papers to hand back . . . but first I would like to read one of them to the entire class."

It was my paper.

Needless to say, I was astonished. And even more so when the professor went on to say, "I have never seen such mature thought in an undergraduate." Of course, it wasn't really *my* thought—it was the Christian worldview analysis I had been learning through L'Abri.[35] Again and again, I tested these ideas in my university classes, and I saw that Christianity really does have the intellectual resources to stand up in a secular academic setting.

God Wins

While still at L'Abri, I had once accosted another student, demanding that he explain why he had converted to Christianity. A pale, thin young man with a strong South African accent, he responded simply, "They shot down all my arguments."

I continued gazing at him somewhat quizzically, expecting something more, well, dramatic. "It's not always a big emotional experience, you know," he said with an apologetic smile. "I just came to see that a better case could be made for Christianity than for any of the other ideas I came here with." It was the first time I had encountered someone whose conversion had been strictly intellectual, and little did I know at the time that my own conversion would be similar.

Back in the States, as I tested out Schaeffer's ideas in the classroom, I was also reading works by C. S. Lewis, G. K. Chesterton, Os Guinness, James Sire, and other apologists. But inwardly, I also had a young person's hunger for reality, and one day I picked up David Wilkerson's *The Cross and the Switchblade.* Now, *here* was a story exciting enough to suit anyone's taste for the dramatic—stories of Christians braving the slums and witnessing supernatural healings from drug addiction. Fired up with the hope that maybe God would do something equally spectacular in my own life, that night I begged Him, if He was real, to perform some supernatural sign for me—promising that if He did, I would believe in Him. Thinking that maybe this sort of thing worked better with an aggressive approach, I vowed to stay up all night until He gave me a sign.

Midnight passed, then one o'clock, two o'clock, four o'clock . . . my eyes were closing in spite of myself, and still no spectacular sign had appeared. Finally, rather chagrined about engaging in such theatrics, I abandoned the vigil. And as I did, suddenly I found myself speaking to God simply and directly from the depths of my spirit, with a profound sense of His presence. I acknowledged that I did not really need external signs and wonders because, in my heart of hearts, I had to admit (rather ruefully) that I was already convinced that Christianity was true. Through the discussions at L'Abri and my readings in apologetics, I had come to realize there were good and sufficient arguments against moral relativism, physical determinism, epistemological subjectivism, and a host of other isms I had been carrying around in my head. As my South African friend had put it, all my own ideas had been shot down.[36] The only step that remained was to acknowledge that I had been persuaded—and then give my life to the Lord of Truth.

So, at about four-thirty that morning, I quietly admitted that God had won the argument.

What I hope you take from my experience is that *worldview* is not an abstract, academic concept. Instead, the term describes our search for answers to those intensely personal questions everyone must wrestle with—the cry of the human heart for purpose, meaning, and a truth big enough to live by. No one can live without a sense of purpose and direction, a sense that his or her life has significance as part of a cosmic story. We may limp along for a while, extracting small installments of meaning from short-term goals like earning a degree, landing a job, getting married, establishing a family. But at some point, these temporal things fail to fulfill the deep hunger for eternity in the human spirit. For we were made for God, and every part of our personality is oriented toward relationship with Him. Our hearts are restless, Augustine said, until we find our rest in Him.[37]

Once we discover that the Christian worldview is really true, then living it out means offering up to God all our powers—practical, intellectual, emotional, artistic—to live for Him in every area of life. The only expression such faith can take is one that captures our entire being and redirects our every thought. The notion of a secular/sacred split becomes unthinkable. Biblical truth takes hold of our inner being, and we recognize that it is not only a message of salvation but also the truth about all reality. God's Word becomes a light to *all* our paths, providing the foundational principles for bringing every part of our lives under the Lordship of Christ, to glorify Him and to cultivate His creation.

SCOLDS AND SCALAWAGS

Looking back after three decades, I've come to appreciate L'Abri more than ever, because it gave me a worldview conception of Christianity right from the beginning of my spiritual life. Schaeffer didn't just *teach* about the Cultural Mandate, he *demonstrated* it. From the moment I arrived at L'Abri, hitchhiking up the mountain and knocking on the door of a quaint Swiss chalet, I was struck by the respect for art and culture evident in even the little things—the simple beauty of a small vase of wildflowers on the dinner table, the natural elegance of the Swiss mountain decor, the depth and range of the conversation, the after-dinner readings in classical literature.[38] Listening to Schaeffer's lectures was an education in itself, as they ranged over politics, philosophy, education, art, and popular culture—showing by example that there can be a Christian perspective in all these areas.

After becoming a Christian, I returned to L'Abri for a longer period of study, and discovered how liberating a worldview approach can be. There is no need to *avoid* the secular world and hide out behind the walls of an evangelical subculture; instead, Christians can *appreciate* works of art and culture as products of human creativity expressing the image of God. On the other hand, there is no danger of being naive or uncritical about false and dangerous messages embedded in secular culture, because a worldview gives the conceptual tools needed to analyze and critique them. Believers can apply a distinctively biblical perspective every time they pick up the newspaper, watch a movie, or read a book.

Schaeffer modeled this balanced approach in his lectures and writings. He would draw attention to the artistic quality of, say, a Renaissance painting, even while critiquing the Renaissance *worldview* of autonomous humanism expressed in it. He would appreciate the color and composition of an Expressionist painting, or the technical quality of a Bergman film, or the musicianship of a piece of rock music—even while identifying the relativistic or nihilistic worldview it expressed.[39]

Artists are often the barometers of society, and by analyzing the world-views embedded in their works we can learn a great deal about how to address the modern mind more effectively. Yet many Christians critique culture one-dimensionally, from a moral perspective alone, and as a result they come across as negative and condemning. At a Christian college, I once took an English course from a professor whose idea of critiquing classic works of literature was to tabulate how many times the characters used bad language or engaged in illicit sexual relations. He seemed blind to the books' literary quality—whether or not they were good *as literature*. Nor did he teach us how to detect the worldviews expressed there. Similarly, a Christian radio personality recently wagged a stern finger at Elvis Presley for the immoral content of his songs, without ever asking whether his songs were good *as music* (which they certainly were), or raising other worldview questions, such as why popular culture has such a powerful impact. When the only form of cultural commentary Christians offer is moral condemnation, no wonder we come across to non-believers as angry and scolding.

Our first response to the great works of human culture—whether in art or technology or economic productivity—should be to celebrate them as reflections of God's own creativity. And even when we analyze where they go wrong, it should be in a spirit of love. Today on religious radio or in ministry fund-raising letters, it is common for Christian activists to attack Hollywood or television or rap music in tones of aggrieved anger, berating their immoral content or mocking the pretensions of postmodern political correctness. But Schaeffer would have none of that. Even when raising serious criticisms, he expressed a burning compassion for people caught in the trap of false and harmful world-views. When describing the pessimism and nihilism expressed in so many movies, paintings, and popular songs, he demonstrated profound empathy for those actually living in such despair. These works of art "are the expression of men who are struggling with their appalling lostness," he wrote. "Dare we laugh at such things? Dare we feel superior when we view their tortured expressions in their art?" The men and women who produce these things "are dying while they live; yet where is our compassion for them?"[40]

Today, Christian activists are quick to organize a boycott or pressure a politician to de-fund some artistic group, and these strategies have their place. But how many reach out to the artists with compassion? How many do the hard work of crafting real answers to the questions they are raising? How many cry out to God on behalf of people struggling in the coils of false worldviews?

IN LOVE WITH CREATIVITY

The best way to drive out a bad worldview is by offering a good one, and Christians need to move beyond *criticizing* culture to *creating* culture. That is the task God originally created humans to do, and in the process of sanctification we are meant to recover that task. Whether we work with our brains or with our hands, whether we are analytical or artistic, whether we work with people or with things, in every calling we are culture-creators, offering up our work as service to God.

A church in Los Angeles that ministers to Hollywood artists includes among its core principles this wonderful statement: "Creativity is the natural result of spirituality."[41] Exactly. Those in relationship with the Creator should be the most creative of all. By creatively developing a biblical approach to their subject area, believers may even transform an entire discipline. Consider a few inspiring examples.

Christian Philosophers Out of the Closet

The philosophical journal *Philo* recently carried an article deploring the way Christians are taking over philosophy departments in universities across the country.[42] At least, that's what the author claims is happening. Quentin Smith is an aggressive proponent of philosophical naturalism (he publicly debates Christian apologists[43]), and in this article he warns his colleagues that the field of philosophy is being "de-secularized." In informal surveys, Smith reports, professors around the country consistently say that one-quarter to one-third of their departments now consist of theists, generally Christians.

Why is this happening? Largely because of the work of one Christian philosopher: Alvin Plantinga. In the past, Christians working in philosophy kept their theism restricted to their "private lives," never mentioning it in "their publications and teaching," Smith says. Then came Plantinga's influential *God and Other Minds,*[44] which demonstrated that theists could match their naturalistic colleagues in "conceptual precision, rigor in argumentation, technical erudition, and an in-depth defense of an original worldview." Other books by Plantinga followed quickly, Smith notes, all showing that Christians are capable of "writing at the highest qualitative level of analytic philosophy."

Soon other forms of theistic realism, most of them influenced by Plantinga, began sweeping through the philosophical community. While in other fields Christian academics still tend to compartmentalize their beliefs from their scholarly work for fear of committing academic suicide, Smith writes, "in philosophy, it became, almost overnight, 'academically respectable' to argue for theism."

He concludes morosely: "God is not 'dead' in academia. He returned to life in the later 1960s and is now alive and well in his last academic stronghold, philosophy departments."

Plantinga's far-ranging influence shows that it is possible for believers to do better work than their opponents, and even begin to reverse the direction of an entire academic discipline. It is an astonishing example of what Christians can do when they obey the command to take every thought captive to Christ. Smith castigates his fellow naturalistic philosophers for "the embarrassment" of belonging to the only academic field being de-secularized, and spends the rest of the article urging them to reverse this pernicious trend.[45] We can pray that, by God's grace, they will not succeed.

Religion: Good for Your Health

Another inspiring example is the work of the late David Larson, who practically single-handedly turned around the medical community on the subject of religion and health. As a graduate student in psychiatry, Larson was actually advised to leave the field. The settled stereotype was that religious belief is associated with mental illness. Ever since Freud had declared belief in God a "universal obsessional neurosis,"[46] it had become dogma that religion is harmful to mental health, and even pathological.

Nevertheless, Larson persisted in his studies, and over time he began to notice that the negative stereotype of religion was not supported by actual research results. In fact, the facts pointed to the *opposite* conclusion: Subjects who were more religious tended to show up in the healthy groups, not the sick groups. Eventually Larson began doing his own research and founded the National Institute for Healthcare Research (NIHR), which has published scores of studies confirming that religious belief (which in America generally means Christianity) actually correlates with better mental health. It is now widely accepted that religious people have lower rates of depression, suicide, family instability, drug and alcohol abuse, and other social pathologies.

How did scientists overlook for so long the fact that religion is a powerful source of mental well-being? How did they even mistake it for a form of mental *disorder*? If the study of mental health is a science, as its practitioners like to claim, this was no "minor oversight," writes Patrick Glynn, in *God: The Evidence*. "It shows to what degree the term 'science' has been abused by the thinkers of modernity to mask what amounts to little more than a prior prejudice against the idea of God."[47]

Even more surprising, religious belief also correlates with better *physical* health—with lower rates of virtually everything from cancer to hypertension to cardiovascular disease. When religious people do get sick, they recover faster. They even have lower mortality rates—that is, they live longer—which is the bottom line for medical professionals. (Modern demographers regard life expectancy as the best indicator of quality of life.) All told, people who attend church regularly are happier, healthier, and even live longer.

What a stunning irony, writes Glynn. The heralds of modernity had "assumed that spirituality would be shown to have a physical basis"—but "instead something like the reverse has occurred: Health has been shown to have a spiritual underpinning."[48]

Only fifteen years ago, research on the topic of religion and health could not even get published. "Research of this type could almost be described as 'anti-tenure' activity," Larson once observed. "Research on religion was almost unheard of and my colleagues considered it hazardous to one's academic health."[49] Yet today it is rapidly gaining acceptance. Even non-Christian researchers are beginning to acknowledge the correlations. Herbert Benson of Harvard, who claims no religious faith, is famous for his catchy saying that we are all "wired for God."[50] Our bodies simply function better, he says, when we believe in God.

Another non-Christian persuaded by the sheer weight of the evidence was Guenter Lewy, author of *Why America Needs Religion*. Interestingly, Lewy started out to write a book on the opposite theme—why America does *not* need religion. Many political conservatives have argued that religion is foundational to morality and social stability, and Lewy intended to prove them wrong. His book would be, in his own words, "a defense of secular humanism and ethical relativism."[51]

But as he examined the evidence, Lewy turned around 180 degrees. He ended up writing a book arguing that religion, particularly Christianity, correlates with lower rates of social pathologies such as crime, drug abuse, teen pregnancy, and family breakdown. Or, to put it positively, Christianity motivates attitudes that signal social health, such as responsibility, moral integrity, compassion, and altruism. "Contrary to the expectations of the Enlightenment," Lewy concludes, "freeing individuals from the shackles of traditional religion does not result in their moral uplift." To the contrary, the evidence now shows clearly that "no society has yet been successful in teaching morality without religion."[52]

Today the facts are in: Science itself confirms that biblical principles work in the real world—which is strong evidence that they are true. The Bible describes the way we were created to function, and when we follow its prescriptions, we are happier and healthier. The best explanation of the positive data is that our lives are lining up with the objective structure of reality.

Benevolent Empire

A final example is Marvin Olasky, who unexpectedly and decisively transformed the welfare debate. A slim, bespectacled former Marxist from a Russian Jewish background, Olasky is a journalism professor and editor of *World* magazine. But in the early 1990s he received a grant to write a book, so he holed up in a small office at the Heritage Foundation in Washington, D.C., just two blocks from where I was living at the time. When I walked over for a visit, he told me about the project that would catapult him to fame a few years later.

American welfare policy had come to an impasse: Though welfare had done some good for those who needed only a temporary boost to get back on their feet, it had also created a permanent underclass—the chronically poor, whose poverty was related to social pathologies such as alcohol addiction, drug abuse, fatherless homes, and crime. Everyone on both sides of the political aisle agreed that welfare needed to be reformed, but no one knew how to do it.

It was Olasky who discovered the answer, and he did it by analyzing the traditional Christian approach to charity. In researching the vast proliferation of Christian charities in the nineteenth century, often dubbed the Benevolent Empire,[53] Olasky found that the churches specialized in personal assistance that fulfilled the literal meaning of *compassion*—"suffering with" others. They didn't just hand out money; they helped people change their lives, focusing on job training and education. They required that the poor do some useful work, giving them a chance to rebuild their dignity by making a worthwhile contribution to society. They helped outcasts to build a social network—to reconnect with family and church for ongoing support and accountability. Most of all, they addressed the moral and spiritual needs that lie at the heart of dysfunctional behavior.

Clearly, this goes beyond what any government can do. In fact, government aid can actually make things worse. By handing out welfare checks impersonally to all who qualify, without addressing the underlying behavioral problems, the government in essence "rewards" antisocial and dysfunctional patterns. And any behavior the government rewards will generally tend to increase. As one perceptive nineteenth-century critic noted, government assistance is a "mighty solvent to sunder the ties of kinship, to quench the affections of family, to suppress in the poor themselves the instinct of self-reliance and self-respect—to convert them into paupers."[54]

The churches' successful approach is described in Olasky's book *The*

Tragedy of American Compassion, where he coined the term *compassionate conservatism.* The book was picked up by former Speaker of the House Newt Gingrich, who liked it so much that he distributed it to all incoming freshmen in Congress. Overnight, Olasky began to be feted as the guru who had discovered a way out of the welfare impasse. He became an advisor to George W. Bush, who campaigned for the presidency on the slogan of "compassionate conservatism," promising to create a special office to support faith-based initiatives. Though policy analysts continue to debate the details, Olasky has brought about a decisive paradigm shift in America's approach to welfare.

The successes of people like Plantinga, Larson, and Olasky can inspire all of us to take our theistic beliefs out of hiding and into the public sphere. If Christianity really is true, then it will yield a better approach in every discipline.

Why do many Christians still compartmentalize their faith in the private sphere? Why do they accept the secular/sacred split that limits the revolutionary impact of God's Word? The only way to break free from this confining grid is to trace it back to its roots—to diagnose where it came from, how it grew over time, and how it came to shape the way most Christians think today. In the next chapter, we will sleuth our own history for clues to why we think the way we do. How can we recover the conviction that Christianity is not only religious truth but total truth?

2

REDISCOVERING JOY

The problem is not only to win souls but to save minds.
If you win the whole world and lose the mind of the world,
you will soon discover you have not won the world.
CHARLES MALIK[1]

By the time Sealy Yates was just twenty-five years old, he had already ful-filled his life's dreams. He had gone to law school, passed the bar exam, landed a great job. He had married a wonderful woman, and they were busy raising their first child. Life was good.

That's when Sealy slumped into a profound depression. He was too young for a midlife crisis, yet he found himself asking all the same questions: Is this all there is? Is this what I want to do for the rest of my life? What's the mean-ing of it all?

Sealy was not naturally depressive, so he probed for some reason behind it. And the answer he discovered was one that no psychologist would have guessed: The key to recovering joy and purpose turned out to be a new under-standing of Christianity as total truth—an insight that broke open the dam and poured the restoring waters of the gospel into the parched areas of his life.

Years ago, at the age of fifteen, Sealy had responded to an altar call at a Baptist church. From that moment on, he knew deep in his bones that what he wanted most was to serve God. At first, he figured that meant doing church work of some kind—becoming a pastor, missionary, or music leader. "I wanted to live for God," Sealy told me,[2] "and the only frame of reference I had said that meant full-time Christian work."

There was only one problem: He didn't have the skills for any church-based profession. In reviewing his aptitude tests, however, a high school guid-ance counselor suggested that he consider becoming an attorney. The idea was electrifying. No one in Sealy's family had even gone to college, let alone law school. The very thought seemed to soar beyond the bounds of possibility. Nevertheless, he prayed, he worked hard, and now . . . he had made it.

So why wasn't he happy? Sealy's impossible dream had come true, yet he was miserable. He maintained a heavy schedule of church activities, but a spiritual hunger still gnawed at his heart. Maybe he had made a mistake? Maybe he really *had* been called to full-time church work but had ignored God's call? Maybe he should drop his job and go to the mission field?

Christians who are seriously committed to their faith often experience this inner tug-of-war. Like Sealy, most of us absorb the idea that serving God means primarily doing church work. If we end up in other fields of work, then we think serving the Lord means piling religious activities on top of our existing responsibilities—things like church services, Bible study, and evangelism. But where does that leave the job itself? Is our work only a material necessity, something that puts food on the table but has no intrinsic spiritual significance? Is it merely utilitarian, a way of making a living?

Sealy discovered that it was just such questions that were driving his depression: He had no idea how to integrate his Christian faith with his professional life. In his law classes at UCLA there had never been any mention of Christianity; none of his professors or classmates had shared his faith commitment; nor did any colleagues at the law firm where he now worked. And since his professional work took up most of his waking hours, that meant a large segment of his life was sealed off from what mattered most to him.

"Where is God in my life?" Sealy found himself asking. What he thought was depression turned out to be an agonized longing for spiritual meaning in his work. Adding church activities to a completely secularized job was like putting a religious frame on a secular picture. The tension between his spiritual hunger and the time demands of a purely "secular" job was tearing him apart inside.

Sealy's search for a solution was finally rewarded when he discovered a Christian study program that taught him how to address clients' spiritual lives. Instantly, a whole new world opened to him, as he came to realize that the law addresses issues connected to the whole person. After all, "people typically come to lawyers when they're in a crisis," he explained. "It's a phenomenal opportunity to help them do what's right." Lawyers can minister to troubled spouses seeking a divorce, counsel misguided teens in trouble with the law, advise ethically conflicted businessmen to do what's right, confront Christian ministries that are compromising biblical principles. The law is not merely a set of procedures or an argumentative technique. It is God's means of confronting wrong, establishing justice, defending the weak, and promoting the public good.

In every profession, the prevailing views stem from some underlying philosophy—basic assumptions about what is ultimately true and right. That means Christians need not feel out of place bringing their *own* assumptions into the field. Sealy began to claim the freedom to bring biblical understandings of justice, rights, and reconciliation into the legal arena.

Sealy's Secret

The dilemma Sealy faced is not uncommon for Christians in any profession. As we saw in the previous chapter, modern society is characterized by a sharp split between the sacred and secular spheres—with work and business defined as strictly secular. As a consequence, Christians often live in two separate worlds, commuting between the private world of family and church (where we can express our faith freely) and the public world (where religious expression is firmly suppressed). Many of us don't even know what it means to have a Christian perspective on our work. Oh, we know that being a Christian means being ethical on the job—as Sealy put it, "no lying or cheating." But the work itself is typically defined in secular terms as bringing home a paycheck, climbing the career ladder, building a professional reputation.

For lawyers like Sealy, success is defined primarily as winning cases. The attitude in today's legal profession is that law has nothing to do with morality. Lawyers are little more than "hired guns" who are expected to defend their clients, right or wrong, with no regard for moral principles of truth or justice. They are admonished to keep their own moral perspective tucked tightly away in the private sphere; in the public sphere, their job is to give strictly legal advice.[3]

But no Christian, in any profession, can be happy when torn in two contrary directions. We all long for our work to count for something more than paying the bills or impressing our colleagues. How can we experience the full power of our Christian faith when it is locked away from the rest of life? How can we lead whole and integrated lives when we're required to shed our deepest beliefs along the way as we commute to work, functioning there from a purely "secular" mindset?

The dichotomies we've been talking about—secular/sacred and public/private—are not merely abstractions. They have a profoundly personal impact. When the public sphere is cordoned off as a religion-free zone, our lives become splintered and fragmented. Work and public life are stripped of spiritual significance, while the spiritual truths that give our lives the deepest meaning are demoted to leisure activities, suitable only for our time off. The gospel is hedged in, robbed of its power to "leaven" the whole of life.

How do we break free from the dichotomies that limit God's power in our lives? How can love and service to God become living sparks that light up our whole lives? By discovering a worldview perspective that unifies *both* secular and sacred, public and private, within a single framework. By understanding that all honest work and creative enterprise can be a valid calling from the Lord. And by realizing there are biblical principles that apply to every field of work. These insights will fill us with new purpose, and we will begin to experience the joy that comes from relating to God in and through every dimension of our lives.

For Sealy, that meant discovering that practicing law is much more than a way to make money and win cases. It is fundamentally a way to execute God's own purposes in the world—to advance justice and contribute to the good of society. "God showed me how to live for him *in* my professional life," Sealy told me. "It's not just about running a business or making a living. In our work, we do the work of God. That's when I rediscovered joy."

CAPITOL HILL GUILT

Probably most of us had not linked together the idea of Christian worldview with finding joy in life. Yet Sealy is right. It is only when we offer up everything we do in worship to God that we finally experience His power coursing through every fiber of our being. The God of the Bible is not only the God of the human spirit but also the God of nature and history. We serve Him not only in worship but also in obedience to the Cultural Mandate. If Christian churches are serious about discipleship, they must teach believers how to keep living for God after they walk out the church doors on Sunday.

Not long ago, after speaking on Capitol Hill, I was approached by a congressional chief of staff who confided, with some frustration, that many of the Christian young people who come to Washington feel "guilty" about their interest in politics.

"Guilty?" The notion was incomprehensible to me. "But why?"

"Well," he explained, "they feel that if they were *really* committed to God, they wouldn't be here. They'd be in the ministry." Though many of these young people were graduates of Christian colleges, they had not been taught a Christian worldview. They still placed their professional work on the *secular* side of the secular/sacred split, regarding it as less valuable than religious activity.

A high-ranking Washington official once lamented how difficult it was to find people for government positions who were committed Christians and at the same time outstanding professionals. The problem, he told me, is that most Christians don't have a biblical sense of calling in their jobs—and thus they fail to treat it as frontline work for the Kingdom. As an example, he related the story of a doctor who had stopped practicing medicine in order to join the staff of a Christian organization.

"I left my medical practice to work in ministry," the doctor told him.

"Hold it," the official broke in. "That's exactly the problem: Your medical practice *was* a ministry, just as much as what you're doing now." Taken aback, the doctor confessed he had never thought of it that way before.

Ordinary Christians working in business, industry, politics, factory work, and so on, are "the Church's front-line troops in her engagement with the world," wrote Lesslie Newbigin. Imagine how our churches would be transformed if we truly regarded laypeople as frontline troops in the spiritual battle. "Are we taking seriously our duty to support them in their warfare?" Newbigin asked. "Have we ever done anything seriously to strengthen their Christian witness, to help them in facing the very difficult ethical problems which they have to meet every day, to give them the assurance that the whole fellowship is behind them in their daily spiritual warfare?"[4] The church is nothing less than a training ground for sending out laypeople who are equipped to speak the gospel to the world.

BECOMING BILINGUAL

In a sense, Christians need to learn how to be bilingual, translating the perspective of the gospel into language understood by our culture. On one hand, we all learn to use the language of the world: If we've gone through the public education system, "we have been trained to use a language which claims to make sense of the world without the hypothesis of God," as Newbigin puts it. But then, "for an hour or two a week, we use the other language, the language of the Bible."[5] We are like immigrants—like my own grandparents, who came to America from Sweden. During the Lutheran church service on Sunday, they spoke their familiar mother tongue; but for the rest of their lives they had to employ the strange-sounding English of the land where they had settled.

Yet Christians are not called to be *only* like immigrants, simply preserving a few customs and phrases from the old country. Instead, we are to be like missionaries, actively translating the language of faith into the language of the culture around us.

The uncomfortable truth is that we don't seem to be doing very well as linguists. Columnist Andy Crouch tells the story of a Christian professor at Cornell University who was concerned about the Christian students in his classes. They "hardly say a thing," the professor complained. The only way I even know that they're fellow believers is when "they come up after class and furtively thank me." Here was a professor actively seeking to create a friendly environment where Christian students would feel free to participate—"but they won't say anything!"[6]

Why not? The answer is that most Christian students simply don't know how to express their faith perspective in language suitable for the public square. Like immigrants who have not yet mastered the grammar of their new country, they are self-conscious. In private, they speak to one another in the mother tongue of their religion, but in class they are uncertain how to express their religious perspective in the accents of the academic world.

THE FAITH GAP

Polls consistently show that a large percentage of Americans claim to believe in God or to be born again—yet the effect of Christian principles is decreasing in public life. Why? Because most evangelicals have little training in how to frame Christian worldview principles in a language applicable in the public square. Though Christianity is thriving in modern culture, it is *at the expense* of being ever more firmly relegated to the private sphere.

Another way to phrase it is that the private sphere has become increasingly religious, while at the same time the public sphere has become increasingly secular. In a 1994 poll, 65 percent of Americans said religion is losing its influence in public life—yet almost the same number, 62 percent, said the influence of religion was actually *increasing* in their personal lives.[7] This means the divide between public and private realms has widened to a yawning chasm, making it harder than ever for Christians to cross over in order to bring biblically based principles into the public arena.

Privatization has also changed the *nature* of religion. In the private realm religion may enjoy considerable freedom—but only because the private sphere has been safely cordoned off from the "real" world where the "important" activities of society take place. Religion is no longer considered the source of serious truth claims that could potentially conflict with public agendas. The private realm has been reduced to an "innocuous 'play area'," says Peter Berger, where religion is acceptable for people who need that kind of crutch—but where it won't upset any important applecarts in the larger world of politics and economics.[8]

By allowing religion to be restricted to a segregated area of life, however, we have undercut one of its primary purposes, which is precisely to provide a sense of life's overarching meaning. As Berger writes, privatization "represents a severe rupture of the traditional task of religion, which was precisely the establishment of an integrated set of definitions of reality that could serve as a common universe of meaning for the members of a society."[9] In fact, many evangelicals no longer even think it *is* the task of religion to provide a "common universe of meaning." Today religion appeals almost solely to the needs of the private sphere—needs for personal meaning, social bonding, family support, emotional nurturing, practical living, and so on. In this climate, almost inevitably, churches come to speak the language of psychological needs, focusing primarily on the therapeutic functions of religion. Whereas religion used to be connected to group identity and a sense of belonging, it is now almost solely a search for an authentic inner life.

People often become very attached to a religion that addresses their emotional and practical needs in this manner. In an increasingly impersonal public world, people are hungry for resources to sustain their personal and private world. Nonetheless, it represents a truncated view of Christianity's claims to be the truth about all of reality. "Secularization did not cause the death of religion," says theologian Walter Kasper, but it did cause it to "become but one sector of modern life along with many others. Religion lost its claim to universality and its power of interpretation."[10] That is, Christianity no longer functions as a lens to interpret the whole of reality; it is no longer held as total truth.

In essence, Christians have accepted a trade-off: By acquiescing in the privatization process, Newbigin says, Christianity "has secured for itself a continuing place, at the cost of surrendering the crucial field."[11] In other words, Christianity has survived in the private sphere, but at the cost of losing the ability to make a credible claim in the public sphere or to challenge the reigning ideologies.

The reason Newbigin was so sensitive to the problem is that he lived for forty years as a missionary in India, which is not plagued by the same secular/sacred, public/private split. The mentality of Indian Christians is that *of course* religion permeates all of life. The same is true of African Christians. "In most human cultures, religion is not a separate activity set apart from the rest of life," Newbigin explains. In these cultures, "what we call religion is a whole worldview, a way of understanding the whole of human experience."

On a global scale, then, the secular/sacred dichotomy is an anomaly—a distinctive of Western culture alone. "The sharp line which modern Western culture has drawn between religious affairs and secular affairs is itself one of the most significant peculiarities of our culture, and would be incomprehensible to the vast majority of people."[12] In order to communicate the gospel in the West, we face a unique challenge: We need to learn how to liberate it from the private sphere and present it in its glorious fullness as the truth about all reality.

DISCONNECTED DEVOTION

The first step in the process is simply identifying the split mentality in our own minds, and diagnosing the way it functions. The dichotomy is so familiar that

Christians often find it difficult *even to recognize* it in their own thinking. This struck me personally when I read about a survey conducted a few years ago by Christian Smith, a sociologist at the University of North Carolina (and himself an evangelical believer).[13] The results of the survey highlight both the good news and the bad news about American evangelicalism.

The good news was that, on several measures of religious vitality, evangelicals came out consistently on top. It's clear that evangelicals are highly committed to their faith; they speak the language of the gospel fluently. On the other hand, when asked to articulate a Christian worldview perspective on *other* subjects—areas such as work, business, and politics—they had little to say. They seemed unable to translate a faith perspective into language suitable for the public square.

The survey compared evangelicals to four other groups: fundamentalists, mainline Protestants, liberal Protestants, and Roman Catholics.[14] Let's look at a few examples of the findings. First, the good news. When asked about their view of the Bible, some 97 percent of evangelicals said it is inspired by God and without errors. Compare that to the other groups surveyed:

97% of evangelicals
92% of fundamentalists
89% of mainline Protestants
78% of liberal Protestants
74% of Catholics

Evangelicals were also the most likely to say they have committed their life to Jesus Christ as personal Lord and Savior:

97% of evangelicals
91% of fundamentalists
82% of mainline Protestants
72% of liberal Protestants
67% of Catholics

Here's the percentage who say their religious faith is very important to them:

78% of evangelicals
72% of fundamentalists
61% of mainline Protestants
58% of liberal Protestants
44% of Catholics

Do absolute moral standards exist? "Yes":

75% of evangelicals
65% of fundamentalists
55% of mainline Protestants
34% of liberal Protestants
38% of Catholics

Do you have doubts about your faith? "Never":

71% of evangelicals
63% of fundamentalists
62% of mainline Protestants
44% of liberal Protestants
58% of Catholics

A question particularly relevant to this book: How important is it to defend a biblical worldview in intellectual circles? "Very important":

63% of evangelicals
65% of fundamentalists
46% of mainline Protestants
49% of liberal Protestants
(Catholics not polled)

The numbers make it clear that on many measures of religious vitality, evangelicalism is doing very well.[15] Historians and sociologists are notorious for predicting the demise of Christianity in the modern world: Most accept the "secularization thesis," which states that as societies modernize, they inevitably secularize. But the secularization of America has been vastly overstated. The evidence shows that evangelicalism is thriving even in today's highly modernized society.

If that's the good news, then what's the bad news? The bad news is that when asked to articulate a biblical worldview perspective on issues in the public square, no one could do it. *Not one person* in the entire survey. Respondents spoke strictly in the language of individual morality and religious devotion; they seemed unable to express a Christian philosophy of business, politics, or culture.[16]

This comes alive if we read a few examples in their own words. When asked how to have a transforming effect on the broader culture, a Baptist woman replied, "I just feel that if each individual lived the Christian life, . . . it influences society. We just need to live the life that Christ wants us to live, the best we can, to influence society in general." A Christian charismatic told the survey takers, "For me, the solution to the world's problems is becoming a Christian, okay?" A Church of Christ man said, "Just believe in Christ and live the best you can the way he wants you to, and that would change the whole world."[17]

These answers contain a great deal of truth, of course; but that truth is limited to individual conversion and personal influence. None of the respondents talked about critiquing the worldviews that shape modern public life, or about developing a Christian theory of social order.

When asked how Christianity should affect the world of work and business, most thought only of injecting religious activities into the workplace. A woman from a seeker church said, "There are opportunities . . . to have Bible study on company time, a prayer breakfast, outreach of some kind." A Pentecostal man (with apparently a tough job), said, "I don't let them cuss excessively on the job. . . . No drinking, no alcohol, no coming to work drunk. Also, we pray most of the time before we start work in the morning."[18]

Other respondents stressed their own moral witness on the job. Christians "should be the most honest employees they have," a Presbyterian man replied. "If you are working for someone, you shouldn't steal or take an extra ten minutes for lunch break." In fact, honesty was the single factor most often mentioned—listed by more than one out of three evangelicals. When survey-takers pressed the issue, asking whether Christians could do anything else for the economy, a Church of Christ man answered, "No, because if everybody would be honest, that's all it would take." A Baptist woman said, "If you [are honest], most everything will take care of itself."[19]

Of course, we have to commend those who start Bible studies in the work place or try to exert a moral influence. But what about a biblical perspective on the work itself? There's something missing when we don't hear any respondents talking about their work itself as service to God or as fulfillment of the Cultural Mandate—the biblical command to subdue the earth (see chapter 1). Even when pressed, none of the respondents offered any biblical principles of economics or seemed aware of the impact of systemic economic forces or institutions.

Finally, what about politics? A woman attending an evangelical Moravian church told the survey, "What can a Christian accomplish in politics? Be a moral presence." A Church of Christ man said, "Why should Christians be active [in politics]? Because I think souls should be saved. . . . If I can help somebody [go to heaven] by being in the government, . . . that would make me feel good."[20]

No one would deny that Christians are called to be evangelists *wherever* they are—including politics. But political office is not just a platform for sharing the gospel. We are also called to work out a biblical perspective on the state and politics. God created the state for a purpose, and we need to ask what that purpose is. How do Christians work to advance justice and the public good?

On occasions when respondents did address specific political issues, they typically mentioned abortion and homosexuality. Why these particular issues? Because they are easy to conceptualize in terms of individual morality. By the same token, solutions to social problems were phrased almost solely in terms of individual voluntary activities—missions of mercy to the poor, the homeless, the addicted. "Worthy as these projects may be," Smith comments, "none of them attempt to transform social or cultural systems, but merely to alleviate some of the harm caused by the existing system."[21]

The study provides a fascinating snapshot of contemporary evangelical Christians, pinpointing with deadly accuracy both their strengths and their weaknesses. On one hand, their hearts are in the right place: They are sincere, serious, committed. On the other hand, their faith is almost completely privatized: It is usually restricted to the area of personal behavior, values, and relationships. Even when evangelicals do try to influence the public sphere, their main strategy is to import activities from the private sphere, like prayer meetings and evangelism. Friends who work on Capitol Hill tell me there are several Christian groups that minister to politicians and staffers, yet virtually all of them limit their ministry to one's personal devotional life—"How's your walk with Jesus?" Few challenge those in politics to think about the issues themselves from a biblical perspective—"What is a Christian political philosophy? How does your faith perspective influence the way you're going to vote today on the bills before Congress?"

Before we can even begin to craft a Christian worldview, we first need to identify the barriers that prevent us from applying our faith to areas like work, business, and politics. We need to try to understand why Western Christians lost sight of the comprehensive call God makes on our lives. How did we succumb to a secular/sacred grid that cripples our effectiveness in the public sphere? To break free of this destructive thought pattern, we need to understand where it came from, identify the forms it has taken, and trace the way it became woven into the pervasive patterns of our thinking. We will discover that, from the beginning, Christianity has been plagued by dualisms and dichotomies of various kinds. And the only way to free ourselves from dualistic thinking is to make a clear diagnosis of the problem.

CHRISTIAN SCHIZOPHRENIA

To make that diagnosis, we must go back to the early church and its encounter with Greek thought. Imagine the earliest believers: Small, embattled groups surrounded by an alien culture with its own established language, literature, culture, civic institutions—and, most powerful of all, the rich intellectual tradition of Greek philosophy. How would the early church defend its faith in the resurrection of Jesus over against the highly developed philosophies of the day?

The classical thinkers taught much that was good. You know the names: Homer, Socrates, Plato, Aristotle. They emphasized the rational order of the universe, which was later to become an important inspiration for the development of modern science. They stood against the materialists and hedonists of their day, asserting the eternal ideals of Truth, Goodness, and Beauty. They argued that knowledge was objective, not merely a social convention. Plato even offered an argument from design based on the goal-directed order in nature.[22] All this and more, Christian thinkers found very congenial, and eventually they began adopting many elements of classical philosophy as intellectual tools to give philosophical expression to their own biblical faith.

Yet the Greek thinkers were pagans, and many of their doctrines were incompatible with biblical truth. Instead of giving a comprehensive description of classical thought, we will zero in on some of these problematic elements. To be fair, the church fathers almost couldn't help absorbing a good bit of Greek thought. It was, after all, the only conceptual language available to them as they sought to address the educated world of their day. But it came with some serious negative baggage—especially what Schaeffer calls a "two-story" view of reality.[23] Classical thought drew a stark dichotomy between matter and spirit, treating the material realm as though it were less valuable than the spiritual realm—and sometimes outright evil. Thus salvation was defined in terms of ascetic exercises aimed at liberating the spirit from the material world so that it could ascend to God.

This may sound abstract, so let's make it concrete by examining the two key figures who had the greatest impact on Christian thought.

Why Plato Matters

The dualism just described was especially strong in Plato, the philosopher who had by far the greatest impact on Christian thinkers through the Middle Ages (especially through a later adaptation known as neo-Platonism).[24] Plato taught that everything is composed of Matter and Form—raw material ordered by rational ideas. Think of a statue: It consists of marble crafted into a beautiful shape according to a design or blueprint in the artist's mind. Matter on its own was regarded as disordered and chaotic. The Forms were rational and good, bringing about order and harmony.

In fact, the realm of pure Form was actually considered *more real* than the material world, strange as that sounds to us today. Plato painted a powerful word picture to suggest that the world of ordinary experience—the world we know by sight and sound and touch—is merely a play of shadows cast on the wall of a cave. Most people are captivated by the shadow show and mistake it for reality, he said. But the philosopher is the enlightened one who manages to escape the cave and discover the genuinely real world of immaterial Forms, the highest being Goodness, Truth, and Beauty. The point of Plato's word picture is that the material world is the realm of error and illusion: The path to true knowledge is to free ourselves from the bodily senses, so that reason can gain insight into the realm of Forms.

Why did Plato view the material world as inferior? As we saw in our discussion of mathematics in chapter 1, Plato regarded Matter as preexisting from all eternity. The role of the creator was merely to impose rational Form upon it. But the preexistence of Matter meant it had independent properties over which the creator had no control; as a result, the deity was never fully successful in forcing it into the mold of the Forms. This explains why there is always some chaos, disorder, and irrationality in the world.

In essence, Plato was offering a twofold origin for the world. Both Form and Matter are eternal: Form represents reason and rationality, while the eternal flow of formless Matter is inherently evil and chaotic. This twofold view of origins led to a two-story view of reality, with *Form* in the upper story and *Matter* in the lower story.

Platonic dualism can be represented like this:

FORM
Eternal Reason

MATTER
Eternal Formless Flux

From a biblical perspective, the problem with Platonic dualism was that it identified the source of chaos and evil with some *part* of God's creation—namely, Matter. Creation was divided into two parts: the spiritual (superior, good) and the material (inferior, bad). This stands in clear opposition to the biblical worldview, which teaches that *nothing* exists from eternity over against

God. Matter is not some preexisting stuff with its own independent properties, capable of resisting God's power. God created it and thus has absolute control over it. This was the operative meaning of the doctrine of creation ex nihilo— that nothing is independent of God, but everything came from Him and is subject to Him.

In contrast to the Greeks, then, the Bible presents the material world as originally good: Since it was created by God, it reflects His good character.[25] The Bible does not identify evil with Matter or with any other part of creation, but with sin, which twists and distorts God's originally good creation. For example, Scripture does not treat the body as inherently sinful or less valuable.[26] When Paul urges us in Galatians 5 to avoid "the lusts of the flesh," he is not referring to the body but is using "flesh" as a technical term for the sinful nature.[27] Indeed, if the body were inherently sinful, the Incarnation would have been impossible, for Jesus took on a human body yet had no sin. The sheer, monumental fact that God Himself took on human form speaks decisively of the dignity of the body. For Greek thinkers, the most shocking claim Christians made was that God had become a historical person, who could be seen, heard, and touched. Rational inquiry could no longer simply reject the world of the senses but had to take account of history—events in time and space like Christ's incarnation, death, and resurrection.[28]

That Rascal Augustine

Another way to put it is that Scripture defines the human dilemma as *moral*— the problem is that we have violated God's commands. But the Greeks defined the human dilemma as *metaphysical*—the problem is that we are physical, material beings. And if the material world is bad, then the goal of the religious life is to avoid, suppress, and ultimately escape from the material aspects of life. Manual labor was regarded as less valuable than prayer and meditation. Marriage and sexuality were rejected in favor of celibacy. Ordinary social life was on a lower plane than life in hermitages and monasteries. The goal of spiritual life was to free the mind from the evil world of the body and the senses, so it could ascend to God.

Does this sound familiar? It describes much of the spirituality of the church fathers and the Middle Ages. The *really* committed Christian was the one who rejected ordinary work and family life, withdrawing to a monastery to live a life of prayer and contemplation. A Christian vocation was conceived of as separate from ordinary human life and community.

These ideas were derived not from the Bible but from Greek philosophy. Many of the church fathers were deeply influenced by Platonism, including

Clement of Alexandria, Origen, Jerome, and Augustine. On one hand, in their writings they took a strong stand for the goodness of creation, rejecting the twofold origin of the world. Every aspect of creation comes from the hand of God and bears the stamp of His handiwork. Yet, on the other hand, in practice most of them absorbed at least some of the Greeks' negative attitude toward the material world.[29]

The most influential was Augustine, a bright but rascally youngster (as he himself tells us) who rebelled against his mother's Christian faith and embarked on an intellectual quest for truth. He was first attracted to Manicheism (there are two gods, one good and the other evil). Later he became a Platonist, then finally converted to Christianity—without, however, ever quite giving up all the elements of Platonism. Most important, he retained an adapted notion of the double creation, teaching that God first made the Platonic intelligible Forms, and afterward made the material world in imitation of the Forms.

The effect of this modified dualism proved devastating. Even though Augustine explicitly affirmed the goodness of creation, his concept of a dual creation had the effect of undercutting what he said and leading to a two-story hierarchy: The immaterial world (the Forms) functioned as his upper story, which he regarded as superior to the material creation in the lower story. "Despite his averrals of the goodness and reality of the created order," says theologian Colin Gunton, "the sensible world is for him manifestly inferior to the intellectual—that Platonic dualism is never long absent from his writing."[30]

This dualistic view of creation led naturally to a dualistic view of the Christian life. Thus Augustine embraced an ethic of asceticism, based on the assumption that the physical world and bodily functions were inherently inferior, a cause of sin. The way to reach the higher levels of spiritual life was by renunciation and deprivation of physical wants. He regarded ordinary work in the world—what he called the "active" life—as inferior to the "contemplative" life of prayer and meditation shut away in monasteries. He also treated marriage as inferior to celibacy, and even recommended that married clergy not live with their wives.[31]

Partly because Augustine was such a towering figure in church history, a kind of Christianized Platonism remained the *lingua franca* among theologians all the way through the Middle Ages. It is a prominent thread woven through the writings of Boethius, John Scotus Erigena, Anselm, and Bonaventure, and was not challenged until the thirteenth century, when the works of Aristotle were reintroduced into Europe.

Aristotle and Aquinas

In fact, the rediscovery of Aristotle's work represented a serious challenge to Christianity itself, for it presented a comprehensive pagan system that included not only philosophy but also ethics, aesthetics, science, and politics. Some Christians were so impressed that they resorted to an extreme two-story dichotomy—the so-called double-truth theory, where the upper and lower stories were regarded as actually contradictory to one another.

For example, Aristotle taught that the world was eternal, while of course Scripture teaches that it was created—and somehow, it was said, *both* are true. The most notorious proponent of the double-truth theory was a French theologian named Siger de Brabant, whose views are described in acid tones by G. K. Chesterton: "There are two truths; the truth of the supernatural world, and the truth of the natural world, which contradicts the supernatural world. While we are being naturalists, we can suppose that Christianity is all nonsense; but then, when we remember that we are Christians, we must admit that Christianity is true even if it is nonsense."[32]

Of course, this itself was nonsense, and the man who rallied to oppose it was a Dominican named Thomas Aquinas. A gentle giant of a man, Aquinas was so taciturn that his friends nicknamed him the Dumb Ox. But his words flowed fluently when he rose to attack the double-truth theory. Aquinas labored mightily to "Christianize" Aristotle's philosophy, rejecting what was clearly unscriptural and seeking to reinterpret the rest in a form compatible with Christianity (just as earlier thinkers had done with Plato).[33]

The end result was that Aquinas retained the dualistic framework of Greek philosophy while changing the terminology. In the upper story he put *grace*, and in the lower story he put *nature*—not nature in the modern scientific sense but in the Aristotelian sense of the "nature of a thing," meaning its ideal or perfect form, its full potential, the goal toward which it strives, its *telos*. In Aristotle's philosophy, all natural processes are *teleological*, tending toward a purpose or goal.[34]

This adaptation of Aristotle had several beneficial effects on Christian thought. For example, Aristotle had taught that natural processes are *good* because they are the means by which things fulfill their "nature" and arrive at their ideal or perfected form—as an acorn grows to become a full-grown oak or an egg matures into a rooster. This argument was picked up by Aquinas and aimed as a weapon against the Platonic idea that the material world (Matter) is inherently inferior. Against that view, Aquinas argued that the creation (nature) is good because it is the handiwork of a good Creator. As one historical account put it, the message of Christian Aristotelianism "was that God is good, His creation is good, [and] the goodness and the causality of the Creation are evidence of the goodness of God."[35]

Thus Aquinas struck a blow at the world-denying asceticism so common during the Middle Ages, and recovered a more biblical view of creation. This had an immediate effect in the arts, where it inspired a more natural and realistic style of painting in the works of artists like Cimabue and Giotto. It also encouraged the study of nature, preparing the ground for the scientific revolution.[36]

Fluffs of Grace

Yet the fact that Aquinas retained a bi-level schema was eventually to undercut much of the good that he achieved. The Aristotelian definition of nature that Aquinas borrowed contained a hidden dynamite that was to blow the system apart. Why? Because it defined the "nature" of things—their goal or purpose or teleology—as immanent within the world. That meant the world did not need God, but was perfectly capable of reaching its purpose or full potential strictly on its own, by its own resources. This was particularly troublesome in the case of human beings: Is the purpose of our lives really circumscribed by the horizons of this world? Don't we have a higher purpose? Can we really live the way we were meant to by our natural faculties alone? Don't we need to be in relationship to God to be truly fulfilled?

The biblical answer, of course, is that all creation is ordered toward relationship with God, as Aquinas knew. But how could he make room for this biblical truth? His solution was to keep the Aristotelian concept of *nature* but restrict it to the lower story. Then, in the upper story, he added God's supernatural *grace*. That is, over and above our natural faculties, God had endowed humans with a supernatural gift or faculty that enables them to be in relationship with God: "In the state of pure nature man needs a power *added to* his natural power by grace . . . in order to do and to will supernatural good."[37] The state of "pure nature" had to be supplemented by an added-on state of grace. In his words, grace was a *donum superadditum*—meaning a gift (donum) that is added on (superadditum).

Aquinas's reworking of the two stories can be diagrammed like this:

GRACE
A Supernatural Add-On

NATURE
A Built-In Ideal or Goal

But this two-tiered schema of nature and grace proved unstable, and after Aquinas the two orders of existence had a tendency to separate and grow increasingly independent. Why? Because there was no real interaction or interdependence between them. Aristotelian "nature" remained complete and sufficient in itself, with grace merely an external add-on. No matter how much icing you spread on a cake, it's still a separate substance. The things of the world and the things of God coexisted on parallel tracks, without relating in any intrinsic way. Those who came after Aquinas (the later scholastics) even tended to speak as though human life had two distinct goals or ends: an earthly one and a heavenly one—a view still held by some Roman Catholic theologians today. Here's a recent expression: "There are in us, then, since there are two ends, one natural, one supernatural, two sets of virtues, two sets of habits, two sets of gifts, the one set natural the other supernatural."[38]

The problem with this radical dichotomy was that it divided human nature itself in half. "Man, such as mediaeval Christendom conceived him, has been split in two," writes Catholic philosopher Jacques Maritain.

> On the one hand, one has a man of pure nature, who has need only of reason to be perfect, wise, and good, and to gain the earth; and on the other, one has a celestial envelope, a believing double, assiduous at worship and praying to the God of the Christians, who surrounds and pads with fluffs of grace this man of pure nature and renders him capable of gaining heaven.

Thus, Maritain comments with heavy irony, "by a sagacious division of labor that the Gospel had not foreseen, the Christian will be able to serve two masters at once, God for heaven and Mammon for the earth, and will be able to divide his soul between two obediences each alike absolute and ultimate—that of the Church, for heaven, and that of the State, for the earth."[39]

The practical impact of this nature/grace dualism was to reinforce the medieval two-tiered spirituality: Laypeople were thought to be capable of attaining only natural, earthly ends, which were clearly inferior, while the religious elites alone were thought capable of spiritual perfection, defined primarily in terms of performing rituals and ceremonies. Thus the religious professionals took over the spiritual duties of those deemed unable to fulfill them for themselves—saying prayers, attending mass, doing penance, going on pilgrimages, and performing acts of charity on behalf of the common folk.

The Reformers Rebel

One of the driving motives of the Reformers was to overcome this medieval dualism and to recover the unity of life and knowledge under the authority of

God's Word. They argued that the medieval scholastics had accommodated far too much to pagan philosophers such as Aristotle, and they urged a more critical attitude toward the alleged truths of reason arrived at apart from divine revelation. (This is how we must understand Luther's overstated charge that "reason is the devil's whore"—he was not against reason per se but against reason applied outside the bounds of God's Word.) The Reformers sought a return to a unified field of knowledge, where divine revelation is the light illuminating all areas of study.

Above all, they soundly rejected the spiritual elitism implied by the nature/grace dualism. They threw out the two-tiered system of religious professionals versus lay believers, replacing it with a robust teaching of the priesthood of all believers (1 Pet. 2:9). Rejecting monasticism, they preached that the Christian life is not a summons to a state of life *separate from* our participation in the creation order of family and work, but is *embedded within* the creation order. Whereas in the Middle Ages the word *vocation* was used strictly of religious callings (priest, monk, or nun), Martin Luther deliberately chose the same term for the vocation of being a merchant, farmer, weaver, or homemaker. Running a business or a household was not the least bit inferior to being a priest or a nun, he argued, because all were ways of obeying the Cultural Mandate—of participating in God's work in maintaining and caring for His creation.

This was backed up theologically by rejecting the definition of grace as something added to nature (*donum superadditum*). That definition assumed that human nature on its own, as God created it, was not fit for relationship with Him but required the infusion of an additional power—which seemed to suggest that human nature was defective in some way. The Reformers were eager to banish any form of dualism that denigrated God's creation, and so they argued that God created human nature as good *in itself*. Grace was not a substance added onto human nature, but was God's merciful acceptance of sinners, whereby He redeems and restores them to their original perfect state.

We get a clearer picture of why this was so revolutionary from the Augsburg Confession, which gives us a window into the attitudes of that time. Prior to the Reformation, it says, "Christianity was thought to consist wholly in the observance of certain holy-days, rites, fasts, and vestures. These observances had won for themselves the exalted title of being the spiritual life and the perfect life." As a result, obedience to God in ordinary life was devalued. As the text explains:

> The commandments of God, according to each one's calling, were without
> honor: namely, that the father brought up his offspring, that the mother bore

children, that the prince governed the commonwealth—these were accounted works that were worldly and imperfect, and far below those glittering observances.

This dual ranking system created genuine distress among spiritually committed lay believers: "This error greatly tormented devout consciences, which grieved that they were held in an imperfect state of life, as in marriage [or] in the office of magistrate. . . . They admired the monks and such like, and falsely imagined that the observances of such men were more acceptable to God."[40] The Reformers' hearts went out to these devout but devalued laypeople, and they strove to restore spiritual significance to the activities of ordinary life, performed in obedience to the Cultural Mandate.

Thus the Reformers contrasted the monastic call *from* the world with the biblical call *into* the world. As Jesus says to the Father in John 17:15, "I do not ask that you take them out of the world, but that you keep them from the evil one" while still in the world. Calvin articulated a view of ordinary work so distinctive that it later came to be called the Protestant work ethic. "He taught that the individual believer has a vocation to serve God in the world—in *every* sphere of human existence—lending a new dignity and meaning to ordinary work," explains theologian Alister McGrath.[41] Calvin taught that Christ was the Redeemer of every part of creation, including culture, and that we serve him in our everyday work.

Despite all this, the Reformers' emphatic rejection of the nature/grace dualism was not enough to overcome an age-old pattern of thought. The problem was that they failed to craft a *philosophical* vocabulary to express their new theological insights. Thus they did not give their followers any tools to defend those insights against philosophical attack—or to create an alternative to the dualistic philosophy of scholasticism.[42] As a result, the successors of Luther and Calvin went right back to teaching scholasticism in the Protestant universities, using Aristotle's logic and metaphysics as the basis of their systems—and thus dualistic thinking continued to affect all the Christian traditions.

ESCAPE FROM DUALISM

Over the centuries, of course, the definition of what is sacred and what is secular, or worldly, has been redefined. Among the Puritans, some defined worldliness in terms of wearing colorful clothing and ruffled collars; to be holy meant wearing dark, plain clothing. Today many older Christians can remember growing up in churches where it was still forbidden to dance, smoke, play cards, chew tobacco, wear makeup, or go to movies. When a friend of mine attended a Christian college several years ago, "mixed bathing" was still forbidden in the college swimming pool. Even now, walk into some fundamentalist churches and you feel like you've been transported back to the 1950s: All the men are in dark suits while all the women wear skirts below the knees with pumps and hose. The congregation might not exactly call it a sin for a woman to wear pants, but they certainly regard it as a "bad witness."

The problem with this secular/sacred dualism is that it does exactly what Plato did so many years ago: It identifies sin with some *part* of creation (dancing, movies, tobacco, makeup). Spirituality is defined as avoiding that part of creation, while spending as much time as possible in another part (church, Christian school, Bible study groups). This explains why work in the spiritual realm as a pastor or missionary is regarded as more important or valuable than being a banker or businessman. No wonder someone like Sealy Yates absorbed the attitude that the only way to really serve God was in full-time Christian ministry.

In *Loving Monday,* a businessman named John Beckett tells how he struggled to overcome this same dualistic thinking. Having come to God as an adult, Beckett soon discovered "a wide gulf" between his new faith and his work life. He realized, of course, that clear moral principles apply across the board. "But by and large," he says, "I found myself living in two separate worlds."[43]

Longing for "a much fuller integration of my two worlds," he began reading books by Francis Schaeffer and discovered, much as we have in this chapter, that ever since the Greeks the world of work and occupations has been demoted to the lower story. The obvious implication of this dualistic outlook was that it was "'impossible' to serve God by being a man or woman in business," Beckett writes. "For years, I thought my involvement in business was a second-class endeavor—necessary to put bread on the table, but somehow less noble than more sacred pursuits like being a minister or a missionary."[44]

Beckett's story reminds us that the Greek perspective is still alive and well, continuing to rob believers of the integrated life God promises. How did he free himself from this pervasive dualism? Through a new understanding of the cosmic scope of Creation, Fall, and Redemption. And you and I can overcome dualistic thinking in the same way, to bring healing and wholeness to our lives.

Creation: God's Fingerprints All Over

Dualism was born, you will recall, because the Greeks thought Matter was preexisting and eternal, capable of resisting the rational order imposed by the Forms. The obvious answer to that dualism, then, is the biblical doctrine that *nothing* is preexisting or eternal except God. He is the sole source of all creation; every part bears His fingerprints and reflects His good character in its original, created form. "The earth is the LORD's and the fullness thereof," writes the psalmist (Ps. 24:1). Everything bears the stamp of its Maker. Genesis presses the point home by repeating over and over again, of the newly created world, "And God saw that it was good" (Gen. 1:4, 10, 12, etc.).

The implication is that no *part* of creation is inherently evil or bad. "Everything created by God is good, and nothing is to be rejected if it is received with thanksgiving," Paul says (1 Tim. 4:4). Being spiritual cannot be defined simply in terms of roping off and avoiding certain parts of creation—whether movies, cards, dancing, or makeup. Once we understand this, Christians will never come across as negative kill-joys. While hating sin, we should exhibit a deep love for this world as God's handiwork, seeing through its brokenness and sin to its original created goodness. We should be known as people in love with the beauties of nature and the wonders of human creativity.

Among the Reformers, it was Calvin who sounded this theme most consistently. Whereas Plato explained the order of the universe in terms of abstract ideals (Matter is ordered by rational Forms), Calvin explained its order as a product of God's word or law or creative decree. The divine word gives things their "nature" or identity, governing both human life (moral law) and the physical universe (laws of nature). Modern people tend to place morality and science in completely different categories, but for Calvin both were examples of God's law. The difference is only that humans must *choose* to obey the moral law, whereas natural objects have no choice but to obey the laws of physics or electromagnetism. If we look at the world through Calvinist eyes, we see God's law governing every element in the universe, God's word constituting its orderly structure, God's truth discoverable in every field.

Fall: Where to Draw the Line

Just as we must insist on the cosmic scope of Creation—that all creation came from God's hand—so too we must insist on the cosmic scope of the Fall. Even the natural world has been affected by human sin, as we are told in Genesis 3 and Romans 8. Because humans were created to be God's deputies exercising dominion over creation, their sin had a ripple effect that has extended into the natural world. This is simply one of the consequences of authority: If a father is harsh, the whole family is unhappy; if a CEO is unethical, the whole company is likely to be corrupt.

Against the Greek conception, we must insist that evil and disorder are not intrinsic in the material world but are caused by human sin, which takes God's good creation and distorts it to evil purposes. "When Adam fell, it was the result of a rebellious will, and not because he had a body," writes philosopher Gordon Clark.[45] That's why Paul can write, "Nothing is unclean in itself"

(Rom. 14:14). It *becomes* unclean only when sinners use it to express their rebellion against God. The line between good and evil is not drawn between one part of creation and another part, but runs through the human heart itself—in our own disposition to use the creation for good or for evil.

For example, music is good, but popular songs can be used to glorify moral perversion. Art is a good gift from God, but books and movies can be used to convey nonbiblical worldviews and encourage moral decadence. Science is a vocation from God, but it can be used to undermine belief in a Creator. Sexuality was God's idea in the first place, but it can be distorted and twisted to serve selfish, hedonistic purposes. The state is ordained by God to establish justice, but it can be perverted into tyranny and injustice. Work is a calling from God, but in American corporate culture it is often an addiction—a frenzied scramble for a higher rung on the corporate ladder, a bigger salary, a more impressive résumé. In every area of life, we need to distinguish between the way God originally created the world, and the way it has been deformed and defaced by sin.

Reformed thinkers label this *structure* versus *direction*. Structure refers to the created character of the world, which is still good even after the Fall— music, art, science, sexuality, work, the state (to use the examples above). Direction refers to the way we "direct" those structures to serve either God or idols. In every enterprise in which we are engaged, we need to ask: (1) What is the original structure that God created, and (2) how is it being distorted and directed to sinful purposes?[46]

Even religious activity can be directed toward sin. We've probably all had the tragic experience of knowing pastors and ministry leaders who, despite impressive God-talk and skillful PR, are actually driven by spiritual pride, using their position as a means for power and influence instead of for service. Spiritual sin can be difficult to spot precisely because we are blinded by the secular/sacred split, which inclines us to classify the spiritual realm as the "good" part of creation. This makes it easy for religious leaders to gloss over wrongdoing by claiming it is necessary "to advance the ministry" or "to reach more people." We need to bear in mind the powerful words of Alexander Solzhenitsyn, when he wrote, "The line separating good and evil passes not through states, nor between classes, nor between political parties either, but right through every human heart."[47]

Redemption: After the Great Divorce

Finally, just as all of creation was originally good, and all was affected by the Fall, so too all will be redeemed. God's ultimate promise is a new heavens and a new earth, which means earthly life is not simply going to end; instead it's going to be fully sanctified. Heaven will not be a place of insubstantial spirits or disembodied minds floating around. Our physical bodies will be resurrected and restored, and we will dwell in a new earth. In the Apostles' Creed we affirm both Jesus' bodily resurrection and our own as well. His resurrection is the guarantee that we too will rise (1 Corinthians 15). As part of God's good creation, the material world will participate in the final redemption. In eternity, we will continue to fulfill the Cultural Mandate, though without sin—creating things that are beautiful and beneficial out of the raw materials of God's renewed creation.

This means that every valid vocation has its counterpart in the new heavens and new earth, which gives our work eternal significance. We cannot know exactly what life will be like in eternity, but the fact that Scripture calls it a new "earth," and tells us we will live there with glorified physical bodies, means that it will not be a negation of the life we have known here on the old earth. Instead it will be an enhancement, an intensification, a glorification of this life. In *The Great Divorce,* C. S. Lewis pictures the afterlife as recognizably similar to this world, yet a place where every blade of grass seems somehow more real, more solid, more substantial than anything experienced here on earth.[48]

A young woman working as a technical writer once told me that her job was merely a way of establishing a financial base to do the things she *really* wanted—which consisted mostly of church activities. "I considered going back to school to learn how to write better," she explained. "But then I realized this won't exist in heaven, so it isn't worth studying." The young woman's commitment to spiritual matters is commendable, but she was mistaken in regarding her earthly vocation as merely a temporary expedient. In our work we not only participate in God's providential activity today, we also foreshadow the tasks we will take up in cultivating a new earth at the end of time. God's command to Adam and Eve to partner with Him in developing the beauty and goodness of creation revealed His purpose for *all* of human life. And after He has dealt with sin once for all, we will joyfully take up that task once again, as redeemed people in a renewed world.

This comprehensive vision of Creation, Fall, and Redemption allows no room for a secular/sacred split. All of creation was originally good; it cannot be divided into a good part (spiritual) and a bad part (material). Likewise, all of creation was affected by the Fall, and when time ends, all creation will be redeemed. Evil does not reside in some part of God's good creation, but in our abuse of creation for sinful purposes (structure versus direction). Paul defined sin as "anything not of faith"—that is, *anything* not directed to God's glory and service. The other side of the coin is that, in redemption, *"all things* are ours" (see 1 Cor. 3:21).

This holistic vision can be wonderfully liberating. When John Beckett finally overcame the secular/sacred split, for the first time he was able to regard his work "as having great worth to God." As "a business person, I was no longer a second-class citizen," he exulted. "Nor did I need to leave my Christian convictions and biblical values outside the office entrance when I headed into work on Monday morning."[49] This same liberating experience can be available to all of us, as we shed dualistic thinking and embrace a holistic Christian worldview.

CHRISTIANITY OUT OF BALANCE

The task of identifying dualistic thinking can be somewhat tricky, because several different forms exist. However, the three-part grid of Creation-Fall-Redemption gives us a powerful tool of analysis. Throughout the history of the church, various groups have tended to seize upon one of these three elements, overemphasizing it to the detriment of the other two—producing a lopsided, unbalanced theology. For example, stressing the Fall too heavily tends toward pessimism and negativism, while overemphasizing Redemption can lead to triumphalism and complacency.

Let's practice using the three-part grid by applying it to some common tendencies among Christian groups. Perhaps the most common imbalance in American evangelicalism is to overemphasize the Fall. Consider the typical evangelistic message: "You're a sinner; you need to be saved." What could be wrong with that? Of course, it's true that we are sinners, but notice that the message starts with the Fall instead of Creation. By beginning with the theme of sin, it implies that our essential identity consists in being guilty sinners, deserving of divine punishment. Some Christian literature goes so far as to say we are nothing, completely worthless, before a holy God.

This excessively negative view is not biblical, however, and it lays Christianity open to the charge that it has a low view of human dignity. The Bible does not begin with the Fall but with Creation: Our value and dignity are rooted in the fact that we are created in the image of God, with the high calling of being His representatives on earth. In fact, it is only *because* humans have such high value that sin is so tragic. If we were worthless to begin with, then the Fall would be a trivial event. When a cheap trinket is broken, we toss it aside with a shrug. But when a priceless masterpiece is defaced, we are horrified. It is because humans are the masterpiece of God's creation that the destructiveness of sin produces such horror and sorrow. Far from expressing a low view of human nature, the Bible actually gives a far *higher* view than the dominant secular view today, which regards humans as simply complex computers made of meat—products of blind, naturalistic forces, without transcendent purpose or meaning.

If we start with a message of sin, without giving the context of Creation, then we will come across to nonbelievers as merely negative and judgmental. After an extended trip through Africa (described in *Dark Star Safari*), the writer Paul Theroux said one of the saddest moments in his journey was "hearing a young woman [missionary] tell me that she was heading for Mozambique and adding, 'They're all sinners, you know.'" Theroux concluded that missionaries only make people "despise themselves."[50] We need to begin our message where the Bible begins—with the dignity and high calling of all human beings because they are created in the image of God.

More Than Sinners

Moreover, in our secularized culture, starting with the Fall renders the rest of our message incoherent. In an earlier age, when most Americans were brought up in the church, they were familiar with basic theological concepts—which meant that the revivalist's simple message of sin and salvation was often adequate. When people heard, "You're a sinner," they had the context to understand what it meant, and many were moved to repentance. But contemporary Americans often have no background in biblical teaching—which means that the concept of sin makes no sense to them. Their response is likely to be, What is *sin?* What right does God have to judge me? How do you know He even exists? Beginning with sin instead of creation is like trying to read a book by opening it in the middle: You don't know the characters and can't make sense of the plot.

As a result, even a pulpit-pounding, fire-and-brimstone sermon is likely to have only a limited effect at best. In my own pilgrimage back to faith as a teenager, I encountered a message of sin and judgment in the unlikeliest of places—in James Joyce's semi-autobiographical book *A Portrait of the Artist as a Young Man*, which was required reading in a high school English class. When I read its description of Father Arnall's hellfire sermons, dwelling in exquisite detail on the suffering of the damned, I had to admit that it was a bit frightening. I was impressed with a sense that *if* Christianity were true, then the decision to believe would be a genuinely life-and-death matter. I began to tell friends that maybe we should reconsider our relaxed relativism: *What if* there really is one single, universal Truth? A small step in the right direction, perhaps, but it certainly did not bring me to faith or repentance. The hellfire images in Joyce's book served as nothing more than a metaphor for the seriousness of the search for truth. Isolated doctrines taken out of their biblical context do not even make sense to modern people, because they no longer have the background to supply the context on their own.

Finally, if we begin with the Fall instead of Creation, we will not be able to explain Redemption—because its goal is precisely to *restore* us to our original, created status. If it were true that we are worthless, and that being sinners is our core identity, then in order to have something of value God would have to destroy the human race and start over again. But He doesn't do that; instead He restores us to the high dignity originally endowed at Creation—recovering our true identity and renewing the image of God in us.

God's Offspring

We can take a lesson from the way the apostles addressed various audiences in New Testament times. Their initial audiences consisted of the Jews of their day—people steeped in the Old Testament, with a firm grasp of key concepts like covenant, law, sin, and sacrifice. When addressing these audiences, the apostles could simply start with Jesus as the supreme sacrifice, the Lamb of God. With people already looking for the coming Messiah, the apostles could simply announce that Jesus was the One they were waiting for.

By contrast, when Paul addressed secular Greek philosophers in Acts 17, the Stoics and Epicureans on Mars Hill, where did he begin? With Creation. Notice how carefully he builds his argument, step by step. First he identifies God as the ultimate origin of the world: "The God who made the world and everything in it" is the "Lord of heaven and earth" (v. 24). Then he identifies this God as the source of our own humanity: "He made from one man every nation of mankind" (v. 26). Finally, he draws the logical conclusion: "Being then God's offspring, we ought not to think that the divine being is like gold or silver or stone" (v. 29). That is, God cannot be akin to material things like idols. Since He made us, He must have at least the qualities we have as personal, moral, rational, creative beings. As water cannot rise above its source, so a nonpersonal object or force could not have produced personal beings like ourselves. It is logical to conclude that God too is a personal Being.

In that case, however, we stand in a personal relationship with God—we owe Him our allegiance, just as children owe honor and allegiance to the parents who brought them into the world. In fact, failure to acknowledge God is a moral fault and calls for repentance: "Now He commands all people everywhere to repent" (v. 30). Notice that it is only *after* having built a case based on Creation that Paul introduces the concepts of sin and repentance. In addressing the pagan Greek culture, he first lays a foundation in the doctrine of creation. As Robert Bellah comments, "In order to preach Jesus Christ and him crucified to the biblically illiterate Athenians, Paul must convince them of the fundamentally Jewish notion of a creator. . . . Only in that context does the incarnation, crucifixion, and resurrection of Jesus Christ make sense."[51]

Today, as we address the biblically illiterate Americans of the twenty-first century, we need to follow Paul's model, building a case from Creation before expecting people to understand the message of sin and salvation. We need to practice "pre-evangelism," using apologetics to defend basic concepts of who God is, who we are, and what we owe Him, before presenting the gospel message.

Jars of Clay

If beginning with sin and judgment has historically been the most typical imbalance among Protestants, it is also possible to tilt in the opposite direction. Some groups weight Redemption more heavily than the Fall, leading to the doctrine of Christian Perfection or Holiness—the idea that we can become completely holy even in this life. For example, a central doctrine in the Wesleyan and Nazarene tradition is "entire sanctification," the teaching that we can be made completely holy or freed from sin in the present life, instead of waiting for eternal life. These churches hold that believers are "made free from original sin, or depravity, and brought into a state of entire devotion to God, and the holy obedience of love made perfect" (in the words of the articles of faith of the Church of the Nazarene).[52]

The error here consists in holding that Redemption overcomes the Fall completely in this life. The Bible teaches that sin will not be completely conquered until Christ returns. On the cross, Christ defeated sin and Satan and won the decisive victory; yet much of the world remains under the power of the enemy until Christ returns as conquering King. We need to hold both of these truths together in proper balance. When the Pharisees asked Jesus when the kingdom would come, He answered, "the kingdom of God is in the midst of you" (Luke 17:21). Yet he also instructed His disciples to pray, "Thy kingdom come," and taught that its coming has not yet been fully accomplished. Between Christ's first and second coming, we must balance both the "already" and the "not yet" aspects of this interim phase.[53]

Picture the world as God's territory by right of Creation. Because of the Fall, it has been invaded and occupied by Satan and his minions, who constantly wage war against God's people. At the central turning point in history, God Himself, the second person of the Trinity, enters the world in the person of Jesus

Christ and deals Satan a deathblow through His resurrection. The Enemy has been fatally wounded; the outcome of the war is certain; yet the occupied territory has not actually been liberated. There is now a period where God's people are called to participate in the follow-up battle, pushing the Enemy back and reclaiming territory for God. This is the period in which we now live—between Christ's resurrection and the final victory over sin and Satan. Our calling is to apply the finished work of Christ on the cross to our lives and the world around us, without expecting perfect results until Christ returns.

This is not an excuse for complacency. We should still strive to develop a character of such quality that people can see a difference between the redeemed and the unredeemed. Our lives should exhibit a supernatural dimension that nonbelievers cannot explain away in terms of merely natural talent or energy.

Paul expressed the proper balance by saying we have a powerful spiritual treasure but it is held in fragile, breakable jars of clay (2 Cor. 4:7). This side of heaven, we should strive to live with all three elements held in balance: recognizing the created goodness of God's world (Creation), fighting the corruption of ongoing sin and brokenness (Fall), and working toward the healing of creation and the restoration of God's purposes (Redemption).

A Higher Consciousness?

Some groups hold an even more extreme imbalance—that Redemption overcomes not only the Fall but even Creation itself. This is the conviction embraced by all sorts of utopian movements, including monasticism: the idea that the highest calling is not to recover God's purpose in Creation but to presage the final Redemption. Monasticism recognized that marriage is part of the creation order; nevertheless it rejected marriage as inferior and aspired instead to prefigure the glorified state, where there will be neither marrying nor giving in marriage, but we will be "like angels in heaven" (Mark 12:25). Thus in the monastic interpretation of this verse, celibacy was exalted as a way to foreshadow the final Redemption.[54]

Similarly, monasticism recognized that owning property is a natural right, rooted in creation and protected by the eighth commandment; nevertheless, by abandoning all property, monks and nuns sought to rise above the natural order to a higher state. Monasticism recognized a natural right to protect oneself, and for a nation to protect itself; yet it claimed for itself the higher calling of pacifism. And so on. Nor are these ideas restricted to monks and nuns: Throughout history, Christianity has seen the rise of various radical, utopian movements that rejected ordinary life, rooted in the creation order, for the sake of some supposed higher spirituality that would be an anticipation of eternity.

The error here is to assume that the order of Redemption destroys the order of Creation. And the antidote is to realize that Redemption is intended not to demolish God's good creation but to fulfill it. As we have seen, this was a theme in the writings of the Reformers, and of Thomas Aquinas before them. The way Aquinas put it was that grace does not *destroy* nature in order to replace it with something higher—instead grace *perfects* nature. He was using the verb "perfect" in the biblical sense of reaching a goal, achieving a purpose, fulfilling an ideal—as when James calls on believers to become "perfect and complete, lacking in nothing" (James 1:4).[55] In Redemption, God does not call us to become something *other* than human but rather to *recover* our true humanity. He empowers us to achieve the purpose for which we were originally created—to fulfill our created nature, which He declared in Genesis to be "very good."

Notice how Jesus Himself replied when the Jewish leaders challenged His teaching on marriage. What was His response? "He who created them from the beginning made them male and female" (Matt. 19:4). In other words, the creation order that God established "from the beginning" remains normative throughout human history. It is not an inferior order to be overcome or destroyed by Redemption. Genesis reveals what God intended for humanity from the start, and what it still means to live a fully human life today.

The Great Drama

The tragedy is that in applying this corrective to medieval thought, Aquinas overcompensated and ended up with a new imbalance. We've talked about what happens when groups overemphasize the Fall or Redemption. But what happens when someone overemphasizes Creation? That's what Aquinas did, and it led to a truncated or incomplete view of the Fall.

Think back to our earlier discussion of Aquinas's nature/grace dualism, which treated grace as an addendum to nature—a suprahuman faculty given to Adam at Creation to supplement his natural faculties. What did this imply for Aquinas's view of the Fall? The answer is that when humans fell into sin, they lost *only* the added-on gift of supernatural grace (the upper story). They fell from the state of grace to the state of pure nature, losing the extra, suprahuman faculties but retaining their human faculties (the lower story) essentially intact and unchanged.[56]

But notice what this implies: If only the upper story fell, then only the upper story needs to be redeemed. The lower story does not. Spiritually, we need a re-infusion of supernatural grace, but our ordinary human nature does not participate in either the Fall or Redemption.[57]

As a result, the gospel was restricted to the upper-story realm of religion and theology. In those areas, humans needed divine revelation and the enlightening of God's Spirit. But in the lower-story realm of science, philosophy, law, and politics, human reason was thought to function quite adequately on its own. Reason was regarded as spiritually neutral or autonomous, not affected by the Fall nor in need of direction from God's Word. In other words, in these subject areas, there was *no distinctively biblical perspective*. Everyone could simply accept whatever "reason" decrees.

This differs sharply from classic Protestant teaching, which defines sin as turning away from God at the core of our being—thus coloring *everything* we think or do. Our entire being is involved in the great drama of sin and redemption. There is no aspect of human nature unaffected by the Fall, no independent realm known by a spiritually neutral reason. Indeed, it's a mistake even to think of reason as neutral, in the sense of being independent of any philosophical or religious commitments. As we saw in chapter 1, all systems of thought begin with some basic premise—some ultimate principle that is regarded as self-existing or divine. Reason is merely the human capacity to reason from those starting premises.

In short, reason is always exercised in service to some ultimate religious vision. People interpret the facts in the light of either biblical revelation or some competing system of thought. When Calvinists use the phrase *total depravity*, this is what they mean: not that humans are hopelessly evil but rather that *every aspect* of human nature has been affected by the Fall, including our intellectual life—and thus *every aspect* needs to be redeemed. Nothing was left pristine and innocent. Even our minds are tempted to worship idols instead of the true God.

Serving Two Masters

This analysis explains why Protestant thinkers have long argued that the medieval nature/grace dualism led to an incomplete view of the Fall. If only the upstairs fell, then the range of God's revelation and redemption is limited to the religious sphere. "By restricting the scope of fall and redemption to the supranatural," writes Herman Dooyeweerd, the nature/grace dualism robbed the Christian message of its integral, all-encompassing character, so that it "could no longer grip man with all its power and absoluteness." In practical terms, the nature/grace dualism implied that we need *spiritual* regeneration in the upper story of theology and religion, but we don't need *intellectual* regeneration in order to get the right view of politics, science, social life, morality, or work. In these areas, human reason is treated as religiously neutral, and we can all go ahead and accept whatever the secular experts decree. It should come as no surprise, then, that this dichotomy led believers to accommodate with the world in these areas. (It also functioned as a stepping-stone to secularism, as we will see in the next chapter.)

Today many Catholic scholars have come to agree with this critique of the nature/grace dualism. For example, Louis Dupré notes that the dualistic scheme allowed *pure nature* (downstairs) to be conceived of as "independent of the historical stages of the fall and redemption." And he praises Reformed theology for expressing "man's *total* involvement in the drama of sin and redemption far more profound than the late medieval theologies with their dual vision of a supernatural order 'added' to nature."[58]

We must never forget, however, that the same dualism permeated the Protestant denominations nearly as thoroughly as it did Catholicism. Because the Protestant Reformers did not craft an alternative philosophy to scholasticism (as we saw earlier), many of their followers slipped back into the same medieval nature/grace dualism. We see the effects today when Christians assume they can attend church and Bible study on the weekends and then, during the week, simply accept whatever concepts and theories are current in their professional field.

In practice, the notion that reason is religiously neutral means that secularism and naturalism are often promoted under the guise of "neutrality." They are presented as objective, rational, and binding on everyone, while biblical views are dismissed as biased private opinions. This equivocation has created enormous pressure on Christians to abandon any distinctively biblical perspective in their professional work. One Christian philosopher goes so far as to insist that it would be "wrong" to apply biblical principles to his work: "I have, myself, definite religious convictions: but I would consider it entirely wrong to make them intrude as tacit presuppositions in the actual process of analysis I undertake."[59] This scholar has clearly acquiesced to the idea that intellectual work can be autonomous of religious or philosophical commitments.

The effect of such a stance, however, is that Christians will abandon the world of ideas to the secularists. They will fail to see that secularism is itself a philosophical commitment—and that if they don't bring *biblical* principles to bear on various issues, then they will end up promoting *nonbiblical* principles. It is impossible to think without some set of presuppositions about the world. This illustrates why it is crucial for Christians to understand the ongoing pitfalls of the nature/grace dualism—so that we can break free from faulty thought patterns and open our whole lives to the transforming power of God's Word.

ALL TOGETHER NOW

What we learn from this brief survey of theological traditions is that Creation, Fall, and Redemption are not only the fundamental turning points of biblical history—they also function as marvelously useful diagnostic tools. A genuinely biblical theology must keep all three principles in careful balance: that all created reality comes from the hand of God and was originally and intrinsically good; that all is marred and corrupted by sin; yet that all is capable of being redeemed, restored, and transformed by God's grace.

These three principles also provide a way to overcome the secular/sacred dichotomy in our lives. The biblical message is not just about some isolated part of life labeled "religion" or "church life." Creation, Fall, and Redemption are cosmic in scope, describing the great events that shape the nature of all created reality. We don't need to accept an inner fragmentation between our faith and the rest of life. Instead we can be integrally related to God on all levels of our being, offering up everything we do in love and service to Him. "Whether you eat or drink or whatever you do, do all to the glory of God," Paul says (1 Cor. 10:31). The promise of Christianity is the joy and power of an integrated life, transformed on every level by the Holy Spirit, so that our whole being participates in the great drama of God's plan of redemption.

Yet when we work to overcome the long-standing secular/sacred dualism in the Christian world, our efforts will run up against powerful dualisms in the *secular* world as well, aimed at privatizing and marginalizing the biblical message. After all, in the West, secular thought grew out of the same stream of intellectual history that we have been surveying. The nature/grace dualism was simply secularized, producing the fact/value dichotomy that remains potent right up to our own times. To liberate Christianity from its cultural captivity, we need to diagnose the modern secular dualism as well. And that is what we will do in the next chapter.

3

KEEPING RELIGION
IN ITS PLACE

When all is said and done, science is about things
and theology is about words.
FREEMAN DYSON[1]

Alan Sears of the Alliance Defense Fund patted his right jacket pocket. "Most Christian lawyers keep their faith in one pocket," he told me. Then he patted his left pocket. "And they keep the law in the other. Their ability to integrate the two is very poor."[2]

Sears was explaining why the ADF had set up a program to train practicing attorneys in a Christian approach to the law. Educated in mainstream law schools, many Christian attorneys simply absorb a secularized view of the law as nothing more than a utilitarian set of procedures that can be manipulated at will to further their client's interests. Their professional lives remain completely separate from their personal walk with the Lord. As Christians, of course, they realize that they should behave morally on the job—not lie or steal. But few have any background in Christian apologetics or worldview that would provide an alternative approach to legal philosophy itself.

"Our first step in the educational programs," Sears explained, "is to deconstruct the legal philosophy these lawyers have absorbed from their secular training." This is done in small groups, he added, "because it is far too painful to be done publicly."

"Painful?" I asked. "Why is that?"

"Because it can be devastating to discover how much they have compromised with the secular mindset," Sears replied. In spite of their personal religious beliefs, in their professional work many Christian lawyers have slipped into a mindset of relativism and pragmatism.

A particularly striking example was a Christian lawyer who worked for a Fortune 500 company. A deacon in his church, he tithed generously, taught

Sunday school, and was in every way a model church member. But on the job, his sole responsibility was . . . to break contracts. Whenever the company decided it was no longer in its interest to work with someone, this man's job was to find a legal loophole that allowed the company to break the contract. He seemed to have no sense that his work involved violating moral principles every day—ideals of truth, integrity, and keeping one's word. He was just "doing his job."

How can even committed Christian believers be so blind? Because they often undergo many years of professional training in a secular setting where they have no opportunity to develop a biblical worldview. In fact, they know that if they *did* express a biblical perspective, it would be a barrier to getting into most graduate schools. And so, most believers learn to compartmentalize their lives, absorbing the reigning secular assumptions in their field of study, while maintaining a devotional life on the side in their private time.

Sears recounted a story about the chief justice of a state supreme court who once told a group of lawyers, "If you think the law has anything to do with morality, you won't last long in this profession." So how *do* most Christians last in the legal profession? By locking away their religious beliefs while on the job and adopting the prevailing concepts and procedures in their field.

In fact, the very concept of being "professional" has come to have connotations of being secular. In the late nineteenth and early twentieth centuries, explains Christian Smith, there was a drive to professionalize all fields—which meant in practice throwing off a Christian worldview and cultivating a secular approach that was touted as *scientific* and *value-free*. The process was nothing less than a "secular revolution," Smith says. In higher education, colleges that used to promote "a general Protestant worldview and morality" were transformed into universities "where religious concerns were marginalized in favor of the 'objective,' a-religious and irreligious pursuit and transmission of knowledge."[3]

This "secular revolution" affected every part of American culture—not only higher education but also the public schools, politics, psychology, and the media. In each of these areas, Christianity was privatized as "sectarian," while secular philosophies like materialism and naturalism were put forth as "objective" and "neutral," and therefore the only perspectives suitable for the public sphere.

Of course, they were nothing of the sort. There is nothing neutral about the claim that the only way to get at truth is to deny God's existence. That is a substantive religious claim, just as it is to affirm God's existence. Yet because of the secular revolution, even many believers came to believe that speaking from a distinctively Christian perspective was biased—that to be truly objective they must bracket their faith and think like nonbelievers in their professional work. To adapt to modernity's professional ethos, Christians found themselves pressured to adopt a naturalistic, secularized approach to the subject matter of their field.

Across the board Christians have been taught (in Alan Sears's image) to keep their faith in one pocket and their work in the other pocket. Many have accepted the idea that the secularized concepts in their field really *do* constitute neutral knowledge, requiring no biblical critique. Faith is often reduced to a separate add-on for personal and private life—on the order of a private indulgence, like a weakness for chocolates—and not an appropriate topic in the public arena.

Today believers are sometimes so intimidated "that they bend over backwards not to sound too 'Christian'," says English professor Kathleen Nielson. Speaking from her experiences in teaching literature in Christian colleges, she says evangelicals are so eager to fit into the standard ideal of neutral scholarship that "we're sometimes afraid to notice a worldview within a novel [even when it] is profoundly un-Christian, or anti-Christian, because we don't want to appear condemnatory or unappreciative of the art."[4] In other words, we don't want to come across as unsophisticated. The rules of professional scholarship rigidly enforce the public/private dichotomy, so that Christians are often made to feel they have no choice but to play by the rules.

Why does this bifurcation between public and private have such force? In the last chapter, we examined the nature/grace dualism that arose within Christianity from the early church through the Middle Ages. In this chapter, we will pick up the story from there and trace the way the dualism became secularized, producing the modern dichotomies between public and private, fact and value. When we think of medieval society, what strikes us most often are the vast differences between that period and our own. For example, despite its dualistic worldview, medieval society remained much more unified and holistic than modern society, which is split institutionally between public and private spheres. In the Middle Ages, moreover, it was the upper story that was valued more highly, whereas in the modern age we have witnessed a stunning reversal. Nevertheless, important continuities link the historical process together, as we will see. In order to craft an effective strategy for bringing Christian truth back into the public sphere, we must understand how secular dualisms arose—so we can strike them right at the root. By tracing their development, we will be equipped to diagnose the way they function today. In the process, we will also develop an effective strategy for evangelism in the postmodern age.

REASON UNBOUND

If we begin with an overview of the process of secularization—the big picture—
then it will be easier to break it down and examine key steps along the way.
We pick up the story with the nature/grace dualism as it developed after
Thomas Aquinas. Recall that *grace* meant theology and the mysteries of faith
(the upper story), while *nature* meant knowledge of this-worldly things, supposedly known by unaided reason apart from divine revelation (the lower
story). But serious problems were raised by the very notion of unaided or
autonomous reason, for if the ordinary affairs of life could be understood and
managed by reason alone, then the realm of grace seemed increasingly irrelevant. Oh, people knew they'd better perform the correct church rituals to make
sure they got into the *next* life on good terms. But in *this* life, Christian truth
began to seem superfluous. Human reason was regarded as perfectly competent on its own for understanding the state, society, science, economics, philosophy—in fact, everything outside of theology. Thus the Christian mind itself
began to be split. God's Word was limited to the upper story, but was deemed
irrelevant and unnecessary in directing the lower story.

Aquinas managed to maintain a balanced synthesis of both stories; but his
synthesis was not to last. Increasingly, religion was seen as nothing more than
a negative check on what reason was allowed to say. Revelation provided a set
of truths that reason was not allowed to contradict, which made it a useful
yardstick for detecting error. But it did not provide any positive guidance in
the lower story.[5] By the time of the later scholastics, faith and reason began to
be split into separate, unrelated categories. Religion was reduced to a matter
of arbitrary faith, while reason was made increasingly autonomous from revelation, as though it were an independent source of truth. We could picture it
by saying that late medieval thinkers thickened the line of demarcation between
the upper and lower stories until it became a dense, impenetrable wall.

Just prior to the Reformation, the separation between faith and reason was
stretched to the breaking point. The key person was William of Ockham, who
denied that God could be understood in rational categories at all. Prior to this,
many Christian thinkers had labored to show that God's plan of salvation was
fitting, suitable, and perfectly reasonable. For example, in the twelfth century
Anselm had offered a case for salvation that was concise and logical: *Because*
human beings sinned, therefore a human being had to render payment.
However, the debt we owe God is so great that only God Himself is able to
pay it. *Therefore* God became a human being in order to pay the price exacted
by divine justice. Anselm's point was that God's plan of salvation makes perfect sense.[6] By contrast, Ockham argued that if we apply rational principles to

God in any way, we deny His absolute freedom. From the perspective of reason, God's plan of salvation is completely arbitrary; God could have chosen a completely different way to save us. Instead of becoming a human being, Ockham said, He could have become a stone or a donkey. In matters of religion, we cannot consider what seems rational; religion derives solely from revelation, accepted by faith.

In short, faith and reason had split into two independent categories. And from this radical dichotomy, it was only a small step to complete secularism. For if virtually everything needed for ordinary life could be known by reason alone, eventually people began to ask why we need revelation at all. A type of rationalism arose that regarded "Reason" as a storehouse of truths known autonomously, apart from divine revelation.[7] In fact, it seemed as though these autonomous truths could even be used to *judge* the claims of religion. Thus the balance of power shifted: Instead of religion functioning as a yardstick of error, reason was now held up as the yardstick of truth. And in applying that yardstick, many concluded that religion failed to measure up.

As the medieval period merged into the Renaissance (beginning roughly in the 1300s), a drumbeat began to sound for the complete emancipation of reason from revelation—a crescendo that burst into full force in the Enlightenment (beginning in the 1700s). The credo of the Enlightenment was autonomy. Overthrow all external authority, and discover truth by reason alone! Impressed by the stunning successes of the scientific revolution, the Enlightenment enthroned science as the sole source of genuine knowledge. Claiming to "liberate" the lower story from the upper story, it insisted that nature was the sole reality, and scientific reason the sole path to truth. Whatever was not susceptible to scientific study was pronounced an illusion. Though reason was touted as philosophically neutral, in reality it began to be identified with scientific materialism.

COLLATERAL DAMAGE

Yet scientific materialism, with its vision of a mechanistic universe, was unattractive to many people, and it galvanized a reaction known as the Romantic movement. For religion was not the only casualty of scientific materialism masquerading as neutral reason. Morality and the arts came under attack as well—after all, things like moral ideals and beauty and creativity are not subject to scientific investigation either. The Romantics responded by trying to preserve some cognitive territory for things that are not reducible to scientific materialism, including religion and morality and the arts and humanities. Romanticism rejected the philosophy of materialism in favor of the philosophy of idealism, which says that ultimate reality is not material but mental or spiritual—usually capitalized as Mind or Spirit or the Absolute.

Yet Romanticism made a fatal concession: It largely conceded the study of nature to mechanistic science, and sought only to carve out a parallel arena for the arts and humanities. Thus scientific materialism continued to reign unchallenged in the lower story, while Romantic idealism was limited to the upper story, leaving the dualistic schema intact.

In a thumbnail sketch, then, the Enlightenment and its intellectual heirs were given jurisdiction over the lower story, where we deal with knowledge that is rational, objective, and scientific—the public sphere. Romanticism and its heirs were given jurisdiction over the upper story, where we deal with religion, morality, and the humanities—the private sphere. We can diagram the division like this:

Modern forms of dualism began with the Enlightenment:

ROMANTICISM
Religion and the Humanities

ENLIGHTENMENT
Science and Reason

This is the overall picture of the secularization process; but to understand it more effectively, we need to trace key steps along the way.

CARTESIAN DIVIDE

The beginning of secular dualism is generally traced to the seventeenth-century French philosopher René Descartes, who proposed a sharp dichotomy between matter and mind. The material world he pictured as a vast machine moving in fixed patterns set by natural laws, subject to mathematical necessity. For Descartes, even animals were machines, and so was the human body. By contrast, the human mind or spirit was the realm of thought, perception, emotions, and will.

Few people realize that in drawing such a sharp opposition between matter and mind, Descartes' purpose was actually to *defend* the realm of mind. As noted in chapter 1, Descartes was a pious Catholic, and by drawing a sharp distinction between the mechanical universe and the human spirit, he hoped to defend belief in the latter. His famous phrase "I think, therefore I am" was intended as a religious affirmation: Since thought is a spiritual activity, he had proved the existence of the human spirit.

But in one of the ironies of history, the enduring impact of Descartes' philosophy was precisely the opposite of what he had intended. What survived
was not his defense of the human spirit but his mechanistic conception of the
universe. Mind was cast into the upper story, where it was reduced to a shadowy substance totally irrelevant to the material world known by science—a
kind of ghost only tenuously connected to the physical body. The novelist
Walker Percy speaks of the "dread chasm that has rent the soul of Western man
ever since the famous philosopher Descartes ripped body loose from mind and
turned the very soul into a ghost that haunts its own house."[8]

The legacy of Descartes' secular dualism can be diagrammed like this:

MIND
Spirit, Thought, Emotion, Will

MATTER
A Mechanical, Deterministic Machine

This "dread chasm" between upper and lower stories grew even wider
after the stunning success of Newtonian physics. Newton's law of gravity sub-
sumed a vast number of natural processes under a single mathematical formula—from the fall of an apple to the orbit of the planets. Nature began to
be pictured as a huge machine, governed by natural laws as strictly as the gears
of a clock. How could there be any room in such a mechanism for the human
soul or spirit? Though these concepts were crucial for religion and morality,
in the conceptual world of science there seemed to be no room for them in
the inn.[9]

If one had to choose between the two, science seemed to promise far
greater certainty than religion or metaphysics. During the religious wars of the
sixteenth century, Christians actually fought and killed one another over religious differences—and the fierce conflicts led many to conclude that universal
truths were simply not knowable in religion. The route to unity lay not in religion but in science. This conviction gave rise to philosophies like positivism and
scientific materialism, which grant science a monopoly on knowledge (downstairs) while consigning everything else to merely private belief and cultural tradition (upstairs).

KANTIAN CONTRADICTION

A pivotal figure in the demotion of the upper story was the great German
philosopher Immanuel Kant. A thin, spare man, Kant ordered his personal life

like clockwork (it was said that his neighbors could set their watches by his daily walks). He also eagerly embraced the Enlightenment's clockwork image of the universe. Deeply absorbed in the new scientific findings of his day, Kant actually spent most of his life writing on science rather than philosophy, developing the first completely naturalistic account of the origin of the solar system (the nebular hypothesis). His interest in philosophy arose only after he encountered the writings of a skeptical Scot named David Hume, who seemed to undermine the credibility of Newtonian science itself.[10] This was an outrage, and Kant turned to philosophy as a tool for defending Newtonian physics from such scandalous skepticism. In the process, he recast the upper and lower stories in terms of *nature* versus *freedom*.[11]

Kant's version of the two-realm theory of truth:

FREEDOM
The Autonomous Self

NATURE
The Newtonian World Machine

What did these terms mean for Kant? *Nature* was no longer the Aristotelian nature of Thomas Aquinas; it now meant the deterministic machine of Newtonian physics. As Kant wrote, it is "necessary that everything which takes place should be infallibly determined in accordance with the laws of nature."[12]

Yet Kant also sensed the beginnings of the Romantic reaction against Newtonian determinism, which explains why he put *freedom* in the upper story. He was intensely aware that the machine image of the universe was becoming distasteful to creative and sensitive people, like artists, writers, and religious thinkers. The machine model implied that the vivid colors and sounds and smells that make the world so beautiful were not real; they were merely the secondary effects of atoms impinging on our senses. Worse, if the machine included everything, even humans, then there could be no such thing as creativity, morality, freedom, or spirit. Enlightenment science, with its clockwork universe, had begun to loom as an enemy of the humane values.

The first person to reject Enlightenment notions of progress and civilization had been Jean-Jacques Rousseau, the flamboyant Swiss rebel who gave birth to Romanticism. Humans are *not* part of the machine, he declared; they are inherently free and autonomous. Rousseau himself fled the courts of Paris for the countryside, where he could throw off cultivated manners and live freely, in harmony with nature.[13] Kant was captivated by Rousseau's idea of autonomy (though he was far too straight-laced to live it out personally). Having been raised in a devout pietistic family, Kant also believed firmly in the need for morality, and morality presupposes the freedom to make moral choices. Thus in the upper story he put freedom or autonomy—defining *autonomy* literally as being subject only to laws imposed on oneself by oneself. (In Greek, *autos* = self, *nomos* = law.) His ideal was to be influenced by nothing but one's own moral will.

This was a radical concept of autonomy. As one theologian comments, "The creation of universal [moral] law was traditionally the function of God alone, and this function is now arrogated to the individual human rational will." Thus one might even say, "Kant has made reason into God."[14]

It is crucial to realize that the two sides in Kant's dichotomy were not just independent but outright contradictory. For if nature really is the deterministic machine of Newtonian physics, then how is freedom possible? Even Kant admitted that this was a paradox (an "antinomy") that he never succeeded in resolving. The trick, he said, is somehow to think of ourselves in both ways at once: On one hand, we operate within a physical world completely determined by natural laws (downstairs); and at the same time, we participate in a conceptual world where we conceive of ourselves as free moral agents (upstairs). In that purely conceptual world, Kant also placed God, the soul, and immortality.

Yet try as he might, Kant could not maintain both sides of the paradox as equally true. For in the lower story he was talking about things that actually exist, the constituents of the real world—while in the upper story he was talking about a realm of concepts or principles that we assume only because they are necessary for morality. Since morality requires freedom of the will, we must *suppose* ourselves to be free, no matter what science says to the contrary. Since the correspondence of happiness with virtue cannot be left to mere coincidence, we must *suppose* there is a God who guarantees it. And since moral perfection cannot be attained in this life, we must *suppose* ourselves to live forever. Kant himself admits that he did "not demonstrate freedom as something actual in ourselves and in human nature," but only something that "we must presuppose." It is "only an idea of reason whose objective reality is in itself questionable."[15]

In short, the lower story is what we *know*; the upper story is what we *can't help believing*.

In the end, Kant threw up his hands and simply insisted that regardless of what science says, we must act "as if" we were free. But that little phrase gives away the store: It implies that we know better, that we're tricking ourselves, and that moral freedom is little more than a useful fiction. In Kant's formulation, says philosopher Colin Brown, freedom, God, and immortality "look suspiciously like pieces of wishful thinking."[16]

INTELLECTUALLY FULFILLED ATHEISTS

Another way to describe Kant's dichotomy is to say that the lower story became the realm of publicly verifiable *facts* while the upper story became the realm of socially constructed *values*. This is the terminology that has become widespread in our own day through the work of social scientists.

The most common terminology today is fact versus value:

VALUE
Socially Constructed Meanings

FACT
Publicly Verifiable Truth

The divide between *fact* and *value* was clinched in the late nineteenth century by the rise of Darwinism. Though Kant and others had speculated on a naturalistic origin of the universe, the picture was not complete until Darwin offered a plausible naturalistic mechanism for the origin of life. He provided the missing puzzle piece that rendered naturalism a complete and comprehensive philosophy. That's why contemporary biologist Richard Dawkins says "Darwin made it possible to be an intellectually fulfilled atheist."[17] As he explains, before Darwin it was certainly possible to be an atheist, but not an intellectually satisfied one—because you could not have a complete, comprehensive worldview. Darwin filled in the final gap in a naturalistic picture of the universe. The lower story was now seamless and self-contained.

As a result, the upper story was now completely cut off from any connection to the realm of history, science, and reason. After all, if evolutionary forces produced the human mind, then things like religion and morality are no longer transcendent truths. They are merely ideas that appear in the human mind when it has evolved to a certain level of complexity—products of human subjectivity. We create our own morality and meaning through our choices.

Of course that means we can also *recreate* them whenever we choose. Nothing justifies the normative definition of, say, marriage as a lifetime union between a husband and a wife. That social pattern is not inherent and original in human nature—because *nothing* is inherent and original in human nature. Cultural patterns emerge gradually over the course of human evolution, arising by naturalistic causes and lasting only as long as they are expedient for survival.[18]

SECULAR LEAP OF FAITH

Today the fact/value dichotomy has become part of the familiar landscape of the American mind. Children pick it up every day in the typical school classroom. Fields like the humanities and social studies have been taken over by postmodernism. In English classes, teachers have tossed out their red pencils, and act as though things like correct spelling or grammar were forms of oppression imposed by those in power.

But paradoxically, if you go down the hallway to the science classroom, you'll find that there the ideal of objective truth still reigns supreme. Theories like Darwinian evolution are *not* open to question, and students are not invited to judge for themselves whether or not it is true. It is treated as public knowledge that everyone is expected to accept, regardless of their private beliefs.

By the time these students go to college, they've learned the lesson very well. Describing the students who troop into his classroom year after year, philosopher Peter Kreeft says, "They are perfectly willing to believe in objective truth in science, or even in history sometimes, *but certainly not in ethics or morality.*"[19] Do you recognize the dichotomy? The vast majority of students arrive in the classroom already convinced that science constitutes *facts* while morality is about *values.*

And what they learn in the college classroom typically reinforces this split. Let's do a close analysis of a few contemporary thinkers to show how widespread the two-realm theory of truth remains today.[20] Take, for example, Steven Pinker of MIT, a leader in the field of cognitive science, and his best-selling book *How the Mind Works*. The message of science, Pinker writes, is that the human mind is nothing more than a data-processing machine, a complex computational device. At the same time, he goes on to say, the very possibility of morality depends on the idea that we are *more* than machines—that we are capable of making free, uncoerced, undetermined choices. Here's how he states the dilemma: "Ethical theory requires idealizations like free, sentient, rational, equivalent agents *whose behavior is uncaused,*" and yet "the world, as seen by science, does not really have uncaused events."[21]

What is Pinker saying here? Let me restate it to make it even clearer: The postmodern dilemma can be summed up by saying that ethics depends on the *reality* of something that materialistic science has declared to be *unreal.*

You might think Pinker is arguing that science has disproved the foundational premise of ethics. At least, you might think that if you had not just read about Kant. For like Kant, Pinker wants to maintain *both* sides of the contradiction—by putting concepts like moral freedom in the upper story. As a scientist, Pinker accepts a materialistic, mechanistic model of human nature: "The mechanistic stance allows us to understand what makes us tick and how we fit into the physical universe." (That's his lower story.) But when he takes off his lab coat and goes home, he reverts to the traditional language of moral responsibility: "When those discussions wind down for the day, we go back to talking about each other as free and dignified human beings." (That's his upper story.)

This is not just a *divided* field of truth, it's an out-and-out contradiction—one that Pinker finds no way to resolve. He simply holds both sides of the contradiction at the same time: "A human being is *simultaneously* a machine *and* a sentient free agent, depending on the purposes of the discussion." Or, as he also puts it, depending on whether we are playing the "science game" or the "ethics game."[22]

We could represent Pinker's two-realm theory like this:

THE ETHICS GAME
Humans Have Moral Freedom and Dignity

THE SCIENCE GAME
Humans Are Data-Processing Machines

We must never forget that this is a real person, not just Exhibit A in a taxonomy of ideas—a person living in sharp existential tension between two contradictory modes of thought. It is impossible for Pinker to conduct his *personal* life on the basis of the philosophy that guides his *professional* life. Real people stubbornly refuse to act according to the mechanistic paradigm. So he is virtually forced to affirm the reality of things like freedom and dignity—*even though there is no basis for them within his own philosophy.*

Schaeffer uses a vivid image to describe this dilemma: He says modern thinkers often make a "leap of faith" from the lower story to the upper story. Intellectually they embrace scientific naturalism; that's their professional ideology. But this philosophy does not fit their real-life experience, so they take a leap of faith to the upper story where they affirm a set of contradictory ideas like moral freedom and human dignity—*even though these things have no basis within their own intellectual system.*

Pinker comes close to calling it a leap as well—he labels it *mysticism.*

"Consciousness and free will seem to suffuse the neurobiological phenomena at every level," he writes. "Thinkers seem condemned either to denying their existence or to wallowing in mysticism."[23] That is, *either* you can try to be consistent with evolutionary naturalism in the lower story—in which case you have to deny the existence of consciousness and free will. Or *else* you can affirm their existence even though they have no basis within your intellectual system—which is sheer mysticism. An irrational leap.

The secular "leap of faith":

POSTMODERN "MYSTICISM"
Moral and humane ideals have no basis in truth,
as defined by scientific naturalism.
BUT WE AFFIRM THEM ANYWAY

SCIENTIFIC NATURALISM
Humans are machines

You can understand why Schaeffer titled one of this books *Escape from Reason.* This is the great intellectual lostness of our age: that many are forced to hang their entire hopes for dignity and meaning on an upper-story realm that they themselves regard as noncognitive and unverifiable.

WAR OF WORLDVIEWS

To show how common this pattern is, let's consider a few more examples. Pinker's colleague at MIT, Marvin Minsky, is famous for his catchy phrase that the human mind is nothing but "a three-pound computer made of meat." But in his book *The Society of Mind,* he too takes a leap of faith. "The physical world provides no room for freedom of will," he writes. And yet, "that concept is essential to our models of the mental realm. Too much of our psychology is based on it for us to ever give it up. [And so] We're virtually forced to maintain that belief, *even though we know it's false.*"[24]

This is an astounding statement. Because people are made in the image of God, they unavoidably and inescapably believe in things like human freedom—yet they "know" these ideas are false, based on materialistic philosophy. The upper story has been reduced to a realm of false but necessary illusions.

Philosopher John Searle says there are two pictures of the universe that "are really at war" with one another. Science gives a picture of the universe as a vast machine, regular and law-like in its behavior. But everyday experience gives a picture of humans as agents capable of conscious, rational decision making. This universal experience is so compelling, Searle says, that "we can't give up our conviction of our own freedom, *even though there's no ground for it.*"[25] No ground, that is, within scientific materialism.

What he's saying is that he has to take a leap into the upper story—where he believes things even though there's no rational ground for them.

This is the tragedy of the postmodern age: The things that matter most in life—freedom and dignity, meaning and significance—have been reduced to nothing but useful fictions. Wishful thinking. Irrational mysticism.

YOUR WORLDVIEW IS TOO SMALL

The key to understanding the dynamics of the two stories is to recognize the symbiotic relationship between them. It is *because* the lower story has been defined in terms of scientific naturalism that there is "no ground" for upper-story beliefs. Naturalism leads to a mechanistic, deterministic model of human nature that reduces ideas like freedom and dignity to useful fictions. We might say that it's *because* modernism is in the lower story that postmodern skepticism has taken over the upper story.

Whenever we hear the language of "separate realms," we can be sure that one of them will be accorded the status of objective truth, while the other is demoted to private illusion. Since the Enlightenment, the *fact* realm has steadily expanded its territory into the *value* realm until there is little or no content left there. It has been reduced to empty words that merely express our irrational wishes and fantasies, with no basis in reality as defined by scientific naturalism. Using graphic terms, Schaeffer warns that the lower story "eats up" the upper story, dissolving away all traditional concepts of morality and meaning.[26]

Again, this is not merely an intellectual analysis. We are talking about a split that divides a person's inner life, creating enormous tension. When we evangelize among people who have accepted a divided field of knowledge, we must press them to face squarely the terrifying reality of this jagged split running through their own thought world. The very fact that they have to make a leap of faith shows that the scientific naturalism they have accepted in the lower story is not an adequate worldview. It does not explain human nature as everyone experiences it—as even they themselves experience it.

When a person's worldview is too "small," there will always be some element in human nature that fails to fit the paradigm. It's like trying to stuff a person into a garbage can, to borrow an analogy from Schaeffer—an arm or a leg will always stick out.[27] Adherents of scientific naturalism freely acknowledge that in ordinary life they have to switch to a different paradigm. That ought to tell them something. After all, the purpose of a worldview is to explain the *world*—and if it fails to explain some part of the world, then there's something wrong with that worldview. "Although man may *say* that he is no more than a machine," Schaeffer writes, *"his whole life denies it."*[28]

In evangelism, our task is to bring people face to face with this contradiction—between what a person *says* he believes and what his *whole life* is telling him. The gospel then becomes good news indeed: The doctrine that we are created in the image of God gives a solid foundation for human freedom and moral significance. We do not have to resort to an irrational upper-story leap. Given the starting point of a personal God, our own personhood is completely explicable. It no longer "sticks out of the garbage can." The Christian worldview provides a firm basis for the highest human ideals.

Now we can see why it's so important that we do not put Christianity in the upper story—because then *we will have nothing to offer to people trapped in the two-story dichotomy.* We will be offering just one more irrational upper-story experience—"true for me" but not universally, objectively true. We have to insist on presenting Christianity as a comprehensive, unified worldview that addresses all of life and reality. It is not just religious truth but total truth.

IMPERIALISTIC "FACTS"

The fact/value dichotomy gives us the tools to explain a host of cultural and intellectual trends. Take, for example, the process of reductionism, or what Schaeffer referred to as the lower story "eating up" the upper story. In our own day, this process has advanced very far indeed. If the upper story has traditionally been the realm for the spirit or soul—or, as moderns say, the self—today these concepts are under heavy shelling from cognitive science (philosophy of mind). At best, our sense of self is regarded as an accidental by-product of the interaction of particles. "The physical world is a perfectly natural place," writes Searle. "It consists of particles organized into systems, some of which have evolved consciousness and intentionality."[29] That is, you and I are merely particles that have somehow evolved consciousness and a sense of personal identity.

Many scientific materialists have even begun to say there is no "self" at all—no central "I" that resides in the body and makes decisions, holds opinions, loves and hates. The popular computational theory of the mind breaks it up into an array of independently evolved modules—a collection of computers, each of which performs a highly specialized function. In a recent public forum, Pinker argued that the concept of a unified self is sheer fiction: "It's only an illusion that there's a president in the Oval Office of the brain who oversees the activity of everything."[30] Appropriately, the forum was titled, "Is Science Killing the Soul?"

One school of thought, called eliminative materialism, goes so far as to dismiss consciousness itself as an illusion. Proponents insist that mental states do not exist; and they urge us to replace language about beliefs and desires with statements about the nervous system's physical mechanisms—the activation of neurons and so on.[31] Searle suggests that we describe the product of brain processes as "mentation," just as the product of stomach processes is digestion. We may *think* that we act deliberately and consciously, but in fact the brain acts on its own, and then deceives us into thinking we acted intentionally. A Harvard psychologist named Daniel Wegner has even written a book called *The Illusion of Conscious Will,* arguing that unconscious forces control all our actions.[32]

Yet in true Kantian form, even eliminative materialists concede that the concept of a self remains a convenient fiction—one that, in practice, we cannot do without. Even though our actions are produced by unconscious forces, Wegner writes, the *feeling* of a conscious will is a useful illusion because it helps us to sort out who did what, so that we can accept moral responsibility for our actions (even though we didn't actually choose to do them).

Do you recognize the leap of faith again? Scientific naturalism rules out the objective existence of conscious will; but in ordinary experience we can't get along without it. And so it is tossed into the upper story with other useful fictions.

In a similar vein, philosopher Daniel Dennett argues that language about purposes, intentions, feelings, and so on, does not belong to science but only to what he calls "folk psychology"—the idiom of ordinary discourse. Yet *there* it is all but indispensable. Predicting people's behavior is much more reliable if we think of them *as if* they had beliefs, desires, and purposes than if we assume they are simply physical mechanisms. (It's easier to predict that Sally will go to the refrigerator if we know that she *wants* milk and that she *believes* it is in the fridge.) But that Kantian phrase *as if* is a dead giveaway that Dennett is describing an upper-story concept—one that is useful but technically false. Folk psychology is useful, says one philosopher, if we keep in mind that it is "a way of looking at things which is strictly speaking, or in some sense, false."[33]

Clearly, the *fact* realm has grown aggressively imperialistic and is rapidly colonizing the *values* realm, reducing traditional concepts of the self and moral responsibility to convenient fictions.

CONFLICTED ON CAMPUS

The dynamic between the upper and lower stories often leads to outright hostility between people representing the two sides. On today's university campus, the antagonism between them is almost palpable. On the *fact* side of the campus, in the hard sciences, an ideal of objective knowledge still holds sway. Many Christians attending secular universities can tell horror stories about Darwinist professors who ridicule students for their religious faith. By contrast, on the *value* side of campus, in the humanities and social sciences, the idea of objective truth is long since passé, and subjectivism rules in the form of postmodernism, multiculturalism, deconstructionism, and political correctness. Here we are told that truth is relative to particular interpretive communities, and that knowledge claims are at best social constructions, at worst nothing but power plays. As a university student, I found that by far the toughest challenge to my newfound faith came from a sociology class: The assumption of relativism was so pervasive that it was tough to maintain hope in the sheer *possibility* of objective truth, let alone the conviction that Christianity was true. In a recent Zogby poll, 75 percent of American college seniors said their professors teach that there is no such thing as right and wrong in a universal or objective sense—that "what is right and wrong depends on differences in individual values and cultural diversity."[34]

We might explain the campus wars by saying that as the *fact* realm grows ever more imperialistic, the *values* realm is fighting back. Postmodernists are taking aim at Enlightenment concepts of rationality and science, debunking them as expressions of Western, white, male power. In feminist algebra, the common idiom of "attacking" mathematical problems is denounced as oppressive and violent. In feminist biology, the concept of DNA as the "master molecule" directing the cell's activities is denounced as a product of masculine bias. The scientific method itself is criticized for incorporating sexist overtones of male dominance and control, which justify the "rape of the earth." Feminist Sandra Harding is notorious for suggesting that Newton's principles of mechanics should be called Newton's "rape manual."[35] Women have often introduced helpful new perspectives into scholarship, but here I'm talking about a radical, ideological feminism that works hand-in-glove with postmodernism and multiculturalism in debunking the very idea of rationality and objectivity.

Why are these movements driven by such hostility to Western rationalism? It's important to recall that the rise of Enlightenment scientism put not only religion on the defensive, but also the arts and humanities. Traditionally, the arts had been regarded as an expression of Truth. Even though they make use

of myth and metaphor, the arts conveyed deep truths about the human condition. In the Enlightenment, however, rationalist critics began to denounce the
arts. They argued that poetry and fairy tales—with their unicorns and dragons, monsters and fairies—were nothing but harmful illusions. The "true
world" revealed by science was contrasted to the "false world" invented by
poets and painters.

"Science had persuaded the intelligent that the universe was nothing but
the mechanical interaction of purposeless bits of matter," writes historian
Jacques Barzun. As a result, "Thoughtful people in the nineties [1890s] told
themselves in all seriousness that they should no longer admire a sunset. It was
nothing but the refraction of white light through dust particles in layers of air
of variable density."[36] By the same token, why *paint* a sunset? It would only
be painting an illusion. At best, art was nothing more than a pleasing falsehood, a Noble Lie.

As the arts lost status and prestige, artists and writers found themselves
adrift, without their historical function in society. Many responded by going
on the offensive, attacking the mechanistic science and industrial society that
they regarded as dehumanizing—and that had made their own status so precarious.[37] Today they continue to seek redress by demonstrating the superiority of their own new analytical tools of literary analysis and deconstruction.
And why not apply these tools even to the sacrosanct area of science? If all
texts can be deconstructed, what makes scientific texts immune to that
process?

I witnessed a fascinating altercation at a conference at Boston University
on science and postmodernism several years ago. Postmodernist philosophers
led off by arguing that "there are no metanarratives," meaning no overarching, universal Truths. Responding on behalf of the scientists was Nobel
Prize–winning physicist Steven Weinberg, who replied: But of course there are
metanarratives. After all, there's evolution—a vast metanarrative from the Big
Bang to the origin of the solar system to the origin of human life. And since
evolution is true, that proves there is at least *one* metanarrative.

To which the postmodernist philosophers responded, ever so politely:
That's just *your* metanarrative. Evolution is merely a social construct, they said,
like every other intellectual schema—a creation of the human mind.

Thus postmodernism reduces even the most cherished scientific theories
to relativistic, culture-bound social constructs. Moreover, it does so in the
name of "liberation" from the dead hand of rationalism—and from the
impersonal, industrialized society that rationalism has produced. Even sheer
irrationality is sometimes portrayed as an escape from the naturalistic
"machine" of the lower story. This explains the celebration of irrationality

that we witnessed in the drug culture of the 1960s, then again in the New Age movement of the 70s, and yet again in today's postmodernism. In 1978, a *New York Times* article commented that California was the first state to shift "from steel to plastic, from hardware to software, from materialism to mysticism, from reality to fantasy."[38] Mysticism? Fantasy? A stunning example of romantic postmodernism offered as a redemptive alternative to the deadening impact of materialism.

As the lower story becomes ever more naturalistic and mechanistic, it seems that the upper story compensates by becoming ever more irrational and fanciful. Flight from logic and rationality has been embraced as an escape to a larger experience of meaning.

LEFTOVERS FROM LIBERALISM

The shift to a two-story view of truth also helps to explain the rise of liberal theology. Liberalism can be tough to pin down, because individual theologians may retain different bits and pieces of historic Christian doctrine. One accepts that Jesus was divine, while another denies it. One accepts the reality of the Resurrection, or the Virgin Birth, or Jesus' miracles, while another denies it. And so on. For a long time, conservative theologians tried to oppose liberalism by scurrying about arguing individual points of doctrine, one after another. But a much more effective way to critique liberalism is to expose its epistemology (theory of truth): The crucial flaw in liberalism is that it adopts the two-layer concept of truth. It accepts a naturalistic account of science and history in the lower story, while relegating theology to the upper story where it is reduced to personal, noncognitive experience.[39]

This explains why liberal theologians insist that Scripture is full of mistakes. After all, naturalistic science and history have decreed that miracles and other supernatural events are impossible.[40] Convinced that they must accommodate to naturalism, liberals either deny the supernatural elements in Scripture or else translate them into naturalistic terms. For example, an Irish clergyman recently wrote an article claiming that "there are possible natural explanations" for all the biblical miracles: "One natural explanation of the loaves-and-fishes miracle is that the people in the crowd, moved by the words of Jesus, so effectively and generously shared the little they had that there was enough for all." Astonishingly, the clergyman intended this as a *defense* of Christianity against scientific detractors. He concludes, hopefully: "If you think about it, this could work."[41] I doubt that his scientific opponents were impressed.

After accepting naturalism in the lower story, liberal theology then tries to rebuild a new form of Christianity strictly in the upper story, cut off from any roots in nature or history. "Creation" is not something God actually did; it is merely a symbolic term for our dependence on God. "The Fall" was not an event in history; it is merely a symbol of pervasive moral corruption. "Redemption" refers to a sense of meaning and purpose that has nothing to do with whether Jesus' tomb was empty as a historical fact. The theology left over after this process is typically so thin that liberalism ends up borrowing an interpretative framework from some other source—from existentialism (neo-orthodoxy) or Marxism (liberation theology) or feminism (feminist theology) or process thought (process theology) or postmodernism. Christian categories are then reinterpreted in terms of this external conceptual framework.

The defining feature of liberalism, then, does not lie in the details of its scriptural interpretation but in its two-realm view of truth. Liberalism rips Christianity from its roots in historical fact and casts it into the upper story, where it is demoted to subjective, contentless symbols and metaphors. It then becomes, in practice, little more than spiritualized window dressing for some other, more substantial system of thought.

This segmentation of the concept of truth is completely alien to historic Christianity, which teaches that spiritual truths are firmly rooted in historical events. Paul went so far as to say that if Christ's resurrection had not happened in real history—if there were no empty tomb—then our faith would be worthless (see 1 Corinthians 15). He even claimed to know of some five hundred people who were eyewitnesses to the fact that Christ was alive after His crucifixion—which meant he was treating religious truth as susceptible to the ordinary means of verification for historical events. Of course, the Resurrection is not *only* a historical event; it also has profound and far-reaching spiritual implications. But the point is that the two are not partitioned off from one another: An event that did not occur can have no spiritual implications. The orthodox Christian holds a unified field of truth, because the God who acts in our hearts is also the God who acts in history.

EVANGELISM TODAY

The holistic unity of Christian truth has to be at the heart of our message when we engage in evangelism in a postmodern age. For many people, the traditional forms of apologetics have become ineffective. For example, arguments based on the historical reliability of the Bible work well when nonbelievers still function within an older framework where religious claims are still considered to be either true or false.[42] But today if you talk about Christianity being true or historically verifiable, many people would be puzzled. Religion is assumed to be a product of human subjectivity, so that the test of a "good" religious belief is not whether it is objectively true but only whether it has beneficial effects in the lives of those who believe it.

During my own agnostic stage, I had absorbed this attitude wholesale. My older brother Karl once quizzed a friend and me about our religious beliefs. Hesitant to admit her doubts openly, the friend was being evasive until finally my brother said, "Look, do you believe in the Resurrection—that Jesus rose historically from the dead?"

My friend paused. "Well, that's the crux of the matter, isn't it?" she replied thoughtfully.

"No, it's not," I jumped in. "The Resurrection could be a kind of parable—not historically true but expressing some spiritual truth for those who believe it." In this exchange, my friend represented the older, rationalist skeptic, who still thought in categories of true and false and empirical verifiability. I was already swept up into postmodern subjectivism, where religion is not even susceptible to such categories anymore. President Eisenhower presaged the same attitude when he said, "Our government makes no sense unless it is founded in a deeply felt religious faith—and I don't care what it is."[43] In a postmodern world, it doesn't matter whether a religion is objectively true but only whether it performs a beneficial function.

Indeed, today people are less likely to talk about *religion* at all, preferring the term *spirituality.* The magazine *American Demographics* noted that five words are rapidly becoming the mantra of the new millennium: "I'm into spirituality, not religion."[44]

What's the difference between the two? *Religion* has come to refer to the public realm of institutions, denominations, official doctrines, and formal rituals—while *spirituality* is associated with the private realm of personal experience. "Spirit is the inner, experiential aspect of religion," explains Wade Clark Roof, "institution is the outer, established form of religion."[45] Isn't it interesting that even the realm of faith itself has now been divided between public and private? And since spirituality is firmly located in the private realm of personal experience, many people find something suspect about the *very notion* of public religious institutions and official religious doctrines. This pervasive sense that faith is by definition individual and subjective may be the prime reason for the loss of credibility on the part of religious institutions in our day.

This cleavage came to light in polls tracking Americans' spiritual response to the terrorist attacks. When surveys asked people how September 11 affected their religious *feelings,* the poll numbers soared. But when surveys were asked about their actual religious *beliefs and practices* (e.g., how often do you go to church or read the Bible?), the numbers dropped down to the same level as before the attacks. "The emerging consensus seems to be that vague, comforting spirituality is healthy," concludes columnist Terry Mattingly, "but that doctrinal, authoritative religion may even be dangerous."[46] The concept of *spirituality* has come to mean an experience devoid of doctrinal content and detached from any testable historical claims—something that belongs strictly in the upper story.

SPIRIT OF THE AGE

In this climate, the crucial challenge is to present Christianity as a unified, comprehensive truth that is not restricted to the upper story. We must have the confidence that it is true on *all* levels—that it can stand up to rigorous rational and historical testing, while also fulfilling our highest spiritual ideals.

Christians are called to resist the spirit of the world, yet that spirit changes constantly. The challenges facing our generation are not the same that faced an earlier generation. In order to resist the spirit of the world, we must recognize the form it takes in our own day. Otherwise, we will fail to resist it, and indeed may even unconsciously absorb it ourselves.[47]

And haven't many of us done just that? Haven't many evangelicals shifted their beliefs to the upper story, holding them as subjective, personalized truths—"true for me" but not universally, objectively true? "A significant percentage of Americans have inherited a theistic world from previous generations which they have 'syncretized' with the cultural elite's relativism," writes Bill Wichterman. As a result, they end up "holding fundamentally incompatible ideas and affirming both simultaneously."[48]

For example, a survey done in the 1970s of the three largest Lutheran synods found that 75 percent of Lutherans agreed that belief in Jesus Christ is absolutely necessary for salvation. But 75 percent also agreed that all roads lead to God and it does not matter which way one takes. Based on these numbers, at least half the Lutherans polled held two mutually exclusive theological positions at the same time. How is that possible? Christians often have "bifurcated minds," explains historian Sidney Mead. "When an American asserts that belief in Jesus Christ is essential for salvation, he speaks as one programmed by exposure to Christendom's orthodox tradition. . . . But when he asserts that all roads lead to God and are equally valid, he speaks as the creature of an eighteenth-century 'Enlightenment' perspective."[49]

Have you and I made faith a matter of the heart, while letting our minds be shaped by an Enlightenment perspective? Far too often the answer is yes, writes Phillip Johnson: "Even conservative Christians have so privatized their faith that they do not regard it as a source of knowledge but as merely theological 'reflection' on topics given by secular academia."[50] As he explains, "The typical strategy is to cede to science the authority to determine the 'facts,' then try to salvage some area of Christian faith in the realm of 'value.'"[51]

But such a strategy is ultimately self-defeating. Since values are not granted the status of genuine knowledge, they end up being dismissed as subjective and arbitrary. The appeal of the term *values,* writes historian Douglas Sloan, is that it seems to refer to "the most important dimensions of human experience," such as right and wrong, good and evil, the beautiful and the ugly. "But this is an illusion," Sloan warns; "in reality it means a capitulation to the modern dualism between . . . value and fact, in which the most important domains of human experience can only be dealt with in arbitrary, irrational, and ultimately dogmatic ways."[52] Christians must find ways to make it clear that we are making claims about reality, not merely our subjective experience.

After I had given a presentation explaining the fact/value dichotomy at an education conference, a teacher stood up and said cheerfully, "In Christian education, we have both: Christianity is about *values* while education is about *facts.* So I think we're doing pretty well." Without realizing it, the teacher had completely absorbed the modern split mindset. If we really understood what those terms mean today, we would utterly reject both. Christians do not promote *values,* because we hold that Christianity is objectively true, not merely our private preference. Nor do we teach *facts* in the modern sense, because that term means "value-free" science—free from any religious framework. What Christianity offers is a unified, integrated truth that stands in complete contrast to the two-level concept of truth in the secular world.

C. S. LEWIS'S TRUE MYTH

Traditional evangelism addressed a person's *moral* "lostness," which can be an effective method when that person is aware of standing guilty before a holy God. But today many people do not believe in a transcendent moral standard; if you speak about guilt, they think you're talking about a psychological problem that requires therapy, not about true moral guilt that requires forgiveness.

Yet there is also a *metaphysical* "lostness" that we can address. The tragedy of the two-story split is that the things that matter most in life—like dignity, freedom, personal identity, and ultimate purpose—have been cast into the upper story, with no grounding in accepted definitions of knowledge. We must never treat the divided concept of truth as merely academic; it produces an inner division between what people *think they know* (that we are merely machines in a deterministic universe) and what they desperately *want to believe* (that our lives have purpose and meaning).

This can be a soul-wrenching dilemma, and it is illustrated dramatically in the life of the well-loved writer C. S. Lewis. As a young man, Lewis abandoned his childhood faith in favor of atheism and materialism. Yet the bracing new philosophies that tantalized his intellect left his imagination hungry. As he wrote later, "Nearly all that I loved [poetry, beauty, mythology] I believed to be imaginary; nearly all that I believed to be real I thought grim and meaningless."[53]

Do you recognize the two-story division? What Lewis *thought* was real was the lower-story world of scientific materialism—but it was "grim and meaningless." What he *wished* were real was the upper-story world of myth and meaning—but he believed it to be only "imaginary."

This inner conflict created such agony that it drove Lewis's religious quest. He became desperate to find a truth that satisfied the whole person, including his longing for meaning and beauty. Eventually he abandoned materialism and adopted philosophical idealism, followed by pantheism, in an earnest effort to bring together the two conflicting realms he called "reason" and "romanticism."

C. S. Lewis spoke of reason versus romanticism:

ROMANTICISM
Beautiful but Imaginary

REASON
Repulsive but Real

What a joy it was when Lewis eventually discovered that Christianity resolved his lifelong struggle. He saw that Christ's incarnation was the fulfillment of the ancient myths that he had always loved—while at the same time a confirmable fact of history. Christianity was "the true myth to which all the others were pointing," explains one biographer. "It was a faith grounded in history and one that satisfied even his formidable intellect."[54]

To use Lewis's own punchy phrase, Christ's resurrection was a myth that became fact. It had all the wonder and beauty of a myth, answering to humanity's deepest needs for contact with the transcendent realm. And yet—wonder of wonders!—it had actually happened in time and space and history:

> The heart of Christianity is a myth which is also a fact. The old myth of the Dying God, without ceasing to be myth, comes down from the heaven of legend and imagination to the earth of history. It happens—at a particular date,

in a particular place, followed by definable historical consequences. We pass from a Balder or an Osiris, dying nobody knows when or where, to a historical Person crucified (it is all in order) under Pontius Pilate.[55]

Ironically, the turning point for Lewis came through a conversation with "the hardest boiled" atheist he'd ever known, who startled him by observing that the evidence for the historicity of the Gospels was surprisingly good: "All that stuff of [mythology] about the Dying God. Rum thing. It almost looks as if it had really happened once."[56]

Those few words brought Lewis's thoughts into sharply concentrated focus: He realized that Christianity rests on historical events that are confirmable by empirical evidence, and that at the same time express the most exalted spiritual meanings. There is no division into contradictory, opposing levels of truth—and therefore no division in a person's inner life either. Christianity fulfills both our reason and our spiritual yearnings. This is truly good news. We can offer the world a unified truth that is intellectually satisfying, while at the same time it meets our deepest hunger for beauty and meaning.

THE WHOLE TRUTH

Are we prepared to make that case to our postmodern neighbors? When we read James's injunction to "keep oneself unstained from the world" (James 1:27), we tend to interpret that in strictly moral terms—as an injunction not to sin. But it also means to keep ourselves "unstained" from the world's wrong ways of thinking, its faulty worldviews. We must learn how to identify and resist the false worldviews dominant at our moment in history. And the most pervasive thought pattern of our times is the two-realm view of truth. If we aspire to engage the battle where it is really being fought, we must find ways to overcome the dichotomy between sacred and secular, public and private, fact and value—demonstrating to the world that a Christian worldview alone offers a whole and integral truth. It is true not about only a limited aspect of reality but about total reality. It is total truth.

How do we go about crafting such a comprehensive Christian worldview? Where do we begin? In the next chapter, you will have a chance to practice hands-on worldview analysis, learning to handle the basic tools for building a Christian worldview. At the same time, you will be equipped with a simple but effective strategy for critiquing nonbiblical worldviews—so you will be ready to be used by God to liberate others from the power of false ideas as well.

4

SURVIVING THE
SPIRITUAL WASTELAND

[A Christian worldview] involves three fundamental dimensions:
the original good creation,
the perversion of that creation through sin,
and the restoration of that creation in Christ.

ALBERT WOLTERS[1]

As a teenager, I once went searching for books on Christianity at the local university library, wandering the aisles like a babe in the woods. I had just finished my senior year in high school, where I had taken an experimental class in intellectual history taught by a teacher who was a militant atheist. That was fine with me, since I had already rejected the Christian faith in which I had been reared, and was searching for my own truth. I had even written a senior paper for the class on why I no longer found Christianity credible.

But to my great surprise, when he read my paper, the same aggressively atheistic teacher urged me to slow down. "Make sure you know what you're rejecting before you try something new," he said. "Why don't you research some books on Christian philosophy before you decide to give it up." He reassured me that it was perfectly possible to be a "liberal-minded Christian"(or conversely a "closed-minded atheist"), so I didn't need to slam the door on my family background in order to pursue an honest, open-minded search for truth.

Having never heard before that there was such a thing as Christian philosophy (as opposed to theology), I promptly made my way to the local university library and looked in the card catalog under "Philosophy—Christian." Going to the shelves, I pulled out a book titled *Behold the Spirit,* by Alan Watts. Those familiar with the counterculture of the 1960s will instantly recognize that I had stumbled into a trap: Watts was a key figure in introducing Eastern religions to the West, and despite the Christian-sounding title, the book's theme was that if you delve under the surface details, Christianity really teaches the same things as Eastern mysticism. In fact, Watts taught that *all* religions are merely cultural window dressing over a common core of beliefs—a "perennial philosophy"—which regards everything as an emanation from the divine Being.

Now, I had gone to church all my life (my parents made sure of that) and also attended Lutheran elementary school. Over the years, I had memorized hymns, Bible verses, the creeds, and the Lutheran catechism, and I remain immensely grateful for that background. Yet I had never been trained in apologetics, or given tools for analyzing ideas, or taught to defend Christianity against competing "isms"—and when I read Watts's book, I was entranced. Through trips to the local bookstore, I brought home more of his books, along with works by Aldous Huxley (who promoted the same "perennial philosophy" in a book by that title) and Teilhard de Chardin (who offered a mystical spiritual evolutionism).[2]

The only person who looked over my shoulder and offered a critical perspective was my troublesome older brother Karl, who was annoying enough to point out that the content of these books deviated far from orthodox Christianity. But of course that was precisely their appeal. If I could explore exotic religious ideas while at the same time holding on to the genuine mystical core of Christianity, as these books promised, so much the better.

The story illustrates one of the most important reasons for developing a Christian worldview: to protect against absorbing alien philosophies unaware. Like so many young people, I had learned my Bible but had no clue how to relate biblical doctrine to the realm of ideas and ideologies. When I first encountered the broader intellectual world beyond the circle of family and church, I was an easy target. I had no conceptual tools to ward off challenges to the faith.

"Always [be] prepared to make a defense to anyone who asks you for a reason for the hope that is in you," Peter says (1 Pet. 3:15). The Greek word for "defense" is *apologia* (the root word in *apologetics*) and it was originally a legal term, meaning the defendant's reply to the prosecutor in a court of law. Later the same term was used of the early Christian apologists—philosophically trained theologians who defended the new faith against the rampant paganism of the Roman Empire.

But defending the faith is not only for professionally trained apologists. Just as all Christians are called to practice evangelism, so all have a responsibility to learn how to give reasons supporting the credibility of the gospel message. By "translating" Christian theology into contemporary language, we can set it side by side with other systems of thought, demonstrating that it offers a more consistent and comprehensive account of reality.

A few months ago I saw a clever advertisement that featured a rumpled, tweedy college professor glaring out at the reader, while the copy said: "Meet your son's first college professor. He is a Marxist, Atheist English professor who eats Christian freshmen for lunch."[3] That's exactly the image that ought to pop up in the minds of Christian parents when they are preparing their teens to go off to secular universities. Today basic apologetics has become a crucial skill for sheer survival. Without the tools of apologetics, young people can be solidly trained in Bible study and doctrine, yet still flounder helplessly when they leave home and face the secular world on their own. The tragedy is replayed over and over again, as Christian teenagers pack their bags, kiss their parents goodbye, and head off to secular universities, only to lose their faith before they graduate, falling prey to the latest intellectual fads.

MYSTIQUE OF THE FORBIDDEN

Like many others caught up in the counterculture of the 1960s and 70s, I plunged into Eastern thought, explored existentialism, read the early feminists, experimented with drugs, and "discovered" that truth was relative and subjective. For some teenagers, of course, the counterculture was merely fun and high jinks, but for me it was a serious search for truth and meaning. I tried mind-altering drugs only after reading books on the subject by philosophers like Aldous Huxley, who recommended drugs as a means of tapping into the cosmic consciousness. In *The Doors of Perception,* he promised that using hallucinogens would open the "reducing valve" of ordinary rationality that restricts our perceptions to the dull, mundane everyday world. Inspired by Huxley, I dipped into psychedelic drugs as part of a philosophic search for wider horizons of truth.[4]

Strange as it seems in retrospect, I first read Francis Schaeffer's *Escape from Reason* because I thought it sounded like yet another book on drugs. Before ever hearing about L'Abri, I happened on the first British edition of the book, which had a slightly eerie-looking cover illustration. And the title seemed to promise exactly what I was looking for—liberation from the dull grid of ordinary rationality. Yes, *I* want to "escape from reason," I thought as I picked up the book. Of course, I soon saw that Schaeffer's theme is precisely the opposite—that postmodern irrationality is a dead end, and that Christianity alone offers a logically consistent answer to the basic philosophical questions of life.

We need to make sure our own children leave home with that same conviction burned deeply into their minds—that Christianity is capable of hold-ing its own when challenged in the marketplace of ideas. It is not enough to teach young believers how to have a personal quiet time, follow a Scripture memory program, and link up with a Christian campus group. We also need to equip them to respond to the intellectual challenges they will face in the classroom. Before they leave home, they should be well acquainted with all the "isms" they will encounter, from Marxism to Darwinism to postmodernism. It is best for young believers to hear about these ideas first from trusted par-ents, pastors, and youth leaders, who can train them in strategies for analyz-ing competing ideologies.

At the very least, these ideologies should be stripped of the mystique of for-bidden ideas. When I was a teenager, my older sister initiated me into some of the mysteries of the wider culture—like evolution and ethical relativism—and I remember how much added allure these ideas had simply because they were something "Mother never told me." The dominant methodology in many Christian schools and churches has been to protect children from nonbiblical ideologies, and in part that is educationally sound. It makes sense to protect children until they are developmentally ready to handle complex ideas. But in many cases students are *never* exposed to competing ideas within their fami-lies, churches, or Christian schools, and as a result they go out into the world unprepared for the intellectual battles they are about to encounter, especially on secular college campuses.

NOT A SMOKESCREEN

When these young people start their classes and are confronted by new, plau-sible-sounding ideas, they may begin to wonder whether the adults in their lives were covering something up. They may suspect that their parents and teachers did not criticize competing ideas because there *are* no good criti-cisms—that they did not demonstrate how to defend Christianity because it is indefensible.

Nor do students get much help from the typical Christian campus group. The group I associated with after my conversion was spiritually committed but hopelessly anti-intellectual. As a new believer, I was still wrestling with the "isms" that had been so seductive in my pre-Christian days, but the fel-lowship group was unable to provide any support. One day, almost over-whelmed by the pervasive relativism taught in a sociology class, I sought the advice of one of the group leaders, asking desperately for some intellectual tools for defending the notion that there is genuine, objective truth—other-wise, how can we be sure that *Christianity* is true? His response was to steer the conversation out of intellectual territory and into familiar spiritual territory: "Nancy, it sounds like you're having a problem with assurance of salvation."

Now, I knew that I had done what was necessary for salvation: At my conversion I had carried out the requisite transaction, asking Jesus to pay the penalty for my sin, which is all that God requires. So my concerns were not theological. Instead I was struggling with doubts and second thoughts about whether God even existed, brought on by the almost smothering atmosphere of relativism in the classroom.

Despite the common stereotype, intellectual questions are not always merely a smokescreen for spiritual or moral problems. To be effective in equipping young people and professionals to face the challenges of a highly educated secular society, the church needs to redefine the mission of pastors and youth leaders to include training in apologetics and worldview. We must refuse to dismiss objections to the faith as mere spiritual subterfuge, but instead prepare ourselves to give what Schaeffer called "honest answers to honest questions."

When America was a young nation, the clergy were often the most highly educated members of the community. The congregation looked up to them and respected their intellectual expertise. But today those sitting in the pews are often as highly educated as the pastor; among the general population the clergy may even be looked down upon as narrowly trained functionaries. In this climate, it is imperative for seminaries to broaden the education of pastors to include courses on intellectual history, training future pastors to critique the dominant ideologies of our day. Pastors must once again provide intellectual leadership for their congregations, teaching apologetics from the pulpit. Every time a minister introduces a biblical teaching, he should also instruct the congregation in ways to defend it against the major objections they are likely to encounter. A religion that avoids the intellectual task and retreats to the therapeutic realm of personal relationships and feelings will not survive in today's spiritual battlefield.

HANDS-ON WORLDVIEW

Let's move now to the heart of this section of the book, giving you a chance to practice hands-on worldview construction. The grid of Creation, Fall, Redemption is not only helpful in diagnosing theological traditions, as we saw in earlier chapters. It also provides the scaffolding for constructing a Christian perspective on any topic, along with a grid for analyzing competing worldviews.

In any field, the way to construct a Christian worldview perspective is to ask three sets of questions:

1. CREATION: How was this aspect of the world originally created? What was its original nature and purpose?

2. FALL: How has it been twisted and distorted by the Fall? How has it been corrupted by sin and false worldviews? Cut off from God, creation tends to be either divinized or demonized—made into either an idol or an evil.

3. REDEMPTION: How can we bring this aspect of the world under the Lordship of Christ, restoring it to its original, created purpose?

Let's apply these categories to a few key areas—to education, the family, and then to a broad Christian social theory.

Repairing the Ruins

In Scripture, parents are repeatedly urged to pass on biblical truths to the next generation. As the Israelites were poised to enter the Promised Land, Moses emphasized the need to pass on their religious heritage to their children: "You shall teach [these words of mine] to your children, talking of them when you are sitting in your house, and when you are walking by the way, and when you lie down, and when you rise" (Deut. 11:19). The language paints an image of families passing on the faith not only through formal instruction but also through everyday conversation.

In every period of history, Christians have taken the charge of education seriously—founding schools, promoting literacy, and preserving the literary heritage of the surrounding culture. After the fall of Rome, it was the monks who carefully preserved the great literary and philosophical masterpieces of the classical world, painstakingly copying ancient manuscripts, along with commentaries and glosses to explain the meaning of the text.[5] The Reformers preached the priesthood of all believers—the responsibility of each person to know and understand the Scriptures—and they founded catechism schools to teach children the principles of the faith from an early age. When the Puritans landed on American shores and began to clear the wilderness, within a mere six years they had founded the first university (Harvard) to train young men for the ministry and for political leadership.

How, then, do we apply the categories of Creation, Fall, and Redemption to education? Creation tells us that children are created in the image of God, which means they have the great dignity of being creatures with a capacity for love, morality, rationality, artistic creation, and all the other uniquely human capabilities. Education should seek to address *all* aspects of the human person. We cannot be content with a behaviorist methodology that treats students as complex stimulus-response machines. Nor can we adopt a constructivist methodology that treats students as organisms adapting to their environment, using concepts merely as tools to organize subjective experience. Christianity gives the basis for a higher view of human nature than any alternative worldview that begins with nonpersonal forces operating by chance.[6]

Yet the biblical view of human nature is also solidly realistic. The doctrine of the Fall teaches us that children are, like all of us, prone to sin and in need of moral and intellectual direction. In the aftermath of the Fall, God gave verbal revelation to enable us to order our lives by timeless and universal truths that would otherwise be unavailable to fallen, finite creatures. Thus Christian educators will not accept the Enlightenment optimism that unaided reason, apart from divine revelation, is capable of achieving a "God's-eye" view of the world. Nor will we accept the Romantic notion that children come to earth naturally innocent, "trailing clouds of glory." Both of these philosophies deny the reality of the Fall and give birth to progressive methods of education that refrain from teaching students true from false, or right from wrong, but instead expect them to discover their own "truths."[7]

Finally, Redemption means that education should aim at equipping students to take up their vocation in obedience to the Cultural Mandate. Each child should understand that God has given him or her special gifts to make a unique contribution to humanity's task of reversing the effects of the Fall and extending the Lordship of Christ in the world. As the poet John Milton once wrote, the goal of learning "is to repair the ruins of our first parents."[8] To do that, every subject area should be taught from a solidly biblical perspective so that students grasp the interconnections among the disciplines, discovering for themselves that all truth is God's truth.

At the same time, we must be alert to the false visions of redemption that shape various theories of education today. Proponents of virtually every ideology seek to gain a foothold in the classroom, because they know that the key to shaping the future is shaping the minds of children. We may have to fend off New Age methods of meditation and guided imagery applied to the classroom (redemption through cultivating a higher consciousness); or the misuse of therapeutic techniques to change students' attitudes to fit some progressive agenda (redemption through psychological adjustment); or programs of political correctness and multiculturalism (redemption through leftist politics).[9] Many educators no longer even define education as helping students learn skills and gain knowledge, but as empowering students to enlist in approved social causes. As American culture moves away from its Christian heritage, the public classroom is becoming a battleground for competing ideologies, so that one of our most important tasks is to teach students how to identify and critique worldviews.

Retooling the Family

How does the grid of Creation, Fall, and Redemption give us tools for crafting a biblical concept of the family? As the foundational social institution, the family has functioned as the laboratory for countless social experiments. Every political visionary dreams up some scheme for retooling the family—often abolishing it altogether in favor of either radical statism or radical individualism.

Statism has been a recurring theme since the dawn of Western culture. To an astonishing degree, Western political and social thought has been hostile to the role of the family in proposed visions of the ideal society. Secular intellectuals from Plato to Rousseau to B. F. Skinner to Hilary Clinton have been enamored with the idea of putting the child directly under the care of the state rather than the family.

To counter such utopian schemes, we must begin with Creation. The biblical doctrine of creation tells us the family is a social pattern that is original and inherent in human nature itself. It is therefore normative for all times and all historical situations. Although there can be variety in the details, its essential nature cannot be remodeled at will. Any utopian scheme that seeks to cast the family into the dustbin of history will find itself working against human nature itself.

Utopians who deny Creation also deny the Fall, totally rejecting the idea that human nature is corrupt and prone to evil. Instead they redefine all social problems as temporary disorders that can be resolved through education and social engineering. "Utopians are motivated by a desire to overcome the effects of the Fall without relying on divine redemption," writes Bryce Christensen in *Utopia Against the Family*. "Most utopians wish to 'be as gods' (Gen. 3:5) through self-will and human engineering, not through the blessings of heaven."[10]

Thus is born a seductive image of Redemption through the creation of a new Eden—a return to the original state of innocence. In B. F. Skinner's famous novel *Walden Two,* the founder describes his utopian community as "an improvement on Genesis."[11]

Yet, ironically, virtually every actual historical attempt to improve on Genesis has ended in a coercive, totalitarian state. Why? Because, contrary to the utopian vision, sin is real and cannot be simply engineered out of existence. Thus the state always finds itself having to *force* people to fulfill its utopian schemes. The destruction of the family is often simply one tool for increasing government power over individuals by eliminating competing loyalties, in an attempt to create total allegiance to the state. To defend the family against statist agendas, we need to make the case that only the biblical drama of Creation, Fall, and Redemption gives a realistic yet humane account of human nature and of the structure and purpose of the family in society.

For the Love of Children

Alongside the tendency toward statism runs what seems a paradoxical tendency to reduce all social relationships to individual choice. A dramatic example can be found in Ted Peters's *For the Love of Children,* which urges a complete overhaul of the American family. Peters recommends that each parent be required to make a legal contract with each of his or her children—preferably with a public ceremony similar to a wedding ceremony. The purpose of this odd-sounding proposal? To shift the foundation of the family from biology to choice.[12]

"Whether we like it or not, the end of the road for a disintegrating liberal society is individual choice," Peters argues, implying that there is no alternative but to go along. As a liberal Lutheran, he urges Christians to discard "any premodern formalism based on divine dicta or traditional authority or natural law that would try to make an end run around choice"[13]—which is to say, not even God's commands ("divine dicta") have any force to stop us from reconfiguring the family on the basis of choice. Peters's proposal would turn the family into a collection of disconnected, atomistic individuals, bound by no attachments or obligations they do not choose for themselves. This is called ontological individualism, which means that individuals are the only ultimate reality. Relationships are not ultimate in the same sense but are derivative, created by individual choice.

It is significant that Peters begins by rejecting the biblical doctrine of creation in favor of the evolutionary approach of Process Theology—which frees him to jettison traditional Christian social philosophy.[14] For Creation implies that we are not merely disembodied wills, forming families by sheer choice; instead we are holistic beings who procreate "after our kind." We exercise our wills by choosing to submit to an objective moral order that God has ordained, not by inventing alternatives to it. The family provides a rich metaphor for the Kingdom of God precisely because it is the primary experience we have of an obligation that transcends mere rational choice, and is constitutive of our very nature.

Mobilizing the Trinity

The tug-of-war between statism and individualism in regard to the family is easier to understand if we jump to a higher level and consider social theory in general. The Rosetta Stone of Christian social thought is the Trinity: The human race was created in the image of God, who is three Persons so intimately related as to constitute one Godhead—in the classic theological formulation, *one in being* and *three in person*. God is not "really" one deity, who only appears in three modes: nor is God "really" three deities, which would be polytheism. Instead, both oneness and threeness are equally real, equally ultimate, equally basic and integral to God's nature.

The balance of unity and diversity in the Trinity gives a model for human social life, because it implies that both individuality and relationship exist within the Godhead itself. God is being-in-communion. Humans are made in the image of a God who is a tri-unity—whose very nature consists in reciprocal love and communication among the Persons of the Trinity.[15] This model provides a solution to the age-old opposition between collectivism and individualism. Over against collectivism, the Trinity implies the dignity and uniqueness of individual persons. Over against radical individualism, the Trinity implies that relationships are not created by sheer choice but are built into the very essence of human nature. We are not atomistic individuals but are created for relationships.

As a result, there is harmony between being an individual and participating in the social relationships that God intended for our lives together. This may sound abstract, but think of it this way: Every married couple knows that a marriage is more than the sum of its parts—that the relationship itself is a reality that goes beyond the two individuals involved. The social institution of marriage is a moral entity in itself, with its own normative definition. This was traditionally spoken about in terms of the common good: There was a "good" for each of the individuals in the relationship (God's moral purpose for each person), and then there was a "common good" for their lives together (God's moral purpose for the marriage itself).

In a perfect marriage unaffected by sin, there would be no conflict between these two purposes: The common good would express and fulfill the individual natures of both wife and husband. In fact, certain virtues necessary for spiritual maturity—such as faithfulness and self-sacrificing love—can be practiced *only* within relationships. That means individuals cannot fully develop their true nature unless they participate in social relationships, such as marriage, family, and the church.[16]

Ever since the Fall, however, societies have tended to tilt toward either the individual or the group. In modern cultures, family bonds are rapidly dissolving in the acids of personal autonomy. By contrast, in some traditionalist cultures, the clan or tribe still takes precedence over the individual. When I attended a Lutheran Bible school in the mid-1970s, a fellow student, a young Japanese woman, was under enormous pressure from her Buddhist family back home to renounce her Christian faith. The main barrier to Christianity in her homeland, she told me, was that most young people refused to adopt a religion different from that of their parents and extended family. This was a novel idea to me since, as a young American, being different from one's parents seemed a good reason in *favor* of adopting a religion, or anything else.

The doctrine of the Trinity has repercussions not only for our concept of the family but also for virtually every other discipline. In philosophy, the triune nature of God provides a solution to the question of the One and the Many (sometimes called the problem of unity and diversity): Ever since the ancient Greeks, philosophers have asked, Does ultimate reality consist of a single being or substance (as in pantheism) or of disconnected particulars (as in atomism)?[17] In politics, the opposing poles play out in the two extremes of totalitarianism versus anarchy. In economics, the extremes are socialism or communism versus laissez-faire individualism.

In practice, of course, most societies shuffle toward some middle ground between the two opposing poles—like America's "mixed" economy today. Yet merely hovering between two extremes is not a theoretically coherent position. A consistent worldview must offer a way to reconcile them within a consistent system. By offering the Trinity as the foundation of human sociality, Christianity gives the only coherent basis for social theory.

Nor is the answer merely theoretical. In Redemption, believers are called to form an actual society—the church—that demonstrates to the world a balanced interplay of the One and the Many, of unity and individuality. In John 17:11, Jesus prays for the disciples He is about to leave behind, asking the Father "that they may be one, *even as we are one.*" Jesus is saying that the communion of Persons within the Trinity is the model for the communion of believers within the church. It teaches us how to foster richly diverse individuality within ontologically real relationships. "The Church as a whole is an icon of God the Trinity, reproducing on earth the mystery of unity in diversity," writes

Orthodox bishop Timothy Ware. "Human beings are called to reproduce on earth the mystery of mutual love that the Trinity lives in heaven."[18] And as we learn to practice unity-in-diversity within the church, we can bring that same balance to all our social relationships—our families, schools, workshops, and neighborhoods.

THE WORLDVIEW NEXT DOOR

Apologetics involves not only defending the Christian faith but also critiquing other faiths or worldviews. Part of the task of evangelism is to free people from the power of false worldviews by diagnosing the points where they fail to stack up against reality. Just as Isaiah had to argue against the wooden idols of Old Testament times, showing how silly it was to bow down to the work of one's own hands (Isa. 44:6ff.), so today we have to deconstruct the conceptual idols that hold so many people captive.

A wonderfully simple and effective means of comparing worldviews is to apply the same grid of Creation, Fall, and Redemption. After all, every worldview or ideology has to answer the same three sets of questions:

1. CREATION: Translated into worldview terms, Creation refers to ultimate origins. Every worldview or philosophy has to start with a theory of origins: Where did it all come from? Who are we, and how did we get here?

2. FALL: Every worldview also offers a counterpart to the Fall, an explanation of the source of evil and suffering. What has gone wrong with the world? Why is there warfare and conflict?

3. REDEMPTION: Finally, to engage people's hearts, every worldview has to instill hope by offering a vision of Redemption—an agenda for reversing the "Fall" and setting the world right again.

Let's practice applying the three-part grid to some of the worldviews we all encounter. In the passages that follow, I will offer brief descriptions and excerpts from representative worldviews, and as you read along, stop and think how *you* would break down these ideas into Creation, Fall, and Redemption.

Marx's Heresy

Marxism fits the three categories of Creation, Fall, and Redemption so neatly that many have called it a religious heresy, which makes it a good sample to start with. It also remains an important philosophy for Christians to understand: Though the Iron Curtain has fallen, Marxism retains a powerful influence in many places of the world—especially on the American university campus. A French political philosopher recently said that nowadays when he wants to debate a Marxist, he has to import one from an American university.

Even more important, all of us encounter various leftist movements such as multiculturalism, feminism, and political correctness. These liberation movements are sometimes called *neo*-Marxist because they apply Marxist forms of analysis to groups identified by race or gender, urging them to raise their consciousness and throw off their oppressors. The characters have changed, but it's still the same play.

How, then, can we use the categories of Creation, Fall, and Redemption to analyze these various forms of Marxism?[19] For Karl Marx, the ultimate creative power was matter itself. This was a new form of philosophical materialism, for earlier versions had been static, picturing the world as a vast machine. The problem with that conception, for Marx, was that it seemed to open the door to the idea of God: Since a machine is designed to fulfill a particular function, it virtually requires a designer, just as a watch implies the existence of a watchmaker.[20] To avoid that conclusion, Marx proposed that the material universe is not static but dynamic, containing within itself the power of motion, change, and development. That's what he meant by *dialectical* materialism. He embedded the Prime Mover within matter as the dialectical law.

In short, Marx made matter into God. His disciple, Vladimir Ilyich Lenin, did not shy away from using explicitly religious language: "We may regard the material and cosmic world as the supreme being, the cause of all causes, the creator of heaven and earth."[21] The universe became a self-originating, self-operating machine, moving inexorably toward its final goal of the classless society.

Marx's counterpart to the Garden of Eden was the state of primitive communism. And how did humanity fall from this state of innocence into slavery and oppression? Through the creation of private property. From this economic "Fall" arose all the evils of exploitation and of class struggle.

Redemption comes about by reversing the original sin—in this case, destroying the private ownership of property. And the "redeemer" is the proletariat, the urban factory workers, who will rise up in revolution against their capitalist oppressors. One historian, though not a professing Christian, brings out the religious overtones nicely: "The savior proletariat [will], by its suffering, redeem mankind, and bring the Kingdom of Heaven on earth."[22]

Let's break this down now by applying the three-part grid. Without looking ahead at the answers, how would you analyze Marx's thought into Creation, Fall, and Redemption?

CREATION

Q: What is Marxism's counterpart to Creation,
the ultimate origin of everything?

A: *Self-creating, self-generating matter*

A crucial subpoint under the category of Creation is one's view of human nature. You see, humanity is always defined by its relationship to God—to whatever is regarded as ultimate reality. In Marxism, then, we are defined by the way we relate to matter—the way we manipulate it and make things out of it to meet our needs. In short, by the means of production. Thus Marx's materialism explains why he embraced economic determinism—why he regarded everything from politics to science to religion as mere superstructure built upon economic relations.

FALL

Q: What is Marxism's version of the Fall,
the origin of suffering and oppression?

A: *The rise of private property*

Notice that Marx does not identify the ultimate source of evil as a moral failing, for that would imply that humans are morally culpable—which means the solution must be forgiveness and salvation. Instead he locates evil in social and economic relations; thus the solution is to change those relations through revolution. Marxism assumes that human nature can be transformed simply by changing external social structures.

REDEMPTION

Q: How does Marxism propose to set the world right again?

A: *Revolution! Overthrow the oppressors*
and recreate the original paradise of primitive communism

The day of judgment in Marxism is the day of revolution, when the evil bourgeoisie will be condemned. Marx and Engels even used the liturgical term *Dies Irae* (the Day of Wrath), looking forward to the day when the mighty would be cast down.[23] Marxism "is nothing less than a program for creating a new humanity and a new world in which all present conflicts will be solved," says theologian Klaus Bockmuehl. It "is a secularized vision of the kingdom of God."[24]

This analysis explains why Marxism continues to have such widespread influence despite its dramatic failure ever to produce a classless society anywhere on earth—and why it keeps spawning neo-Marxist movements. By incorporating all the elements of a comprehensive worldview, it taps into a deep religious hunger for redemption. Marx's idea of the end of history, when communism will triumph and conflict will vanish from the world "is transparently a secular mutation of Christian apocalyptic beliefs," writes philosopher John Gray. It is "myth masquerading as science."

Of course, that's why it is far more powerful than science. It takes otherworldly religious hope and secularizes it into this-worldly revolutionary zeal.[25] "Like Christianity, Marx's thought is more than a theory," writes philosopher Leslie Stevenson. "It has for many been a secular faith, a vision of social salvation."[26]

Rousseau and Revolution

Let's go back before Marx to one of the sources of his ideas—Jean-Jacques Rousseau. Most of the ideologies that bloodied the twentieth century were influenced by Rousseau. His writings inspired Robespierre in the French Revolution, as well as Marx, Lenin, Mussolini, Hitler, and Mao. Even Pol Pot, who massacred a quarter of the population in Cambodia, was educated in Paris and read his Rousseau. So if you get a grip on Rousseau's thinking, you have a key to understanding much of the modern world.

What exactly was it that made his worldview so revolutionary? Rousseau said the way to grasp the essence of human nature was to hypothesize what we would be like if we were stripped of all social relationships, morals, laws, customs, traditions—of civilization itself. This original, pre-social condition he called the "state of nature." In it, all that exists are lone, disconnected, autonomous individuals, whose sole motivating force is the desire for self-preservation—what Rousseau called self-love (*amour de soi*). Social relationships are not ultimately real; instead they are secondary or derivative, created by individual choice.

What did that mean for Rousseau's view of society? If our true nature is to be autonomous individuals, then society is *contrary* to our nature: It is artificial, confining, oppressive. That's why Rousseau's most influential work, *The Social Contract,* opens with the famous line, "Man is born free, and everywhere he is in chains." He did not mean chains of *political* oppression, as we Americans might think: For Rousseau, the really oppressive relationships were *personal* ones like marriage, family, church, and workplace.

This line of thought represented a stark break from traditional Christian social theory, which takes the Trinity as the model of social life (as we saw above). The picture of ultimate origins given in the Bible is not one of disconnected solitary individuals wandering under the trees in a state of nature. Instead, the picture is one of a couple—male and female—related from the beginning in the social institution of marriage, forming the foundation of social life.

The implication of the doctrine of the Trinity is that relationships are just as ultimate or real as individuals; they are not the creation of autonomous individuals, who can make or break them at will. Relationships are part of the created order and thus are ontologically real and good. The moral requirements they make on us are not impositions on our freedom but rather expressions of our true nature. By participating in the civilizing institutions of family, church, state, and society, each with its own "common good," we fulfill our social nature and develop the moral virtues that prepare us for our ultimate purpose, which is to become citizens of the Heavenly City.

This explains why it was so revolutionary when Rousseau proposed that individuals are the sole ultimate reality. He denounced civilization, with its social conventions, as artificial and oppressive. And what would liberate us from this oppression?

The state. The state would destroy all social ties, releasing the individual from loyalty to anything except itself. Rousseau spelled out his vision with startling clarity: "Each citizen would then be completely *independent* of all his fellow men, and absolutely *dependent* on the state."[27] No wonder his philosophy inspired so many totalitarian systems.

Let's run these ideas through the three-part grid.

CREATION

Q: What is the starting point for Rousseau's philosophy,
his substitute for the Garden of Eden?

A: *The state of nature*

Rousseau was not alone in starting with the concept of a state of nature. Other early modern political thinkers like Thomas Hobbes and John Locke had proposed the concept as well, picturing the original human condition in terms of disconnected, atomistic individuals. They were taking their cue from seventeenth-century mechanistic physics, which pictured the material world in terms of atoms combining and recombining under the force of attraction or repulsion. Reflecting the same model in the social world, these early political thinkers recast society in terms of human "atoms" who are logically prior to the social arrangements in which they "bond."

The notion of a state of nature was clearly an alternative to the Garden of Eden, a new account of human origins. It "is a new myth of origins at variance with the account in Genesis," says philosopher Nancey Murphy.[28] Standing at the dawn of modernity, these thinkers sensed that in order to propose a new view of civil society, they needed to begin by offering a new creation myth. Because they were writing prior to Darwin, they were ambiguous about whether they were offering an actual historical account or merely a thought experiment. But in any case they realized that to propose a new political philosophy, they had to ground it in a new creation story.

Rousseau went further than either Hobbes or Locke, however: In his state-of-nature scenario the individual is stripped not only of social ties but of human nature itself. The earliest human is unformed, indeterminate, nothing more than a beast—a gentle, peaceful, and happy beast (in contrast to Hobbes), but a beast nonetheless. Thus Rousseau's definition of human nature is, paradoxically, not to have a nature at all—to be free to create oneself.[29] Humans have the distinctive ability to develop and transform themselves. The reason social relationships are oppressive is that they interfere with the individual's freedom to create himself.

With this concept of human nature, revolution in the modern sense became possible—not just revolt against a political regime but the attempt to destroy the entire social order and rebuild an ideal one from scratch, one that would transform human nature itself and create "the New Man." As Rousseau put it, the ideal legislator "should feel within himself the capacity to change human nature."[30] For if human nature is indeterminate and can no longer be defined positively, then there is an unlimited space for the state to impose its own definition of human nature.

FALL

Q: For Rousseau, what is the Fall, the source of oppression and suffering?

A: *Society or civilization*

In the state of nature, human beings are autonomous selves, with no ties to others except those they choose for themselves. Virtually by definition, then, any relationships *not* a product of choice are oppressive—such as the biological bonds of family, the moral bonds of marriage, the spiritual bonds of the church, or the genetic bonds of clan and race.

The only social bond where individuals retain their pristine autonomy is the contract—because there the parties are free to choose for themselves how they wish to define the terms and the extent of their agreement. The terms are not preset by God, church, community, or moral tradition but are strictly voluntary.[31] That's why Rousseau, Hobbes, and Locke all called for a state based on a "social contract." In it, all social ties would be dissolved and then reconstituted as contracts, based on choice. This was always presented in terms of liberating the individual from the oppression of convention, tradition, class, and the dead hand of the past.[32]

REDEMPTION

Q: What is the source of Redemption for Rousseau?

A: *The state*

The idea that the state could be a liberator was completely novel. In actual experience, of course, the state is a locus of power, authority, and coercion. No one had ever suggested before that it might be a liberator. Thus one Christian political theorist says Rousseau gave birth to "the politics of redemption."[33]

Historians tell us the twentieth century was the bloodiest ever, but the problem is not that large numbers of people suddenly underwent some mysterious moral degeneration. The problem is that they adopted worldviews based on faulty definitions of Creation, Fall, and Redemption.[34]

It may seem paradoxical that a philosophy of radical individualism would lead to radical statism. But as Hannah Arendt points out in *The Origins of Totalitarianism,* disconnected, isolated individuals are actually the most vulnerable to totalitarian control because they have no competing identity or loyalties.[35] That's why one of the best ways to protect *individual* rights is by protecting the rights of *groups* such as families, churches, schools, businesses, and voluntary associations. Strong, independent social groupings actually help to limit the state because each claims its own sphere of responsibility and jurisdiction, thus preventing the state from controlling every aspect of life. Neo-Calvinist political philosophy describes the independence of the social spheres using the term *sphere sovereignty,* meaning the right of each to its own limited jurisdiction over against the other spheres.[36] Catholic social thought uses the term *subsidiarity* for basically the same idea. Contrary to Rousseau, protecting moral, social, and kinship bonds actually protects individual freedom.

Unfortunately, most American political thought—both liberal and conservative—continues to rest on the atomistic view that society is made up of autonomous individuals. It is the unconscious assumption that students bring into the classroom today, says one Christian professor: "Without ever having read a word of Locke, they could reproduce his notion of the social contract without a doubt in the world."[37]

In fact, I suggest that the assumption of autonomous individualism is a central factor in the breakdown of American society today. Take public policy: In *Democracy's Discontent,* Michael Sandel says the background belief of modern liberalism is the concept of the "unencumbered" self—by which he means "unencumbered by moral or civic ties they have not chosen."[38] In liberalism, the individual exists prior to its membership in moral communities such as marriage, family, church, and polity. The self is even prior to any definition of its own nature. Thus for liberalism the core of our personhood is our ability to choose our own identity—to create ourselves. This is why relationships and responsibilities are often considered separate from, and even contradictory to, our essential identity—why individuals often feel they need to break free from their social roles (as husband, wife, or parent) in order to find their "true self."[39] It is Rousseau redux.

Or take legal philosophy: In *Rights Talk*, Mary Ann Glendon says modern American law typically depicts the "natural" human person as a solitary creature. Our law is "based on an image of the rights-bearer as a self-determining, unencumbered individual, a being connected to others only by choice."[40] In other words, relationships are not constituent of our identity but are creations of individual choice—a direct echo of Rousseau's "state-of-nature" theory.

Finally, political philosophy: In *Modern Liberty and Its Discontents*, Pierre Manent says the basic tenet of liberalism is that no individual can have an obligation to which he has not consented. All human attachments are to be dissolved, and then reconstituted on the basis of choice—that is, contracts. "Through the contracts that he makes with his fellows, each individual is the author of his every obligation."[41] We now understand why Ted Peters wanted to dissolve the biological base of the family to reconstitute it on the basis of sheer choice.

Ideas like these do not remain purely abstract and academic. They filter down from professors to their students, who may well put them into practice. For example, with marriage reduced to sheer choice, many students are deciding that saying "I do" has become too risky—that it's not worth the trade-off involved in giving up their autonomy. A study from the National Marriage Project at Rutgers University found that today's young people view marriage "as a form of economic exposure and risk, largely due to the prevalence of divorce." This is the deadly fruit of the atomistic view of society. Instead of being reverenced as a social good, marriage is now feared as an economic risk. "Today's singles mating culture is not oriented to marriage," the study says. "Instead it is best described as a low-commitment culture of 'sex without strings, relationship without rings'."[42] Clearly, the ontological individualism of Hobbes, Locke, and Rousseau remains at the heart of America's social and political crisis. (For more on this subject, see appendix 1, "How American Politics Became Secularized.")

Sanger's Religion of Sex

Having raised the subject of "sex without strings," let's apply a worldview analysis to some of the cutting-edge social issues of our day. The left-right split in American politics used to be over economic issues, such as the distribution of wealth. But today the split tends to be over issues of sex and reproduction:

abortion, homosexual rights, no-fault divorce, the definition of the family, fetal experimentation, stem cell research, cloning, sex education, pornography.

In fact, a few years ago, *The Boston Globe* reported that college students have a new way to make the grade—by watching pornographic movies. Many colleges now offer courses where students analyze hard-core pornography. They're even required to shoot their own explicit films as homework to show in class. It's a new trend called "porn studies."[43]

How did students go from studying Homer to studying "Debbie Does Dallas"? The answer is that sexual liberation itself has become nothing less than a full-blown ideology, with all the elements of a worldview.

Just listen to some of the architects of the sexual revolution, like Margaret Sanger, the founder of Planned Parenthood. Most of us know Sanger as an early champion of birth control, but not everyone knows that she also wrote several books expounding a complete worldview. Sanger was a committed Darwinist, a champion of Social Darwinism and eugenics, which was very much in vogue in the early part of the twentieth century. Her goal was to construct a "scientific" approach to sexuality based squarely on Darwinism.

Sanger portrayed the drama of history as a struggle to free our bodies and minds from the constraints of morality—what she called the "cruel morality of self-denial and sin." She touted sexual liberation as "the only method" to find "inner peace and security and beauty." She even offered it as the way to overcome social ills: "Remove the constraints and prohibitions which now hinder the release of inner energies [her euphemism for sexual energies], [and] most of the larger evils of society will perish."[44]

Finally, Sanger offered this sweeping messianic promise: "Through sex, mankind will attain the great spiritual illumination which will transform the world, and light up the only path to an earthly paradise."[45]

Clearly this is a religious vision if there ever was one. Let's run it through the three-part grid:

CREATION

Q: What functions as Sanger's creation myth?
Where did humans come from?

A: *Evolution: She was an avid proponent of both biological and Social Darwinism*

What did this mean for Sanger's view of human nature? If we are products of evolution, then our ultimate human identity is located in the biological, the natural, the instinctual—especially the sexual instincts. A few years ago, the *New Yorker* ran an article on "porn studies," and even interviewed some of the professors who teach these courses. As one of them explained: "Sex is now seen as the motive force of our beings"—our "ultimate" identity.[46]

In Sanger's day, scientists were just discovering the glands, and she concluded that healthy human development depended on the free functioning of the reproductive glands. This suggested to her that sexual restraint was actually physiologically harmful. Today those older notions have been debunked—no one knowledgeable in the field believes that sexual restraint is physically harmful. Yet sexologists do continue to believe that sexual liberation is the foundation of healthy personality development.

FALL

Q: For Sanger, what is the source of our social and personal dysfunctions?

A: *The rise of Christian morality*

It is Christianity, with its repressive morality, that prevents people from finding their true sexual identity, which is the core of their being—and this in turn causes all sorts of other dysfunctions. Sanger condemned "the 'moralists' who preach abstinence, self-denial, and suppression."[47]

Of course, not all sexual liberals come right out and condemn Christian morality so openly. A more common strategy is to claim that they simply want to be scientific, and that science requires a morally neutral stance. For example, Alfred Kinsey opened his major study *Sexual Behavior in the Human Male* by complaining about scientists who divide human behavior into categories of normal and abnormal. "Nothing has done more to block the free investigation of sexual behavior" than the acceptance of this moral distinction, he fumed; and he urged scientists to describe all forms of human behavior "objectively," without ethical comment. Repeatedly he emphasized that sex is "a normal biologic function, *acceptable in whatever form it is manifested.*"[48]

But of course, that statement itself expresses a moral stance. Kinsey was completely committed to a form of ethical relativism based on Darwinian naturalism—and he was smuggling in his *own* values masked as objective and neutral science. Kinsey often insisted that science is only descriptive—that it cannot prescribe what people should do. But in reality, writes historian Paul Robinson, he "had very strong opinions about what people should and should not do, and his efforts to disguise those opinions were only too transparent." The very categories of analysis he chose to use "clearly worked to undermine the traditional sexual order." Indeed, Kinsey sometimes spoke as if the introduction of a Bible-based sexual morality were *the* watershed in human history[49]—a sort of "fall" from which we must be redeemed.

REDEMPTION

Q: What do people like Sanger and Kinsey offer as means of healing and wholeness?

A: Sexual liberation

In the *New Yorker* article on porn studies, one professor explained that "the cultural left" has turned from changing society to "inner change"—defined primarily as discovering the true nature of one's sexuality.[50] In short, sexual liberation has itself become a moral crusade, in which Christian morality is the enemy and opposition to it is a heroic moral stance.

This is a difficult concept for Christians to get their minds around, because when we hear the word *morality* we think of biblical morality. But for many secularists, biblical morality is nothing less than the source of evil and dysfunction—while their own position has all the fervor and self-righteousness of a moral call to arms.

The conservative Jewish film critic Michael Medved learned this the hard way. He once publicly praised the work of a couple who were both Hollywood film producers. They had been together for fifteen years, had two children, and he spoke of them as a married couple. Immediately he heard from friends of the couple, who said they were certainly *not* married—and that they would be "offended" to hear themselves described that way.[51]

Offended? Why would anyone consider it an insult to be regarded as married? By rejecting marriage, you see, this couple meant to take a high-minded stand for freedom against an oppressive moral convention. The philosopher John Stuart Mill once wrote, "The mere example of nonconformity, the mere refusal to bend the knee to custom, is itself a service."[52] By giving an example of liberation, folks like this Hollywood couple feel they are performing a service to humanity. When Madonna was asked in a recent interview why she had published her raunchy book *Sex* back in 1992, she responded, "I thought I was doing a service to mankind, being revolutionary, liberating women."[53]

This attitude explains why it is so difficult to stop the sexualizing of our culture. Sexual liberation is not just a matter of sensual gratification or titillation: It is a complete ideology, with all the elements of a worldview. To stand against it, we cannot simply express moral disapproval or say, *That's wrong.* We have to remember that morality is always derivative—it stems from one's worldview. In order to be effective, we have to engage the underlying worldview.

Buddhist in the Sky

On an airplane I once found myself sitting beside a sweet-faced, black-haired woman from Thailand who was a devout Buddhist. Determined not to miss this opportunity to learn more about an Eastern religion firsthand, I peppered her with questions—and discovered that the real article is vastly different from the version that is trendy among Hollywood celebrities. Take reincarnation. In the Westernized version, cycling through ever-higher levels has the optimistic ring of evolutionary progress.[54] But for a real Buddhist, reincarnation is the wheel of *suffering*. The whole purpose of life is to escape from it.

How? Through self-denial and detachment from the things of the world. This earnest Thai woman traveled to a Buddhist monastery for a week out of each month to live in a hut with a dirt floor and no electricity in order to practice meditation. Through long hours of practice, she explained, your "muddy mind" (full of worldly concerns) can be transformed into a "clear mind" (free from all earthly attachments). And if you finally attain that level of consciousness, you will break free from the cycle of suffering. Few succeed within a single lifetime, the woman told me—mostly monks, because they have rejected the attachments of marriage and family. Yet out of hundreds of thousands of monks, maybe only one will make it.

"What about you?" I asked, knowing that she was married and had children. "Haven't you already blown it, then?"

"I don't worry about that; I just keep practicing meditation," the woman replied. She went on to explain the law of karma: "Bad thoughts attract bad things, good thoughts attract good things."

"What if you are good, and bad things still happen?" I asked.

"Then you are paying for what you did in a previous life." It struck me that Buddhism is a pretty bleak religion. Everything bad that happens is your own fault—caused by what you did either in this life or in an earlier one. There is no grace, no real hope of redemption in this lifetime. And meditation is not contact with a God who responds by listening and loving; it's merely a set of mental exercises to train the mind to detach from the material world.

In fact, there *is* no personal God in Eastern religions like Buddhism and Hinduism. The divine is a nonpersonal, noncognitive spiritual force field. The ultimate goal in these religions is not so much happiness as relief from the burden of the self: Nirvana is the merging of the individual spirit with the universal spiritual substratum to all things—losing your individuality in the pantheistic One.

When Eastern thought came to America in the 1960s, it combined with Western elements to form the New Age movement. But the core pantheistic concepts remain essentially the same. So let's apply our three-part grid to New Age thought.

CREATION

Q: What is the ultimate reality, the origin of all things, in New Age pantheism?

A: *The Absolute, the One, a Universal Spiritual Essence*

In pantheism, ultimate reality is a unified mind or spiritual essence pervading all things. It is an undifferentiated Unity beyond all human categories of thought—beyond the divisions of good and evil, subject and object. This is not a personal Being with consciousness and desires, but a nonpersonal spiritual essence of which we are all part. In fact, a personal God like the Christian deity is regarded as inferior because personality implies differentiation, which to the Eastern mind suggests limitation. The biblical idea of a God who is *both* personal *and* infinite is regarded as incomprehensible.

FALL

Q: In pantheism, what is the source of evil and suffering?

A: *Our sense of individuality*

In pantheism, the great dilemma of human existence is not sin—after all, an unconscious spiritual essence cannot care about what humans do to each other. The human dilemma is that we *don't know* we are part of god. We think we're individuals, with separate existences and identities. This is what gives birth to greed and selfishness, conflict and warfare. In Hinduism, our sense of individuality is even called "maya," which means illusion. The goal of spiritual exercises is to free our minds from the illusion of individuality.

REDEMPTION

Q: How does pantheism tell us to solve the problem of evil and suffering?

A: *By being reunited with the Universal Spiritual Essence*
from which we all came

The goal of Eastern religious exercises is to reunite with the god within—to recover a sense that we are all god. This analysis helps make sense of the bewildering proliferation of techniques in the New Age movement—yoga, transcendental meditation, crystals, centering, tarot cards, diets, guided imagery, and all the rest. In spite of their vast variety, the purpose of all these techniques is to dissolve the boundaries of the self and recover a sense of universal oneness.

One reason it is important to learn how to do worldview analysis is to protect ourselves and our children from being taken in by false worldviews. A few years ago a friend of mine, a very committed Christian woman, recommended a book to me. "It's a classic," she said. "You must read it." But when I bought it, I was stunned to find that it featured a clear statement of Eastern pantheism in story form. It is a book sure to be familiar to most of you: *The Secret Garden,* by Frances Hodgson Burnett.

The main character is a ten-year-old boy named Colin, and Burnett uses him as the main mouthpiece for her pantheistic philosophy. Colin tells the other characters in the story that everything in the world is made of a single spiritual substance, which he calls "Magic." The word is always capitalized in the book—a dead giveaway that it is a code word for the divine. Colin says, "Everything is made out of Magic, leaves and trees, flowers and birds. . . . The Magic is in me. . . . It's in every one of us."[55] This Magic has marvelous, even miraculous, powers—it makes things grow, heals the sick, and makes people good. It is the ultimate power in the universe, for as one character in the book says, there could not be any "bigger Magic." Significantly, Colin even borrows explicitly Christian language: "Magic is always . . . making things out of nothing."[56]

It turns out that this is not a personal God who loves us but an impersonal force to be tapped, like electricity. As Colin puts it, "We need to get hold of Magic and make it do things for us, like electricity and horses and steam."[57] (Burnett was writing back in 1911.) And the way to "get hold" of this power is through spells and incantations. The children in the story cross their legs, "like sitting in a sort of temple," and Colin begins to chant "in a High Priest tone": *"the Magic is in me—the Magic is in me. . . . Magic, Magic, come and help."*[58]

If this isn't outright religion, I don't know what is. Yet I have known countless Christian parents and teachers who have read the book with their children—*without detecting the Eastern pantheistic worldview.* After reading the book, I wrote an article analyzing its not-so-hidden religious themes,[59] and not long afterward, my own son was assigned to read it . . . in a Christian school.

Several years later I researched Burnett's life, and learned that she was involved in Spiritualism and Theosophy (a Buddhist-inspired philosophy involving concepts such as karma, reincarnation, and pantheism).[60] But even if readers do not know her personal history, the Eastern worldview is recognizable throughout the book. It is a prime illustration of the principle that if we do not learn how to do worldview analysis—and teach our children as well—we will have no defense against the alien worldviews we encounter in the surrounding culture. And then we are likely to absorb them without even being aware of it. (For more detail on the New Age movement, see appendix 2.)

WORLDVIEW MISSIONARIES

In thinking about why we need a Christian worldview, I suggest that it is nothing less than obedience to the Great Commission. As Christians we are called to be missionaries to our world, and that means learning the language and thought-forms of the people we want to reach. In America we don't have to master a new language, but we *do* have to learn the thought-forms of our culture.[61] We need to speak to philosophers in the language of philosophy, to politicians in the language of public policy, and to scientists in the language of science.

A student in international relations once told me that the courses she was taking, designed to prepare professionals to work in other cultures, focused almost entirely on worldviews. Learning another language was considered only a preliminary step, she explained; to communicate effectively, the most impor-

tant requirement was to know the habits of thought in a culture. It is no accident that Paul says Christians are called to be "ambassadors" for the heavenly
King to an alien culture (2 Cor. 5:20). To be effective ambassadors, we need to
prepare ourselves as thoroughly as any professional in international relations.

If the grid of Creation, Fall, and Redemption provides a simple and effective tool for comparing and contrasting worldviews, it also explains why the
biblical teaching of Creation is under such relentless attack today. In any worldview, the concept of Creation is foundational: As the first principle, it shapes
everything that follows. Critics of Christianity know that it stands or falls with
its teaching on ultimate origins.

To become more effective ambassadors for Christ, then, we must learn
how to defend the biblical view of Creation, both scientifically and philosophically. That is the theme of the next four chapters (Part 2).[62] As you work
through these chapters, you will learn how to defend your faith against the
challenges of Darwinian naturalism while also crafting a positive case for
Intelligent Design. You will learn how a Darwinian worldview helped propel
a host of damaging cultural trends, from the legalization of abortion to the
decline in public education. To communicate a Christian worldview, the first
step is learning how to make a winsome case for creation.

PART TWO

STARTING AT THE BEGINNING

5

DARWIN MEETS
THE BERENSTAIN BEARS

[Darwinism] is supported
more by atheistic philosophical assumptions
than by scientific evidence.
HUSTON SMITH[1]

It was Darwinism that first raised doubts about my faith," recalls Patrick Glynn, author of *God, the Evidence*.[2] Raised in a Catholic home, Glynn describes himself as a serious child who was "very devout." He became an altar boy at a younger age than was officially permitted, and recalls that at the Catholic school he attended, a good half of the books in the library consisted of lives of the saints.

In seventh grade, however, the teacher presented the theory of evolution, and like the clear-sighted child in *The Emperor's New Clothes*, young Patrick immediately recognized that it contradicted all his prior religious teaching. "I stood up in class and asked the nun, If Darwin's theory is true, then how can the creation story in the Bible be true?" The poor nun was flummoxed . . . and thus the seeds of doubt were planted.

Patrick's mother urged him to talk to a local priest, who took the boy to a baseball game, bought him a hot dog, and took the opportunity to have *the talk*. Between innings, the priest explained how to reconcile Genesis with an evolutionary origin of the human race: "You don't have to believe that Adam and Eve were the *only* beings around at the time," he said. "You only have to believe that God took them and gave them souls." This seemed such an obviously ad hoc strategy that it only reinforced the boy's growing doubts.

"By the time I became a student at Harvard, I was ripe for its atmosphere of naturalism and secularism," Glynn says. In his classes, it was simply assumed that religious belief had become impossible for any rational human being. After all, "Darwin had demonstrated that it was not necessary to posit a God to explain the origin of life." If natural causes working on their own are capable of producing everything that exists, then the obvious implication is that there's nothing left for a Creator to do. He's out of a job. And if the existence of God no longer serves any explanatory or cognitive function, then the only function left is an emotional one: Belief in God is reduced to an escape hatch for people afraid to face modernity. At Harvard, Glynn says, religion was regarded as a human construct invented by primitive cultures as a defense mechanism to help them cope with the rigors of surviving. By the end of his graduate studies, he had reached the conclusion that there was no God, no soul, no afterlife, no inherent justice in the universe. "I prided myself on being realistic, even Machiavellian, in my view of the world."

It was some twenty years later, after a personal crisis, that Glynn began to question his settled certitudes of rationalism and naturalism. In *God, The Evidence* he recounts the various lines of argument that finally persuaded him that God exists after all, including the stunning evidence for design in the physical universe (which we will cover in chapter 6).

Glynn's personal story illustrates the foundational role played by a theory of origins in the formation of a worldview. As we have seen, every worldview starts with an account of Creation, which shapes its concepts of the Fall and Redemption.[3] As a result, whoever has the authority to shape a culture's Creation myth is its de facto "priesthood," with the power to determine what the dominant worldview will be. To break the power of today's secular "priesthood," Christians need to have a basic grasp of the origins controversy, with its wide-ranging impact on American thought.

As we will discover over the next four chapters, the major impact of Darwinian evolution does not lie in the details of mutation and natural selection, but in something far more significant—a new criterion of what qualifies as objective truth. As one historian explains, Darwinism led to a naturalistic view of knowledge in which "theological dogmas and philosophical absolutes were at worst totally fraudulent and at best merely symbolic of deep human aspirations."[4] Let's unpack that phrase: If Darwinism is true, then both religion and philosophical absolutes (like Goodness, Truth, and Beauty) are strictly speaking false or "fraudulent." We can still hold on to them if we really want to, but only if we're willing to place them in a separate category of concepts that are not genuinely true but "merely symbolic" of human hopes and ideals.

Do you recognize the two-story division of truth? A naturalistic view of knowledge places Darwinism in the lower story of public *facts,* while relegating religion and morality to the upper story where they are merely symbols of private *values.* As one philosophy textbook tells the story, prior to Darwin, most thinkers in America assumed "the fundamental unity of knowledge" based on the conviction of a single universal order established by

God—encompassing both the natural and the moral order. The impact of Darwinian evolution "was to shatter this unity of knowledge," reducing religion and morality to "noncognitive subjects."⁵ In short, Darwinism completed the cleavage between the upper and lower stories. Today the two stories run along on parallel tracks, never meeting or merging. As you read through Part 2, you will see how this bifurcation was solidified and cemented in place, until in our own day it has become a potent instrument for debunking the objectivity of religious truth claims.

To start off, we will examine the key scientific claims and counterclaims. The current chapter will bring you up to date on the scientific case against Darwinism, while the next chapter will equip you to make a positive case in favor of Intelligent Design. After that, we will trace the broad implications of the origins controversy across all of Western culture—from ethics to education, from movies to music. Virtually every part of society has been affected by the Darwinian worldview, and in order to be effective worldview missionaries, you and I need to be prepared to show why it is mistaken, while offering a credible alternative.

A UNIVERSAL ACID

For some three hundred years after the scientific revolution, Christianity and science were thought to be completely compatible and mutually supporting. Most scientists were Christian believers, and a parson collecting biological specimens was a common sight in the countryside. The stunning complexities of nature unveiled by science were not feared as a challenge to belief in God but hailed as confirmation of His wisdom and design. Scholars as diverse as Copernicus, Kepler, Newton, Boyle, Galileo, Harvey, and Ray felt called to use their scientific gifts in praise to God and service to humanity. The application of science in medicine and technology was justified as a means of reversing the effects of the Fall by alleviating suffering and tedium.⁶

Secularizing trends eventually began to threaten the harmony between science and religion, but its final collapse came abruptly in the late nineteenth century when Charles Darwin published his theory of evolution. Darwinism was implacably naturalistic, explaining life's origin and development by strictly natural causes. It was (as we saw in chapter 3) the missing puzzle piece that completed a naturalistic picture of reality. This is when historians began concocting images of "warfare" between science and religion—especially historians who hoped the victor in the conflict would be science.

Many people are surprised to learn how recently the warfare stereotype was constructed, because today it is part of folk culture. I was once preparing a lecture while sitting outside my son's karate class. (This is how mothers of

young children get much of their work done—by the playground or the soccer field.) Another mother came over to chat, and when she heard that my topic
was Christianity and science, her eyebrows shot up in surprise: "Why? Aren't
religion and science always in conflict? Don't they disagree on just about everything?" More recently, a graduate student in aerospace engineering told me
that when her unchurched roommate learned she was a believer, her first
response was, "How can you be a Christian and study science?" Stories like
these remind us that many people still unthinkingly assume that science and
religion are in deadly opposition to one another.

To be fair, it's a stereotype deliberately cultivated in some quarters. A few
years ago, a friend of mine decided to educate himself on the origins issue, and
browsing in a bookstore he came across a book titled *Darwin's Dangerous
Idea*. "Just the thing," he thought, "for a good critique of Darwinism."

To his chagrin, my friend discovered that far from offering a critique, the
book actually gives an enthusiastic *endorsement* of Darwinism. The theory is
"dangerous" only to irrational superstitions, like traditional religion and
ethics, says the author Daniel Dennett. He calls Darwinism a "universal acid,"
an allusion to the children's riddle about an acid so corrosive that it eats
through everything—including the flask in which you are trying to contain it.
The point is that Darwinism is likewise too corrosive to be contained. It spreads
through every field of study, corroding away all traces of transcendent purpose
or morality. As Dennett puts it, Darwinism "eats through just about every traditional concept and leaves in its wake a revolutionized world-view."[7]

Public schools are urged to revolutionize their students' worldviews by
applying Darwin's "universal acid" to the beliefs they bring in from home. And
what if meddlesome parents persist in teaching their children that Darwinism
is *not* the whole story of human origins? In that case, Dennett growls, "we will
describe your teachings as the spreading of falsehoods, and will attempt to
demonstrate this to your children at our earliest opportunity." As a final insult,
he suggests putting traditional churches and rituals in "cultural zoos," along
with other artifacts from defunct cultures.[8]

Obviously, what Dennett is promoting here is not objective science but his
own personal philosophy of evolutionary materialism or naturalism. Making
an appearance in the eight-part PBS series "Evolution," Dennett informed the
audience that Darwin's great accomplishment was to reduce the design of the
universe to a product of "purposeless, meaningless matter in motion."[9] But
think about it: Is there any possible way such a statement could be tested scientifically? Any laboratory test that could confirm that the universe arose from
"meaningless matter in motion"? Clearly not. It is not a scientific theory at all,
but merely Dennett's personal philosophy.

Yet it is the philosophy that has become official orthodoxy in the public square. Half a century ago G. K. Chesterton was already warning that scientific materialism had become the dominant "creed" in Western culture—one that "began with Evolution and has ended in Eugenics." Far from being merely a scientific theory, he noted, materialism "is really our established Church."[10]

To defend a Christian worldview in our generation, we must learn how to challenge this "established Church." And a crucial first step is to demonstrate precisely that it *is* a church—a belief system or personal philosophy. Much of what is packaged and sold under the label of *science* is not really science at all but philosophical materialism. Which is to say, it is not objective truth but merely the expression of someone's personal "values." We can use the fact/value dichotomy to turn the tables, arguing that evolution itself belongs in the sphere of private, subjective "values"—which means the rest of us have no reason to regard it as authoritative. Scientists may have authority to tell us how to hybridize corn or manufacture medicines, but they have no special expertise to tell us what worldview to believe. They have no valid claim on us when they leave the bounds of science and issue metaphysical proclamations that the universe is a product of "purposeless, meaningless matter in motion." We need to develop sales resistance to such aggressive philosophical proselytizing.

KINDERGARTEN NATURALISM

These days, even young children need to be primed to think critically. Several years ago I picked up a science book for my little boy Michael, and was shocked to discover that along with the science it gave a whopping dose of philosophical naturalism. Titled *The Bears' Nature Guide*,[11] the book featured the Berenstain Bears from the extremely popular children's picture book series. As the book opens, the Bear family invites us to go on a nature walk; and after turning a few pages, we come to a two-page spread with a dazzling sunrise and the words spelled out in capital letters: "Nature . . . is all that IS, or WAS, or EVER WILL BE!"

Where have we heard those words before? You might remember them from Carl Sagan's PBS program "Cosmos." Its trademark slogan was: "The Cosmos is all that is or ever was or ever will be."[12] Those who attend a liturgical church will recognize that Sagan was offering a substitute for the *Gloria Patri* ("As it was in the beginning, is now, and ever will be").[13] Clearly, if nature is all that ever *has* existed or ever *will* exist, then there is no supernatural, and nature itself functions as the divine—the eternal, uncaused cause.

And just in case a child misses the naturalistic message, at the bottom of the page the authors have drawn a bear pointing out at the reader, saying, "Nature is you! Nature is me!"

The point is that if philosophical naturalism is appearing in books even for young children, then you *know* it has permeated the entire culture. Under the guise of teaching science, a philosophical battle is being waged. And if Christians do not frame the philosophical issues, someone else will do it—and they will not balk at preaching their message even to small children.

SPINMEISTERS IN SCIENCE

To grasp the defining role played by naturalistic philosophy, all we have to consider is how limited the evidence for Darwinian evolution really is. When pressed for observable, empirical support for the theory, Darwinists invariably reach into the same grab bag and pull out their favorite stock examples, which you can easily master. Let's look at a few of them, following loosely the lead of Jonathan Wells in *Icons of Evolution*,[14] which analyzes the illustrations used most frequently in high school and college textbooks. These are images familiar to all of us—and probably to our children as well—which means it is crucial that we learn how to evaluate them.

Darwin's Beaks

One of the most widely cited pieces of evidence for evolution is the variation among finches on the Galapagos Islands off the coast of South America. The finches are small, rather dull-looking birds, whose main claim on our interest is that their beak size differs according to the habitats where they live—suggesting that they have adapted to differing conditions. Virtually every biology textbook repeats the story of Darwin's voyage to the Galapagos as a young naturalist,[15] and contemporary biologists have gone back there to confirm his theory.

Sure enough, one study found that during a period of drought, the average beak size among the finches actually increased slightly. Apparently the only food available in the dry period were larger, tougher seeds, so that the birds with slightly larger beaks survived better. Now, we're talking about a change measured in tenths of a millimeter—about the thickness of a thumbnail. Yet it was hailed enthusiastically as confirmation of Darwin's theory. As one science writer exulted, this is evolution happening "before [our] very eyes."[16]

But that was not the end of the story. Eventually the rains returned, restoring the original range of seeds. And what happened then? The average beak size returned to normal. In other words, the change that Darwinists were so excited about turned out to be nothing more than a cyclical fluctuation. It did not put the finches on the road to evolving into a new kind of bird; it was simply a minor adaptation that allowed the species to survive in dry weather.

Which is to say, the change was a minor adjustment that allowed the finches *to stay finches* under adverse conditions. It did not demonstrate that they originally evolved from another kind of organism, nor that they are evolving into anything new (see fig. 5.1).[17]

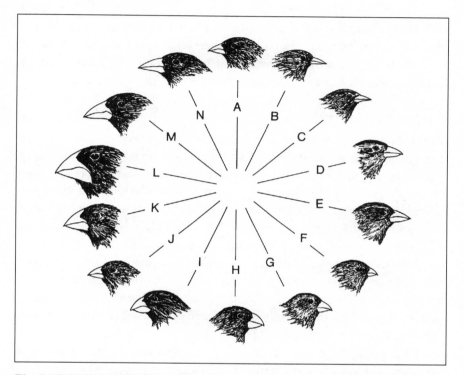

***Fig. 5.1* DARWIN'S FINCHES:** The change in beak size was a cyclical variation that allowed the birds to *stay finches* under adverse conditions. *(Copyright Jody Sjogren. Used with permission.)*

When the National Academy of Sciences (NAS) put out a booklet on evolution for teachers, it decided this story really needed a more positive spin. And so the booklet *did not mention* that the average beak size returned to normal. Instead it speculated what might happen if the change were to continue indefinitely for some two hundred years—whether the process would even produce a "new species of finch."[18]

This was clearly a misleading treatment of the facts, suggesting that the change was directional instead of reversible. The *Wall Street Journal* responded with an apt rejoinder by Phillip Johnson: "When our leading scientists have to resort to the sort of distortion that would land a stock promoter in jail," he said, "you know they are in trouble."[19]

Nor is the problem limited to finch beaks. Examples of minor, reversible diversification are the stock-in-trade of textbooks on biological evolution.

Another frequent example is the development of resistance to antibiotics. A highlight of the PBS "Evolution" series was a section explaining how the HIV virus becomes resistant to the drug used in treatment, due apparently to a mutation. Once again, this was hailed as evolution in action. But once again, as soon as the drug was removed, the change was reversed, and the virus returned to normal. (It became drug sensitive again.)[20] Such limited, reversible change is hardly evidence for a theory that requires *un*limited, directional change.[21]

Dysfunctional Fruit Flies

To come up with better evidence than nature offers, scientists have tried producing mutations in the laboratory, typically using fruit flies. These tiny insects reproduce in a matter of only days, which means researchers can expose them to radiation or toxic chemicals and then observe the resulting mutations over several generations. What kinds of mutations have they produced? Larger wings. Smaller wings. Shriveled wings. No wings. They even get oddities like a fly with legs growing out of its head instead of antennae.

So what does it all add up to? To be frank, dysfunctional fruit flies. After half a century of bombarding fruit flies with radiation, scientists have not coaxed them into becoming a new kind of insect—or even a new and improved fruit fly. None of the mutated forms fly as well as the original form, and probably would not survive in the wild.

There's only one mutation that could even appear to be an improvement: The PBS "Evolution" series featured a mutation that produces four wings instead of two (see fig. 5.2). Now, *that* might seem to be an evolutionary advance. But if you were watching the program, and looked closely at the television screen, you would have seen that the extra wings don't actually move. That's because they don't have any muscles; they just hang motionless, weighing down the fly like a suit of armor. If mutations are the engine that drives evolution, as Darwinism claims,[22] they certainly don't seem to be *taking* evolution anywhere.

The key to Darwin's theory is an extrapolation: It assumes that the same kind of small-scale changes we see in nature today can be extrapolated backward in time, allowing us to explain the major differences between taxonomic groups by the slow accumulation of minor changes. The problem is that minor changes simply do not add up the way the theory requires. After experimenting with fruit flies for nearly half a century, geneticist Richard Goldschmidt finally threw up his hands and said that even if you could accumulate a thousand mutations in a single fruit fly, it would still be nothing but an extremely odd fruit fly.[23] To produce a new species, you cannot simply accumulate changes in the details. Instead you need a new overall design.

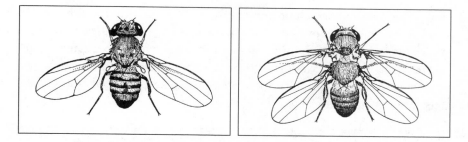

Fig. 5.2 **NORMAL and FOUR-WINGED FRUIT FLIES:** Because the mutated forms are weaker, they are *less* likely to survive in the wild. *(Copyright Jody Sjogren. Used with permission.)*

The limited nature of organic change has been common knowledge among farmers and breeders for centuries. You can breed for faster horses or larger apples, but eventually you reach a boundary that cannot be crossed, no matter how intensively you continue the breeding program. A horse will never be as fast as a cheetah, or an apple as large as a pumpkin. What's more, as you approach the boundary, organisms become progressively weaker and more prone to disease, until eventually they become sterile and die out. This has been the bane of breeding efforts since the dawn of time. Luther Burbank, possibly the most famous breeder of all times, suggested that there might even be a natural law that "keeps all living things within some more or less fixed limitations."[24]

An enormous amount of research has been carried on within the Darwinian paradigm over the past century and a half, yet success has been limited to changes *within* those "fixed limitations," like mutations in fruit flies. Research has cast virtually no light on the really important questions, like how there came to be fruit flies in the first place.[25] As one wag put it, Darwinism might explain the *survival* of the fittest, but it fails to explain the *arrival* of the fittest.

Doctored Moths

The case for naturalistic evolution has been seriously damaged in recent years by reversals in key evidence. Take the peppered moths in England, which most of us remember from photos in our high school science textbooks. The moths appear in two variants—a light gray and a darker gray—and the standard textbook story goes like this: During the Industrial Revolution, the new factories poured out smoke and soot, which darkened the tree trunks where the moths perched and made it easier for birds to see the lighter variety and eat them. Over time this process led to a larger proportion of the darker moths. This has long been touted as *the* showcase example of natural selection.

In recent years, however, a small problem has come to light: Peppered moths don't actually perch on tree trunks in the wild. (They are thought to perch in the upper canopy of trees.) How, then, do we explain the photographs we see in the textbooks? It turns out that they were staged: To create the photos, scientists glued dead moths onto the tree trunks. One scientist who helped make a television documentary acknowledged that he glued dead moths on the trees in producing the film (see fig. 5.3).[26]

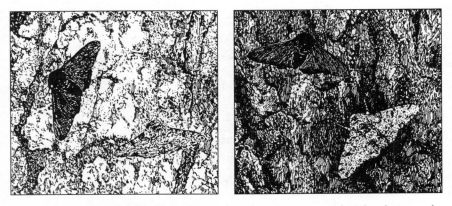

Fig. 5.3 **PEPPERED MOTHS ON TREE TRUNKS:** It turns out that the photographs were staged. *(Copyright Jody Sjogren. Used with permission.)*

Why was such a shoddy piece of scientific research accepted in the first place? And how did it attain to iconic status in evolutionary biology? Because scientists desperately wanted to believe it, says journalist Judith Hooper in a recent exposé. The problem with Darwin's theory is that evolutionary change requires thousands or millions of years, so we never actually see it happening. In the case of the peppered moth, however, for the first time evolutionary change seemed fast enough to be actually observed. It was just what Darwinists had been waiting for, and before long it had become "an irrefutable article of faith."[27]

The scandal has now been thoroughly aired in the scientific literature, to the great embarrassment of evolutionists. The peppered moth was a "prize horse in our stable of examples," lamented one well-known evolutionary biologist. Learning the truth, he said, was like learning "that it was my father and not Santa Claus who brought the presents on Christmas Eve."[28]

Yet amazingly, the moths continue to appear in science textbooks. One enterprising reporter interviewed a textbook writer who admitted he *knew* the photos were faked—but used them anyway. "The advantage of this example," the writer said, "is that it is extremely visual." "Later on," he added, students "can look at the work critically."[29] Apparently even falsified evidence is acceptable, if it reinforces Darwinian orthodoxy.

Most Famous Fake

As a junior high student, I was immensely impressed when my parents took me to a museum featuring an exhibit sure to be familiar to everyone: It showed vertebrate embryos lined up side by side—fish, amphibian, reptile, bird, and human. The point of the exhibit was to show how similar the embryos are, in order to suggest common ancestry. Darwin himself said the similarity among vertebrate embryos was "by far the strongest single class of facts in favor of" his theory.[30]

But it turns out that Darwin was misled. The embryo series was created by one of his most ardent supporters, a German scientist named Ernst Haeckel. His goal was to support a polysyllabic slogan he had coined—*ontogeny recapitulates phylogeny*—which means each individual embryo replays all the prior stages of evolution (see fig. 5.4).

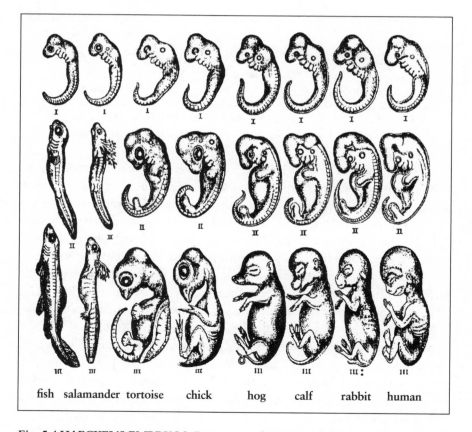

fish salamander tortoise chick hog calf rabbit human

Fig. 5.4 HAECKEL'S EMBRYOS: Darwin was fooled by a supporter who was overly eager to "confirm" evolutionary theory.

Shocking as it may seem, however, Haeckel fudged his sketches, making them look far more similar than they really are. Compare his illustrations with the more accurate ones in fig. 5.5.

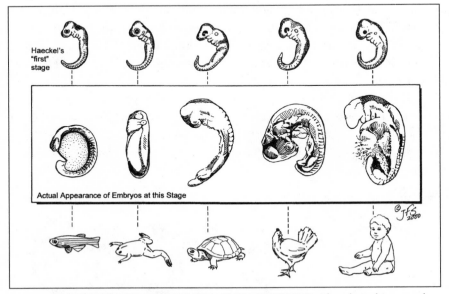

Fig. 5.5 HAECKEL'S DRAWINGS VS. REAL EMBRYOS. Already in his own day, Haeckel was accused of fraud. *(Copyright Jody Sjogren. Used with permission.)*

Even more shocking, in Haeckel's own day, more than a hundred years ago, scientists *already knew* that he had faked the sketches—and his colleagues accused him of fraud. Yet only recently has the scientific community begun to expose the falsehood publicly. An embryologist writing in the journal *Science* called Haeckel's drawings "one of the most famous fakes in biology."[31] Yet the same drawings, or similar ones, continue to be used in biology textbooks.

Haeckel's principle of recapitulation (that the human embryo replays the steps of evolution) has likewise been debunked, yet it continues to live a kind of postmortem zombie existence—often in arguments used to justify abortion. ("After all, at that stage it's only a fish or a reptile.") Columnist Michael Kinsley even used it in an attempt to support embryonic stem cell research. Technically speaking, Kinsley acknowledged, the principle of *ontogeny recapitulates phylogeny* has been discredited. Nevertheless, he argued, it contains a kernel of truth: Restated in ordinary language, in the development of the individual human being, "something similar" to evolution really does happen— namely, "that we each start out as something less than human, that the transformation takes place gradually."[32]

But if a principle is false, then restating it in the vernacular does not make it true. Biologically speaking, it is simply incorrect to say that we all start out as something less than human. The embryo is human from day one—a self-integrating organism whose unity, distinctness, and identity remain intact as it develops.

It is no coincidence that Haeckel, with his low view of life in the womb, supported race-based eugenics, and is often considered a progenitor of National Socialism. But it is odd that a contemporary liberal like Kinsley would resurrect the long-defunct argument of a racist German scientist.

BALONEY DETECTORS

How have Darwinists responded to the debunking of their icons?[33] Astonishingly, most have closed ranks to defend the use of falsified stories. For example, Bassett Maguire, a biology professor at the University of Texas, admits that the moths were staged, the embryos exaggerated. But, he told a reporter, the examples don't really matter so much as the concepts they teach. The icons represent flawed but nevertheless historic moments in science, he said, and the concepts they illustrate remain valid.[34]

This certainly shatters the idealized image of scientists as noble seekers after truth. Instead they are coming across as propagandists ready to employ useful lies.

My children have the advantage (if you can call it that) of having a mother who was a science writer for many years, and even as youngsters their antennae were super-alert to evolutionary messages. When my older son Dieter was only about six years old, he picked up an endearing habit of singing out, every time he encountered Darwinian concepts in library books or television nature programs, "Hey, Mom—evo-LOO-shun!" Together we would then examine the claims being made, contrasting them to what the evidence really shows. My goal was to help my children develop finely tuned "baloney detectors" (to borrow a phrase from Phillip Johnson[35]) to equip their young minds to evaluate the claims made on behalf of evolution.

Let's get out our own "baloney detectors" and identify the flaws in the standard Darwinian argument. The essence of Darwin's theory is that minor adaptations (sometimes called *micro*evolution) can be extrapolated over vast periods of time to explain the major differences dividing taxonomic groups (*macro*evolution). But as we have seen, small changes simply don't add up the way the theory requires. What's more, this has been public knowledge since at least 1980.

I recall the shock of opening a copy of *Newsweek* that year and reading about a landmark conference titled "Macroevolution," held at Chicago's Field Museum of Natural History.[36] What made the conference such a watershed was that the paleontologists bravely told the biologists what they least wanted to hear: that the fossil record does not, and never will, support the Darwinian scenario of a smooth, continuous progress of life forms, nicely graded from simple to complex. Instead the rocks show a pervasive pattern of gaps: New life forms appear suddenly, with no transitional forms leading to them, followed by long periods of stability during which they show little or no change at all. The late Stephen Jay Gould of Harvard dubbed this "the trade secret of paleontology"—revealing, perhaps inadvertently, how powerful the peer pressure can be among scientists. (Why did they feel the need to keep it secret?)

Darwin himself acknowledged that the most damaging evidence against his theory was the discontinuous nature of the fossil record—the lack of intermediate forms. However, he held out the hope that someday all the missing links would be discovered. And when that happened, the fossil record would finally reveal the continuous stream of transitional forms that his theory predicted.

What made the Macroevolution conference so significant was that many paleontologists finally seemed to be throwing in the towel. Since Darwin, fossil hunting has been carried on intensively for more than a century, but instead of filling in the gaps, new findings have actually made the gaps more pronounced than ever. Why? Because the fossil forms tend to fall *within* existing groups, leaving clear gaps *between* groups—just as there are clear gaps between modern animals like horses and cows, dogs and cats. Put another way, variation tends to be limited to change *within* groups, instead of leading gradually from one group to another.

Given this consistent pattern in the rocks, the paleontologists at the Macroevolution conference announced that it is irrational to keep hoping that the gaps will one day be filled in. It's time to recognize that they are here to stay. The standard picture of evolution will simply have to be revised: Instead of a smooth, continuous chain of life forms, evolution must be reconfigured as an erratic, leap-frog process. The new view was dubbed *punctuated equilibrium* (irreverently shortened to "punk eek") to denote an overall pattern of stability broken by occasional eruptions in which new forms appear suddenly out of nowhere. "Most species exhibit no directional change during their tenure on earth," Gould explained. "They appear in the fossil record looking much the same as when they disappear."[37]

This is a far cry from classic Darwinian gradualism, and it sent biologists scurrying to identify some new mechanism capable of generating sudden, large-scale, systemic changes—a search that continues to this day.[38] To use an image from Aesop's fables, evolutionary change was once modeled on the tortoise (slow and steady), but is now modeled on the hare (sudden spurts, followed by a long nap). Yet there seems to be no genetic mechanism capable of producing such a herky-jerky pattern. Large-scale mutations are usually deleterious, and often fatal. (Think: birth defects.) Thus evolution is, as the title of one influential book puts it, *A Theory In Crisis*.[39] Darwinian gradualism has been discredited, but there is as yet no broadly accepted alternative mechanism to replace it.

PUNK SCIENTISTS

With all this ferment going on, it's astonishing to see how leading scientists respond when challenged publicly—like during the public school controversies in Kansas and Ohio a few years ago. Immediately they trot out all the old examples of limited variation, like finch beaks and fruit flies and antibiotic resistance, as though they had never heard about the macroevolution controversy. The point of the controversy, after all, was that minor variations like these are *not* the engine driving macroevolution. "The central question of the Chicago [Macroevolution] conference was whether the mechanisms underlying microevolution can be extrapolated to explain the phenomena of macroevolution," wrote Roger Lewin in *Science*. With some qualifications, "the answer can be given as a clear No."[40]

Yet rather than admit that all the classic evidence is now irrelevant, the scientific establishment papers over the controversy by using the word *evolution* to cover two very different processes. On one hand, the term is applied to *limited* variation within *existing* groups, like finches and fruit flies, which is readily observed and which no one denies. On the other hand, the term is also applied to *un*limited change leading to the creation of *new* groups, which has no observational support and is completely speculative. This seems to be a deliberate equivocation of terms, a verbal trick designed to enhance the credibility of speculative evolutionary scenarios by linking them with minor variations familiar to everyone. Our baloney detectors should start ticking loudly whenever we encounter this ruse.

Nor does the newer paradigm of "punk eek" solve the problem. If you point out the problems with classic Darwinism in a typical science classroom, you will quickly be reassured that punctuated equilibrium has solved them all. But since there is no known mechanism capable of producing sudden, large-scale evolutionary change, most biologists sneak classic Darwinism in the back door. The typical tactic is to say that Darwinist evolution occurs very rapidly, and in very small populations, so that it leaves no record in the fossils. In short, the mechanism is still Darwinian variation plus natural selection, with the process merely speeded up until it is invisible. In that case, however, punk eek is nothing but a variation on the same old theme, and is subject to the same problems as classic Darwinism.[41]

BIRDS, BATS, AND BEES

Where, then, is the evidence that natural selection has the power to create the vast diversity of living things on earth? Where do we see that creative power at work? Certainly not in the standard examples cited in the typical biology textbook.

And that is a clue that something else is at work—that it is not really the evidence that persuades. The reason people can find such minor, reversible change persuasive is that they are already persuaded on other grounds—on philosophical grounds—that nature alone *must* be capable of creating all life forms. In other words, they are already persuaded of philosophical naturalism: that nature is all that exists, or at least that natural forces are all that may be invoked in science. And once people have made that philosophical commitment, they can be persuaded by relatively minor evidence.[42]

The place to focus our attention, then, is not on the scientific details but on the philosophy of naturalism. Should the definition of science restrict inquiry to natural causes alone? Or should inquiry be free to follow the evidence wherever it leads—whether it points to a natural or an intelligent cause?

Most ordinary people hold an idealized image of science as impartial, unbiased empirical investigation that attends strictly to evidence. That's the official definition found in the standard science textbook, bristling with objective-sounding words like *observation* and *testing*. The problem is that, in practice, science has been co-opted into the camp of the philosophical naturalists, so that it typically functions as little more than applied naturalism.

How do we know that? Because the only theories regarded as acceptable are naturalistic ones. Consider these words by the well-known science popularizer Richard Dawkins: *"Even if there were no actual evidence* in favor of the Darwinian theory . . . we should still be justified in preferring it over all rival theories."*[43] Why? Because it is naturalistic.

Here's the same argument, flipped over. A Kansas State University professor published a letter in the prestigious journal *Nature*, stating: *"Even if all the data point to an intelligent designer,* such an hypothesis is excluded from science because it is not naturalistic."*[44] Pause for a moment and let that sink in: Even if there is *no* evidence in favor of Darwinism, and if *all* the evidence favors Intelligent Design, still we are not allowed to consider it in science. Clearly, the issue is not fundamentally a matter of evidence at all, but of a prior philosophical commitment.

A few more examples drive the point home. During the Ohio controversy, one of the drafters of the controversial state guidelines wrote a letter to *Physics Today,* insisting that, in order to be considered at all, *"the first criterion* is that any scientific theory must be naturalistic."[45] In other words, unless a theory is naturalistic, it will be ruled out before any consideration of its merits. The editor in chief of *Scientific American* then entered the fray, stating that "a central tenet of modern science is methodological naturalism—it seeks to explain the universe purely in terms of observed or testable natural mechanisms."[46] But who says we have to accept naturalism as a "central tenet" of science? As one professor I know retorted, "Who made up that rule? I don't remember voting on it."

In other words, why should we acquiesce in letting philosophical naturalists prescribe the definition of science itself? The only reason for restricting science to *methodological* naturalism is if we assume from the outset that *philosophical* naturalism is true—that nature is a closed system of cause and effect. But if it is not true, then restricting science to naturalistic theories is not a good strategy for getting at the truth.[47]

Today a naturalistic definition of science is taught as unquestioned dogma throughout the public education system, even to young students who lack the background to challenge it. Read this quotation from a typical high school textbook: "Many people believe that a supernatural force or deity created life. That explanation is not within the scope of science."[48] Notice that the book does not say creation has been proven false or discredited by facts, but only that it falls outside a certain definition of science. It has been ruled out by definition.

Another high school textbook says, "By attributing the diversity of life to natural causes rather than to supernatural creation, Darwin gave biology a sound scientific basis."[49] Note how the text equates "sound" science with philosophical naturalism.

One more example, this time from the college level: "Biological phenomena, including those seemingly designed, can be explained by purely material causes, rather than by divine creation."[50] An aggressive assertion of materialism like this is deemed acceptable in a college textbook. But a parallel passage asserting design would be deemed unacceptable.

Clearly, philosophy has gained primacy over the facts. The first question many scientists ask is not whether a theory is true, but whether it is naturalistic. They no longer consider it appropriate to ask *whether* life evolved by natural forces, but only *which* natural processes were at work. And once science has been defined in terms of naturalism, then something very close to Darwinism has to be true.[51]

Anyone who believes in naturalism or materialism "must, as a matter of logical necessity, also believe in evolution," writes Tom Bethell. "No digging for fossils, no test tubes or microscopes, no further experiments are needed." He goes on to explain:

> For birds, bats, and bees do exist. They came into existence somehow. Your consistent materialist has no choice but to allow that, yes, molecules in motion succeeded, over the eons, in whirling themselves into ever more complex conglomerations, some of them called bats, some birds, some bees. *He 'knows' that is true, not because he sees it in the genes, or in the lab, or in the fossils, but because it is embedded in his philosophy.*[52]

Precisely. Evolution wins the debate by default. Getting an exact theory of how the process happened is secondary.

Surprisingly, Darwin himself was willing to countenance alternative theories of evolution—so long as they were naturalistic. He was not wedded to his own theory of natural selection as the only mechanism of evolution, but regarded any mechanism as acceptable as long as it got rid of the concept of divine creation. "If I have erred" by exaggerating the power of natural selection, he wrote, "I have at least, as I hope, done good service in aiding to overthrow the dogma of separate creations." After listing some of the other theories offered in his day, he added: "Whether the naturalist believes in the views given by [these other writers] or by myself, signifies extremely little in comparison with the admission that species have descended from other species, and have not been created immutable."[53] It's clear that, for Darwin, evolution was not so much a specific theory as a philosophical stance—a stance that could be described as, *any mechanism is acceptable, as long as it is naturalistic.* Darwinian evolution is not so much an empirical finding as a deduction from a naturalistic worldview.

DIVINE FOOT IN THE DOOR

Harvard biologist Richard Lewontin gave the game away in a highly revealing article in the *New York Review of Books* a few years ago. Lewontin starts out by admitting the darker side of science (it makes extravagant claims, causes environmental problems, and so on). And yet, he quickly adds, we must still prefer science to any form of supernaturalism. Why? Because, "we have a prior commitment, a commitment to materialism."

This is a stunning admission that what drives the show is not the facts but the philosophy. (And who is this *we* Lewontin keeps addressing? Clearly he is assuming that his audience consists of the elites who have made that "prior commitment to materialism.")

"It's not that the methods and institutions of science somehow compel us to accept a material explanation" of the world, Lewontin explains. "On the contrary," he says, "we are forced by our *a priori* adherence to material causes to create an apparatus of investigation and a set of concepts that produce material explanations." Translation: We first accepted materialism as a philosophy, and then refashioned science into a machine for cranking out strictly materialist theories.

Finally, he warns that this materialism must be "absolute, for we cannot allow a divine foot in the door."[54] That final phrase points to what's really at stake in the evolution controversy. Why does Lewontin urge us to define science as applied materialism? Because otherwise we might let a "divine foot in the door." And we all know what happens then: When a salesman gets his foot in the door, pretty soon his brooms and brushes are all over your living room. If a "divine foot" ever got in the door of science, that would provide the groundwork for the entire Christian worldview, with its theology and biblical morality. That's what sends a shiver of fear up the spine of many secularists.

The famous duo who discovered the double-helix structure of DNA, Francis Crick and James Watson, freely admit that anti-religious motivations drove their scientific work. "I went into science because of these religious reasons, there's no doubt about that," Crick said in a recent interview. "I asked myself what were the two things that appear inexplicable and are used to support religious beliefs." He decided the two things that support religion were "the difference between living and nonliving things, and the phenomenon of consciousness."[55] He then aimed his own research specifically at demonstrating a naturalistic view of both.

Religion is just so many "myths from the past," Watson chimed in during the same interview. The discovery of the double helix, he said, gives "grounds for thinking that the powers held traditionally to be the exclusive property of the gods might one day be ours."[56]

Steven Weinberg was even more aggressively anti-religious when addressing the aptly named Freedom From Religion Foundation. "I personally feel that the teaching of modern science is corrosive to religious belief, and I'm all for that!" he said. The hope that science would liberate people from religion, he went on, is "one of the things that in fact has driven me in my life." If science helps bring about the end of religion, he concluded, "it would be the most important contribution science could make."[57] Clearly, the motives driving many evolutionists have as much to do with religion as with science.

EVOLUTION GETS RELIGION

We could even say that Darwinism itself often functions as an alternative religion. In fact, that's exactly what philosopher of science Michael Ruse does say. Ruse is a pugnacious and aggressive evolutionist, who testified in court against an Arkansas creationist statute back in 1982. While there, however, he had a conversation with the well-known creationist Duane Gish that brought him up short. "The trouble with you evolutionists is that you just don't play fair," Gish told him. You accuse us of teaching a religious view, he said, but "you evolutionists are just as religious in your way. Christianity tells us where we came from, where we're going, and what we should do on the way. I defy you to show any difference with evolution. It tells you where you came from, where you are going, and what you should do on the way."[58] In short, evolution itself functions as a religion.

The comment rankled Ruse, and he couldn't get it out of his mind. Eventually, he decided that Gish was right—that evolution really *is* "more than mere science," as he put it in a recent article. "Evolution came into being as a kind of secular ideology, an explicit substitute for Christianity." Even today, it "is promulgated as an ideology, a secular religion—a full-fledged alternative to Christianity, with meaning and morality."

Ruse hastens to reassure his readers that he himself remains "an ardent evolutionist and an ex-Christian." And yet, "I must admit that in this one complaint . . . the [biblical] literalists are absolutely right. Evolution is a religion. This was true of evolution in the beginning, and it is true of evolution still today."[59]

Ruse announced his new insight at the 1993 annual meeting of the American Association for the Advancement of Science (AAAS), where his presentation was met by stunned silence. A conference report published by an evolution advocacy group wondered, "Did Michael Ruse Give Away the Store?"[60]

But Ruse wasn't making wild allegations. He backed them up with solid examples, citing people like Stephen Jay Gould, who once claimed that evolution "liberates the human spirit." For sheer excitement, Gould added, evolution "beats any myth of human origins by light years." Since evolutionary history is entirely contingent, "in an entirely literal sense, we owe our existence, as large and reasoning mammals, to our lucky stars."[61]

"If this is not a rival to traditional Judaeo-Christian teaching," Ruse comments wryly, "I do not know what is."[62]

Ruse's analysis certainly throws new light on the controversy over teaching evolution in the classroom. Critics typically accuse Intelligent Design supporters of trying to inject religion into the classroom. For example, during the

Ohio controversy an editorial in a Columbus newspaper said, "The problem is that intelligent-design proponents want to bring religion into science classes, where it doesn't belong."[63]

The correct response is that religion is *already* in the classroom—because naturalistic evolution is itself a religion or worldview. "The so-called warfare between science and religion," wrote historian Jacques Barzun, should really "be seen as the warfare between two philosophies and perhaps two faiths." The battle over evolution is merely one incident "in the dispute between the believers in consciousness and the believers in mechanical action; the believers in purpose and the believers in pure chance."[64] To promote one faith in the public school system at public expense, while banning the other, is an example of viewpoint discrimination, which the Supreme Court has declared unconstitutional in a wide variety of cases.[65]

BERKELEY TO THE RESCUE

If the evolution controversy really is a "warfare between two philosophies," the next question is whether Christians are prepared to fight it. As we saw in Part 1, American evangelicals have not historically had a robust intellectual tradition. When I first started writing on science and worldview back in 1977, the Christian world had splintered over the issue. Most people involved had been trained as scientists, and while they were doing (and continue to do) excellent work in developing critiques of evolutionary theory, they were still losing the battle. Why? Because they did not think in terms of underlying worldviews.

As a result, instead of joining together to oppose the hegemony of the naturalistic worldview, Christians often got caught up in fighting each other. The bitterest debates were often not with atheistic evolutionists but among believers with conflicting scientific views: young-earth creationists, old-earth creationists, flood geologists, progressive creationists, "gap" theorists, and theistic evolutionists. There were endless arguments over theological questions like the length of the creation "days" and the extent of the Genesis flood.

Meanwhile, secularists were happy to fan the flames. As Phillip Johnson once put it, "They all but said, 'Let us hold your coats while you fight.'"[66] For if Christians were going to endlessly divide, then it was clear that secularists would conquer.

It was Johnson himself, more than anyone else, who refocused the debate and brought about a rapprochement of the warring camps under the umbrella of the Intelligent Design movement.[67] Johnson converted to Christianity in his late thirties, at the peak of a highly successful career as a law professor at the

University of California at Berkeley. Perhaps he was suffering the malaise of those to whom success has come too easily and too early, for he was already asking the classic midlife questions: Is this all there is to life? Then his wife got caught up in the trendy feminism of the seventies and walked out, leaving him with the house and kids. Disillusioned with both his professional and his personal life, Johnson began to look for something more than the pragmatic success ethic that had governed his thinking so far, and he began considering the case for Christianity.

That meant taking on Darwinism. If you want to know whether the Christian worldview is "fact or fantasy," Johnson said in a recent interview, then "Darwinism is a logical place to begin because, if Darwinism is true, Christian metaphysics is fantasy." More than any other factor, Darwinism is the reason Christianity is marginalized and dismissed in mainstream academia.[68]

Johnson's critiques of evolution (in books like *Darwin on Trial* and *Reason in the Balance*)[69] have had an enormous impact. Having spent much of his life as a cynical secularist, Johnson was well versed in the latest intellectual fads and knew how to speak the language of secular academia. Equally important, Johnson crafted a new battle strategy that has proven remarkably effective in winning a respectful hearing for the concept of Intelligent Design. What made his strategy so effective is that Johnson did not come into the fray with yet another position to defend. Instead he introduced a paradigm shift: He urged Christians to stop fighting *each other* and to rally together behind the crucial point of confrontation with the *secular* world—namely, its embrace of naturalistic philosophy.

Luther once said that if we fight on all fronts except the one actually under attack at the moment, then we are not really fighting the battle. And what is the point under attack today? Mainstream evolutionists may disagree with one another over the precise mechanism and timing of evolution (whether natural selection needs to be supplemented by other mechanisms); but they all agree that it happened by blind, undirected natural causes. On the other side of the divide, Christians may argue with one another over secondary questions like *when* God created the universe (whether it is young or old); but they all agree that the universe is the handiwork of a personal God. Thus the heart of the battle is whether the universe is the result of Intelligent Agency or of blind, noncognitive forces—and that's where we must direct our energies. Christians need to bracket peripheral issues and focus on the crucial point of whether there is evidence for Intelligent Design in the universe.[70]

CLOSED SYSTEM, CLOSED MINDS

Johnson's way of framing the debate parallels in many ways the approach Francis Schaeffer crafted for cultural apologetics. When long-haired, bearded young people began flocking to his chalet in the Alps in the 1960s and 70s seeking answers to life, Schaeffer sketched in stark outline what the basic choices are. When it comes to first principles, he noted, there are not really many viable options—in fact, only two: Either the universe is a closed system of cause and effect, or it is an open system, the product of a Personal Agent. Everything that follows stems from that fundamental choice.

During the course of my own studies at L'Abri, I listened to a tape of one of Schaeffer's best-known lectures, "Possible Answers to the Basic Philosophical Questions"[71]—replaying the tape several times because it simplified so neatly the quest for truth. Every worldview has to start somewhere, Schaeffer said, and either we can start with "time plus chance plus the impersonal" or we can begin with a Personal Being who thinks, wills, and acts. Once we grasp these two basic categories and all their implications, then worldview analysis is greatly streamlined. By showing that a nonpersonal starting point fails to account for the world, we can eliminate a vast variety of philosophical systems that fall within that category—materialism, determinism, behaviorism, Marxism, utilitarianism—without needing to investigate the myriad details that distinguish them.

In a similar way, the Intelligent Design argument wonderfully streamlines the debate over origins. It cuts through the conflicting claims of a vast variety of positions by grouping them within two basic categories: Either nature is a closed system, and science is permitted to consider only blind, material forces; or else nature is an open system, and intelligence is an irreducible reality alongside natural forces. Darwinism functions as the scientific underpinning for the first view: that the universe is a closed system. That is why the cultural ruling class will not allow it to be seriously questioned.

The website for Internet Infidels greets visitors with an unusually candid statement of their beliefs: "Our goal is to promote a nontheistic worldview, which holds that the natural world is all that there is, a closed system in no need of a supernatural explanation and sufficient unto itself."[72] That certainly puts the matter bluntly. The fundamental question is whether the universe is a closed system or an open system, and focusing on this basic antithesis will help us follow Luther's dictum to direct our forces to the actual point of attack.

WINNING A PLACE AT THE TABLE

If the key issue is naturalistic philosophy, then the main *consequence* of naturalism, as we saw at the beginning of the chapter, is a new view of knowledge. Historically speaking, it was Darwinism more than anything else that barred the door on any consideration of Christianity as objective truth. It cemented in place the two-story division of truth that pushed religion into the upper story of *values*, defined as the irrational beliefs of certain reactionary subcultures.

As one historian explains, Darwinism caused a shift "from religion as *knowledge* to religion as *faith.*" Since there was no longer any function for God to carry out in the world, "He was, at best, a gratuitous philosophical concept derived from a personal need." If you still wanted to believe in God, that was fine, so long as you realized that your belief was "private, subjective, and artificial."[73]

Unless we understand this shift, we will not be able to decipher the debates going on all around us. For example, see if you can detect the two-story divide in these words from a position paper put out by the Arkansas Science Teachers Association (ASTA) in 2001: "Science strives to explain the nature of the cosmos while religion seeks to give the cosmos and the life within it a purpose."[74] Notice that, in this definition, religion doesn't give any actual *knowledge* about the cosmos; it addresses only questions of "purpose." Even then, it doesn't *reveal* the purpose of the cosmos but instead "gives" it one—language implying that purpose is not objectively real but only a human construction that we impose upon the material world.

Logically enough, the ASTA paper concludes that religion-based views are relativistic, and should be restricted to the private realm within "the home or within the context of religious institutions." By contrast, naturalistic evolution is universally true and should be taught to everyone in the public schools: "The goal of science is to discover and investigate universally accepted natural explanations. This process of discovery and description of natural phenomena should be taught in public schools."[75]

Thus the first hurdle for Christians is simply reintroducing the very concept that religion can be genuine knowledge. Julian Huxley once said, "Darwinism removed the whole idea of God as the Creator . . . from the sphere of rational discussion."[76] We must learn how to bring God back into the sphere of rational discussion—to win a place at the table of public discourse. We must find a way to talk about Christianity as objective knowledge, not our personal values. We must stake out a cognitive territory and be prepared to defend it.

WHAT EVERY SCHOOLCHILD KNOWS

It is unwise for Christians even to use the terminology of *values* in referring to our beliefs. Many evangelicals have become active in the public arena today, proclaiming the need to defend "Christian values." Some groups have even adopted the term in their name, like the Values Action Team in the U.S. Congress. These groups often do excellent work, yet by adopting the label *values* they unwittingly pick up baggage that could ultimately discredit their efforts. As one historian explains, "Values are for the modern mind subjective preferences, personal and social, over against the objective realities provided by scientific knowledge."[77] Allan Bloom (author of the best-seller *The Closing of the American Mind*) puts it more tersely: "Every school child knows that values are relative," and not objectively true.[78] If this meaning of the word is so obvious to "every school child" in the secular world, why haven't Christians picked up on it?

When we use the term *values*, we are broadcasting to the secular world a message that says *we are talking only about our own group's idiosyncracies, which the rest of society should tolerate as long as it doesn't upset any important public agendas.* After all, everyone knows that ethnic subcultures often hold irrational beliefs and quaint customs, and these can be accommodated as long as we all understand that no one really believes that stuff anymore—rather like humoring an eccentric old aunt.

Some Christians don't just use the lingo but have actually capitulated wholesale to the fact/value dichotomy. Delaware was recently in the news for instituting a particularly aggressive program for teaching evolution in high schools. The reporter asked a fifteen-year-old Christian student what effect the course had on her religious beliefs. It didn't really have *any* effect, the student replied. Why not? "Religion is what you believe because of *faith,*" she explained. "With science, you need *evidence* and need to back it up."[79] Notice the assumption that religion has nothing to do with evidence or reason.

In another recent example, the website for the PBS "Evolution" series includes a statement from two young people identified as science students attending a conservative Christian college. The statement says, "Science deals with the material world of genes and cells, religion with the spiritual world of value and meaning."[80] Do you see how the students have absorbed the fact/value dichotomy? Science is about facts; religion is about values. This is not even accurate: Christianity does make claims about the material world— about the origin of the cosmos, the character of human nature, and events in history, preeminently the Resurrection. Yet these students were willing to deny that their faith has any cognitive content, reducing it to subjective questions of "value and meaning."

When Christians are willing to reduce religion to noncognitive categories, unconnected to questions of truth or evidence, then we have already lost the battle. We have thrown away our chance of evangelizing people who long for a unified truth that escapes the pervasive fact/value dichotomy.

If the broader impact of Darwinism was to remove Christianity from the sphere of objective truth, then the broader significance of the Intelligent Design movement will be to bring it back. By providing evidence of God's work in nature, it restores Christianity to the status of a genuine knowledge claim, giving us the means to reclaim a place at the table of public debate. Christians will then be in a position to challenge the fact/value dichotomy that has marginalized religion and morality by reducing them to irrational, subjective experience.

To accomplish that goal, however, we must go beyond negative critiques of naturalistic evolution and lay out the positive evidence for design, putting forward a viable research program. Let's turn now to the exciting new ways Christians are crafting a positive case for Intelligent Design in the public square.

6

THE SCIENCE
OF COMMON SENSE

When I first started studying,
I saw the world as composed of particles.
Looking more deeply I discovered waves.
Now after a lifetime of study,
it appears that all existence is the expression of information.
JOHN WHEELER[1]

In a public library in Toronto, I was once chatting with a recent émigré from
Ukraine named Bogdan about an article I was writing on evolution.
Suddenly he looked around furtively, as if afraid of being overheard, dropped
his voice, and asked, "Do you believe in Darwinism?"

Startled, and assuming that he was probably a Marxist materialist, I
launched into a rambling discussion about the lack of a plausible mechanism
. . . when he cut me short, leaned closer, and asked in more urgent tones, "But
do you *believe* in Darwinism?"

I paused, then shook my head. "Uh. No."

Bogdan smiled ever so slightly, looked around again, and then said conspiratorially, "Neither do I."

This was 1986, before the fall of the Berlin Wall, and prior to emigrating
to Canada this man had been an officer in the KGB, the Soviet secret police.
Handpicked at an early age, Bogdan had been educated at the Marxism-
Leninism University in Moscow, from which he had emerged as a true believer
in atheistic communism. That is, until he traveled to Canada, ostensibly to visit
family members but in fact on a KGB mission. Having been steeped in Marxist
propaganda all his life, the experience of seeing the West firsthand destroyed all
his prior mental categories, and soon after returning to Moscow he put in an
application to emigrate. His wife promptly divorced him and he was shunted

off to a dead-end job. But this was after the Stalin era (when he would have been summarily executed), and after many years he was finally permitted to emigrate.

As I got to know Bogdan, I learned that he was in the process of painfully dismantling the atheistic ideology that had formed the bones and sinews of his thinking for his entire life. And the crucial foundation for it all was evolution. For decades, communist authorities had held up Darwinian evolution as the trump card supporting an atheistic, materialist worldview.

"No," Bogdan repeated thoughtfully. "I don't *believe* it." And he began to talk about the obvious design and complexity of the world. His sense of design was intuitive, and he had not yet worked out all the implications. He was just beginning to open his mind to the possibility that there were more things in heaven and earth than Marx had dreamed of. But of one thing he was certain: Darwinism, along with the entire edifice of atheistic materialism that it supported, was simply false.

A sense that the universe was designed is an intuitive awareness found in virtually all cultures from the beginning of time. Even the Soviets' official state policy of atheism could not completely stamp it out. Here in America, a 1998 survey by the Skeptics' Society found that among highly educated Americans the number one reason for believing in God was seeing "good design" and "complexity" in the world. Design was cited by almost a third of respondents—29 percent—while only 10 percent said they believed in God because religion was comforting or consoling. The results were quite surprising, especially for the skeptics who had conducted the study, because it shot down the common stereotype that religion is nothing but an emotional or psychological crutch. On the contrary, for most believers the ground for faith is an essentially rational intuition: They are convinced that there is a God because the universe seems so highly ordered that it suggests the hand of a conscious Mind or Creator.[2]

That conviction would certainly have resonated with the founders of the scientific revolution—figures like Copernicus, Kepler, Newton, and Galileo—all of whom were inspired in their scientific discoveries by the conviction that they were revealing the intricate plan of a Divine Artisan.[3] If the intuition of design is so common and compelling, can we restate it in rigorous scientific terms? Can we formalize it as a scientific research program? That, in a nutshell, is the aim of the Intelligent Design movement.

LITTLE GREEN MEN

The heart of design theory is the claim that design can be empirically detected. When you think about it, this is something we do all the time in ordinary life. We distinguish readily between the products of nature and the products of intelligence. Walking on the beach, we may admire the lovely pattern of ripples running across the sand, but we know it is merely a product of the wind and the waves. If, however, we come across a sand castle with walls and turrets and a moat, do we assume it too was created by the wind and waves? Of course not. The material constituents of the castle are nothing but sand and mud and water, just like the ripples all around it. But we intuitively recognize that those starting materials have a different kind of order imposed upon them. Design theory merely formalizes this ordinary intuition—just as all of science is largely formalized common sense.[4]

An illustration that design theorists often use is Mount Rushmore. If you were driving through the mountains in South Dakota, and suddenly came upon the faces of four famous presidents carved into the rock, you would not think for a moment that they were the product of wind and rain erosion. You would instantly recognize the handiwork of an artist.

A friend of mine once took a ship up the West Coast to Canada, where he was greeted by a colorful display of flowers spelling out "Welcome to Victoria." It was a sure guarantee that the seeds were not blown there randomly by the wind.[5]

Critics say the concept of design does not belong in science. They argue that it is a "science-stopper" that puts an end to scientific investigation. The head of an evolution advocacy group recently told CNN that design theory is "not a very good science, because it's basically giving up and saying: We can't explain this; therefore, God did it."[6]

But that accusation is based on a misunderstanding. The process of detecting design is thoroughly empirical. In fact, it is already an important element in several areas of science. Back in 1967, I was startled to read a newspaper headline announcing that astronomers may have discovered radio messages coming from outer space. They dubbed the signals "LGM" to signify "Little Green Men." Later, however, they realized that the radio pulses were coming in a regular, recurring pattern like the flashing of a lighthouse, not an irregular pattern like the sequence of letters in a message. What they had discovered were not aliens but pulsars—rotating stars.

Today astronomers involved in the search for extraterrestrial intelligence (SETI) have worked out extensive criteria for recognizing when a radio signal is an encoded message and when it is just a natural phenomenon, like a pulsar. In other words, they have developed criteria for distinguishing between products of design and products of natural causes.

The same distinction is made in several other fields:

- Detectives are trained to distinguish murder (design) from death by natural causes.
- Archeologists have criteria for distinguishing when a stone has the distinctive chip marks of a primitive tool (design), and when its shape is simply the result of weathering and erosion.
- Insurance companies have steps for deciding whether a fire was a case of arson (design) or just an accident.
- Cryptologists have worked out procedures to determine whether a set of symbols is a secret message (design) or merely a random sequence.

Across all the scientific disciplines, researchers also need to know how to identify the telltale signs that an experiment has been rigged, that someone has tampered with the results. There is even a U.S. Office of Research Integrity, dubbed the Fraud Squad, which has the job of scrutinizing scientific research for signs that the data has been fudged—graphs that are a bit too neat, random numbers that are not completely random, protein blots that look too similar, and so on.[7]

A bizarre case of detecting design involved a standardized test used in the Washington state school system in 2001. Students were asked to identify a bus route based on the distances among four cities, with the correct answer being a sequence of city names: Mayri, Clay, Lee, and Turno. A perceptive tenth-grader thought the sequence sounded suspiciously like the name of Mary Kay Letourneau, a teacher who had been convicted of child molestation. When authorities investigated the company that had produced the test, sure enough, they confirmed that it was an intentional act and tracked down the culprit.[8] The student who had spotted the pattern was making a design inference—correctly, as it turned out.

It should be possible to formalize the thinking process used in all these examples, which is exactly what design theory does. Its central tenet is that the characteristic marks of design can be empirically detected. As the title of one book puts it, in nature we can uncover *Signs of Intelligence.*[9]

BLIND WATCHMAKER?

In one sense, the concept of design in nature is completely uncontroversial. Evidence for design shows up in laboratories all the time. Biologists have found that the best way to tease out the functions of various molecules in the cell is to practice "reverse engineering"—the same backward reasoning we would use if we wanted to figure out how some gadget was manufactured. Working in their laboratories, biologists take apart the complicated "molecular machines" within the cell, and then try to reconstruct the "blueprints" by which they were designed.[10]

If you listen carefully to nature programs on television, you'll often hear language that is sprinkled with references to design or biological engineering. "Every couple of minutes the narrator was talking about 'the designs of nature' and 'the blueprint of life,'" a friend of mine commented after watching a PBS nature program. "It seems scientists can't get away from the language of design."

Surprisingly, Darwin himself never denied the evidence for design. His goal, however, was to show that the same evidence could be accounted for by purely natural forces. In other words, he hoped to demonstrate that living things only *appear* to be designed, while actually being products of noncognitive forces. Natural selection was proposed as an automatic, mechanistic process that could *mimic* the effects of intelligence. As one historian puts it, Darwin hoped to show "how blind and gradual adaptation could *counterfeit* the apparently purposeful design" that seemed so obviously "a function of mind."[11]

In fact, design is such a defining feature of living things that biologist Richard Dawkins begins one of his books with this startling sentence: "Biology is the study of complicated things that give *the appearance of having been designed for a purpose.*"[12] Being an evolutionist, he then spends the rest of the book seeking to demonstrate that this prima facie "appearance" of design is false and misleading.

Titled *The Blind Watchmaker,* Dawkins's book plays off a famous metaphor formulated two hundred years ago by a clergyman named William Paley. If you find a gadget like a watch lying on the ground, Paley said, you don't have any trouble deciding that it is a product of human manufacture—made by a watchmaker. For a watch has all the diagnostic signs of design: It is a set of interconnecting, coordinated parts all directed toward a purpose (to tell time). In living things we find the same type of integrated, purposeful structures: The purpose of the eye is to see, the ear to hear, the fin to swim. Thus, Paley argued, they must likewise be products of an intelligent agent. Dawkins's claim is that Paley's intelligent agent can be replaced by a blind, unconscious process—one that produces purposeful structures without itself having any purpose or intention. Natural selection is a "blind watchmaker."

The same claim was put in remarkably clear language by George Gaylord Simpson, sounding rather like Paley except for a tendency to speak of "apparent" purpose instead of the real thing. It does seem obvious, Simpson conceded, that organisms are designed for a purpose—that "fishes have gills in order to breathe water, that birds have wings in order to fly, and that men have brains in order to think." Echoing Paley, Simpson admits that living things remind us forcefully of machines:

> A telescope, a telephone, or a typewriter is a complex mechanism serving a particular function. Obviously, its manufacturer had a purpose in mind, and the machine was designed and built in order to serve that purpose. An eye, an ear, or a hand is also a complex mechanism serving a particular function. It, too, looks as if it had been made for a purpose. This *appearance of purposefulness* is pervading in nature.

Accounting for this "apparent purposefulness," Simpson says, is a central problem for biology. But not to worry, he hastens to conclude, because Darwin has already solved it. Natural selection "achieves the aspect of purpose *without* the intervention of a purposer, and it has produced a vast plan *without* the concurrent action of a planner."[13]

In other words, both sides of the evolution debate agree that, taken at face value, living things look for all the world as though they are designed. To salvage the notion of evolution, its proponents have to show that this obvious design is not real but is instead a deceptive illusion produced by natural selection. Design theorists, on the other hand, have the advantage that design is prima facie plausible, and all they have to do is identify reliable empirical markers of intelligent agency.

MARKS OF DESIGN

There are three main areas where exciting new evidence for design is being uncovered: (1) the world of the cell (biochemistry), (2) the origin of the universe (cosmology), and (3) the structure of DNA (biological information). Let's get acquainted with the major lines of argument being developed in each of these areas.

Roller Coaster in the Cell

As a young man, Darwin was greatly impressed by Paley's argument for a watchmaker; in fact, he even formulated his own theory explicitly to counter it. So let's examine Paley's reasoning more closely. When we inspect a watch, he wrote, we perceive "that its several parts are framed and put together for a purpose," namely, to tell time. The intricate interplay of parts makes no sense apart from the purpose it serves. Hence, Paley concluded, "the inference we think is inevitable, that the watch must have had a maker . . . who comprehended its construction and designed its use."

Now, living systems likewise are made of interconnected parts that are ordered toward a purpose, Paley noted; thus it is reasonable to conclude that they too were designed by a Maker. As he put it, "The marks of design are too strong to be got over."[14]

Paley adduced many examples, some of which did not support his argument well, with the result that his work was eventually discredited. Yet the core of his reasoning continues to have a great deal of validity. Paley's central argument "has actually never been refuted," says Michael Behe in his influential book *Darwin's Black Box*.[15] Behe himself has gone on to refine and update the design argument with new findings from the field of biochemistry.

Behe is a short, personable fellow with a disarming, aw-shucks manner, who is rarely seen wearing anything but his trademark jeans and plaid shirt. As a Roman Catholic, he was taught evolution as a youngster in parochial schools, and thus had no religious motivation for rejecting it. Instead it was his work in biochemistry that caused him to question Darwinian orthodoxy, by revealing the almost unthinkable complexity contracted into the tiny space of the living cell.

More than a hundred years ago, Darwin thought the living cell was extremely simple—nothing but a bubble of jelly (protoplasm). Over the past few decades, however, new technologies like the electron microscope have produced a revolution in molecular biology. We now know that the cell bristles with high-tech molecular machinery far more complex than anything devised by mere humans. Each cell is akin to a miniature factory town, humming with power plants, automated factories, and recycling centers. In the nucleus is a cellular library, housing blueprints and plans that are copied and transported to factories, each of which is filled with molecular machines that function like computerized motors. These manufacture the immense array of products needed within the cell, with the processes all regulated by enzymes that function as stopwatches to ensure that everything is perfectly timed.[16]

"The cell is thus a minute factory, bustling with rapid, organized chemical activity," writes Francis Crick of DNA fame. "Nature invented the assembly line some billions of years before Henry Ford."[17] The outside surface of the cell is studded with sensors, gates, pumps, and identification markers to regulate traffic coming in and out. Today biologists cannot even describe the cell without resorting to the language of machines and engineering.

Behe piles example upon example, but consider just one. Each cell has an automated "rapid transit system" in which certain molecules function as tiny monorail trains running along tracks to whisk cargo around from one part of the cell to another. Other molecules act as loading machines, filling up the train cars and attaching address labels. When the train reaches the right "address" in another part of the cell, it is met by other molecules that act as docking machines, opening them up and removing the supplies. To frame a mental image of the cell, picture it as a large and complex model train layout, with tracks crisscrossing everywhere, its switches and signals perfectly timed so that no trains collide and the cargo reaches its destination precisely when needed.[18]

For kids raised on computer games, a good image might be the highest level on Roller Coaster Tycoon. This is a level of complexity Darwin never dreamed of, and his theory utterly fails to account for it. Why? Because a system of coordinated, interlocking parts like this can only operate *after* all the pieces are in place—which means they must appear simultaneously, not by any gradual, piece-by-piece process. Behe coined the term *irreducible complexity* to refer to the minimum level of complexity that must be present before such a tightly integrated system can function at all.

Behe's favorite illustration is the humble mouse trap. You cannot start with the wooden base and catch a few mice . . . then add the spring and catch a few more mice . . . then add a hammer and catch even more mice. No, all the parts have to be assembled at once, or you don't catch *any* mice at all. You cannot get gradual improvement in function by adding the pieces incrementally, one at a time. Instead, the entire system has to be in place from the beginning in order to perform at all.

You see, natural selection is said to work on tiny, random improvements in function—which means it does not kick in until there is at least *some* function to select from. But irreducibly complex systems don't have *any* function until a minimum number of parts are in place—which means those parts themselves cannot be products of natural selection. We're talking about a minimum number of interacting pieces that must be present before natural selection even begins to operate.

As an example, consider the tiny string-like flagellum attached like a tail to some bacteria. As the bacterium swims around in its environment, the flagellum whips around exactly like a propeller, and from a diagram, you would think you were looking at some kind of tiny motorized machine (see fig. 6.1). It is a microscopic outboard rotary motor that comes equipped with a hook joint, a drive shaft, O-rings, a stator, and a bi-directional acid-powered motor that can hum along at up to 100,000 revolutions per minute. Structures like these require dozens of precisely tailored, intricately interacting parts, which could not emerge by any gradual process. Instead the coordinated parts must somehow appear on the scene all at the same time, combined and coordinated in the right patterns, for the molecular machine to function at all.

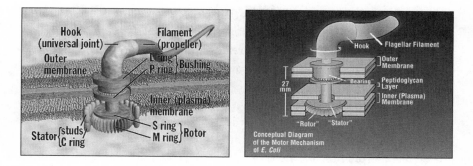

***Fig. 6.1* MOLECULAR MACHINES:** Many structures within the cell bear an uncanny resemblance to manufactured gadgets. *(Reprinted with permission from Access Research Network, www.arn.org.)*

"More so than other motors, the flagellum resembles a machine designed by a human," writes biologist David DeRosier.[19] That resemblance suggests that the tiny molecular machines within the cell were designed by an intelligent agent.

Behe and the Black Box

In Darwin's day, scientists knew next to nothing about biochemistry. Living things were "black boxes," their inside workings a mystery—hence the title of Behe's book. It was easy to speculate about large-scale scenarios where fins gradually turned into legs, or legs into wings, since no one had a clue as to how limbs and organs actually worked from the inside. It's as though we were to ask how a stereo system is made and the answer was: by plugging a set of speakers into an amplifier and adding a CD player, radio receiver, and tape deck.[20] What we really want to know is how things like speakers and CD players themselves were assembled. What is *inside* those plastic boxes?

Today, through the use of the electron microscope, the "black box" of the cell has been opened, and biologists are intimately familiar with its inside workings. The older broad-stroke speculations about fins becoming legs won't cut it anymore. Today any theory of life's origin must explain molecular systems.

Darwin himself once admitted that the existence of irreducible complexity (though he didn't use that term) would stand as a refutation of his theory. He even offered it as a test: "If it could be demonstrated that any complex organ existed which could not possibly have been formed by numerous, successive, slight modifications, my theory would absolutely break down."[21] With the explosion of knowledge from molecular biology, it appears that Darwin's theory has indeed broken down.

Critics charge that irreducible complexity is nothing more than an argument from "personal incredulity." As they see it, people like Behe are simply saying, *We can't imagine any naturalistic way to explain this high level of complexity, so there isn't one.* If that were really all Behe meant, then his argument would only reveal the poverty of his own imagination. After all, there was a time when no one thought it would be possible to fly, either.

But the critics are missing the point. The argument from irreducible complexity is not a statement about what is psychologically possible to imagine. Instead, it is a *logical* argument about how wholes are constructed from parts. An *aggregate* structure, like a pile of sand, can be built up gradually by simply adding a piece at a time—one grain of sand after another. By contrast, an *organized* structure, like the inside of a computer, is built up according to a preexisting blueprint, plan, or design. Each interlocking piece is structured to contribute to the functioning of the whole—which in turn becomes possible only after a minimal number of pieces are in place.

The logical question, then, is whether living structures are aggregates or organized wholes. And the answer is clear: Not only on the level of body systems, but also within each tiny cell, living structures are incredibly complex organized wholes. The most plausible theory, then, is that the pieces were put together according to a preexisting blueprint.[22]

A Universe Built for You

Until recently, the controversy over evolution has centered on design in biology. But today evidence of design is being uncovered in physics and cosmology as well. The cosmos itself is exquisitely fine-tuned to support life.

Cosmologists have discovered that the universe's fundamental forces are intricately balanced, as though on a knife's edge. Take, for example, the force of gravity: If it were only slightly weaker, all stars would be red dwarfs, too cold to support life. But if it were only slightly stronger, all stars would be blue giants, burning too briefly for life to develop. (The margin of error in the universe's expansion rate is only 1 part in 10^{60}.) Cosmologists speak of "cosmic coincidences"—meaning that the fundamental forces of the universe just *happen* to have the exact numerical value required to make life possible. The slightest change would yield a universe inhospitable to life.[23]

This is sometimes dubbed the Goldilocks dilemma: How did these numerical values turn out not too high, not too low, but just right?

What makes the question so puzzling is that there is no physical cause explaining why these values are so finely tuned to support life. "Nothing in all of physics explains why its fundamental principles should conform themselves so precisely to life's requirement," says astronomer George

Greenstein.[24] And since there is no known *physical* cause, it looks suspiciously as though they are the product of *intention*—as though someone designed them that way. "Why is nature so ingeniously, one might even say suspiciously, friendly to life?" asks astrophysicist Paul Davies. "It's almost as if a Grand Designer had it all figured out."[25]

To make the logic clearer, imagine that you found a huge universe-creating machine, with thousands of dials representing the gravitational constant, the strong nuclear force, the weak nuclear force, the electromagnetic force, the ratio of the mass of the proton and the electron, and many more. Each dial has hundreds of possible settings, and you can twirl them around at will—there is nothing that pre-sets them to any particular value. What you discover is that each of the thousands of dials *just happens* to be set to exactly the right value for life to exist. Even the slightest tweak of one of the cosmic knobs would produce a universe where life was impossible. As a science reporter puts it, "They are like the knobs on God's control console, and they seem almost miraculously tuned to allow life."[26]

Since the "knobs" are not constrained by any natural law, they have all the earmarks of being a product of design or intention. "I am not a religious person, but I could say this universe is *designed very well* for the existence of life," says astronomer Heinz Oberhummer. "The basic forces in the universe are tailor-made for the production of . . . carbon-based life."[27]

Nobel Prize–winner Arno Penzias, who has a Jewish background, is quick to see the religious implications: "Astronomy leads us to a unique event, a universe which was created out of nothing, one with the very delicate balance needed to provide exactly the conditions required to permit life, and one which has an underlying (one might say 'supernatural') plan."[28] In fact, he says, "The best data we have are exactly what I would have predicted, had I had nothing to go on but the five books of Moses, the Psalms, the Bible as a whole."[29]

Cosmic Coincidences

Critics admit that the fine-tuning of the universe suggests design, but they grope around for an alternative explanation. Astronomer Fred Hoyle is often quoted as saying, "A common sense interpretation of the facts suggests that a super-intellect has monkeyed with the physics."[30] But who is that "superintellect"? Adamantly opposed to the Christian teaching of creation, Hoyle proposed that it was an alien mind from another universe.[31]

Others have proposed the quasi-pantheistic notion that the universe itself is intelligent, with a mind of its own. For example, Greenstein starts out *appearing* to agree with Christianity: "As we survey all the evidence, the thought insistently arises that some supernatural agency—or, rather Agency—must be involved. Is it possible that suddenly, without intending to, we have stumbled upon scientific proof of the existence of a Supreme Being? Was it God who stepped in and so providentially crafted the cosmos for our benefit?"

Yet, no matter how "insistently" this thought arises, Greenstein firmly suppresses it. He wants no part of a personal God. Instead, making a wild extrapolation from quantum mechanics, Greenstein says the universe could not fully exist until human beings emerged to observe it—and thus, in order to become fully real, the universe decided to evolve human consciousness. The "cosmos does not exist unless observed," he writes, and thus "the universe brought forth life in order to exist."[32]

This implausible notion has proven surprisingly popular. Sounding like an Eastern mystic, the Nobel Prize–winning biologist George Wald said the reason intelligent life evolved is that "the universe wants to be known."[33] And physicist Freeman Dyson, noting "the many accidents of physics and astronomy that have worked together to our benefit," wrote these eerie-sounding words: "It almost seems as if the Universe must in some sense have known that we were coming."[34] How ironic that scientists who dismiss the idea of design as unscientific will turn around and embrace the bizarre, almost mystical notion of a conscious universe that "knew" we were coming.

Less mystical astronomers take a different tack to explain away the "cosmic coincidences," proposing to beat the low probabilities by inflating the number of possibilities. They stack the deck by suggesting that there are multiple universes besides our own (the "Many Worlds" hypothesis). Most of these universes would be dark, lifeless places, but a few might possibly have the right conditions for life—and ours just happens to be one of them. This is sheer, unbridled speculation, of course, since it is impossible to know if any other universes actually exist. "The multiverse theory requires as much suspension of disbelief as any religion," comments Gregg Easterbrook. "Join the church that believes in the existence of invisible objects 50 billion galaxies wide!"[35] The only reason for proposing such a far-fetched idea is that it makes our own universe seem a little less like a freak improbability.

Surveying all these bizarre speculations, physicist Heinz Pagels remarks that scientists seem reluctant to draw the most straightforward inference from the evidence—that "the reason the universe seems tailor-made for our existence is that it *was* tailor-made."[36] The design inference is the simplest, most direct reading of the evidence. It's amazing what exotic theories some scientists will propose in order to avoid that inference. David Gross, director of the Kavli Institute for Theoretical Physics, recently admitted that his objection to the concept of fine-tuning is "totally emotional": It's a dangerous idea because "it smells of religion and intelligent design."[37] Convoluted theories of a conscious cosmos, or of countless unknowable universes, are little more than desperate attempts to avoid the obvious evidence for design.

Who Wrote the Genetic Code?

The most powerful evidence for design in my own view is the DNA code. You may remember the burst of publicity a few years ago, when scientists announced that they had decoded the human genome. At a White House press conference, all the ceremonial language crafted for the occasion stressed the analogy between DNA and a written language. The director of the National Human Genome Research Institute, Dr. Francis Collins, an evangelical Christian, said: "We have caught the first glimpses of our instruction book, previously known only to God." Not to be outdone, then-President Clinton resorted to God talk as well: "Today we are learning the language in which God created life."[38]

These are actually very apt analogies. The DNA molecule is built up of four bases that function as chemical "letters"—adenine (A), thymine (T), cytosine (C), and guanine (G)—which combine in various sequences to spell out a message. The discovery of this chemical code means we can now apply the categories of information theory to DNA. "What has happened is that genetics has become a branch of information technology," writes Dawkins. "The genetic code is truly digital, in exactly the same sense as computer codes. This is not some vague analogy, it is the literal truth."[39]

The result is that the origin of life has now been recast as the origin of biological information: How do we get highly specified, complex biological information?

In ordinary life, when we find a message, we don't have any doubt where it came from. We *know* that natural causes do not produce messages. I once took my little boy to a park, where we sat under a large old beech tree with hearts and slogans carved into the bark—"George loves Wendy" and "Class of '95." It was a sure sign that the squiggles were not the product of natural forces. When Egyptian hieroglyphics were discovered, no one knew how to decipher them for 1,400 years (until the Rosetta Stone was discovered in 1799). Yet everyone knew without a doubt that the hieroglyphs were made by an intelligent agent, and were not patterns etched into the rock by some naturally occurring acid.

An amusing episode took place shortly after September 11 in Palm Beach, Florida. A minor panic broke out when residents spied a crop duster flying overhead, using skywriting to spell out, "God is great." Afraid that the pilot might be a terrorist praising Allah, several people called the cops. But the pilot turned out to be a Christian, who periodically uses his skywriting skills to send inspirational messages—and who was rather amused by all the furor.[40]

The point is that when you see a message, a language, you immediately conclude that it is not a product of natural causes. When the citizens of Palm Beach saw fluffy white shapes that looked like letters in the sky, they did not for a moment start discussing interesting patterns of water condensation. They correctly inferred that the pattern was the product of an intelligent agent—though they were a little worried about *who* the agent was!

This kind of reasoning is intuitive—it seems to be natural to the human mind. But how do we make it logically and scientifically rigorous? What are the empirical markers of design? Under what conditions do we draw the design inference? And can we apply the same reasoning to nature?

Explanatory Filter

We begin by distinguishing among three types of events: those that occur by chance, by law, and by design. Back in 1970, the French geneticist Jacques Monod wrote a book titled *Chance and Necessity*,[41] which achieved cult-like status among college students at the time. (I still have my dog-eared copy from those days.) Monod was presenting standard Darwinian theory, but he did so in a manner that was strikingly streamlined—conceiving it as the interplay between chance (randomness) and necessity (law). Intelligent Design theory adopts the same simplified schema but adds a third category: design.

Thus, (1) some things are the result of random processes, occurring by chance; (2) others are the result of regular, predictable processes which can be formulated as laws of nature; (3) still others are the result of design—like houses, cars, computers, and books.

Which category best explains the origin of life? William Dembski has formulated a rigorous mathematical analysis of the reasoning we use to assign things to each category, which he calls the Explanatory Filter, described in his book *The Design Inference*.[42] His explanation is highly complex, as befits a book published by Cambridge University Press. But I'm going to offer a much simpler treatment, using the analogy of Scrabble letters. After all, if DNA is made up of chemical "letters," like a language, then it is the *sequence* of those "letters" that makes biological function possible, just as the sequence of letters on this page makes its message intelligible. How can we best account for the origin of complex specified sequences in DNA—by chance, by law, or by design?

UP FROM CHANCE

If we have an infinite number of monkeys sitting at typewriters, and an infinite amount of time, eventually they will type out the works of Shakespeare. So goes the theory, at least. But researchers in England recently put the theory to the test. They placed a computer in a cage with six monkeys to see what would happen. The monkeys' main response was to bang the computer with stones; for some reason many of them also found it appealing as an outhouse. When a few actually got around to pressing the keys, the result was a lot of *s*'s, along with about four other letters. After a month the monkeys had not written anything even close to a word of human language. Shakespeare? Not a chance.[43]

The experiment was done partly as a gag, but it does suggest that a bit of skepticism is in order about the standard assumption that life arose by sheer chance. Darwin himself did not write much about the origin of life (his main interest was the origin of species), but in a private letter he once dropped a casual comment about life arising by random chemical interactions in a "warm little pond." When spelled out in greater scientific detail by others, this became the dominant view until recent decades. Ask ordinary people what the theory of evolution is, and typically they will say it's the theory that life arose by pure chance. Yet, among professional scientists, chance-based theories have been all but completely rejected.

The heyday of chance theories was in the early 1950s, when scientists first discovered that they could produce a few simple organic compounds (like amino acids—the building blocks of proteins) in laboratory experiments. But those heady days are over. The early successes have petered out; the excitement has died down. Having created a few simple building blocks, researchers found it much more difficult to create the larger molecules (macromolecules like proteins and DNA) that are crucial for life.[44] It has become clear that simply mixing chemicals in a flask and sparking them with an electrical charge does not produce any biologically significant results.[45]

But if the core of life is biological information, this is exactly what we should expect. Why? Because chance processes do not produce complex information. Take our Scrabble analogy: Imagine that you put a blindfold over your eyes, then pull out a random string of Scrabble letters. Are they going to spell out an intelligible sentence? Of course not. You might get a few short words like "it" or "can," but a random process will not produce Shakespeare's *Hamlet*. Chance simply does not give rise to complex, specified information. Theologian Norman Geisler once offered a spunky illustration: "If you came into the kitchen and saw the Alphabet cereal spilled on the table, and it spelled out your name and address, would you think the cat knocked the cereal box over?"[46]

In fact, instead of *creating* information, chance events tend to *scramble* information. Think of random typos sprinkled throughout a page of text: They are much more likely to make nonsense than better sense. Applied to origin-of-life theories, this means that if any short chains of molecules *did* arise by chance processes in that warm little pond, they would quickly break down again—because the same chance processes would go on to insert "typos" into the chemical "text." It's as though every time your string of Scrabble letters spelled out "it" or "can," a mischievous child grabbed some of the letters and replaced them with new random letters. The upshot is that chance interactions of chemicals will never accumulate any significant concentrations of biologically important compounds. The primeval pond would be as dilute as the Atlantic Ocean is today.[47]

This is not an argument from probability, because the point is not merely that the odds are against the chance formation of life. The point is that, *in principle,* chance events do not create complex information. As a result, virtually all origin-of-life researchers today have abandoned theories based on chance.

AGAINST THE LAW

The second possibility is that the origin of life can be accounted for by some law of nature. This is the most popular view among scientists today—that life arose by natural forces within the constituents of matter itself. The idea is that every time the right preconditions exist, life will arise automatically and inevitably. It is no coincidence that one of the most widely used graduate textbooks expounding this view is titled *Biochemical Predestination.*[48] But instead of God, it was some force within matter itself that "predestined" the chemical compounds to line up in just the right sequences to create the building blocks of life.

The theory is based on the fact that chemical compounds react more easily with certain substances than with others, and it proposes that these chemical preferences are responsible for the highly specified sequences in protein and DNA. Yet the predestinarians turned out to be better biologists than theologians. When the textbook's authors, Dean Kenyon and Gary Steinman, conducted experiments to confirm their theory of biochemical predestination, the chemicals appeared to be Arminians with wills of their own: They stubbornly refused to line up in the proper sequences to form biologically significant results. When I interviewed Kenyon in 1989, he told me, "If you survey the experiments to date, designed to simulate conditions on the early earth, one thing that stands out is that you do not get ordered sequences of amino acids. These simply do not appear among the products of any experiments." And he added wryly: "If we thought we were going to see a lot of spontaneous ordering, something must have been wrong with our theory."[49]

When the experiments failed, Kenyon faced the implications squarely: Eventually he repudiated his own theory and became a proponent of Intelligent Design.[50]

Once again, however, if life consists in information, then Kenyon's failed experiments are exactly what we should expect—because, *in principle*, laws of nature do not give rise to information. Why not? Because laws describe events that are regular, repeatable, and predictable. If you drop a pencil, it will fall. If you put paper into a flame, it will burn. If you mix salt in water, it will dissolve. That's why the scientific method insists that experiments must be repeatable: Whenever you reproduce the same conditions, you should get the same results, or something is wrong with your experiment. The goal of science is to reduce those regular patterns to mathematical formulas. By contrast, the sequence of letters in a message is *ir*regular and *non*repeating, which means it cannot be the result of any law-like process.

NO RULES FOR *HAMLET*

To illustrate the point, let's invoke our imaginary Scrabble game again, but this time when you organize the letters, you decide to follow a certain formula or rule (an analogy to laws of nature). For example, the formula might require that every time you have a D, it is followed by an E. And every time you have an E, it's followed by a S, then an I, then a G, and an N. The result would be that every time you started with D, you would get DESIGN, DESIGN, DESIGN, over and over again. Obviously, if the letters in a real alphabet followed rules like that, you would be limited to spelling only a few words—and you could not convey very much information. The reason a real alphabet works so well is precisely that the letters do *not* follow rules or formulas or laws. If you know that a word begins with a T, you cannot predict what the next letter will be. With some minor exceptions (in English, *q* is always followed by *u*), the letters can be combined and recombined in a vast number of different arrangements to form words and sentences.

When I was a youngster and computers were still new, my father used the huge, whiz-bang computer at work to create wrapping paper with "Happy Birthday" printed all over. It was a novelty at the time, though today you can easily do the same thing on your PC using a macro. It's a matter of programming the computer to write "Happy Birthday," and then cycle back and do the same thing—over and over again. The result is an ordered pattern, but one that conveys very little information. The entire page contains only as much information as the first two words. On the other hand, if you want your computer to write out Shakespeare's *Hamlet,* there is no rule or formula you can program it to follow. Instead, you have to specify each individual letter one by one.

The same is true of the DNA code. If the chemical "letters" in DNA followed some law or formula, they would line up automatically into only a few repeated patterns, storing very little biological information. But in fact, every cell in your body contains more information than the entire thirty volumes of the *Encyclopedia Britannica.* Why is that possible? Because with some minor exceptions, there are no laws of chemical attraction and repulsion that cause the "letters" in DNA to link up in any particular pattern. If you were to decode one section of DNA, there is no rule or formula determining what comes next. Instead the chemical "letters" are free to combine and recombine in a vast variety of sequences.[51]

What holds the DNA molecule together is a sugar-phosphate chain that functions like a backbone, and of course there is a chemical bond that makes the "letters" (bases) stick to that backbone. But there are no chemical bonds connecting one letter to the next in order to form a particular sequence. "DNA is like the magnetic letters your kid sticks on the refrigerator," says Steve Meyer. "The magnetic force explains how the letters stick to the fridge, but it doesn't explain how the letters are sequenced to spell 'I love Daddy.'"[52]

Thus it is futile for scientists to keep looking for some natural law or force within matter to explain the origin of life. It's not just that experiments to create life in a test tube have failed so far; it's that, *in principle,* law-like processes do not generate high information content.

Nor is the problem solved by the newer theories of complexity that are so fashionable these days. At the Santa Fe Institute, Stuart Kauffman holds out the hope that complexity theory will finally uncover the laws that make life inevitable. Kauffman and his colleagues have found that they can construct intricate structures on their computer screens that resemble frost and ferns and snowflakes. This has been touted as evidence that the complexity of life might be the result of self-organizing forces in matter.[53]

The problem, however, is that these structures represent the same kind of order as the birthday wrapping paper—they are products of a simple instruction that cycles back on itself again and again. In Kauffman's own words, they are constructed by the application of a few "astonishingly simple rules," repeated over and over again.[54] While the patterns on the computer screens may look impressive, they lack high information content.

THE MEDIUM IS NOT THE MESSAGE

If neither chance nor law accounts for complex biological information, the final option is design. The distinctive feature of design is an irregular sequence that fits a prescribed pattern—the kind of order found in Scrabble games, books, magazines, and radio scripts. The sequence of letters and words you are reading right now convey information because it fits the prescribed pattern of the English language.

The most popular analogy, however, is a computer program. DNA is the "software" that makes the cell operate, and the sequence of its bases carries information in the same way that sequences of 0 and 1 carry information in a computer code. "The machine code of the genes is uncannily computer-like," writes Dawkins. "Apart from differences in jargon, the pages of a molecular biology journal might be interchanged with those of a computer engineering journal."[55]

The upshot is that we can now apply information theory to biology, which opens whole new vistas on the origin of life.[56] For example, information theory tells us that a message is independent of the material medium used to convey it. The words you are reading right now were printed with ink on paper, but they could also be written with crayon or paint or chalk, or even scratched into sand with a stick. The message remains the same, no matter what kind of material you use to store and transmit it.

But if information is independent of the material medium, *then it was not created by the forces within that medium.* The words on this page were not created by chemical forces within the ink and paper. If you see "Math Test Today" written on a chalkboard, you do not think the message is a product of the chemical properties of calcium carbonate. Applied to the origin of life, this principle means the message encoded in DNA was not created by chemical forces within the molecule itself.

We can now explain why all the experiments to create life in a test tube have failed—because they tried to build life from the bottom up, by assembling the right materials to form a DNA molecule. But life is not about matter, it's about information. "Evolutionary biologists have failed to realize that they work with two more or less incommensurable domains: that of information and that of matter," writes George Williams (himself an evolutionary biologist). "The DNA molecule is the medium, it's not the message."[57] And information theory tells us that the medium does not write the message.

This becomes even clearer if we press the analogy a step further. DNA is a "genetic databank" that transmits information using the genetic code, writes Paul Davies. As a result, he concludes:

> Trying to make life by mixing chemicals in a test tube is like soldering
> switches and wires in an attempt to produce Windows 98. *It won't work
> because it addresses the problem at the wrong conceptual level.*[58]

This is a devastating critique of the dominant origin-of-life scenarios.
Proposing that matter gave rise to life is not just mistaken; it is addressing the
question "at the wrong conceptual level."

The argument from information theory was developed by the late A. E.
Wilder-Smith, a brilliant British-Swiss scientist with multiple earned doctor-
ates.[59] I had the good fortune to meet Wilder-Smith when he was teaching in
Ankara, Turkey, and I had just graduated from high school. (My father was
teaching at the Middle East Technical University in Ankara.) I was still in a
rebellious stage where I wanted nothing to do with Christians—and to my
great surprise, that made Wilder-Smith very interested in talking to me. He had
a broad, genial face, with eyes that twinkled intently through wire-rimmed
spectacles. And unlike most of the Christians I knew, he did not condemn me
for my lack of faith but showed genuine interest in my questions and objections. I was impressed that he would take the time to talk to a somewhat hostile teenager about things like DNA and information theory.

As a consequence, after becoming a Christian, I immediately sought out
his books and studied them intensively. That's when I realized that he was pioneering what would become the heart of the design argument: that information does not arise from natural forces within matter but has to be imposed
upon matter from outside by an intelligent agent.

Testing Positive

Negative evidence that matter does not write messages will not clinch the case,
however. We also need to identify positive evidence for an intelligent agent.
And once again, information theory provides the key: The tell-tale sign of
design is what information theorists call *specified complexity.*[60]

To translate that phrase into simple English, we can once again use
the three-part Explanatory Filter to compare chance, law, and design.
(1) Chance alone may account for simple order (in our Scrabble example,
short words like "it" and "can")—but products of design are *complex.*
(2) Laws describe regular patterns ("DESIGN, DESIGN, DESIGN")—but
products of design exhibit an irregular pattern. (3) That pattern is pre-
selected, or *specified* in advance. Hence the distinctive mark of design in
specified complexity.

Take the example of a language. There is no law of nature that determines
the meaning of a sequence of sounds like G-I-F-T. In English the sequence means

present; in German it means *poison;* in Norwegian it means *married.* A language takes what is an otherwise arbitrary sequence of sounds like G-I-F-T and confers meaning on it through a linguistic convention—formalized in dictionaries, rules of grammar, and so on. Out of all the possible combinations of sounds, a language selects only a few and confers meaning on them.

The DNA code is precisely parallel. The sequences of chemical "letters" are chemically arbitrary. There is no natural force that determines the meaning of certain combinations. Out of all the possible combinations of chemical "letters," somehow only a few carry meaning. But where did the cell's linguistic convention come from?

Clearly, linguistic conventions and rules of grammar do not arise out of chemical reactions. They come from the mental realm of information and intelligence.

The concept of specified complexity was first applied to the origins debate by Charles Thaxton and his coauthors, Walter Bradley and Roger Olsen, in their groundbreaking book *The Mystery of Life's Origin.*[61] Many years before the book came out, I had heard Charlie make the case when he was on staff at L'Abri and I was still an agnostic. Lecturing in the wood-paneled chapel, with the snow-covered Alps blazing through the windows, Charlie covered an easel with symbols for amino acids and proteins and DNA molecules, while I madly scribbled notes. I came away knowing that whatever other objections I might still harbor against Christianity, I could no longer cavalierly argue that it was disproved by science.

What made Thaxton an innovator in the design movement was that he was unwilling to stop short with building a negative case against evolution. Since Darwin's day, a wide variety of people (not only creationists) had rejected evolution, but no one had built a *positive* case for Intelligent Design. Thaxton argued that it is not enough to show the inadequacies of *natural* causes; we must go on to demonstrate the plausibility of *intelligent* causes. And the hallmark of intelligence is that elusive quality we just discussed: specified complexity. The structure of DNA is precisely parallel to the structure of languages and computer programs. Can we infer that specified complexity in DNA is likewise the product of an intelligent agent? Unless we define science from the outset in terms of naturalistic philosophy, the answer should be yes.

Three to Get Ready

Notice that the design inference is not an argument from ignorance: It does not say, *We don't know* the cause of a certain phenomenon, so we just throw up our hands and invoke a miracle. Instead, the argument is based on what we *do* know about the kinds of structures produced by chance, law, and design.[62] Faced with any phenomenon, a scientist can run it through the Explanatory Filter: Is it a random event? Then all we need to invoke is chance. Does it occur in a regular, repeated pattern? Then it is an instance of some natural law. Is it a complex, specified pattern? Then it exhibits design, and was produced by intelligence.

The Explanatory Filter is also useful for cutting through the surface detail in order to see what competing theories are really proposing. Take, for example, Darwin's theory. Stripped of the details, its core claim is that science should be limited to the first two categories of explanation—chance and law. In fact, its goal is precisely to eliminate design as a permissible category within science. How? By showing that chance and law, working together, can substitute for design. Darwinism proposes that when random mutations (chance) are run through the sieve of natural selection (law), then over time organisms become better and better adapted until they *appear* to be designed. In this way, the theory claims, a wholly naturalistic process can mimic the effects of Intelligent Design—which means design is no longer required as a separate category. As one philosopher puts it, Darwin was offering "a scheme for creating Design out of Chaos without the aid of Mind."[63]

This explains why Darwin himself had no patience with theistic, or God-guided, evolution. In his theory, natural selection functions to sift out any harmful variations, while letting only beneficial variations through. If God were guiding the process, however, then He would create only good variations in the first place—in which case the sifting action of natural selection would be unnecessary. In Darwin's words, "The view that each variation has been providentially arranged seems to me to make Natural Selection entirely superfluous, and indeed takes the whole case of the appearance of new species out of the range of science."[64]

Notice that Darwin was offering two objections to design. First, that it makes natural selection "entirely superfluous." In other words, if you invoke natural selection *plus* design, then one of the two is redundant and unnecessary. And Darwin intended to make sure it was design that would be rejected as redundant. Thus a widely used college textbook says, "By coupling undirected, purposeless variation [chance] to the blind, uncaring process of natural selection [law], Darwin made theological or spiritual explanations of the life processes superfluous."[65]

Second, and more importantly, Darwin's remarks show that he wanted to transform the definition of science itself. That's why he objected that attributing the origin of species to providential purpose would take it "out of the range of science." The implication is that science cannot countenance intelligent causation in any form. In Darwin's mind, theistic or divinely ordained evolution was no different in principle from direct creation—and neither was admissible in science. To use our three categories, chance and law were permitted in science, but design was not. As one philosopher of science explains, "Darwin insisted on telling a totally consistent naturalistic story or none at all."[66]

Today, however, it is clear that the naturalistic story did not succeed. Chance and law do not mimic design. Applying the Explanatory Filter to life's origin, we find that the sequence in DNA is neither random (chance) nor regular (law). Instead, it exhibits specified complexity, the hallmark of design. Chance and law may explain many other events in the history of the cosmos. But to explain the origin of life, we need to include an additional tool in the scientist's tool chest.[67]

It's beginning to look like the key to interpreting the organic world is not natural selection but information. In science we are hearing echoes of John 1:1, "In the beginning was the Word." The Greek word *Logos* means intelligence, wisdom, rationality, or information. Modern genetics seems to be telling us that life is a grand narrative told by the divine Word—that there is an Author for the text of life.

CHRISTIAN RELATIVISTS

If Darwin's goal was to get rid of design, then clearly his motivation was not strictly scientific but also religious. We should avoid the misleading dichotomy that says evolution is scientific, while design is religious. Darwinism and design theory are not about different subjects—science versus religion. Instead they are competing answers to the *same* question: How did life arise in the universe? Both theories appeal to scientific data, while at the same time both have broader philosophical and religious implications.

Christians will only be able to make this case effectively, however, when we challenge the science/religion dichotomy in our own thinking. We must be confident that the biblical teaching on creation is objectively *true* and not just a matter of religion—in the modern sense of merely personal, subjective values. Consider the Bible's opening claim: "In the beginning God created the heavens and the earth." Is this true or false? For many people, even asking such a question amounts to making a category mistake.[68] Genesis is religion, they might say, which is not a matter of true or false. Religion is a personal commitment, a way of life, a source of ultimate meaning. And of course, Christianity *is* all these things. But are we also prepared to say it is *true*?

Many Christians have come to think of religion as a matter of experience rather than truth. I discovered this shortly after my conversion, after I had returned to the States from L'Abri. Living in New Mexico, I heard about a

Christian "crash pad" in Albuquerque. (Do you even *remember* that term? It
meant a household that took people in for the night as a ministry.) Immediately
I hitched a ride to Albuquerque, and ended up living in the household all summer. Those who lived or gathered regularly at His House, as it was called, were
all ex-hippies, "Jesus freaks." But because of my studies at L'Abri, I talked
about my recent conversion in terms of becoming convinced that Christianity
is *true*—that it answers the basic philosophical questions better than any other
system of thought.

My new friends, with their long hair and granny dresses, looked puzzled.
They would often go to the park to evangelize among teens tripping on drugs,
and they said, "We tell the people, 'Jesus works for me. Why don't you try
Him.' Isn't that good enough?"[69]

It's *not* enough, of course, and the weakness of reducing Christianity to
"what works" came home to me when I joined my friends in their witnessing
expeditions. One evening I had a long, engaging discussion with a young
teenager who expressed interest in converting. When I asked if he was convinced that Christianity was true, however, he frowned and burst out, "Well,
of course it's true. If you believe it, it's true for you!"

Clearly, the evangelistic message was being sieved through a relativistic
grid that reduced all truth claims to whatever is "true for you." The reason
Christians often fail to break through that relativistic framework is partly that
we ourselves have absorbed a form of religious relativism—in practice, even if
not in belief. By accepting the fact/value dichotomy, many of us have come to
think of religion and morality in terms of a privatized, upper-story experience.

FAIRY DUST

If we privatize our faith, however, we will play right into the hands of the philosophical naturalists, who likewise relegate religion to the upper story. Rather
than attacking religion directly as *false,* which would risk arousing public
protest, philosophical naturalists deftly relegate it to the "values" realm—
which keeps the question of true and false off the table altogether. As Johnson
writes, religion is consigned "to the private sphere, where illusory beliefs are
acceptable 'if they work for you.'"[70]

Unless Christians tackle this attitude head on, our message will continue
to pass through a grid that reduces it to an expression of merely psychological
need. I witnessed a breathtaking example a few years ago at a scientific conference at Baylor University. One of the speakers was the Nobel Prize–winning
physicist Steven Weinberg, and he opened his presentation by announcing that
he intended to lump together all spiritual beings—whether Buddha or Jesus or

whoever—under a single rubric, which he would call "fairies." And then he would explain why as a scientist he did not believe in "fairies." A murmur of awkward laughter rippled through the audience, many of whom were Christians. And no wonder: It's pretty tough to defend your beliefs with any dignity when they've just been labeled nothing more than fairy tales.

Yet Weinberg was only bluntly stating the logical consequence of redefining religion in terms of noncognitive experience—exactly what many Christians themselves do, at least implicitly, when they accept the fact/value dichotomy.

OUT OF THE NATURALIST'S CHAIR

Some even do it explicitly. Consider Christians who are theistic evolutionists: Though they would never agree with atheists that nature is all that exists (*metaphysical* naturalism), they do agree that science must be limited to natural causes (*methodological* naturalism). As philosopher Nancey Murphy of Fuller Theological Seminary writes: "Christians and atheists alike must pursue scientific questions in our era without invoking a Creator." Why? Well, because that's what atheists have decided: "For better or worse, we have inherited a view of science as *methodologically* atheistic."[71]

But who says that we have to play by the rules set down by atheists? If Christianity is true, then it's not at all obvious that valid science can be done only by making the counterfactual assumption that atheism is true. Theistic evolutionists generally accept exactly the same scientific theories as atheists or naturalists; the only thing they ask is that they be allowed to propose a theological meaning behind it all—known only by faith, and not detectable by scientific means. In essence, they allow atheists to define scientific knowledge, so long as theology is allowed to put a religious spin on whatever science comes up with.

In that case, however, what does this theological meaning amount to? It is reduced to a subjective gloss on the story told by naturalistic science. God's existence doesn't make any difference scientifically because He does not act in ways that can be detected. As a result, theology is no longer regarded as an independent source of knowledge; it is merely an overlay of *value* on otherwise value-free facts.

"As the scientific concept of truth came to dominate modernity," explains theologian Ellen Charry, "theologians came to assign religious claims to the realm of myth and meaning." Theology lost its status "as genuine truth and knowledge," while "a small space was carved out for theological claims as symbolic terms that render life meaningful."[72] A merely symbolic religion does not threaten the ruling regime of materialistic science, and hence the scientific establishment is generally willing to tolerate it. It is seen as a harmless delusion for those who need that kind of crutch—provided they keep it contained within Sunday worship and don't bring it into the science classroom, where we talk about what *really* happened. The attitude is summed up in H. L. Mencken's aphorism: "We must respect the other fellow's religion, but only in the sense and to the extent that we respect his theory that his wife is beautiful and his children smart."

Theistic evolutionists tend to be content with this arrangement, but secularists understand very well that it is an untenable halfway house. John Maddox, former editor of *Nature* and a self-identified atheist, put the matter bluntly when he reviewed a book by a liberal churchman: "The religious explanation of the world is not free standing, but an optional add-on," he wrote. In other words, religion is not an independent source of knowledge, but merely an optional emotional overlay to what we already know from science—like adding a color overlay to a photograph.[73]

The attempt to accommodate to philosophical naturalism was illustrated nicely by Francis Schaeffer in an image of two chairs. Those who sit in the naturalist's "chair," he said, view the world filtered through a lens that limits their sight to the natural world. But those who sit in the supernaturalist's "chair" view the world through a much larger lens that makes them aware of an unseen realm that exists in addition to the seen realm. Christians are called to live out their entire lives, including their scientific work, from the perspective of the supernaturalist's chair, recognizing the full range of reality.[74] This is what it means to "walk by faith, not by sight" (2 Cor. 5:7), with a day-by-day awareness of the unseen dimension of reality.

Sadly, however, even sincere believers keep wandering over to the naturalist's chair. They may embrace biblical doctrine with their minds, and follow biblical ethics in their practical behavior—and yet still conduct their day-to-day professional lives on the basis of a naturalistic worldview. You might say that in confessing their beliefs they sit in the supernaturalist's "chair," but in pursuing their professional work, they walk over and sit in the naturalist's "chair." This is what happens when Christians accept methodical naturalism in science.

By contrast, design theory demonstrates that Christians can sit in the supernaturalist's "chair" even in their professional lives, seeing the cosmos through the lens of a comprehensive biblical worldview. Intelligent Design steps boldly into the scientific arena to build a case based on empirical data. It takes Christianity out of the ineffectual realm of *value* and stakes out a cognitive

claim in the realm of objective truth. It restores Christianity to its status as genuine knowledge, equipping us to defend it in the public arena.

Finally, by challenging naturalism in science, it provides the basis for challenging naturalism in theology, morality, politics, and every other field. And
none too soon, because naturalism is spilling over the banks of science and
making deep inroads into the rest of culture. In the next chapter we will see
how naturalistic evolution is being transformed into a universal worldview that
is aggressively taking over every aspect of human life and society.

7

TODAY BIOLOGY,
TOMORROW THE WORLD

What is in our genes' interests
is what seems "right"—morally right.
ROBERT WRIGHT[1]

A first-grader came home from school one day and asked: "Who's lying, Mom—you or my teacher?" That day, it turned out, the teacher had informed the class that humans and apes are descended from a common ancestor. Little Ricky was bright enough to figure out that this didn't square with what his mother had taught him from the Bible, so he figured one of them must be making things up. Surely, it couldn't be the teacher; after all, in his young eyes she was the expert, the professional. No, the person he decided to doubt was his mother. With sorrow, she realized that she had better start on a long process of counter-education.

It is because of incidents like this, repeated over and over in the classroom, that the controversy over teaching evolution refuses to die. When Ohio debated the topic in 2002, the Department of Education received more public response than to any previous issue. The public senses intuitively that there's much more at stake than just science—that when naturalistic evolution is taught in the science classroom, that will lead to a naturalistic view of ethics and religion being taught down the hallway in the history classroom, the social studies classroom, the family life classroom, and all the rest of the curriculum. A leader in the Ohio controversy put it well: "A naturalistic definition of *science* has the effect of indoctrinating students into a naturalistic *worldview.*"[2]

The public is right to be concerned, and the purpose of the next two chapters is to show why.[3] Darwinism functions as the scientific support for an overarching naturalistic worldview, which is being promoted aggressively far beyond the bounds of science. Some even say we are entering an age of "universal Darwinism," when it will no longer be just a scientific theory but a comprehensive worldview. In order to have a redemptive impact on our culture, Christians need to engage Darwinian evolution not only as science but also as a worldview.

UNIVERSAL DARWINISM

I'd like to begin with a sentence from one of Francis Schaeffer's books. The central reason Christians have not been more effective in the public square, he says, is that we tend to see things in "bits and pieces." We worry about things like family breakdown, violence in schools, immoral entertainment, abortion and bioethics—a wide array of *individual* issues. But we don't see the big picture that connects all the dots.

And what *is* that big picture? All these forms of cultural dissolution, Schaeffer writes, have "come about due to a shift in worldview . . . to a worldview based on the idea that the final reality is impersonal matter or energy shaped into its current form by impersonal chance."[4] In other words, long before there was an Intelligent Design movement, Schaeffer saw that everything hangs on your view of origins. If you start with impersonal forces operating by chance—in other words, naturalistic evolution—then over time (even if it takes several generations) you will end up with naturalism in moral, social, and political philosophy.

Many evolutionists today would agree with that. In fact, one of the fastest-growing disciplines today is the application of Darwinism to social and cultural issues. It goes by the name of evolutionary psychology (an updated version of sociobiology), and its premise is that if natural selection produced the human body, then it must also account for all aspects of human belief and behavior. Evolutionary psychology is spreading rapidly to virtually every subject area, with new books appearing on the shelves almost faster than you can keep up with them. Let's run through a smattering of recent titles, just to get a flavor of what's coming out on the subject.

One of the topics tackled most frequently is morality. After all, if human behavior is ultimately programmed by "selfish genes" (as Dawkins argues in *The Selfish Gene*), then it becomes enormously difficult to explain unselfish or altruistic behavior. Thus new books keep being churned out with titles like *The Moral Animal* and *Evolutionary Origins of Morality*, seeking to explain morality as a product of natural selection. The theme is that we learn to be kind and helpful only because that helps us survive and produce more offspring.[5]

"The basis of ethics does not lie in God's will," write E. O. Wilson and Michael Ruse. Ethics is "an illusion fobbed off on us by our genes to get us to cooperate." For some unexplained reason, humans simply "function better if they are deceived by their genes into thinking that there is a disinterested objective morality binding upon them, which all should obey."[6] In other words, evolution practices a kind of benign deception to get us to be nice to one another.

If natural selection is the reason we're good, it's also the reason we're bad. So says a new book called *Demonic Males: Apes and the Origins of Human Violence*. The authors take aim at the biblical teaching of "original sin," insisting that even the September 11 attacks had nothing to do with moral "evil"—they merely show that a predisposition to violence "is written in the molecular chemistry of DNA." Their genes made them do it.[7]

Religion is another favorite target, and recent books include *In Gods We Trust* and *Religion Explained: The Evolutionary Origins of Religious Thought*. The basic theme is that religion is a malfunction to which brains are susceptible when the nervous system has evolved to a certain level of complexity.[8]

EVOLUTION FOR EVERYMAN

If you are interested in politics, there are books like *Darwinian Politics: The Evolutionary Origin of Freedom*. For economists, there's *Economics as an Evolutionary Science*. Lawyers may want to consult *Evolutionary Jurisprudence* or *Law, Biology and Culture: The Evolution of Law*.[9]

For educators, there's *Origins of Genius: Darwinian Perspectives on Creativity*. The book defines intelligence as a Darwinian process of generating a variety of ideas, then selecting those that are "fittest." There are even books targeted specifically to English teachers, like *Evolution and Literary Theory*.[10]

If you work in medicine, a slew of new books have come out, such as *Evolutionary Medicine* and *Why We Get Sick: The New Science of Darwinian Medicine*. Mental health workers can choose either *Darwinian Psychiatry* or *Genes on the Couch: Explorations in Evolutionary Psychology*.[11]

If you're a woman, there's *Divided Labours: An Evolutionary View of Women at Work*. For parents, there's *The Truth About Cinderella: A Darwinian View of Parental Love*. If you're a businessman, there's even something for you: *Executive Instinct: Managing the Human Animal in the Information Age*. The author asks, How do we manage people whose brains were hardwired in the Stone Age?[12]

Of course, to really sell books you have to talk about the racier topics, and scientists have not been shy about doing so. A sampling of recent titles includes *The Evolution of Desire: Strategies of Human Mating* and *Ever Since Adam and Eve: The Evolution of Human Sexuality*.[13] Science seems to be descending to the level of soap opera.

The PBS "Evolution" series featured an evolutionary psychologist named

Geoffrey Miller, author of *The Mating Mind: How Sexual Choice Shaped the Evolution of Human Nature.*[14] On the program Miller told the audience that the origin of the human brain "wasn't God, it was our ancestors . . . choosing their sexual partners." As he was talking, you could hear the strains of Handel's "Messiah" playing in the background, while a voice-over explained that even artistic expression began as a form of sexual display.

After September 11, evolutionary psychologists suddenly had a real-world opportunity to apply their theory. Pundits of every stripe rushed to offer some explanation for the terrible tragedy, and even the science desk at the *New York Times* got into the act. It claimed that the heroism of the rescue workers was a product of evolution—akin to the cooperative instincts of ants and bees.

Selfless behavior is a product of "kin selection," the article said—the idea that your genes are passed on not only to your own children but also to close relatives. As a result, you can enhance your own reproductive success by caring for a wider group of genetic relatives.[15] A leading evolutionist, J. B. S. Haldane, once explained the calculus of kin selection by saying he was prepared to sacrifice his life for two brothers, or possibly eight cousins.[16]

Other theories of altruistic behavior are based on game theory, which shows that cooperative strategies—"tit for tat"—work best in getting what we want. Of course, neither of these explanations accounts for altruism in the ordinary sense; they are merely extended forms of self-interest. They tell us that what *appears* to be sacrificial behavior—for example, on the part of a mother for her child—is *really* just a strategy for passing on her own genes.

We could go further and argue that genuine altruism actually provides a powerful apologetic argument for Christianity. Heroic self-sacrifice of the type we witnessed on September 11 can *only* be explained by the Christian understanding of human nature as genuinely moral beings, made in the image of God.[17]

DARWINIAN FUNDAMENTALISM ON RAPE

If Christians remain skeptical of the claims of evolutionary psychology, they are in good company. Many mainstream scientists are likewise critical. After all, it's easy to come up with imaginary scenarios of how some behavior *might* be adaptive under certain circumstances, and then jump to saying it *was* adaptive—even when there is no actual evidence. The literature of evolutionary psychology is full of "cocktail party" speculation devoid of any real data from genetics or neurology. Some critics have dismissed the theory as "Darwinian fundamentalism"—a provocative phrase implying that Darwinism itself has become a rigid orthodoxy.[18]

"The ugly fact is that we haven't a shred of evidence that morality in humans did or did not evolve by natural selection," says geneticist H. Allen Orr. Evolutionary psychologists have constructed a host of hypothetical scenarios on questions like *What would happen if we had a gene that said be nice to strangers?* "But, in the end, a thought experiment is not an experiment," Orr states acerbically. The reality is, "We have no data."[19]

We have to realize, however, that once someone has accepted the evolutionary premise, the question of evidence becomes all but irrelevant. Applying Darwinian explanations to human behavior is a matter of simple logic. After all, if evolution is true, then how else did the mind emerge, if *not* by evolution? How else did human behavior arise, if *not* through adaptation to the environment?

This became clear a few years ago when a book appeared offering an evolutionary account of sexual assault. It was titled *The Natural History of Rape: Biological Bases of Sexual Coercion,* and the authors were two university professors who made the rather inflammatory claim that rape is not a pathology, biologically speaking. Instead it is an evolutionary adaptation for maximizing reproductive success. In other words, if candy and flowers don't do the trick, some men may resort to coercion to fulfill the reproductive imperative. The book calls rape "a natural, biological phenomenon that is a product of the human evolutionary heritage," akin to "the leopard's spots and the giraffe's elongated neck."[20]

Demonstrating how insulated many scientists are, the authors said they were genuinely surprised by all the controversy the book caused. After all, to a Darwinist it is simple logic that any behavior that survives today *must* have conferred some evolutionary advantage—otherwise it would have been weeded out by natural selection. So the authors were virtually forced to identify some benefit even in the crime of rape.[21]

When one of the authors, Randy Thornhill, appeared on National Public Radio, he found himself deluged by angry calls, until finally he insisted that the logic is inescapable: If evolution is true, then "every feature of every living thing, including human beings, has an underlying evolutionary background. *That's not a debatable matter.*"[22] Three times during the program, he hammered home the same phrase: It's "not a debatable matter."

This explains why opponents of evolutionary psychology have failed to halt its rapid growth: Many accept the same evolutionary premise, which means ultimately they have no defense against its application to human behavior. For example, critics of the rape thesis tended to focus their arguments at the level of details: Many victims of rape are either too young or too old to bear children—and in some cases, are even males (e.g., prison rape)—which clearly undercuts the idea that rape is driven by a biological imperative to reproduce. The entire theory, said *Nature*, rests on "statistical sleight of hand."[23]

Yet the critics were hamstrung by the fact that most of them accept the same evolutionary assumptions as the book—which left them no principled means of opposing its conclusion. To borrow an elegant phrase from Tom Bethell, "The critics were disarmed by their shared worldview."[24]

There was an amusing episode in the NPR program when Thornhill faced off against a leading feminist, Susan Brownmiller, who authored an influential book on rape many years ago called *Against Our Wills*. Not surprisingly, she objected strenuously to the rape thesis, and Thornhill fired back with the worst insult he could dream up: He said she was starting to sound just like "the extreme religious right."

No doubt she *was* insulted, but the underlying point was actually serious. Thornhill was saying that *evolution* and *evolutionary ethics* are a package deal. If you accept the premise, then you must accept the conclusion. And if you don't like it, you may as well join the "religious right" and challenge evolution itself. It's just as Schaeffer said: All the dots connect back to your view of origins.

MOTHERS RED IN TOOTH AND CLAW

A few years ago, Steven Pinker wrote an article in the *New York Times* applying evolutionary psychology to another troubling moral issue—infanticide. This was shortly after the news media had picked up the story about a teenage girl, dubbed the "Prom Mom," who delivered her baby at a school dance, then dumped it in the trash. At around the same time, an unmarried teen couple killed their newborn as well. The public was shocked, and so Pinker arose to reassure them with the wisdom of science.

We must "understand" teenagers who kill their newborns, Pinker began, because infanticide "has been practiced and accepted in most cultures throughout history." Its sheer ubiquity implies that it *must* have been preserved by natural selection—which in turn means it *must* have an adaptive function. Speaking of human mothers in terms more suitable to cats, Pinker said, "If a newborn is sickly, or if its survival is not promising, they may cut their losses and favor the healthiest in the litter or try again later on." Thus, "the emotional circuitry of mothers has evolved" to commit infanticide in certain situations. Because of natural selection, "a capacity for neonaticide is built into the biological design of our parental emotions."[25]

Pinker's interpretation should have come as no surprise to anyone who remembered an earlier article that appeared in *Newsweek* back in 1982 under the startling title "Nature's Baby Killers." It was a report on the first major symposium studying infanticide among animals, convened with the hope that it might explain similar behavior in humans. Many of the participating scientists agreed that "infanticide can no longer be called 'abnormal.' Instead it is as 'normal' as parenting instincts, sex drives and self-defense," and may even be a beneficial evolutionary adaptation.[26]

But all this is little more than smoke and mirrors. There is no evidence that neonaticide is a genetic trait to begin with, let alone one selected by evolution. "Where are the twin studies, chromosome locations, and DNA sequences supporting such a claim?" demands Orr. "The answer is we don't have any. What we do have is a story—there's an undeniable Darwinian logic underlying the murder of newborns in certain circumstances." And it's this logic, more than any factual evidence, that drives the theory: The evolutionary story sounds persuasive; evolution requires genes; therefore, the behavior is genetic. "The move is so easy and so seductive," Orr says, "that evolutionary psychologists sometimes forget a hard truth: a Darwinian story is not Mendelian evidence. A Darwinian story is a story."[27]

The "Darwinian logic" is so compelling that even Darwin himself was taken in by it. In *The Descent of Man* he argued that the "murder of infants has prevailed on the largest scale throughout the world, and has met with no reproach." Indeed, "infanticide, especially of females, has been thought to be good for the tribe."[28] More than a century ago, Darwin already understood where the logic of his theory led.

Ultimately, the fatal weakness of evolutionary psychology is that it is so elastic that it can explain anything. Evolution is said to account for mothers who kill their newborn babies—but if you were to ask why most mothers do *not* kill their babies, why, evolution accounts for that too. A theory that explains any phenomenon and its opposite, too, in reality explains nothing. It is so flexible that it can be twisted to say whatever proponents want it to say.

PETER SINGER'S PET THEME

In the past, it was Christians who warned that Darwinian evolution would ultimately destroy morality, by reducing it to behavioral patterns selected only for their survival value. Back then, evolutionists would often respond with soothing reassurances that getting rid of God would not jeopardize morality—that "we can be good without God." But in recent years, evolutionists themselves have begun bluntly declaring that the theory undercuts the basis of morality.

For example, biologist William Provine of Cornell travels the lecture circuit telling university students that the Darwinian revolution is still incomplete, because we have not yet embraced all its moral and religious implications. What are those implications? Provine lists them: "There is no ultimate foundation for ethics, no ultimate meaning in life, and no free will."[29] Thus evolutionary psychologists are simply completing the Darwinian revolution by drawing out its full implications. They are connecting the dots, by showing what consistent Darwinism means for morality.

The results can be quite abhorrent. A few years ago, conservative commentators around the country gave a collective gasp when an article appeared by a Princeton University professor supporting—of all things—sexual relations between humans and animals. The professor was Peter Singer, already notorious for his support of animal rights. (Apparently we didn't realize what kind of rights he meant . . .)

The article was titled "Heavy Petting," and in it Singer makes it clear that his real target is biblical morality. In the West, he writes, we have a "Judeo-Christian tradition" that teaches that "humans alone are made in the image of God." "In Genesis, God gives humans dominion over the animals." But evolution has thoroughly refuted the biblical account, Singer maintains: Evolution teaches us that "We are animals"—and the result is that "sex across the species barrier [isn't that a scientific-sounding euphemism?] ceases to be an offence to our status and dignity as human beings."[30]

These sentiments do not remain carefully contained within academia, but trickle down into popular culture—where they have a much greater impact on the public. In 2002 a play opened on Broadway to rave reviews called *The Goat, or, Who Is Sylvia?* featuring a successful architect who confesses to his wife that he has fallen in love with someone else. The object of his affection turns out to be a goat named Sylvia.[31] Apparently, playwrights no longer feel that they can get enough dramatic tension out of an ordinary affair; to really create drama, they must probe the theme of bestiality.

A culture is driven by a kind of logic: It will eventually begin to express the logical consequences of the dominant worldview. If evolution is true—if there really is an unbroken continuity between humans and animals—then Singer is absolutely right about what he calls "sex across the species barrier."

Once again, all the dots connect back to your view of origins.

In another example, few years ago a song by a group called the Bloodhound Gang soared to number 17 on Billboard's top 200 chart. It featured a catchy refrain punched out over and over again: "You and me baby ain't nothin' but mammals; so let's do it like they do on the Discovery Channel." The video featured band members dressed up as monkeys in antic sexual poses.[32]

Back in the 1940s, Alfred Kinsey, himself a committed Darwinist, said the only source of sexual norms for humans is what the other mammals do—whatever fits within "the normal mammalian picture."[33] What Kinsey stated in academic jargon half a century ago is now showing up in punchy rhymes for teenagers.

And not just teenagers. A friend tells me he heard two young boys belting out a song while playing in the park, and as he came closer he could make out the words—"You and me baby ain't nothing but mammals." The boys were only about eight years old.

DARWINIZING CULTURE

In the past, most social scientists tried to limit the implications of evolution by erecting a wall between biology and culture. Evolution created the human body, they said, but then humans created culture, which is independent of biology.[34] This conviction was a key plank in defending against biological determinism. Today, with the rise of evolutionary psychology, that wall is crumbling. Scientists realize they can no longer put any arbitrary limit on the logic of evolution. Consistency requires that they apply it across the board—to religion, morality, politics, everything.

For a fascinating example of the change in outlook, consider the dramatic turnabout that brought Singer into the sociobiology camp. When the theory first appeared, Singer went into fierce opposition mode. As he later explained, sociobiology raised hackles because it was regarded as a revival of Social Darwinism with its "nasty, right-wing biological determinism." Social Darwinism had long harnessed the idea of the survival of the fittest to the ruthless pursuit of self-interest; and sociobiology, it seemed, merely replaced the selfish individual with the selfish gene.[35]

In his recent book *A Darwinian Left*, however, Singer makes an astounding reversal, pressing liberals and leftists to accept sociobiology's offshoot, evolutionary psychology. The left must "face the fact that we are evolved animals," he intones, "and that we bear the evidence of our inheritance, not only in our anatomy and our DNA, but in our behavior too."[36]

Singer seems to have realized that it is impossible to limit the implications of Darwinian evolution. There is no way to cordon off politics or morality or whatever you happen to care most about, and say, *This* is immune to the implications of evolution. Once you accept the Darwinian premise, there is logical pressure to be consistent, applying it to every aspect of culture. Today evolutionary psychologists are putting out books with all-encompassing titles like *The Evolution of Culture* and *Darwinizing Culture,* which contend that culture can no longer be separated from biology, but is itself merely a product of evolutionary forces.[37]

In other words, Darwinists are connecting all the dots, tracing everything back to origins. And that's why Christians had better connect the dots as well. If *they* offer "universal Darwinism," then *we* had better offer "universal Design," showing that design theory gives scientific support for an all-encompassing Christian worldview.

THE ACID BITES BACK

Given that evolutionary psychology often leads to morally outrageous conclusions, as we have seen, why is it gaining such rapid acceptance? The reason is that, for many people, it promises to provide a morality based on the solid ground of science instead of the myths of religion. Some twenty years ago, sociologist Howard Kaye wrote what is now a classic critique of sociobiology, in which he calls it nothing less than a secularized natural theology—an attempt to use nature to justify a secular worldview. Evolutionary psychology engages in a two-part process: First it debunks traditional morality by reducing it to genetic self-interest ("an illusion fobbed off on us by our genes"); then it offers to construct a new morality with all the authority of science. Extending Darwinian principles from bodies to behavior, it claims that adaptive forms of behavior survive, while maladaptive ones are weeded out by natural selection.[38]

But it is painfully clear from the examples we have surveyed that literally *any* behavior that is practiced today can be said to have survival value—after all, it has *survived* to our own times. Evolution fails as a moral guide because it provides no standard for judging any existing practices.

The logical flaw in the theory, however, is that it undercuts itself. For if all our ideas are products of evolution, then so is the idea of evolutionary psychology itself. Like all other constructs of the human mind, it is not true but only useful for survival. Daniel Dennett may call Darwinism a "universal acid" that dissolves away traditional religion and ethics (as we saw in an earlier chapter)—but it is the height of wishful thinking for him to presume that the acid will dissolve only *other* people's views, while leaving his own views untouched.[39] Once the very possibility of objective truth has been undermined, then Darwinian evolution itself cannot be objectively true.

Once when I was presenting these ideas at a Christian college, a man in the audience raised his hand and said, "I have only one question: These guys who think all our ideas and beliefs evolved . . . , do they think *their own* ideas evolved?" The audience burst into laughter, because of course the man had nailed the crux of the matter in a single, punchy question. If all ideas are products of evolution, and not really true but only useful, then evolution *itself* is not true either. And why should the rest of us pay it any attention?

To use philosophical labels, a statement that undercuts itself is self-defeating or self-referentially absurd. Other examples would include using logical arguments to refute the validity of logic; or stating (in English) that you cannot speak English; or arguing that there are absolutely no moral absolutes; or saying "My brother is an only child." Discovering that a philosophy is self-referentially absurd is a sure sign that it is fatally flawed.

TELLING GENES TO JUMP IN THE LAKE

Another way to evaluate a theory is by submitting it to the practical test: Can we live by it? Does it fit our experience of human nature? Many proponents of evolutionary psychology admit that it is a dark doctrine, with repugnant implications. After all, if humans are nothing more than "gene machines" or "robots" programmed to behave in certain ways by natural selection, then what becomes of moral freedom and human dignity? Ironically, when evolutionary psychologists reach that point, they will suddenly turn around and contradict everything they have just said—urging us to act *against* our genetic programming by embracing traditional moral ideals of love and altruism.

Our earlier discussion of the two-story view of truth helps us recognize the dynamic taking place here. As ever-greater areas of life are absorbed into the lower story of Darwinian determinism, the only way to defend any concept of moral freedom is to leap to the upper story—no matter how self-contradictory and irrational it renders the resulting theory.

A prime example is *The Moral Animal,* where Robert Wright starts with the premise that "our genes control us"—that "we are all machines, pushed and pulled by [physical] forces." Even our noblest beliefs are products of natural selection: "We believe the things—about morality, personal worth, even objective truth—that lead to behaviors that get our genes into the next generation." The implications of all this are as clear as they are troubling: "Free will is an illusion," a "useful fiction," part of an "outmoded worldview." Darwinism even calls into question "the very meaning of the word *truth.*" All truth claims "are, by Darwinian lights, raw power struggles." Wright doesn't flinch from concluding that Darwinism leads to utter "cynicism."[40]

But then, ignoring all he has just said, he takes a grand leap of faith by urging us to work on "correcting the moral biases built into us by natural selection" and practicing the ideal of "brotherly love."[41] But if we really are "machines" created by natural selection, how can we "correct" the force that created us?

Dawkins gives a similar display of stunning inconsistency in *The Selfish Gene*. Again and again he insists that the genes "created us, body and mind"; that we are their "survival machines"—merely sophisticated "robots" built by the genes to perpetuate themselves. Yet astonishingly, he then turns around and issues a stirring declaration of independence from our genetic masters: "We have the power to defy the selfish genes of our birth," he says with rhetorical flourish. Although "we are built as gene machines, . . . we have the power to turn against our creators. We, alone on earth, can rebel against the tyranny of the selfish replicators."[42]

But where does this power to rebel come from? How does a machine rise up against its creator? Like all of us, Dawkins knows from actual experience that we do make genuine choices. Yet there is nothing in evolutionary psychology to account for this power of choice—and so he simply makes a leap of faith to a conclusion totally unwarranted by his own philosophy.

What these examples tell us is that evolutionary psychology fails the practical test: No one can live by it. Since universal human experience confirms the reality of moral choice, evolutionary psychologists cannot actually live on the basis of their own deterministic theory. They may try to, but when the contradiction between theory and life grows too pressing, they suddenly abandon the theory and proclaim their autonomy from the power of the genes. As Steven Pinker once wrote, noting that his choices contradicted the genetic imperative, "If my genes don't like it, they can go jump in the lake."[43]

A rather humorous example came to light back when former president Bill Clinton was in trouble for various escapades, and it became fashionable to offer evolutionary explanations for his behavior couched in terms of "alpha males." Dawkins jumped on the bandwagon, explaining that our evolutionary ancestors were not monogamous (like Canada geese), but instead were harem builders (like seals and walruses), where any male who monopolized power and wealth could also monopolize females, thus ensuring the survival of his genes. Ergo, Clinton's behavior was simply a fossilized remnant from our genetic past.

At this point, Dawkins seemed to grow uncomfortable about offering a genetic excuse for immorality. So he confided to readers that he himself had made the "un-Darwinian personal decision" to be "deliberately monogamous."[44] But think about this for a moment—if we really are programmed by our genes through Darwinian selection, how *could* anyone make an "un-Darwinian" decision? In fact, how could anyone make free moral decisions at all? The notion that we are free to act in un-Darwinian ways is completely irrational within the Darwinian worldview.

The reason people are compelled to take an irrational leap is that no matter what they believe, they are still made in the image of God. Even when they reject the witness of Scripture, they still face the constant witness of their own human nature. At some point, even the most adamant scientific materialists find that their own humanity resists the deterministic implications of the Darwinian worldview—that human nature stubbornly refuses to remain within the cramped confines of any mechanistic philosophy (the lower story). When that happens, they simply issue a declaration of independence from the power of the selfish genes, and take a leap of faith to a traditional concept of moral freedom and responsibility (the upper story), even though it is completely unwarranted within their own worldview.[45]

Ironically, critics often dismiss Christianity as irrational—yet it does not require any irrational, self-contradictory leap of faith. Because it begins with a personal God, Christianity provides a consistent, unified worldview that holds true *both* in the natural realm *and* in the moral, spiritual realm. The biblical doctrine of the image of God gives a solid basis for human dignity and moral freedom that is compatible with the compelling witness of human experience. Unlike the evolutionary psychologist, Christians can live consistently on the basis of their worldview because it fits the real world.

MENTAL MAPS

Since the leap of faith is endemic in the way people think today, let's analyze one final example in greater detail. The theme of Singer's book *A Darwinian Left* is that people along the entire political spectrum must now accept a Darwinian account of human nature. Yet at the end of the book Singer contradicts everything he has just said, by pronouncing that morality must be based on a power that *transcends* Darwinian forces. What power is that? Human reason. In a way not explained, natural selection has made us "reasoning beings"—which, paradoxically, enables us to transcend the impulses instilled by natural selection. Through reason, he promises, we will develop genuine altruism, not merely the pseudo-altruism of evolutionary psychology (the enlightened self-interest of kin selection or tit for tat). "We do not know," he writes wistfully, "to what extent our capacity to reason can . . . take us beyond the conventional Darwinian constraints on the degree of altruism that a society may be able to foster."[46]

Singer does not account for this novel capacity that frees us from "Darwinian constraints"—he simply pulls it out of a hat. Reason may eventually even "overcome the pull of other elements in our evolved nature," he hopes, until we embrace "the idea of an impartial concern for all of our fellow humans." To that end, we are urged to consider "deliberately cultivating and nurturing pure, disinterested altruism—something that has no place in nature, something that has never existed before in the whole history of the world."[47]

If *this* isn't a leap of faith, I don't know what is. Reason is presented as a mysterious capacity capable of creating something de novo, something that has never existed before—one might even say ex nihilo. This godlike power will enable us to rise above our evolutionary origins. Here reason is treated as far more than a utilitarian instrument: It is nothing less than the means of achieving freedom—metaphysical and moral freedom. "In a more distant future that we can still barely glimpse," Singer writes, scientific knowledge "may turn out to be the prerequisite for a new kind of freedom."[48]

Translation: Singer finds no basis for morality and altruism within the Darwinian worldview in the lower story—so he takes a leap to a hypothetical upper-story realm far beyond the constraints of "our evolved nature." Somehow the evolutionary process has produced a power that liberates us from the evolutionary process. Singer has cut humanity completely loose from its Darwinian anchor in biology, and set it free to soar to dizzying heights. But his philosophy is left behind in a hopeless crumple of contradictions.

Taking a leap of faith is a sure sign that a person's philosophy fails to explain human nature *as he himself experiences it.* When his worldview points in one direction while his lived experience points in another direction, then he cannot consistently live on the basis of his professed worldview.

This in turn is a reliable indicator that the worldview itself is faulty. After all, a worldview is a mental map of the *world*—and if it is accurate, it will enable us to navigate reality effectively. Most of us have a mental map of our bedroom, for example, so that if we get up at night, we can walk around in the dark and not bump into things. But if we're spending the night in an unfamiliar place, then we're liable to hit our shin on the furniture or knock our nose on the door frame. Our mental map of the new place isn't accurate yet—it doesn't fit reality. And so we find ourselves bumping up against reality in painful ways.

By the same token, if our worldview doesn't fit the larger reality we are trying to explain, then at some point we will find that we cannot follow it—that it is not a workable guide for navigating the world. C. S. Lewis once wrote, "The Christian and the Materialist hold different beliefs about the universe. They can't both be right. The one who is wrong will act in a way which simply doesn't fit the real universe."[49] That's why it is a potent criticism of evolutionary psychology to point out that proponents cannot live consistently on the basis of their own theory. Because they act in ways that don't "fit the real universe," at some point, they bump up against reality. And when they find the consequences too painful, they tell their genes to go jump in the lake—then take a leap to the upper story where, in some subjective way, human values can still be affirmed.

BEWARE SCIENTISTS BEARING VALUES

The rise of evolutionary psychology makes it clear that the debate over Darwinism is not just over scientific facts but over conflicting worldviews—the mental maps we use to navigate the world. "The Darwinian revolution was not merely the replacement of one scientific theory by another," wrote zoologist Ernst Mayr, "but rather the replacement of a worldview, in which the supernatural was accepted as a normal and relevant explanatory principle, by a *new worldview* in which there was no room for supernatural forces."[50] Worldview clashes are far too important to leave to scientists to adjudicate. All of us need to understand the debate over Darwinian evolution and be prepared to discuss it with our family and neighbors, and in the public square. It is nothing less than a debate over how we should order our personal lives and our corporate lives—and the stakes are very high indeed.

For if Darwinism is true, then religion and morality are nothing more than irrational, upper-story beliefs inhabiting the realm of *value* rather than *fact*. We are sometimes reassured that this is not a bad thing, because after all the subjectivity of the *value* realm renders it immune to rational scrutiny. The marketing pitch can be quite seductive: Scientific naturalists say they will acknowledge that there are certain moral and religious feelings that science cannot account for—if, in return, theology will agree not to intrude into realms investigated by science. In other words, if Christians would just relinquish all claims to objective truth, then they would be granted an arena where their beliefs are secure from criticism.

But it has become evident that such a bargain offers a false security. So great is the intellectual imperialism of naturalistic evolution that it will not leave the *value* realm in peace. Evolutionary psychology is recklessly invading the *value* territory and claiming ground once off-limits to science—seeking to explain moral behavior, human relationships, cultural customs, and yes, even religion, as products of natural selection. A recent book by Dawkins denounces religion as a virus of the mind—a "malignant infection" that invades the mind like a computer virus.[51] Clearly, the *fact* realm is mounting a continued siege on the *value* realm.

That's why it is dangerous to engage in any cognitive bargaining that relegates Christianity to the *value* realm. The human mind has a natural drive toward unity and consistency, and for the Darwinist, that means dragging everything down into the lower story so that evolution itself may become a unified, holistic system. The only way to counter that system is to show that Christianity is equally holistic. It is not an irrational, upper-story leap, but a comprehensive truth that meets the human hunger for an overarching, consistent worldview. As Christians we must make it clear that we are not offering a subjective, private faith that is immune to rational scrutiny. We are making cognitive claims about objective knowledge that can be defended in the public arena.

DILEMMA OF LEO STRAUSS

The historic Christian conception of morality rests on a cognitive claim about human nature. It says humans were designed for a purpose—to be conformed to spiritual ideals of holiness and perfection, so that we may live in love with God and our fellow creatures. Moral rules are simply the instructions telling us how to fulfill those ideals, how to reach that goal, how to live according to that divine purpose. In the Fall we went off the track, but in salvation God puts us back on course and empowers us to resume the journey to developing our full humanity, to become the people He originally intended us to be. To use a technical term, Christian morality is *teleological,* based on the concept of human progress toward the purpose or ideal (*telos*) for which we were designed.

Under the Darwinian regime, however, the very concept of purpose or teleology has come under attack. For if the world itself was not designed, then there can be no design or purpose for human life either. Morality is reduced to a product of biology—an expression of our subjective desires and impulses, programmed into us by natural selection. That's why the political philosopher Leo Strauss once said "the fundamental dilemma" in locating a moral basis for public life today "is caused by the victory of modern natural science." For "the teleological view of the universe, of which the teleological view of man forms a part, would seem to have been destroyed by modern natural science."

Just so. If evolution is correct in portraying a world without purpose, then the traditional teleological conception of morality cannot be sustained. (For more on this subject, see appendix 3.) Now, Strauss took Darwinian evolution to be an irrefutable fact, and he tried to work around it by grounding morality in the realm of Platonic ideals. Yet that was not "an adequate solution to the problem," as he himself recognized, because it implied a two-story view of knowledge—the "fundamental, typically modern, dualism of a nonteleological natural science" (in the lower story), along with "a teleological science of man" (in the upper story).[52]

The liberating message of Design theory is that we don't have to take Darwinian evolution as an irrefutable fact, nor resign ourselves to the "typically modern dualism." As we saw in the previous chapter, design and purpose have once again become core concepts in explaining nature itself—both in the organic world (the cell and DNA) and in the physical world (the fine-tuning of the universe). Design theory thus provides the scientific basis for the recovery of a holistic, teleological worldview. It releases us from the modern dualism, making it reasonable once again to speak of morality as a form of objective knowledge.

BORN-AGAIN DARWINISTS

The destructive impact of the Darwinian worldview on religion and morality has become so commonplace that it hardly even registers as news anymore. For example, when yet another article came across my desk about someone challenging the Boy Scouts' exclusion of atheists and homosexuals, I nearly set it aside without reading it. But then a small item caught my eye. It turned out that an Eagle Scout was being threatened with ejection because he was an atheist, counter to the Scout pledge, and the significant phrase read like this: The young man, who was nineteen, "has been an atheist since studying evolution in the ninth grade."[53] The fact was reported as though it were perfectly normal, even routine, for kids to lose their religious faith when they encounter the theory of evolution in science classes.

Admittedly the pattern is distressingly common. "In my senior year of high school I accepted Jesus as my Savior and became a born-again Christian," says one writer. "I had found the One True Religion, and it was my duty—indeed it was my pleasure—to tell others about it, including my parents, brothers and sisters, friends, and even total strangers."[54] But this young man's religious conviction did not survive a serious encounter with evolutionary theory: He underwent a "deconversion in graduate school six years later when I studied evolutionary biology."[55] Who is the writer? Michael Shermer, the director of the Skeptics Society and publisher of *Skeptic* magazine. Shermer now makes a cottage industry of debunking Christianity, while defending Darwinism against design theorists.

Another prominent atheist tells a similar story. "I was a born-again Christian. When I was fifteen, I entered the Southern Baptist Church with great fervor and interest in the fundamentalist religion." But once again, the religious fervor did not survive its confrontation with evolution. "I left [the church] at seventeen when I got to the University of Alabama and heard about evolutionary theory."[56] The encounter was nothing less than an "epiphany." "I was enthralled, couldn't stop thinking about the implications evolution has . . . for just about everything."[57] Who is this? Harvard professor E. O. Wilson, the founder of sociobiology. After losing his Christian faith, he says, science itself became the object of his religious longings, and he sought to channel the power of religion into the service of materialism. Religion itself "had to be explained as a material process, from the bottom up, atoms to genes to the human spirit. It had to be embraced by a single grand naturalistic image of man."[58]

THE KITCHEN AS CLASSROOM

This is the metaphysical motivation that drove sociobiology, and that now drives its offspring, evolutionary psychology—the desire to craft "a single grand naturalistic image of man." The only way to stand against such a comprehensive naturalistic worldview, as Abraham Kuyper said, is by articulating a Christian worldview "of equally comprehensive and far-reaching power."[59] We must prepare young people *before* they leave for college by teaching them that Christianity is not just religious truth but the truth about all reality. It is total truth.

One of the most inspiring models I've encountered was my own grandfather, Oswald Overn. With five rambunctious children close in age, he was determined to prepare them all to defend their faith by the time they left home. And so he turned the evening dinner table into a classroom—a place for serious teaching and discussion. "My father would bring books and articles to the dinner table, to read and discuss with us," recalls my uncle Bill Overn. "He taught us Latin, physics, math. He also had us memorize the creeds, the Lutheran catechism, and passages from the Bible." In fact, that's how all five children learned how to read: "We would read a passage by going around the table, and everyone from the oldest to the youngest had their verses to read."

He also created opportunities for one-on-one discussions. "My father would take one of the children with him when he went into town, and always he would expound on some topic," Bill says. "It was a three-mile walk into town, and he made use of every minute." As a physicist, my grandfather was especially attuned to the sciences, and he would often bring clippings of recent science news to the dinner table to discuss. He taught the children how to counter the standard evidences for evolution, so that by the time Bill went off to college to study physics, following in his father's footsteps, he was solidly grounded in apologetics and knew in his bones that the Christian faith was intellectually defensible.[60]

Unless we give our children that same level of confidence, they will not survive the cognitive warfare they face in the secular world today. Evolutionary psychologists, with their blatant, in-your-face applications of Darwinism, are the shock troops of evolution. Yet there is also a more hidden impact of Darwinism on American thought—and precisely because it is hidden, it is more pervasive and thus more dangerous. In the next chapter I will take you behind the scenes, so to speak, to reveal how Darwinism has permeated the American mind at a deeper level—even reshaping America's social, educational, and legal institutions. If Christians hope to speak effectively to modern culture, we need to diagnose the way these ideas have rippled out far beyond the sciences.

8

DARWINS OF THE MIND

They mean to tell us all was rolling blind
Till accidentally it hit on mind . . .
ROBERT FROST[1]

The impact of Darwin on worldview came home to me starkly one day while I was homeschooling my son. One of the joys of teaching your own children is that you get a chance to read all the wonderful books you missed when you were growing up. Thus it was that when Dieter was in junior high, we were reading together several young adult biographies of famous people—including Joseph Stalin. Suddenly I came across a startling dialogue from the days when the young Stalin was a seminary student, studying to become a priest in the Russian Orthodox Church. As one of his friends relates, they were discussing religion:

> "Joseph heard me out, and after a moment's silence, said: "'You know, they are fooling us, there is no God. . . .'"
> "I was astonished at these words. I had never heard anything like it before.
> "'How can you say such things, Soso?' I exclaimed.
> "'I'll lend you a book to read; it will show you that the world and all living things are quite different from what you imagine, and all this talk about God is sheer nonsense,' Joseph said.
> "'What book is that?' I enquired.
> "'Darwin. You must read it,' Joseph impressed on me."[2]

We all know what happened after that: Having become an atheist, Stalin went on to murder literally millions of his own people in his attempt to construct an officially atheistic state.

Here in the West, the impact of Darwinism has been more subtle, yet it runs far deeper than most of us imagine. In the 1950s a group of scholars produced a thick volume titled *Evolutionary Thought in America* surveying its impact across the curriculum. The book included chapters on the influence of evolution on sociology, psychology, economics, political thought, moral theory, theology, and even literature.[3] Simply reading the table of contents hammers home the wide-ranging impact Darwinism has exerted on virtually every field of study. It is impossible to understand twentieth-century America unless we grasp the implications of evolutionary thinking.

In fact, in the late nineteenth century when Darwinism crossed the Atlantic, it was welcomed to American shores by a group of scholars who founded an entire school of philosophy upon it. The school was called philosophical pragmatism, and its core assumption was that if *life* has evolved, then the human *mind* has evolved as well—and all the human sciences must be rebuilt on that basis: psychology, education, law, and theology.[4] Pragmatism is America's only "home-grown" philosophy (most of the others were imported from Europe), and for that reason alone it has been enormously influential. By taking a closer look at philosophical pragmatism, we will get a good handle on the way Darwinism has altered not only the way Americans think but also the very structure of American social institutions.

HOLMES LOSES HIS FAITH

The central figures in developing philosophical pragmatism were John Dewey, William James, Charles Sanders Peirce, and Oliver Wendell Holmes, Jr. Their goal was to expand Darwinian naturalism into a complete worldview to rival traditional religion. As one historian explains, the pragmatists "sought ways of preserving some of the heart values of the older religion"—not by retaining any of the actual *content* of religion, but by finding "rich and inspiring versions of naturalism to replace it." Which is to say, by turning Darwinian naturalism itself into a comprehensive philosophy that would satisfy the need to make sense of life.[5]

The pragmatist's core beliefs can be illustrated in a dramatic way in the personal odyssey of Oliver Wendell Holmes, Jr. As a Harvard student prior to the Civil War, Holmes held conventional religious views. He joined a student group called the Christian Union, and wrote school essays on themes such as "the relations of man to God" and the need to base morality on ideas "in the mind of the Creator" instead of on arbitrary human concepts.[6] Later he became deeply involved in the abolitionist cause, and when war broke out he risked his college degree by dropping out right before graduation to enlist in the Massachusetts Militia.

But the horrors of war proved almost too much for Holmes—the blood, the chaos, and everywhere the dead and wounded bodies. He watched many of his friends die, and was wounded himself three times. The third time, he was shot in the foot and hoped desperately that it would have to be amputated, so he could be discharged. That's how much he had come to hate the war.

Somewhere along the way he began losing his Christian faith, a process that reached a crisis the first time he was wounded. Bleeding profusely, he was told by hospital personnel that he might die. And so, lying in a makeshift field hospital, with soldiers dying all around him, Holmes commenced a reexamination of his personal beliefs—or rather, by this time, his lack of beliefs. It struck him forcefully, as he later wrote, that "the majority vote of the civilized world declared that with my opinions I was *en route* to Hell"—and he was terrified. Should he undergo a deathbed conversion? Upon reviewing the options, he decided against it, feeling that conversion would be "nothing but a cowardly giving way to fear." Instead he determined to adopt the rather simplistic credo, "whatever shall happen is best." And with a whispered prayer, "God forgive me if I'm wrong," he went to sleep.[7]

Holmes had gone off to fight because of his moral beliefs (abolitionism), but he came home a moral skeptic. "The war did more than make him lose those beliefs," writes one historian. "It made him lose his belief in beliefs."[8] That is, he emerged from his wartime experience with the firm conviction that firm convictions lead only to conflict and violence. While recovering from his third war wound, he began reading books by Herbert Spencer, the enormously influential popularizer of Social Darwinism, and became a convinced Darwinist. From then on he began to argue that evolution applies not only to physical organisms but also to the sphere of beliefs and convictions. The great, towering principles that have shaped civilizations are not transcendent truths, he wrote, but simply those that won out in the "struggle for life among competing ideas."[9] These were to become the core teachings of philosophical pragmatism.

DARWIN'S NEW LOGIC

At its heart, pragmatism is a Darwinian view of knowledge (epistemology). The pragmatists asked, What does Darwinian naturalism mean for the way we understand the human mind? And they answered, It means the mind is nothing more than a part of nature. They rejected the older view that the human mind is *transcendent to* matter, in favor of the Darwinian view that mind is *produced by* matter.

In a single stroke, this assumption subverted both traditional and liberal forms of theism. Why? Because both forms make mind prior to matter. In traditional theology, a transcendent God creates the world according to His own design and purpose; in liberal theology, an immanent deity externalizes its purposes through the historical development of the world. Either way, mind precedes matter, shaping and directing the development of the material world.

Darwin reversed that order: In his theory, mind emerges very late in evolutionary history, as a product of purely natural forces. Mind is not a fundamental, creative force in the universe but merely an evolutionary by-product. In short, Darwin "naturalized" the mind.[10]

For the pragmatists, this naturalizing of the mind was the most revolutionary impact of Darwinian theory. It seemed to imply that mental functions are merely adaptations for solving problems in the environment. Ideas originate as chance mutations in the brain, parallel to Darwin's chance variations in nature. And the ideas that stick around and become firm beliefs are those that help us adapt to the environment—a sort of mental natural selection. Concepts and convictions develop as tools for survival, no different from the lion's teeth or the eagle's claws.

John Dewey even wrote a famous essay called "The Influence of Darwin on Philosophy," in which he said Darwinism gives us a "new logic to apply to mind and morals and life."[11] In this new evolutionary logic, ideas are nothing more than mental tools for getting things done. We don't decide if a tool is any good by judging it against a transcendent, eternal ideal; instead we test it by how successfully it does the job, how well it works in coping with the environment. If a fork works, Dewey said, you go ahead and use it. If you're trying to eat soup and it doesn't work, you don't engage in philosophical disquisitions on the essential "nature" of forks; instead you go get a spoon.[12]

CASH VALUE OF AN IDEA

The pragmatists were highly influenced by the experimental psychologists of their day, who were engaged in a similar project of applying Darwinism to the mind. Through most of the nineteenth century, psychology had been understood as the science of the soul, and its method was introspection—the examination of consciousness. But the new experimental approach was behavioristic, claiming that the mind could be known only through external actions of the body that can be observed and measured. These ideas reinforced the pragmatists' view that mind is not a distinct spiritual substance but merely part of nature.

William James, for example, was quite impressed by the laboratory work of one of his students, Edward Thorndike, who put chickens and other tame animals in boxes, then measured how long it took them to learn to press a lever to open a door and get food pellets. You may remember this from a Psychology

101 course. Sure enough, over time the chickens learned to press the lever as soon as they were in the box. The pattern had been imprinted. James decided that ideas were imprinted in the human mind the same way. If believing something produces results—if it gets us "pellets" that we want—then over time that belief is imprinted in our minds. In his famous phrase, truth is the "cash value" of an idea: If it pays off, then we call it true.[13]

In short, beliefs are not reflections of reality but rules for action.[14] Peirce liked to say that beliefs are a kind of prediction—a bet. When we say something is true, we are merely predicting that if we perform a certain action we will get a certain response. The model for this definition was scientific knowledge: If we say quartz is hard, we mean it will not be scratched if we rub it with wood or cork or plastic. Given the meaning of the word *hard*, we may predict the outcome of various operations on a lump of quartz. For Peirce, a successful belief is simply a winning bet.[15]

To understand how revolutionary all this was, we must realize that until this time the dominant theory of knowledge was based on the biblical doctrine of the image of God. It is because human reason reflects the divine reason that we can trust human knowledge to be generally reliable. God created our minds to "fit" the universe that He made for us to inhabit; and when our cognitive faculties are functioning properly, they are designed to give us genuine knowledge. Even thinkers who moved outside the sphere of traditional Christian theology still retained the philosophical assumption that the human mind is akin to a higher Mind, an absolute Mind, as the guarantee of human knowledge.[16]

But the pragmatists faced squarely the implications of evolution: If blind, undirected natural forces produced the mind, they said, then it is meaningless to ask whether our ideas reflect reality. Ideas are simply mental survival strategies—continuations of the struggle for existence by other means. "'The true' is only the expedient in the way of our thinking," James wrote, "just as 'the right' is only the expedient in the way of our behaving."[17]

WHAT'S RELIGION WORTH TO YOU?

James was even tolerant toward religious beliefs, at least more so than some of the other pragmatists. His father had converted to Christianity during the Second Great Awakening, then converted just as enthusiastically to Swedenborgianism, with the result that James never quite shook off an awareness of the spiritual realm. His view was that if a religion gives some sense of happiness and meaning, then it is "true." In his words, "If the hypothesis of God works satisfactorily in the widest sense of the word, it is true."[18]

True, at least, for the individual who believes it. James was perhaps the most personable of the pragmatists—charming, creative, emotionally effusive, and totally maddening to his colleagues because of his extreme individualism. The other pragmatists all held that knowledge is a social construction; individuals don't create knowledge, groups do. By contrast, James was willing to let each individual decide what "works satisfactorily" for him, and then believe accordingly.

In some passages, James even seemed to say that any system of thought, scientific or religious, is "true" insofar as it meets a person's needs. Presented with a complex world, he wrote, humans naturally wonder what its ultimate nature is: "Science says molecules. Religion says God." How do we decide which is true? Well, on one hand, James answered, "science can do certain things for us." (By that he meant that scientific reasoning enables us to "deduce and explain" events.) Yet on the other hand, "God can do other things" for us. (Religion can "inspire and console" us.) So the question each individual must ask is: "*Which things* are worth the most?"[19] Whatever you decide, that's your truth.

James was toying with ideas we now call postmodern, and it evoked a stinging rebuke from the British philosopher Bertrand Russell. James's pragmatic defense of religion "simply omits as unimportant the question whether God really is in His heaven," Russell objected; "if He is a useful hypothesis, that is enough." What a ridiculously narrow frame of reference, he fumed: The pragmatists act as though all that matters is the effect ideas have "upon the creatures inhabiting our petty planet."[20] Plainly, beliefs can be useful and yet be false, Russell pointed out; thus it really does matter whether a religion is true, not just how it makes us feel.

There is a kernel of truth in pragmatism, of course. If a belief system is true, then it ought to work in the real world, as we argued in the previous chapter. One of the ways we can check out a truth claim is to submit it to the practical test. But pragmatic success does not *make* a claim true. As with all "isms," pragmatism fastens upon one aspect of reality and elevates it into a system that reduces everything else to a single dimension.

TOUGH VERSUS TENDER

To understand any philosophy, it is crucial to ask what question people were trying to answer. The problem the pragmatists wanted to solve was the division of knowledge that has plagued Western thought for centuries. They wanted to bridge the gap between fact and value—to merge the lower and upper stories—and bring about a reunification of knowledge.

Recall the thumbnail sketch given in chapter 3: When the two-story dichotomy was secularized, the downstairs was occupied by the Enlightenment and the upstairs by Romanticism. What did these categories mean in the late nineteenth century? In the lower story, the Enlightenment had given rise to British empiricism and utilitarianism. Society was reduced to a collection of individuals held together by sheer choice (atomism). And individuals in turn were reduced to complex mechanisms.

Meanwhile, the upper story was taken over by Romantic idealism. Here we're talking about people like Hegel, who taught that the material world is the outworking of an Absolute Spirit or Mind or God. Romanticism was fiercely opposed to the Enlightenment: In contrast to utilitarianism, it upheld moral idealism. Instead of atomism, it offered holism. Instead of physical reductionism, it affirmed the reality of Spirit.

This dualism was even reflected in the university curriculum, in a division between the sciences and the humanities. As the sciences were taken over by philosophical naturalism, the humanities adopted philosophical idealism and historicism (the Absolute externalizes itself over time through the historical process).[21]

The two-tiered truth led to a division within the university curriculum:

THE ARTS AND HUMANITIES
Philosophical Idealism

THE SCIENCES
Philosophical Naturalism

By the late nineteenth century, these two contradictory streams stood in tense opposition to one another. Nor was it merely an academic problem. The two contradictory pictures of reality were experienced by thoughtful people as an agonizing internal division, a painful tension that cried out to be resolved.[22] This was the existential dilemma that drove the pragmatists, especially Dewey and James.

"Dewey's condemnation of dualism was the central feature of his philosophy," says one philosopher; "he vigorously attacked this in virtually everything he wrote."[23] Dewey traced the dichotomy back to the Form/Matter dualism of the ancient Greeks (just as we did in chapter 2). Then he offered pragmatism as a "via media," a middle way that would overcome the dichotomy that pitted naturalism in the lower story against idealism in the upper story.[24]

William James experienced the inner conflict even more intensely.[25] He was particularly sensitive to the imperialism of science in the lower story. While respecting legitimate science, James despised what he saw as an aggressive naturalistic philosophy masquerading as science, which led to "determinism, atheism, and cynicism." It undercut the objective status of values, driving students to agnostic despair (here James spoke from painful personal experience).[26] Caught in the conflict, he spiraled into a profound depression, which finally precipitated what he described as a "collapse."

James would later describe his spiritual crisis as a tension between the Tough-Minded (who care only about science and facts) and the Tender-Minded (who long for meaning and values).[27] The pragmatists hoped their own philosophy would bridge the gulf: "You want a system that will combine both things," James wrote: "the scientific loyalty to facts . . . but also the old confidence in human values." The two have become "hopelessly separated," he went on, but "I offer the oddly-named thing pragmatism as a philosophy that can satisfy both kinds of demand."[28]

DISCIPLES OF DARWIN

How did the pragmatists hope to accomplish this reunification of knowledge? By taking a little from each of the two conflicting streams of thought and melding them together. From Romantic idealism (the upper story), the pragmatists took its historicism—the definition of ideas as products of evolving custom. For if reality was the unfolding of an Absolute Mind, then everything was in a process of constant change and evolution—not only living things but also cultures, customs, and concepts.

From British empiricism (the lower story), the pragmatists took its instrumentalism—the definition of ideas as tools for achieving social goals. By combining these two approaches, the pragmatists transformed Hegel's historicism from a *spiritual* process into a thoroughly *naturalistic* process.

As a result, however, they never actually succeeded in combining *fact* and *value,* but only offered a new flavor of naturalism. The model for their strategy was Darwin, who had effected virtually the same merging of the two philosophical traditions within biology. Darwin's theory of evolution was in part a product of Romantic historicism applied to biology (there are no stable essences; everything is in constant flux). But being a good British empiricist, he gave the evolutionary process a completely materialistic mechanism. In other words, he melded historicism with naturalism. As one historian puts it, "Darwin gave Hegel the respectability of science."[29] That's exactly what the pragmatists aspired to do in areas *beyond* biology—take over Hegel's cultural evolutionism, but give it the respectability of science by rendering it completely naturalistic.

The pragmatists were not the only ones who wanted to naturalize Hegelian historicism. Many of the early anthropologists and other social scientists of the nineteenth century had tried to do the same thing, the most notable being Karl Marx. (That's why it is often said that Marx turned Hegel on his head.) The difference was that these earlier thinkers tended to be determinists: They decreed that all societies everywhere must pass through the same inevitable stages of cultural evolution, governed by unchanging "laws" of social evolution. (For Marx, the stages were based on economic relationships.) What made the pragmatists unique is that they rejected determinism outright, and instead conceived of history as completely contingent—spontaneous, unpredictable, open to genuine novelty.

Why did the pragmatists break the mold of deterministic thinking? The answer, again, was the influence of Darwin. As we saw in chapter 6, Darwin's theory consists of two elements: chance and law. The pragmatists seized on the role of chance and turned it into the basis for a philosophy of indeterminacy, freedom, and innovation. In their interpretation, the "openness" of the world takes the form of *chance* at lower levels of complexity, and takes the form of *choice* at the human level.[30] An incomplete and indeterminate world left room for humans to play a role in creating reality by their free choices.

TRANSFORMING AMERICA

How do these ideas affect the world we live in today? The answer is that they have radically reshaped American social institutions. Let's focus on four crucial areas: theology, law, education, and philosophy.

Let God Evolve

In theology, the pragmatists asked: What kind of God is compatible with evolution? And they answered that *if* you keep any notion of God at all, it has to be an immanent God—a finite deity evolving in and with the world. "With the advent of evolution," writes one philosopher, "the tendency of those who took science seriously was to conceive of God increasingly as immanent in the world process."[31]

Among the pragmatists, the most influential in this area was Charles Sanders Peirce. The quirkiest of the group, Peirce had a prickly, arrogant character that made it difficult for him to keep a job. He violated prevailing moral sensibilities by getting divorced and then living with his second wife before marrying her. Back then, this kind of scandal was enough to shut the door on teaching positions at the universities, and often Peirce had to rely on the generosity of his friends just to keep body and soul together. But he was a brilliant abstract thinker and made significant contributions to logic and probability theory.

Peirce felt strongly about religion, but despised traditional and orthodox forms of it. Instead, he proposed a form of panpsychism (everything in the universe has a mind or consciousness). He envisioned the entire cosmos evolving toward Mind or the Absolute or God, in a teleological process he called "evolutionary love."[32]

Where do we hear these ideas in our own day? In Process Theology, which some say is the fastest-growing movement in mainline seminaries today. Its founder, Charles Hartshorne, said Peirce was one of the few thinkers who had the greatest influence on him.[33]

Process Theology teaches that God and the world are both in a process of constant change and evolution. God is a divine spirit evolving in and with the world, the soul of the world, the evolving cosmic life of which our lives are a part. This is not strictly speaking *pantheism* (all is God), but rather *panentheism* (all is *in* God), where the physical world is a concrete emanation of God's own essence.[34] Process Theology teaches that as we make the choices that shape our lives and experiences, we also shape God and His experiences, since our lives give concrete form to the divine life. In short, we are not only co-creators *with* God, we are also co-creators *of* God. When we die, then, the life we have lived merely becomes a past stage in God's own ongoing life, while we as individuals cease to exist. There is no afterlife.

By placing God Himself within the evolutionary nexus, Process Theology breaks sharply with traditional theism. It holds that God is limited—He does not know in advance what is going to happen (He is not omniscient), nor does He have the power to prevent evil from happening (He is not omnipotent). Instead, He simply evolves along with the world over the course of history.

Surprisingly, some of these same themes have spilled over into evangelical circles as well, in what is known as Open Theism, promoted by Clark Pinnock and others. The term itself echoes the pragmatists' language when they described an evolving universe as an "open" universe—a world of novelty, innovation, emergence, and unpredictable possibilities, which cannot be known in advance, even by God.[35]

Clearly, one reason for challenging evolutionary *science* is that otherwise we may find our churches and seminaries teaching evolutionary *theology*.[36]

Why Judges Make Law

Oliver Wendell Holmes, Jr., influenced legal thought more than anyone else in the twentieth century. Applying philosophical pragmatism to the law, he founded a movement called—not surprisingly—legal pragmatism. As we saw at the beginning of the chapter, Holmes was greatly influenced by Herbert Spencer, and he often sprinkled Social Darwinist concepts throughout his writings, speaking of the law as merely a product of the "survival of the fittest" among competing interest groups.[37] But Holmes did more than just use Darwinian metaphors. Earlier we saw how pragmatism followed the Darwinian model by weaving together German idealism with British empiricism—and Holmes followed exactly the same strategy in the field of jurisprudence. He took the historical school of jurisprudence (from German idealism) and wove it together with the analytical school of jurisprudence (from British empiricism).[38]

From the historical school, Holmes took the idea that the source of law is nothing but evolving custom. Whereas traditional Western legal philosophy had based law on an unchanging source (on natural law, derived ultimately from divine law), Holmes treated law as a product of evolving cultures and traditions, completely relative to particular times and cultures. In fact, the whole reason for doing historical research, he said, was not to defend traditional concepts of law against would-be reformers, but precisely the opposite: By tracing legal ideas over the course of history, we can see for ourselves that they are *not* based on any unchanging, universal moral order, but are always the product of a particular local culture and its unique history. Once we grasp this, Holmes said, then judges will be liberated from the past and free to change the law to reflect whatever social policy they think works best. As Holmes put it, "History sets us free and enables us to make up our minds dispassionately" as to whether the old legal rules still serve any purpose.[39]

And how do we determine whether the old rules still serve any purpose? By their practical consequences. From the analytical school of jurisprudence Holmes took the idea that the criterion for law is social utility, as measured by the social sciences. In his words, the law should be established "upon accurately measured social desires."[40] This is the source of one of Holmes's famous aphorisms: "The man of the future is the man of statistics and the master of economics."[41] In other words, the law should be judged by what works—and what works is determined by empirical studies done by social scientists. Law is reduced to a tool for social engineering. The justification for any given law, Holmes wrote, is "not that it represents an eternal principle" such as Justice, but "that it helps bring out a social end which we desire."[42]

In practice, of course, this means a social end that the *judge* desires. Holmes unabashedly agreed that judges do not merely interpret the law but make law.

Where have we seen these ideas at work in our own day? The idea that law is about enacting social policies? That judges don't just interpret the law but make law?[43] The most significant example is the 1973 *Roe v. Wade* abortion decision. Even supporters of the decision agree that the court essentially legislated from the bench. In the majority opinion, Justice Harry Blackmun wrote that abortion must be considered in relation to "population growth, pollution, poverty, and racial" issues. In other words, the Court made its decision not by what the *law* said but by the social outcomes it favored.[44]

This is the heritage of legal pragmatism. And it will shape the way the courts deal with a host of new bioethical issues on the horizon, unless we challenge the underlying Darwinian worldview.

Dewey's Dilemmas

John Dewey did more to shape educational methodology than anyone else in the twentieth century. Born in 1859, the same year Darwin published his *Origin of Species*, Dewey grew up in an evangelical home (Congregational) and was profoundly influenced by his devout mother. In his early twenties, he underwent a conversion—a "mystic experience," he called it—and afterward he attended church regularly and even taught Bible classes.[45]

Eventually, however, Dewey embarked on a slow and gradual process of losing his faith—so gradual that it never seemed to cause him any mental trauma. That may have been due partly to his inherent temperament, for Dewey had a phlegmatic, unflappable, almost colorless personality. In any case, his spiritual decline began in college, where he encountered a liberal form of theology shaped by German idealism. Later he was to say that Hegel "left a permanent deposit in my thinking." His early writings are attempts to meld Hegel and Darwin by proposing an immanent God embodied in matter, like the soul in the body—similar to Process Theology. Later Dewey accepted the Social Gospel, which redefined salvation as social progress. God did not impart grace to individuals, he argued, but was immanent in culture; if the culture embraced Christian values, the individual would be redeemed.[46]

In his thirties, Dewey shed even this attenuated form of Christianity and adopted a consistently naturalistic philosophy. He stopped being active in church and student religious associations, and his children stopped attending Sunday school.[47] Naturalism itself would now be his religion. He offered himself "as a quiet-spoken evangelist of a redeeming form of humanism and naturalism," says one historian.[48] Dewey even presented his "redeeming" naturalism in a book titled *A Common Faith,* urging his followers to cultivate a "religious" devotion to social ideals. This was a form of religion consistent with his belief that humans were merely biological organisms seeking to control the environment through scientific inquiry.

These ideas then became the basis of Dewey's educational philosophy. He recast intellectual inquiry as a form of mental evolution, and said it should proceed on the same pattern as biological evolution: by posing problems and then letting students construct their own answers based on what works best—a kind of mental adaptation to the environment. Teachers are not instructors but "facilitators," guiding students as they try out various pragmatic strategies to discover what works for them.[49] Of course, this is inherently relativistic: After all, what works for me may not work for you. (In fact, it might not even work for *me* all the time.) Thus pragmatism inevitably leads to a pluralism of beliefs, all of them transient and none of them eternally or universally true.

Does this sound familiar? Dewey is the source of much of today's moral education, where all values are treated as equally valid and students simply clarify what they personally value most. Teachers are rigorously instructed not to be directive in any way, but only to coach students in a process of weighing alternatives and making up their own minds. Any value that students choose is deemed acceptable, whether or not it comports with accepted moral standards, as long as they have gone through the prescribed series of steps. Why? Because, as one textbook puts it, "None of us can be certain that our values are right for other people."[50] Each individual has to become an autonomous decision maker, determining his values strictly on his own.

The underlying assumption of this approach is philosophical naturalism. A naturalistic approach to ethics does not acknowledge any transcendent standard, so that the only standard available is whatever the individual in fact values. As Dewey argued, we all experience things as good or bad, pleasurable or painful, rewarding or disturbing. And since science is supposed to be based on experience, moral inquiry must begin by analyzing our experience. We first clarify what we in fact value, and then weigh various courses of action to decide which will lead most reliably to consequences that match our values.

The first step—clarifying what we value—sounds easy, but in reality it may not be so simple, Dewey said. For our experience is often distorted by religious and moral dogmas telling us what we *ought* to want or do. Thus it becomes crucial to disentangle our thoughts and feelings from preexisting moral dog-

mas in order to clarify what we *really* want. This explains why most programs
of moral education start by presenting students with difficult moral dilemmas:
These are designed to jolt students out of their preexisting moral framework,
absorbed from family and church and other sources, so they can probe their
true feelings about right and wrong.

For example, one mother tells of a dilemma used in her daughter's class,
where students were required to imagine they were planning to murder their
best friend. What alternatives could they come up with for accomplishing that
goal? Some students were appalled, objecting that they would not choose *any*
methods because murder is wrong. Period. But that answer was not acceptable. The teacher required students to leave behind their preexisting moral
convictions, by mentally rehearsing behavior they held to be wrong. The goal
of such activities is to detach students from the moral teachings absorbed from
outside, so that they will get in touch with their own personal, authentic
values.

HAMSTRUNG TEACHERS

By "liberating" students from the moral standards they bring in from home
and church, however, the inquiry approach leaves them with nothing higher
than their own subjective likes and dislikes—or worse, the pressures of the
peer group. Thomas Lickona, an education professor, relates the story of a
teacher who used the values clarification strategy with a class of low-achiev-
ing eighth-graders. Having worked through the requisite steps, the students
concluded that their most valued activities were "sex, drugs, drinking, and
skipping school." The teacher was hamstrung: Her students had clarified
their values, and the method gave her no leverage for persuading them that
these values were morally wrong.[51] Moral education no longer means teaching students about the great moral ideals that have inspired virtually all civilizations, but training them to probe their own subjective feelings and
values.

In spite of such criticisms, the inquiry approach remains immensely popular among educators. Another professor of education, William Kilpatrick,
speaks frequently to parent and teacher groups around the country, and he
often poses the following question: Which approach would you prefer at your
own school—Model A, where students are encouraged to develop their own
values, with no right or wrong answers; or Model B, where students are
encouraged to develop specific virtues like courage, justice, and honesty, with
inspiring illustrations from literature and history? The vast majority of *parents*
choose Model B, Kilpatrick reports. By contrast, *teachers* almost invariably

prefer Model A, and many "say they would not use the second approach under any circumstances"![52] Clearly, a wide chasm separates the educational establishment from the public on the sensitive issue of moral education.

Kilpatrick tells the story in a book aptly titled *Why Johnny Can't Tell Right from Wrong*. American educators have imbibed deeply at the well of Dewey, and many toe the professional line even when their own experience shows that the method does not work.

INVENTING YOUR OWN REALITY

The same teaching method is being applied to other subject areas as well. One of the trendiest fads today is called constructivist education. If knowledge is a social construction, as Dewey said, then the goal of education should be to teach students how to *construct* their own *knowledge*. Read this description by a proponent of the method:

> Constructivism does not assume the presence of an outside objective reality that is revealed to the learner, but rather that learners actively *construct their own reality*.[53]

That's a pretty tall order: Before kids are big enough to cross the street, they're supposed to learn how to "construct their own reality." Teachers are not to tell students that their ideas are right or wrong, either, but merely to encourage them "to clarify and articulate their own understandings." Just as in values clarification, the teacher is left with no mechanism to adjudicate between the answers students come up with. Thirty different students may well offer thirty different answers, but each must be considered viable. After all, there are many different possible ways to construct the world, and constructivism cannot rule out any viable theory that encapsulates personal experience.[54]

This explains why schools now have classes where children construct their own spelling systems ("invented spelling"), their own punctuation and grammar rules, their own math procedures, and so on. In one state, the history standards say that by high school, students "should have a strong sense of how to reconstruct history."[55] Isn't *that* an Orwellian phrase?

When I began writing on educational issues back in 1982 for a statewide citizens group, I would send my articles to my mother, who has a doctoral degree in education. "But, Nancy," she would say, "these things are taught to teachers as merely the latest teaching techniques"—as instructional methodologies based on practical experience in the classroom. But actually most educational theories are *not* inspired by teaching experience. Instead they are applications of a philosophy, and constructivism is no exception: It is a direct application of Dewey's evolutionary epistemology.[56] As one prominent constructivist writes, "To the biologist, a living organism is viable as long as it manages to survive in its environment. To the constructivist, concepts, models, theories, and so on are viable if they prove adequate in the contexts in which they were created."[57] Notice that the passage speaks of ideas being *viable*, not *true*. Constructivism is based on the assumption that we are merely organisms adapting to the environment, so that the only test of an idea is whether it works.

Astonishingly, even some Christian teachers have accepted constructivism, apparently without discerning its philosophical roots. After I spoke on the subject at an education conference, a Christian school superintendent came up to me and said, "All my teachers are constructivists—all of them."

"But don't they realize what that means for their faith?" I asked in surprise. "If knowledge is a social construction, then that applies to Christianity as well—it's just a product of social forces."

"I know, I know," the superintendent replied. "But constructivism is what they learned at the university under the auspices of the 'experts,' and they don't question it. They just keep their religious beliefs in a separate mental category from their professional studies." As a result of this compartmentalization, the teachers had unwittingly embraced a radical postmodernism that reduces all truth claims to merely social constructions.[58]

"Keeping Faith" with Darwin

If this is starting to sound like postmodernism in the classroom, that's exactly what it is. One of the most influential philosophers in America today is the postmodernist Richard Rorty—and the interesting thing is that he calls himself a *neo*-pragmatist. If you spell out the logical consequences of Dewey's pragmatism, he says, you end up with a postmodernism very much like the thought of Jacques Derrida, Martin Heidegger, and Michel Foucault.[59]

For Rorty, the key slogan of postmodernism is, "Truth is made, not found." In other words, it is not "out there," objective, waiting to be discovered. Beliefs are merely human constructions, like the gadgets of modern technology. And they function the same way as commodities in the marketplace: Echoing James's economic metaphor of the "cash value" of an idea, Rorty says we accept ideas when they "pay off"—when we find them "profitable."[60]

Like Dewey, Rorty bases his philosophy ultimately on Darwinian evolution. He once wrote that "keeping faith with Darwin" (a telling phrase in itself) means understanding that all our beliefs and convictions "are as much products of chance as are tectonic plates and mutated viruses."[61] Ideas arise by random variations in the brain, just like Darwin's random variations in nature.

Thus Rorty reduces all the great formative ideas of Western culture to evolutionary accidents: Just as "a cosmic ray scrambles the atoms in a DNA molecule" to produce a mutation, so too the great work of Aristotle or St. Paul or Newton could be "the results of cosmic rays scrambling the fine structure of some crucial neurons in their respective brains."[62] The reason these ideas have exhibited great staying power is not that they reflect reality, but that they help people organize their experience and get ahead in the struggle for existence. Thus the human species is not oriented "toward Truth" (note the capital T) but only "toward its own increased prosperity." The very notion of Truth, he says, frankly is "un-Darwinian."[63]

TOM WOLFE AND DARWIN'S DOUBT

What this means is that, despite postmodernism's rejection of the notion of objectivity, paradoxically there is *one* idea that it treats as unquestioned truth—namely, Darwinism itself. Evolution is treated as an objective fact and not merely a human construction—because unless it is true, there's no reason for accepting postmodernism. If the mind is a product of Darwinian evolution, then ideas and words are merely tools for controlling the environment, including other people. As Rorty says, language evolved because it is a "useful tactic in predicting and controlling [people's] future behavior."[64]

I once attended a luncheon with the well-known writer Tom Wolfe, who understood very well what Rorty was saying. According to postmodernism, Wolfe said, "language is merely one beast using words as tools to get power over another beast."

Precisely.

The most devastating argument we can use against this radical reductionism is that it undercuts itself. If ideas and beliefs are not true but only useful for controlling the environment, then that applies to the idea of postmodernism itself. And if postmodernism is not *true*, then why should the rest of us give it any credence?

Interestingly, Darwin himself wrestled with the same question—not just once, but several times—calling it his "horrid doubt." In one typical example he wrote, "With me, the horrid doubt always arises whether the convictions of man's mind, which has been developed from the mind of the lower animals, are of any value or at all trustworthy."[65] But of course, Darwin's own theory was likewise one of "the convictions of man's mind," and so he was cutting off the branch he himself was sitting on.

In short, Darwinian evolution is self-refuting. "What evolution guarantees is (at most) that we *behave* in certain ways—in such ways as to promote survival," explains Alvin Plantinga. But "it does not guarantee mostly true or verisimilitudinous beliefs."[66] British philosopher Roger Trigg agrees: For evolution, "it does not matter if a belief is true or false, as long as it is useful, from a genetic point of view."[67]

Thus postmodernists like Rorty are merely showing us where a consistent naturalistic view of knowledge ends up.[68] Once again we see the symbiotic nature of the two stories: It's *because* Darwinian naturalism was put in the lower story that we now have postmodernism (or neo-pragmatism) in the upper story:

The symbiotic relationship between the two stories:

NEO-PRAGMATISM
Truth Is What Works

NATURALISM
The Mind Evolved by Natural Selection

Some find it hard to take postmodernism and its radical implications seriously, shrugging them off as the antics of campus radicals. But ways of thinking that strike us as strange and out of the ordinary may have their roots in very ordinary worldview assumptions. People often do not understand the full implications of the ideas they have picked up from their education and the culture around them.

That's why an effective method of apologetics can be to compel people to face the logical conclusions of their own premises. Francis Schaeffer called this strategy "taking the roof off"—removing the shield of denial that people erect to protect themselves from the dangerous and unsettling implications of their own views, which might otherwise storm in on them.[69] In talking with nonbelievers, we need to press them to recognize the logical conclusions of naturalism. If they were utterly consistent, those who hold naturalistic premises would end up holding postmodern skepticism in science, morality, and every other field of knowledge. The fact that most people are *not* postmodern skeptics means they disagree with the consequences of their own premises—which is a good reason to go back and reconsider those premises. (To read more about Darwinism and pragmatism, see appendix 3.)

TRUTH FROM THE BARREL OF A GUN

"There is an old joke among philosophers that the problem with pragmatism is that it doesn't work," writes Phillip Johnson. After all, "Who wants to rely upon people who think that the only truth is that we should employ the most effective means to get whatever it is we happen to want?"[70] The only measure that pragmatism offers for evaluating an idea is whether it works—whether it achieves social desires and goals. But how do we know whether those goals *themselves* are good or bad, right or wrong?

As a result, in practice, pragmatism easily leads to an endorsement of whatever values a particular society happens to hold.[71] Or, more ominously, whatever the powerful happen to want.

Holmes, the most cynical of the pragmatists, saw these implications clearly—and endorsed them. He was willing to support the powerful even when the consequences were socially destructive: "I quite agree that a law should be called good if it reflects the will of the dominant forces of the community, even if it will take us to hell." And: "Wise or not, the proximate test of a good government is that the dominant power has its way."[72] Applying the same principle to international relations, he famously defined truth as "the majority vote of the nation that can lick all the others."[73]

In short, a rule based on what the pragmatists called "social desires" turns out to be the rule that the most powerful come out on top. If pragmatism has its way, Bertrand Russell warned darkly, then "ironclads and Maxim guns must be the ultimate arbiters of metaphysical truth."[74]

HE IS THERE AND HE IS NOT SILENT

In a remarkable passage, Rorty admits that the very notion of capital-T Truth is coherent only within the context of a Christian worldview. "The suggestion that truth . . . is out there" (that is, objective and universal), he says, "is a legacy of an age in which the world was seen as the creation of a being who had a language of his own," a "nonhuman language" written into the cosmos.[75] Here Rorty is harkening back to an image that Christians have used since the church fathers—the idea of two books: the book of God's word (the Bible) and the book of God's world (nature). His point is that objective truth is possible only if the world itself is a kind of book, created by God's word—language, Logos—so that there is an objective message and meaning in the universe itself.

Of course, that's precisely what science is proving to be the case, as we saw in chapter 6. The discovery of DNA, the coded instructions in every cell of every living thing, means that at the heart of life is a language, a message, information. In other words, the organic world really *is* a book, packed with complex biological information. And not only the organic world—information has become the key for interpreting the physical universe as well. The fine-tuning of the fundamental forces bespeaks a designing intelligence.

"Ask anybody what the physical world is made of, and you are likely to be told 'matter and energy,'" said a recent article in *Scientific American*. "Yet if we have learned anything from engineering, biology, and physics, information is just as crucial an ingredient." Indeed, some physicists now "regard the physical world as made of information, with energy and matter as incidentals."[76]

And where does information come from? In all of human experience, information is generated not by blind material forces but only by an intelligent agent. The reality of the Logos in the material realm underscores the reality of the Logos *beyond* the material—an Intelligent Agent who is the source of its order and rationality.

Rorty agrees that the very idea of objective truth and morality is possible only on the basis of the Logos doctrine. As he puts it, the idea of a truth beyond human subjectivity "is a remnant of the idea that the world is a divine creation, the work of someone who had something in mind, *who Himself spoke some language in which He described His own project.*"[77] In other words, objective truth is possible only if there is a Creator who has spoken to us—giving us divine revelation. As Schaeffer put it in the title of one of his books, only if *He Is There and He Is Not Silent.*[78] The only way of escape from postmodern skepticism is if God has revealed something of His own perspective to us—not about spiritual matters only, and not just a noncognitive emotional experience, but revelation of objective truth about the cosmos we live in.

In short, the biblical doctrine of revelation is the only way to close the gap between fact and value, between the upper and lower stories. The pragmatists sought to bring the two together, but their noble enterprise failed. Once they had put Darwinian evolution in the lower story, then ideas were reduced to mental mutations selected only for their survival value. Instead of uniting the two stories, pragmatism cast the net of naturalism over the upper story and drew it down into the lower story, leaving only postmodern irrationalism and skepticism on top.

Rorty states the choice with utter clarity: Either we "keep faith with Darwin" and embrace postmodernism, or we keep faith with a personal God who is not silent—whose Logos is the source of unified, universal, capital-T Truth.

THE COGNITIVE WAR

It has become commonplace to say that Americans are embroiled in a culture war over conflicting moral standards. But we must remember that morality is always derivative—it stems from an underlying worldview. If Christians hope to engage effectively in the *culture* war, we must be willing to engage the underlying *cognitive* war over origins. Darwinism was the turning point that sealed a naturalistic worldview in the lower story, while reducing religion and morality to noncognitive, upper-story categories.

Thus the key to restoring a unified concept of truth is to recover a robust concept of creation. Christianity has always taught that there is "a single reality" because it was created by a single omnipotent and all-wise God, explains one historical account. *"Given this creation story,* it followed that knowledge, too, comprised a single whole."[79] It was the doctrine of creation that undergirded confidence in the unity of truth.

To be loyal to the great claims of our faith, we can no longer acquiesce in letting Christianity be shunted aside to the *value* sphere. We must throw off metaphysical timidity, be convinced that we have a winning case, and take the offensive. Armed with prayer and spiritual power, we need to ask God to show us where the battle is being fought today, and enlist under the Lordship and leadership of Christ.

Why are evangelicals so prone to metaphysical timidity? Why don't we have a strong and robust intellectual tradition? To advance, we sometimes first need to go backward, retracing our steps to discover where we went wrong, so we can identify negative patterns and replace them with more positive ones. In the next section, we will dig into the history of American evangelicalism to uncover what went wrong on the intellectual front. We will ask why Christians have not had a strong worldview tradition, and what we can do about it. A better understanding of where we have come from can help us adjust the compass, set a better direction, and then go forward confidently to make a difference in our world today.

PART 3

HOW WE
LOST OUR MINDS

9

WHAT'S SO GOOD
ABOUT EVANGELICALISM?

Is Christianity a felt thing?
If I were converted would I feel and know it?
JAMES MCGREADY[1]

When Denzel was a teenager, he prayed fervently that he would lose his virginity. A basketball star in an inner-city high school, Denzel was tired of telling lies about his nonexistent sex life to impress his teammates. "All my friends had a lot more sexual experience than I did, and I didn't want them to think I was unpopular with the girls," he told me. "I had this idea that God just wanted me to be happy. So I kept praying that I would lose my virginity."[2]

Growing up, Denzel had attended church only sporadically with his mother and brother. (His father was a drug dealer, who had been sent to prison for robbing a credit union when Denzel was very young.) "I thought of church as a wonderful, holy place—the Sunday clothes, the choir, the rituals, the baptisms. But I didn't really know anything about God." Clearly not, if he thought God would answer a prayer in favor of fornication.

Eventually Denzel would learn to know this God better, but only after undergoing a personal conversion experience. He did not harbor any intellectual objections against Christianity. He respected the church and accepted the foundational principles taught there: that the Bible is God's Word, that Christ rose from the dead, that we need to be saved. What brought about his conversion was a simple message of sin and repentance, which won over his heart. In many ways, Denzel's story illustrates both the strengths and weaknesses of the old-fashioned evangelical message, and provides a helpful entrée into understanding its history and heritage.

We can begin Denzel's story of sin and salvation in his senior year of high school, when he finally found that girlfriend he'd been praying for. By that time, he was also drinking heavily. ("My friends considered me an alcoholic.") After high school, he tried college but after the first semester he dropped out. He tried working but after six months he was fired. Then his girlfriend announced that she was pregnant.

The news hit Denzel hard. So hard that it drove him, for the first time in his life, to take stock of his actions. "I was seventeen, and I thought, *I can't raise a child*. But most important, I knew it would hurt my mother, and I didn't want to do that."

His mother had gone through several bad relationships with men, who always ended up being drug addicts or alcoholics. Denzel longed to protect her somehow. And she in turn was fiercely protective of her two sons. For years, she had been cutting ethical corners just to put food on the table and a roof over their heads—writing bad checks, falsifying her financial status, opening new accounts under a relative's name. Every few years, things would catch up with her, and she and her sons would be evicted again. Eventually she tried starting her own business, but it was not going well. At just the time Denzel was facing the greatest personal crisis of his young life, she was facing an accusation of financial mismanagement. It looked likely that she would be convicted and end up behind bars.

The thought of his mother being gone, leaving him totally on his own, made Denzel panic. And as one crisis after another pressed in on him, he began praying again—this time in agonizing earnestness. "Many nights I would hide out in the bathroom and cry for hours. I didn't know how to pray, so I would read the Psalms as prayers."

As the court date loomed, his mother decided they needed to resort to drastic measures: She announced that they would go to church. Denzel quickly agreed. "As I got dressed, it somehow became very real to me that this is where I would meet God—the same God I'd been trying to pray to every night. My heart was almost shivering with excitement and fear." As he and his mother slipped into a pew, he could not hold back tears. "I cried through the whole service. I don't remember a thing that was said."

His mother ended up with a six-month prison sentence, and since his older brother was working, Denzel was alone in the house all day with his grief and desperation. Reaching out to God, he sat and read the Bible for hours every day. "One day I read the book of Revelation, and I was struck forcefully by the beauty of the new heavens and the new earth. But I was also struck by the fact that I knew I wasn't going there. Though no one had told me, somehow I knew that fornication was wrong, that I was drinking too much, that I was not living for God. I felt so guilty. I dropped to my knees and cried out, '*God, forgive me! God, forgive me!*'"

Suddenly Denzel recalled an old box of books left behind by his father many years ago, shoved into the corner of a dark closet. He pulled the box out, rummaging around until he uncovered a few dusty Christian books and tracts. One tract caught his eye: It presented a simple, old-fashioned message of guilt and forgiveness, along with a prayer. "I read the tract, prayed the prayer, and immediately I sensed God's forgiveness. I was overwhelmed with joy—I knew now that I could go to heaven." From that moment on, Denzel was utterly and totally committed to his newfound faith.

Denzel's conversion is a classic evangelical story of sin and repentance. He wasn't struggling with questions about positivism or postmodernism; he just knew he was a sinner. He didn't need a complicated apologetic to persuade him that God exists; he just wanted assurance of forgiveness. He couldn't unravel the theological subtleties that divide the denominations; he just longed to know he was going to heaven. His conversion was spiritual and emotional—a profound experience that Christ's atonement applied to *him* personally. In that sense, it was not unlike the conversion of the great evangelist John Wesley, who wrote, "I felt my heart strangely warmed. . . . And an assurance was given me, that [Christ] had taken away *my* sins, even *mine,* and saved *me* from the law of sin and death."[3] In the same way, Denzel's conversion involved personally appropriating God's forgiveness for his own sins. (Later that day he told his girlfriend, with more enthusiasm than theological precision, "God *did* something to me!")

Historically, evangelicalism began as a renewal movement within the churches, not as a separate denomination—and that explains why at first it did not develop an independent intellectual tradition. It didn't need to. It could take for granted the inherited theological and ecclesiastical structures within the denominations where it arose. Like the pietists before them, evangelicals focused on the personal appropriation of theological teachings like sin and atonement. Their goal was to cultivate a *subjective* experience of *objective* biblical truths.[4] As a result, when evangelicalism became dominant within various groups—or when evangelical groups broke away from existing denominations altogether and became independent—they suffered from a certain theological weakness. Evangelical groups tended to downplay the role of theology in favor of practical application such as personal devotion, moral living, and social reform.

DENZEL ASKED THE DEACON

Soon after Denzel's conversion, he began to sense the missing cognitive element in the churches he sought out. Having felt God move in his soul, he was now eager to learn more about *who* this God was. By the time I met Denzel two years later, he had developed an insatiable hunger for spiritual knowledge and was attending three services every Sunday—at three different churches!—in his eagerness to discover what the various denominations teach. (His girlfriend, a preacher's daughter, wanted nothing to do with his newfound faith; as they broke up, she revealed that she had not been pregnant after all.)

Unfortunately, Denzel's hunger for theological knowledge went largely unmet. "At my baptism, I asked the deacon about the Trinity. She told me, just believe Jesus is God, and don't worry about the details." He tried to engage pastors, Sunday school teachers, anyone he could buttonhole in the church hallway, but few had answers to the flurry of questions that came tumbling out.

The pressure to find answers grew even stronger after Denzel got a job. Many of his coworkers were Muslims or Jehovah's Witnesses who were quite vocal about their beliefs. "Everyone at work was able to defend their spiritual convictions—except the Christians. They were the only ones who seemed to have no answers." It became clear to Denzel that in a pluralistic society, Christians need to master apologetics in order to defend their faith in the public arena.

Finally he came up with the idea of applying for a job at a Christian bookstore, to gain access to serious spiritual reading. There he became friends with my son Dieter, who had undergone his own spiritual awakening a few months earlier and had come on staff for the same purpose! Through the world of books, both young men finally tracked down writers on theology and apologetics who helped slake their deep intellectual thirst—Francis Schaeffer, C. S. Lewis, R. C. Sproul, James Montgomery Boice, and J. I. Packer. Browsing the web, Denzel also dug up classic works by Augustine, Aquinas, Luther, Calvin, and Spurgeon.

Denzel's story of sin and salvation illustrates both the fortes and the flaws of American evangelicalism. When he unearthed that dusty, dog-eared tract and read the simple gospel message, he immediately felt freedom from his burden of guilt. Assurance of salvation swept over his soul like a life-giving stream. His church welcomed him, baptized him, and gave him a place to worship. But when he began looking for more solid intellectual food—theological teaching and apologetics—he had to search long and hard to find resources to satisfy his hunger. Today he is still trying to track down a church that ministers to the whole person, including the mind.

Why are evangelical churches typically weak in apologetics and worldview? To answer that question, we need to open up the archives on the history of the evangelical movement. In Part 1, we traced the crucial importance of having a Christian worldview—of not letting ourselves be "conformed to this world" (Rom. 12:1) with its two-story division of truth. In Part 2 we identified the crucial role that Darwinian naturalism plays in maintaining the two-tiered fact/value split—by reducing religion and morality to meaningless products of a mindless process. Now, in Part 3, we will dig into the history of American evangelicalism in order to discover why it has largely acquiesced in the two-story division of truth. Why did evangelicalism largely accept the secular/sacred split that locks Christianity into the upper story of merely personal experience? How did we lose a full-bodied conception of Christianity as truth about all reality—as total truth? Only by backtracking over the path that brought us here will we be equipped to chart a better course for the future.

FORWARD TO THE PAST

Questions about the history of evangelicalism became pressing for me personally after I had finished my work on *How Now Shall We Live?* Having immersed myself in the theme of Christian worldview through the writing process, the burning question that arose at the end was *why* this is such a difficult message to communicate. What are the mental barriers people have against worldview thinking? Why have evangelicals accepted a largely privatized faith? This was not merely an academic question but also a personal one, because I was trying to understand how to communicate the book's themes to the real people I encountered.

I began digging into books on evangelicalism, and as I identified various paradigms from the past, all the pieces fell into place. Many of the trends we confront today were characteristic of the evangelical movement right from the beginning, and if we trace them down from colonial times, they come alive as never before. Often we do not recognize patterns even in our own thinking unless we gain some outside vantage point, just as a fish can't tell you what water is, because it is all the fish has ever known. Getting a historical perspective is like going up high for an aerial shot, and as we look down through the scope of time we can detect various trends unfolding gradually, which makes them much easier to recognize—and gives us insight into our own time as well. After all, we are heirs to more than two hundred years of American history, and these inherited habits of thought shape our ideas and practices still today.

I will not be giving anything like a comprehensive historical account, but only looking for clues to diagnose the intellectual weakness of the church today. Our goal is to pinpoint patterns that throw light on the contemporary situation of the church. A book by Alister McGrath includes a chapter titled, "The Dark Side of Evangelicalism,"[5] and in a sense that is our theme here as well. Though there is much that is good and praiseworthy within evangelicalism, our focus will be on elements in our history and heritage that continue to pose barriers to Christian worldview thinking.

Historically, the evangelical movement divided roughly into two wings. The first we might call populist: It had a strong revivalist style that downplayed doctrine and appealed to ordinary folk. Strongest in the Southern states, this stream included mostly Baptists, Methodists, and the Restoration movement (the Churches of Christ, the Disciples of Christ, and the "Christian" Churches). The second wing was rationalist and scholarly. Centered in the North, it included evangelicals within the Congregationalist, Presbyterian, and Episcopalian churches, who united evangelical fervor with these denominations' traditional emphasis on theology and scholarship.[6]

In this chapter and the next, we'll examine the populist stream, which has become dominant today in terms of sheer numbers and influence within the churches. We will bring this tradition to life with colorful anecdotes of lively camp meetings and impassioned revivalists. Then in chapter 11 we will turn to the scholarly stream, getting acquainted with some of the most interesting and inspiring figures in the history of American thought. Finally, in chapter 12, we will take a fascinating side trip to see how religion in America was reshaped by changes in social and economic life. After all, religion is not just about abstract ideas. It is part of the fabric of concrete reality, and new ideas about religion were woven in with new ideas about the family, the church, work, and even the relationship between men and women.

IDENTITY CHECK

What does it mean to be evangelical? Most of us probably apply the term to all Christians who are Bible-believing and personally committed. I certainly used the word in this broad sense for many years. Thus when I began researching the subject, I was puzzled to turn up literature by conservative Lutheran clergy (the church I grew up in) insisting that they were certainly *not* evangelical—and warning darkly that evangelicalism was seeping into the Lutheran churches!

So what *does* the term mean? American historians typically use it in a more technical sense to refer to a movement that grew out of the First and Second Great Awakenings, embracing a revivalist style of preaching and an emphasis on personal conversion (the "New Birth").[7] Because it was a renewal movement within the church, its goal was not so much to convert nonbelievers as to enliven the faith of nominal believers—to bring individuals to a subjective experience of the saving truths of the gospel.

Classic Protestantism stemming from the Reformation defined the

Christian life largely in terms of participation in the church's corporate worship and liturgy. A church expressed its identity through creeds and confessions, maintained by the authority of clerical office. But the revival movement cast much of that aside. It stressed the individual's direct access to God apart from any church, defining the Christian life primarily in terms of individual devotion and holiness. Thus the rhetoric of revival tended to have an anti-authoritarian and anti-traditionalist flavor, denouncing liturgy and ceremonies as empty, external ritualism. Even today, says one historian, we must not "lose sight of this central point, namely, that any Protestant who emphasizes the subjective and ethical aspects of Christianity, rather than its official and churchly characteristics, is an evangelical."[8]

Some religious groups stood aloof from the revivalist movement, notably Catholics, Lutherans, German Reformed, Dutch Reformed, and Old Side Presbyterians. These are sometimes called the confessional churches. Yet the boundaries are not watertight: Even within the confessional churches, some groups were more sympathetic to revivalism.[9] Moreover, the very fact that today groups like Lutherans need to patrol their borders so diligently is evidence of how pervasive the evangelical style of spirituality has become. For good or ill, over a period of more than two hundred years of American history, populist evangelicalism has triumphed over the confessional churches.

"Evangelicals now constitute the largest and most active component of religious life in North America," says historian Mark Noll.[10] And not only here but also across the globe. In *The Next Christendom*, Philip Jenkins shows that the fastest-growing Christian groups in Africa, Asia, and Latin America tend to exhibit the characteristics of populist evangelicalism as well (experiential, theologically conservative, with an emphasis on personal conversion and supernatural signs and wonders).[11] That's why the populist branch of evangelicalism is something we all need to grapple with, no matter what our own denominational background, if we hope to communicate a worldview message to those around us.

AND THE WINNER IS

In evaluating the impact of evangelicalism, we might say there is good news and bad news. The good news is that the evangelical movement has been remarkably effective in "Christianizing" American society. Look at fig. 9.1, which shows church membership in America from the colonial era. The graph is from *The Churching of America*, by Roger Finke and Rodney Stark,[12] and surprisingly it shows that religious adherence in America has actually *increased* significantly since the colonial period. The common stereotype that

in colonial times virtually everyone belonged to a church turns out to be
false.[13] And the correlative stereotype that in the modern world religion is
withering away is likewise false. In terms of adherents, churches are doing
very well today.

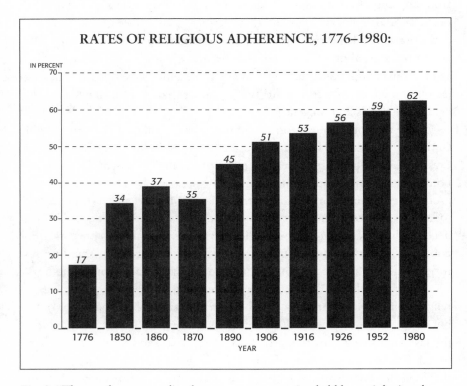

Fig. 9.1 The numbers contradict the common assumption held by sociologists that as
societies modernize, they inevitably secularize. *(Finke and Stark, 16, adapted with
permission.)*

The sheer rise in numbers doesn't tell the whole story, however. Turn to
fig. 9.2, which shows the sizes of various denominations between 1776 and
1850 (from the American Revolution to the climax of the Second Great
Awakening).[14] Notice the stunning reversals in fortune. At the time of the
Revolution, more than half of Americans who belonged to a religious group
(55 percent) were Congregationalist, Episcopalian, or Presbyterian. At the time
it seemed almost certain that these groups would remain dominant. Yet by
1850, Congregationalism had virtually collapsed. The Episcopalians had suffered greatly (partly because they supported England during the War; many
returned to the homeland). The Presbyterians enjoyed some growth, but the

increase shown in the graph only kept pace with the growing population; they actually lost ground in terms of "market share"—percentage of religious adherents. The Catholics grew, but through immigration, not conversion.

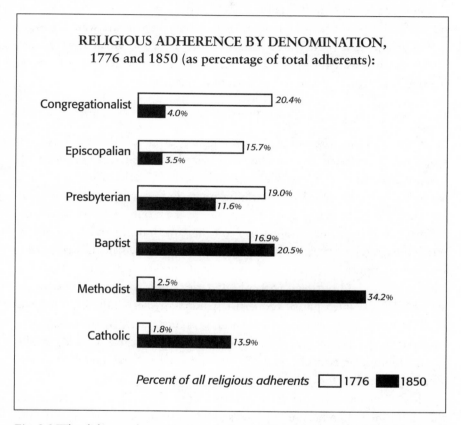

RELIGIOUS ADHERENCE BY DENOMINATION,
1776 and 1850 (as percentage of total adherents):

Congregationalist — 20.4% / 4.0%
Episcopalian — 15.7% / 3.5%
Presbyterian — 19.0% / 11.6%
Baptist — 16.9% / 20.5%
Methodist — 2.5% / 34.2%
Catholic — 1.8% / 13.9%

Percent of all religious adherents   ☐ 1776   ■ 1850

Fig. 9.2 Why did some denominations decline, while others grew rapidly? *(Finke and Stark, 55, adapted with permission.)*

The most striking growth took place among the Baptists and the Methodists. During the Revolutionary War, most Methodist preachers returned to England at John Wesley's command, so they were starting over again—yet even so, they enjoyed phenomenal success. By 1850, they had become the largest Protestant denomination, accounting for 34 percent of all church members in the country. Some historians even call the nineteenth century "the Methodist Age." In 1906 they were overtaken by the Baptists, which tells us that *their* growth rate continued steadily as well.

When we talk about the "growth" of religion in America, then, we need to understand that it was not uniform: After the nation gained its independence, some groups went into decline, while others grew like wildfire, especially the Baptists and Methodists, and also (though not on the chart) the Churches of Christ.

How do we explain this pattern? Why did some churches flourish, while others declined? The answer, in a nutshell, is that the winners were the evangelical groups that participated in the First and Second Great Awakenings, while the losers were the established churches that largely failed to compete in the free marketplace of religion that arose in the new nation.

WHEN GOVERNMENT HELP HURTS

We sometimes forget that, in pre-Revolutionary America, the religious landscape was dominated by churches that rested on legal establishment: the Congregationalists in New England, and the Episcopalians in New York, Virginia, Maryland, North and South Carolina, and Georgia. What exactly did legal establishment mean? It is so far removed from our own experience that we may not realize what an intensive role the government played in administering the churches. Typically, the state collected tithes (which all citizens were legally required to pay, whether they attended the established church or not). The state also laid out new parish boundaries, subsidized new church construction, maintained parish properties, paid clergymen's salaries, hired and fired them, and even took measures to suppress dissenters. (Baptist preachers, for example, were sometimes jailed and beaten. Yes, here in America!) Finally, in many states, government positions were limited to church members—there were religious tests for office.[15]

It might seem that having the government on their side would have given the established churches quite an edge, and to some extent it did. But ultimately, it weakened them. Monopolies tend to be lazy, whether we're talking about businesses or schools or churches. The established clergy often lived like members of the gentry (the class that did not work but lived off of investments and rents), enjoying ample time for leisure activities. For example, in Scotland's state church, which was Presbyterian, Thomas Chalmers observed that after holding worship services, "a minister may enjoy five days in the week of uninterrupted leisure."[16]

By contrast, the evangelical ministers were enthusiastic activists, throwing themselves into ceaseless efforts to spread the gospel. They set up additional worship services, started Sunday schools, taught Bible classes, made personal visits, established charities, and founded missionary societies. Chalmers himself later became an evangelical, after which he is reputed to have visited

11,000 homes in his Glasgow parish during a single year! Becoming an evangelical made a significant difference in one's style of ministry.

People at the time were keenly aware of the difference in ethos. A document from 1837 (after all American churches had been disestablished), describes the vivid contrast between America's free churches and England's established church. Having seen both firsthand, the writer observed that legal establishment made the clergy "indolent and lazy," since a person with a guaranteed income would never "work as hard as one who has to exert himself for a living." As a result, the writer concluded, the Americans had a threefold advantage: "they have *more* preachers; they have more *active* preachers, and they have *cheaper* preachers than can be found in any part of Europe."[17]

A monopoly faith breeds religious indifference not only among the clergy but among members as well. This is one reason rates of religious adherence were lower in colonial days than we typically suppose. A modern analogy might be societies like Sweden where everyone is putatively Lutheran, or Italy where everyone is Roman Catholic. The level of religious participation in these countries is astonishingly low compared to that in America.[18]

Finally, the established churches tended to be the first to drift into theological liberalism. The wealthier the church, the more likely its clergy were to enjoy social status and formal academic training—and thus also the more likely to welcome the liberalism emerging from European universities at the time. Well before the American Revolution, leading scholars at Harvard and Yale had become Unitarian. Instead of exhorting their congregations to repent and be saved, they delivered elegantly styled lectures on "reasonable religion," with the supernatural elements increasingly stripped away. When the First and Second Great Awakenings broke out, the liberal clergy firmly opposed them, declaring themselves on the side of "Reason" against the revivalists' "religion of the heart."

That was a sure recipe for failure. It is a common assumption that, in order to survive, churches must accommodate to the age. But in fact, the opposite is true: In every historical period, the religious groups that grow most rapidly are those that set believers at odds with the surrounding culture. As a general principle, the higher a group's tension with mainstream society, the higher its growth rate.

"Religious organizations are stronger to the degree that they impose significant costs in terms of sacrifice and even stigma upon their members," write Finke and Stark. Why? Because religions that demand a lot also give a lot. A frankly supernatural religion may demand more from adherents than a watered-down gospel of "reasonable religion" or social activism. But in turn it gives much greater rewards in terms of doctrinal substance, intense spiritual experience, and a sense of direct access to God. As Finke and Stark comment dryly, people go to church "in search of salvation, not social service."[19]

WILD WEST RELIGION

While these principles hold true in any society, they apply especially to American history—because throughout most of our nation's history, there has been a large frontier. The map in fig. 9.3 shows the percentage of religious adherents in America in 1850, at the height of the Second Great Awakening (the same year the previous chart ended). Notice that the country is only half settled! To make these dates concrete, I remind myself that I was born in the 1950s, which means this map shows conditions a mere hundred years before my birth. And notice which states are on the frontier: Michigan, Missouri, Texas! This means that *most* of American history can be mapped as the gradual westward movement of the frontier—a process that lasted nearly three hundred years. The dynamics of frontier life continued to shape much of American culture right up to the dawn of the twentieth century.

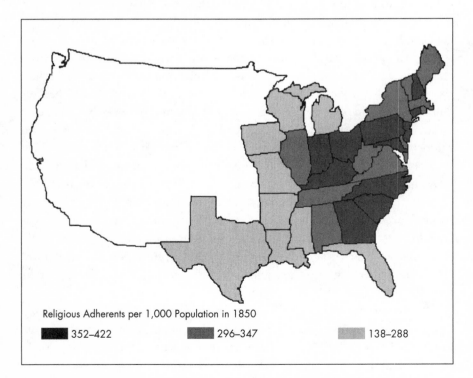

Religious Adherents per 1,000 Population in 1850

■ 352–422   ■ 296–347   138–288

Fig. 9.3 Throughout most of America's history, there has been a frontier to evangelize. *(Finke and Stark, 68, adapted with permission.)*

What were conditions like on the frontier? First, it was rough and dangerous. Think of it this way: People were moving west faster than social institutions could keep up with them. Often there were no schools, no churches, no local governments, not even families (large numbers of single men went west).[20] Many who went west were drifters and people in trouble with the law, fleeing their past. Listen to this firsthand account from 1840 by the French nobleman Alexis de Tocqueville, a perceptive observer of American culture. Those going west, he noted, were "adventurers impatient of any sort of yoke, greedy for wealth, and often outcasts from the States in which they were born. They arrive in the depths of the wilderness without knowing one another. *There is nothing of tradition, family feeling, or example to restrain them.*"[21]

So when you think of the frontier, think Dodge City. As Finke and Stark write, you should picture "towns filled with male drifters, gamblers, confidence tricksters, whores, and saloon keepers, and *without* churches, schools, or respectable women."[22]

The question facing the Christian churches, then, was how do you make an effective religious appeal to such uncivilized, rough-hewn people? How do you bring religion to Dodge City? And the answer is that you do exactly what the Methodists and Baptists did in the revival movements: You grab people by the throat with an intense emotional experience to persuade them of the power of the supernatural—then you tell them to stop drinking, stop shooting each other, and live straight.

This kind of intense emotional conversion experience is exactly what the camp meetings of the First and Second Great Awakenings aimed to produce. No profound teaching, no high church ceremonies, no theological subtleties, no solemn hymns. Instead the revivalists used simple, vernacular language and catchy folk tunes, delivered with lively theatrics to catch people's attention and move their emotions. Evangelical preachers broke with the older pattern of using sermons to instruct, and began to use their sermons to press hearers to a point of crisis, in order to produce a conversion experience. Instead of talking about a gradual growth in faith through participation in a church, evangelicals began to treat a one-time conversion event as the only sufficient basis for claiming to be a Christian.[23]

RIDERS IN THE STORM

Another key to success on the frontier is that you have to *be* there. You have to be willing to sacrifice the comforts of the settled cities in order to minister among rough people living rough lives. As a rule, the established clergy were not willing to do that. In the state-supported churches (and in wealthier churches generally), the training for pastors was a long, expensive process that led to a chronic shortage of clergy, thus giving them considerable bargaining power over salary and location. Many simply refused to go to the unsettled frontier areas.

Fig. 9.4 METHODIST CAMP MEETING, March 1, 1819: People flocked from miles around to hear the revivalists' message of sin and grace. *(Engraving. Library of Congress, Prints and Photographs Division [LC-USZC4-772].)*

By contrast, the Methodist circuit preachers became a legend on the frontier. They traveled constantly, virtually living in the saddle. They were willing to preach to tiny frontier outposts, even to individual households. Most were single (they were on the road too often to maintain a family), worked for almost no money, and literally died young from the sheer hardship of their lives. One minister dubbed them God's "light artillery," perfectly adapted to the frontier. They had a reputation for braving terrible conditions and bad weather, so that during particularly bad storms it used to be said, "There's nobody out tonight but crows and Methodist preachers."[24]

Similarly, most Baptists preachers were simple farmers, ministering to their own neighbors. Many had only minimal theological education, speaking the same language as the people they were trying to reach. It was not unusual for someone to be converted at one revival meeting, then turn around and immediately start helping to run others, picking up a little theological education along the way only if he had the time and money.[25]

This was a complete novelty. We often forget that ever since Christianity was made the state religion of the Roman Empire in the fourth century, the church had been associated with the ruling class. As America was becoming a nation, most European countries still had state churches, in which church authorities wielded considerable political power—often even holding government office. In England, for example, Anglican bishops sat in the House of Lords (and still do). Even in colonial America, clerical and government authority were intertwined, since things like tithing and Sunday attendance were matters of legal coercion. Typically ministers were also the most highly educated in a community, which meant they were given deference as leaders.

This elitism was utterly abhorrent to the revivalists, and they set out to "popularize" religion. Fired by a profound concern for ordinary people, they pronounced the right of the unlearned to investigate religion for themselves. They made the gospel accessible by using simple language and spontaneous preaching. They delivered sermons that were emotive and extemporaneous— a refreshing novelty at a time when it was customary for clergy to simply *read* sermons written out ahead of time. In John Wesley's words, the revivalists wanted to preach nothing but "plain truth for plain people."[26] Ordinary believers were no longer regarded as passive recipients, as they were under the old hierarchical model, but as active participants.

The revivalists' concern for the poor and outcast reached even to slaves. At the time of the Revolutionary War, few blacks, whether slave or free, were Christians. "Well into the nineteenth century Episcopalians and Presbyterians were still wringing their hands about their failure to Christianize their own slaves," says historian Nathan Hatch.[27] Over the next three decades, however, thousands of African-Americans turned to the gospel. What attracted them? The simple, colloquial preaching style of the revivalists. "Other denominations preached so high-flown that we were not able to comprehend their doctrine," said Richard Allen, founder of the African Methodist Episcopal Church.[28] But the preaching style of the Methodists and Baptists was simple, direct, and dramatic. Instead of imposing a solemn, restrained style of worship, they encouraged spontaneous singing, chanting, and shouting, affirming the rich heritage of folk expression among African-Americans.

When we consider the growth of religious affiliation in America, then, the most striking thing is that it did *not* take place among the respectable or established churches, but among the evangelical groups—the "upstart" groups, as they were called at the time. This is the good news about evangelicalism. Later, the revivalist techniques that had been honed on the frontier were adapted to the cities by men like Charles Finney. He took the camp meeting style, dressed it in a suit, upgraded to a more urbane language, and pitched his appeal to the professional classes (lawyers and businessmen).[29]

Meanwhile, what happened to the established churches? They went into a slow but steady process of decline that has continued to our own day. For a long time they were able to mask their decline: The overall population in America was growing so fast that their numbers continued to increase in absolute terms, even though they were not actually keeping pace with the population increase. To leap ahead for a moment, by the 1960s the mainline churches could no longer hide the fact that even absolute numbers were falling. In 1972 Dean Kelley, an executive of the theologically liberal National Council of Churches, wrote a book called *Why Conservative Churches Are Growing*,[30] which stated frankly for the first time that mainline and liberal churches were dying. Kelley's colleagues excoriated him for airing unpleasant truths in public, but today even liberals admit that evangelical denominations have confounded all predictions by refusing to die out in the modern world, but instead continuing to grow and thrive.[31]

Overall, the Great Awakenings are largely responsible for the fact that America remains the most religious of the industrialized nations. By popularizing Christianity, evangelicalism permeated all the social classes. "In 1790 something like only 10 percent of Americans professed membership in a Christian church," writes Noll, "but by the time of the Civil War [1861], the proportion had multiplied several times." And the main cause of this dramatic increase was "the active labors of the revivalists."[32]

FRONTIER FALLOUT

If that is the good news about the populist wing of evangelicalism, what's the bad news? What happened along the way to the evangelical mind? Why did the evangelical movement become largely anti-intellectual, with little sense of how to relate to the mainstream culture? Ironically, the answer lies in some of the same factors that made it so successful. Let's outline some of the major factors, and then watch them unfold more dramatically in a series of short narratives through the rest of this chapter and into the next.

First, the focus on an intense conversion experience was highly effective in bringing people to faith. But it also tended to redefine religion in terms of emotion, while contributing to a neglect of theology and doctrine and the whole cognitive element of belief. This tendency did enormous damage by reinforcing a conception of Christianity as a noncognitive upper-story experience.

Second, the use of vernacular language and simple folk songs was highly effective in reaching ordinary people. But the revivalists often went much further, practically wearing their ignorance on their sleeves, as though being theologically educated equated with being spiritually dead. One of their favorite themes was poking fun at the educated clergy "back east."

Third, addressing individuals apart from their family or church was very effective in forcing a crisis of faith. But it could also lead to a radically individualistic view of the church that rejected the intellectual riches developed over the centuries by the great minds throughout church history—including the distillations of doctrine in corporate statements of faith, such as creeds and confessions. Many evangelicals uncritically absorbed the individualism that was coming into vogue in American *political* life, and simply transferred it to the church. An atomistic, voluntaristic ecclesiology was born that did not reflect biblical teaching so much as the political philosophy of the day.

Finally, revivalism led to a new model of leadership. The pastor was no longer a teacher who instructs a covenanted congregation, but a celebrity who is able to inspire mass audiences.

Of course, these trends were not embodied by all evangelical groups, nor did they appear full-blown right from the beginning. We will find seeds of the new attitudes being planted in the first Awakening (the rest of this chapter), coming to full fruition only in the second Awakening (the topic of the next chapter). See if you can spot the characteristic themes as I flesh them out with a few historical sketches.

Whitefield Across America

The First Great Awakening began when a young English evangelist named George Whitefield made a sensational appearance in the American colonies. He preached in the open air, in the fields, in the streets—anywhere he could gather an audience. Having been an actor as a youngster, Whitefield always retained a love for dramatic flair, which he now employed in his passion to build God's kingdom. One biographer even titles his book *The Divine Dramatist,* and says Whitefield pioneered a new preaching style: "an actor-preacher, as opposed to a scholar-preacher."[33] He raised his arms, stamped his feet, acted out Bible stories, and wept aloud.

To recapture the novelty of all this, we have to realize how contrary it was to the somber, reserved preaching fashion of the day. Living in Europe, I once got a taste of the old-world preaching style when we visited a seven-hundred-year-old Lutheran church in rural Sweden. The pastor literally read an hour-long sermon in a monotonous tone of voice, rarely even looking up at the congregation. It was the revivalists who pioneered extemporaneous preaching, aimed at evoking an emotional response and changing hearts. Whitefield's delivery was so effective, people joked he could bring an audience to tears just by the way he pronounced the word *Mesopotamia*.

To promote his tours, Whitefield pioneered the use of mass marketing, borrowing heavily from marketing techniques in the commercial world of his day. I had always assumed that the huge crowds attracted to Whitefield's evangelistic crusades were spontaneous gatherings, but most were carefully orchestrated: When he planned to visit a city, he would send out assistants—up to two years in advance—to distribute flyers and line up the facilities. He also issued a constant stream of advance publicity, from press releases to newspaper ads to printed copies of his sermons. He "followed a strategy of self-promotion and publicity that was unheard of in religious circles" of his day, says one historian. He would sometimes even "inflate the numbers to generate greater attention in the press," or "stage events again to draw crowds and publicity in newspapers."[34] All told, these were some of the best publicized events in colonial America.

Historian Harry Stout sums up Whitefield's novelty by calling him America's "first modern celebrity." In what sense? In the sense that his claim to influence did not rest on institutional validation—things like degrees and ordination, by which a church or denomination qualifies a person to represent it. Instead his claim to credibility rested on personality and popularity—the sheer ability to move a crowd. Unlike local pastors, revivalists like Whitefield did not address regular congregations who knew them personally. Instead they drew mass audiences made up of strangers who had no way of knowing them personally, and who therefore could only be attracted by publicity and advertising.[35]

Do you recognize some of our themes emerging here? The focus on an emotional response; the celebrity-style leader; the engineered publicity; the individual detached from his local congregation. Again, my purpose is not to give a complete historical account but only to highlight key patterns that help explain the loss of a Christian mind in our own day. There is no question that in both Awakenings, God performed a mighty work in the land. Great numbers of people became aware of their sin, then discovered the joys of forgiveness and grace. One cannot read firsthand accounts by Whitefield and other revivalists without being impressed by their fervent love for God and their hunger to see people brought into the Kingdom. But if we hope to make an unflinching diagnosis of the anti-intellectualism in our midst, we must recognize that crucial seeds were being sown.

Heart Versus Head

Contemporary Christians tend to have such a positive picture of the great Awakenings that it is difficult to grasp why they provoked such bitter contention at the time. In the First Great Awakening, some churches, like the Presbyterians, actually split between revivalist and confessional groups, while other groups broke away entirely to become independent (often Baptist). What drove the two sides was a disagreement over the role of emotion or experience in conversion.

Opponents of the Awakening treated the Christian life as a gradual growth in faith and holiness by what they called "Christian nurture," through participation in the rituals and teaching of the church. It was, they insisted, a thoroughly rational growth in knowledge. As one critic put it, "The Acts of the Soul in Conversion" are "the most rational Acts."[36] This reflected the Enlightenment view (revived from classical Greek culture) that humans are preeminently rational creatures. The "passions" were distrusted as forces that interfere with reason. The critics often charged that the revivalists were subverting the social order by rousing the passions of the ignorant rabble.

By contrast, supporters of the Awakening insisted that a merely intellectual assent to theological propositions was not enough. What was needed was "a Change of Heart" or a "New Birth." This theme came from European pietism, which had rejected the Enlightenment focus on reason to embrace the emerging Romantic focus on feelings. "Our people do not so much need to have their heads stored, as to have their hearts touched," wrote Jonathan Edwards, the preeminent theorist of the First Great Awakening, in 1743.[37] One of his protégés described the best preacher as one "whose heart is ravished with the glory of divine things."[38]

The emphasis on emotion was perhaps inevitable, given that most people in the colonial era were at least nominally Christian, which meant that the primary goal of the Awakenings was to counter spiritual coldness and indifference. With few outright atheists to address, the revivalists did not seek to convert people to Christianity so much as to what they called "experimental religion"—the idea that religious truth should not merely be believed but also experienced.

Consider a typical conversion account from very early in the second Awakening. James McGready was studying for the Presbyterian ministry when it struck him that, even though his theological beliefs were orthodox and his moral behavior impeccable, these things were not enough. "When he came to examine *his feelings,* to try them by such passages as, being 'filled with the Spirit; filled with joy; filled with the Holy Ghost; joy of the Holy Ghost . . . ,' it seemed to him that he did not understand these things experimentally," wrote an early historian.[39] After being ordained, McGready said the goal of his own preaching was to get people to ask themselves, "Is Christianity a *felt* thing? If I were converted would I *feel* and know it?" [40]

The emphasis on making Christianity "a felt thing" did not mean evangelicals were outright anti-intellectual—not in the early stages, at least. What they opposed was a *merely* intellectual knowledge of God. Many succeeded in maintaining a balance between piety and rationalism, Edwards being the outstanding example. Highly educated, Edwards maintained an admirable blend of theological learning and spiritual fervor. Even secular historians count him as one of the greatest minds in American history. Supporters of the revival also founded several universities, including Princeton, Rutgers, Brown, and Dartmouth.

And yet, the New Birth was consistently described in emotional terms, as producing "sudden rapturous joys" and "boundless felicity." A convert at the time called it the surest "Way to Happiness." One historian comments, somewhat sarcastically, that the incessant search for emotional rapture through the New Birth "represented the evangelical version of the pursuit of happiness."[41] We could say that Protestantism was being split into two stories, with the revivalists pushing for emotional conversions (upper story) while their opponents defended reasonable religion (lower story).[42]

Defiant Individualism

Moreover, the revivalists of the first Awakening engaged in an attack on church authority that tended to undercut, in the long run, even the natural authority of learning and scholarship. Although many were themselves well-born and well-educated, ironically they tended to identify themselves as outsiders. At every opportunity they pictured their opponents as "the Noble and Mighty" elders of the church, while identifying themselves with the poor and the "common People."[43]

Unlike the local pastor ministering to his own covenanted congregation, the revivalist often preached to crowds of people drawn together from across several congregations and denominations. This was a significant change, for it meant the individual was addressed *as an individual,* apart from his membership in a church. In fact, the revivalists often went further, explicitly urging people to leave their local churches to find ministers who were truly converted—an idea that was shocking in light of Puritan covenant theology.

To understand why this message was so unsettling, we have to realize that the seventeenth-century view of social order was highly communal and organic. A person simply did not conceive of himself apart from the family, church, local community, and so on. When a pastor was called to a local parish, it was almost like a marriage proposal: He was expected to bond permanently with the congregation and stay there for life.[44] By the same token, members were bound by a covenant to the local parish.

Thus it was a radical departure when the revivalists directed their message to individuals, exhorting them to make independent decisions in regard to religion—and to act on those decisions regardless of their effect on the larger society. "Piety was no longer something inextricably bound up with local community and corporate spirituality," explains Stout. "The emphasis shifted to a more individualistic and subjective sense of piety that found its quintessential expression in the internal, highly personal experience of the 'New Birth.'"[45]

To wrench individuals free from tenacious traditional bonds, the revivalists often adopted a contentious, even defiant tone. For example, Samuel Finley, who later became president of the College of New Jersey (Princeton), urged his listeners to take sides immediately for or against their parish ministers: "Away with your carnal Prudence! And either follow *God* or *Baal*. *He that is not actually with us, is against us.*" He then urged parishioners to act on their decisions even if it "rends the Church; divides Congregations and Families; [and] sets People at Variance"—even if "your Neighbours growl against you, and reproach you."[46] His words illustrate what one historian calls "the new spirit of defiant individualism that was one of the most radical manifestations of the Awakening."[47]

Partisans of the revival also gave vent to harsh denunciations of the local clergy, pronouncing them spiritually dead and carnal. One of the most famous sermons in the first Awakening was a flaming address by a leader of the New Side Presbyterians named Gilbert Tennent, titled "The Danger of an Unconverted Ministry," urging people to exercise their Christian liberty by deserting their parish minister for ministers who had been genuinely converted by undergoing a "New Birth." Not surprisingly, such declarations of religious independence were especially popular among young people. Taunting religious authorities became so widespread on college campuses that in 1741 the trustees at Yale University had to pass a college law forbidding students to call college officers "carnal" or "unconverted."[48]

The shock and outrage these actions produced at the time can be sensed in these anguished words from an opponent of the Awakening: "You have no liberty, no right, to forsake the communion of these churches . . . you cannot do it without breaking the covenant . . . and incurring the awful guilt of schism."[49] What was emerging was a new theology of conversion: The older view that believers are nurtured *within* the corporate church as whole persons, including the mind (through study and catechesis), was giving way to a new view that individuals undergo a one-time emotional decision that takes place *outside* the church.

The focus on individual choice and experience would eventually contribute to the idea that Christian belief is a noncognitive, upper-story phenomenon. Despite the overall positive legacy of the First Great Awakening, we cannot avoid the conclusion that seeds of anti-intellectualism were being planted. They did not come into full bloom, however, until the Second Great Awakening.[50] The two Awakenings were divided historically by the Revolutionary War, and so we will divide our narrative at this point as well, to resume our account with the dawning of the Second Great Awakening.

10

WHEN AMERICA MET CHRISTIANITY— GUESS WHO WON?

We have it in our power to begin the world over again.
THOMAS PAINE[1]

After moving to a new suburb a few years ago, my family began the search for a church home, visiting a Bible church not far down the road. In the middle of the sermon, the pastor launched into the most blatant expression of anti-intellectualism I had ever encountered. "In college I once took a philosophy course," he said, "and when I tried to read the textbook, I discovered it was pure nonsense. Gobbledygook."

He smiled expansively at the congregation, as though proud of his discovery. "From that time on, I knew Christians didn't have to worry about reading books on philosophy or any of that intellectual stuff. Those philosophers don't know what they're talking about."

My husband and I exchanged looks of utter amazement. Yet the attitude we were witnessing—a disdain for the things of the mind—had already begun to take root in the First Great Awakening, as we saw in the previous chapter. And it was to grow even more pronounced in the Second Great Awakening. In this chapter, we pick up the story again and trace its enduring legacy. The purpose is not to give a complete or comprehensive history, but only to zero in on patterns that help us understand why so much of the Christian world finds itself trapped in a two-story view of truth today.

As the Second Great Awakening got underway, open-air camp meetings became huge affairs. People would come from miles around to live in tents for days, even weeks, at a time. Paintings from the time show row upon row of peaked white tents filling a forest clearing, with a speaker's stand in the middle, surrounded by wooden benches. Several speakers' stands might even be

scattered throughout the camp, so that at virtually any time *someone* could be
heard preaching.[2]

Fig. 10.1 **THE SECOND GREAT AWAKENING:** In the Second Great Awakening,
camp meetings became huge social gatherings. *(The Camp Ground, courtesy of the
Billy Graham Center Museum, Wheaton, Ill.)*

In many ways, the second Awakening carried forward the themes of the
first Awakening, so as we tell some of its stories, bear in mind the major characteristics listed in the previous chapter: the focus on an intense emotional conversion experience; the celebrity model of leadership; a deep suspicion of
theological learning, especially as embodied in creeds and confessions; and an
increasingly individualistic view of the church, which borrowed heavily from
the political philosophy of the day. In fact, if there is one factor especially distinctive of the second Awakening, it is a surprising lack of critical distance from
the political ideology of the American Revolution. This provides a handy way
to remember what distinguishes the two Awakenings: the first came *before* the
American Revolution, while the second came *after* it—at a time when the
Revolution was becoming the template for the way people thought about virtually every area of life. It became common for leaders in the second
Awakening to transfer the rhetoric of independence uncritically from the political sphere to the religious sphere.

For example, in the first Awakening, revivalists had not attacked church
structure or learning per se, but only the abuses that had turned the clergy into

a privileged class. By contrast, in the second Awakening, church authority itself was denounced as "tyranny." Creeds and liturgies were nothing but "popery" and "priestcraft." (Charles Finney denounced the Westminster Confession as a "paper pope.") Many began to argue that the American Revolution was not yet complete: We have cast off *civil* tyranny, they said, but now we need to cast off *ecclesiastical* tyranny. The priesthood of all believers was taken to mean religion of the people, by the people, and for the people.

This assault on authority and learning was part of a general "democratization of truth," says historian Gordon Wood. The concept of "unalienable rights" was transferred from the political realm to the realm of ideas, where it meant the right of ordinary people to think as they pleased without deferring to the judgments of the well-bred and well-educated. As a result, "Americans of the early Republic experienced *an epistemological crisis* as severe as any in their history," Wood writes. Truth itself seemed to be shattered, and everything was left to the individual—the voter, the buyer, the religious believer—to make decisions strictly on his own.[3]

Unfortunately, many evangelicals were caught up in the same "epistemological crisis." They absorbed the American ethos, and in some respects even led the way to an anti-authoritarian, anti-historical, individualistic outlook—which, as we will see, had devastating consequences for the Christian mind.

DEMOCRACY COMES TO CHURCH

One way to bring these themes to life is by telling stories, which Nathan Hatch does remarkably well in *The Democratization of American Christianity*. His book will be our major source as we draw vignettes of some of the key figures in the Second Great Awakening.

A Politician for a Priest

Lorenzo Dow played a significant role in the growth of Methodism. He traveled more miles, preached to more people, and attracted larger crowds to camp meetings than any other preacher of his day. Cultivating a John-the-Baptist image, he sported long, loose hair, unkempt clothes, and a weather-beaten face. Theatrical in the extreme, he could hold an audience spellbound, bringing them to tears or laughter with his vivid stories. He was a master of the vernacular style in preaching and had a rollicking sense of humor—which he used especially to make fun of the genteel educated clergy.

The most striking thing about Dow, however, was that his religious views were thoroughly intertwined with his political views. He was a radical

Jeffersonian who would begin a sermon by quoting Tom Paine. He railed against "the galling yoke of Tyranny and priest-craft"—putting political oppression side by side with church authority. In one of his many pamphlets Dow wrote, "if all men are 'BORN EQUAL,' and endowed with unalienable RIGHTS by their CREATOR . . . then there can be no just reason . . . why he may or should not think, and judge, and act for himself in matters of religion."[4] Notice how he applies the words of the Declaration of Independence to the church. The title of the pamphlet was the *Rights of Man*, an Enlightenment phrase if there ever was one. Instead of offering a distinctively biblical perspective on the current political culture, many evangelicals virtually equated spiritual liberty with political liberty.[5]

Do you detect our themes emerging? The appeal to the emotions; the distrust of learning; the lack of critical distance from the secular philosophies of the day. In fact, the borrowing of political slogans was so common among the revivalists that when Tocqueville visited America, he wrote that you would "meet a politician where you expected to find a priest."[6]

Fetters for Our Children?

Another key person in the Second Great Awakening was John Leland, one of the most popular and controversial Baptists in the early nineteenth century. Leland, too, was a fervent Jeffersonian, taking the concept of self-government in *politics* to imply personal autonomy in *religion*. "We will be free, we will rule ourselves," he wrote. It is fitting that the inscription on Leland's tombstone praises him for protecting both civil and religious rights. (It reads, "Elder John Leland, who labored . . . to protect piety and to vindicate the civil and religious rights of men.")

Leland took the concept of religious autonomy so far that he was even opposed to parents teaching their own children. He warned that "it is very iniquitous [for a man] to bind the consciences of his children." And to show that he did not mean only adult children, he went on: "to make fetters for them before they are born, is very cruel."[7] This was a radically individualistic conception of the divine economy: He urged people to make a deliberate effort to free themselves from all natural authorities, whether church, state, teachers, or even the family.

Leland's rejection of religious authority led him to insist that the simple and the ignorant are actually *more* competent than the learned clergy to read and understand the Bible: "Is not the simple man, who makes nature and reason his study, a competent judge of things?"[8] Here we see an early expression of the Baptist concept of *soul competency*.

The troubling thing about all this is that Christianity was not shaping the culture so much as the culture was shaping Christianity. In the classic Protestant churches—Lutheran, Reformed, Anglican—corporate statements of faith such as creeds, confessions, and formal liturgies were considered necessary means of expressing communal identity and structuring communal worship. But now all theological formulations were denounced as nothing but man-made devices to keep the people "under the thumb of clerical tyrants."[9] As liberal individualism was taking root in politics, it was being uncritically applied to the churches, producing a highly individualistic and democratic ecclesiology. Modern values like autonomy and popular sovereignty became simply taken for granted in evangelical churches.

Half American

The Disciples of Christ, Churches of Christ, and "Christian" Churches merged to form the first indigenous American denomination, and one of its most fascinating figures was Elias Smith. Starting out as a Baptist minister, Smith fell under the spell of a radical Jeffersonian political writer—and then began translating the idea of popular sovereignty from the political sphere to the religious sphere. He resigned from his church as a manifesto of his liberty, and began denouncing formal religion of every kind.

In one pamphlet Smith wrote, "Many are *republicans* as to *government,* and yet are but half republicans, being in matters of religion still bound to a catechism, creed, covenant, or a superstitious priest." In other words, the American Revolution was only a halfway measure: We've thrown off political tyranny, now we must throw off ecclesiastical tyranny. (Smith is using the word *republican* to mean essentially what we would call *democratic*.) And he ended with this heady challenge: "Venture to be as independent in things of religion, as those which respect the government in which you live."[10]

Notice again how the paradigm is borrowed from politics. Similarly with Barton Stone (who founded the Disciples of Christ): When he broke away from the Presbyterian Church where he had been a pastor, he couldn't resist calling it the "declaration of our independence."[11] Thus the American Revolution was taken as a precedent for toppling authority and elitism of all kinds. A letter published in a "Christian" newspaper drew an explicit parallel: The conflict to free the Bible from "creeds and confessions," it said, was "perfectly analogous to the revolutionary war between Britain and America."[12] So deeply intertwined were democratic themes with biblical themes that any real political analysis was short-circuited.

Salvation on the Spot

To be fair, the borrowing did not go one way only. Key phrases like "inalienable rights" were actually first developed by religious dissenters. The difference in usage was this: Prior to the Revolution, slogans about rights and autonomy were used primarily by dissenting *groups* against coercive state churches. After the Revolution, the same slogans were used by dissenting *individuals* against their own churches.[13] Many began to declare the right of each person to reject historic churches, ancient creeds, and theological scholarship in order to decide strictly on his own what the Bible really teaches. For example, Elias Smith argued that each individual Christian had an "unalienable right" to follow "scripture wherever it leads him"—even if he ended by embracing positions "contrary to what the Reverend D.D.'s call Orthodoxy."[14]

What was emerging in the populist branch of evangelicalism was a new individualistic, even atomistic, view of the church. The shift can be illustrated by a new theology of conversion. In early New England, to become a member of a church, a candidate went through a long process of learning the Bible, the creeds, the Lord's Prayer, the Ten Commandments, the catechism. Then he or she was required to submit to an initial examination by the church elders and minister. After that, he had to present a credible narrative of his conversion experience before the entire congregation. Next came an investigation of the candidate's life and moral conduct: The townspeople would be questioned about his character and reputation. And so on. Only if the candidate passed these various tests was he or she received into the covenant. The whole process was "a kind of community rite."[15]

The conversion experience alone was expected to take years of struggle before a person sensed the inner testimony of the Holy Spirit, giving assurance of being forgiven and counted among the elect. Memoirs of the time show that some people suffered through years of haunting doubt and anxiety before gaining assurance of salvation.[16]

By contrast, the revivalists offered assurance of salvation on the spot. Instead of going through a lengthy process, the individual made a decision—and he was saved instantly.[17] Instead of being taught and tested by the church, the convert announced to others what he had experienced.

Eventually, of course, some procedures for membership had to be recreated, but the American mind had been altered. What need was there for things like catechism, liturgy, or sacraments if what counted for salvation was the crisis of conversion? The church was no longer an organic community into which one was received, and certainly not a spiritual authority to which one submitted. Rather, it was a collection of equal, autonomous individuals coming together by choice.

AMERICA THE NATURAL

If you have read chapter 4, that last sentence should set off loud bells in your mind: Populist evangelicals were sounding the same note as the early social contract theorists—Hobbes, Locke, and Rousseau—who regarded social structures as the creation of sheer choice, formed by the consent of autonomous individuals living in a "state of nature." (For more detail, see appendix 1.) After the Revolution, social contract theory gained enormous plausibility among Americans, because it seemed to describe what they were actually experiencing. Even Christians echoed similar themes in their views of the church.

Back when social contract theories were first proposed, the state of nature had been offered as a merely hypothetical scenario, a myth of how society might have originated in the misty past. After all, no one has actual experience of a state of nature; we are all born into a preexisting family, church, clan, village, nation. And yet, the settlement of the New World broke the norm, and actually seemed to fit the hypothetical paradigm. Here in America, some began to say, a genuine state of nature had existed; then a society of independent farmers and entrepreneurs had come together and formed a state through deliberation and choice—just as social contract theory prescribes. The people themselves had created the structures of government, distributing power as they wished.[18]

In short, in America it seemed that the state of nature had been real and historical. Here at last was a genuine natural equality among independent individuals. Here at last humanity had the chance to start over and build civil society from the ground up. For many Americans, the meaning of the Revolution was not just that they had eliminated a king but that they had started a new world from scratch. "We have it in our power to begin the world over again," Thomas Paine exulted. "A situation similar to the present has not happened since the days of Noah until now."[19] This was an astonishing comparison—as though in the New World, the earth itself had been swept clean so that human civilization could begin again.

For the first time, in other words, social contract theory seemed to fit people's actual experience instead of being merely hypothetical—and as a result, liberalism became the dominant political philosophy. As Wood explains, many Americans adopted an atomistic image of civil society based on "isolated and hostile individuals" who exist intrinsically "outside all governments" (that is, in a state of nature), and who then come together and create power by their own choices.

This was a new and exhilarating view of society. In the colonial period, the dominant political philosophy had been classical and Christian republicanism, which was highly communal. It called on individuals to submit to a set of preexisting, normative social structures—family, church, state—instituted and sanctioned by the Creator. Virtue consisted in accepting the responsibilities attached to one's prescribed role within the social organism, practicing self-sacrifice for the common good. But in the new liberalism, social structures were not instituted by God; they came into being only when individuals created them in order to protect their interests. The ethos of self-sacrifice was replaced by one of self-assertion and self-interest.[20]

LEAPFROGGING 1,800 YEARS

This was a momentous intellectual revolution, and soon the ideas were echoing throughout every sphere of society, including the churches. Instead of analyzing the new ideas from a biblical perspective, many evangelicals embraced them uncritically. If the people could form their own state, why not their own church as well? There was a widespread conviction that the rise of democracy was the most significant historical event in two millennia—a *novus ordo seclorum* ("new order of the ages," the phrase on the back of our dollar bills). And just as Americans felt they were establishing a "new order" politically, so many also hoped that they could start a new church. They would sweep away the rubble of the ages and start over from scratch, recreating the church of New Testament times.

There arose a conviction that Christianity had become hopelessly corrupted sometime after the apostolic age, and that the great task at hand was to leapfrog back over 1,800 years of history to restore the original purity of the primitive church. This is sometimes called the assumption of the "fallen" church—that the visible church has suffered a great falling away. Various groups located the fall at different points in history: Some placed it at the age of Constantine, with its merging of state and church; others placed it at the time the papacy was established; and so on. The common theme, however, was that the forms and practices that had developed over the ages within the church were not normative, nor even valuable. Instead they represented a process of corruption and degeneration in which the purity of primitive Christianity had been lost.[21] Things like creeds and ceremonies were merely human inventions that had crusted over the gospel like barnacles on a ship, which must be scraped away so that authentic New Testament worship could be restored.

This attitude is sometimes called primitivism, and it stands in striking contrast to the stance of Catholics, Orthodox, and Anglicans, who vie with one another even today in claiming an unbroken historical continuity back to the apostolic age, which is regarded as a mark of authenticity. It was the Reformation that first introduced the new theme—the idea that the past was a morass of corruption and that the true church could be found only by throwing out centuries of historical development to recover an earlier, purer pattern. For populist evangelicals, however, even the Reformers' work was inadequate; after all, they had still retained a host of churchly trappings like creeds and liturgies. Evangelicals wanted to go much further: They vigorously denounced creeds, confessions, ceremonies, and ecclesiastical structures as violations of Christian liberty that must be stripped away.

"The fresh start in the New World was seen as a providential chance to begin over again at a selected point in history where it was thought the Christian Church had gone astray," writes historian Sidney Mead.[22] Admittedly, this was more rhetoric than reality, for most evangelicals in fact retained the basic teachings of Christian orthodoxy spelled out in such statements as the Apostles' and the Nicene Creeds. Yet there was a heady sense that just as the American Revolution had started the world over again, so evangelicals would start the church over again—rebuilding it, plank by plank, on the New Testament alone.

On one hand, this kind of primitivism could be liberating: It put the individual on notice that he could no longer passively accept whatever his church taught, but had to conduct his own independent study of the Bible. The focus on the early church also inspired a wealth of empirical study of the New Testament's original linguistic and cultural context. On the other hand, however, the cavalier rejection of the past stripped the church of the rich resources of centuries' worth of theological reflection, Scriptural meditation, and spiritual experience. It inculcated an attitude that there was nothing to be gained from grappling with the thought of the great minds of the past—Augustine and Tertullian, Bernard of Clairvaux and Thomas Aquinas, Martin Luther and John Calvin. It was an approach doomed, almost by definition, to anti-intellectualism and theological shallowness.

I am not making a theological point about whether tradition should be accorded religious authority, but only a historical point about the effects that an anti-historical attitude had on the life of the mind. "The greatest danger besetting American Evangelical Christianity is the danger of anti-intellectualism," warned Charles Malik at the dedication of the Billy Graham Center at Wheaton College. Evangelicals are in a hurry to preach the gospel, Malik said, but "they have no idea of the infinite value of spending years of leisure in con-

versing with the greatest minds and souls of the past, and thereby ripening and
sharpening and enlarging their powers of thinking."[23] This cavalier rejection
of the past had roots in the great Awakenings. Evangelicals were eagerly "liberating" themselves from their own Christian heritage, without recognizing
how impoverished this left them.

CHRISTIANS FOR JEFFERSON

Why did these ideas become so popular? Why did this atomistic, anti-historical conception of the church spread like wildfire? In many ways, evangelicals
were caught up in the great transformations taking place in the culture around
them. Ideas take hold when they seem to match people's experience, and the
most common experience in America was that of an expanding democracy—
in both the political and the economic spheres.

First, the political sphere. Prior to the Revolution, as we have mentioned,
most colonials held the classical republican view of society: Social institutions
like family, church, and state were thought of as organic wholes, each with a
common good transcending the interests of its individual members. In this context, certain words had a completely different meaning from the way we understand them today. For example, virtue was primarily public, not private: It
meant fulfilling the responsibilities laid on the individual through his or her role
within a social group—husband and wife, parent and child, pastor and laity,
magistrate and citizen. (Think of the way Paul ends many of his New
Testament letters with instructions to each of these groups.) Liberty was
defined in public terms as well, as the right of each social institution to govern
itself. Leadership was an "office" with divine sanction; and the person in office
was called upon to be "disinterested," sacrificing his personal interests and selfish ambitions in order to protect and promote the common good of the group.

As we know all too well, such sacrifice and selflessness are not typical of
human nature, and so classical republicanism was typically hierarchical and
elitist: Only certain classes of persons were qualified by birth, breeding, and gender to practice the high ideal of disinterested leadership.[24] The great masses were
considered hopelessly self-interested, fractious, and incapable of self-government.
This seemed to accord with the biblical teaching that people are prone to sin,
making civil order difficult to maintain. As a result, a kind of Christian republicanism was widespread among the Calvinists who predominated in colonial
America. Wood even calls it a "secularized version" of Puritanism.[25]

After the Revolution, however, many Americans began to reject classical
republicanism (represented politically by the Federalists) and to replace it with
modern liberalism (represented by the Jeffersonians). Based on social contract

theory, liberalism regarded civil society as a voluntary gathering of individuals. There was no organic "whole" beyond the individuals involved. As a result, there was no common good either—no purposes or values for the group beyond the discrete aims of individual members—and thus no need for a leadership class responsible for *protecting* the common good. With this logic, liberals rejected the elitism of classical republicanism.

They also began to attack the biblical doctrine of sin because it was now associated in their minds with the idea that people were incapable of governing themselves, which had provided a rationale for elitism and paternalistic government.[26] In place of the old elitism, liberals promoted a new confidence that ordinary people are perfectly capable of making rational, constructive choices for themselves, if only they are given their freedom. Liberalism denied that government was a locus of public virtue, called upon to execute Justice; instead, the state was a product of individual choices—which meant its worth was merely functional, measured in terms of how effectively it facilitated the individual pursuit of happiness and prosperity.[27]

Of course, these new ideas took hold only gradually, so that republican and liberal ideas were often combined in various blends. Yet, against this backdrop, it is easier to understand why the populist branch of evangelicalism spread so quickly. Most *opponents* of the revival movement, whether orthodox Calvinists or Unitarians, tended to be Federalist in political philosophy, holding to the older view of classical republicanism. By contrast, *supporters* of the revival movement, especially Methodists, Baptists, and Disciples, tended to be Jeffersonian, sharing its deep aversion to elitism and its trust of the common folk. They knew that Jefferson himself was a deist, who took a scissors to the New Testament and snipped out all the supernatural elements, leaving only Jesus' moral teaching intact; yet they supported Jefferson's presidential bid in 1800. Their attitude was summed up by Samuel Miller, an evangelical Presbyterian, who announced that he would "much rather have Mr. Jefferson President of the United States than an aristocratic Christian." Isaac Backus, a leader of the New England Baptists, even regarded Jefferson's election as a harbinger of the millennium.[28]

In this context, it is understandable why popular evangelicalism rejected the older conception of the church as organic and hierarchical (reflecting classical republicanism), in favor the church as atomistic and egalitarian (reflecting liberalism). This is sometimes called a believers-church or free-church ecclesiology, and it shares the liberal conception of social institutions as merely collections of their members, with no overarching organic "whole." Noll speaks of "the triumph of the believers' church, defined as the sum of its members, whose own choices brought it into existence."[29] Church authority was no longer thought of as a spiritual gift conferred by God through the office itself, but merely as a functional difference among equals.

NO TRAFFIC COP

This egalitarian revolution in *political* philosophy was supported by an *economic* revolution occurring at the same time. Throughout the vast scope of human history, most societies have lived at the subsistence level, with some 90 percent of the people's labor being required just to produce food for the community. This gave rise to an organic view of society, focusing on the survival of the whole rather than the liberty of the individual. With little defense against bad weather and poor harvests, "the survival of the whole was clearly linked to the diligence of each member," says one historian. And "with so many lives always at risk, concern for the public good predominated." The precariousness of life justified authoritarian control of economic relations.[30]

With the rise of capitalism and the Industrial Revolution, however, for the first time many people were freed from the fear of want and hunger—a truly historic benchmark. What's more, the new economic network crisscrossing the country was being created by ordinary men and women: farmers, craftsmen, traders, merchants, shopkeepers, cattle drovers. It began to seem that, contrary to the old Calvinist pessimism concerning human nature, ordinary people were quite capable of making rational choices to advance their own interests. And when they did, lo, they created wealth all around. Adam Smith's *The Wealth of Nations* was only the clearest expression of what by that time had become a common "discovery"—that ordinary people, operating freely and autonomously, were quite competent and capable after all.

Astonishingly, by the middle of the eighteenth century in the larger American colonies, per capita wealth was far higher than anywhere else in the world.[31] There was no longer any need for an authoritarian government to stand as traffic cop over limited resources. In fact, opportunities for enterprise were growing at a much more rapid rate than the government's capacity to oversee them. "It was increasingly clear that no one was really in charge of this gigantic, enterprising, restless nation," writes Wood. And yet, order seemed to emerge spontaneously as individuals pursued their own self-interest. "The harmony emerging out of such chaos was awesome to behold, and speaker after speaker and writer after writer commented on it."[32] In this economic climate, radical theories about individual liberty suddenly acquired plausibility. They seemed to make sense of the real conditions of life that people were experiencing.

Against this backdrop, we can better understand why Christianity became a matter of "making a decision for Christ." The focus was on individual choice, not on fitting into an inherited tradition. It is no coincidence that the populist branch of evangelicalism flowered in the age of Thomas Jefferson in politics and Adam Smith in economics.[33] People's experience in these other realms made them open to a religious message that rejected elitism and authority, while championing the right of ordinary people to assert themselves and make their own decisions. Instead of critically challenging the emerging culture of modernity, populist evangelicals were reshaping Christianity to fit the categories of the modern experience.

SELF-MADE PEOPLE

We can make this more concrete with a word picture suggested by sociologist Gary Thomas. In post-Revolutionary America, Thomas says, a Calvinist minister might stand in the pulpit on a Sunday morning and preach to his congregation that they were morally corrupt by nature and slaves to sin, that they did not have the capability to choose salvation, that God had chosen some and rejected others, and that there was nothing they could do about it. The trouble is, this Calvinist message would not fit the congregation's actual experience. They were no longer born into a static society, where people had no choice about their status, and where virtue was defined in terms of the duties attached to one's unchanging station in life. Instead, they were active participants in a mobile society, which they were creating by their own choices. They were self-made men and women in an expanding economy where success rested largely on their own choices, drive, and ambition. A Calvinist message, says Thomas, "would run counter to the individual's self-determinism in the everyday life of market and polity," and as a result, the sermon simply would not seem plausible. It would not make sense.

On the other hand, a traveling Methodist revivalist might ride into town and address the same people that night in an open-air revival meeting. He might preach that they had the power to choose God, that their salvation hung upon their own decision, and that salvation was open to any who chose to call upon the Lord. Given their everyday experience, this message would make sense. An Arminian message and a free-church ecclesiology fit with their experience as independent, autonomous actors in a democratic polity and an expanding capitalist economy.[34]

This explains why historians often characterize evangelicalism as a quintessentially modern religion. At first blush, that claim might seem implausible, running contrary to the typical stereotype that Christianity is a conservative, even reactionary, force in Western society. But consider: Though populist evangelicalism preached the age-old message of sin and salvation, at the same time its spirituality and ecclesiology were thoroughly modern—anti-historical, anti-authoritarian, individualistic, and voluntaristic (hinging on the individual's decision). Thus Wood writes that "by challenging clerical unity, shattering the communal churches, and cutting people loose from ancient religious bonds," the religious revivals became "a massive defiance of traditional authority."[35] On a similar note, Michael Gauvreau says evangelicalism actually helped to assert "the independence of the individual from the social constraints of the old order" while promoting "a rival vision of community based upon the free association of equal, autonomous individuals."[36] In short, evangelicalism did not provide a critical stance from which to evaluate the new developments in politics and economics, but was itself in many ways a powerful force for modernization.[37]

PREACHER, PERFORMER, STORYTELLER

The new model of human community called forth a new model of leadership as well. When Richard Hofstadter wrote his Pulitzer Prize–winning book *Anti-Intellectualism in American Life*, whom do you suppose he highlighted as Exhibit A? Right: evangelicals. Tracing the history of revivalism, much as we have done, he concluded that one of its most significant results was a new style of leadership. The populist branch of the evangelical movement cast aside an older model of leaders as holy men and instead gave rise to leaders who were entrepreneurs—pragmatic marketers who were willing to use whatever worked to get conversions. Hofstadter quoted the evangelist Dwight L. Moody, who once said, "It makes no difference how you get a man to God, provided you get him there." And the Congregationalist divine Washington Gladden said his theology was "hammered out on the anvil for daily use in the pulpit. The pragmatic test was the only one that could be applied to it: 'Will it work?'"[38] Long before pragmatism was developed into a full-blown American philosophy (see chapter 8), it had already been formulated and practiced by evangelical leaders.

Revivalism altered the seminaries as well: "The Puritan ideal of the minister as an intellectual and educational leader was steadily weakened in the face of the evangelical ideal of the minister as a popular crusader and exhorter," Hofstadter writes.[39] Theological education began to focus more on practical techniques and less on intellectual training.

Even the style of preaching was transformed: Expository preaching on biblical texts gave way to topical sermons on the felt needs of the congregation. "Earlier, a minister had been expected to provide his congregation with a comprehensive intellectual [theological] system," explains historian Donald Scott. The traditional sermon was essentially a formal argument—moving point by point through a logical progression in order to show that a particular doctrine was grounded in Scripture, then concluding with an application. But now congregations no longer expected to be taught theology; they wanted a minister who would move them emotionally and give them practical guidance for daily living. The pastor was no longer "expected to articulate a general intellectual structure by which life in all its facets could be comprehended." Instead, "the pastoral role had become almost exclusively a devotional and confessional one."[40]

Scott offers a striking example in a well-known sermon by the famous Congregationalist preacher Henry Ward Beecher, titled "How to Become a Christian." Beecher portrayed conversion as a simple step that required absolutely no doctrinal knowledge or assent. The sermon consisted almost entirely of an extended word picture of Jesus inviting the hungry to eat at a banquet. Don't "wait for somebody to explain it," Beecher urged his listeners. "Try it yourself today." The sermon was virtually free of theological content, focusing on the pragmatic appeal to simply "try it."[41]

Increasingly, the populist preacher became a performer, stringing together stories and anecdotes, often from his own life. This method engaged the audience's emotions, while subtly enhancing the speaker's own image by highlighting his own ministry and spiritual experiences.

CELEBRITY STYLE

The outcome of all this was the rise of personality cults, the celebrity system that has become so entrenched in evangelicalism. The traditional clergy had earned authority by going through a long process of training and certification; they were ordained by a recognized religious body and spoke on its behalf. But the leaders of the populist evangelical movement made an end run around denominational structures and built movements based on sheer personality—on their ability to move people and win their confidence. Starting with Whitefield, as we saw earlier, they became Christian celebrities: Their authority came not from having met accepted standards of education or training but from their magnetism and ability to gather a large following. As one account puts it, the revivalists went forth "armed only with a sense of divine calling and the sheer talent of being able to move people," relying on little besides "presence and charisma."[42] No wonder Hofstadter could say that "the 'star' system prevailed in religion before it reached the theater."[43]

These self-appointed leaders tended to be shrewd entrepreneurs and talented entertainers, adept at arousing (or manipulating) people's emotions. They honed the sermon into an effective "recruiting device,"[44] using language peppered with provincial expressions and colloquialisms. They were also quick to make use of the growing technology of print journalism to publish vast quantities of newspapers, books, and pamphlets, which resulted in many becoming well-known far beyond any local congregation.

The local rootedness of the traditional clergy had provided at least some measure of genuine accountability: Their character was known and tested in ongoing, long-term contact with a regular congregation. By contrast, the evangelist addressed mass audiences made up of strangers, who could not possibly judge his character by personal knowledge. He could dazzle them with sheer image-making and marketing hype. Many evangelical leaders became "successful, polished politicians," says Hofstadter, "well versed in the secular arts of manipulation."[45]

IN PR WE TRUST

Some evangelicals even began to speak as though revivals could be produced simply by applying the right techniques in a near-mechanical fashion. During the first Awakening and earlier stages of the second, most regarded revivals as movements of the Spirit that could not be predicted or controlled; as a result, no one even considered using special techniques to spark them. Many of the preachers had been laboring in the pulpit for years when revival suddenly erupted, surprising them as much as anyone else. Jonathan Edwards spoke for many when he called the Awakening a "Surprizing Work of God."[46]

As the Second Great Awakening proceeded, however, preachers began to employ methods calculated to pressure people into making a decision. The most aggressive was Charles Finney, a lawyer-turned-evangelist who toned down the revivalist style and added a note of rational persuasion to make it palatable to educated, middle-class audiences. His innovations also included several high-pressure tactics, however, that were to become quite controversial. Finney "had a flair for pulpit drama," Hofstadter comments. "But his greatest physical asset was his intense, fixating, electrifying, madly prophetic eyes,"[47] which he used to great effect in confronting sinners by name in his revival meetings. That was one of his special tricks. Another was the use of the "anxious seat" at the front of the crowd: Those who felt convicted of sin were urged to come forward and sit on a bench, a technique that focused everyone's attention on them, creating pressure to reach a resolution (an early form of the altar call, an innovation that also began around this time).

By coming down to the front, converts became visible—which meant for the first time they could be counted. Not surprisingly, the practice of counting converts only fed the results-oriented mentality. Already in 1817 a critic of the revivalists could write, "They measure the progress of religion by the numbers, who flock to their standard; not by the prevalence of faith, and piety, justice and charity."[48]

Finney insisted that revivals had to be carefully staged. "A revival is not a miracle," he stated flatly; it is merely "the result of the right use of the appropriate means." Using the right methods, he said, a revival can be produced just as certainly as farmers using scientific methods can "raise grain and a crop of wheat." His recommendations included techniques such as holding "protracted" meetings (nightly gatherings for several weeks), ensuring good ventilation, making effective use of music, and so on, in order to engineer mass conversions. One of Finney's famous sayings was, "Religion is a work of man"—and clearly he regarded *revivals* of religion as a work of man as well.[49]

Supporters said Finney was merely pointing out that a revival must use the means God had ordained. And God apparently blessed his efforts: Finney was instrumental in the conversion of thousands of people, in addition to inspiring a surge of social reform movements. But his "new measures," as they were called, aroused considerable opposition and were ultimately rejected by many of the other revivalists, especially among his fellow Presbyterians. In the face of criticism, his defense was largely pragmatic: "The results justify my methods."[50] That same pragmatic attitude lives on today, as Christian organizations build large internal PR machines relying heavily on the latest secular marketing and publicity techniques. The natural outcome of this mechanical mentality, both then and now, is a tendency to measure success by numbers and impact, instead of by the minister's personal virtue and faithfulness to the gospel.

PULLING STRINGS

One of the dangers in personality cults is that they lead easily to demagoguery. The revivalists were often strong-willed leaders who, ironically, ended up exercising an even higher degree of dogmatism and control than pastors in traditional denominations, whom they denounced. A critic of the Awakening at the time, a Reformed theologian named John Nevin, argued that the revivalists' "high-sounding phrases" of liberty and free inquiry were merely masks for a new form of domination. Though they called loudly for "liberty," he said, most evangelical groups pressed every member into "thinking its particular notions, shouting its shibboleths and passwords, dancing its religious hornpipes, and reading the Bible only through its theological goggles." Nevin compared these restrictions to "so many wires, that lead back at last into the hands of a few leading spirits, enabling them to wield a true hierarchical despotism over all who are thus brought within their power."[51] Thus, ironically, the magnetic leaders who encouraged people to break away from traditional theological structures often ended up becoming authoritarian leaders within their own groups, sometimes verging on demagoguery.

Yet this was an almost inevitable result of having revamped the role of the Christian leader. The traditional minister relied upon the institutional authority of his office to influence his flock. But since the revivalists rejected the notion of institutional authority, all they had to rely on was personal charisma and power. Thus Henry Ward Beecher once insisted that sermons should aim not to impart knowledge so much as to gain "direct power on men's minds and heart." As one historian writes, the minister became not so much a spiritual teacher as "a personality exercising power."[52]

NOT A ROGUES' GALLERY

How do the patterns we have traced throw light on evangelicalism today? Not long ago, I met a young man who had moved to Washington, D.C., as part of the advance team for an event to be hosted by a major evangelist, scheduled to take place two years from then. Two years? I thought I must have heard wrong. Yes, he assured me, the speaker's organization sent out full-time, paid staffers a full two years in advance to set up the event. I could not help thinking how the earliest revivalists first began orchestrating events a year or two in advance. The pattern was set right from the beginning. Contemporary practices become easier to understand when we trace their emergence through history.

How should we evaluate the enduring impact of the populist branch of evangelicalism? On one hand, with their simple language and emotional appeals, the revivalists were wildly successful in Christianizing broad segments of the population. They imparted a sense of dignity and independence to the laity. "A compelling theme in popular preaching throughout this era was the Jeffersonian notion that people should shake off all servile prejudice and learn to prove things for themselves," writes Hatch.[53] The revivalists' deep concern for the poor and the downtrodden continues to inspire respect in all who know of their work.

Even critics have been turned around. Catholic writer Ronald Knox was highly critical when he began research on his book *Enthusiasm* (an older derogatory term applied to the revivalist movement). At the outset, he intended the book to be a "broadside, a trumpet-blast," a "rogues' gallery" of disheveled, eccentric, wild-eyed preachers sowing confusion. But to his great surprise, as he came to know his subjects—great men like Wesley and Whitefield—he could not help respecting their sincerity and single-mindedness, their commitment to truth, their concern for simple folk. By the time Knox finally finished writing *Enthusiasm,* he had painted a highly positive portrayal of the early evangelicals.[54] Afterward he even translated the Catholic Bible into more accessible English, in the hope of inspiring a little more "enthusiasm" among Catholics!

On the other hand, as America moved beyond being a nation of settlers and farmers and small towns, a "religion of the heart" was not enough to respond to the intellectual challenges emerging in the nineteenth century, especially Darwinism and higher criticism. Later evangelists like Dwight L. Moody and Billy Sunday tried to counter the new ideas with sheer revivalist fervor. The fervor, however, began to take on a brittle, defensive edge. And the more Christians sought to prop up their faith with mere emotional intensity, the more it appeared to be an irrational belief that belonged in the upper story of private experience.

Unable to answer the great intellectual questions of the day, many conservative Christians turned their back on mainstream culture and developed a fortress mentality. This led to the fundamentalist era of the early twentieth century, when separatism was adopted as a positive strategy, and Christianity was reduced to the jargon of a distinct subculture. "The result was a near-abdication of any voice in academe at a time when the intellectual foundations of Judeo-Christian theism were being questioned as never before," writes historian Joel Carpenter. "Fundamentalist leaders were caught unprepared to respond to the critiques of scientific naturalism, whether applied to natural history [Darwinism] or the study of the Bible [higher criticism]."[55]

This is not to overlook the fundamentalist movement's enormous vitality and worthy accomplishments. In its zeal to protect the basic teachings of historic Christian orthodoxy, it founded large numbers of schools, seminaries, radio programs, youth organizations, Bible study groups, missions, and so on. Yet fundamentalism tended to be marked by an attitude of defiant defensiveness against mainstream culture.

Today evangelicalism is still emerging from the fundamentalist era—still working to regain a more holistic understanding of the Lordship of Christ over all of life and culture.[56] In recent decades, evangelicals have moved up the social and economic ladder. We are more likely to be educated and have high incomes. Yet I would suggest that in our churches and parachurch ministries, we still encounter many of the basic patterns from an earlier age—the tendency to define religion primarily in emotional terms; the anti-creedal, anti-historical attitude that ignores the theological riches of the past; the assertion of individual choice as the final determinant of belief; the atomistic view of the church as merely a collection of individuals who happen to believe the same things; the preference for social activism over intellectual reflection. Most of all, perhaps, evangelicalism still produces a celebrity model of leadership—men who are entrepreneurial and pragmatic, who deliberately manipulate their listeners' emotions, who subtly enhance their own image through self-serving personal anecdotes, whose leadership style within their own congregation or parachurch ministry tends to be imperious and domineering, who calculate success in terms of results, and who are willing to employ the latest secular techniques to boost numbers.[57]

Through the lens of history we can see these patterns more clearly, which helps us to identify the way they persist in our own churches and parachurch groups. "Today we rail against the celebrity system within Christianity, thinking it was imported from Hollywood culture," a university student recently said to me. "But when we look back historically, we find that the star system began in Christian circles." Exactly. Only by recognizing the source of various trends can we craft the tools to correct them. We need to diagnose the way historical patterns continue to shape the way we operate our churches and ministries. History holds up a mirror to the way we think and act today.

RISE OF THE SOVEREIGN SELF

The populist branch represents the dominant form of evangelicalism in North America in our day. "We are now entering a new chapter of evangelical history," Carpenter wrote in 1997, "in which the pentecostal-charismatic movement is quickly supplanting the fundamentalist-conservative one as the most influential evangelical impulse today." By *pentecostal-charismatic,* he meant populist, experiential, anti-creedal.[58] Especially in some megachurches and seeker churches, the evangelical worship style is becoming less doctrinal, more experiential, more geared to contemporary tastes.

This same worship style is even crossing religious boundaries. "We are all evangelicals now," says a provocative new book by sociologist Alan Wolfe. What he means is that the evangelical pattern is becoming dominant in all religions in America—a pattern he describes as "more personalized and individualistic, less doctrinal and devotional." Evangelicalism is growing "theologically broad to the point of incoherence," he adds; we may even be witnessing "the gradual disappearance of doctrine."[59]

This style may not be so much distinctively Christian as it is distinctly American, Wolfe says—in the sense that its individualism and experientialism align closely with the modern American ethos.[60] In many churches, the individual alone with his Bible is regarded as the core of the Christian life. A poll taken in the mid-1990s by sociologist Wade Clark Roof found that 54 percent of evangelical Christians said "to be alone and meditate" was more important than "to worship with others." And more than half agreed that "churches and synagogues have lost the real spiritual part of religion." Roof concluded that "the real story of American religious life in this half-century is the *rise of a new sovereign self* that defines and sets limits on the very meaning of the divine."[61] In other words, instead of challenging modern liberalism's notion of the autonomous self, evangelicalism tends to reflect the same theme in religious language.

As Wolfe puts it, "In every aspect of the religious life, American faith has met American culture—and American culture has triumphed."[62] Evangelicalism has largely given in to the two-story division that renders religion a matter of individual experience, with little or no cognitive content.

If we hope to retain what is best in the evangelical heritage, we must also soberly assess its weaknesses, praying for wisdom and strength to bring about reformation. And one of the best places to seek help is from other resources within evangelicalism itself—from its more scholarly branch. In the next chapter, we will meet some of the intellectual leaders in the history of evangelicalism—teachers and professors who sought to shape the thought of the entire nation from their positions at universities and seminaries. To diagnose what happened to the evangelical mind, let's take a closer look at those who did the most to cultivate it. Did they succeed in breaking out of the two-story division of truth? What resources did they develop that could help us today in developing a Christian worldview?

11

EVANGELICALS'
TWO-STORY TRUTH

Religious forces accepted a division of labour;
they were boxed in.
MARTIN MARTY[1]

Several years ago, a lively controversy flared up in the pages of the *Christian Scholar's Review* over the correct way to define evangelicalism. Which groups are included? Who should be allowed to lay claim to the label?

Two historians faced off against each other, while others cheered along the sidelines. On one side was Donald Dayton, who traced a "Methodist" lineage for evangelicalism. Starting with the Reformation, this line moves through European pietism, John Wesley in England, the Great Awakenings in America, through Dwight L. Moody to Billy Graham—with a focus on individual conversion and the subjective experience of faith. By now, you recognize this pattern: Dayton was identifying evangelicalism with the populist branch described in the previous two chapters.

Taking the other side in the journal debate was George Marsden, who traced a "Presbyterian" lineage for evangelicalism. Starting with the Reformation, this line moves through Protestant Orthodoxy, to the Old School Presbyterians, especially Charles Hodge and B. B. Warfield at Princeton, to J. Gresham Machen at Westminster Seminary. The focus of this line has been on theological orthodoxy and biblical authority.[2]

Which definition of evangelicalism is correct? Answer: Both are. As we mentioned at the outset, historically the evangelical movement has consisted of two wings, one populist and the other scholarly—and we need to be familiar with both in order to craft an effective strategy for reviving the evangelical mind in our own day. Surveying the populist wing revealed the roots of long-standing patterns of anti-intellectualism. Surveying the scholarly wing will reveal why even a rational approach was not fully successful in confronting the challenges from secular academia. Yet we will also discover important resources within our heritage for reviving a Christian worldview in our day.

The scholarly wing of evangelicalism actually included more than the "Presbyterian" line that Marsden traced. As the decades passed, the populist wing of evangelicalism outgrew its adolescent stage of rebuffing all religious authority and began giving rise to its own scholars. Alongside fiery preachers there appeared distinguished professors, teaching at seminaries and universities. Together with stalwarts among the Old School Presbyterians, they labored to develop moral and political philosophies; honed apologetics arguments against Deists, Unitarians, and infidels; responded to the latest scientific theories; and in general sought to relate the evangelical faith to the intellectual currents of the day.

And to a large degree, they were successful. The scholarly wing of evangelicalism, says one historian, became "the most powerful shaping influence" in nineteenth-century American culture.[3] The Presbyterians alone established forty-nine universities prior to the Civil War—more than any other denomination—thereby dominating American education. Though in terms of sheer numbers they were quickly overtaken by the populist wing, in terms of influencing American public life they were far more effective. "Conservative Presbyterians were zealous campaigners against the anti-intellectualism" pervasive during this period, says one historian. They "considered themselves missionaries to the American intellect."[4]

What can we learn today by getting to know these "missionaries to the intellect"? In every age, Christians have sought to address the issues of their day by "translating" timeless biblical truths into contemporary language. They have commended the ancient faith by using up-to-date terms understood by the people around them. The trick is to find a language that communicates effectively *without* compromising the gospel in the process. How well did nineteenth-century evangelicals succeed at this task? What philosophical language did they adopt, and did it compromise their spiritual message? What enduring legacy did they leave for us today?

SCOTCH TIP

To give philosophical expression to their faith, most evangelicals of the eighteenth and nineteenth centuries called on the services of a philosophy imported from Scotland called Common Sense realism, which was immensely popular across the entire intellectual landscape in America at the time. It was embraced by both supporters and critics of the Awakenings. It was held by Unitarians and other theological liberals. It was even adopted by deists (who denied all supernatural elements in the Bible) like Thomas Jefferson. "The Scottish Enlightenment was probably the most potent single tradition in the American Enlightenment," concludes one account.[5] Common Sense realism has even been called "the official philosophy of nineteenth-century America."[6]

How many of you know about this aspect of our history? When I was studying philosophy at the university, we read about the great European thinkers—Descartes, Kant, Hegel, and so on. But we never read about the philosophy that was dominant for more than a century in our own country.[7] This is an astonishing oversight, and crucial gap to fill in, if we want to understand our own history.

Common Sense realism was imported to America by John Witherspoon, who left Scotland in 1768 to become president of Princeton University (then called the College of New Jersey). From Princeton, Common Sense philosophy spread throughout the academic world of the day. "It became an *evangelical worldview* that permeated every classroom and which eventually influenced hundreds of ministers, countless schoolmasters, and dozens of practicing scientists and physicians," says one historian. It "became practically identified with the evangelical point of view."[8]

If this was nothing less than the "evangelical worldview" for such a long time, then certainly we should know more about it. What was this philosophy and why was it so popular?

Common Sense realism was crafted by the Scottish philosopher Thomas Reid in response to the radical skepticism of a fellow Scot, David Hume (discussed briefly in chapter 3). In fact, Hume's skepticism was so radical that Immanuel Kant famously said it roused him from his "dogmatic slumbers." It seems to have roused Reid as well, because he aimed his own philosophical efforts at refuting Hume and formulating a new foundation for knowledge. The way to avoid skepticism, Reid proposed, is to realize that some knowledge is "self-evident"—that is, it is forced upon us simply by the way human nature is constituted. As a result, no one really doubts or denies it. It is part of immediate, undeniable experience.

For example, no one really doubts that he or she exists (not in practice, at least). No one doubts that the material world is real (we all look both ways before crossing the street). Nor do we doubt our inner experiences like memories or pain. (If I say I have a headache, you don't ask, *How do you know?*) If anyone does deny these basic facts, we call him insane—or a philosopher. And even philosophers deny them only theoretically: Hume himself said that, after reasoning his way to radical skepticism in the solitude of his study, he would clear his mind by playing a good game of backgammon with his friends.[9]

In practical life, everyone has to simply take a good many propositions for granted. As Reid put it, "The statesman continues to plod, the soldier to fight, and the merchant to export and import, without being in the least moved by the demonstrations that have been offered of the non-existence of those things about which they are so seriously employed."[10]

The core claim of Common Sense realism was that these undeniable or self-evident truths of experience provide a firm foundation upon which to build the entire edifice of knowledge—like the foundation of a house. (By "common sense," Reid did not mean practicality or horse sense, as we use the term today, but rather those truths known by universal human experience—*common* to all humanity.) Most nineteenth-century thinkers included among the self-evident truths many of the basic teachings of Christianity, such as God's existence, His goodness, and His creation of the world. These were taken to be self-evident to reasonable people.

Having laid a foundation in self-evident truths, how did Common Sense realism build the house on top? For this task, Reid recommended the work of Francis Bacon, a seventeenth-century thinker often credited with establishing the inductive method of science.[11] The reason earlier ages got their science all wrong, Bacon had said, was that they deduced their ideas about nature from metaphysical speculations. Genuine science must start not with philosophy but with facts, then reason strictly by induction. "Taught by Lord Bacon," Reid wrote, people had at last been freed from the treadmill of medieval "deductivism," and set on "the road to the knowledge of nature's works."[12]

To a wide range of Americans, this linkage of Common Sense realism with Baconian induction seemed an unbeatable combination for countering the skepticism of Hume and other radical Enlightenment philosophers. Soon it was being applied to virtually every field of thought: science, political philosophy, moral theory, and even biblical interpretation (hermeneutics). Its central concept was even enshrined in the Declaration of Independence: "We hold these truths to be self-evident." Where did the idea of self-evident truths come from? From Common Sense realism.[13]

To evaluate these ideas, let's first zero in on how the Baconian method was applied to biblical studies and various other disciplines. Then we will back up for a wider perspective on Common Sense realism as a whole, focusing on how it has continued to be developed by Christians right up to our own day. I will not be attempting in any way to give a comprehensive description of these ideas or the figures who propounded them. Our goal here is to draw out key patterns that contributed to the decline of the evangelical mind, in order to get a better handle on how to bring about intellectual revival in our own day.

THE SCIENCE OF SCRIPTURE

What did Baconianism mean when applied to biblical interpretation? For Bacon, standing at the dawn of the scientific revolution, the main enemy had been Aristotelian philosophy. Thus he taught that science must start by clearing the decks—by liberating the mind from all metaphysical speculation, all received notions of truth, all the accumulated superstition of the ages. "With minds washed clean from opinions" (in his words), we sit down before the facts "as little children" and let the facts speak for themselves—then compile them inductively into a system.[14]

The very notion that facts can "speak for themselves" would send contemporary philosophers into babbling fits about *paradigm shifts* and *conceptual frameworks*. Yet this positivistic approach to knowledge became a powerful ideal among virtually all Enlightenment thinkers. Applied to biblical interpretation, the Baconian method stipulated that the first step is to free our minds from all historical theological formulations (Calvinist, Lutheran, Anglican, or whatever). With minds washed clean from merely human speculations, we confront the biblical text as a collection of "facts" that speak for themselves—and then compile individual verses inductively into a theological system. Statements in Scripture were treated as analogous to facts in nature, knowable in exactly the same way.

Among the most influential to embrace the Baconian method were the Old School Presbyterians at Princeton. For example, James Alexander said, "The theologian should proceed in his investigation precisely as the chemist or the botanist proceeds"—which "is the method which bears the name of Bacon."[15] Charles Hodge even compared the propositions in the Bible with the "oceans, continents, islands, mountains and rivers" studied by geography. That's why he could say: "The Bible is to the theologian what nature is to the man of science. It is his store-house of facts."[16]

It is important to realize that the term *science* had not yet acquired the narrow, specialized meaning it has today. Instead, it meant any form of systematized knowledge (Latin for *knowledge* is *scientia*), so that the term was applied even to subjects like politics, morality, and theology ("the queen of the sciences"). This explains why so many clergymen at the time assumed that a scientific method like Bacon's could be applied to theology. It did not necessarily mean they were selling out to scientism, as some critics have suggested.

It did mean, however, that they were seeking to meet the challenge of modern science in part by arguing that theology followed the same inductive method. In other words, they were trying to co-opt the Enlightenment. After the American Revolution, all traditional and inherited authorities were discredited as "tyranny" and "oppression." The only public authority to which one could credibly appeal was science because, ideally at least, science was democratic. By following the scientific method, one was not supposed to bow to any established authority; each individual could examine the evidence and decide for himself. Applied to theology, the Baconian method claimed that the Bible was accessible to everyone who cared to look at its "facts"—an idea that appealed to a newly born democratic culture.[17]

CAMPBELL'S RATIONALIST SOUP

Let's flesh out some of these themes through a personal vignette. Few embraced Baconian hermeneutics more enthusiastically than members of the Restoration movement (Disciples of Christ, Churches of Christ, and the "Christian" Church). In fact, theologians within this tradition continue to debate the merits of the method even today. When I ran an Internet search on "Baconian" and "hermeneutics" a few years ago, half a dozen articles from the *Restoration Quarterly* popped up. So we're talking about a question that is still a live issue.

One of the founders of the Restoration movement was Alexander Campbell. Born in Ireland, Campbell underwent an intense conversion experience as a young man. After weeks of wandering the fields alone in prayer, he writes, "finally, after many strugglings, I was enabled to put my trust in the Saviour, and to *feel* my reliance on him as the only Saviour of sinners."[18] Several years later, he set off for America and began to preach.

In many respects, then, Campbell was as evangelical as any of the revivalists we have discussed. Like them, he treated the American Revolution as a paradigm for inaugurating a new age within the church, insisting that America's "political regeneration" gave her the responsibility to lead an "ecclesiastical renovation" as well. Thoroughly anti-clerical and populist, he called for "the inalienable right of all laymen to examine the sacred writings for themselves." He even favored abolishing the traditional distinction between clergy and laity: "Liberty is no where safe in any hands excepting those of the people themselves."[19]

Yet Campbell was critical of the emotionalism of the revivalist movement, and he became known for a highly rationalist approach to theology—based on an application of Baconian hermeneutics. "We are in science and philosophy Baconians," he asserted proudly. "We build on Bible facts and documents and not on theories and speculations."[20] Like so many others in his day, Campbell described the Bible as a book of "plain facts," defining "its science or doctrine [as] merely the meaning of its facts, . . . inductively gathered and arranged by every student for himself."[21]

The main attraction of the Baconian method for Campbell was its promise of creating Christian unity. The overriding goal of the Restoration movement was to reverse the splintering of the denominations, reuniting them within a single church. And his model of unity was science: "Great unanimity has obtained in most of the sciences, in consequence of the adoption of certain rules of analysis and synthesis," he wrote; "for all who work by the same *rules,* come to the same *conclusions.*"[22] Campbell was convinced that the main cause of disunity in the church was that everyone read Scripture from the perspective of a particular theological system. That was like reading through "colored glasses," he said—it distorts our perception. If we would clean the glasses (clear our minds), then we would all observe the facts of the Bible correctly and arrive at the same interpretation. Using himself as a happy example, Campbell wrote: "I have endeavored to read the scriptures as though no one had read them before me."[23] The Baconian doctrine of the perspicuity of nature for science seemed to underscore the Protestant doctrine of the perspicuity of Scripture for theology.[24]

OLD BOOKS FOR MODERN MAN

What are some of the enduring effects of evangelicals' embrace of a Baconian hermeneutic? The method suffered from several serious weaknesses, which we need to grasp in order to understand how it continues to shape the way we read the Bible today.[25] First, the very notion that Christians needed a "scientific" exegesis of Scripture represented a degree of cultural accommodation to the age. By embracing the most widely held scientific theory of their day—and even applying it to theology—evangelicals came close to losing the critical distance that Christians are called to have in every age.

Moreover, the empiricist insistence that theology was a collection of "facts" led easily to a one-dimensional, flat-footed interpretation of Scripture. Metaphorical, mystical, and symbolic meanings were downplayed in favor of the "plain" meaning of the text. And by treating Bible verses as isolated, discrete "facts," the method often produced little more than proof-texting— pulling out individual verses and aligning them under a topical label, with little regard for literary or historical context, or for the larger organizing themes in Scripture.[26]

Perhaps most serious, however, was the Baconian hostility to history—its rejection of the creeds and confessions that had been hammered out by the church over the course of centuries. When Campbell admonished believers to remove the "colored glasses" and read the Scriptures "as though no one had read them before," he was suggesting that each individual had to start over from scratch to figure out what the Bible teaches. But notice what this means: It means the church loses the wisdom of the luminous intellects that have appeared throughout church history—Augustine, Aquinas, Luther, Calvin. By adopting the Baconian method, many American evangelicals lost the intellectual riches of two millennia of theological reflection. As we noted in the previous chapter, the idea that a single generation can reject wholesale all of Christian history and start over again is doomed to theological shallowness. The very language and concepts in currency today—like *Trinity* or *justification*—were defined and developed over centuries of controversy and heresy-fighting, and unless we know something of that history we don't really know the meaning of the terms we are using.

Moreover, in our own age, with its keener sense of the historical context of knowledge, we recognize that it is unrealistic to think people are capable of approaching Scripture with minds swept clean, like blank slates. Those who attempt to jettison the past are likely to simply sanction their own current prejudices and preconceptions as unquestioned truth. They lose the critical distance afforded by checking their ideas against those of Christian scholars across a wide range of different cultures and historical periods. Instead of seeing farther by standing on the shoulders of giants, they are limited to what they are able to see from their own narrow perspective within a tiny slice of history.

That's why C. S. Lewis urged Christians to read "old books," not just contemporary ones. It is difficult *not* to be taken in by the prejudices of our own age, he wrote, unless we have access to another perspective—which is what old books provide.[27] The great figures in church history are our brothers and sisters in the Lord, members of the Body of Christ extended across the ages, and we can learn much by honing our minds on the problems they wrestled with and the solutions they offered.[28]

SOLA SCRIPTURA?

At first blush, it may seem that nineteenth-century evangelicals were simply following the Reformation principle of *sola Scriptura*. Not so: Their anti-historical individualism was a far cry from the Reformation meaning of the phrase. In spite of their insistence that the Bible was plain to anyone, the Reformers retained an allegiance to the ecumenical creeds and councils of the church's first five centuries (including the Apostles' Creed, the Nicene Creed, the Athanasian Creed, and the councils of Chalcedon, Orange, and Constantinople), where fundamental doctrines like the Trinity and the deity of Christ were deliberated and defined. Moreover, after their break with Rome, the Reformers and their followers promptly set to work writing their own confessions and catechisms (including the Augsburg Confession, the Westminster Confession, the Belgic Confession, the Lutheran Catechism, and the Heidelberg Catechism).[29] For the Reformers, *sola Scriptura* meant that Scripture was the final authority, but clearly it did not mean a radical rejection of history or of corporate statements of faith.

Nor did the Reformers deny the importance of theological study or the natural authority of scholarship and learning. To the radical egalitarians of his day, Luther responded sarcastically that from Scripture alone one might prove anything: "Now I learn that it suffices to throw many passages together helter-skelter whether they fit or not," he said. "If this is the way to do it, I certainly shall prove with Scripture that Rastrum beer is better than Malmsey wine." John Calvin likewise stood against the idea that anyone's private reading of Scripture is as valid as another's: "I acknowledge that Scripture is a most rich and inexhaustible fountain of all wisdom; but I deny that its fertility consists in the various meanings which any man, at his pleasure, may assign."[30]

In short, among the Reformers, the principle that the Bible is the final authority was not intended to deny other forms of religious authority. Thus when nineteenth-century evangelicals urged common people to cast aside the rich heritage of creeds, confessions, and theological systems, they were embarking on a radical departure from the Reformation heritage. The most distinctive principle among evangelicals was "No creed but the Bible,"[31] which clearly goes far beyond the Reformers' position.

THE VIEW FROM NOWHERE

Ironically, after nineteenth-century evangelicals had thoroughly embraced the Baconian method, to their great consternation scientists themselves began to discard it. At the dawn of the scientific revolution, when Francis Bacon had first proposed his empiricist approach to knowledge, it probably did good service in drawing people's attention away from theoretical speculations to focus on the facts of nature. As a full-blown philosophy of science, however, it had serious shortcomings. For one thing, science does not proceed by sheer induction—by collecting and organizing facts. It proceeds by proposing hypotheses and then testing them (the hypothetico-deductive method), and theories are accepted based on a wide range of factors, from simplicity to how well they cohere with existing knowledge.[32]

More fundamentally, the very idea that our minds can be "washed clean from opinions," as Bacon put it, was eventually rejected as an illusory Enlightenment ideal. The Baconian method assumes that it is possible to shed all metaphysical commitments and stand outside our limited slot in history and culture in order to observe the unadorned "facts," stripped of any philosophical framework. This imaginary stance is sometimes called the "God's-eye view" or "the view from nowhere," as though individuals were capable of transcending their particular location in time and space to gain a universal perspective on reality. Such godlike objectivity is clearly impossible for unaided human reason. To think at all, we have to make at least some initial assumptions. Even scientific investigation always proceeds under the guidance of control beliefs—a set of premises that indicates which ideas are worth pursuing, and then provides a framework for interpreting the results.

Moreover, by stressing the need to shed all presuppositions, the Baconian ideal of objectivity blinded people to the presuppositions they actually continued to hold. Thus, in the nineteenth century, religious groups would often charge that *everyone else* imposed a preexisting, humanly constructed framework of interpretation on the Bible, but *they* did not; *they* merely accepted the self-evident meaning of the text. As one historical account explains, their "reliance on Baconianism had convinced them that they had escaped the constraints of history, culture, and tradition and simply stood with the apostles in the first Christian age," understanding the text precisely as the apostles originally intended.[33]

The paradox is that the very notion that we are capable of freeing ourselves from human systems of thought was itself the product of . . . a human system—one inherited from Francis Bacon. Historians have pointed out "the irony of claiming to overturn all human traditions and interpretive schemes while at the same time being wedded to an empirical theological method drawn from early Enlightenment thought." For example, Campbell and his colleagues "never quite saw that in addition to being Disciples of Christ they also had become disciples of Baconian empiricism."[34]

The enduring legacy of Baconianism, then, was an anti-historical and somewhat positivist view of biblical interpretation—the idea that we may safely ignore the wisdom of the church's heritage over the centuries; that the best way to read the biblical text is to approach it as an isolated individual. The beauty and wonder of God's personal approach is that He often *does* speak to individuals as they come to Him in humility and openness, simply reading the Scripture as they understand it. The Holy Spirit graciously enlightens our hearts to apply biblical truth to our personal lives. As a formal method of determining what biblical truth is in the first place, however, Baconianism was unrealistic and self-deceptive—while also tending to reinforce the same primitivism and disdain for history we found so prominent in populist evangelicalism.

The defining theme in nineteenth-century American Christianity, says one historian, was a profound sense of "historylessness."[35] Artistic people picked up on this attitude and portrayed it in the literature of the time: In Anthony Trollope's novel *Barchester Towers,* an evangelical minister repeatedly announces that the time has come for "casting away the useless rubbish of past centuries."[36] We might say that evangelicalism became characterized by a rejection of C. S. Lewis's advice about reading old books.

BECOMING DOUBLE-MINDED

Applied to other fields, Baconianism led to even more pernicious results. Its primary effect was to reinforce the two-story division of truth, by promoting a kind of methodological naturalism in the lower story. By promising that knowledge could be based on empirical facts unfiltered through any religious or philosophical grid, Baconianism persuaded Christians to set aside their *own* religious framework. At the same time, it allowed *alien* philosophical frameworks, like naturalism and empiricism, to be introduced under the banner of "objectivity" and "free inquiry." By insisting that science operated without any philosophical framework, Baconianism disarmed evangelicals by blinding them to these new anti-Christian frameworks . . . until it was too late.

Another way to picture the process is that Baconianism drove Christian perspectives out of the lower story, where we deal with subjects like science and history, and into the upper story. The Baconian ideal of knowledge as religiously neutral made believers feel that it was illegitimate to bring their faith into the classroom or the science lab—for that would mean they were biased. To be objective and unbiased, one must treat the world as though it were a naturalistic system known by strictly empirical methods. The upshot was that religion was limited to the upper story, while methodological naturalism was given free rein in the lower story.

A Science of Duty

Let's flesh out the way this worked by looking at a few examples, starting with moral philosophy. The heyday of evangelicals' influence was in the mid-nineteenth century, when they controlled many of the nation's universities. At that time, the capstone of a student's university career was a course in moral philosophy—or, as it was called, "moral science." Generally taught by the college president, it was a senior course intended to draw together everything the student had learned, integrating it into an uplifting moral vision for life.

But that label *science* is a dead giveaway that the very definition of morality had shifted. A new approach to moral philosophy had arisen that rejected the Aristotelian ethic (which had been taught by Christian scholasticism up to that time) in favor of what was heralded as a scientific approach. And that meant a Baconian approach. An effort was made, says Mark Noll, "to construct ethics as Francis Bacon had defined the doing of science."[37] The starting data would be our sense of right and wrong; by examining the moral sense, one could gather the data into general laws to create a science. Thus, in 1859 a Methodist college president wrote that moral philosophy was a "science of duty" for investigating the "laws of morality" through rational methods.[38]

To turn morality into a science, it was assumed that cause and effect operate there exactly as in Newtonian physics—that virtue leads to health and happiness, while vice causes misery. Thus Witherspoon urged that progress could be made by "treating moral philosophy as Newton and his successors have done natural [philosophy]."[39] And Francis Wayland, a Baptist minister who became president of Brown University, taught that the laws of morality consist of "sequences connected by our Creator" (behaviors followed by reward or punishment) that are "just as invariable as an order of sequence in physics."[40]

Labeling ethics a *science* was a good public relations move, because it gave Christian clergy a credibility boost in an age when traditional and historical authorities were being cast aside. Claiming to be scientific put them "in a position to prescribe a Christian moral order without looking *too* Christian," as one historian comments wryly.[41] They did not appeal to the Bible or revelation, but tried to base ethics on induction from experience. For example, Witherspoon described his own moral philosophy as one that proceeded "by reason, as distinct from revelation."[42]

As a result, however, what evangelical scholars offered to the public was *an ethic not explicitly grounded in a Christian worldview.* "Wayland's text and others like it also written by clergymen did not expound a specifically Christian ethics," explains one account. "They found the basis of ethics . . . in the natural order and in the experience of rational creatures rather than in the revealed will of God."[43]

In one sense, of course, there was nothing new in this approach. It was just putting "scientific" window dressing on the age-old concept of natural law. From ancient times, Christians have acknowledged that all humans, because they are created in the image of God, have a basic sense of right and wrong. C. S. Lewis referred to it as the Tao—the conviction found in virtually every culture that there is an objective moral order, and that wisdom consists in aligning our personal lives with that order.[44]

Yet the moral sense itself is not enough to ground a full-blown moral philosophy. Our sense of right and wrong is merely a datum of experience—which must be explained and accounted for by an overarching worldview. And if the

Christian worldview is ruled out as an explanatory framework, then anti-Christian worldviews will rush in to fill the vacuum.

Historically, that is exactly what happened. Because of their Baconian view of knowledge, nineteenth-century evangelicals tried to build a moral science that was religiously autonomous—a lower-story science based on empirical and rational grounds alone. It was, as one philosophy textbook puts it, an approach based "on *an entirely naturalistic view of human nature.*"[45] Of course, evangelical scholars assumed that the findings of moral science would turn out to be parallel to the teachings of the Bible—and thus would provide confirmation of Christianity. But within the discipline itself, they adopted a form of methodological naturalism.

In doing so, however, they opened the door to full-fledged *philosophical* naturalism (nature is all that exists). And it was not long before scholars who embraced that philosophy walked right through the door that had been opened for them. They abolished the courses on moral philosophy, replacing them with empirically oriented courses on experimental psychology and sociology that spelled out the full implications of a naturalistic view of human nature. The American university was being secularized.

Celestial Mathematician

The same secularization process was proceeding apace in the natural sciences. Ever since Isaac Newton established classical physics, science seemed to be creating an image of the universe as a huge clockwork, wound up at the beginning but ever since running by mechanistic forces. Inevitably, tension emerged between this machine model of the universe, which portrayed God as a kind of celestial mathematician, and the belief in a personal God who lovingly supervises every event by His direct providence. If all physical phenomena could be explained by natural law, what room was there for divine causality? It began to seem that the natural world operated autonomously by inbuilt natural laws known by science (the lower story), while the supernatural world was limited to the invisible realm of the spirit, known only by religion (the upper story).

The outcome was what one historian calls "a schizophrenic conception of God." On one hand, "intellectual assurance came from the Divine Engineer," while on the other hand, "personal religious experience assumed the Heavenly Father." Yet the relationship between them was far from equal, for science had been defined as the sole source of genuine knowledge, which meant religion was demoted to subjective feelings. Thus as science progressed, eventually "the personal God retreated into an impalpable spiritual world."[46]

In short, a chasm was opening in the minds of believers. Many struggled to keep the upper and lower stories connected, insisting that in the end the two realms would prove complementary—that scientific knowledge would harmonize with biblical teachings. The design argument was immensely popular during this period, especially William Paley's analogy that the universe is like a finely-made watch, and thus requires a watchmaker. Yet this did not prevent Christianity from being reduced eventually to little more than a ceremonial benediction pronounced over the results of science. At the end of his research, the typical scientist would round off with a flourish by praising God for His wise and benevolent design; but he denied that biblical assumptions were foundational in making science possible in the first place, or that they played any role as control beliefs in directing his scientific work.

"By the end of the eighteenth century, American Protestants of almost all sorts had adopted this two-tiered worldview, founded on an empiricist epistemology, with the laws of nature below, supporting supernatural belief above," writes George Marsden.[47] Christians were treating fields outside theology as essentially autonomous disciplines, operating by the methodology of "value-free" science. This was reflected in the increasing specialization within the university curriculum, so that when the Duke of Argyll gave his inaugural address as chancellor of the University of St. Andrews in 1852, he warned that theology no longer provided an overarching unity of knowledge: "An absolute separation has been declared between science and religion; and the theologian and the [scientist] have entered into a sort of tacit agreement that each is to be left free and unimpeded by the other within his own walk and province." This was a dangerous development, he warned, for if the true meaning of nature and history is not recognized, then "a false one will be invented."[48]

Just so. If a Christian philosophy does not provide the control beliefs for science, then false philosophies will fill the vacuum—naturalism and materialism. The Enlightenment claim that science can operate without any philosophical premises proved, in the end, to be a cover for discarding Christian premises while smuggling in naturalistic ones. As Marsden writes, the ideal of "free inquiry" became merely a tactic for debunking traditional religion, while science itself was elevated to "the new orthodoxy."[49]

Blinded by Bacon

Unfortunately, once again the Baconian view of science prevented many Christians from recognizing what was happening. An example is the way some responded to the appearance of Darwinism in 1859. The reason Darwinian evolution was so revolutionary was not its concept of natural selection but its definition of knowledge, or epistemology. The older epistemology assumed an open universe, where concepts like design and purpose (teleology) made sense and were considered perfectly rational. But as we saw in chapter 6, Darwin wanted to establish a naturalistic epistemology that assumed a closed system of cause and effect—one that ruled design and purpose out of bounds. Thus the heart of the conflict revolved around two rival epistemologies: Which definition of knowledge should govern in science?[50]

The tragedy is not just that evangelicals failed to meet the challenge: For the most part they did not even recognize it. As good Baconians, evangelicals denied the role of philosophical assumptions in science—and thus they were powerless to critique and counter the new assumptions when they appeared on the intellectual horizon. A great many of them simply took the *facts* that Darwin presented and inserted them into the older *philosophy* of nature as an open system—not realizing, apparently, that *the older philosophy was precisely what was under attack*. In the late nineteenth century, explains historian Edward Purcell, the majority of thinkers failed to realize that Darwinism implied "a fully naturalistic worldview." They inserted Darwinism into a religious and providential framework, trying to somehow fit it into a "belief in nature as part of a comprehensive divine order, and in science as part of a larger and morally oriented natural philosophy."[51]

An example was the Princeton theologian B. B. Warfield. As a young man, he had bred shorthorn cattle on his father's ranch, where he noticed that wild cattle developed distinctive traits through interaction with their environment. In short, he had witnessed natural selection. Thus when he encountered the concept of evolution, he accepted it easily, describing himself as "a Darwinian of the purest water." Yet when Warfield explained what he *meant* by evolution, he spoke of the constant supervision of divine providence, punctuated by "occasional supernatural interference."[52] Anyone expressing those views today would be branded a flaming creationist.

Princeton president James McCosh likewise called himself a Darwinian. Yet he held that several pivotal events could not be explained by natural causes alone—that God worked by "immediate fiat" at the origin of life, intelligence, and morality.[53] Finally, one of the most influential theistic evolutionists of the nineteenth century, Asa Gray, also inserted Darwin's concept of natural selection into the older theistic cosmology open to divine supervision and design. He apparently failed to understand that Darwin's intention was to replace that cosmology with a naturalistic one.[54]

One of the few to recognize what was at stake philosophically was Charles Hodge. "The distinctive element" in Darwinism, he wrote, is not natural selection but the denial of design or purpose. And "the denial of design in nature is virtually the denial of God."[55]

Despite Hodge's protest, the debate was not really engaged on the level of philosophy until the rise of the Intelligent Design movement in our own day. When I began writing on science and worldview back in the 1970s, the debate was still being carried on almost solely at the level of scientific details (fossils, mutations, geological strata). One reason the Intelligent Design movement has had such a powerful impact is that Phillip Johnson finally succeeded in shifting the argument to Darwin's naturalistic definition of science. "Christians often think the controversy is primarily a dispute about scientific facts, and so they become trapped into arguing scientific details rather than concentrating on the fundamental assumptions that generate the evolutionary story," Johnson writes in his latest book.[56] The rise of the Intelligent Design movement signals that Christians are finally moving beyond a Baconian view of science, recognizing the formative role that philosophical assumptions play in what counts as genuine knowledge. As we saw in Part 2, factual evidence is important, but it will not persuade unless at the same time we challenge the reigning naturalistic epistemology in science.

Religion on the Side

As the nineteenth century progressed, the Baconian two-story schema filtered down from the realm of abstract ideas and began to be expressed in the institutional structure of the university itself. Universities that had been founded as Christian schools, like Harvard, Princeton, and Yale, began pushing theology off into a separate department instead of allowing it to permeate the curriculum as a whole. Religion became an extracurricular activity that students pursued in their private time on the side—like going to chapel or participating in Christian student groups. The public/private split was becoming part of the institutional structure: Religion was being removed from the curriculum, where we teach public knowledge, and relegated to the private sphere of subjective experience.

In the curriculum, religion was replaced by the humanities, which were supposed to fill the vacuum by dealing with higher questions of meaning, morality, and the spiritual life. But the humanities remained strictly in the upper story, leaving the lower story to science. In 1906 Daniel Coit Gilman, the first president of Johns Hopkins University, wrote, "While the old line between the sciences and the humanities may be invisible as the equator, it has an existence just as real." The difference between them, he said, is that science is "true everywhere and all the time" whereas the humanities depend on "our aesthetic preferences, our intellectual traditions, our religious faith."[57] Notice that by this time Gilman can simply assume the fact/value split: Science is universally true, but the humanities are a matter of preferences, traditions, and faith.

The bi-level division of truth began to be internalized by individuals as well. As the world of the intellect became secularized and divorced from spiritual experience, Christians began talking about a schism between the *head* and the *heart*. A German man spoke for many educated people in 1817 when he said, I "am a heathen in my reason and a Christian with my whole heart."[58]

It is nothing less than tragic that Christians themselves were partly responsible for the privatizing of religion, by accepting the Baconian definition of science as religiously neutral. Evangelicalism fostered a split, says historian Douglas Sloan, between "an emotional conversion experience as the heart of religion" (upper story) and "a narrow, technical utilitarian reason for dealing with this world" (lower story).[59] In other words, for the things of this world, they adopted a form of *methodological* naturalism, which eventually opened the door to *metaphysical* naturalism. After all, if you can interpret the world perfectly well without reference to God, then His existence becomes a superfluous hypothesis, and those who are intellectually honest and courageous will dump it altogether. Historically, that is exactly what happened: "The naturalistic definition of science," Marsden writes, was "transformed from a *methodology* into a dominant academic *worldview.*"[60]

To bring about a restoration of the Christian mind, we would do well to follow the Intelligent Design movement in challenging the Baconian model of autonomous or neutral knowledge in every field. We must reject the presumption that holding Christian beliefs disqualifies us as "biased," while the philosophical naturalists get a free pass by presenting their position as "unbiased" and "rational." Most of all, we need to liberate Christianity from the two-story division that has reduced it to an upper-story private experience, and learn how to restore it to the status of objective truth.

MAKING SENSE OF COMMON SENSE

We can draw resources for the task from some of the other strands within nineteenth-century thought. The Baconian method was just one element of Common Sense realism, and as we raise our sights to a higher level, we will discover new intellectual terrain yielding valuable insights and strategies for today.

In nineteenth-century America, as we saw earlier, Scottish realism became immensely popular. It was applied to virtually every discipline in the college curriculum, becoming the *lingua franca* of the day. What exactly did it teach? Thomas Reid said all knowledge begins with those things we cannot help believing because of the very way the human mind is constituted (self-evident truths). Our inner awareness of pain and pleasure, our moral sense of right and wrong, our instinctive belief in the reality of the physical world—things like these do not need any philosophical justification. They are virtually forced upon us by the constitution of our own nature in order to function in the world God created.[61]

You might say that Common Sense realism is not so much a philosophy as an anti-philosophy[62]—because it actually describes the experiential knowledge that forms the raw material for formal philosophy. Using the image of a plant, Reid said philosophy "has no other root but the principles of Common Sense; it grows out of them, and draws its nourishment from them."[63] Common Sense is the *pre-theoretical experience* that provides the starting material for our *theories* in philosophy, science, morality, and so on. The role of philosophy is to explain *why* it is possible to know the things we already know by experience.

This experiential knowledge also serves as a touchstone for error. When philosophers concoct abstract systems that contradict the self-evident truths of Common Sense, we can be sure that something has gone wrong. After all, the purpose of philosophy is to *explain* what we know by direct experience, not to contradict or deny it. "When a man suffers himself to be reasoned out of the principles of common sense, by metaphysical arguments," Reid said, "we may call this metaphysical lunacy."[64] That is, embracing a philosophy that denies the truths known by experience is sheer craziness.

Scottish realism was particularly attractive to Christians because it was a theistic philosophy, resting on the assumption of divine creation. Reid was a moderate Presbyterian clergyman, and he argued that the reason our minds and senses are trustworthy is that God designed them to work reliably in the world He created. James Henley Thornwell, an Old School Presbyterian, explained that God created the mind to know truth, just as He made "the eye to see, the ear to hear, or the heart to feel."[65]

REID ROMANS 1

What is the legacy of Scottish realism for our own day? Critics charge that it fostered a type of intellectual laziness among nineteenth-century evangelicals, by short-circuiting careful theoretical reflection. It seemed to imply that they did not need to invest in the hard work of defending their core beliefs— because, after all, those beliefs were undeniable and self-evident. "For much of the history of the United States," writes Noll, "evangelicals denied that they *had* a philosophy. They were merely pursuing common sense."[66] What's worse, they included in that category a good number of theological propositions that, to a later generation, did not seem at all self-evident—beliefs that very much required defending in a new, more hostile intellectual climate.

Yet Common Sense philosophy has continued to have remarkable vitality, and has even enjoyed somewhat of a resurgence in our own day, especially among Reformed thinkers. Since the late nineteenth century, there have been essentially two major strands within Reformed thought. Common Sense realism was the *Scottish* Reformed tradition. It fostered an evidentialist form of apologetics, emphasizing truths knowable by believer and unbeliever alike, which function as testing grounds to evaluate competing worldviews. A later strand is the *Dutch* Reformed tradition, consisting of the neo-Calvinism of Abraham Kuyper and Herman Dooyeweerd. It fostered a presuppositionalist form of apologetics, emphasizing the formative impact of worldviews themselves and the need to evaluate them as unified wholes—starting with first principles and tracing out their logical conclusions. "In almost every field today," Marsden notes, "evangelical scholars are divided basically into [these] two camps, with some hybrids in between."[67]

One hybrid was proposed by Francis Schaeffer, who showed how evidentialist and presuppositionalist elements can actually work in tandem in practical evangelism.[68] His method proved remarkably effective for an entire generation of young people. I personally found it persuasive many years ago after arriving on the doorstep at L'Abri as a nonbeliever. And today whenever I give my testimony in public, invariably half a dozen people come up afterward with their own stories of how Schaeffer's ministry and writings brought them to conversion, or helped them through a crisis of faith. Let's do a closer analysis of his hybrid method, then, to see how he crafted a method of apologetics that is still relevant and workable today.

On one hand, Schaeffer agreed with the basic tenet of Common Sense realism that everyone has immediate, pre-theoretical knowledge derived from direct experience. We are all made in the image of God, live in God's universe, and are upheld by God's common grace—and thus we share certain universal experiences, insights, and ways of thinking. Most basic would be the truths of common sense—our fundamental sense of personal identity, right and wrong, the rules of logic, and so on.

Yet these truths do not interpret themselves. They are merely *data* that need to be explained and accounted for by an overall metaphysical system. And so, on the other hand, Schaeffer agreed with neo-Calvinism that even our basic beliefs must be interpreted within a Christian framework. When speaking with nonbelievers, our goal is to show them that Christianity is the only *theoretical* system that accounts for the truths we know by *pre-theoretical* experience. All truth is God's truth, wherever we may find it, as the church fathers said so long ago; but those truths make sense only within a Christian worldview.

This approach is based on Romans 1:19-20. The passage starts by asserting that everyone has genuine knowledge of God through the world He has made: "what can be known about God is plain to them, because God has shown it to them. For his invisible attributes, namely, his eternal power and divine nature, have been clearly perceived, ever since the creation of the world, in the things that have been made. So they are without excuse." In other words, the most pervasive, inescapable experiences—of our own human nature and of an orderly and beautiful universe—give ample reasons for believing in God. Why? Because only His revelation accounts for those experiences.

Nonbelievers try to "suppress" their knowledge of God, Romans goes on to say, by inventing all sorts of alternative explanations for the world. Yet none of these explanations is adequate—and as a result, at some point the nonbeliever's account of the world will be contradicted by his lived experience. That ought to tell him something. The term rendered "without excuse" (v. 20) literally means "without an apologetic." The task of evangelism starts with helping the nonbeliever face squarely the inconsistencies between his professed beliefs and his actual experience. As philosopher Roy Clouser explains, one test of a worldview involves "seeing whether certain data can have *any plausible account at all* on its standpoint."[69] After showing that the nonbeliever's worldview cannot give "any plausible account" of the data of experience, we can then present Christianity as the only worldview that gives a consistent and logical answer.

Or, to turn the argument around, we want to help people see that if their worldview contradicts commonsense experience, then it cannot be true. As Dooyeweerd put it, experience is "a pre-theoretical datum" and "any philosophical theory of human experience which cannot account for this datum in a satisfactory way must be erroneous."[70] To borrow Reid's colorful phrase, it is metaphysical lunacy.

Colors and Shapes

What are some practical examples of how we might use this line of argument in apologetics? Common Sense realism points out that no one can really deny the testimony of the senses. To function at all in the world, we must have a basic trust in the things we see and hear. The entire scientific enterprise is based on the trustworthiness of sense data, and would collapse without the assurance that our sensations provide a reliable picture of reality. Yet how do we know that the images or impressions from our senses match up with the real world? The fatal flaw in any empiricist philosophy is that we cannot step *outside* our sensations and gain some independent vantage point, from which we can test sense data against the external world. How, then, can we explain the trustworthiness of our senses?

The only adequate basis for our confidence is the biblical teaching that there is a Creator who designed our mental capacities to function reliably in the world He created. The doctrine of creation is the epistemological guarantee that the constitution of our human faculties conforms to the structure of the physical world. As Alvin Plantinga writes, it is part of the "human design plan" to trust our own sense perceptions. When our perceptual faculties are in good working order, and functioning in the environment for which they were designed, we naturally trust that the colors and shapes we perceive represent real objects in a real world.[71]

Udo Middelmann (Schaeffer's son-in-law) uses a wonderful phrase to explain why the Christian can have epistemological confidence: Because God created us in His image, to function in His world, there is a "continuity of categories" between God's mind, our minds, and the structure of the world.[72]

The concept of creation or design is the crucial assumption that believers of the nineteenth century overlooked when they thought the sciences could proceed without any distinctively Christian presuppositions. Apart from the doctrine of creation or design, there is no basis for trusting that the ideas in my mind have any correlation to the world outside. If the human mind is a product of chance events, preserved by natural selection, then there is no basis for trusting any of our ideas. Recall Darwin's "horrid doubt" that the human mind could be trusted at all, if it is a product of evolution (chapter 8). The non-Christian pursuing his research has no choice but to rely on his senses, just as everyone else does; but he has no philosophical *basis* for doing so. He is being inconsistent with his own worldview.

Just a Habit?

Take another example. No one can function in daily life without assuming regular patterns of cause and effect. All our actions are based on the conviction that if we perform action A, we will produce effect B. If we put food on the stove, we expect it to cook. If we put fuel in our car, we expect it to run. Science likewise depends on the reality of a consistent order in nature. "Belief in the absoluteness of nature's laws is a deeply-rooted part of the scientific culture," writes an astrophysicist. "To do science, you have to have faith that something is sacrosanct and utterly dependable."[73]

Yet skeptics have argued that our belief in causation is merely a habit, resulting from the flow of sense impressions in our head. When we perceive event A followed by event B, then over time we come to expect the pattern to continue. There is no real basis for that expectation, however, for we cannot know that nature has any plan or order that justifies our thinking. If the universe is a product of chance, then there is no guarantee that the sun will rise tomorrow, or that *any* of the regularities we observe today will hold in the future.

Hume states the problem in a famous passage: "The bread which I formerly ate, nourished me . . . but does it follow that other bread must also nourish me at another time?"[74] In other words, the sheer fact that in the past we have always experienced that bread nourishes us, or that the sun rises, or that fires burns, gives no ground for projecting the same pattern into the future. The tendency to think inductively, Hume says, is grounded in nothing but "custom" and "habit." It has no rational justification.

Science offers mathematical formulas to express the cause-and-effect relationships in nature, but that only intensifies the dilemma. For if the universe evolved by blind, material forces acting randomly, why should it fit so neatly into the mathematical formulas we invent in our minds? In short, why does math work? In a famous essay titled "The Unreasonable Effectiveness of Mathematics in the Natural Sciences," Eugene Wigner says the fact that math works so well in describing the world "is something bordering on the mysterious." Indeed, "there is no rational explanation for it."[75]

No explanation *within scientific materialism,* that is. But within the Christian worldview there is a perfectly rational explanation—namely, that a reasonable God created the world to operate as an orderly progression of events. This was the conviction that inspired the early modern scientists, says historian Morris Kline: "The early mathematicians were sure of the existence of mathematical laws underlying natural phenomena and persisted in the search for them because they were convinced *a priori* that God had incorporated them in the construction of the universe."[76]

By the same token, it was God who outfitted humans with the ability to discover that order in nature. Our instinctive tendency to draw predictions for the future based on the past is part of the human "design plan."[77] In order to function in the world, the nonbeliever has no choice but to reason inductively, but his worldview gives no *basis* for believing in cause-and-effect regularities. To live in the real world, he has to be inconsistent with his own worldview.

Are You Nobody?

The same argument can be applied to our sense of personal identity or selfhood. "I take it for granted that all the thoughts I am conscious of, or remember, are the thoughts of one and the same thinking principle, which I call *myself* or my *mind,*" Reid wrote. "Every man has an immediate and irresistible conviction, not only of his present existence, but of his continued existence and identity as far back as he can remember."[78]

That seems to be an obvious point, but the reason Reid made an issue of it was that skeptics were contesting it. His nemesis, Hume, had pointed out that, on strictly empirical premises, we cannot justify believing even in something as basic as the existence of a unified self. Scanning the contents of our consciousness, all we can detect is an ever-flowing series of perceptions and impressions. "When I enter most intimately into what I call *myself*, I always stumble on some particular perception or other, of heat or cold, light or shade, love or hate, pain or pleasure," Hume wrote. "I never can catch *myself* at any time without a perception, never can observe any thing but the perception."[79] As we saw in chapter 3, some cognitive scientists today side with Hume, denying the reality of a single unified self.

But the purpose of a worldview is to *explain* the data of experience—not to *deny* it. Any philosophical system that fails to offer a plausible account of our sense of personal selfhood should be rejected as inadequate. And that includes both scientific materialism (which defines reality in terms of nonpersonal *natural* forces) as well as Eastern and New Age thought (which defines reality as nonpersonal *spiritual* forces).[80] Any system that begins with nonpersonal forces must, in the end, reduce persons to components of an unconscious matrix of being.

Only Christianity, with its teaching of a personal Creator, provides an adequate metaphysical explanation of our irreducible experience of personhood. It alone accounts for the raw material of experience within a comprehensive worldview. In the modern world, with its large, impersonal institutions where people are treated as ciphers in the machine, the Christian message is good news indeed. Ultimate reality is not the machine; it is a personal Being who loves and relates to each individual in a personal manner.

Mere Chemistry?

Indeed one of the central characteristics of human nature is the capacity for relationships of love and self-giving. Young children deprived of love do not thrive. Yet reductionists tell us that feelings of "love" are merely the effects of chemical reactions in the brain—or, as cognitive science puts it, an illusion caused by patterns of neural activity.

Evolutionary psychologists (as we saw in chapter 7) tell us that altruistic behavior is merely a calculated strategy of helping others so they will help us in return. Tit for tat. It is a strategy of "reciprocal altruism," programmed into our genes by natural selection so that we will get along and survive better. It would be more candid, however, to call this "pseudo-altruism" (as Daniel Dennett does)[81] because the assumption is that individuals practice cooperation and self-control only when it secures their larger interests. Every good deed is ultimately selfish.

What do these same scientists do when they take off their lab coats and go home to their families? Do they treat their love for their spouses and children with the same skepticism? If they have ordinary human emotions, they are all but forced to live inconsistently with the philosophy they have embraced professionally.

The only worldview that supports the highest aspirations of the human heart is Christianity. It gives a basis for believing that love is real and genuine because we were created by a God whose very character is love. The Bible teaches that there has been love and communication between the members of the Trinity from all eternity. Love is not an illusion created by the genes to promote our evolutionary survival, but an aspect of human nature that reflects the fundamental fabric of ultimate reality. Moreover, by submitting to God's plan of salvation and becoming His children, we have the astonishing possibility of participating in that eternal love.

DISINFORMATION MINISTER

The principle running through these examples is that, on one hand, Common Sense realism was right to argue for universal, undeniable human experiences. Human nature is constituted in such a way that we can't help functioning as though our senses are reliable, that cause-and-effect relationships are real, that we have a personal self, and so on. Believer and nonbeliever alike, we were all created in God's image, to live in God's universe, supported by God's common grace, and thus we all share certain fundamental experiences. It rains on the just and the unjust alike.

But the truths of experience are not self-explanatory. Instead they merely constitute the data that cries out to be explained within an overarching worldview. *Why* is it that the bits of matter we call our bodies have consciousness and are able to navigate the world so effectively? *Why* are we capable of building societies with some measure of justice and compassion? As I write, NASA has just released stunning new photographs of the surface of Mars—but why is it possible for humans to calculate a trajectory and land a spacecraft on another planet? What kind of world permits these fascinating achievements? Our claim as Christians is that only a biblically based worldview offers a complete and consistent explanation of why we are capable of knowing scientific, moral, and mathematical truths. Christianity is the key that fits the lock of the universe.

Moreover, since all other worldviews are false keys, we can be absolutely confident, when talking with nonbelievers, that they themselves know things that are *not accounted for* by their own worldview—whatever it may be. Or, to turn it around, they will not be able to live consistently on the basis of their own worldview. Since their metaphysical beliefs do not fit the world God created, their lives will be more or less inconsistent with those beliefs. Living in the real world requires them to function in ways that are not supported by their worldview.

This creates a state of cognitive dissonance, and at that point of tension, the gospel may find an opening. In evangelism we can draw people's attention to the conflict between what they *know* on the basis of experience and what they *profess* in their stated beliefs—because that is a sure sign that something is wrong with their beliefs.[82]

The level of tension will depend on how logically consistent the person is. During the invasion of Iraq, the Iraqi Minister of Information appeared daily before a bank of microphones to repeat over and over again: "There are no American infidels in Baghdad! Never!" This, as American soldiers were taking over government buildings a few blocks away. Presuming that the minister was not simply lying, he was being utterly, unshakably consistent in the face of contrary evidence.

Most people, however, are less consistent. They may hold a philosophy of materialism or Darwinian naturalism, yet in practice they live in ways that contradict those worldviews. After all, who really treats their convictions as the products of natural selection, and not really true but only useful for survival? Who could survive emotionally if they really believed that self-sacrificing love is nothing but "pseudo-altruism"? Because nonbelievers are created in the image of God, the force of their own human nature compels them to live in ways that are inconsistent with their professed worldview. In evangelism, our goal is to highlight that cognitive dissonance—to identify the points at which the nonbeliever's worldview is contradicted by reality. Then we can show that only Christianity is fully consistent with the things we all know by experience to be true. (For more on how this works, see appendix 4.)

PHILOSOPHICAL "CHEATING"

Often people are not fully aware of the logical conclusions of their own beliefs—in which case we may have to press them to follow them out to the end. We cannot let them "cheat" by sneaking in conclusions that are not rationally supported by their starting premises. I recall the regular Saturday night discussions in the L'Abri chapel, where Schaeffer would sit before the large stone fireplace interacting with students and guests, many of them seekers or nonbelievers. Often they would try to defend some purely secular basis for morality or freedom or whatever—and relentlessly he would press them back to their starting premises. "If you want to maintain that something is real, then you have to say what it is and where it came from," as he put it during one discussion. A closed system of naturalistic cause and effect simply gives no basis for things like moral freedom or human dignity—as B. F. Skinner stated so forcefully in the title of his book *Beyond Freedom and Dignity*. In fact, if nonbelievers were utterly consistent, they would all be amoral skeptics.

Yet in reality very few people in the West are either completely amoral or completely skeptical. Why not? Because they "cheat" by borrowing ideas from the Christian heritage.

A recent example is Dennett's latest book, *Freedom Evolves,* in which he seeks to reconcile Darwinism with a belief in moral freedom. British philosopher John Gray penned a scathing review accusing Dennett of being inconsistent with his self-professed philosophy of naturalism. After all, Gray explained, "the notion that humans are free in a way that other animals are not does not come from science. Its origins are in religion—above all, in Christianity." He charged Dennett with "seeking to salvage a view of humankind derived from Western religion."[83]

To use our terminology, Dennett is "cheating" by borrowing concepts from the Christian heritage that have no basis within his own naturalistic system.

This is far more common than we might think. Gray argues that the whole of Western liberalism is actually parasitic on Christianity. The high view of the human person in liberalism, he says, is derived directly from Christianity: "Liberal humanism inherits several key Christian beliefs—above all, the belief that humans are categorically different from all other animals." No other religion has given rise to the conviction that humans have a unique dignity.

Think of it this way: If Darwin had announced his theory of evolution in India, China, or Japan, it would hardly have made a stir. "If—along with hundreds of millions of Hindus and Buddhists—you have never believed that humans differ from everything else in the natural world in having an immortal soul, you will find it hard to get worked up by a theory that shows how much we have in common with other animals." The West's high view of human dignity and human rights is borrowed directly from Christianity. "The secular world-view is simply the Christian take on the world with God left out," Gray concludes. "Humanism is not an alternative to religious belief, but rather a degenerate and unwitting version of it."[84]

Do we believe this ourselves? Are we convinced that concepts like moral freedom and human dignity have no basis outside of Christianity? We need to press people to stop "cheating" and face squarely the bankruptcy of their own belief systems. For postmodern people, this may be what the Holy Spirit uses to create an awareness of their need—and an openness to the biblical answer. A realization of their "metaphysical lostness" may be the means by which God brings them to salvation.

SIGNS OF INTELLIGENT LIFE

Francis Schaeffer's method of evangelism, which we have just described, was highly effective with the stream of seekers who stopped in at his chalet in Switzerland. Yet his was not the only possible adaptation of Common Sense realism. In chapter 1 we told the story of Alvin Plantinga's stunning success in restoring theistic philosophy to academic respect in recent years—but what we did *not* mention was that the philosophy he has expounded so brilliantly is an updated version of Thomas Reid's realism. "Human beings are constructed according to a certain design plan," Plantinga argues—including our cognitive faculties. We don't need to construct a complex philosophical defense of the basic beliefs of common sense. Those beliefs are warranted if our cognitive faculties are functioning properly in the environment for which they were designed.[85] This revival of Common Sense philosophy is shared by other Reformed thinkers (such as William Alston and Nicholas Wolterstorff), and their approach has been labeled Reformed Epistemology.

The work of Schaeffer, Plantinga, and many others testifies to the fact that both Scottish Common Sense realism and Dutch neo-Calvinism remain viable philosophical traditions among evangelical thinkers today, capable of sustaining substantial philosophical work. Even outsiders have begun to sit up and take notice. A few years ago, *Commonweal* ran an article titled "The Evangelical Mind Awakens,"[86] remarking that the majority of evangelical scholars who have achieved academic recognition in mainstream academia have ties to neo-Calvinism. Three historians mentioned in the article—George Marsden, Mark Noll, and Nathan Hatch—are so prolific in their scholarship that a Yale professor has even warned that an "evangelical thesis" may be taking over the study of American history![87]

Ordinary believers are expressing a hunger to recover a richer heritage as well, by acquainting themselves with the spiritual classics. When I visited a small Christian bookstore near my home, the owner told me that the shelf he can't restock fast enough is the one devoted to the older classics, from Augustine to St. John of the Cross—an encouraging sign of a new interest in worshiping God with our minds as well as our hearts.

BOXED-IN BELIEVERS

Let's summarize what we've learned from the history of American evangelicalism over the past three chapters. To begin with, we cannot help recognizing its overall positive impact. By inspiring an intensely personal commitment to Christianity, it is the main reason America remains the most religious nation in the industrialized world today. Yet we also need to realize that evangelicalism did not overcome the age-old two-story division of knowledge—on the contrary, it intensified the split. The populist branch of evangelicalism contributed to the idea that religion is a private emotional experience (upper story), while the scholarly branch reinforced the idea that public knowledge must be religiously neutral and autonomous (lower story). As a result, religion was removed from the public realm and shunted off into the private realm. There it might flourish, as in fact it has. But it would be carefully kept in its cage. Meanwhile, secular ideologies took advantage of the vacuum and quickly filled the public arena.

What happened in the nineteenth century, explains historian Martin Marty, was that religion in America "accepted a division of labour." On one hand, "religion acquiesced in the assignment to address itself to the personal, familial, and leisured sectors of life" (the private dimension). On the other hand, "the public dimensions—political, social, economic, cultural—were to become autonomous," and were eventually taken over by non-Christian ideologies.[88]

This division of labor was "a momentous concession," Marty says, and yet today Americans have grown so used to it that we no longer realize what a novel development it was. He calls it the Modern Schism and says it was a complete "novelty in Western culture." Of course, Christian thought had been marked by the two-story dichotomy for centuries, as we have seen. But in the nineteenth century that dichotomy began to be expressed externally in social institutions. Society was divided into "an outer, encompassing culture," on one hand, and on the other hand "an inner, sequestered largely ecclesiastical religious culture within."[89] Individual believers began to inhabit two worlds, commuting from one to the other across the Modern Schism.

No longer were religious leaders the public spokesmen of society, as they had once been. Instead, they were permitted to appear in public only to perform the limited role of inspiring and legitimating the larger culture. They could perform invocations and benedictions—like opening prayers in Congress—but they were not welcome to comment on the substance of legislation; that would be "meddling" in politics. Visitors from other countries were amazed at the way the clergy in America were boxed in. The ever-observant

Tocqueville commented, "In America, religion is a distinct sphere, in which the priest is sovereign but out of which he takes care never to go."[90]

The overall pattern of evangelicalism's history is summarized brilliantly by Richard Hofstadter in a single sentence. To a large extent, he writes, "the churches *withdrew* from intellectual encounters with the secular world, *gave up* the idea that religion is a part of the whole life of intellectual experience, and often *abandoned* the field of rational studies on the assumption that they were the natural province of science alone."[91] Let's break that sentence down, for it sums up the entire story of what happened to the evangelical mind. Notice that Hofstadter mentions three factors: One, churches and seminaries themselves largely *withdrew* from intellectual confrontation with the secular world, limiting their attention to the realm of practical Christian living. Two, they *gave up* the idea that Christianity gives a comprehensive framework to interpret all of life and scholarship, allowing it to become boxed into the upper story. Three, in the process, they *abandoned* an entire range of intellectual inquiry to the lower story. They gave in to the demand that the academic disciplines must be religiously and philosophically autonomous, without realizing that it was just a cover to introduce *new* philosophies like positivism and naturalism.

Yet that is not the whole story. Ideas do not remain in the realm of the abstract; they also influence the concrete ways people construct their society and its institutions. The Modern Schism was not just a set of ideas about religion, it was also a profound change in the way real people lived and organized their lives. It was part of a larger reordering of society that affected the structure of the workplace, the family, and even the relations between the sexes. Turn to the next chapter for a fascinating excursion into the personal and social consequences of the public/private split in American life—consequences that include religion but also go far beyond it.

12

How Women Started the Culture War

Modernization brings about
a novel dichotomization of social life.
The dichotomy is between
the huge and immensely powerful institutions
of the public sphere . . . and the private sphere.
PETER BERGER[1]

I had just spoken on a panel at a large secular university when a woman in the audience stood up and said, "I'm not a feminist, but . . ." That was a pretty good tip-off that she was about to say something from a feminist perspective.

"Why didn't this program mention any women? None of the speakers cited works by women. Why are you ignoring half the human race?" The woman glared around the room, then added: "Don't bother to answer." She began to stalk out of the auditorium, staging a dramatic exit.

I grabbed the microphone. "Don't leave," I said. That night I had talked about the divided concept of truth that runs like a chasm through all of Western thought. "The fact/value split is not merely academic," I said. "It has been incarnated in modern social institutions as a split between public and private life—which affects even the relationships between men and women."

That got her attention, and the room grew hushed. I explained that the two-story conception of knowledge has restructured not only the university curriculum but also the home, the church, and the workplace. This is an important aspect of the two-tiered division of truth, because it reminds us that it is not just a matter of ideas but also a powerful force reshaping the way we live.

WOMEN AND THE AWAKENING

Come with me back to the middle of the Second Great Awakening. In 1838, a controversial article appeared urging laypeople to "think for themselves" in matters of religion.[2] Ordinarily, a message like that would hardly have caused a ripple. As we have seen, the call to ordinary people to read and interpret the Bible for themselves was a central theme in the evangelical movement of the time. What made this article so controversial, however, was that it was written by a woman—and she was calling on *women* to read the Bible for themselves: "I believe it to be the solemn duty of every individual to search the Scriptures for themselves, with the aid of the Holy Spirit, and not be governed by the views of any man, or set of men."[3]

Once the evangelical movement had embraced spiritual populism, it was difficult to contain the logic of equality to white males. In terms of sheer numbers, the Awakenings reached more women than men, especially younger women. The revivalists also permitted women to pray and speak publicly, and even to become "exhorters" (teaching assistants), which scandalized critics. Moreover, because the revivalists stressed the emotional side of religion, their message seemed to be pitched especially to women. They began to speak of women as being more naturally religious than men, and urged wives to be the means of converting their more worldly husbands.

Like the other trends we have traced, this one has continued into our own day. American churches still typically attract more women than men, giving rise to the stereotype that religion is for women and children. This pattern is so widespread that some have spoken of the "feminization" of the church. "Men still *run* most churches," one study concludes, but "in the *pews* women outnumber men in all countries of Western civilization."[4]

Interestingly, this is not true of other faiths: In Eastern Orthodoxy, the membership is roughly balanced, and in Judaism and Islam men actually predominate.[5] So the pattern cannot be explained by saying that men are just naturally less religious than women. Instead, Western Christianity is unusual in this regard. Why is that?

The answer is found in the split between the public and the private, fact and value, which cast Christianity into the upper story. This was not merely a change in ideas about religion; it involved changes in the material world as well—in the institutional structures of society. Once we grasp this process, it will shed new light not only on the state of evangelicalism today but also on issues like the role of the church in society and the roles of men and women in the home.[6]

HOUSEHOLDS AT WORK

Historically speaking, the key turning point was the Industrial Revolution, which eventually divided the private realm of family and faith from the public realm of business and industry. To grasp these changes more clearly, let's start by painting a picture of life *before* the Industrial Revolution.

In the colonial period, families lived much the way they have lived for millennia in traditional societies. The vast majority of people lived on farms or in peasant villages. Productive work was done in the home or its outbuildings.[7] Work was done not by lone individuals but by families or households. A household was a relatively autonomous economic unit, often including members of the extended family, apprentices, servants, and hired hands. Stores, offices, and workshops were located in a front room, with living quarters either upstairs or in the rear.[8] This meant that the boundary between home and world was highly permeable: The "world" entered continually in the form of clients, business colleagues, customers, and apprentices.

This integration of life and work actually survives in pockets of modern society. When I was twelve years old, my family lived for a year in a small village outside Heidelberg, Germany. To go shopping we would take a large basket and walk down the street to the baker, then the butcher, then the grocer, and so on. Each storefront was located in the front room of a house, with the family living upstairs or in the back rooms. Husband and wife worked together all day, and school let out at noon (all the way through high school), so the kids could come home and help out too, stocking shelves and running the cash register. Each business was a genuine family enterprise.

One evening when I visited a small gift shop down the street, a woman came out of a back room with a baby on her hip. She waited on me holding her baby in one arm, then waved goodbye and went back to making dinner. As late as the 1960s, in German villages, one could still experience the pre-industrial form of the family enterprise.

What did the colonial integration of work and life mean for family relationships? It meant that husband and wife worked side by side on a daily basis, sharing in the same economic enterprise. For a colonial woman, one historian writes, marriage "meant to become a co-worker beside a husband . . . learning new skills in butchering, silversmith work, printing, or upholstering— whatever special skills the husband's work required."[9] A useful measure of a society's treatment of women is the status of widows, and historical records show that in colonial days it was not uncommon for widows to carry on the family enterprise after their husbands died—which means they had learned the requisite skills to keep the business going on their own.[10]

Of course, women were also responsible for a host of household tasks requiring a wide range of skills: spinning wool and cotton; weaving it into cloth; sewing the family's clothes; gardening and preserving food; preparing meals without preprocessed ingredients; making soap, buttons, candles, medicines. Many of the goods used in colonial society were manufactured by women, and, as Dorothy Sayers writes, they "worked with head as well as hands."[11]

Now, the fact that all this took place in the home meant that mothers were able to combine economically productive work with raising children. It also meant that *fathers* were much more involved in raising children than they are today. In fact, we cannot understand changes in women's roles unless we consider changes in men's roles at the same time.

COMMUNAL MANHOOD

In the colonial period, the husband and father was regarded as the head of the household—and headship had a highly specific definition: It was defined as a divinely sanctioned office that conferred a duty to represent *not* his own individual interests but those of the entire household. This was an extension of the classical republican political theory discussed in chapter 10, in which a social institution (family, church, or state) was regarded as an organic unity where all shared in a common good. There was a "good" for individuals, but there was also a "good" of the whole, which was more than the sum of its parts—and this latter was the responsibility of the one in authority. He was called to sacrifice his own interests—to be *dis*interested—in order to represent the interests of the whole.[12] Husbands and fathers were not to be driven by personal ambition or self-interest but to take responsibility for the common good of the entire household.

We might say that the culturally dominant definition of masculinity was "communal manhood," a term coined by Anthony Rotundo in *American Manhood*. It meant that a man was expected to rank duty above personal ambition. To use a common phrase of the time, he was to fulfill himself through "publick usefulness" more than through economic success.[13]

In their day-to-day life, fathers enjoyed the same integration of work and childrearing responsibilities that mothers did. With production centered on the family hearth, fathers were "a visible presence, year after year, day after day" as they trained their children to work alongside them. Being a father was not a separate activity to come home to after a day at work; rather, it was an integral part of a man's daily routine.[14] Historical records reveal that colonial literature on parenting—like sermons and child-rearing manuals—were not addressed to mothers, as the majority are today. Instead, they were typically addressed to *fathers.* Fathers were considered the primary parent, and were held to be particularly important in their children's religious and intellectual training.[15]

Each household was a small commonwealth, headed by a Hausvater (literally: "house father"). In the mid-nineteenth century, writes historian John Gillis, "Not only artisans and farmers but business and professional men conducted much of their work in the house, assisted by their wives and children." As a result, "There was no difference between [the Hausvater's] time and that of his wife, children, and servants. They all ate and prayed together; they got up and went to bed on the same schedule." Indeed, surprising as it may seem, "Males . . . were as comfortable in the kitchen as women, for they had responsibility for provisioning and managing the house. Until the nineteenth century, cookbooks and domestic conduct books were directed primarily to them, and they were as devoted to décor as they were to hospitality."[16]

In terms of the father's constant presence in the home, nineteenth-century America was actually closer to the world of Martin Luther than to our own. "When a father washes diapers and performs some other mean task for his child, and someone ridicules him as an effeminate fool," Luther wrote, he should remember that "God with all his angels and creatures is smiling."[17]

This is not to idealize colonial life, which was often a rugged life of backbreaking labor. Yet in terms of family relations, there is no doubt that families benefited from an integration of life and labor that is extremely rare in our fragmented age.

HOME AS HAVEN

All of that changed with the Industrial Revolution. The main impact of the Industrial Revolution was to take work out of the home. This apparently simple change—in the physical location of work—set off a process that led to a sharp decline in the social significance accorded the home, drastically altering the roles of both men and women.

Industrialization took place in America at breakneck speed, roughly between 1780 and 1830. In the early stages, whole families went to work in the factories or did piecework at home—after all, they were used to working together as a unit. But it soon became evident that industrial work was shockingly different from the older family-centered work culture.

Since we've grown used to an industrialized workplace, we have to use a bit of historical imagination to grasp the differences. The old pattern was based on *personal* relations between a farmer and his sons and hired hands, or between craftsman and apprentices. In the Industrial Revolution, that gave way to *impersonal* relations based on wages. Or again, in the old handcraft tradition, a single craftsman would plan, design, and then carry out a project. But under capitalism there arose an ever-increasing class of managers and contractors, who took over all the creative planning and decision making, while leaving workers with mechanical tasks divided into simple, repetitive steps—the assembly line. In the traditional agrarian society, farming and handcrafts were "task-oriented," structured by human need and seasonable requirements. But in an industrial society, factory work was "time-oriented," structured by the clock and the regularity of the machine.

The new workplace fostered an economic philosophy of atomistic individualism, as workers were treated as so many interchangeable units to be plugged into the production process—each struggling to advance himself at the expense of others. To many, the world of industry seemed to be a Social Darwinist war of each against all. (Some have even suggested that Darwin's concept of the struggle for existence was merely an extrapolation into biology of the competitive ethos of early industrialism.[18])

It was not long before a great social outcry was raised against this new and alien work style, while large-scale efforts were mobilized to restrict its dehumanizing effects. The primary strategy was to delineate one outpost where the "old" personal and ethical values could be protected and maintained—namely, the home. It came to stand for enduring values and ideals that people desperately wanted to maintain in the face of modernity: things like love, morality, religion, altruism, and self-sacrifice.

To protect these endangered values, laws were passed limiting the participation of women and children in the factories. This was followed, beginning in the 1820s, by an outpouring of books, pamphlets, advice manuals, and sermons that delineated what historians call a doctrine of separate spheres: The public sphere of business and finance was to be cordoned off from the private sphere of home and family—so that the home would become a refuge, a haven, from the harsh and competitive world outside, a place of solace and spiritual renewal.[19]

WHY MEN LEFT HOME

How did these changes affect men and women? The most obvious change is that men had little choice but to follow their work out of households and fields, and into factories and offices. As a result, their physical presence around the household dropped sharply. It became difficult for them to fulfill their traditional responsibilities in the home. Fathers simply no longer spent enough time with their children to educate them, enforce regular discipline, or train them in adult skills and trades.

As a result, the most striking feature of child-rearing manuals of the mid-nineteenth century is the disappearance of references to fathers. For the first time we find sermons and pamphlets on the topic of child-rearing addressed exclusively to mothers rather than to fathers or both parents.[20] Men began to feel connected to their children primarily through their wives. The story is told of one Victorian father with sixteen children, who failed to recognize his own daughter at a parish Christmas party: "And whose little girl are you?" he asked. To which the miserable child replied, "I am yours, Daddy." The incident was probably exceptional, yet there is no doubt that middle-class fathers were becoming disconnected from their children.[21]

The impact on women was, if anything, even more dramatic. After the Industrial Revolution, the home eventually ceased being the locus of production and became a locus of consumption—which meant that women at home were gradually reduced from producers to consumers. Household industries with their range of mutual services were replaced by factories and waged labor. Instead of developing a host of varied skills—spinning, weaving, sewing, knitting, preserving, brewing, baking, and candle-making—women's tasks were progressively reduced to basic housekeeping and early childcare. Instead of enjoying a sense of economic indispensability, women were reduced to dependents, living off the wages of their husbands. Instead of working in a common economic enterprise with their husbands, women were shut off in a world of private "retirement." Instead of working with other adults throughout the day—servants, apprentices, clients, customers, and extended family—women became socially isolated with young children all day.[22]

Indeed, the role of mothers in childrearing actually became *more* salient than it had been in the past, when they had shared the task with other adults in the household—grandparents, single relatives, older siblings, servants, and especially fathers. As these others left home for the workplace, raising children became almost solely the mother's responsibility.

In a nutshell, women experienced a drastic *decrease* in the range of work available to them in the home—while, at the same time, experiencing a dramatic *increase* in responsibility for the narrow range of tasks that remained. Historical records give evidence of the dramatic change: Women "vanished more or less entirely from a number of occupations; they appeared less frequently in public records as printers, blacksmiths, arms-makers, or proprietors of small business concerns."[23] As I mentioned earlier, colonial widows often took over the business when their husbands died—but no longer. "By the early nineteenth century," writes one historian, "widows were conventionally viewed as pitiful charity cases,"[24] lacking the work skills to support themselves.

THE PASSIONATE MALE

Even the portrayals of masculine and feminine character came in for social redefinition. In the older ideal of "communal manhood," the key word was *duty:* duty to one's superiors and to God. Manly virtue was defined as keeping one's "passions" in submission to reason (with *passion* defined primarily as self-interest and personal ambition). The good man was one who exercised self-restraint and self-sacrifice for the sake of the common good.

But the emerging world of industrial capitalism fostered a new definition of virtue. The capitalist world seemed to require each man to function as an individual in competition with other individuals. In this new context, it was appropriate, even necessary, to act under the impulse of self-interest and personal ambition. Economic theories appeared—like Adam Smith's *The Wealth of Nations*—that treated self-interest as a universal natural force, analogous to the force of gravity in physics.

At the same time, political theory was shifting from the household to the individual as the basic unit of society. Classical republican political philosophy—with its organic view of an overarching, unifying common good—gave way to an atomistic view of society as an aggregate of warring, self-interested individuals. There emerged a new vision of the individual as free from settled social bonds, free from generational ties to the past, free to find his own place in society through open competition.[25]

We discussed these trends earlier in relationship to the evangelical movement, but they also had an enormous impact on the family. Eventually the values of the colonial period were actually turned upside down: The Puritans had viewed the "passions" as a threat to social order, requiring control and self-restraint for the public good. But by the end of the nineteenth century, male "passions" and self-interest had come to be viewed in a positive light—as the source of equality and economic prosperity.

In fact, the word *competitive* now entered the English language for the first time. Until then, English did not even have a word for a person who relished the challenge of a contest. But by the end of the nineteenth century, competition had become an obsession among American men. It was firmly believed that free competition was the engine of prosperity and political life.[26] "By a remarkable inversion," writes Lesslie Newbigin, people began to find "in covetousness not only a law of nature but the engine of progress by which the purpose of nature and nature's God was to be carried out."[27] And as men went forth to do battle in the tough, competitive world of commerce and politics, the masculine character itself was redefined as morally hardened, competitive, aggressive, and self-interested.

Taming Men

For women, however, the doctrine of separate spheres meant an entirely different story. They were called on to maintain the home as an arena cordoned off from the competitive, dog-eat-dog ethos of economics and politics. Women were to cultivate the softer virtues—of community, morality, religion, self-sacrifice, and affection. They were urged to act as moral guardians of the home, making it a place where men could be renewed, reformed, and refined—a place of "retirement" from the competitive, amoral world outside. As Frances Parkes wrote in 1829, "The world corrupts; home should refine."[28]

Thus the public/private split was reflected in a sharp contrast between the sexes as well. As Kenneth Keniston of MIT writes: "The family became a special protected place, the repository of tender, pure, and generous feelings (embodied in the mother) and a bulwark and bastion against the raw, competitive, aggressive, and selfish world of commerce (embodied by the father)."[29]

This was a startling reversal. In colonial days, husbands and fathers had been admonished to function as the moral and spiritual leaders of the household. But now men were being told that they were naturally crude and brutish—and that they needed to learn virtue from their wives. And many men acquiesced to the new ethos. For example, during the Civil War, General William Pender wrote to his wife, "Whenever I find my mind wandering upon bad and sinful thoughts I try to think of my good and pure wife and they leave me at once. . . . You are truly my good Angel."[30] Women were called upon to be the guardians of morality—to make men virtuous.

This is the origin of the double standard, and on the surface, it may appear to empower women. After all, it accorded them the status of enforcers of virtue. But the underlying dynamic was actually very troubling: As Rotundo explains, in essence America was releasing men from the requirement to be virtuous. For the first time, moral and spiritual leadership were no longer viewed as masculine attributes. They became women's work. "Women took men's place as the custodians of communal virtue," Rotundo writes, but in doing so, they "were freeing men to pursue self-interest."[31] In other words, men were being let off the hook.

In the long run, this "de-moralizing" of the male character would not be in women's best interest, as we will see. Nor was it in men's best interest, either, for they were becoming content with a stunted definition of masculinity as tough, competitive, and pragmatic, which denied their moral and spiritual aspirations.

FEMINIZING THE CHURCH

Where was the Christian church in all this? Did it stand firmly against the "demoralization" of the male character? Sadly, no. Instead the American church largely acquiesced in the redefinition of masculinity. After centuries of teaching that husbands and fathers were divinely called to the office of household headship, the church began to pitch its appeal primarily to women. Churchmen began to speak of women as having a special gift for religion and morality. If you look carefully at illustrations of camp meetings, you often see women dominating the front rows, swooning and fainting (see fig. 12.1). In many evangelical churches, women began to outnumber men, often by two to one. When the British novelist Francis Trollope visited America in 1832, she commented that she had never seen a country "where religion had so strong a hold upon the women or a slighter hold upon the men."[32]

Fig. 12.1 THE "FEMINIZATION" OF CHRISTIANITY: The awakenings tended to attract more women than men. *(Library of Congress, Prints and Photographs Division [LC-USZC4-4554].)*

Even the tone of religion became feminized. In a classic book on the subject, *The Feminization of American Culture*, Ann Douglas writes that the ministry lost "a toughness, a sternness, an intellectual rigor which our society then and since has been accustomed to identify with 'masculinity,'" and instead took on "feminine" traits of care, nurturing, sentimentalism, and retreat from the harsh, competitive ethos of the public arena.[33] The trend was especially typical of liberal churches. "Religion in the old virile sense has disappeared, and been replaced by a feeble Unitarian sensibility," lamented Henry James, Sr., father of the famous novelist.[34] A Congregationalist minister complained that "the sword of the spirit" has been "muffled up and decked out with flowers and ribbons."[35]

The underlying dynamic is that the church was adopting a defensive strategy vis-a-vis the culture at large. Many churchmen simply retreated from making cognitive claims for religion that could be defended in the public sphere. Instead, they transferred faith to the private sphere of experience and feelings—which put it squarely into the domain of women. In 1820 the Unitarian minister Joseph Buckminster wrote,

> I believe that if Christianity should be compelled to flee from the mansions of the great, the academies of the philosophers, the halls of legislators, or the throng of busy men, we should find her last and purest retreat with women at the fireside; her last altar would be the female heart.[36]

The operative word here is "flee." There was a presumption that religion was on the run from the public realm of hard-headed men, retreating to the private realm of soft-hearted women.

In short, instead of challenging the growing secularism among men, the church largely acquiesced—by turning to women. Churchmen seemed relieved to find at least one sphere, the home, where religion still held sway. Whereas traditional church teaching had held that fathers were responsible for their children's education, in the early 1800s, says one historian, "New England ministers fervently reiterated their consensus that mothers were *more* important than fathers in forming 'the tastes, sentiments, and habits of children,' and more effective in instructing them."[37] As a result, "mothers increasingly took over the formerly paternal task of conducting family prayers."[38]

Once again, we detect a disturbing dynamic: The churches were releasing men from the responsibility of being religious leaders. They were turning religion and morality into the domain of women—something soft and comforting, not bracing and demanding. Charles Eliot Norton of Harvard spoke for many at the time when he complained of the intellectual flabbiness—he called it the "unmanliness"—of religion.[39]

MORALS AND MERCY

A similar transformation was taking place in the arena of social reform. If women were the moral guardians of the home, it seemed logical that they should be the guardians of society as well. After all, many women began to argue, it was impossible to hermetically seal off private life from public life.

Public vices like drunkenness and prostitution have private consequences. As the leader of the Women's Christian Temperance Union put it, women must seek to "make the whole world Homelike."[40]

Thus it was largely women who fueled the widespread reform movements of the progressive era in the nineteenth century. Working first through churches, women set out to reform the public sphere by dispensing Christian benevolence. They joined or started societies to feed and clothe the poor. They supported the Sunday school movement and missionary societies. They joined or founded organizations to abolish slavery, to outlaw prostitution and abortion, to stop public drunkenness and gambling. They supported orphan asylums and societies such as the YWCA to assist single women in the cities. They initiated movements to abolish child labor, establish juvenile courts, and strengthen food and drug laws.

This interlocking network of reform societies has been dubbed the Benevolent Empire, and one prominent reformer at the time credited its construction largely to women: "Scarcely without exception," he said, "it has been the members of the women's clubs . . . who have secured all the advanced legislation . . . for the protection of home and the child."[41]

The progressive era marked the birth of the secular feminist movement as well, which I will discuss later. But most of these early crusaders were definitely *not* feminists: They did not base their claim to work outside the home on the now-familiar argument that there are no important differences between men and women. Just the opposite: They accepted the doctrine that women are more loving, more sensitive, more pious—but then they argued that it was *precisely those qualities* that equipped them for benevolent work beyond the confines of the home. As one woman put it at the time, the affairs of government and industry have "been too long dominated by the crude, war-like, acquisitive, hardheaded, amoral qualities of men," and they "should no longer be deprived of the tempering influence of women's compassion, spirituality, and moral sensitivity."[42]

The locus of many of these reform activities was the church, and they were eagerly supported by the clergy, who declared that women's naturally pious influence was crucial for society. Again Joseph Buckminster gives an eloquent example:

> We look to you, ladies, to raise the standard of character of our own sex [i.e., men]; we look to you, to guard and fortify those barriers which still exist in society, against the encroachments of impudence and licentiousness. We look to you for the continuance of domestick purity, for the revival of domestick

religion, for the increase of our charities, and the support of what remains of religion in our private habits and publick institutions.[43]

But notice the same dangerous dynamic we noted before: When "ladies" are given responsibility for "raising the standard of character" among men, then men are freed to be less responsible. They are let off the hook. "The care of dependent populations" was "once the civic duty of town fathers and poor masters," writes one historian. But in the nineteenth century, it became "known as charity . . . and became the province of women."[44]

FEMALE STANDARDS, MALE RESENTMENT

Eventually the double standard created tensions in relationships between men and women. After all, who were the objects of all these reform movements? Who were the scoundrels so debauched that women must take them in hand? They were, well, . . . men. The temperance movement mobilized wives and mothers against hard-drinking husbands and fathers, to drive them out of the tavern and back to the hearth. The rhetoric of female abolitionists focused on male slave masters who took sexual advantage of slave women.[45] The movement to outlaw prostitution and abortion cast fallen women as victims and men as cruel seducers. Historian Mary Ryan sums up the gender dimension to the reform movements: "Almost all the female reform associations were implicit condemnations of males; there was little doubt as to the sex of slave masters, tavern-keepers, drunkards and seducers."[46]

The message sent by the doctrine of separate spheres was "that women must control men morally," explains historian Carl Degler. Women were urged to "work together to control the male tendency toward lasciviousness." For if the mother was "moral arbiter in the home," that role "vouchsafed to women the right—nay, obligation—to regulate men's sexual behavior."[47]

The ideology of separate spheres was nothing less than "a plan for female government of male passions," Rotundo agrees. But then he notes that it had a paradoxical effect: "It gave men the freedom to be aggressive, greedy, ambitious, competitive, and self-interested, then it left women with the duty of curbing this behavior."[48]

These themes were even reflected in the literature of the day. In the early nineteenth century, a full third of all novels published in the United States were written by women (inspiring Nathaniel Hawthorne's famous outburst that America had been taken over by a "mob of scribbling women").[49] One of the most common themes in these novels is the triumph of women against evil men. "The major repeated story," writes an English professor, "is that of the struggle of the good woman against the oppression and cruelties, covert and blatant, of men."[50] The message was that men are inherently coarse and immoral—and that virtue is a womanly trait, imposed upon men only through great travail. The very concept of virtue, which had once been primarily a masculine trait, defined as courage and disinterested civic duty, was transformed into a feminine trait, focused primarily on sexual purity.[51]

MANLY MEN

Ultimately, however, the attempt to make women the moral reformers of men was self-defeating. Why? Because when virtue is defined as a *feminine* quality instead of a *human* quality, then requiring men to be virtuous is seen as the imposition of a feminine standard—a standard that is alien to the masculine nature. Being virtuous took on overtones of being effeminate instead of manly. The Unitarian minister William Ellery Channing was once praised by a friend who described him as "almost feminine" and admired his "womanly temperament."[52]

By the late nineteenth and early twentieth century, a reaction set in and men began to rebel against female efforts to reform them. A new word entered the American language: *overcivilized*. Men began to worry that boys were now growing up far too exclusively under the tutelage of mothers and female teachers, with the result that they were becoming soft and effeminate.[53]

In reaction, a new emphasis was laid on the wild, untamed masculine nature. This is when legends of the lost frontier became popular—the lives of Davy Crocket and Daniel Boone. Theodore Roosevelt went west and began to celebrate the "strenuous life" of the outdoorsman. Ernest Thomas Seton dressed up in an Indian costume and founded the American Boy Scouts. A 1914 Scout manual expressed the new philosophy vividly:

> [The] Wilderness is gone, the Buckskin man is gone, the painted Indian has hit the trail over the Great Divide, the privations and hardships of pioneer life which did so much to produce sterling manhood are now but a legend, and we must depend on the Boy Scout movement to produce the MEN of the future.[54]

Literary works began to sound a tone of male rebellion against female standards of virtue. Around the turn of the century, says one historical account, there arose "new genres of cowboy and adventure fiction, written by such authors as Owen Wister [author of the first Western] and Jack London"—books that "celebrated the man who had escaped the confines of domesticity."[55] So-called "bad boy" books became a popular genre, the best-known being Mark Twain's *Tom Sawyer* and *Huckleberry Finn*. The latter ends with Huck taking off for lands unknown "because Aunt Sally she's going to adopt me and sivilize me, and I can't stand it." Note that "sivilizing" is something done by old maid aunts. Twain's books express a poignant ambivalence of "both reverence for and resentment of the home and female standards."[56]

Some writers began to celebrate the male as primitive and barbarian, praising his "animal instincts" and "animal energy." The Tarzan books, featuring a wild man raised by apes, became immensely popular. This new definition of masculine virtue reflected in part the influence of Darwin's theory of evolution. For if humans evolved from the animal world, the implication was that the animal nature is the core of our being. This was a startlingly new concept: From antiquity, virtue had been defined as the exercise of restraint of the "lower" passions by the "higher" faculties of the rational spirit and the moral will. But now, in a stunning reversal, the animal passions were held up as the true self. "It is a new sensation to come to see man as an animal—the master animal of the world," wrote John Burroughs (son of the author of *Tarzan*).[57] The rise of Social Darwinism exalted "the triumph of man over man in primitive struggle."[58]

Even churches sensed a problem and began recasting religion in a more masculine tone. Too long religion had been the domain of women, tinged with sentimental piety. In 1858 an *Atlantic Monthly* article scolded parents, saying that if a son was "pallid, puny, sedentary, lifeless, joyless," then he was directed to the ministry—while on the other hand the "ruddy, the brave, and the strong" were directed to secular careers.[59] The answer? "Muscular Christianity"—a concept that combined hardy physical manliness with ideals of Christian service.

The best-known advocate of muscular Christianity was the evangelist Billy Sunday, who proclaimed that Jesus was "no dough-faced, lick-spittle proposition" but "the greatest scrapper that ever lived." Sunday offered followers a "hard-muscled, pick-axed religion," not some "dainty, sissified, lily-livered piety."[60] Books appeared with titles like *The Manliness of Christ, The Manly Christ*, and *The Masculine Power of Christ*. A church-based movement appeared called the Men and Religion Forward movement, which lasted until the 1950s, stressing an image of Jesus as the Successful Businessman or Salesman. Organizers bought ads on the sports pages, alongside ads for cars and whisky, and proclaimed that women "have had charge of the Church work long enough." They promoted a manly religion that emphasized strength and social responsibility.[61]

ROMPER ROOM DADS

This welcome emphasis on male strength was tainted, however, by the continuing theme that genuine masculinity is attained only by resisting "feminine" standards. In 1926 an influential book called *The Mauve Decade* opened with a savage attack on what the author called "the Titanesse"—the American woman as arbiter of public taste and morals. The author worried about the masculinity of boys growing up in woman-dominated homes and schools.[62]

In the 1940s, Philip Wylie penned a best-selling book called *A Generation of Vipers,* in which he accused women of "Momism"—of smothering, controlling, and manipulating their sons.[63] I still remember as an adolescent seeing articles in women's magazines on the dangers of "Momism." In the 1950s, *Playboy* made its appearance, warning that women are economic parasites and that marriage is a trap that will "crush man's adventurous, freedom-loving spirit."[64] An early issue showed a full-page spread of a smiling bride and groom—but on the next page, the bride's nose and chin are elongated, her veil sticks out like spikes, and the poor man discovers he's married a harpy. The theme was that family life and values are imposed by women, but are oppressive to men.

For the first time it became socially acceptable for fathers not to be involved with their families. By the 1920s and 30s in urban areas, the father had become the secondary parent who covered the "extras": hobbies, sports, trips to the zoo. As one historian describes it, fathers were reduced to entertainers—Romper Room dads.[65]

There emerged the now-familiar image of fathers as incompetent bumblers in the home, who are patronized by long-suffering wives and clever children[66]—the image popularized today in the comic strip figure Dagwood Bumstead, Al Bundy on "Married with Children," and the beleaguered Father Bear in the popular Berenstain Bears picture-book series. When Mother Bear decides the family must stop eating junk food, it's Papa Bear who sneaks his favorite snacks. When Mother Bear decides the family must give up TV, it's Papa Bear who sneaks downstairs at night to watch the tube. The books present a stereotype where mothers impose rules, and childish fathers break them. Even the children scold Papa Bear for his infractions. It's all presented as humorous, of course. Ha-ha! Let's teach children to feel superior to their incompetent fathers.

When I was attending seminary, a professor opened class one day by telling a story of how he was left alone—*alone!*—with his two small sons one Saturday morning while his wife went shopping. Unable to restrain their lively behavior, he finally imposed order by settling one boy at one end of the couch, the other boy at the other end, while he stationed himself rigidly between them, forbidding them to move or talk until his wife returned and rescued him. The (male) students in the class all laughed. And I wondered: When did it become socially acceptable for a Christian man to admit that he is incompetent as a father?

As fatherhood lost status, not surprisingly, men showed a decreasing investment in being fathers. From 1960 to 1980 there was a striking 43 percent reduction in the amount of time men spend in a family environment where young children are present.[67] For many women today, on a personal level, the problem is not male dominance so much as male desertion.

FEMINIST FURY

As we noted earlier, the secular feminist movement began at roughly the same time women were swelling the ranks of the Benevolent Empire, so let's back up now to see where it fits into the cultural pattern. From the beginning, this form of feminism was marked by considerable anger and envy—not toward individual men so much as toward the fact of the opportunities available to men in the public sphere. In 1912 one feminist wrote,

> Not since I started to do my own thinking have I been in any doubt as to which sphere most attracted me. The duties and pleasures of the average woman bore and irritate. The duties and pleasures of the average man interest and allure.[68]

Since the problem began when work was removed from the home, the solution, as feminists saw it, was obvious: Women should follow their work into the public arena. That's what men had done; why not women? Even science supported the idea of getting out of the house. The Social Darwinists of the day explained that the reason men were superior to women (a premise they did not question) was that, from their brute beginnings, males had fought for survival out in the world, where they were subject to competition and natural selection—a process that weeds out the weak and inferior. By contrast, women were at home nurturing the young, out of the reach of natural selection, with the result that they evolved more slowly.[69]

Ironically, even those who defended women against the Social Darwinist theories of biological inferiority did so by denigrating the home. Sociologist Lester Frank Ward argued that women were not *inherently* inferior; their faculties were merely underdeveloped because of their restriction to the home. Since nothing of significance happens in the home, those who spend time in it have only trivial matters upon which to exercise their minds, so it's no wonder they are stunted in their development.[70]

Radical feminists like Charlotte Perkins Gilman (a student of Ward's) concluded that women would never undergo evolutionary progress as long as they remained isolated in the pre-scientific environment of the home. Gilman urged that all the functions remaining in the home should be removed and put under the care of scientifically oriented professionals. Only when taken out of the amateurish hands of the housewife, she said, would any progress be made in cooking, cleaning, or childcare.[71] That may have sounded radical at the time but in our own day many women in essence follow Gilman's recommendations: Many rely on prepackaged foods or fast-food restaurants for much of their family's food; they hire crews to clean their houses; and hand their children over to be raised by day care workers.

WHAT HATH WOMAN LOST?

How does this historical perspective give us a better understanding of contemporary "women's issues"? What principles can we draw out for crafting a more biblical view of marriage and family?

First, it is clear that we cannot understand the changes in women's roles and circumstances without relating them to parallel changes in men's roles. The two are intertwined in a dynamic interaction. The Industrial Revolution caused both men's and women's work to contract and become more specialized; the work of both sexes lost range and variety, and became more intensely focused. Men lost their traditional integration into the life of the household and family (no more of those cookbooks written for men!). They lost the close contact they once enjoyed with their children throughout the day, and as a result experienced a sharp reduction in their function as parent and teacher in the home.

For their part, women at home lost their former participation in economic production, along with the wide range of skills and activities that once involved. The loss of women's traditional productive role placed them in a new economic dependence: Whereas the preindustrial household was maintained by an interplay of mutual services, now women's unpaid service stood out as unique, feeding into a stereotype of women's character as selfless and giving— or more negatively, as dependent and helpless. Women also became more isolated: They lost their easy contact with the adult world, while at the same time, their responsibility for childrearing actually increased, since it was no longer shared by fathers and other adults in the household.

It might be asked why, since both sexes lost much of the integration of life and labor characteristic of the preindustrial household, only women protested.

Why has there been a women's movement but no men's movement (at least, not until recently)? The answer is that the contraction of women's sphere was more onerous because they were confined to the private sphere—which means they suffered from the *general devaluation* of the private sphere. The home was cut off from the "real" work of society, isolated from intellectual, economic, and political life, at the same time that the church was.[72] I suggest that just as it is not good for religion to be compartmentalized in the private realm, it is not good for women either.

REMORALIZING AMERICA

A second theme we can draw from history is that the goal of the reform movements of the Benevolent Empire was to "remoralize" the public sphere with the values of the private sphere—of religion and family. We could even say this was an early stage of today's "culture war": Politics, economics, and academia were beginning to declare autonomy from the old controls of religion and morality, and evangelical Christians were fighting back.

Yet there was a gender dimension to this conflict: Since men worked in the public sphere, they were the first to absorb the ethos of modernity—while social reform was largely fueled by the efforts of women (backed by the clergy). Thus, to be more precise, it was largely an attempt by *women* to remoralize the public sphere and draw men back to traditional values.

A third theme should be obvious: This strategy did not work and ought to be abandoned. Men perceived the attempt at remoralization as an attempt to impose "feminine" values, which they were bound to resist. The consequent male rebellion against religion and family led to a devaluation of both—a trend that continues even today.

Despite the adverse consequences, astonishingly, some social commentators persist in holding women responsible for "taming" men. In an article titled "Women Taming Men," columnist William Raspberry says crime and drugs among African-American men are the fault of . . . African-American women! "As long as women tolerate this behavior in men, it will continue," Raspberry writes. In support, he argues that it was women who "created marriage" and "domesticated" men, and who "are the civilizers of the society."[73]

Yet the historical record in America shows that this approach did not work. The truth is that men will be drawn back into family life only when they are convinced that being a good husband and father is a *manly* thing to do; that parental duty and sacrifice are masculine virtues; that marital love and fidelity are not female standards imposed upon men externally, but an integral part of the male character—something inherent and original, created by God.

NO DOUBLE STANDARD

Finally, the failure of the strategy of separate spheres illuminates why the feminist movement grew rapidly in the 1960s. It meant that many women were no longer willing to be the "moral guardians" of men or to "regulate men's sexual behavior." In short, they refused to maintain the double standard. Nor were they willing to remain isolated in a private sphere that had been devalued and emptied of much of its productive and personally fulfilling work. Secular feminists urged women to leave the empty husk of the home and to stake out a claim in the public arena, where "real" work was done and where they could regain some respect.

Of course, there was only one small problem—or actually several small problems: young children. Who would take care of the children? That's why it became so important to radical feminists to gain control of their reproductive lives through contraception and abortion; and when they did have children, to demand state-sponsored day care. These measures seemed crucial to gaining relatively equal access with men to the public realm.

Clearly, these "solutions" are morally objectionable to most evangelical Christians. Yet few have suggested realistic alternatives to the historical and economic trends that gave rise to them. In conservative circles, writes Dorothy Sayers, women are often simply "exhorted to be feminine and return to the home from which all intelligent occupation has been steadily removed."[74]

RECONSTITUTING THE HOME

A better course would be to challenge the trend toward emptying the home of its traditional functions. On the conceptual level, we need Christian economists willing to rethink the modern economy from the ground up, and creatively craft a biblically inspired philosophy of economics. What is the proper function of the family and of economic institutions, and how can they interrelate in ways that support rather than hinder each sphere's proper calling before the Lord?

Christians also need to challenge the "ideal-worker" standard in American corporate culture, which decrees that an employee should be available for full-time (even overtime) work without permitting his personal and family life to interfere—because he has turned all that over to a home-based spouse.[75] The ideal-worker standard did not function well even when wives and mothers were still home-based, filling in for absent fathers. Among the many causes of the rebellious youth culture of the 1960s was a great deal of "father hunger." The ideal-worker also helped create America's rootless, mobile society because it required workers to be willing to move anywhere at any time—tearing apart extended families and stable neighborhood communities. Family life became impoverished and more difficult to sustain without that traditional network of support systems.

Christian organizations ought to be the first to debunk the ideal-worker standard as harmful to families. They should be on the forefront in offering practical alternatives for reintegrating family responsibilities with income-producing work—through such things as home-based work, part-time work positions with prorated benefits, flexible hours, and telecommuting.

Heidi Brennan of Mothers At Home, a national group headquartered in Virginia, says the single most frequent question the organization receives from mothers around the country is, How can I earn an income and still be home with my family? Many women are finding that an effective way to combine work and family is to start a home-based business, and today women-owned small businesses are growing at a rapid pace. Home-based work has the added benefit of providing a means for children to participate, so that parents once again fulfill the role of training their children in basic work skills and values, just as in the preindustrial household.[76]

Nor are these suggestions just for women. One poll found that men (age 20 to 39) with young children said having time with their family was the most important issue in their jobs. A full 82 percent said a family-friendly schedule was "very important," while only 56 percent wanted more job security, 46 percent mentioned a high salary, and 27 percent mentioned status.[77]

What about single mothers, families living in poverty, and others who have no choice but to work? Even they would benefit from measures that allow them to integrate work with raising children, instead of putting them in day care. Some groups have discovered that strategies first developed among the poorest of the poor in places like Bangladesh work equally well in America's inner cities. For example, the Women's Self-Employment Project in Chicago works with poor women—mostly single mothers—using a rotating loan system developed in Third World countries in order to support the creation of "microenterprises" based in the home. Many work-training programs offered to low-income women channel them into hotel cleaning, data entry, and other positions that offer relatively little scope for creativity or responsibility. By contrast, self-employment gives women the opportunity to develop initiative and to take charge of their lives. It also gives them much more flexibility in working around their family responsibilities.[78]

At the same time, Christians must not fall into the trap of assuming that paid employment is the only thing that will give women a sense of dignity. That's a mistake secular feminists often make. Instead Christians need to challenge the prevailing ideology of success by insisting that individuals are most fulfilled when they enjoy a sense of calling or vocation—whether in paid *or* unpaid work. We all long for a sense that we are contributing to something larger than ourselves, to a greater good, to God's purposes in the world.

PRIVATE AND PERSONAL

To summarize the historical changes we have traced, in the nineteenth century the two-realm theory of truth came to be reflected in a deep social divide. Whereas in colonial times the social order was viewed as an organic whole, by the mid-nineteenth century it had splintered into a set of separate domains. Society was segmented, says Donald Scott, into "sacred and secular, domestic and economic, masculine and feminine, private and public."[79]

Yet these were all aspects of a single fundamental cleaveage. "The fissure in society divided the sexes," explains Newbigin: "the man dealt with public facts, the women with personal values." Read that sentence again and notice how succinctly it covers the split between public and private, facts and values, men and women.[80] We can better understand secular feminism by realizing that it was an attempt by women to cross this troubling chasm in order to join men in the public sphere. A better route, however, would be to find ways to *close* the gap itself, recovering some measure of integration of work and worship for both men and women.

Obviously, we could also raise exegetical questions about the way Scripture deals with the relations of husbands and wives, women's leadership in the church, and so on. But such questions go beyond the scope of this book. My goal has been to show how the social and intellectual context shapes the very way those questions are conceived. Though we no longer live in the nineteenth century, the tension between the public and private spheres continues to have profound personal consequences, especially for women. Most women today are trained, like men, for life and work in the public sphere. As a result, they may not even have much contact with the private sphere until they have children, which can then be a difficult and even traumatic transition.

My own interest in this subject grew out of the conflicts I experienced upon becoming pregnant with my first child. As a seminary student, I was profoundly ambivalent about this pregnancy. What would having a child mean for my future? How could I have children and still grow professionally? The only way I knew to pursue my deepest interests, to fulfill my calling before the Lord, was in the world of ideas, through academic study. But having a child seemed to pose a profound threat to the possibility of continuing my studies. I felt as though I were facing a black hole of uncertainty.

To jump ahead, I want to say that I greatly enjoyed becoming a mother, even homeschooling our son because I wanted to be intensely involved in his life. In addition, for most of my career, I have worked part-time and from a home office, which allows me to combine work and parenting responsibilities. Yet in my student days, unable to foresee all this, I went through an agonizing dilemma—and it was this experience that caused me to begin thinking about the pressures women face when they become mothers.

Let me highlight the issue by turning it around: My husband was about to become a father for the first time, but *he* did not have to wrestle with fears of giving up a central source of fulfillment, and the exercise of his gifts, for a significant portion of his life. When men have families, most are able to continue working in their chosen fields (though admittedly, they often do make difficult trade-offs between family and career advancement). At the time, I confess, it struck me as decidedly unfair that women should experience such intense pressure to choose between the two major tasks of adult life—between pursuing a calling and raising the next generation.

Rachel Cusk, in her book *A Life's Work,*[81] says many women describe becoming a mother as a "shock." Their lives are turned upside down by the constancy of a baby's demands. At the same time, they are astonished by the intensity of the love bond they form with their newborn. They feel like aliens entering a strange new world of home and childrearing.

Why does all this come as such a surprise? Because through young adulthood, most of us have been carefully primed for participation in the *public* world—while growing out of touch with the private world of babies and families. We probably haven't even baby-sat a neighbor's kids since we were teenagers. Our identity and sense of self-worth has been built primarily on our public persona and accomplishments, especially at work. By contrast, motherhood is still individual, personal, and private. As Cusk puts it, "In motherhood, a woman exchanges her *public* significance for a range of *private* meanings" for which she has not been prepared. Modern child-care manuals, she comments, "begin with a sort of apocalyptic scenario in which the world we know has vanished, replaced by another in whose principles we must be educated."[82]

Here the yawning gap between public and private spheres becomes a personal issue, as women find themselves catapulted into a new world that is not only unfamiliar but also undervalued. If they are feminists, as I was when I had my first child, they may even feel guilty about taking on "traditional" female roles and responsibilities in the home.[83] Women often face intense pressure from the outside world, including former colleagues urging them to return to the "real" world of professional work. Because of the unusually high percentage of professional women in the Washington, D.C., area where I live, there are no less than three support organizations that help mothers who want to leave the workplace, or at least cut back, while they have young children at home. The pressure is so relentless on professional women to stay in the work-force and put in long hours away from their families that women who want more time with their children need support from others who understand the strain.

BLUEPRINT FOR LIVING

Not only this topic but all the topics we have discussed up to this point have profound personal implications. These are not merely abstract intellectual mat-ters fit for philosophers and historians to debate in the rarified atmosphere of academia. Ideas and cultural developments affect real people, shaping the way they think and live out their lives. That's why it is crucial for us to develop a Christian worldview—not just as a set of coherent ideas but also as a blueprint for living. Believers need a roadmap for a full and consistent Christian life. We also need to understand enough of modern thought to identify the ways it blocks us from living out the gospel the way God intends—both in terms of intellectual roadblocks and, as we have seen in this chapter, in terms of eco-nomic and structural changes that make it harder to live by scriptural princi-ples. It is enormously difficult for fathers in a modern industrialized society to function in the strong parental role that Scripture calls them to—and as they *did* in earlier historical periods. It is likewise difficult for mothers to raise their children well, and still be faithful in honing their other gifts in a Christian call-ing. The distance between home and workplace, between public and private spheres, means most of us are required to specialize in either one or the other, at least for a substantial period of our lives.

The personal dimension to living out a Christian worldview typically gets short shrift in most books on the subject, yet it is by far the most important. What ultimate benefit do we gain from investing time and effort to develop a Christian worldview, if it is only a new way to think? A mental exercise? A slick set of arguments? New ideas have limited value unless they transform the way we actually live—the day-to-day decisions we make, the way we interact with other people, the way we run our organizations. The practical application of Christian worldview is so important that it is the subject of the next chapter. We cheat ourselves terribly unless we take the final step and restructure our entire lives by the life-giving truths in God's Word.

PART 4

WHAT NEXT?
LIVING IT OUT

13

TRUE SPIRITUALITY
AND CHRISTIAN WORLDVIEW

Moral character is assessed not by what a man knows
but by what he loves.

ST. AUGUSTINE[1]

As Tony unfolded his life story,[2] I wondered how anyone who had suffered so greatly had ever come to faith in God. Where had he encountered a witness that was authentic and powerful enough to cut through all the pain he had endured?

Tony's parents claimed to be Christians, but they seemed content to do little more than go through the ritual of strict church attendance. In fact, the tone of their home life could not have been better calculated to make atheists of all their children. Which it pretty nearly did.

Tony's father was a workaholic, so driven to getting ahead professionally that he was seldom home. And when he *was* home, he seldom stopped working there either. He organized the children in a constant round of chores and home-building projects. A quiet, contemplative boy, Tony rarely seemed capable of pleasing his quick-tempered father—whose response was to beat him. "I was awkward and uncoordinated, and when I was unable to meet his expectations, my reward was the fist."

Tony's own words tell the story with a grim repetitiveness that mirrors the abuse he endured:

I was often punished. I was punished for misunderstanding what my father wanted me to do. I was punished when I asked a question for clarification. I was punished when I didn't work fast enough. I was punished when my awkwardness caused me to knock things over or drop things. I was punished when I told the truth, and when I told a lie trying to avoid more punishment. I was punished! I was punished!

Tony's story, with its tragic refrain, echoed in my memory long after we had talked together. In time, he came to live in terror of his father. And it wasn't just the beatings. Along with the physical abuse came a constant torrent of verbal abuse. His father would tower over the trembling boy, his face contorted in rage, shouting what a stupid, incompetent idiot he was—as he punched him again and again.

By the time he reached high school, Tony had decided to commit suicide. "My parents told me that I was bad, and that a good Christian boy would obey them. But I just couldn't meet their expectations, and eventually I gave up trying. My life was misery. I could see no hope." The only thing that stopped him short was the thought that God might be real—and might send him to hell for killing himself. "The only way I could see out of my misery was suicide, but I was scared of the possibility of hell. That fear was the one thing that stayed my hand."

So Tony began to search out the question of God's existence—not with any hope of salvation but only to methodically clear the deck for taking his life. "I had to find out: Is there a God? Not that I'd seen any evidence of His existence, but suicide gives no second chances. So before I killed myself, I had to be sure."

One Sunday a gaunt, shabby man with a strong foreign accent appeared on the doorstep of the church where Tony, at the insistence of his parents, still attended. Tony showed him the way into the sanctuary, little knowing that this tall stranger held the key to the answers he was seeking. The man had good reason to look so haggard, for he had survived fourteen years in that hell on earth known as a communist prison camp in Romania. For what? For the crime of being a Lutheran pastor. On the minister's neck and head, Tony could see deep scars from the torture he had endured at the hands of his communist captors.

The man's name was Richard Wurmbrand, and he had only recently been released from communist Romania. The stories he related about communist persecution shocked Americans, who at that time knew little about conditions behind the Iron Curtain. (This was long before Alexander Solzhenitsyn smuggled out his massive *Gulag Archipelago*, documenting the Soviet Union's extensive prison camp system.) Later Wurmbrand would give a riveting testimony to a U.S. Senate subcommittee, which was picked up by the media and reported across the country.[3]

As Tony listened to Wurmbrand's account of his years behind bars, a faint glow of hope flickered within him. Here was a man who had been beaten just as he had been—in fact, far worse—and who understood what it meant to endure pain so searing that you don't want to live anymore. Yet he had come back from the edge of the abyss with a profound faith in a good God who loves us. "Humanly speaking, he should have been full of fury at his captors who had treated him so unjustly," Tony told me. "That I could understand. But instead he had responded in love."

Here was something entirely alien to Tony's experience: "This wasn't just a Sunday morning ritual. This was a life-giving power." He quickly recognized that it was the only power that could salvage his own damaged life. "I already knew a person's natural reaction to unjust suffering. But here was something new—something that opened up an alternative to what I had experienced." After that memorable Sunday, Tony began to read the Bible, and over time he too discovered a faith strong enough to bring him back from the edge of the abyss. "After this experience of seeing the reality of Christ in a person's life, I slowly started growing in the faith."

WURMBRAND'S FREEDOM

One reason I was so fascinated by Tony's story is that I, too, had seen Richard Wurmbrand shortly after his release from Romania—in fact, within only a few weeks. Wurmbrand was freed in 1965, when the Norwegian Lutheran Mission paid a $10,000 ransom to the Romanian government to purchase his liberty, and shortly afterward he traveled to Norway. My family was living in Oslo at the time, and on Wurmbrand's first Sunday there, since he could not speak Norwegian, he decided to visit the American Lutheran Church where we attended.

With hollow cheeks and sunken eyes, outfitted in secondhand clothing, Wurmbrand and his wife (who had also been imprisoned) stood out sharply from the well-heeled Western diplomats who made up most of the English-speaking congregation. Yet the couple radiated a strong personal magnetism that irresistibly drew attention. When they witnessed the sight of people worshiping freely and without fear of persecution, they broke down and wept uncontrollably.

That did it. The pastor of the church turned the service over to Reverend Wurmbrand to tell his strange tale of unspeakable persecution. The most vivid picture that remains in my mind is of the tears running down his face when he visited the Sunday school and saw children openly taught the Word of God. Openly! In Romania that was against the law. Many believers were in prison at that very moment because they had been caught secretly teaching young people about Christianity.

Though only thirteen at the time, I have never forgotten the terrible stories Wurmbrand told—of prisoners branded by red-hot irons, or hung upside down from a pole while their feet were beaten into a bloody mass, or locked into narrow closets with metal spikes in the walls. For religious prisoners, there were special tortures: Wurmbrand told of pastors forced to give the Lord's Supper in the form of urine and feces. He himself endured the worst trial of all: three years in solitary confinement in a cell thirty feet underground.

Casting my mind back to these memories, I could understand why Wurmbrand's testimony had worked so strongly upon Tony's heart. The Romanian pastor's message carried authenticity and conviction because he had suffered—and had come through it with a new spirit. His character was a testimony to the biblical principle that suffering is a crucible that tests the quality of a person's faith.

"We suffer with him in order that we may also be glorified with him," Paul writes (Rom. 8:17). Western Christians like to jump ahead to the second half of the verse, to the assurance that we will share in His glory. But spiritual growth doesn't work that way. Genuine sanctification begins with suffering and dying with Christ. "I have been crucified with Christ," Paul writes. "It is no longer I who live, but Christ who lives in me" (Gal. 2:20). Notice the order again: Only when we have faced trials so severe that we are crucified spiritually to this world can Christ truly give us His resurrection life.

Ultimately, this experience is the goal of developing a Christian worldview—not just studying and debating ideas, but dying and rising again in union with Christ. Without this inner spiritual reality, everything we have said about worldviews can become little more than a mental exercise—a way to solve intellectual puzzles, or, worse, a way to impress others by sounding smart and well-educated. Virtually anyone can learn to parrot high-sounding phrases, pronounce certain shibboleths, repeat a few punchy quotations, in order to craft an image of being cultured and sophisticated. Even worldview studies can become a seedbed for pride instead of a process of submitting our minds to the Lordship of Christ.

In fact, I would go even further and say that the first step in conforming our intellect to God's truth is to die to our vanity, pride, and craving for respect from colleagues and the public. We must let go of the worldly motivations that drive us, praying to be motivated solely by a genuine desire to submit our minds to God's Word—and then to use that knowledge in service to others.

We may do a great job of arguing that Christianity is total truth, but others will not find our message persuasive unless we give a visible demonstration of that truth in action. Outsiders must be able to see for themselves, in the day-to-day pattern of our lives, that we do not treat Christianity as just a private retreat, a comfort blanket, a castle of fairy-tale beliefs that merely make us feel better.

It is all but impossible for people to accept new ideas purely in the abstract, without seeing a concrete illustration of what they look like when lived out in practice. Sociologists call this a "plausibility structure"—the practical context in which ideas are fleshed out. The church is meant to be the "plausibility structure" for the gospel. When people see a supernatural dimension of love, power, and goodness in the way Christians live and treat one another, then our message of biblical truth becomes plausible.

But what if people see Christians practicing injustice and compromising with the world? Then who will believe our message? A verbal presentation of a Christian worldview message loses its power if it is not validated by the quality of our lives.

SCHAEFFER'S CRISIS

In doing research for this book, I reread several of the Christian classics that had shaped my thinking in the early years after my conversion some thirty years ago. Among them was Francis Schaeffer's *True Spirituality*, which he considered foundational to the rest of his writings. Why? Because it explains how to apply biblical principles to daily experience. He knew that without integrity at the personal level, a Christian worldview easily deteriorates into a lifeless set of ideas or a bare cognitive system. And while it is true that Christianity offers the best cognitive system for explaining the world, it is never *just* a system. *Knowing* the truth has meaning only as a first step to *living* the truth day by day.

And how do we drive our beliefs down into the reality of daily experience? By dying to ourselves, that we may live for God. From my earlier readings of *True Spirituality*, I did not remember that it opens with the theme of suffering. Spiritual giants like Richard Wurmbrand are not the only ones who grow spiritually through suffering. All of us discover at some point that the most profound spiritual growth typically comes through crises. Because we are fallen creatures living in a fallen world, the winnowing of our character is usually a painful process.[4]

Schaeffer himself underwent a crisis of faith after having been a pastor, then a mission worker, for more than ten years. At that point, he grew frustrated by the lack of spiritual reality in the lives of so many Christians he knew—including himself—and began to ask, How can we know experientially the Christian life described in the New Testament? How do we grasp hold of the love, the power, the abundant life that God promises?

"I walked in the mountains when it was clear," Schaeffer later recalled, "and when it was rainy I walked backward and forward in the hayloft we had in the old chalet in which we lived."[5] Pacing and praying, he retraced his thinking all the way back to the agnosticism he had held as a young man, reconsidering such basic questions as whether or not the Bible is true. After coming to a new confidence that it *is* true, he then asked God to show him how its redemptive message could become demonstrably real in his own life.

Over time he discovered that the key to inner transformation is the application of Christ's work on the cross for *this* life, not only for the life to come. Theologically speaking, he had discovered that Christ's death and resurrection are the basis not only for justification but also for sanctification—the growth in holiness that is meant to take place in believers here and now.

IDOLS OF THE HEART

A pervasive theme throughout the New Testament is that Christ's death and resurrection were not merely objective events that happened in history— though certainly they were *that* first of all. We should never give up our conviction that the objective truths of Christ's death and resurrection are the basis for our justification. But the next step is to take Christ as the ongoing model for our lives. As the medieval spiritual writers put it, we are called to practice "the imitation of Christ." Not in a moralistic sense of trying to mold our behavior by certain ethical precepts, but rather in a mystical sense that our own suffering becomes a participation in Christ's suffering. That's why Paul wrote, "Our old self was crucified with him" (Rom. 6:6); and, "The world has been crucified to me, and I to the world" (Gal. 6:14).

Only *after* sharing in Christ's death is there a promise of sharing in His resurrection power. Again, the order is crucial. "Therefore we were buried with him by baptism into death," Paul writes, "that, as Christ was raised from the dead by the glory of the Father, so also we may walk in newness of life" (Rom. 6:4). It is impossible for us to receive a new life until we have truly given up the old one. We do that at our conversion, of course, in a once-for-all transaction where God, as the Judge, declares us forgiven of our sins and adopts us into His family. But being declared righteous in a judicial sense is only the beginning. After that, we are called to begin a process in which we die spiritually, day by day, to deeply ingrained sinful patterns, so that we can be liberated from sin and grow spiritually into a new person.

Moment by moment, we must learn to say no to sin and worldly motivations. In a world of moral relativism, where everything is reduced to personal choice, simply saying no is in itself a very hard teaching. If it does not seem hard, then we are probably accommodating to the world without realizing it. If we are not saying no in ways that bring us to our knees to seek God's enabling power, then it's likely that we are not standing against the sinful system of the world as we ought.

The principle of dying to worldly systems applies beyond obvious sins. In a culture that measures everything in terms of size, success, and influence, we have to say no to these worldly values as well. In a culture of material affluence, we have to say no to coveting a better house, a sleeker car, a more upscale neighborhood, a more impressive ministry. In a culture that judges people by reputation and achievements, we have to resist the lure of living for professional recognition and advancement. Not that these things are wrong in themselves. But when they fill our hearts and define our motivations, then they become barriers to our relationship with God—which means they become sin for us. As Paul says, *anything* not of faith is sin, because it blocks our single-minded devotion to God and hinders our growth in holiness.

God calls such barriers "idols of the heart" (see Ezek. 14:1-11)—and they can even include genuine needs that are completely right and proper in themselves. This is where the principle becomes really difficult. When our natural needs become a cause of anger and bitterness, or a reason to oppress or attack others, then we must say no to them as well. For example, it's perfectly proper to want intimacy and respect in our marriage. But people are sinners, and at times even Christian spouses may find themselves lonely and unloved. Then one of two things will happen: Either we will become angry and reject the other person—or we will learn how to die to even our valid personal needs, and trust God to work good even in an imperfect situation. Again, it is proper and right to want a job that fulfills our God-given talents, where we enjoy the respect of colleagues and supervisors. But in a fallen world, we may have to accept work that is less than fulfilling; we may not be successful; or we may work for bosses who are demeaning and exploitive. What then? Either we will find ourselves shaking our fist at God—or we will put our talents on the altar and die to them, trusting God to honor our sacrifice to Him.

Putting our valid needs on the altar does not mean shutting our mouths and closing our eyes to a sinful situation. If someone is truly in the wrong, then the loving response is not to give in but to confront the person. It is not an act of love to allow someone to sin against you with impunity. Sin is a cancer within the other person's soul, and genuine love must be strong and courageous in bringing that sin to the light, where it can be diagnosed and dealt with.

Yet it is all too easy to do the right thing in the wrong spirit. Only as we offer up to God our anger, fear, and drive for control do we develop the kind of spirit God can use in confronting others. "Christ also suffered for you, leaving you an example, so that you might follow in his steps," Peter writes—with the ultimate purpose "that He might bring us to God" (1 Pet. 2:21; 3:18). So, too, when we suffer, even unjustly, the ultimate purpose is to equip us to bring others to God. Moment by moment, as we suffer the effects of sin and brokenness in a fallen world, we need to ask Him to use those trials to unite us to Christ in His sacrifice and death—so that we can then be used to bring others to repentance and renewal.

THEOLOGY OF THE CROSS

Peter is telling us that the cross of Christ is a model for the deep structure of our own spiritual progress. Jesus makes this connection Himself in the Gospels: "The Son of Man must suffer many things and be rejected by the elders and chief priests and scribes, and be killed, and on the third day be raised." Immediately afterward He adds: "If anyone would come after me, let him deny himself, and take up his cross daily and follow me" (Luke 9:22, 23).

Notice the sequence: rejected and slain come first, before we can be raised.[6] In Jesus' case, the rejection came from the corrupt religious leaders of His day, whose hearts, hidden under their religious robes and their pious God-talk, were driven by worldly ambition and jealousy. They thus represented the world itself, in its rebellion against God and its rejection of His Son. In our own lives, too, rejection may come either from the world or from religious believers with worldly motivations in their hearts—parents who are neglectful or abusive, like Tony's; a spouse who is unloving or unfaithful; a child who rebels against his Christian upbringing; a church that is unwelcoming; a boss who is disrespectful and demeaning; a close friend who betrays you. Living in a world still under the dominion of sin, each of us will be rejected and wounded in some way.

As Martin Luther put it, Christians embrace a theology of the cross, not a theology of glory.[7] The mystery of our salvation was effectuated by Jesus' descent to earth not as a conquering hero but as a suffering servant—mocked, beaten, hung on a cross. True knowledge of Christ comes only as we are willing to give up our dreams of glory, praying to be identified with Him on the cross. While homeschooling my son Dieter, I taught him to play the recorder, and we used to play this moving hymn as a duet:

> Jesus, I my cross have taken,
> All to leave and follow Thee;
> Destitute, despised, forsaken,
> Thou from hence my all shall be.[8]

Try applying this outlook in the Washington, D.C., area, where I live, or any other place where the pressure is relentless to get ahead, make a good impression, pursue the right contacts, advance your cause. Destitute? Despised? Are we really willing to let God take us through times of defeat and despair, when we experience communion with Him in His crucifixion?

The wonder of God's goodness is that He can use these "crosses" for our sanctification, just as He used the death of Jesus to advance His redemptive plan. "You meant evil against me, but God meant it for good," Joseph told his brothers (Gen. 50:20). Christians sometimes think it a matter of piety to deny the evil done to them—to cover it up, say it wasn't so bad, wear a smile in public. But Joseph did not shrink from calling his brothers' actions *evil*, and neither should we. In this world, we too will be rejected by people with sinful motives, and for the sake of truth we should call it what it is. But we can also turn it to good by realizing that suffering gives us a chance to enter spiritually upon the journey that Jesus mapped out for us: rejected, slain (spiritually), and, finally, raised.

REJECTED, SLAIN, RAISED

In a fallen world, where nature itself has been thrown out of harmony, the greatest source of suffering for some people may be physical. The force that disrupts and threatens the normal course of life may be illness or injury. Over the past few years, a dear friend has suffered from cancer—at one point hovering between life and death for several months. Knowing that she is a spiritually sensitive person, I asked what she had learned from this harrowing experience. "I learned that I had to be willing to die," she replied, her eyes misting. "I was desperately holding on to life, to my family, and I had to let go and be willing to let God take everything from me."

That is exactly the point to which God has to bring each of us. Whether the suffering is physical or psychological, the way God brings us to see what we are *really* basing our life upon is to take it away. When we lose our health or family or work or reputation, and our lives come crashing down and we feel lost and empty—that's when we realize how much our sense of purpose and identity was actually bound up in those things. That's why we have to be willing to let Him take them away. We have to be "willing to die."

This principle may sound overly negative, and certainly there are strains of Christianity that teach a stern, tight-lipped asceticism—as though holiness consisted simply in saying no to fun and pleasure. But genuine spiritual death doesn't have a whiff of asceticism about it. It has nothing to do with monastic flight from the world. It is choosing to obey God's commands across the whole of life even when it is painful or costly. It is crying out to Him when our hearts are crucified by betrayal or oppression. It is letting go of the things we love or want the most, if hanging on to them is causing us to grow angry at God or to strike out against others. It is believing in God's goodness, sometimes by a sheer act of the will, in the face of overwhelming evil. And it is the whispered prayer that God would grant us to be united to Christ as we submit ourselves to the model He gave us—rejected, slain, raised.

We tend to have a limited concept of spiritual death as saying no only to things we want or covet—our guilty pleasures and selfish ambitions. But in reality it means dying inwardly to whatever has *control* over us. And the thing that really controls us may not be what we want; it may be what we fear. Fear can dominate our lives just as strongly as desire. It may be anger. Or pride. Or even futile wishes—a person disappointed in life may simply keep wishing that things had been different, and may find it all but impossible to let go of those dashed hopes and ruined dreams. Whatever it is that controls you, *that* is what you must place on the altar to be slain. Only then will we be released from our inner compulsions and be able to discover the freedom in which nothing but "the love of Christ controls us" (2 Cor. 5:14).

LIFE-PRODUCING MACHINES

Offering up the idols of our heart is only one step in the process, however. The next is to pray for spiritual deliverance. For whenever we give in to long-term, ingrained patterns of sin, we give Satan a foothold in our inner self—and become spiritually enslaved to him. As Paul writes, our bodies themselves can become "instruments for unrighteousness" (Rom. 6:13). This is a sobering thought: It means that it is possible for even a Christian to be controlled by Satan and do his work. There is no neutral ground in the spiritual battle between the forces of God and the forces of the devil. If some area of our lives is not fully submitted in obedience to God, then in practice we are under the control of Satan in that area—giving him the allegiance that belongs to God alone.

Paul seems to realize that this is a hard saying for Christians to accept, for he expounds further on the principle. "Do you not know that if you present yourselves to anyone as obedient slaves, you are slaves of the one whom you obey, either of sin, which leads to death, or of obedience, which leads to righteousness?" (Rom. 6:16). Paul is saying that even those saved by Christ can, in their day-to-day words and actions, produce either life or death. The terrible reality is that we may attend church regularly, read the Bible diligently, even work in a Christian ministry, yet still be what Schaeffer calls "death-producing machines"—"living contrary to our calling, yielding ourselves to the devil and therefore producing death in this poor world."[9]

How do we know whether we are producing life or death? By whether our lives exhibit the beauty of God's character. When people see the way you live, are they drawn closer to God or are they alienated from God? When they observe the way you treat others, do they find the gospel more credible or less credible? That is the standard by which we should measure our actions. Christians are called to be "life-producing machines," demonstrating by our actions and character that God exists. We may preach a God of love, we may even have opportunities to reach thousands through our ministries and church programs, but if nonbelievers do not observe *visible love* within those ministries and churches and Christian organizations, then we undermine the credibility of our message.

"The medium *is* the message," to use Marshall McLuhan's famous phrase. And for Christians, the medium is the way we treat one another. "By this all people will know that you are my disciples," Jesus said, "if you have love for one another" (John 13:35). God's strategy for reaching a lost world is for the church to function as a visible demonstration of His existence.

HIS WORK, HIS WAY

When Christians talk about the importance of developing a worldview message, they typically mean learning how to argue persuasively against the "isms" of the day. But having a Christian worldview is not just about answering intellectual questions. It also means following biblical principles in the personal and practical spheres of life. Christians can be infected by secular worldviews not only in their *beliefs* but also in their *practices*.

For example, a Christian church or ministry may be biblical in its *message* and yet fail to be biblical in its *methods*. Hudson Taylor, the great missionary to China, said that the Lord's work must be done in the Lord's way, if it is to have the Lord's blessing. We must express the truth not only in *what* we preach but also in *how* we preach it. A Christian organization may be doing the Lord's work—but if it is acting on human zeal and willpower, using secular methods of promotion and publicity, without visible love among staff and coworkers, then it is merely another form of human achievement, accomplishing little for the Kingdom of God.

Think back to the image of two chairs (discussed in chapter 6). For the nonbeliever sitting in the naturalist's chair, all that exists is a closed system of natural causes. The very definition of what counts as knowledge is limited by naturalism and utilitarianism. But for the believer sitting in the supernaturalist's chair, the natural world is only part of reality. A complete perspective includes both the seen and the unseen aspects of reality. Christians are called not merely to assent intellectually to the existence of both parts of reality but also to *function practically* on that basis. Day by day, they are to make choices that would make no sense unless the unseen world is just as real as the seen world.

Scripture gives a dramatic illustration of the two chairs in the account of Elisha when he was surrounded by Syrian troops (2 Kings 6:15-17). "Do not be afraid, for those who are with us are more than those who are with them," Elisha said to his anxious servant. But the servant could see no one. Then God opened the servant's eyes, and he saw that "the mountain was full of horses and chariots of fire all around Elisha." The same concept is echoed in the New Testament: "he who is in you is greater than he who is in the world" (1 John 4:4). We are called to make our decisions knowing that the unseen world has a powerful effect on the seen world, playing an active role in human history.

What does this mean in practice? It means we sometimes act in ways that seem irrational to those sitting in the naturalist's chair, who see only the physical world. It means we do what is right even at great cost, because we are convinced that what we gain in the unseen realm is far greater than what we lose from a worldly perspective.

Sadly, many Christians live much of their lives as though the naturalist were right. They give cognitive assent to the great truths of Scripture, but they make their practical, day-to-day decisions based only on what they can see, hear, measure, and calculate. When confessing their religious beliefs, they sit in the supernaturalist's chair. But in ordinary life, they walk over and sit in the naturalist's chair, living as though the supernatural were not real in any practical sense, relying on their own energy, talent, and strategic calculations. They may sincerely *want* to do the Lord's work, but they do it in the world's way— using worldly methods and motivated by worldly desires for success and acclaim.

The Bible calls this living in the "flesh" instead of in the Spirit, and Paul addresses the problem in the book of Galatians: "Having begun in the Spirit, are you now being perfected by the flesh?" (Gal. 3:3). Many believers act as though *becoming* a Christian were a matter of faith, but *being* a Christian afterward were a matter of their own drive and willpower. They are striving to be "perfected by the flesh."

Working in the flesh, they may well produce impressive results in the visible world. Churches and parachurch ministries may generate a great deal of publicity, hold glamorous conferences, attract huge crowds, bring in large donations, produce books and magazines, and wield political influence in Washington. But if that work is done in the flesh, then no matter how successful it appears, it does little to build God's kingdom. When the Lord's work is done in merely human wisdom, using human methods, then it is not the Lord's work any longer.[10]

The only way the church can establish genuine credibility with nonbelievers is by showing them something they cannot explain or duplicate through their own natural, pragmatic methods—something they can explain only by invoking the supernatural.

GOLD, SILVER, PRECIOUS STONES

If we find ourselves thinking we can do the Lord's work in the world's way, as though worldly weapons were adequate, then we have drastically underestimated the nature of the battle. For the real battle is not in the seen world only, but chiefly in the unseen world. The battle is not "against flesh and blood," Paul says (Eph. 6:12), and if we try to fight it in the flesh, we will be merely shadowboxing. Sheer activism may bring about results that look impressive to those sitting in the naturalist's chair, whose only frame of reference is the visible world—but they will not be the results the Lord wants.

We can go so far as to say that if Christians win their battles by worldly methods, then *they have really lost*.[11] Visible results can be deceptive. In the seen world, we may appear to make a great advance—win professional recognition, attract people to our cause, raise money for our program, distribute tons of literature, win passage of an important bill. But if it was done by humanistic reliance on technical methods, without the leading of the Spirit, then we have accomplished little of value in the unseen world.

The opposite is likewise true: If Christians use the weapons God has ordained—if we lay our talents at His feet, dying to our own pride and ambition, obeying biblical moral principles, empowered by His Spirit, guided by a Christian worldview perspective—then even if by external standards we seem to have lost, *we have really won*. Outsiders looking on may conclude that we have failed. Even Christian friends and leaders may shake their heads disapprovingly and advise us that we've made a mistake. But if we have genuinely given our lives over to God's purposes and are being led by Him, then we have won a battle in the unseen world.

An old spiritual classic says the Christian life really begins when we understand by hard experience that "apart from me you can do nothing" (John 15:5). It's a verse many of us have memorized and can quote at the drop of a hat. But it rarely becomes real in practice until we encounter an overwhelming crisis that pushes us to the end of our own resources. For people with a lot of resources, that may not be until midlife or even later. But at some point, the realization crashes in on us that life is not what we had hoped for, and we ask,

Is this all there is? We realize that in a fallen world, even the good things cannot fully satisfy our deepest hungers, and everything we have loved and lived for turns to sawdust and slips through our fingers. If we are honest, we have to admit that our personal relationships are often driven by what *we* want and need from others, not by a genuinely unselfish love for them. Even our efforts at Christian ministry are often motivated more by personal zeal and ambition than by God's Spirit. And the greater our natural zeal, the greater the crisis God has to allow in order to bring us to the end of our rope. Only after dying to everything we have ever lived for do we genuinely come to believe, as a practical reality, that "apart from Me you can do nothing." And only then can God really pour His life and power into our work.

When life ends and we stand at the believers' judgment described in 1 Corinthians 3, some of our most successful and impressive projects may prove to be nothing but wood, hay, and stubble—devoured by the flames. But the activities that were truly led and empowered by God, in obedience to His truth, whether the results were visible or not, will sparkle as gold, silver, and precious stones. And God will set them as jewels in our heavenly crown.

RESULTS GUARANTEED

Looking back over the history of evangelicalism, we can understand better why there has been a strong temptation to split belief from practice—to do the Lord's work but in the world's way. As we saw in chapter 11, in the nineteenth century, evangelical scholars adopted methodological naturalism in dealing with subjects in the lower story, treating them as religiously neutral—as merely technical subjects where biblical truth did not apply in any integral way. As a result they tended to accept a largely functional and utilitarian approach to areas like science, engineering, politics, business, management, and marketing.

In the late nineteenth century, evangelicals even stopped sending their children to Christian liberal arts colleges, where the classics were still taught (they were suspicious of those pagan Greeks!). Instead they sent their children in droves to the newly founded state universities, to receive the technical training required to succeed in an increasingly technological society. Studies show a steady decline in church-related colleges, while the numbers in state institutions boomed. And the students attending those state colleges were predominantly evangelicals—Methodists, Baptists, Disciples of Christ, Presbyterians.[12] "Ironically," says historian Franklin Littell, "it was the misguided piety of revivalist Protestantism which . . . gave the first great impetus to the state colleges and universities."[13]

Littell calls it "misguided" precisely because it was shaped by the two-story division of knowledge. Christian students were avoiding fields like philosophy and literature and the classics, where they would have to deal with ideas, while avidly seeking technical and vocational training in fields that they thought were safely neutral. They were willing to accept an exclusively technological and utilitarian concept of knowledge in the technical fields (the lower story), as long as they were allowed to supplement their studies with campus religious activities designed to nurture the spiritual life (the upper story).

This explains why many Christian churches and ministries today continue to treat areas like business, marketing, and management as essentially neutral—technical fields where the latest techniques can simply be plugged into their own programs, without subjecting them to critique from a Christian worldview perspective. Start the business meeting with prayer, by all means, but then employ all the up-to-date strategies learned in secular graduate schools. Douglas Sloan calls this "the inner modernization of evangelicalism."[14] That is, we have resisted modernism in our *theology* but have largely accepted modernism in our *practices*. We want to employ the latest techniques and quantitative methods, where the results can be calculated and predicted.

For example, a Christian ministry once hired a young man who had just received his master's degree in marketing to head up its fundraising department. Immediately he set about implementing the standard techniques he had learned in his courses, including a sharp increase in the number of fundraising letters sent out. When other staff members questioned the new strategy, asking whether increased mailings were a good use of funds given sacrificially to the ministry, his response was, *but this works*. Brandishing graphs and studies, he said: "Statistics show that if you send out X number of letters, you will get Y rate of return—guaranteed."[15]

But if any secular organization can achieve the same results using the same "guaranteed" methods, where is the witness to God's existence? How does relying on statistically reliable patterns persuade a watching world that God is at work?

Doing the Lord's work in the Lord's way means forging a biblical perspective even on the practical aspects of running an organization, instead of relying on mechanical formulas derived from naturalistic assumptions. We may reject naturalism as a philosophy, but if our work is driven by the rationalized methods we have learned from the world, then we are naturalists *in practice*, no matter what we claim to believe.

"The *central* problem of our age is not liberalism or modernism," Schaeffer writes—or even hot-button social issues like evolution, abortion, radical feminism, or homosexual rights. The primary threat to the church is the "tendency to do the Lord's work in the power of the flesh rather than the Spirit." Many church leaders crave a "big name," he continues: They "stand on the backs of others" in order to achieve power, influence, and reputation—instead of exhibiting the humility of the Master who washed His disciples' feet. They "ape the world" in its publicity and marketing techniques, manipulating people's emotions to induce them to give more money.[16] No wonder outsiders see little in the church that cannot be explained by ordinary sociological forces and principles of business management. And no wonder they find our message unconvincing.

MARKETING THE MESSAGE

What are some examples of "aping the world"? In their marketing strategies, many Christian organizations borrow heavily from commercial enterprises, creating idealized images of their "product" to motivate people to "buy" it. For a familiar example, think of the ubiquitous fundraising letters that sound like they were all written by the same person—because they were ghostwritten by staffers all trained in the same techniques. Each letter creates a crisis mentality that is enhanced by melodramatic anecdotes, fake highlighting in the margins, and a signature produced by a machine. Often a little card is enclosed announcing a premium, a gimmick to induce us to reach for our checkbooks.

Where is the authenticity in all this? The name of a ministry leader appears at the bottom of the letter, but clearly it is not an authentic message from that person. It was produced by a committee of writers, marketers, and fund development professionals, carefully calculated to elicit a response. As often as not, the crisis is half-manufactured and the anecdotes half-fictionalized for greater emotional impact. A young man who traveled on staff with a respected Christian leader once told me that when their experiences were written up later as fundraising anecdotes, the stories were so heavily slanted, they were "practically unrecognizable to anyone who was actually there."

Should we shrug this off as benign deception? Or is it a serious moral failing that could spread corruption through an entire ministry? Can we compromise the truth without undermining our effectiveness for the Lord?

Several months ago, a fundraising letter arrived in my mailbox inviting me to "have your morning coffee with So-and-So," a well-known Christian leader. The wording was obviously meant to stir up warm feelings associated with an intimate, personal chat around the kitchen table. But the reality? The ministry was offering a product that involved daily readings—something completely different from the image in the marketing pitch. What's more, the readings themselves were prepared by staff writers. The image of sipping coffee together with the author was a complete fabrication aimed at manipulating readers' emotions.

Where is our passion for truth and authenticity? Where is our respect for the reader as a person made in the image of God, not a mass of emotions to be manipulated? In short, where is a Christian worldview perspective on marketing and fundraising? *This is just as important as framing a worldview perspective on the "isms" of our day.*

Yet its importance is often overlooked in discussions of Christian worldview. Because evangelicals have historically accepted methodological naturalism in the lower-story, in their minds there *is* no distinctively Christian perspective in fields like marketing and management—and thus they have uncritically accepted whatever methods and techniques the secular world develops. In doing so, however, they have unwittingly limited their own thinking to the conceptual categories allowed within naturalism. They have absorbed what H. Richard Niebuhr calls a "depersonalized and disenchanted" perspective that lacks even the conceptual vocabulary to deal adequately with the human person. In this naturalistic framework, persons become merely "objects for objective manipulation in the market and the political arena."[17] Though Christians would never accept naturalism as a philosophy, many have absorbed a naturalistic approach to marketing, adopting techniques that treat a target audience essentially as passive "consumers" to be manipulated into buying a "product."

MORE MONEY, MORE MINISTRY

I once addressed a group of Christian graduate students earning advanced degrees from some of the nation's top universities in fields like philosophy, literature, and political theory. When I raised the need to develop a Christian worldview approach to practical fields as well, like business and marketing, they were startled. Having defined worldview study in terms of *ideas,* they had never even considered its relation to practical areas. Yet practical fields are not religiously neutral; they are shaped by fundamental assumptions about reality just as much as any other area of life.

By overlooking this fact, many ministry leaders have uncritically absorbed a nonbiblical view of business and success. "They are deeply infused with an American capitalist culture concerning the gospel," writes historian Joel Carpenter. They unconsciously assume "that God measures success by the numbers, that more money means more ministry, which means more success for God's kingdom. So they tend to measure their own success as disciples and servants of the Lord by the size of their ministry."[18]

Do we recognize a pattern here? We are witnessing history come home to roost. In earlier chapters on revivalism, we watched the seeds being sown. The appeal to the emotions. The pragmatic attitude of using whatever works. The habit of borrowing marketing techniques from the commercial world. The celebrity style of leadership. The focus on measurable results. "Religion is a work of man," Charles Finney said, meaning that conversions can be induced simply by manipulating the right conditions. All too often, today's ministries exhibit the same naturalistic attitude, the only difference being that they have access to vastly more sophisticated marketing and promotional techniques.

"The nonprofit economy has become more like the for-profit world," writes Thomas Berg. Religious fundraising has become "extremely fast-paced and sophisticated, relying more and more on high technology [and] carefully targeted direct-mail campaigns."[19] Many large religious organizations have entire departments of trained and credentialed marketers to create a constant flow of fundraising letters and promotionals. They conduct marketing surveys on how to position their "product" better. They organize focus groups to determine where to aim their efforts. They angle for articles and profiles in Christian magazines. They hire ghostwriters to write copy under the leader's name for columns, newsletters, daily devotionals, and websites. The overriding question is not, "Is this morally and spiritually right?" but rather, "Will it sell?"

Sometimes the marketing hype shades into subtle deception. Statistics are cited with no control group to make the numbers scientifically reliable. Successes are highlighted, while failures are swept under the carpet. Ken Blue tells the story of a ministry he started, which began including only the most striking success stories in its reports—until eventually he began to feel guilty about creating a "distorted image" of the ministry's impact. When he sought counsel from another pastor, however, the pastor only looked puzzled. "What's the problem?" he asked. "No one in ministry tells the unvarnished truth. We automatically take exaggeration into account."

But if that is true, Blue notes, "then the church regularly lies to itself and condones using people for its public relations needs."[20]

This is the ultimate danger of doing the Lord's work in the flesh: It may eventually lead to outright sin. We can be so driven by ministry goals that we are blinded to the use of unethical methods. Without really thinking, we begin to stretch the truth to enhance our image and attract donors. A former high-ranking executive at a parachurch organization told me he had resigned after discovering an internal "culture of lying"—a regular pattern of shading the truth and cutting ethical corners in order to look better and win influence—all for the good of the ministry, of course. It is a modern form of thinking we can "speak lies in the name of the Lord" (Zech. 13:3).

Imagine that you were to wake up tomorrow morning, Schaeffer says, and that by some magic, everything the Bible teaches about prayer and the empowering of the Holy Spirit was gone—it was erased from history and had never been said. Would that make any difference in practice in the way we run our churches and organizations? The tragic fact, Schaeffer says, is that in many Christian organizations, "there would be *no difference whatsoever.*" We function day by day sitting in the naturalist's chair, as though the supernatural were not real.[21]

OPERATING INSTRUCTIONS

The same contradictory pattern often emerges in the way Christian churches and organizations function—in their management of the workplace itself, treatment of employees, and leadership style. Many groups are Christian in what they *profess* but not in the way they *operate.*

Consider, for example, ministries that demand excessively long hours on the job. This common practice produces a line of destructive domino effects: It breaks up marriages, erodes family life, and eliminates outside sources of renewal, like involvement in a local church. Cut off from external emotional resources, a person often becomes overdependent on relationships at work and thus vulnerable to control and manipulation.

After working eight years in the U.S. Congress, a talented office manager switched to an executive position at a Christian parachurch ministry. "I wanted to get away from the typical congressional office, where everyone was so focused on the Big Name politician," she told me. "The staff was expected to sacrifice their personal lives, their families, their professional identities." And she added, "I hate to use the language of the recovery movement, but many staff really had codependent relationships with their member of Congress. They lived derivative lives, feeding off his fame and public identity."

When she started her new job, however, she was disappointed to discover exactly the same dynamics at the parachurch ministry. "Staff members were expected to live for the ministry—work long hours, have no outside life, make all their social relationships within the organization. It was the same codependent relationship with a Big Name." The emotionally unhealthy pattern was all too recognizable, and wisely she left the new position after only two months.

These patterns can be *physically* unhealthy as well, producing stress-related ailments that result in absenteeism and reduced productivity. An executive at a Washington think tank once worked at a Christian ministry where the atmosphere was so negative that he developed stress-related physical symptoms. When he sought medical treatment, the doctor said, "Why is it that everyone I see with this particular ailment *works at that same ministry?*"

Negative experiences are so common in churches and parachurch groups that a genre of self-help books has appeared on the market with titles like *The Subtle Power of Spiritual Abuse* and *Healing Spiritual Abuse*.[22] These books describe the signs of an unhealthy organizational system, marked by controlling, domineering leaders who drive people to perform in order to build a celebrity image. Believers who find themselves in such a system, whether in unpaid volunteer work or in a paid position, often find themselves subject to many of the classic forms of workplace abuse.

FROM GOOD TO GREAT

Happily, there are many positive counter-examples, and a study done in 2003 by the Best Christian Workplaces Institute[23] identified several of them. The study uncovered forty organizations that rank highest in worker satisfaction. It found that the most effective leaders are those who regard workers as part of their mission, not merely as a means to larger goals. Instead of asking, What can this person do for my ministry? they ask, What can I do to help this person develop spiritually and professionally?

In the top organizations, the study found, employees consistently described their leaders in terms like *humble, approachable, caring,* and *godly.* At Phoenix Seminary, President Darryl DelHousaye is known for asking his staff, "How can I help you? How can I bless you? How can I help you succeed?"[24] The best organizations regard the nurturing of their own employees as a spiritual mandate.

At Whitworth College, another top organization identified in the study, President Bill Robinson says, "I am trying to lead 'from amongst'." The reference is to John 1:14 ("the Word became flesh and dwelt among us, . . . full of grace and truth"). Robinson has a habit of wandering into the dining hall unannounced and sitting down with students to find out what they think of the college. "I hope it can be said of me that I dwelt among the people, bringing grace and speaking truth."[25]

Examples like these give concrete evidence that servant leadership is not an abstract ideal; it is completely practical and workable. Having a Christian worldview means being utterly convinced that biblical principles are not only true but also work better in the grit and grime of the real world.[26]

Even secular businesses are starting to recognize these principles. The bestseller *Good to Great,* popular in Christian management circles these days, is based on a study of business leaders who started with a *good* business but turned it into a *great* one, propelling it to the highest echelons of success. Contrary to the common stereotype, says author Jim Collins, these successful leaders "are not charismatic, nor are they celebrities." They are not "hard charging" leaders who feel they have to whip up employees to perform. Instead they are humble, modest, even self-effacing people, who share decision making with their staff.[27] One of the most damaging trends in recent history has been the tendency to select dazzling celebrity leaders, Collins concludes. It's a strategy that typically creates mediocre businesses, which eventually go into decline.

Clearly, biblical principles are not just Sunday school pieties. Because they are true to the real world, they actually work better in making people and companies more productive.

LOVING ENOUGH TO CONFRONT

Another common workplace abuse involves taking credit for another person's work or ideas. In the 1988 film *Working Girl,* starring Harrison Ford, Melanie Griffith, and Sigourney Weaver, a bright secretary named Tess comes up with a creative idea for a deal with a client. After winning her trust, however, her boss steals the idea, intending to pass it off as her own. At stake, of course, is not just a single project but also Tess's entire career, which could finally take off if clients had a chance to recognize her gifts.

Hard as it may be to believe, Christians sometimes exploit their workers in similar ways, denying them recognition for their God-given gifts. It can happen among coworkers—when someone discusses an idea with a colleague, who then presents it to the boss as his own. It can happen when a leader or supervisor takes credit for the success of a program without mentioning the creative work of team members. Or it can happen when a boss claims authorship of a work written by a staff writer. In every case, the offender is essentially co-opting someone else's spiritual gifts and calling by claiming them as his own.

In a journalism class I once taught, one of the students was agonizing over what to do. Fresh from earning a master's degree, she had landed a job doing policy analysis for a state-level Christian organization. On her first big project, she had worked for months analyzing the data and preparing an outstanding report. But when she was finished, to her shock, the boss announced that he was going to put his name on the final product.

"The message will get out better with my name on it," he said. "We'll get more attention, sell more copies, have greater impact." No matter that claiming to be the author was false and deceptive to the public. No matter that the woman who had done the real work was essentially reduced to a ghostwriter. Worse, the dishonesty was rationalized in religious language as the best way to "advance the ministry." Eventually the boss "graciously" agreed to include the writer's name on the cover as well, but the public was still misled into thinking that the ideas were his, while she was nothing but a staff writer.

It is scandalous that Christian ministries and publishing houses often turn a blind eye to this form of deception—especially when it involves top-selling names. Not long ago an editor at a major Christian publishing house told me that he had managed to get a Big Name to write a foreword to a forthcoming book—then added casually, "But of course he didn't really write it."

I recently met a conference speaker and author who once worked for a prominent ministry leader. To my amazement, she revealed that staff workers wrote everything that went out under his name—books, articles, radio programs. "The attitude among the staff is, let's not bother him with these projects. We'll just take care of them for him." Meanwhile the public is deceived into thinking they are getting this revered leader's own thoughts and insights.

Clearly, any practice that deceives the public ought to be off-limits—no matter how much money it brings in for the ministry. "Better is a little with righteousness than great revenues with injustice" (Prov. 16:8). There is nothing shameful in hiring someone to do things that you cannot do for yourself, says top-ranking journalist David Aikman. Hiring a professional writer to help you is like hiring an accountant to do your tax returns. But it *is* morally wrong to pretend to the public that you wrote something yourself when you did not.[28] When a Christian organization violates ethical principles in order to get results, it cannot expect God to use those results. We cannot "structure sin into our method of doing business" (to use a phrase my husband once coined), and then expect God to bless it.

NO LITTLE PEOPLE

The operative principle is that each member in the Body of Christ has been given unique gifts—and the Body as a whole functions best when each is recognized, honored, and allowed to flourish. A Christian organization should aim to cultivate each worker's gifts, not stifle them or build up leaders at the expense of others. As Schaeffer put it, "with God there are no little people"—which means we cannot treat anyone as a mere means to other goals.[29]

A high-profile political commentator was approached by a Christian publisher to write a novel. "But I'm a columnist," he protested, "not a novelist."

"Don't worry," the publisher responded. "We'll get someone to write it for you."

To his credit, the columnist turned down the offer. But the incident reveals how willing many publishers are to use writers as mere means to putting a Big Name on a book cover. They seem to have forgotten that Christian leaders are called to nurture and build up the "little people," not to use them for personal gain.[30]

If you want to know what a Christian leader is really like, don't ask his peers or board members or adoring fans. Ask how he treats his support staff. That is a lesson Jerram Barrs presses upon seminary students at the Francis Schaeffer Institute at Covenant Seminary. "When I come to visit your church someday, I will not ask people about what a great preacher or leader you are," Barrs says. "Rather I will talk to the secretaries, the office staff, the janitors and cleaners and ask them what it is like to work with you. That will tell me far more about the kind of ministry taking place in the church, and whether you are the kind of leader Christ desires for His Church."[31]

To use biblical language, God charges shepherds (whether in the pulpit or in other forms of leadership) to feed the sheep, not to fleece them. He thunders against the leaders of ancient Israel: "You eat the fat, you clothe yourselves with the wool, and slaughter the fat ones, but you do not feed the sheep" (Ezek. 34:3). Bad shepherds are those who exploit other people's gifts and talents to meet their own needs and advance their own agendas, instead of asking what is good for the sheep themselves.

Paul was scrupulous in refusing to take credit for what others had accomplished: "We do not boast . . . in the labors of others" (2 Cor. 10:15). In the Body of Christ, the eye is not the ear (1 Cor. 12:14ff.), and it should not *pretend* to be, by claiming the ear's work as its own.

We can take a lesson from the political realm, where it is now standard for people to give public recognition to speechwriters. Everyone knows that President Bush's main speechwriter is Michael Gerson, because there have been several magazine and newspaper profiles about him. There is no attempt to hide the fact. A few years ago, I went to hear a lecture by Senator Rick Santorum at the Heritage Foundation. "Before I begin," he said, "I want to thank the two people on my staff, Mark Rodgers and Sydney Leach, who did the research for this lecture and wrote it." He then proceeded to deliver the lecture.[32] There are many ways to speak truthfully in order to build up those around us.

The other side of the coin is that it is quite proper for members of the Body to claim ownership of their own work. Psalm 95:5 is a key verse in a biblical defense of private property: "The sea is his, for he made it, and his hands formed the dry land." The implication is that the earth belongs to the Lord *because* He made it. The same principle applies to humans, who are made in God's image: What we create belongs to us. Taking responsibility for our own work—accepting both the credit and the blame, the benefits and the losses— is a crucial element in human dignity. Our work is one of the most important ways we express our inner self and character in external form—it is a principal "fruit" by which others can know who we really are. That is why it is profoundly dehumanizing to separate a person from the "fruit" of his work. Time and again in Scripture, a sign of God's blessing is that "you will eat the fruit of your own labor," whereas a sign of His chastisement is that "others will eat what you have planted" (for example, Deut. 28:30; Mic. 6:15; Mic. 4:4; Ps. 128:2). In the New Testament, Paul advises, "Let each one test his own work, and then his reason to boast will be in himself alone and not in his neighbor" (Gal. 6:4).

The overarching biblical principle is that we have a responsibility to practice stewardship of the gifts God has given us. Once when King David wanted to build an altar in a farmer's field, the farmer offered to simply give it to him, along with the bulls and the wood for the offering. But David refused to take any of it, and he presented this compelling reason: "I will not take for the LORD what is yours, nor offer burnt offerings that cost me nothing" (1 Chron. 21:24). The application to our own day is that we cannot "take for the Lord" work done by another person. Nor can we make an offering that "costs me nothing." Whoever does the actual work pays the cost in term of organizing the project, research, creative analysis, and so on— not to mention probably years of sacrificial study and preparation brought to the job in the first place. Each of us has a responsibility to develop our own gifts, and we cannot excuse exploitive practices by saying "but it's for the Lord."

The consequences of exploitive and deceptive practices ripple in ever-widening circles. There are many "little people" whom God has gifted with an important message or ministry that could benefit a wider segment of the church—if their work were properly recognized and better known. But who can compete with the head of an organization with the resources to hire half a dozen writers, editors, and PR professionals to put out material under a celebrity name? A larger-than-life standard is set up that attracts financial and other forms of support from donors and foundations that might otherwise have gone to worthier causes. The church as a whole then loses the benefit of their gifts. The purpose in assigning proper credit is to identify gifts within the Body of Christ, for the sake of more effective ministry.

REAL LEADERS SERVE

When Kurt Senske was only thirty-six years old, he took over leadership of a company that was losing money rapidly. Yet in only three years, he pulled together a team that turned the company around. The key to their success? "We followed sound Christian leadership strategies that included incorporating the principles of servant leadership from the bottom up, creating a healthy culture that valued its employees."

What is a servant leader? It is someone who, in Senske's words, refuses to use people as means to an end—who always asks, "Am I building people up, or am I building myself up and merely using those around me?" A servant leader creates an atmosphere of "transparency" in which all relevant information is shared openly, so that everyone has an opportunity to make responsible decisions. Finally, a servant leader lets go of command-and-control methods, and creates a culture that allows everyone to grow into leaders, stretching their own God-given talents.[33]

None of these biblical principles were merely fine phrases for Senske. He devoted months of sweat and prayer and sleepless nights to making them real. And his efforts paid off in terms of business success.

Every Christian needs to be equally convinced that biblical principles are true not only in some abstract sense but in the reality of our work, business, and personal lives. If we become aware that a ministry or business is violating biblical principles, we need to stop being enablers and start calling people to accountability—even if it means paying a price. An employee who takes a stand may not ultimately succeed in changing anything. In fact, he may run the risk of losing his job. The church's task is to make sure that he does not bear that risk alone. As Lesslie Newbigin writes, fellow Christians should stand ready to support those who speak the truth to power and pay a price for it, even providing financial assistance to those whose moral courage costs them their livelihood.[34]

We must never forget that going along with unbiblical practices is not only wrong, it is unloving. Acquiescing in an unjust situation typically stems not from love but from fear of possible negative repercussions. If we aspire to a godly, holy love for others, we must be willing to take the risk and practice loving confrontation.

There is too much at stake to be complacent. If you and I do not have the courage to confront worldly and sinful practices in our own ranks, what makes us think we will have the courage to stand against powerful secular leaders? If we cannot run with the footmen, we are fooling ourselves to imagine we will be able to run with the horses (see Jer. 12:5). Only by sitting in the supernaturalist's chair will we have the courage to do what's right even when it costs.

GETTING IT RIGHT BY DOING IT "WRONG"

It was just this kind of courage that Schaeffer demonstrated when he gave up everything to start L'Abri. In doing so, he developed an alternative model of ministry that remains instructive for us even now. Let's look beyond what he wrote and consider the practical model he constructed through his life and work.

In comparison with the strategies employed by many ministries today, we could say that *Schaeffer did everything wrong.* He shunned the celebrity circuit, and was willing to minister on the other side of the ocean in an obscure village that no one had ever heard of. While many Christian leaders are obsessed with getting publicity, visibility, and name recognition in order to raise money, Schaeffer was willing to start a small ministry completely invisible to the public, hidden away in the Swiss Alps. When he wrote about "dying" to our natural ambitions, he was not merely parroting a theological doctrine; his insights grew out of hard-won personal experience.

Nor did he use mass marketing techniques to get his name out and build a constituency. He did not have a fund-development department to churn out an endless flood of fundraising letters, advertising copy, and premium offers. Instead he started with a modest list of prayer supporters, while his wife, Edith, typed personal letters to send out.[35]

Even more remarkable, he was willing to get started by simply talking to his kids' friends. As his children grew older, they went down the mountain to Lausanne to attend university, and when their friends raised spiritual questions, they would say, "You ought to talk to my dad." Since their home was so inaccessible—a chalet perched on the side of the mountain—once students arrived, they would have to spend the night. Later they would tell *their* friends about the earnest little man with the goatee and a powerful message, hidden away in the Alps. And *they* would tell *their* friends, and after a while the Schaeffers had students sleeping everywhere—on couches, on floors, and in the hallways.

This is how L'Abri grew into a home-based ministry: It was a completely organic process, as the Schaeffers talked to real people about real questions. No five-year marketing plans, no lists of goals and objectives, no pumping donors for major gifts, no PR campaign to project an image. The ministry grew almost completely by word of mouth, as the Schaeffers prayed that God would bring to them the people of His choice.

Many of Schaeffer's former colleagues thought he was crazy to give up opportunities in the States to speak before large audiences and build a mega-organization. Some were angry and critical, accusing him of wasting his gifts. What kind of ministry is that, they asked, just *talking* to people? Later Schaeffer was to say in a sermon that if we can speak to thousands, we may have to die to that, and be willing to speak to one or two at a time. Clearly, his insights were not abstract, but were the fruit of his courage to follow God's leading in the face of sometimes vicious criticism.

This unique ministry was possible only because L'Abri was a team effort. Francis and Edith worked side by side, inviting people into their home and making themselves available as whole persons. Unfailingly gracious, Edith brought a touch of elegance and beauty to everything she did, always serving meals with candles and fresh-cut flowers on the table. She also labored alongside her husband in their evangelistic ministry, teaching and counseling and holding people's hands as they came down off drugs or agonized over the meaning of life. One of my closest friends at L'Abri was a fellow musician (we played duets together) who had once been a lesbian, using drugs and practicing the occult. It was Edith who had brought her to the Lord, through a stormy session of tears and prayers.

When a celebrity drops in to speak at a conference and then disappears, the audience has no way of knowing whether his personal character matches his message. But the Schaeffers lived alongside students day in and day out, providing a living demonstration that the Christian message is genuine under the tough pressures of real life. That's why their ministry eventually helped transform an entire generation of young people. When students left, many said the experience of genuine Christian community was at least as significant in their conversion as the intellectual answers given in lectures and discussions.

In many ministries, there is relentless pressure for constant growth: Every year, the numbers have to be bigger, the results more impressive, so that donors will be moved to write another check. By contrast, I once heard Schaeffer speak at a conference where he was asked what would happen if, someday, the money didn't come in. He responded simply, "I guess we'll be smaller." The conference hall erupted into applause at such a refreshing lack of pretentiousness. His mentality was that God had a time and a purpose for L'Abri, and when it had fulfilled that purpose, it might simply end.

How different from the driven, success-oriented attitude that pervades so many ministries today. Perhaps that's why Schaeffer had to leave, says philosopher John Vander Stelt—why he "had to 'flee' to the mountains of Switzerland, in order to be able to penetrate the citadels of our Western culture."[36] In both his message and his methods, Schaeffer left behind a compelling model that is even more relevant today than it was in his own lifetime.

TRUE SPIRITUALITY

A recent Zogby/Forbes ASAP poll asked respondents, What would you like most to be known for? For being intelligent? Good looking? Having a great sense of humor? A full half of respondents checked off an unexpected answer: They said they would like a reputation for "being authentic."[37] In a world of spin and hype, the postmodern generation is searching desperately for something real and authentic. They will not take Christians seriously unless our churches and parachurch organizations demonstrate an authentic way of life—unless they are communities that exhibit the character of God in their relationships and mode of living.

Advertising techniques that merely convey an image may bring in the money, but they are not the means to accomplishing a genuine spiritual work. The church's "manner of speaking the truth must not be aligned to the techniques of modern propaganda," writes Newbigin, "but must have the modesty, the sobriety, and the realism which are proper to a disciple of Jesus."[38] The church is called to be a witness to the gospel through an authentic demonstration of love and unity.

In the days of the early church, the thing that most impressed their neighbors in the Roman Empire was the community of love they witnessed among believers. "Behold how they love one another," it was said. In every age, the most persuasive evidence for the gospel is not words or arguments but a living demonstration of God's character through Christians' love for one another, expressed in both their words and their actions. The gospel is not meant to be "a disembodied message," Newbigin writes. It is meant to be fleshed out in "a congregation of men and women who believe it and live by it"—who exhibit in their relationships the beauty of God's character.[39]

In one sense, this chapter should have been the first, because its message is the pathway to everything else. The spiritual reality of *rejected, slain, raised* lies at the heart of everything in the Christian life, including the work of developing a Christian mind. Only as we cooperate with God in dying to sin and self are we open to receiving "the mind of Christ" (1 Cor. 2:16). May God give us the grace to be worldview missionaries, building lives and communities that give an authentic witness of His existence before a watching world.

APPENDICES

Appendix 1
HOW AMERICAN POLITICS BECAME SECULARIZED

Social contract theory remains at the heart of political liberalism in America today. In chapter 4 we discussed Rousseau's version of the social contract, and in chapters 10 and 11 we talked about the enormous impact the theory had on America after the birth of our nation. We saw how a liberal view of society, with its atomistic individualism, was embraced by many evangelicals, and in chapter 12 how it altered the shape of the American family. Thus it is crucial that we understand this philosophical tradition more deeply.

And the most important point to grasp is why it was developed in the first place. The driving motivation behind the rise of social contract theory was the secularizing of political thought.

Throughout the Middle Ages, a constant tug-of-war was waged between church and state, between pope and emperor, with one gaining predominance for a period, then the other redressing the balance. An important turning point came after the Reformation. The split in the medieval church had fractured the religious unity of Christendom, yet both sides continued to hold a territorial view of the church. They simply assumed that everyone living within a certain nation or geographical region should belong to the same religion. As a result, for more than a hundred years, beginning in the late sixteenth century and continuing throughout most of the seventeenth century, Europe found itself embroiled in religious wars. Many people had to flee persecution in their homeland, becoming religious refugees.[1]

How did a century of religious warfare affect people's attitudes toward morality and politics? When people saw that Christians *were willing to shed blood over religious differences,* they began searching for an alternative basis for the social order. They sought a purely secular arena of discourse, autonomous from religion, that would function as "neutral" territory to bring peace to warring religious factions. As Jeffrey Stout explains, many came to think they could "contain the violent effects of religious disagreement only by creating *non*religious means for discussing and deciding matters of public importance."[2]

Up until this time, the state had been regarded as a moral and spiritual entity even though it was institutionally independent of the church. Ordained by God, its duty was to protect the "common good" of the body politic, conceived in moral terms like Justice, Mercy, and Righteousness (with the definition of these terms ultimately derived from divine revelation). Rulers regarded themselves as mediating, or participating in, God's own righteous rule over the nations—which included the duty of protecting "true religion" and upholding the church.

After the Reformation, however, people began to ask, *Which church?* Then, after a hundred years of warfare between conflicting churches, many began to answer that the state should not have the job of upholding *any* church. They even began to contest the moral function of the state: Since morality is derived from religion, any religious conception of the "common good" that was proposed might well be challenged by a competing religion. No, a purely secular basis would have to be found.[3]

The first to rise to the challenge was Thomas Hobbes. He proposed that the ultimate basis for the political order was the fear of violent death. The "state of nature," as Hobbes pictured it, was hostile and violent—a war of all against all. The threat of death hangs over everything and (in his famous phrase) life is "solitary, poor, nasty, brutish, and short." Each individual has a natural "right" to preserve his own life, taking whatever he needs, even if that means stealing or killing. The state arises when individuals decide that life would be more pleasant if they would give up certain rights, such as the right to defend themselves, and transfer those rights to a civil authority. This transferring of rights is called a contract, and for Hobbes it becomes the basis of all moral obligations.

The crucial point is that social duties no longer arise from a "common good" for civil society, constituted by transcendent principles such as Justice. Instead they are simply the product of individual choice—when people decide it is in their interests to contract away some of their own rights. This is a form of pre-Darwinian naturalism, where the foundation of civic society is not a higher good but merely the individual's biological urge for self-preservation.

John Locke presented a similar scenario, except that for him the ultimate source of the civil order is hunger. The most basic right is the right to eat, and the threat of death does not come from other people (as it did for Hobbes) but rather from hunger. By exerting his labor to find food, or to grow it himself, the individual creates private property—and to protect his property more effectively, he enters into a social contract with others. Now, Locke assigned a much more limited role to the state than either Hobbes or Rousseau did, which is why he became the favorite of political conservatives. Yet like the other social contract theorists, he did not base civil society on any higher good. Instead he portrayed it as the creation of individuals, motivated by enlightened self-interest. Locke's picture of society is atomistic, where all that exists ultimately are individuals and their needs or wants.

Rousseau, as we saw in chapter 4, derived civil society from the natural instinct of "self love" (*amour de soi*) or self-preservation. Thus for all the social contract theorists, the ultimate basis for the political order is purely secular. They based civil society not on moral ideals derived from religion but strictly on the natural, biological instinct of self-preservation. The sole source of political legitimacy is the consent of isolated, autonomous individuals.

Ironically, social contract theory presupposes a completely unrealistic conception of human nature. The atomistic creature that populates the state-of-nature scenarios appears to be an independent, fully developed, autonomous individual. "The theory starts with an image of, say, a 21-year-old adult male," comments Christian political theorist Paul Marshall.[4] Obviously, no one actually comes into the world that way. Each of us begins life as a dependent, helpless baby, born into a family and a complex social, religious, and civil order. Only through the love and sociality exercised toward us by others do we grow into mature, independent creatures. As Bertrand de Jouvenal once commented, social contract theories "are the views of childless men who must have forgotten their childhood."[5] Biology and history both teach that humans are intrinsically social beings.[6]

Yet, despite its unrealistic starting premise, social contract theory became the dominant political theory in America—while at the same time a powerful force for secularization. As we have seen, what united the various versions of social contract theories was their rejection of transcendent moral ideals, to be replaced by a lowest-common-denominator biological urge as the foundation of the political order. Religious perspectives were marginalized, while the state took over as the central institution in modern society.

Perhaps the greatest tragedy is that many evangelicals in the eighteenth and nineteenth century failed to recognize what was happening. Having embraced a two-story concept of truth, they assumed that political philosophy was a lower-story "science" that could be pursued apart from any distinctively Christian perspective. As a result, many evangelicals at the time simply adopted secular political philosophies—especially that of John Locke. Whatever Locke's personal religious faith was (which is endlessly debated), there can be no doubt that his political theory was at root secular, grounding civil society not in moral goods like Justice and Right but merely in individual self-interest.

How did evangelicals miss that? As George Marsden explains, "Locke's contract theory of government was, in practice, sufficiently like the Puritan concept of covenant that no one in the revolutionary era seems to have thought it significant to criticize its essentially secular theoretical base."[7] By treating the lower story as philosophically neutral, Christians failed to recognize *alien* philosophies—and sometimes even adopted them without being aware of it.

In our own day, this same secularization process explains why politics leaves so many people disillusioned and spiritually dissatisfied. "The liberalism of Hobbes and Locke is founded upon the relatively 'low' human goals of self-preservation and the desire for wealth," writes Stanley Kurtz—which accounts for "the chronic disenchantment at the heart of modernity."[8] At the core, humans are moral beings, and we long to see our highest moral ideals expressed in our corporate life. Ultimately the secular version of civic life fails to satisfy the human longing to live together in moral communities, committed to Justice and Righteousness.

Appendix 2
MODERN ISLAM
AND THE
NEW AGE MOVEMENT

Christians sometimes find it easy to dismiss the New Age movement as the loony trappings left over from the counterculture of the 1960s. But that would be a dangerous underestimation. The core of the movement is a pantheistic religion (see chapter 4) deriving from an extraordinarily broad religious tendency that has appeared in virtually every age and culture—West, East, and Middle East (Islamic). In the aftermath of September 11, as the world focuses attention on Islamic cultures, Christians need to be equipped to identify this broader religious tendency in order to make sense of current cultural and political events.

Starting with the West, the quasi-pantheistic ideas we are talking about took root in the third century with the ancient Greeks. This was a period when Asian religions became fashionable in ancient Greek culture, much as they did in America in the 1960s. The result was a school of thought known as neo-Platonism, which merged Plato's philosophy with Indian pantheism. "Neo" means new, of course, so you might think of it as the ancient world's form of the New Age movement.

The main spokesman for this melding of East and West was Plotinus,[1] who taught that the world was an "emanation" or radiation of being from a non-personal Spirit or Absolute—somewhat as light is a radiation from the sun. The lowest level of this radiation was matter; and because it was farthest away from Infinite Goodness, that made it evil. In other words, having a physical, material body was itself regarded as a kind of sin, something negative from which we must be saved. How? By ascetic practices that suppress bodily desires. The goal was to liberate the spirit from the "prison house" of the body in order to be reabsorbed into the Infinite from which it came.

These ideas have obvious parallels with Eastern pantheism, and indeed some modern Hindus recognize Plotinus as a kindred spirit. Swami Krishnananda writes, "Plotinus, the celebrated mystic, comes nearest in his views to the Vedanta philosophy, and is practically in full agreement with the Eastern sages."[2] Other scholars agree: A book of essays titled *Neo-Platonism and Indian Philosophy* notes the "remarkable similarity between the philosophical system of Plotinus (205–270 A.D.) and those of various Hindu philosophers in various centuries."[3] For both, God is not a personal being but a nonpersonal essence.

From the beginning, neo-Platonism was not just a philosophy but also a mystical religion. In fact, it was crafted in part in opposition to Christianity—as a weapon to be wielded by ancient paganism in its polemical battle against Christianity. In the fourth century, the emperor Julian the Apostate even tried to oust Christianity as the official religion of the Roman Empire by replacing it with neo-Platonism.

Surprisingly, many of the early Christians were nevertheless sympathetic to neo-Platonism and were greatly influenced by it—notably Clement of Alexandria, Origen, and Augustine. At the end of the fifth century this semi-Eastern philosophy was actually synthesized with Christianity by an unknown writer posing as a first-century convert of St. Paul's called Dionysius the Areopagite. Later known as pseudo-Dionysius, he presented a Christianized form of neo-Platonism that became enormously influential in the Middle Ages. His writings were translated into Latin by John Scotus Eriugena about the middle of the ninth century, and from then neo-Platonism became the major conduit of Greek thought to later ages. It greatly affected many mystical movements in the West, including those of Meister Eckhart and Jacob Boehme. It was popular among Renaissance humanists like Ficino and Pico della Mirandola. Even many of the early modern scientists held a neo-Platonist philosophy of nature, which inspired much of their scientific work.[4]

Later, neo-Platonism became an important influence on the Romantic movement of the nineteenth century with its philosophical idealism, in which ultimate reality was said to be Spirit, Mind, or the Absolute. In German historicism, the Absolute was given an evolutionary twist—it was said to evolve through a series of stages from lower levels of being to ever higher ones. In the early twentieth century, this notion was modernized in Process Thought, in which God Himself became embedded in the evolutionary process—an immanent, quasi-pantheistic deity that evolves along with the world (see chapter 8). Around the same time, a new blend of Eastern religion and Western occultism was launched under the name *perennial philosophy*—the same ideas I encountered in my teens when I read Aldous Huxley's book *The Perennial Philosophy* (see chapter 4).

The point of this rapid-fire historical survey is that long before the Beatles became disciples of the Maharishi, various forms of quasi-pantheistic thought were already prominent strands within the Western cultural tradition. The New Age movement was merely a more recent expression of a long-standing tendency to import Eastern pantheism into Western culture, which began with Plotinus and neo-Platonism.

What about the Middle East? Many of us do not realize that, historically, Islamic thinkers drew on ancient Greek sources just as heavily as Western thinkers did, so that neo-Platonism spread to Arabic cultures as well.[5] During the Golden Age of Islam in the seventh and eighth centuries, Muhammad's armies swept out from the Arabian peninsula, annexing territory from Spain to Persia. In the process, we might say, they also annexed the works of Plato, Aristotle, Plotinus, and other Greek thinkers. As a result, the Arab world had a rich tradition of commentary on the Greek philosophers long before Europe did. In college history courses, we often learn that the Renaissance was sparked by the recovery of ancient classical writings. But we rarely learn that it was *Muslim* philosophers who had preserved those texts and who reintroduced them to the West.

As a consequence, neo-Platonism became a strong influence on Islamic thought. Today several leading Muslim philosophers have embraced perennial philosophy, with its merging of Western and Eastern pantheism. In fact, the early proponents of this philosophy, who were Europeans, all ended up converting to Islam![6] To complete the circle, the man who launched perennial philosophy (a Frenchman named René Guenon) believed there was actually a common core uniting all three: neo-Platonism in the West, Hinduism in the East, and Islam in the Middle East.

Since September 11, we have heard it said again and again that Islam is just another Abrahamic faith—as though it were not really very different from Christianity. So it may come as a surprise to learn that the God of Islam is actually more akin to the nonpersonal Absolute of neo-Platonism and Hinduism than to the God of the Bible.

Yet it is true, and the central reason is that Islam rejects the Trinity. Without that concept, it cannot hold a fully personal conception of God. Why not? Because many attributes of personality can be expressed only within a relationship—things like love, communication, empathy, and self-giving.

Traditional Christian doctrine maintains a personal conception of God because it teaches that these interpersonal attributes were expressed from all eternity among the three Persons of the Trinity. A genuinely personal God requires distinct "Persons," because that alone makes it possible for love and communication to exist within the Godhead itself.

Islam denies the Trinity, however, which means there is no way for its conception of God to include these relational attributes. (At least, not until He created the world—but in that case He would be dependent on creation.) That's why it is correct to say, as some Islamic philosophers do, that Islam is actually akin to neo-Platonism and Hinduism.

This nonpersonal conception of God also explains why Muslims express their faith in near-mechanical rituals: Muslim believers recite the Koran over and over, in unison, word for word, in the original Arabic. They don't pray to God as a personal being, pouring their hearts out to Him as David did, or arguing with him as Job did. As one Muslim website puts it, "understanding [the Koran] is secondary" to recitation and ritual,[7] which makes sense only if God is not a personal being. As sociologist Rodney Stark explains, religions with nonpersonal gods tend to stress precision in the performance of rituals and sacred formulas; by contrast, religions with a highly personal God worry less about such things, because a personal Being will respond to a personal approach through impromptu supplication and spontaneous prayer.[8]

In our efforts to defend Christianity, we can easily be overwhelmed by the vast number of religions and philosophies being hawked in the marketplace of ideas today. The task becomes easier, however, when we realize they can all be grouped into two fundamental categories: The most crucial distinction falls between systems that begin with a personal God and those that begin with a nonpersonal force or essence. Typically we use the term *nonpersonal* to refer to secular "isms" like naturalism and materialism. But we should bear in mind that the same category includes religious beliefs as well—ones that begin with a nonpersonal spiritual essence. And although naturalism is fashionable among the highly educated, among ordinary people a vague generic spiritualism may actually be more widespread.

Indeed, it was so widespread already half a century ago that C. S. Lewis said we often find ourselves opposed "not by the *ir*religion of our hearers but by their *real* religion"—by which he meant some diluted form of pantheism. People tend to like the idea that God is not a personal being but rather "a great spiritual force pervading all things, a common mind of which we are all parts, a pool of generalized spirituality to which we can all flow." So pervasive is this concept that Lewis considered it "the natural bent of the human mind"—"the attitude into which the human mind automatically falls when left to itself" apart from divine revelation.[9] If Lewis is right, then pantheism will always reemerge as a natural opponent of Christianity.

Over the long term, then, secularism is unlikely to last. Since humanity is naturally religious, ultimately Western culture will probably become spiritualized again. Having served its purpose in undercutting Christianity, secularism itself will die off, giving way to a pantheistic spirituality that is already at the core of so much thinking across the board in the West, the East, and the Middle East. It is crucial for Christians to learn how to analyze these nonpersonal, pantheistic worldviews—both to protect ourselves and to reach out in evangelism to the spiritually lost.

Appendix 3
THE LONG WAR BETWEEN
MATERIALISM AND CHRISTIANITY

Some of the most important figures in American history for Christians to understand are the pragmatists, because they did so much to work out the philosophical implications of Darwinism (see chapter 8). And one way to gauge the impact of their ideas is to situate them within a larger historical context. Charles Sanders Peirce sometimes attributed his ideas about chance to the philosopher Epicurus[1]—a comment that directs us all the way back to the ancient Greek thinkers. Seen through a wider historical lens, pragmatism was one stage in a long war between materialism and Christianity that began with the ancient Greeks.

Virtually every conceivable philosophical position can be found in some form at the dawn of Western culture among the Greek philosophers. In chapter 2, we traced the enormous impact that Plato and Aristotle had on Christian thought. But there was also another stream of Greek thought, represented by Epicurus and Democritus (and later the Roman poet Lucretius). They were the materialists of ancient times, who taught that the universe consisted solely of atoms in motion, combining and recombining to form living things by sheer chance. As Lucretius declared in *On the Nature of the Universe,* living things were brought about by "the purposeless congregation and coalescence of atoms."[2]

This sounds strangely modern, very much like the materialism of our own day. And except for lacking Darwin's mechanism of natural selection, ancient materialism *did* have all the same basic elements: especially the core idea that matter is capable of producing everything we see around us by chance collisions of atoms, without plan or purpose.

In fact, already in ancient times, Epicurus had mapped out a complete worldview based on materialism. First, if matter is all that exists, then we must be empiricists: Knowledge is limited to what we know through the senses (atoms impinging upon our sense organs). Second, morality must be based on the senses too: Good and evil are defined by sensations of pleasure and pain. The sole principle of morality is that we ought to maximize pleasure and minimize pain—in a word, hedonism. Students coming into Epicurus's garden, where he held his classes, were greeted by an inscription on the gate that read: "Stranger, here you will do well to tarry; here our highest good is pleasure." Yet Epicurus did not equate the term *hedonism* with unbridled indulgence, as we do today. He urged moderation and even asceticism, on the grounds that most pleasures bring pain in their wake (like drinking too much). Still, the main feature of his morality was that it was not based on any transcendent standard of the Good; instead it was based on our natural preference for certain sensations.

These ideas were as controversial in the ancient world as they are today. After the Hellenistic period (when Epicurus lived), philosophy once again fell under the sway of classical thought (Plato and Aristotle), whose followers vigorously opposed Epicurean materialism. They argued that if the world really did consist of chance configurations of atoms, then knowledge would be impossible. The constant stream of impressions coming into our minds through the senses would not be ordered in any rational patterns, but would be a meaningless scattershot of sights, sounds, tastes, and textures. The reason we can know anything at all, they said, is precisely that reality is *not* a random flow of atoms but is ordered into intelligible patterns—which they called Forms or Ideas. It is this rational order that our minds apprehend. Living things do not result from a chance collation of atoms; they consist of matter organized by intelligible Forms, which in Latin is *species*. (Recall the Form/Matter dualism discussed in chapter 2.)

What's more, classical philosophers argued, this rational order is teleological—directed by a goal or purpose (Greek *telos*). When an acorn becomes an oak, or an egg grows into a chicken, its development is a directed process that unfolds according to a built-in plan or purpose. The final goal or Form is the full-grown tree or the adult hen. (Aristotle had a pretty clear commonsense understanding of what we now call genetics.[3])

According to classical thought, the same teleological reasoning holds for morality. Morality is not based on the senses (pain and pleasure), as the Epicureans taught; it is based on transcendent Forms like Goodness and Justice. These are teleological in the sense that they express the purpose or ideal toward which humans ought to be developing: We should be striving to become ever more good and just.[4]

The intellectual world of ancient times was a battleground between these competing philosophies (along with several others), until Christianity appeared on the scene. When the early Christian thinkers surveyed the ongoing debate, they had no doubt which side was in the right: They aligned themselves firmly with Plato and Aristotle, while forcefully attacking Epicurean materialism. Indeed, Epicurus became a favorite whipping boy among the early Christian apologists.[5] Against his materialism, they affirmed the reality of the spiritual realm, along with the ability of the mind to know abstract ideals beyond the empirical world—Truth, Goodness, and Beauty. The concept of intelligible Forms was reinterpreted as "ideas in the mind of God"—the plans or designs He used in creating the world. The result was a kind of Christianized classicism that became the dominant philosophical position in Europe from late antiquity all through the Middle Ages and beyond, while Epicureanism was nearly forgotten.

Then, more than a millennium later, at the dawn of the scientific revolution, a seismic shift took place. Seeking to frame a new philosophy of nature, some of the early modern scientists began cautiously reconsidering Epicurean atomism. Many were Christians who broke with the negative judgment that early Christian apologists had pronounced on Epicureanism. Optimistically, these scientific thinkers hoped that atomism could be extracted from its materialistic philosophical context and baptized into a Christian worldview. The first to revive Epicurean atomism was the priest Pierre Gassendi, followed by the devout chemist Robert Boyle and the incomparable Isaac Newton.[6]

By resurrecting Epicurean atomism in *science*, however, they cracked open the door to Epicurean materialism in *philosophy*. In short order, materialism burst the door open and came charging through. Finally, with the evolutionary theory of Charles Darwin, materialism got the upper hand in Western thought. Darwin tossed out the concept of intelligible Forms (recall that the Latin word for Form is *species*), arguing that there are no real species in nature, but only a constantly shifting flux of individuals. The reason there *appear* to be species is only that evolutionary change is so slow—just as the earth appears to be flat only because its curve is so gradual. It is ironic that Darwin's book was titled *On the Origin of Species* because his purpose was actually to deny the real existence of species. He regarded taxonomic categories merely as useful mental constructs that *we* impose on the flux of nature. The organic world consists ultimately of individuals in constantly shifting chance interactions.[7] It is no exaggeration to say that Darwinism represents the triumph of Epicurean atomism in modern times.[8]

And if there are no species or Forms in nature, then there are none in morals or metaphysics either—no eternal ideals of Goodness, Truth, or Beauty. It was the pragmatists who took this next step: What Darwin did to species, they did to ideas. Tossing out the concept of Forms or Ideas, they concluded that all we know is the constantly shifting flux of experiences. In his famous essay "The Influence of Darwin on Philosophy," John Dewey said we must abandon the classical Greek approach of explaining things by reference to intelligible Forms, and replace it with knowledge that is "genetic and experimental."[9] Everything would now be explained as originating through historical processes ("genetic") that are knowable by empirical investigation ("experimental").

For example, instead of basing morality on human nature in its original and ideal form (the way God created us from the beginning), pragmatism explains morality as something that arises over time by a naturalistic process: As humans experiment with various behaviors, those that produce satisfactory results become imprinted in their brains. After all, according to evolution, there *is* no original and ideal human nature, normative for all times and places. Instead, moral practices come into being over the course of history as responses to environmental pressures, and are retained only if they pass the test of expedience and pragmatic results.

By the same token, as evolution proceeds and conditions change, then moral practices must change as well. The important thing is not to identify enduring normative principles but to learn strategies for managing change. For if species are not real, then the boundaries defining human nature become plastic and malleable—and who can assign humans any special moral status? Why not take control of the course of human evolution through social engineering? "Man, as he is, is obsolescent," announced Mary Calderone, former executive director of the Sexuality Information and Education Council of the United States (SIECUS), in 1968. The main question facing educators, she said, is "what kind [of man] do we want to produce in his place and how do we design the production line?" Calderone called on schools to begin producing "quality human beings by means of such consciously engineered processes as society's own best minds can blueprint."[10]

Such unvarnished calls for social engineering are chilling. Worse, we may soon have the scientific capacity to perform *genetic* engineering—which will put far greater power into the hands of technocrats eager to take charge of evolution. "Human nature disappears as a concept from neo-Darwinism," explains embryologist Brian Goodwin, "and so life becomes a set of parts, commodities that can be shifted around."[11] If there is no normative human nature, why *not* experiment? Why *not* shift genes around and manipulate life forms in any way that seems expedient?

By tracing the debate over Darwinism all the way back to Epicurus, we can place the theory within a much larger context. Darwinism was not entirely new, invented out of whole cloth. In many ways, it represented a revival of ancient Epicureanism. Having been decisively defeated by the early Christian apologists, Epicurean materialism lay dormant for a millennium and a half, only to rise once again to do battle with Christianity in modern times.[12] The pragmatists then applied Darwinism to the life of the mind. Thus pragmatism represents one stage in the long war between materialism and Christianity.

Appendix 4

ISMS ON THE RUN:
PRACTICAL APOLOGETICS
AT L'ABRI

When I first arrived at L'Abri, trudging through the early spring snow to the tiny alpine village nestled in the Alps, I had developed a motley set of "isms"—from determinism to subjectivism to moral relativism. But as I settled into a round of study and discussions, I was shocked to find those beliefs under constant and vigorous assault. Looking back, I realize that what finally persuaded me of the truth of Christianity was Schaeffer's apologetic method, which was a unique hybrid of Common Sense realism and Dutch neo-Calvinism (see chapter 11).

How did this method play out in actual apologetics with a skeptic—me, for example? In a nutshell, Schaeffer would argue that one way to test truth claims is to measure them against the standard of what we all know by direct experience—or as he put it, universal human experience (Common Sense realism). Then he would endeavor to show that Christianity alone gives an adequate *theoretical* account of what we know by *pre-theoretical* experience (Dutch neo-Calvinism). To borrow a phrase from a contemporary philosopher of science, the truths known by experience are "conclusions in search of a premise."[1] To make sense of them, we have to find a "premise" or systematic worldview that accounts for them.

SURVIVAL MACHINES?

To get a better grasp of this line of argument, walk with me through a few examples. How might we respond to the reductionism and determinism so widespread today, especially in the field of cognitive science? Just recently an article in *Nature* recited the current orthodoxy, insisting that the mind is "a survival machine with predetermined choices" and that free will is a subjective illusion.[2]

"The real causal story behind human behavior is deterministic," agrees another recent article. Free will is self-deception, for "we are experts at deluding ourselves that we are ideal agents. . . . We confabulate stories that keep the self in the driver's seat."[3]

Daniel Dennett, whom we met in earlier chapters, does not flinch at dismissing consciousness itself as an illusion. Since our brains are nothing but complicated computers, he reasons, we are merely robots—and like any robot, we can function perfectly well without subjective awareness (what we call mind, soul, or consciousness). Thus he concludes that humans are essentially zombies—not the movie monsters but "philosopher's zombies," creatures that exhibit all the behavior of a human being but without any consciousness.[4]

When I arrived at L'Abri, these were some of the ideas I had come to accept. What changed my mind? The counterargument is that determinism contradicts the data of experience. We all have an immediate awareness of being in situations where we must deliberate on alternative courses of action, and then select one of them. It is often exhilarating, and just as often agonizing, but in practice no one can really deny the direct awareness that we make choices.

"We find it impossible *not* to believe that we are radically free and responsible in our choices and actions," says philosopher Galen Strawson. In ordinary life, we find ourselves forced to believe that we have "ultimate, buck-stopping responsibility for what we do, of a kind that can make blame and punishment and praise and reward truly just and fair."[5] Moreover, we find testimony to this belief in the literature of all ages and cultures throughout history. It is part of universal human experience.

To be consistent, the determinist is forced to deny the testimony of experience. But that is not a valid move in the worldview game: The point of offering a worldview is to *explain* the data of experience, not to *deny* it. Anything less is ducking the issue. Thus we can be confident that any philosophy that leads to determinism is simply false. It fails to account for the reality of human nature as we experience it.

Another way to frame the argument is to say that no one can live consistently on the basis of a deterministic worldview. In everyday life, we are forced to operate on the assumption that freedom and choice are real, no matter what we believe theoretically. This creates a point of tension for the nonbeliever. "The conviction of freedom is built into our experiences; we can't just give it up," said philosopher John Searle in an interview. "If we tried to, we couldn't live with it. We can say, OK, I believe in determinism; but then when we go into a restaurant we have to make up our mind what we're going to order, and that's a free choice."[6] In his professional writings, Searle reduces all reality to particles moving by blind physical forces—yet when he leaves his laboratory and tries to function in the real world, he cannot live on that basis. His experience provides a practical contradiction of his philosophy.

By contrast, Christianity is completely consonant with human experience. It offers a rationally consistent explanation of human freedom as one aspect of the image of God. If ultimate reality is a personal God who wills and chooses, then the human person is no longer a misfit in a deterministic world. Christianity explains not only freedom but also the *other* dimensions of human personality that derive from freedom: creativity, originality, moral responsibility, and even love. The whole range of human personality is accounted for only by the Christian worldview, because it begins with a personal God. We don't need to make an irrational leap to the upper story in order to affirm the highest ideals of human nature; they are utterly logically consistent with the Christian worldview.

BUMPING UP AGAINST REALITY

What about subjectivism? During my second visit to L'Abri, I had the privilege of staying in the home of Udo and Debby Middelmann. One of Udo's frequent themes during dinner conversations was the objectivity of truth. It's a lesson we find ourselves learning, like it or not, from the time we are born, Udo would say. When a baby crawls to the edge of the crib and bumps his head against the wooden bars, he learns in a painful way that reality is objective. When a toddler tilts his high chair back until it falls to the floor, he learns that there is an objective structure to the universe. Reality does not bend itself to our subjective desires—a lesson that can be painful to learn even for adults. Thus we can confidently reject any philosophical position that leads to subjectivism. Why? Because it fails to account for what ordinary experience teaches us day by day. It is in tension with the data of experience.

Christianity, by contrast, treats truth as objective and explains why—because the world is the creation of God, not of my own mind. The doctrine of creation gives logical grounds for our belief that an objective, external world exists, with its own inherent structure and design.

What's more, the Creator is not silent. He has spoken, giving us divine revelation in Scripture. Since God sees and knows everything as it truly is, what He communicates in His Word is an objective, trustworthy basis for knowledge.

This is a revolutionary claim in today's postmodern world, with its pervasive subjectivism and relativism. We are not locked into the "prison house of language," as postmodernists put it. By *language* they mean belief systems, which are expressed in language, and which they regard as nothing more than products of history and cultural evolution. Over against this radical form of historicism, Christianity claims that we have access to *trans*historical truth, because God Himself has spoken.

IT'S NOT FAIR

If there is one prevailing characteristic of modern culture, it is moral relativism. Yet this is one of the "isms" that is easiest to shoot down. Why? Because, despite what a person says he believes, no one faced with genuine cruelty remains a moral relativist.

After World War II, when the atrocities of the Nazi concentration camps came to light, it created a crisis among many educated people. Steeped in the cynicism and relativism typical of their class, they perceived for the first time in a visceral way that evil is real. Yet their own secular philosophies gave them no basis for making objective, universal moral judgments—because those philosophies reduced moral judgments to merely personal preferences or cultural conventions. Thus they found themselves trapped in a practical contradiction, which created tremendous inner tension.

The dilemma is that humans irresistibly and unavoidably make moral judgments—and yet nonbiblical worldviews give no basis for them. When nonbelievers act according to their intrinsic moral nature by pronouncing something truly right or wrong, they are being inconsistent with their own philosophy—and thus condemn it by their own actions. "Whenever you find a man who says he does not believe in a real Right and Wrong, you will find the same man going back on this in a moment later," writes C. S. Lewis. "He may break his promise to you, but if you try breaking one to him he will be complaining 'It's not fair' before you can say Jack Robinson."

"It seems, then, we are forced to believe in a real Right and Wrong," Lewis concludes. "People may be sometimes mistaken about them, just as people sometimes get their sums wrong; but they are not a matter of mere taste and opinion any more than the multiplication table."[7] Yet what is the logical ground for this unavoidable belief in right and wrong? The only basis for an objective morality is the existence of a holy God, whose character provides the ultimate foundation for moral standards. Christianity explains why we are moral creatures, and establishes the validity of our moral sense.

These were some of the issues that I had to wrestle with personally in my studies at L'Abri before becoming a Christian. The form of apologetics I encountered there treated common human experience as the touchstone. The purpose of a *worldview* is to explain our experience of the *world*—and any philosophy can be judged by how well it succeeds in doing so. When Christianity is tested, we discover that it alone explains and makes sense of the most basic and universal human experiences. This is the confidence that should sustain us when we bring our faith perspective into the public arena, whether in personal evangelism or in our professional work.

NOTES

INTRODUCTION

1. *How Now Shall We Live?* was coauthored by Charles Colson and published by Tyndale (Wheaton, Ill., 1999) and is hereafter cited as *How Now?* I would also like to recognize the contribution of Harold Fickett, an outstanding writer and storyteller, who wrote the chapters in *How Now?* consisting of extended stories. In offering the current book in part as an advance on themes developed in *How Now?* I'd like to clarify that all citations of that earlier volume refer solely to chapters that I authored.

2. Bill Wichterman, in discussion with the author. Wichterman develops his thesis in greater detail in "The Culture: Upstream from Politics," in *Building a Healthy Culture: Strategies for an American Renaissance,* ed. Don Eberly (Grand Rapids, Mich.: Eerdmans, 2001), 76-101. "While cultural conservatives bemoan judicial activism that reinterprets the plain meaning of the written Constitution, they forget that the courts are only finishing on parchment a job already begun in the hearts of the American people. . . . Politics is largely an expression of culture."

3. Cited in Mary Passantino, "The Little Engine that Can," a review of Phillip Johnson's *The Right Questions* (foreword by Nancy Pearcey), in *Christian Research Journal,* April 2003.

4. Peter Berger, *Facing Up to Modernity: Excursions in Society, Politics, and Religion* (New York: Basic Books, 1977), 133.

5. Francis Schaeffer deals with the divided concept of truth in *Escape from Reason* and *The God Who Is There* (in *The Complete Works of Francis A. Schaeffer* [Wheaton, Ill.: Crossway, 1982]).

6. Phillip E. Johnson, *The Wedge of Truth: Splitting the Foundations of Naturalism* (Downers Grove, Ill.: InterVarsity Press, 2000), 148, emphasis added. See also my review of the book: "A New Foundation for Positive Cultural Change: Science and God in the Public Square," *Human Events* (September 15, 2000, at http://www.arn.org).

7. Lesslie Newbigin, *A Word in Season: Perspectives on Christian World Missions* (Grand Rapids, Mich.: Eerdmans, 1994), see especially the essay titled, "The Cultural Captivity of Western Christianity as a Challenge to a Missionary Church."

8. "Reeve: Keep Religious Groups Out of Public Policy," The Associated Press, April 3, 2003, emphasis added.

9. Michael Goheen, *"As the Father Has Sent Me, I Am Sending You": J. E. Lesslie Newbigin's Missionary Ecclesiology* (Zoetermeer: Uitgeverij Boekencentrum, 2000), 377.

10. Albert M. Wolters, *Creation Regained: Biblical Basics for a Reformational Worldview* (Grand Rapids, Mich.: Eerdmans, 1985), 4.

11. For a brief history of the term *worldview* from a Christian perspective, see Albert M. Wolters, "On the Idea of Worldview and Its Relation to Philosophy," in *Stained Glass,* ed. Paul Marshall, Sander Griffioen, and Richard J. Mouw (Lanham, Md.: University Press of America, 1989), 65-80. For a more detailed account, see David K. Naugle, *Worldview: The History of a Concept* (Grand Rapids, Mich.: Eerdmans, 2002). For a brief history from a non-Christian perspective, see the first two sections of Eugene F. Miller, "Positivism, Historicism, and Political Inquiry," *American Political Science Review* 66, no. 3 (September 1972): 796-817; at http://members. shaw.ca/compilerpress1/Anno%20Miller.htm. Miller writes: "All human expressions point beyond themselves to the characteristic worldview *(Weltanschauung)* of the epoch or culture to which they belong. This underlying impulse or spirit makes the culture a whole and determines the shape of all thought and evaluation within it. We grasp the documentary meaning of human objectifications by seeing them as unconscious expressions of a worldview. Even theoretical philosophy is but a channel through which the spirit of the age finds expression."

12. The first three parts of this book were delivered as three presentations at the Leadership Academy of the Association of Christian Schools International, June 22-26, 2001, under the titles "The Nuts and Bolts of a Christian Worldview" (part 1), "A Worldview Approach to Science" (part 2), and "Facing Our Past: Whatever Happened to the Christian Mind?" (part 3). They were later updated and presented at a L'Abri conference, February 6-7, 2004 in Rochester, Minnesota.

13. Nancy Pearcey, "Anti-Darwinism Comes to the University: An Interview with Phillip Johnson," *Bible-Science Newsletter,* June 1990. See also Nancy Pearcey, "Foreword," in

Phillip E. Johnson, *The Right Questions: Truth, Meaning, and Public Debate* (Downers Grove, Ill.: InterVarsity Press, 2002).

14. In *How Now?* material from the *Bible-Science Newsletter* contributed extensively to the chapters on science in part 2 and the chapters on redemption in part 4, among others. Readers interested in pursuing the original sources will find them referenced there (third printing) and more extensively throughout the present book.

CHAPTER 1: BREAKING OUT OF THE GRID

1. John D. Beckett, *Loving Monday: Succeeding in Business Without Selling Your Soul* (Downers Grove, Ill.: InterVarsity Press, 1998), 52.
2. "Sarah," in discussion with the author. The name has been changed to protect her privacy, but otherwise the story is completely true and accurate.
3. Francis Schaeffer explains this phenomenon in *A Christian Manifesto,* in *The Complete Works of Francis A. Schaeffer,* vol. 5 (Wheaton, Ill.: Crossway, 1982), 424-425: "Many Christians do not mean what I mean when I say Christianity is true, or Truth. They are Christians and they believe in, let us say, the truth of creation, the truth of the virgin birth, the truth of Christ's miracles, Christ's substitutionary death, and His coming again. But they stop there with these and other individual truths. When I say Christianity is true I mean it is true to total reality—the total of what is. . . . Christianity is not just a series of truths but *Truth*—Truth about all of reality."
4. Harry Blamires, *The Christian Mind* (New York: Seabury, 1963), 3, emphasis added.
5. Michael Weiskopf, "Energized by Pulpit or Passion, the Public Is Calling: 'Gospel Grapevine' Displays Strength in Controversy Over Military Gay Ban," *The Washington Post,* February 1, 1993, A1.
6. Blamires, *Christian Mind,* 3-4, emphasis in original.
7. Charlie Peacock, *At the Crossroads: An Insider's Look at the Past, Present, and Future of Contemporary Christian Music* (Nashville: Broadman & Holman, 1999).
8. Cited in Allen C. Guelzo, "The Return of the Will," in *Edwards in Our Time: Jonathan Edwards and the Shaping of American Religion,* ed. Sang Hyun Lee and Allen C. Guelzo (Grand Rapids, Mich.: Eerdmans, 1999), 133.
9. Martin Marty, *The Modern Schism: Three Paths to the Secular* (New York: Harper & Row, 1969), 40. See also 57, 92, 96.
10. Sidney Mead, *The Old Religion in the Brave New World: Reflections on the Relation Between Christendom and the Republic* (Los Angeles: University of California Press, 1977), 4.
11. Dorothy L. Sayers, *Creed or Chaos?* (Manchester, N.H.: Sophia, 1949), 77.
12. Bob Briner, *Roaring Lambs* (Grand Rapids, Mich.: Zondervan, 2000), 17-18.
13. Terry Mattingly, "Veggies Attack the Funny Gap," Scripps Howard News Service, October 2, 2002.
14. Fritjof Capra, *The Tao of Physics* (Boston: Shambhala, 2000).
15. Despite this discouraging conversation, I did end up writing that article on the new physics for the *Bible-Science Newsletter*—in fact, two articles: Nancy Pearcey, "The New Physics and the New Consciousness," parts 1 and 2, *Bible-Science Newsletter,* October 1986 and November 1986. I later expanded the material to form two chapters in a book on the history and philosophy of science, *The Soul of Science.* See chapter 8 on relativity theory, "Is Everything Relative? The Revolution in Physics," and chapter 9 on quantum mechanics, "Quantum Mysteries: Making Sense of the New Physics." I was joined in the project by Charles Thaxton, who provided scientific expertise and review (Nancy Pearcey and Charles Thaxton, *The Soul of Science: Christian Faith and Natural Philosophy* [Wheaton, Ill: Crossway, 1994], hereafter cited as *Soul of Science*).
16. See H. Evan Runner, *The Relation of the Bible to Learning* (Toronto: Wedge, 1970), 16.
17. "I will sprinkle clean water on you, and you shall be clean from all your uncleanness, and from all your idols" (Ezek. 36:25).
18. On these developments in the philosophy of science, see Nancy Pearcey, "The Science of Science," *Bible-Science Newsletter,* August 1983; Nancy Pearcey, "From Tyrant to Tool: A New View of Science," *Bible-Science Newsletter,* April 1986. For a later treatment, see *Soul of Science,* especially chapter 2.
19. Roy Clouser, *The Myth of Religious Neutrality: An Essay on the Hidden Role of Religious Belief in Theories* (Notre Dame, Ind.: University of Notre Dame Press, 1991), 87.

20. John Gray, "Exposing the Myth of Secularism," *Australian Financial Review,* January 3, 2003, at http://afr.com/review/2003/01/03/FFX9CQAJFAD.html.

21. R. G. Collingwood, *An Essay on Metaphysics* (Chicago: Regnery, 1972; orig., London: Oxford University Press, 1940), 253-257. "Matter in the Platonic sense, which must be 'prevailed upon' by reason, will not obey mathematical laws exactly: [On the other hand,] matter which God has created from nothing may well strictly follow the rules which its Creator has laid down for it. In this sense I called modern science a legacy, I might even have said a child, of Christianity" (Carl von Weizsacker, *The Relevance of Science* [New York: Harper & Row, 1964], 163).

22. For a historical account of the relationship between Christianity and mathematics, see Nancy Pearcy, "Mind Your Mathematics: A Two-Part Series on the Role of Mathematics in Science," *Bible-Science Newsletter,* March 1990; Nancy Pearcey, "The Rise and Fall of Mathematics," *Bible-Science Newsletter,* April 1990. I later expanded this material into two chapters in *Soul of Science* (chapters 6 and 7). A good treatment of the philosophy of mathematics can be found in Roy Clouser, *Myth of Religious Neutrality,* chapter 7.

23. *Getting to Know "Connected Mathematics Project,"* April 30, 1996, Teacher's Guide, 17; cited in Michael Chapman, "Worldview War in the Classroom," in *No Retreats, No Reserves, No Regrets,* ed. Brannon Howse (St. Paul, Minn.: Stewart, 2000), 149. Connected Mathematics Project is a complete grades 6–8 mathematics curriculum developed at Michigan State University with funds from the National Science Foundation.

24. *Minnesota State Statutes Governing the Licensing of Teachers,* 106, 111. Cited in ibid.

25. Reality is multilayered, and at levels where reality is simpler, agreement between Christians and non-Christians will be broader. The simplest level is sheer quantity—the level of mathematics. At a somewhat higher level is the application of mathematics to the physical world—physics—where theoretical constructs play a greater role. At a higher level yet is biology, where disagreements grow wider still. The most complex levels are the human sciences, and here the divergences are greatest—in subjects like psychology, morality, and finally religion. The higher you go up the scale, the greater the role played by philosophical and faith commitments, and hence the greater the differences in perspective. Herman Dooyeweerd calls this the "modal scale," and distinguishes fourteen levels: numerical, spatial, physical, biotic, psychical, logical, historical, linguistic, social, economic, aesthetic, juridical, moral, and pistic (faith). Each level is represented by an academic discipline. For a readable introduction, see L. Kalsbeek, *Contours of a Christian Philosophy: An Introduction to Herman Dooyeweerd's Thought,* ed. Bernard and Josina Zylstra (Toronto: Wedge, 1975). Dooyeweerd taught at the Free University of Amsterdam, which is housed in a building fourteen stories high, with each floor devoted to one of the levels in Dooyeweerd's "modal scale." The top floor houses the theology department; just under it is philosophy, then law, and so on. See David Caudill, "A Calvinist Perspective on the Place of Faith in Legal Scholarship," in Michael McConnell, ed., *Christian Perspectives on Legal Thought* (New Haven, Conn.: Yale University Press, 2001), 313.

26. Os Guinness, *The Gravedigger File: Papers on the Subversion of the Modern Church* (Downers Grove, Ill.: InterVarsity Press, 1984), 43, 44, emphasis added.

27. Clouser, *Myth of Religious Neutrality,* 80.

28. Other passages on this theme include Isaiah 6:9-10; 42:18-20; 43:8; Matthew 15:14; 23:16ff.; 2 Peter 1:9.

29. When I lecture on the Cultural Mandate, many people say that they have never encountered the concept before. Thus readers may benefit from my more detailed treatment of the Cultural Mandate in "Saved to What?" chapter 31 in *How Now?*

30. C. S. Lewis, *The Last Battle* (New York: HarperCollins, 1994), 211.

31. Francis Schaeffer makes this point in *True Spirituality,* in *Complete Works,* vol. 3, 200-201.

32. Gene Edward Veith, *God at Work: Your Christian Vocation in All of Life* (Wheaton, Ill.: Crossway, 2002). See also Veith's *The Spirituality of the Cross* (St. Louis: Concordia, 1999), 71ff.

33. Veith, *Spirituality of the Cross.* See also D. G. Hart, *Recovering Mother Kirk: The Case for Liturgy in the Reformed Tradition* (Grand Rapids, Mich.: Baker, 2003), chapter 12, "What Can Presbyterians Learn from Lutherans?"

34. "This small, intense man from the Swiss mountains delivered a message unlike any heard in evangelical circles in the mid-1960s. At Wheaton College, students were fighting to show films like Bambi, while Francis was talking about the films of Bergman and Fellini. Administrators

were censoring existential themes out of student publications, while Francis was discussing Camus, Sartre, and Heidegger. He quoted Dylan Thomas, knew the artwork of Salvador Dali, listened to the music of the Beatles and John Cage" (Michael Hamilton, "The Dissatisfaction of Francis Schaeffer" [*Christianity Today,* March 3, 1997], at http://www.antithesis.com/features/dissatisfaction.html).

35. Schaeffer has been criticized by some academic specialists for various aspects of his treatment of intellectual history. However, one need not agree with Schaeffer's analyses at every point in order to appreciate the way he conceptualized basic themes in philosophy, art, and culture so that questioning students and other seekers could understand and apply them. Many of those students went on to earn advanced degrees, specializing in various areas of scholarship. Thus Schaeffer played an important "bridging" role in leading young people into the intellectual and cultural world.

36. The apologetics arguments that I encountered at L'Abri, and that I eventually found persuasive, are woven throughout the rest of this book, especially in chapters 3, 7, and 11, and in appendix 4.

37. Augustine, *Confessions,* I.1.

38. This everyday artistry was a conscious attempt to express our relationship with a God of beauty. Edith Schaeffer explained her philosophy of finding beauty in ordinary life in *Hidden Art* (Wheaton, Ill.: Tyndale, 1972). For a shorter treatment, listen to her lecture titled "The Art of Life and the Courage to Be Creative," at http://www.soundword.com.

39. See, for example, Francis Schaeffer, *The New Super-Spirituality,* in *Complete Works,* vol. 3, 388; and *The God Who Is There,* in *Complete Works,* vol. 1, 27-31.

40. Schaeffer, *God Who Is There,* in *Complete Works,* vol. 1, 34.

41. The church is pastored by Erwin McManus, author of *An Unstoppable Force* (Loveland, Colo.: Group, 2001); and *Seizing Your Divine Moment* (Nashville: Nelson, 2002). See McManus's essay, "Fulfilling the Vision," at http://www.mosaic.org.

42. Quentin Smith, "The Metaphilosophy of Naturalism," in *Philo* 4, no. 2 (Fall/Winter 2001), at http://www.philoonline.org/library/smith_4_2.htm.

43. Smith debates William Lane Craig in *Theism, Atheism and Big Bang Cosmology* (New York: Oxford University Press, 1995).

44. Alvin Plantinga, *God and Other Minds: A Study of the Rational Justification of Belief in God* (Ithaca, N.Y., Cornell University Press, 1967, 1990).

45. Smith, "Metaphilosophy of Naturalism."

46. Sigmund Freud. *The Future of an Illusion,* trans. and ed. James Strachey (New York: Norton, 1961), 43.

47. Patrick Glynn, *God, The Evidence: The Reconciliation of Faith and Reason in a Postsecular World* (Rocklin, Calif.: Prima, 1997), 62.

48. Glynn, *God, The Evidence,* 20. I have described much more of the medical evidence supporting a positive relation between faith and health in, "Don't Worry, Be Religious," chapter 32 in *How Now?* See also Dale A. Matthews, Michael E. McCullough, David B. Larson, Harold G. Koenig, James P. Swyers, and Mary Greenwold Milano, "Religious Commitment and Health Status: A Review of the Research and Implications for Family Medicine," in *Archives of Family Medicine* 7, no. 2 (March/April 1998), at http://archfami.ama-assn.org/issues/v7n2/ffull/fsa6025.html.

49. Cited in a press release from the International Center for the Integration of Health and Spirituality, "Scientists, Doctors Gather to Define and Measure Spirituality," January 15, 1997, at http://www.nihr.org/programs/archivedreleases.cfm.

50. See, for example, the interview with Benson by John Koch in *The Boston Globe Magazine,* November 9, 1997, at http://www.boston.com/globe/magazine/11-16/interview/.

51. Guenter Lewy, *Why America Needs Religion* (Grand Rapids, Mich.: Eerdmans, 1996), x.

52. Ibid., 132-133.

53. For more on this topic, see chapter 12.

54. Cited in Marvin Olasky, *The Tragedy of American Compassion* (Washington, D.C.: Regnery; Wheaton, Ill.: Crossway, 1992), 48. See online at www.olasky.com/Archives/toac/03%20 (word5).pdf. Chapter 3, page 8.

CHAPTER 2: REDISCOVERING JOY

1. Charles Malik, *The Two Tasks* (Westchester, Ill.: Cornerstone, 1980), 32.
2. Sealy Yates, in discussion with the author.
3. See Joseph G. Allegretti, *The Lawyer's Calling: Christian Faith and Legal Practice* (Mahwah, N.J.: Paulist, 1996). For an analysis of Christian approaches to law, see *Christian Perspectives on Legal Thought*, ed. Michael McConnell (New Haven, Conn.: Yale University Press, 2001).
4. Lesslie Newbigin, *Our Task Today*. An unpublished paper given to the fourth meeting of the diocesan council, Tirumangalam, India, December 18-20, 1951. Cited in Michael Goheen, "The Missional Calling of Believers in the World: Lesslie Newbigin's Contribution," at http://www.deepsight.org/articles/goheenb.htm.
5. Lesslie Newbigin, *Truth to Tell: The Gospel as Public Truth* (Grand Rapids, Mich.: Eerdmans, 1991), 49.
6. Andy Crouch, "Christian Esperanto: We Must Learn Other Cultural Tongues," in *Christianity Today*, April, 2003.
7. Wade Clark Roof, *Spiritual Marketplace: Baby Boomers and the Remaking of American Religion* (Princeton, N.J.: Princeton University Press, 1999), 7.
8. Peter Berger, *Facing Up to Modernity: Excursions in Society, Politics, and Religion* (New York: Basic Books, 1977), 18. Berger is referring specifically to the private sphere of the family, but it is an apt description of the private sphere generally.
9. Peter Berger, *The Sacred Canopy: Elements of a Sociological Theory of Religion* (New York: Doubleday, 1967), 134.
10. Walter Kasper, "Nature, Grace, and Culture: On the Meaning of Secularization," in *Catholicism and Secularization in America: Essays on Nature, Grace, and Culture*, ed. David L. Schindler (Huntington, Ind.: Our Sunday Visitor, Communio Books, 1990), 38.
11. Lesslie Newbigin, *Foolishness to the Greeks: The Gospel and Western Culture* (Grand Rapids, Mich.: Eerdmans, 1986), 31.
12. Lesslie Newbigin, *The Gospel in a Pluralist Society* (Grand Rapids, Mich.: Eerdmans, 1989), 172.
13. In 1995, Smith and his team conducted 130 two-hour interviews. In 1996, they conducted 2,591 telephone surveys (2,087 of which were with churchgoing Protestants). Later in 1996 they conducted intensive face-to-face interviews with 178 people who had identified themselves in the survey as evangelical Protestants, 8 people who called themselves fundamentalists, and 6 liberal Protestants. See Christian Smith, with Michael Emerson, Sally Gallagher, Paul Kennedy, and David Sikkink, *American Evangelicalism: Embattled and Thriving* (Chicago: University of Chicago Press, 1998), 17.
14. The labels were based on self-definition: e.g., if someone identified himself as an evangelical Presbyterian, he was placed in the "evangelical" category, while if he identified himself as a liberal Presbyterian, he was slotted into the "liberal" category. As a result, the number of evangelicals is smaller (7 percent of the population) than in most other surveys, where subjects are identified according to standards selected by the survey-taker, such as denominational affiliation or specific doctrinal beliefs.
15. Surprisingly, evangelicals outrank even fundamentalists on all but one measure. The reason, Smith suggests, may be that fundamentalists tend to embrace a subculture mentality—remaining culturally isolated in their churches, schools, and parachurch organizations. Moreover, the doctrine of premillennial dispensationalism, which is more common among fundamentalists, is sometimes interpreted to imply that the world is on a downward slide, and thus that reform is useless. (Why polish the brass on a sinking ship?) This lack of engagement with the outside world may be the reason that fundamentalists demonstrated a slightly greater complacency about their faith as compared to evangelicals, who place more emphasis on reaching out to the surrounding culture. Regular confrontation with a hostile culture, Smith suggests, may actually make for a more alert and active faith commitment (Smith, *American Evangelicalism*, 145-147).
16. This is a result of an atomistic view of society, which conceives of social groups as merely aggregates of individuals. To understand the sources of this individualistic social philosophy among evangelicals, see part 3.
17. Smith, *American Evangelicalism*, 188, 190.
18. Ibid., 203.

19. Ibid., 204, 205, 206.

20. Ibid., 194.

21. Ibid., 201, 198.

22. Plato, *Complete Works,* ed. John M. Cooper (Indianapolis: Hackett, 1997), Laws, book 10, 1542-1566.

23. Schaeffer critiques the two-story concept of truth in *Escape from Reason* and *The God Who Is There* (in *The Complete Works of Francis A. Schaeffer,* vol. 1 [Wheaton, Ill.: Crossway, 1982]), though he begins with Aquinas instead of the Greeks. Schaeffer's critique is similar to the more detailed analysis offered by Herman Dooyeweerd in *Roots of Western Culture: Pagan, Secular, and Christian Options* (Toronto: Wedge, 1979; orig., Zutphen, Netherlands: J. B. van den Brink, 1959); and *In the Twilight of Western Thought* (Nutley, N.J.: Craig, 1972; orig., Presbyterian & Reformed, 1960).

24. To be precise, we will be dealing with the religious interpretation of Plato, which began with the Jewish philosopher Philo and came to its fullest expression in the third century in the work of Plotinus. When I say "Plato," I will be referring to this religious interpretation of Plato, often referred to as neo-Platonism, which was the most powerful conduit of Greek thought to later centuries. (For greater detail, see appendix 2.) Historically, there was considerable merging and overlapping of Platonic with Aristotelian thought, though for simplicity's sake we will consider them separately here. For an accessible discussion of Plato and Aristotle and their impact on Christian thought, see Arthur Holmes, *Fact, Value, and God* (Grand Rapids, Mich.: Eerdmans, 1997).

25. See Charles Norris Cochrane, *Christianity and Classical Culture: A Study of Thought and Action from Augustus to Augustine* (New York: Oxford University Press, 1957), 342, 390, 417.

26. See J. P. Moreland and Scott B. Rae, *Body and Soul: Human Nature and the Crisis in Ethics* (Downers Grove, Ill.: InterVarsity Press, 2000).

27. Pastor and author John Piper says, "I've tried to define the flesh as Paul uses it. Most of the time . . . it does not simply refer to the physical part of you. (Paul does not regard the body as evil in itself.) The flesh is the ego which feels an emptiness and uses the resources in its own power to try to fill it. Flesh is the 'I' who tries to satisfy me with anything but God's mercy" (from a sermon titled "The War Within: Flesh Versus Spirit," at http://www.soundof grace.com/piper83/061983m.htm).

28. Robert Louis Wilken, *The Spirit of Early Christian Thought: Seeing the Face of God* (New Haven, Conn.: Yale University Press, 2003), chapter 1, passim.

29. For a readable account of the way many Christian thinkers were influenced by the dualistic thinking of Greek philosophy, see Brian Walsh and J. Richard Middleton, *The Transforming Vision* (Downers Grove, Ill.: InterVarsity Press, 1984), chapter 7.

30. Colin Gunton, *The One, the Three, and the Many: God, Creation, and the Culture of Modernity* (New York: Cambridge University Press, 1993), 2, 138.

31. Henry Chadwick, *Augustine: A Very Short Introduction* (Oxford: Oxford University Press, 2001), 64-65, 122.

32. G. K. Chesterton, *Saint Thomas Aquinas, "The Dumb Ox"* (1933; reprint, Garden City, N.Y.: Doubleday, 1956), 92.

33. Anglican philosopher Langmead Casserly says that Aquinas is best regarded as an apologist rather than as a philosopher per se: "The Aristotelian revival had put the Faith on the intellectual defensive in Europe for the first time since the collapse of the Western Empire." Thus Aquinas was not merely engaging in detached, objective philosophical inquiry; rather, "He is first and foremost an apologist, coping with a desperate intellectual situation. . . . He was the first apologist to perceive that the very essence of the strategy of apologetics is to concede as much as possible to one's opponent and to base one's argument on his assumptions. . . . This essential Thomistic strategy has been adopted by all wise Christian apologists since his time." In short, Aquinas's goal was to show the Aristotelians of his day that *even on their own premises* Christianity could account better for what they themselves believed to be true (J. V. Langmead Casserly, *The Christian in Philosophy* [New York: Scribner's, 1951], 77, 81-82).

34. Aquinas did not originate the juxtaposition of nature and grace; it was already part of the vocabulary of medieval theologians. An early example was a book by Augustine. Having read a work by Pelagius titled *Nature,* Augustine answered with his own *Nature and Grace.* See

Garry Wills, *Saint Augustine* (New York: Penguin, 1999), 125. What was innovative about Aquinas was that he gave "nature" an Aristotelian definition.

35. Roger French and Andrew Cunningham, *Before Science: The Invention of the Friars' Natural Philosophy* (Aldershot, Hampshire, UK: Ashgate, 1996), 202. The authors are describing the outlook of the Dominicans as a group, especially of Aquinas's teacher Albertus Magnus. For a summary, see Nancy Pearcey, "Recent Developments in the History of Science and Christianity," and "Reply," *Pro Rege* 30, no. 4 (June 2002): 1-11, 20-22.

36. French and Cunningham, *Before Science*, 183-202.

37. Thomas Aquinas, *Summa Theologica* I-II, q. 109, art. 2.

38. Michael Lapierre, S.J., "Grace in Thomas Aquinas," at http://www.catholic-church.org/grace/western/scholars/lap1.htm. Lapierre is endorsing this radical dualism.

39. Jacques Maritain, *Integral Humanism: Temporal and Spiritual Problems of a New Christendom,* trans. Joseph Evans (New York: Scribner's, 1968), 22.

40. Philip Melanchthon, *The Augsburg Confession* (1530), art. 26, "Of the Distinction of Meats," at http://www.iclnet.org/pub/resources/text/wittenberg/concord/web/augs-026.html.

41. Alister McGrath, "Calvin and the Christian Calling," *First Things* 94 (June/July 1999): 31-35.

42. John Kok, *Patterns of the Western Mind: A Reformed Christian Perspective* (Sioux Center, Ia.: Dordt College Press, 1998), 124, 125.

43. John D. Beckett, *Loving Monday: Succeeding in Business Without Selling Your Soul* (Downers Grove, Ill.: InterVarsity Press, 1998), 53.

44. Ibid., 58, 68, 69.

45. Gordon Clark, *Thales to Dewey: A History of Philosophy* (Boston: Houghton Mifflin, 1957), 192.

46. Albert M. Wolters, *Creation Regained: Biblical Basics for a Reformational Worldview* (Grand Rapids, Mich.: Eerdmans, 1985), 49ff.

47. Alexander Solzhenitsyn, *The Gulag Archipelago, 1918–1956: An Experiment in Literary Investigation,* III-IV (New York: Harper & Row, 1973), 615.

48. C. S. Lewis, *The Great Divorce* (New York: Macmillan, 1946), 28.

49. Beckett, *Loving Monday,* 72.

50. Paul Theroux, interview by Susan Olasky, "Agents of Virtue," *World,* March 15, 2003.

51. Robert Bellah, "At Home and Not at Home: Religious Pluralism and Religious Truth," *The Christian Century,* April 19, 1995, 423-428.

52. A brief description of the Holiness movement can be found in "American Holiness Movement," at http://mb-soft.com/believe/text/holiness.htm. The idea of perfection arose as a reaction against Roman Catholicism with its two-tiered spirituality, where ordinary believers were expected to fulfill only the minimum requirements of morality and religion, while the professionally religious (monks, nuns, priests) were to follow what were called the "counsels of perfection." (The phrase is based on Matthew 19:21, "If you would be perfect, go, sell what you possess and give to the poor.") Protestants rejected the Catholic two-tiered conception by insisting that *all* Christians are called to total commitment to God, and *all* are admonished to "Be perfect, as your heavenly Father is perfect" (Matt. 5:48). However, most Protestants do not think we are capable of fulfilling that calling this side of heaven.

53. Wolters, *Creation Regained,* 62-63.

54. The same argument is offered today by some Catholics to support priestly celibacy. "The triumph of celibacy is a holy anticipation of eternity 'where there is neither marrying nor giving in marriage, but all are like the angels of God,' those perfect heralds of his Word and doers of his Will" (Fr. Vincent Miceli, S.J., review of *Celibacy and the Crisis of Faith,* by Dietrich von Hildebrand, at http://www.ewtn.com/library/PRIESTS/HILDEBRA.HTM); "Celibacy, in the Church, thus draws attention to the new order of the gospel, whereas marriage has its roots in the old order. . . . [Celibacy] is a sign of the world to come" (Max Thurian, "The Theological Basis for Priestly Celibacy," at http://www.vatican.va/roman_curia/congregations/cclergy/documents/rc_con_cclergy_doc_01011993_theol_en.html). Of course, one may embrace singleness and celibacy for reasons that do *not* denigrate marriage, such as the freedom to give oneself wholly to ministry.

55. Paul denotes "perfect" with the term *teleios* (Col. 1:28; 4:12—ESV "mature"), which he contrasts to *nepios,* "childish" (1 Cor. 3:1), which denotes moral immaturity and deficiency.

The "perfect man," *teleion,* is the stable person who reflects "the measure of the stature of the fullness of Christ," in contrast to the children (*nepioi*) who are tossed about by every new wind of doctrine (Eph. 4:13-14).

56. One way this is reflected in Catholic theology is that original sin is conceived primarily as a *deprivation* of the super-added grace, leaving human nature weakened and vulnerable to disordered appetites but not morally corrupt, as Protestantism teaches. That is, according to Catholicism, sin is a subtraction from an original good, not the addition of a positive force of rebellion and evil. The *Catechism of the Catholic Church* says, "Adam and Eve transmitted to their descendants human nature wounded by their own first sin and hence deprived of original holiness and justice; this deprivation is called 'original sin'" (art. 417).

57. Hermann Dooyeweerd describes the nature/grace dualism (which he rejects) in these words: "Man lost this gift [of superadded grace] at the fall, and as a result he was reduced to mere 'human nature,' with all its weaknesses. But this human 'nature,' which is guided by the natural light of reason, was not corrupted by sin and thus also does not need to be restored by Christ" (*Roots of Western Culture,* 116-117; see also Dooyeweerd, *In the Twilight of Western Thought,* 191-194).

58. Louis Dupré, "Nature and Grace: Fateful Separation and Attempted Reunion," in *Catholicism and Secularization in America,* 59, 62, 61. Put another way, the nature/grace dualism implied "the assumed continuity of nature throughout the historical stages of innocence, fall, and redemption." (That is, the lower story is not affected by the fall and redemption.) The result was the idea of "an independent, quasi-autonomous natural order," a concept that "continued to hold sway over Catholic theology until the second half of the twentieth century" (61). In the mid-twentieth century there arose a school of thought within Catholicism (called *nouvelle theologie*) that rejected the nature/grace dualism. Excellent discussions by Catholic thinkers, echoing Schaeffer's imagery of "two stories," can be found in several of the essays in *Catholicism and Secularization in America.* For example, Walter Kasper describes the development of a "dualistic and separatist conception" of nature and grace, which he calls a "two-story system" ("Nature, Grace, and Culture," 41).

Similarly, in *Does God Exist?* (London: Collins, 1980), Hans Küng writes, "Cartesianism and Thomism clearly divide the two ways of knowing (natural reason and grace-inspired faith), two planes of knowledge (natural truth and grace-given revealed truth), two sciences (philosophy and theology). . . . Two spheres, even—as it were—like two floors of a building" (21). See also 23-24, 35-38, 67, 511, 518-522.

Catholic critics generally believe the problem lay not in Aquinas's formulation of nature and grace but in later scholasticism, as the two stories became increasingly independent and autonomous, e.g., in Cajetan, Molina, and Suarez. See Fr. Wojciech Giertych, OP, "Fundamental Moral Theology," at http://www.cfpeople.org/Books/Moral/cfptoc.htm; and International Catholic University, "Nature and Grace: Lesson One: The Natural Desire to See God—History," at http://icu.catholicity.com/c01601.htm. (Contrary to misreadings of his work, Francis Schaeffer was careful not to charge Aquinas with the dualism of later thinkers— see Ronald Nash's sensitive analysis in "The Life of the Mind and the Way of Life," in *Francis A. Schaeffer: Portraits of the Man and His Work,* ed. Lane Dennis [Westchester, Ill.: Crossway, 1986], 59-60.)

59. Cited in Richard Russell, "Biblical Foundations for Philosophy," at http://www.biblical creation.org.uk/theology_philosophy/bcs069.html.

CHAPTER 3: KEEPING RELIGION IN ITS PLACE

1. Freeman J. Dyson, "Is God in the Lab?" *The New York Review of Books,* May 28, 1998, emphasis added.

2. Alan Sears, in discussion with the author, December 30, 2002.

3. Christian Smith, "Introduction: Rethinking the Secularization of American Life," in *The Secular Revolution: Power, Interest, and Conflict in the Secularization of American Public Life,* ed. Christian Smith (Los Angeles: University of California Press, 2003), 2-3.

4. Kathleen Nielson, private correspondence, April 28, 2003.

5. See Roy Clouser, *The Myth of Religious Neutrality: An Essay on the Hidden Role of Religious Belief in Theories* (Notre Dame, Ind.: University of Notre Dame Press, 1991), 86-87.

6. Anselm of Canterbury, *Why God Became Man.* A similar defense had been made in the fourth

century by Athanasius. For readable introductions to both, see Tony Lane, *Exploring Christian Thought* (Nashville: Nelson, 1984).

7. Some contemporary Catholic thinkers concur with Protestant critics that the nature/grace dualism led to secularism. For example, Walter Kasper writes, "the two-story system . . . favored a humanism without God as well as a Christianity that had become alienated from the world. . . . In this way, the Baroque and neo-Scholastic understanding of the relation between nature and grace was one of the sources of modern secularization" ("Nature, Grace, and Culture: On the Meaning of Secularization," in *Catholicism and Secularization in America: Essays on Nature, Grace, and Culture*, ed. David L. Schindler [Huntington, Ind.: Our Sunday Visitor, Communio Books, 1990], 41).

8. Walker Percy, *Love in the Ruins* (New York: Avon, 1978), 181.

9. On the broad impact that Descartes' mechanistic philosophy had historically, see my discussion extended throughout several chapters in *Soul of Science* (chapters 1, 3, 4, and 6). The history of science gives a good handle on intellectual history generally, since every major system of thought includes a philosophy of nature, which is often foundational to everything else. (Regarding Newton, ironically, he himself did not hold what came to be called the Newtonian worldview. See *Soul of Science*, chapter 4.)

10. Hume pointed out that if we are strict empiricists, limiting our claims to what appears to the senses, then we cannot defend even concepts that are fundamental to science, such as causality. For we never perceive a cause as such; all we actually perceive are events following one another. We may say that fire "causes" heat, but all we actually perceive is the sight of fire followed by the sensation of heat. See *Soul of Science*, 138-139.

11. On Kant's nature/freedom dichotomy, see Francis Schaeffer, *Escape from Reason*, in *The Complete Works of Francis A. Schaeffer*, vol. 1 (Wheaton, Ill.: Crossway, 1982), 227-229; and Herman Dooyeweerd, *Roots of Western Culture: Pagan, Secular, and Christian Options* (Toronto: Wedge, 1979; orig., Zutphen, Netherlands: J. B. van den Brink, 1959), 171.

12. Immanuel Kant, *Groundwork of the Metaphysic of Morals* (New York: Harper & Row, 1964), 123.

13. Rousseau's thought is analyzed in greater detail in chapter 4.

14. Colin Gunton, *Enlightenment and Alienation: An Essay Towards a Trinitarian Theology* (Grand Rapids, Mich.: Eerdmans, 1985), 61.

15. Immanuel Kant, *Groundwork of the Metaphysic of Morals* (New York: Harper & Row, 1964), 116, 123.

16. Colin Brown, *Philosophy and the Christian Faith* (Downers Grove, Ill.: InterVarsity Press, 1968), 105. Arthur Holmes offers a more positive interpretation of Kant in *Fact, Value, and God* (Grand Rapids, Mich.: Eerdmans, 1997), chapter 10.

17. Richard Dawkins, *The Blind Watchmaker* (New York: Norton, 1986), 6.

18. See chapters 7 and 8 for a more detailed discussion of these themes.

19. Peter Kreeft, in an interview at http://www.christianbook.com/Christian/Books/cms_content/92165368?page=364779&insert=7843899&event=ESRC>100f743.jpg. Emphasis added.

20. For a briefer treatment, see Nancy Pearcey, "The Transforming Power of a Christian Worldview," delivered October 11, 2003, as part of a lecture series titled "Developing a Gospel Worldview," sponsored by Manna Christian Fellowship, Princeton University.

21. Steven Pinker, *How the Mind Works*, 55, emphasis added. See Phillip Johnson's discussion of Pinker in *The Wedge of Truth: Splitting the Foundations of Naturalism* (Downers Grove, Ill.: InterVarsity Press, 2000).

22. Pinker, *How the Mind Works*, 55-56, emphasis added.

23. Steven Pinker, *The Blank Slate: The Modern Denial of Human Nature* (New York: Viking, 2002), 240.

24. Marvin Minsky, *The Society of Mind* (New York: Simon & Schuster, 1985), 307, emphasis added.

25. Transcript of a television interview with John Searle from a program titled "Thinking Allowed: Conversations on the Leading Edge of Knowledge and Discovery," with Dr. Jeffrey Mishlove, at http://www.williamjames.com/transcripts/searle.htm, emphasis added.

26. Schaeffer, *Escape from Reason*, in *Complete Works*, vol. 1, 212. When Schaeffer was writing, the term *postmodernism* had not been coined yet, but clearly he was dealing with the same concept when he spoke about a "line of despair" (despair of finding rational grounds for

human morality and meaning), followed by a "leap of faith" to an irrational, upper-story experience. Millard Erickson notes Schaeffer's anticipation of postmodernism in *Postmodernizing the Faith: Evangelical Responses to the Challenge of Postmodernism* (Grand Rapids, Mich.: Baker, 1998), chapter 4.

27. Schaeffer, *True Spirituality,* in *Complete Works,* vol. 3, 172-173.

28. Schaeffer, *The God Who Is There,* in *Complete Works,* vol. 1, 122, emphasis added. This argument is developed in greater detail in chapter 11 of the present book.

29. John Searle, interview by Terry McDermott, "No Limits Hinder UC Thinker," *The Los Angeles Times,* December 28, 1999.

30. The forum is available at http://www.edge.org/3rd_culture/dawkins_pinker/debate_p1.html. Pinker makes similar claims in his latest book, *The Blank Slate: The Modern Denial of Human Nature* (New York: Viking, 2002).

31. See Paul M. Churchland and Patricia Churchland, *On the Contrary: Critical Essays, 1987–1997* (Cambridge, Mass.: Bradford/MIT Press, 1998). See also Phillip Johnson's analysis in *Wedge of Truth,* 118.

32. Daniel Wegner, *The Illusion of Conscious Will* (Cambridge, Mass.: MIT Press, 2002). For an excellent analysis of eliminative materialism from a Christian perspective, see Angus Menuge, *Agents Under Fire: Materialism and the Rationality of Science* (Lanham, Md.: Rowman & Littlefield, 2004).

33. This quotation is from a discussion of Dennett's views by Teed Rockwell, *Dictionary of Philosophy of Mind,* at http://www.artsci.wustl.edu/~philos/MindDict/eliminativism.html. See Daniel Dennett, *The Intentional Stance* (Cambridge, Mass.: Bradford, 1987).

34. The poll was taken for the National Association of Scholars and is discussed by John Leo in "Professors Who See No Evil," at http://www.usnews.com/usnews/issue/020722/opinion/22john.htm.

35. See Paul Gross and Norman Levitt, *Higher Superstition: The Academic Left and Its Quarrels with Science* (Baltimore: Johns Hopkins University Press, 1994).

36. Jacques Barzun, *The Use and Abuse of Art* (Princeton, N.J.: Princeton University Press, 1974), 53. Another good source on the subject is M. H. Abrams, *The Mirror and the Lamp: Romantic Theory and the Critical Tradition* (Oxford: Oxford University Press, 1953).

37. See Nancy Pearcey, "The Touch of Cold Philosophy: Darwinism and the Arts," paper presented at the Second Wedge conference at Biola University, December 12, 2003. I have touched on the same themes within a broader treatment of the relationship between Christianity and the arts in "Soli Deo Gloria," chapter 42 in *How Now?*

38. William Thompson, "The Imagination of Jerry Brown," *The New York Times,* February 24, 1978, op-ed page.

39. See Schaeffer, *God Who Is There,* in *Complete Works,* vol. 1, 51-55. I am using the term *liberalism* broadly to include both the earlier theological liberalism stemming from Friedrich Schleiermacher and the later neo-orthodoxy of figures like Karl Barth, Paul Tillich, Rudolf Bultmann, and the Niebuhr brothers (Richard and Reinhold). Though the neo-orthodox theologians sought to recover a richer grasp of biblical *content,* they never broke free from the two-realm *epistemology.* For a detailed discussion, see Douglas Sloan, *Faith and Knowledge: Mainline Protestantism and American Higher Education* (Louisville: Westminster John Knox, 1994). Sloan defines the two-realm theory of truth as "the view that on the one side there are the truths of knowledge as these are given predominantly by science and discursive, empirical reason. On the other side are the truths of the faith, religious experience, morality, meaning, and value." The problem is that "the latter are seen as grounded not in knowledge but variously in feeling, ethical action, communal convention, folk tradition, or unfathomable mystical experience" (ix). In short, for the neo-orthodox theologians, faith remained an upper-story, "existential leap into the unknown" (114).

40. For an example of the way history has been identified with philosophical naturalism, see Crane Brinton, *Ideas and Men: The Story of Western Thought,* 2nd ed. (Englewood Cliffs, N.J.: Prentice-Hall, 1963). As a historian, Brinton says he offers a "naturalistic-historical" study of Christianity (108-109), and a "naturalistic or positivistic explanation" of both Judaism and Christianity (78). "For the purposes of historical analysis," Brinton says he assumes that both religions are "products of human culture in historic time" (77). Brinton seems to assume that, when speaking as a professional historian, he must squeeze religion into naturalistic categories, reducing it to subjective belief, a product of the human mind.

41. William Reville, "God Knows, Richard Dawkins Is Wrong," *The Irish Times,* March 13, 2003.

42. See Schaeffer, *God Who Is There,* in *Complete Works,* vol. 1, 7-8.

43. Cited in Peter Berger, *Facing Up to Modernity: Excursions in Society, Politics, and Religion* (New York: Basic Books, 1977), 155.

44. Richard Cimino, "Choosing My Religion," *American Demographics,* April 1, 1999, at www.demographics.com/publications/ad/99_ad/9904_ad/ad990402.htm.

45. Wade Clark Roof, *A Generation of Seekers: The Spiritual Journeys of the Baby Boom Generation* (San Francisco: Harper, 1993), 30. See also Robert Fuller, "Spiritual, but Not Religious: More than One Fifth of Americans Describe Themselves With This Phrase. What Does It Mean?" at http://www.beliefnet.com (excerpted from Robert C. Fuller, *Spiritual, But Not Religious: Understanding Unchurched America* [New York: Oxford University Press, 2002]).

46. Terry Mattingly, "September 11's Impact on America's Faith Faded Fast," Scripps Howard News Service, September 13, 2002.

47. See Schaeffer, *God Who Is There,* in *Complete Works,* vol. 1, 11.

48. Bill Wichterman, "The Culture: Upstream from Politics," in *Building a Healthy Culture: Strategies for an American Renaissance,* ed. Don Eberly (Grand Rapids, Mich.: Eerdmans, 2001), 79.

49. Sidney Mead, *The Old Religion in the Brave New World: Reflections on the Relation Between Christendom and the Republic* (Los Angeles: University of California Press, 1977), 18-19.

50. Phillip E. Johnson, "Is God Unconstitutional? The Established Religious Philosophy of America," at http://www.arn.org/docs/johnson/unconst1.htm.

51. Nancy Pearcey, "Wedge Issue: An Intelligent Discussion with Intelligent Designer's Designer," *World,* July 29, 2000.

52. Sloan, *Faith and Knowledge,* 190.

53. C. S. Lewis, *Surprised by Joy* (New York: Harcourt Brace 1955), 170.

54. David Downing, *The Most Reluctant Convert* (Downers Grove, Ill.: InterVarsity Press, 2002), 148.

55. C. S. Lewis, *God in the Dock: Essays on Theology and Ethics,* ed. Walter Hooper (Grand Rapids, Mich.: Eerdmans, 1970), 66-67.

56. C. S. Lewis, *Surprised by Joy,* 235.

CHAPTER 4: SURVIVING THE SPIRITUAL WASTELAND

1. Albert M. Wolters, *Creation Regained: Biblical Basics for a Reformational Worldview* (Grand Rapids, Mich.: Eerdmans, 1985), 11.

2. Alan Watts, *Behold the Spirit* (New York: Pantheon, 1947); Aldous Huxley, *The Perennial Philosophy* (New York: Harper, 1945); Teilhard de Chardin, *The Phenomenon of Man* (New York: Perennial Library, 1959); and *Building the Earth* (Wilkes-Barre, Pa.: Dimension, 1965). The most prominent proponent of perennial philosophy today is Huston Smith, considered the premier scholar of world religions. For more on perennial philosophy, see appendix 2, "Modern Islam and the New Age Movement."

3. The ad was placed by Worldview Academy, based in New Braunfels, Texas.

4. Aldous Huxley, *The Doors of Perception* (New York: Harper & Row, 1963). When I first read Schaeffer's *The God Who Is There,* I was astonished to discover that, unlike most evangelical leaders at the time, he understood the philosophic motivation for using drugs: "This overwhelming desire for some nonrational [upper-story] experience was responsible for most of the serious use of the drugs LSD and STP in the 1960s. For the sensitive person, drugs were then not usually used for escape. On the contrary, he hoped that by taking them he would experience the reality of something which would give his life some meaning" (in *The Complete Works of Francis A. Schaeffer,* vol. 1 [Wheaton, Ill.: Crossway, 1982], 22). Similarly, in *The Church at the End of the Twentieth Century,* Schaeffer writes that every "serious" experimenter with drugs was following Aldous Huxley in looking for an "upper-story hope" (in *Complete Works,* vol. 4, 17).

5. For a charming account, see Thomas Cahill's *How the Irish Saved Civilization* (New York: Doubleday, 1995). You can also read my summary of Cahill's book in "Saved to What?" chapter 31 in *How Now?*

6. On behaviorism, see Nancy Pearcey, "Sensible Psychology: How Creation Makes the Difference," *Bible-Science Newsletter*, February 1986. Constructivist education is treated in greater detail in chapter 8 of the present book.

7. I have treated these themes in much greater detail in "Still at Risk," chapter 34 in *How Now?*

8. John Milton, "Of Learning" (1644), in *Tractate on Education* in *The Harvard Classics*, vol. 3, part 4 (New York: Collier, 1909–1914), at http://www.bartleby.com/3/4/1.html.

9. On New Age techniques in the classroom, see Nancy Pearcey, "East Meets West in Education," *Missourians for Educational Excellence*, April/May 1983; on bringing techniques from psychotherapy into the classroom, see Nancy Pearcey, "Classroom 'Therapy' and Family Alienation," *Missourians for Educational Excellence*, January/February 1983.

10. Bryce Christensen, *Utopia Against the Family: The Problems and Politics of the American Family* (San Francisco: Ignatius, 1990), 3, 11. Christensen writes from a Mormon perspective.

11. B. F. Skinner, *Walden Two* (New York: Macmillan, 1968), 297.

12. Ted Peters, *For the Love of Children: Genetic Technology and the Future of the Family* (Louisville: Westminster John Knox, 1997). For a review, see Nancy Pearcey, "I Take You . . ." in *First Things* 80 (February 1998): 48-53. On a similar note, British sociologist Anthony Giddens says that marriage and family should require separate contracts, such that each parent would sign an individual contract with each child. See Anthony Giddens, *The Third Way* (Cambridge: Polity, 2000).

13. Peters, *For the Love of Children*, 11, 31.

14. Process Theology is discussed in greater detail in chapter 8.

15. Francis Schaeffer, *True Spirituality*, in *Complete Works*, vol. 3, 344. See also Cornelius Van Til, *Christian Apologetics*, 2nd ed. (Phillipsburg, N.J.: Presbyterian & Reformed, 2003), 8; *The Defense of the Faith* (Philadelphia: Presbyterian & Reformed, 1955), 25; John D. Zizioulas, *Being As Communion: Studies in Personhood and the Church* (Crestwood, N.Y.: St. Vladimir's Seminary Press, 1985); Miroslav Volf, *After Our Likeness: The Church as the Image of the Trinity* (Grand Rapids, Mich.: Eerdmans, 1998), especially chapter 5, "Trinity and Church."

16. People who are not married can and should participate in other forms of relationship, preeminently in the church, in order to experience the spiritually maturing effects of being morally committed to others.

17. In epistemology (how we know things), the issue is phrased in terms of universals versus particulars. A universal is a common type or pattern used to interpret or make sense of the individual. For example, ideals such as Justice and Goodness function to organize and interpret a great number of particular experiences. When I encounter a particular event and ask, Is this just? my understanding of Justice provides the meaning or interpretation of the individual event. The ancient world regarded universals as "more real" than concrete particulars. In reaction, modern philosophy, starting with the nominalism of William of Ockham, insists that particulars alone are real; universals have been demoted to mere mental constructions.

18. Timothy Ware, *The Orthodox Church* (London: Penguin, 1997), 240; Kallistos [Timothy] Ware, *The Orthodox Way* (Crestwood, N.Y.: St. Vladimir's Seminary Press, 2002), 38-39.

19. For more detail, see Nancy Pearcey, "Religion of Revolution: Karl Marx's Social Evolution," *Bible-Science Newsletter*, June 1986; Nancy Pearcey, "Liberation, Yes . . . But How? A Study of Liberation Theology," *Bible-Science Newsletter*, July 1988. For a later treatment, see "Does It Liberate?" chapter 24 in *How Now?*

20. Historian John Hermann Randall explains that the Newtonian image of the universe as a finely tuned machine "practically forced men, as a necessary scientific hypothesis, to believe in an external Creator" (*The Making of the Modern Mind* [New York: Columbia University Press, 1976], 276).

21. Cited in Francis Nigel Lee, *Communism Versus Creation* (Nutley, N.J.: Craig, 1969), 28.

22. Robert G. Wesson, *Why Marxism? The Continuing Success of a Failed Theory* (New York: Basic Books, 1976), 30.

23. Ibid., 25.

24. Klaus Bockmuehl, *The Challenge of Marxism* (Leicester, UK: InterVarsity Press, 1980), 17.

25. John Gray, "Exposing the Myth of Secularism," *Australian Financial Review*, January 3, 2003, at http://afr.com/review/2003/01/03/FFX9CQAJFAD.html. On the religious character of neo-

Marxist feminist and multicultural movements, see Stanley Kurtz, "The Church of the Left: Finding Meaning in Liberalism," National Review Online, May 31, 2001; and "The Faith-Based Left: Getting Behind the Debate," National Review Online, February 5, 2001.

26. Leslie Stevenson and David L. Haberman, *Ten Theories of Human Nature* (New York: Oxford University Press, 1998), 147.

27. Cited in Robert Nisbet, *The Quest for Community: A Study in the Ethics of Order and Freedom* (1953; reprint, San Francisco: Institute for Contemporary Studies Press, 1990), 127, no source listed. Emphasis added. For greater detail on Rousseau and the other early modern political philosophers, see Nancy Pearcey, "The Creation Myth of Modern Political Philosophy," presented at the sixth annual Kuyper Lecture, the Center for Public Justice, 2000, at http://arn.org/pearcey/nphone.htm.

28. Nancey Murphy, *Anglo-American Postmodernity: Philosophical Perspectives on Science, Religion, and Ethics* (Boulder, Colo.: HarperCollins, 1997), 180. See also Nancey Murphy, *Beyond Liberalism and Fundamentalism: How Modern and Postmodern Philosophy Set the Theological Agenda* (Valley Forge, Pa.: Trinity Press International, 1996), 151.

29. Pierre Manent, *An Intellectual History of Liberalism* (Princeton, N.J.: Princeton University Press, 1994), 29.

30. Jean-Jacques Rousseau, *The Social Contract* (Chicago: Henry Gateway, 1954), 57. See also Manent, *Intellectual History,* 72.

31. For a discussion of the contrast between Christian and contractual views of marriage, see John Witte, Jr., *From Sacrament to Contract: Marriage, Religion, and Law in the Western Tradition* (Louisville: Westminster John Knox Press, 1997).

32. One source of Rousseau's philosophy of the state may well have been his personal decision to abandon all five of his children to a state orphanage. The state in essence liberated him from the moral demands of being a parent. I have recounted this sordid story in "Synanon and Sin," chapter 17 in *How Now?*

33. Glenn Tinder, *Political Thinking: The Perennial Questions* (New York: HarperCollins, 1995), 198-199. Henry May calls Rousseau a "prophet" who delivered the redemptive message that "the Fall was quite real but reversible" (Henry May, *The Enlightenment in America* [New York: Oxford University Press, 1976], 165). In France, in some quarters, May writes, Rousseau was "elevated into the status of . . . a new Christ, preaching a revolutionary redemption" (170).

34. Nancy Pearcey, "Century of Cruelty: Making Sense of Our Era," *Boundless,* December 1999.

35. "The masses grew out of the fragments of a highly atomized society. . . . The chief characteristic of the mass man is not brutality and backwardness, but his isolation and lack of normal social relationships" (*The Origins of Totalitarianism* [New York: Harcourt Brace, 1951], 310-311).

36. On neo-Calvinist political philosophy, see the writings of James Skillen, especially *The Scattered Voice: Christians At Odds in the Public Square* (Grand Rapids, Mich.: Zondervan, 1990); *Recharging the American Experiment: Principled Pluralism for Genuine Civic Community* (Grand Rapids, Mich.: Baker, 1994); and *Political Order and the Plural Structure of Society,* ed. James Skillen and Rockne McCarthy (Grand Rapids, Mich.: Eerdmans, 1991). See also Jonathan Chaplin, "Subsidiary and Sphere Sovereignty: Catholic and Reformed Conceptions of the Role of the State," in *Things Old and New: Catholic Social Teaching Revisited,* ed. Francis McHugh and Samuel Natale (Lanham, Md.: University Press of America, 1993).

37. Eric O. Springsted, *The Act of Faith: Christian Faith and the Moral Self* (Grand Rapids, Mich.: Eerdmans, 2002), x.

38. Michael J. Sandel, *Democracy's Discontent: America in Search of a Public Philosophy* (Cambridge, Mass.: Harvard University Press, 1996), 6, 12.

39. See ibid., especially chapter 4, "Privacy Rights and Family Law." On a similar note, Alasdair MacIntyre writes, "In many premodern, traditional societies it is through his or her membership in a variety of social groups that the individual identifies himself or herself and is identified by others. I am brother, cousin and grandson, member of this household, that village, this tribe. These are not characteristics that belong to human beings accidentally, to be stripped away in order to discover 'the real me.' They are part of my substance" (Alasdair MacIntyre, *After Virtue: A Study in Moral Theory,* 2nd ed. [Notre Dame, Ind.: University of Notre Dame Press, 1997], 33-34).

40. Mary Ann Glendon, *Rights Talk: The Impoverishment of Political Discourse* (New York: Free Press, 1993), 48.

41. Pierre Manent, *Modern Liberty and Its Discontents* (Lanham, Md.: Rowman & Littlefield, 1998), 158. See also Pierre Manent, "Modern Individualism," *Crisis* (October 1995): 35.

42. The study is summarized in Elana Ashanti Jefferson, "Sex 101: College Students Increasingly Casual About Bedfellows, Just as Casual About Condoms," *Denver Post,* October 24, 2002.

43. David Abel, "Porn Is Hot Course on Campus: Professors Seek Meaning Behind Flourishing Market," *Boston Globe,* August 20, 2001.

44. Margaret Sanger, *The Pivot of Civilization* (New York: Brentano's, 1922), 232. For greater detail on Sanger, Kinsey, and other architects of the sexual revolution, see Nancy Pearcey, "Creating the 'New Man': The Hidden Agenda in Sex Education," *Bible-Science Newsletter,* May 1990. For a later treatment, see "Salvation Through Sex?" chapter 25 in *How Now?* Sanger literally believed that sexual restraint caused a vast variety of physical and psychological dysfunctions—even mental retardation. If our sexuality were given full and free expression, she promised, we would literally become geniuses. "Modern science is teaching us that genius is not some mysterious gift of the gods. . . . Rather is it due to the removal of physiological and psychological inhibitions and constraints which makes possible the release and the channeling of the primordial inner energies of man into full and divine expression" (Sanger, *Pivot of Civilization,* 232-233).

45. Sanger, *Pivot of Civilization,* 271.

46. James Atlas, "The Loose Cannon: Why Higher Learning Has Embraced Pornography," *The New Yorker,* March 29, 1999, 60-65.

47. Margaret Sanger, *Pivot of Civilization,* 238.

48. Alfred Kinsey, Wardell Pomeroy, and Clyde Martin, *Sexual Behavior in the Human Male* (Philadelphia: W. B. Saunders, 1948), 7, 263, emphasis added.

49. Paul Robinson, *The Modernization of Sex,* 2nd ed. (Ithaca, N.Y.: Cornell University Press, 1988), 49-50, 85.

50. Atlas, "Loose Cannon."

51. Michael Medved, "Hollywood Chic," *The Washington Post,* October 4, 1992.

52. John Stuart Mill, *On Liberty* (Indianapolis: Hackett, 1978), 12.

53. Dominic Mohan, "In Bend with Madonna," *The Sun,* March 11, 2003.

54. On the "Westernizing" of Eastern pantheism, especially the way it has been merged with optimistic evolutionary views of progress, see Nancy Pearcey, "East Meets West in Science," *Bible-Science Newsletter,* February 1985; Nancy Pearcey, "Spiritual Evolution? Science and the New Age Movement," presentation at the National Creation Conference, Cleveland, Ohio, August 14-16, 1985. For a later treatment, see "The New Age Religion," chapter 28 in *How Now?*

55. Francis Hodgson Burnett, *The Secret Garden* (New York: Harper & Row, 1911), 250, 254.

56. Ibid., 236, 267, 251, 250. At one point in the story, several characters agree that whether you worship using the Christian doxology, or use the term *Magic* or some other name, "they are both the same thing" (285, 290).

57. Ibid., 250.

58. Ibid., 253-254, emphasis added.

59. Nancy Pearcey, "New Age for Kids," *Bible-Science Newsletter,* December 1988. This article gives additional documentation of the Eastern religious elements in the book.

60. Theosophy was the name given by Madame Blavatsky to Eastern religious teachings she learned in Tibet in the late 1800s. Burnett was highly influenced not only by Madame Blavatsky but also by Mind Healing and Christian Science. Her conception of the divine as a unified mind or spirit permeating all things was borrowed from these spiritualist philosophies. So were her ideas about the healing powers of the mind, which became a crucial motif in several of her books, including *The Secret Garden.*

Clearly not all stories that include magic incorporate a pantheistic worldview. For example, C. S. Lewis and J. R. R. Tolkein were Christian fantasy writers who used magic in the classic fairy tale manner—as a means of suggesting that there is more to reality than the mundane, ordinary, material world, while sparking a hunger for an unseen, transcendent spiritual realm. We cannot judge a piece of literature simply by whether it uses a particular term, like *magic,* but need to identify the underlying worldview.

61. See Francis Schaeffer, *Escape from Reason,* in *Complete Work,* vol. 1, 207-208.
62. Unfortunately, space does not permit the same kind of detailed analysis of the concepts of Fall and Redemption. However, readers might want to consult the relevant sections in *How Now?* Briefly, the section on the Fall (chapters 15, 17-21) describes what happens when the biblical doctrine of sin is denied, giving rise to various forms of utopianism, usually enforced by coercive means. The last of these chapters outlines the Bible's unique answer to the problem of evil and suffering. The Redemption section (chapters 23-29) shows that most modern ideologies are variations on the myth of progress—what philosopher Mary Midgely calls "the Escalator Myth"—including Marxism, sexual liberation, New Age thought, and so on. (On Midgely and the Escalator Myth, see Nancy Pearcey, "What Do You Mean, Evolution Is a Religion?" *Bible-Science Newsletter,* April 1988.)

CHAPTER 5: DARWIN MEETS THE BERENSTAIN BEARS

1. See "Huston Smith Replies to Barbour, Goodenough, and Peterson," *Zygon* 36, no. 2 (June 2001): 223-231.
2. Patrick Glynn, in discussion with the author. Glynn also talks about his personal experience in the first chapter of *God, The Evidence: The Reconciliation of Faith and Reason in a Postsecular World* (Rocklin, Calif.: Prima, 1997).
3. On the centrality of creation to the Christian worldview, see Nancy Pearcey, "Creation and the Unity of Scripture: Making the 'Simple Gospel' Simple," *Bible-Science Newsletter,* July 1984; Nancy Pearcey, "Did It Really Happen? Genesis and History," *Bible-Science Newsletter,* March 1987; Nancy Pearcey, "Everything You Wanted to Know About Evolution: But Don't Have Time to Read Up On," *Bible-Science Newsletter,* June 1988.
4. Edward A. Purcell, Jr., *The Crisis of Democratic Theory: Scientific Naturalism and the Problem of Value* (Lexington: University Press of Kentucky, 1973), 8, 21. See also Nancy Pearcey, "Darwinian Naturalism: Cultural and Philosophical Implications," Veritas Forum at UC Santa Barbara, October 25, 2003.
5. Elizabeth Flower and Murray G. Murphey, *A History of Philosophy in America,* vol. 2 (New York: Putnam, 1977), 553. On the unity of knowledge, I have written elsewhere: "Despite the differences among them all major civilizations have believed in a divine order that lays down the law for both natural and human realms. In the Far East it was called *Tao;* in ancient Egypt it was called *Ma'at;* in Greek philosophy it was called *Logos.* . . . John's Gospel borrows the Greek word for this universal plan of creation *(logos)* and, in a startling move, identifies it with a personal being—Jesus Christ himself. . . . In other words, Jesus himself is the source of the comprehensive plan or design of creation" (*How Now,* 297-298; see also C. S. Lewis, *The Abolition of Man*).
6. Nancy Pearcey, "The Birth of Modern Science," *Bible-Science Newsletter,* October 1982; Nancy Pearcey, "How Christianity Gave Rise to the Modern Scientific Outlook," *Bible-Science Newsletter,* January 1989. I later expanded this material into a major theme throughout *Soul of Science,* especially chapter 1, "An Invented Institution: Christianity and the Scientific Revolution."
7. Daniel Dennett, *Darwin's Dangerous Idea* (New York: Simon & Schuster, 1995), 63. See the review by Phillip Johnson in *The New Criterion,* October 1995.
8. Ibid., 519, 520. Nick Humphrey, professor of psychology at the New School for Social Research, uses even stronger language. In an Amnesty Lecture on human rights, he said, "Children have a right not to have their minds addled by nonsense. And we as a society have a duty to protect them from it. So we should no more allow parents to teach their children to believe in the literal truth of the Bible . . . than we should allow parents to knock their children's teeth out or lock them in a dungeon" ("What Shall We Tell the Children?" Amnesty Lecture, Oxford, February 21, 1997. Cited in Andrew Brown, *The Darwin Wars: The Scientific Battle for the Soul of Man* [New York: Simon & Schuster, 1999], 172).
9. PBS, "Evolution, Episode 1: Darwin's Dangerous Idea." See the critique of the series by the Discovery Institute: "Getting the Facts Straight: A Viewer's Guide to PBS's 'Evolution,'" at www.reviewevolution.com.
10. G. K. Chesterton, *Eugenics and Other Evils* (New York: Dodd, Mead, 1927), 98.
11. Stan and Jan Berenstain, *The Bears' Nature Guide* (New York: Random House, 1975). For a whimsical and well-written children's book giving the opposite position, see William Steig, *Yellow and Pink* (New York: Farrar, Straus, & Giroux, 1984). The story is about two wooden

marionettes who debate whether they were formed by natural processes or by Intelligent Design. See my review of the book in *Critique*, March/April 1985 (a publication of Ransom Fellowship), reprinted under the title "In the Language of Children," in the *Bible-Science Newsletter*, August 1985. A summary of the story is found in *How Now?* 94-95.

12. See Carl Sagan, *Cosmos* (New York: Random House, 1980), 4.

13. For a fuller discussion, see Nancy Pearcey, "Canonizing the Cosmos: Carl Sagan's Naturalistic Religion," *Bible-Science Newsletter*, October 1984. See also Norman Geisler, *Cosmos: Carl Sagan's Religion for the Scientific Mind* (Dallas: Quest, 1983). For a later discussion, see "Shattering the Grid," chapter 6 in *How Now?*

14. Jonathan Wells, *Icons of Evolution* (Washington, D.C.: Regnery, 2000).

15. See Nancy Pearcey, "The Galapagos Islands: A World All Its Own," *Bible-Science Newsletter*, February 1984; Nancy Pearcey, "The Origin of the Origin: Or, What Did Darwin Really Find?" *Bible-Science Newsletter*, December 1986.

16. Jonathan Weiner, "Kansas Anti-Evolution Vote Denies Students a Full Spiritual Journey," *Philadelphia Inquirer*, August 15, 1999.

17. See Phillip E. Johnson, *Reason in the Balance: The Case Against Naturalism in Science, Law, and Education* (Downers Grove, Ill.: InterVarsity Press, 1995). For a review of the book, see Nancy Pearcey, "Naturalism on Trial," *First Things* 60 (February 1996).

18. "If droughts occur about once every ten years on the islands, a new species of finch might arise in only about 200 years" (*Teaching About Evolution and the Nature of Science*, National Academy of Sciences, 1998, chapter 2, page 19, at http://www.nap.edu/readingroom/books/evolution98.).

19. Phillip E. Johnson, "The Church of Darwin," *Wall Street Journal*, August 16, 1999.

20. The reason is that the mutated form is less fit, so that the unmutated viruses quickly take over again. What happens is that a few unmutated viruses hide out in cells while the mutated, drug resistant varieties begin to dominate. When the coast is clear—that is, when drug treatment is stopped and the selective pressure is removed—these sequestered wild types quickly take over the population again because the drug resistant forms are much less fit. The PBS program does mention that drug resistance is completely reversible, but presents it misleadingly as evidence *for* evolution rather than as evidence *against* it.

21. See Nancy Pearcey, "What Species of Species? Or, Darwin and the Origin of *What?*" *Bible-Science Newsletter*, June 1989.

22. Technically, we are talking about neo-Darwinism here, rather than the classical version of the theory. Darwin did not know how variations in living things arise, and he was unfamiliar with the theory of genes that had already been developed by Gregor Mendel. Neo-Darwinian theory, which proposes genetic mutations as the source of new variations, arose in the 1930s and 40s and is sometimes called the "modern synthesis."

23. See the discussion of Goldschmidt in Norman Macbeth, *Darwin Retried* (New York: Dell, 1971), 33, 154.

24. Luther Burbank, quoted in ibid., 36. See Nancy Pearcy, "Progress and Limitations in Plant and Animal Breeding," *Bible-Science Newsletter*, November 1982; Nancy Pearcey, "Everybody Can Know: The Most Powerful Evidence Against Evolution," *Bible-Science Newsletter*, June 1987; and "Darwin in the Dock," chapter 9 in *How Now?*

25. Nancy Pearcey, "Natural Selection, the Point that Moved the World," *Bible-Science Newsletter*, November 1984. See also M. W. Ho and P. T. Saunders, "Beyond Neo-Darwinism—An Epigenetic Approach to Evolution," *Journal of Theoretical Biology* 78 (1979): 573-591.

26. In some cases, live moths were used, since they tend to be torpid during the day.

27. Peter D. Smith, "Darwinism in a Flutter," review of *Of Moths and Men: Intrigue, Tragedy, and the Peppered Moth*, by Judith Hooper, *The Guardian*, May 11, 2002.

28. Jerry Coyne, "Not Black and White," review of *Melanism: Evolution in Action*, by M. E. N. Majerus, *Nature* 396 (November 5, 1998): 35.

29. Bob Ritter, a Canadian textbook writer, was quoted in "Moth-eaten Darwinism: A Disproven Textbook Case of Natural Selection Refuses to Die," *Alberta Report Newsmagazine*, April 5, 1999. "High school students are still very concrete in the way they learn," Ritter said. "The advantage of this example of natural selection is that it is extremely visual." He went on: "we want to get across the idea of selective adaptation. Later on, they can look at the work critically." See Nancy Pearcey, "Creation Mythology: Defenders of Darwinism Resort to Suppressing Data and Teaching Outright Falsehoods," *World*, June 24, 2000.

30. From a letter to Asa Gray, September 10, 1860, in *The Life and Letters of Charles Darwin,* vol. 2, ed. Francis Darwin (New York: D. Appleton, 1896), 131.

31. Michael Richardson, quoted in Elizabeth Pennisi, "Haeckel's Embryos: Fraud Rediscovered," *Science* 277 (September 5, 1997): 1435.

32. Cited in Nancy Pearcey, "Michael Kinsley Out on a Limb: Stem-Cell Rationale Recalls Ideas of Debunked Scientist," *Human Events,* September 8, 2000.

33. In 2000, another piece of faked evidence emerged: an alleged feathered dinosaur. "National Geographic convened a press conference last October, heralding the fossil as a crucial missing link, the first solid evidence for a new theory that birds evolved from dinosaurs (contrary to an older theory that they evolved separately). But the prestigious journal soon had egg on its face. Chinese farmers have grown adept at gluing fossils together in ways that increase their black-market value, and in this case, the body turned out to be from an early toothed bird while the tail was from a dinosaur" (Nancy Pearcey, "The Missing Link that Wasn't: National Geographic's 'Bird Dinosaur' Flew Against the Facts," *Human Events,* March 10, 2000).

34. Melissa Ludwig, "New Force in the Fray on State's Textbooks: 'Intelligent Design' Adherents Use Science to Question Evolution," *Austin American-Statesman,* Wednesday, July 9, 2003.

35. Phillip E. Johnson, *Defeating Darwinism by Opening Minds* (Downers Grove, Ill.: InterVarsity Press, 1997), 37.

36. Jerry Alder and John Carey, "Is Man a Subtle Accident?" *Newsweek,* November 3, 1980, 95-96. See Nancy Pearcey, "Evolution After Darwin: What's Left?" *Bible-Science Newsletter,* August 1985.

37. Stephen Jay Gould, "Evolution's Erratic Pace," in *Natural History* 86 no. 5 (May 1977): 14.

38. The same year as the Macroevolution conference, Gould wrote that the neo-Darwinian synthesis "as a general proposition, is effectively dead, despite its persistence as textbook orthodoxy" ("Is a New and General Theory of Evolution Emerging?" *Paleobiology* 6, no. 1 [January 1980]: 120). Today, more than two decades later, the same "dead" proposition is still being flogged, largely because of the difficulty in finding anything with which to replace it: "A number of microbiologists, geneticists, theoretical biologists, mathematicians, and computer scientists are saying there is more to life than Darwinism. . . . I call them the 'postdarwinians.' . . . Their disagreement is with the very sweeping nature of the Darwinian argument, the fact that in the end it doesn't explain much, and the emerging evidence that Darwinism alone may not be sufficient to explain all we see. . . . [W]hat else is operating within or beyond evolution as we understand it?" (Kevin Kelly, *Out of Control: The New Biology of Machines, Social Systems, and the Economic World* [Cambridge, Mass: Perseus, 1994], 365-366).

39. See Michael Denton, *Evolution: A Theory In Crisis* (Bethesda, Md.: Adler & Adler, 1986).

40. Roger Lewin, "Evolutionary Theory Under Fire," in *Science* 210 (November 21, 1980): 883-887.

41. See Nancy Pearcey, "Fact vs. Theory: Does Gould Understand the Difference?" *Bible-Science Newsletter,* April 1987. "The required rapidity of the change implies either a few large steps or many and exceedingly rapid smaller ones. Large steps are tantamount to saltations and raise the problems of fitness barriers; small steps must be numerous and entail the problems discussed under microevolution. The periods of stasis raise the possibility that the lineage would enter the fossil record, and we reiterate that we can identify none of the postulated intermediate forms. Finally, the large numbers of species that must be generated so as to form a pool from which the successful lineage is selected are nowhere to be found. We conclude that the probability that species selection is a general solution to the origin of higher taxa is not great, and that neither of the contending theories of evolutionary change at the species level, phyletic gradualism or punctuated equilibrium, seem applicable to the origin of new body plans" (J. Valentine and D. Erwin, "Interpreting Great Developmental Experiments: The Fossil Record," in Rudolf A. Raff and Elizabeth C. Raff, eds., *Development as an Evolutionary Process* [New York: Alan R. Liss, 1987], 96).

42. Nancy Pearcey, "Foreword," in Phillip E. Johnson, *The Right Questions: Truth, Meaning, and Public Debate* (Downers Grove, Ill.: InterVarsity Press, 2002), 13.

43. Richard Dawkins, *The Blind Watchmaker* (New York: Norton, 1986), 287, emphasis in original.

44. S. C. Todd, "A View from Kansas on That Evolution Debate," *Nature* 401 (September 30, 1999): 423.

45. Mano Singham, a physicist at Case Western Reserve University, writing in *Physics Today,* June

2002, emphasis added. To buttress his argument, he quoted paleontologist George Gaylord Simpson, who wrote, "The progress of knowledge rigidly requires that no nonphysical postulate ever be admitted in connection with the study of physical phenomena. . . . the researcher who is seeking explanations must seek physical explanations only" (*Tempo and Mode in Evolution* [New York: Columbia University Press, 1944], 76).

46. John Rennie, "15 Answers to Creationist Nonsense," *Scientific American,* June 17, 2002.

47. See Del Ratzsch, *The Battle of Beginnings: Why Neither Side Is Winning the Creation-Evolution Debate* (Downers Grove, Ill.: InterVarsity Press, 1996), 167. For a more recent, and more academic, discussion of philosophical issues, see Del Ratzsch, *Nature, Design, and Science: The Status of Design in Natural Science* (New York: SUNY Press, 2001).

48. *BSCS Biology: A Molecular Approach,* 8th ed., Jon Greenberg, revision editor (Everyday Learning Corporation, 2001), 446.

49. Neil A. Campbell, Jane B. Reece, and Lawrence G. Mitchell, *Biology,* 5th ed. (Reading, Mass.: Addison Wesley, 1999), 426. A helpful analysis of textbooks can be found in Norris Anderson's "Education or Indoctrination 2001," at http://www.alabamaeagle.org/education_or_indoctrination_2001.htm.

50. Douglas Futuyma, *Evolutionary Biology,* 3rd ed. (Sunderland, Mass.: Sinauer, 1998), 15. See Jonathan Wells, "Opinions," *Topeka Capital-Journal,* November 23, 1999, at http://www.cjonline.com/stories/112199/opi_science.shtml.

51. Historian Neal Gillespie says Darwin's central innovation was a positivist definition of science that restricted it to natural causes. Once such a definition had been accepted, it "simply nullified special creation as a scientific idea." Put the other way around, "It was the prior success of positivism in science that assured the victory of evolution in biology." There was no need to directly attack religion, Gillespie explains, but only to adopt "positivism as the epistemological standard in science. And this eventually took God out of nature (if not out of reality) as effectively as atheism" (*Charles Darwin and the Problem of Creation* [Chicago: University of Chicago Press, 1979], 152, 146, 153. For more on this history, see Nancy Pearcey, "You Guys Lost," in *Mere Creation: Science, Faith, and Intelligent Design,* ed. William A. Dembski [Downers Grove, Ill.: InterVarsity Press, 1998], 73-92).

52. Tom Bethell, "Against Sociobiology," *First Things* 109 (January 2001): 18-24, emphasis added.

53. Charles Darwin, *The Descent of Man and Selection in Relation to Sex,* 2nd ed. (1871; reprint, London: John Murray, 1922), 92. The term "immutable" reveals that Darwin was reacting in part against an inadequate view of creation held by some in his day that all species came directly from the hand of God—that no new ones had ever appeared, nor had any died out (i.e., there was no extinction). In opposing this particular theory of creation, however, Darwin was also opposing the concept of creation or design per se.

54. Richard Lewontin, "Billions and Billions of Demons," *The New York Review of Books,* January 9, 1997, 28.

55. Cited in Roger Highfield, "Do Our Genes Reveal the Hand of God?" *Daily Telegraph* (London), March, 20, 2003, at http://www.telegraph.co.uk.

56. Cited in ibid.

57. Weinberg's comments were reported in "Free People from Superstition," *Freethought Today,* April 2000, at http://www.ffrf.org/fttoday/april2000/weinberg.html.

58. Cited in Michael Ruse, "Saving Darwinism from the Darwinians," *National Post,* May 13, 2000, B-3.

59. Ruse, ibid. Ruse makes the same argument in his most recent book, *Mystery of Mysteries: Is Evolution a Social Construction?* (Cambridge, Mass.: Harvard University Press, 1999).

60. See Tom Woodward, "Ruse Gives Away the Store, Admits Evolution Is a Philosophy," at http://www.leaderu.com/real/ri9404/ruse.html.

61. Cited in Ruse, "Saving Darwinism from the Darwinians." Elsewhere, Gould explicitly described Darwinism as a substitute for religion: "Evolution substituted a naturalistic explanation of cold comfort for our former conviction that a benevolent deity fashioned us directly in his own image" (Stephen Jay Gould, "Introduction," in Carl Zimmer, *Evolution: The Triumph of an Idea* [New York: HarperCollins, 2001], xi).

62. Ruse, "Saving Darwinism from the Darwinians."

63. Editorial, *Columbus Dispatch,* June 14, 2002.

64. Jacques Barzun, *Darwin, Marx, Wagner: Critique of a Heritage* (Chicago: University of Chicago Press, 1941), 37.

65. See Nancy Pearcey, "Scopes in Reverse," *Washington Times,* July 24, 2000.

66. Cited in Pearcey, "Foreword," in Johnson, *Right Questions,* 7-25.

67. For a general overview of the history of the Intelligent Design movement, see Nancy Pearcey, "The Evolution Backlash: Debunking Darwin," *World,* March 1, 1997, 12-15; Nancy Pearcey, "We're Not in Kansas Anymore: Why Secular Scientists and Media Can't Admit that Darwinism Might Be Wrong," *Christianity Today,* May 22, 2000.

68. Phillip E. Johnson, interview by James M. Kushiner, "Berkeley's Radical: An Interview with Phillip E. Johnson," *Touchstone,* June 2002, at http://www.touchstonemag.com/docs/issues/15.5docs/15-5pg40.html.

69. Phillip E. Johnson, *Darwin on Trial* (Downers Grove, Ill.: InterVarsity Press, 1993); *Reason in the Balance: The Case Against Naturalism in Science, Law, and Education* (Downers Grove, Ill.: InterVarsity Press, 1995).

70. I am often asked about the difference between creationism and Intelligent Design theory. The difference lies largely in the method of approach. Creationism starts with the Bible, and asks, What does the Bible say about science? That is a perfectly valid inquiry, just as we ask what the Bible implies for politics or the arts or any other field. But it is not the way to do apologetics. In speaking to a non-Christian culture, we must start with data that our audience finds credible. Thus Intelligent Design theory does not begin with the Bible—it begins with the scientific data and asks, Does the data itself give evidence of an intelligent cause? It makes the case that design be detected empirically.

71. L'Abri tapes are available at http://www.soundword.com/frontlabri.html.

72. "The Secular Web," at http://www.infidels.org/index.shtml.

73. Gillespie, *Charles Darwin and the Problem of Creation,* 16, emphasis added.

74. The position paper is posted at http://www.aristotle.net/~asta/science.htm. Interestingly, ASTA put out an earlier statement, in 1999, that still treated religion as a form of genuine knowledge: "People have many ways of knowing about their world including scientific knowledge, societal knowledge, religious knowledge and cultural knowledge. Science differs from these other ways of knowing in important ways" (posted on the same website). In only two years, religion was demoted from a type of knowledge to merely a social construction.

75. Ibid.

76. Huxley went on to say, "Darwin pointed out that no supernatural designer was needed; since natural selection could account for any new form of life, there is no room for a supernatural agency in its evolution" ("At Random: A Television Preview," in *Evolution After Darwin* [Chicago: University of Chicago Press, 1960], 41).

77. Douglas Sloan, *Faith and Knowledge: Mainline Protestantism and American Higher Education* (Louisville: Westminster John Knox, 1994), 190.

78. Allan Bloom, *The Closing of the American Mind* (Chicago: Chicago Review Press, 1989). This quotation is from *The Republic of Plato,* translated with notes and an interpretative essay by Allan Bloom (New York: Basic Books, 1968), x.

79. Cited in Victor Greto, "Delaware a Leader in Teaching Evolution," *The News Journal* (Wilmington, Del.), February 25, 2003, emphasis added.

80. Backgrounder for the PBS program "Evolution," titled "Emi and Nathan: Personal Testimonies," at www.pbs.org/wgbh/evolution/library/08/1/l_081_07.html.

CHAPTER 6: THE SCIENCE OF COMMON SENSE

1. Cited in Gerald Schroeder, "Can God Be Brought into the Equation?" review of *Science and Religion: Are They Compatible?* ed. Paul Kurtz and Barry Karr, in the *Jerusalem Post,* May 23, 2003, 13-B; at http://www.jpost.com/servlet/Satellite?pagename=JPost/A/JPArticle/ShowFull&cid=1\054002499080.

2. The survey was conducted by *Skeptic* editor Michael Shermer and MIT professor Frank Sulloway, and though it was sent out to a random sample of Americans, for unknown reasons respondents included a higher-than-average percentage of highly educated people. Results are reported in Michael Shermer, *How We Believe: The Search for God in an Age of Science* (New York: W. H. Freeman, 2000), 74-88. Ironically, when respondents were asked why *other* people believe in God, the number one reason cited was emotional comfort. In other words,

respondents claimed that they themselves had rational grounds for belief, but they regarded *everyone else* as being motivated by psychological need.

3. For a recent treatment of this theme, see Nancy Pearcey, "Shooting Down the Warfare Myth," Megaviews Forum, Los Alamos National Laboratory, September 24, 2003; Nancy Pearcey, "The War that Wasn't," Veritas Forum at USC, February 18, 2004; Nancy Pearcey, "How Science Became a Christian Vocation," in *Reading God's World: The Vocation of Scientist,* ed. Angus Menuge, forthcoming from the Cranach Institute, Concordia University in Milwaukee. For a brief introduction, see "The Basis for True Science," chapter 40 in *How Now?*

4. The difference between science and common sense is a matter of degree, not kind, says W. V. O. Quine, in *Ontological Relativity and Other Essays* (New York: Columbia University Press, 1997), 129.

5. This example is from my colleague Steve Meyer, director of the Center for Science and Culture at the Discovery Institute.

6. Eugenie Scott (executive director of the National Center for Science Education, Inc.), CNN Newsroom, May 3, 2001, at http://www.cnn.com/TRANSCRIPTS/0105/03/nr.00.html.

7. Michael Stroh, "The Office of Research Integrity—a.k.a., the Fraud Squad—Is on the Case," *Popular Science,* December 2003, at http://www.popsci.com/popsci/science/article/ 0,12543,519782,00.html. The article begins with an example:

> Cancer researcher Kenneth Pienta was flipping through a paper written by a promising young postdoc in his University of Michigan laboratory when he spotted something that made his stomach sink: two protein blots that looked remarkably similar.
>
> Too similar.
>
> Pienta knew there could be only one explanation for the identical images: The woman had doctored the data.

As this example shows, there are empirical markers of design—including unethical design!

8. David Postman, "Letourneau Lands on WASL as Answer, Raising Questions," *The Seattle Times,* April 27, 2001.

9. William A. Dembski and James M. Kushiner, eds., *Signs of Intelligence: Understanding Intelligent Design* (Grand Rapids, Mich.: Baker, 2001).

10. See Nancy Pearcey, "We're Not in Kansas Anymore," *Christianity Today,* May 22, 2000.

11. Neal C. Gillespie, *Charles Darwin and the Problem of Creation* (Chicago: University of Chicago Press, 1979), 83-85.

12. Richard Dawkins, *The Blind Watchmaker* (New York: Norton, 1986), 1, emphasis added.

13. George Gaylord Simpson, "Plan and Purpose in Nature," *Scientific Monthly* 64 (June 1947): 481-495; cited in Simpson *This View of Life: The World of an Evolutionist* (New York: Harcourt Brace, 1964), 190-191, 212, emphasis added. Simpson's best-known assertion is, "Man is the result of a purposeless and natural process that did not have him in mind. He was not planned" (Simpson, *The Meaning of Evolution: A Study of the History of Life and of Its Significance for Man* [1949; reprint, New Haven, Conn.: Yale University Press, 1960], 344).

14. William Paley, *Natural Theology,* is in the public domain and available online at http://www.hti.umich.edu/cgi/p/pd-modeng/pd-modeng-idx?type=HTML&rgn= TEI.2&byte=53049319.

15. Michael Behe, *Darwin's Black Box: The Biochemical Challenge to Evolution* (New York: Touchstone, 1996), 213. See also my review: Nancy Pearcey, "The Biochemical Challenge to Evolution," in *Books and Culture* (November/December 1996), at http://www.arn.org/docs/ pearcey/np_bc1296.htm; and "Darwin in the Dock," chapter 9 in *How Now?* Traditional arguments for design are discussed in Nancy Pearcey, "Design: The Oldest Argument for God," *Bible-Science Newsletter,* December 1982.

16. Nancy Pearcey, "Strangely Familiar: The New, but Not So New, World of the Cell," *Bible-Science Newsletter,* July 1987.

17. Francis Crick, *Life Itself: Its Origin and Nature* (New York: Simon & Schuster, 1981), 70-71. Similarly, Bruce Alberts writes, "The entire cell can be viewed as a factory that contains an elaborate network of interlocking assembly lines, each of which is composed of a set of large protein machines" (Bruce Alberts, "The Cell as a Collection of Protein Machines: Preparing the Next Generation of Molecular Biologists," *Cell* 92 [February 6, 1998]: 291-294).

18. See Ronald D. Vale, "The Molecular Motor Toolbox for Intracellular Transport," in *Cell* 112 (February 21, 2003): 467-480. "A cell, like a metropolitan city, must organize its bustling community of macromolecules. Setting meeting points and establishing the timing of transactions are of fundamental importance for cell behavior. The high degree of spatial/temporal organization of molecules and organelles within cells is made possible by protein machines that transport components to various destinations within the cytoplasm" (467).

19. David J. DeRosier, "The Turn of the Screw: The Bacterial Flagellar Motor," *Cell* 93 (April 3, 1998): 17

20. Behe, *Darwin's Black Box,* 39.

21. Charles Darwin, *On the Origin of Species,* facsimile of the first edition (Cambridge, Mass., and London: Harvard University Press, 1964), 189.

22. For a defense of Behe's argument, see William A. Dembski, "Evolution's Logic of Credulity: An Unfettered Response to Allen Orr," at http://www.designinference.com/documents/2002.12.Unfettered_Resp_to_Orr.htm.

23. Nancy Pearcey, "The Heavens Declare: The Origin of the Universe," *Bible-Science Newsletter,* September 1986; Nancy Pearcey, "A Universe Built for Us: The Anthropic Principle," in *Bible-Science Newsletter,* October 1990; and Nancy Pearcey, "The Anthropic Principle: The Closest Atheists Can Get to God," in *Bible-Science Newsletter,* November 1990. For a later treatment, see "Let's Start at the Very Beginning," chapter 7 in *How Now?*

24. George Greenstein, *The Symbiotic Universe: Life and Mind in the Cosmos* (New York: William Morrow, 1988), 85-90.

25. Paul Davies, "A Brief History of the Multiverse," *The New York Times,* April 12, 2003. Elsewhere Davies writes that "the seemingly miraculous concurrence of numerical values" for nature's fundamental contrasts is "the most compelling evidence for an element of cosmic design" (*God and the New Physics* [New York: Simon & Schuster, 1983], 189). For more on fine-tuning, see Dean Overman, *A Case Against Accident and Self-Organization* (Lanham, Md.: Rowman & Littlefield, 1997); Hugh Ross, *The Fingerprint of God* (New Kensington, Pa.: Whitaker, 2000); John Horgan, "Between Science and Spirituality," *Chronicle of Higher Education* 49, no. 14 (November 29, 2002), at http://chronicle.com/free/v49/i14/14b00701.htm; Guillermo Gonzalez and Jay Richards, *The Privileged Planet: How Our Place in the Cosmos Is Designed for Discovery* (Washington, D.C.: Regnery, 2004).

26. Dennis Overbye, "Zillions of Universes? Or Did Ours Get Lucky?" *New York Times,* October 28, 2003. See also John Barrow, *The Constants of Nature: From Alpha to Omega—The Numbers That Encode the Deepest Secrets of the Universe* (London: Jonathan Cape, 2002).

27. Heinz Oberhummer, "Stellar Production Rates of Carbon and Its Abundance in the Universe," *Science* 289 (July 7, 2000): 88-90, emphasis added. Cited in Nancy Pearcey, "Our 'Tailor-made Universe,'" *World,* September 2, 2000.

28. Arno Penzias, "Creation Is Supported by All the Data So Far," *Cosmos, Bios, Theos: Scientists Reflect on Science, God, and the Origins of the Universe, Life, and Homo sapiens,* ed. Henry Margenau and RoyAgraham Varghese (Chicago: Open Court, 1992), 83.

29. Arno Penzias, interview by Malcolm Browne, "Clues to the Universe's Origin Expected," *The New York Times,* March 12, 1978. See also Jerry Bergman, "Arno A. Penzias: Astrophysicist, Nobel Laureate," in *Perspectives on Science and Christian Faith* 46, no. 3 (September 1994): 183-187; also available online at http://www.asa3.org/ASA/topics/Astronomy-Cosmology/PSCF9-94Bergman.html#Penzias.

30. Fred Hoyle, "The Universe: Some Past and Present Reflections," *Annual Review of Astronomy and Astrophysics* 20 (1982): 16.

31. In a 1971 news conference, Hoyle said, "Human beings are simply pawns in the game of alien minds that control our every move. They are everywhere, in the sky, on the sea, and in the Earth. . . . It is not an alien intelligence from another planet. It is actually from another universe which entered ours at the very beginning and has been controlling all that has happened since." Cited in L. K. Waddill. "On Tip Toes Before Darwin," *Power of the Mind Magazine,* 1998, at http://www.btinternet.com/~meirionhughes/Pub/page14.htm.

32. Greenstein, *Symbiotic Universe,* 26-27, 223.

33. George Wald, quoted in Dietrick E. Thomsen, "A Knowing Universe Seeking to Be Known," *Science News* (February 19, 1983): 124.

34. Freeman Dyson, *Disturbing the Universe* (New York: Harper & Row, 1979), 250.

35. Gregg Easterbrook, "The New Convergence," *Wired*, December 2002, at www.wired.com/wired/archive/10.12.

36. Pagels concludes, with an ironic twist, that the anthropic principle "is the closest that some atheists can get to God" ("A Cozy Cosmology," *The Sciences* [March/April, 1985], 35-38).

37. Cited in Overbye, "Zillions of Universes?"

38. Nancy Pearcey, "Copying the Human Script: Genome Project Raises Hopes, Fears," *World*, July 8, 2000.

39. Richard Dawkins, "Genetics: Why Prince Charles Is So Wrong," Checkbiotech.org, January 28, 2003, at http://www.checkbiotech.org/root/index.cfm?fuseaction=news&doc_id=4575&start=1&control=173&page_start=1&page_nr=101&pg=1.

40. Scott McCabe and Alex Navarro, "Writer in Sky Sends Wrong Message," *Palm Beach Post*, January 2, 2002, 1A. See Nancy Pearcey, "*Which* God Is Great?" Salem radio editorial.

41. Jacques Monod, *Chance and Necessity: An Essay on the Natural Philosophy of Modern Biology*, trans. Austryn Wainhouse (New York: Knopf, 1971).

42. William A. Dembski, *The Design Inference* (Cambridge: Cambridge University Press, 1998). A more accessible form of his argument is given in his *Intelligent Design: The Bridge Between Science and Theology* (Downers Grove, Ill.: InterVarsity Press, 1999). Briefer treatments can be found in William A. Dembski, "Science and Design" in *First Things* 86 (October 1998): 21-27; at http://www.firstthings.com/ftissues/ft9810/articles/dembski.html; and William A. Dembski, "Redesigning Science," in *Mere Creation*, excerpted at http://www.arn.org/docs/dembski/wd_explfilter.htm.

43. David Adam, "Give Six Monkeys a Computer, and What Do You Get? Certainly Not the Bard," *The Guardian*, May 9, 2003.

44. The reason is that the production of simple compounds, like amino acids, are "downhill" processes, thermodynamically speaking, which means they involve chemical reactions that occur easily in nature, while the production of macromolecules, like protein and DNA, are "uphill" processes, which means they do not occur readily in nature. See Nancy Pearcey, "Running Down and Falling Apart: Thermodynamics and the Origin of Life," *Bible-Science Newsletter*, September 1987; Nancy Pearcey, "Code for Life: An Interview with Walter Bradley," *Bible-Science Newsletter*, February 1989.

45. A recent book arguing against the chance origin of life is David Swift, *Evolution Under the Microscope: A Scientific Critique of the Theory of Evolution* (Stirling University Innovation Park, UK: Leighton Academic, 2002). Swift writes that "biologically active proteins are such tiny and isolated islands of utility in a boundless ocean of possible but useless amino acid sequences, that it is not credible they could be happened upon by fortuitous drifting around" (183).

46. Norman Geisler, interview by Nancy Pearcey, in "Geisler's Rebuttal: An Appeal to Common Sense," *Bible-Science Newsletter*, March 1985.

47. See Charles Thaxton, Walter Bradley, and Roger Olsen, *The Mystery of Life's Origin* (Dallas: Lewis and Stanley, 1992; originally published by Philosophical Library, 1984). See also Nancy Pearcey, "The First Step—Chemical Evolution (an Interview with Charles Thaxton)," *Bible-Science Newsletter*, October 1985; and Nancy Pearcey, "A Science of Origins: An Interview with Charles Thaxton," *Bible-Science Newsletter*, January 1987.

48. Dean Kenyon and Gary Steinman, *Biochemical Predestination* (New York: McGraw-Hill, 1969). Kenyon also studied under a chemist named Melvin Calvin, though that probably *is* a coincidence.

49. Nancy Pearcey, "Up from Materialism: An Interview with Dean Kenyon," *Bible-Science Newsletter*, September 1989.

50. Like Behe, Kenyon is Catholic and had no religious motivation for questioning evolution; it was the scientific weaknesses of the theory that motivated his quest for an alternative. He is a low-voiced, irenic man who would never willingly attract controversy; yet his altered views cast him into a hostile tug-of-war with authorities at San Francisco State University, where he used to teach. When university officials heard that he had embraced Intelligent Design theory, they actually forced him out of his teaching responsibilities, despite his stature as a leader in his field. He was reinstated only after a long and acrimonious appeal process, during which both the university's Academic Freedom Committee and the American Association of University Professors agreed that Kenyon's academic freedom had been violated. These groups defended a professor's right to question orthodox opinion on the subjects he teaches. The story

is told in Phillip E. Johnson, *Reason in the Balance: The Case Against Naturalism in Science, Law, and Education* (Downers Grove, Ill.: InterVarsity Press, 1995), 29-30; and in John Myers, "A Scopes Trial in Reverse," at http://www.leaderu.com/real/ri9401/scopes.html. University officials held out until public opinion was stirred by a *Wall Street Journal* article that drew attention to the irony of the situation: "Unlike Scopes, the teacher was forbidden to teach his course not because he taught evolutionary theory (which he did) but because he offered a critical assessment of it" (Steve Meyer, "Danger: Indoctrination—A Scopes Trial for the '90s," *The Wall Street Journal,* December 6, 1993).

51. In fact, if the sequence in DNA *were* a regular, repeating pattern, describable by some law or formula, then mapping the human genome would have been a comparatively simple task: Merely find the formula and you've solved the puzzle. The reason the genome is so difficult to map is precisely that there *is* no general formula. Each individual chemical "letter" has to be specified, one by one.

52. Cited in Nancy Pearcey, "Phillip Johnson Was Right: The Unhappy Evolution of Darwinism," *World,* February 24, 2001.

53. The hope that complexity theory may provide an answer to the origin of life is still just that: a hope, not an accomplishment. Yet complexity theory is often cited as though it had already provided an answer. For example, the editor in chief of *Scientific American,* in opposing critics of evolution, writes, "Researchers into nonlinear systems and cellular automata at the Santa Fe Institute and elsewhere have demonstrated that simple, undirected processes can yield extraordinarily complex patterns. Some of the complexity seen in organisms may therefore emerge through natural phenomena that we as yet barely understand. But that is far different from saying that the complexity could not have arisen naturally" (John Rennie, "15 Answers to Creationist Nonsense," *Scientific American,* July 2002). Translation: We don't know what processes were involved, but we are absolutely sure they were natural. This is an example of the way evolutionists rely on philosophy to get over the gaps in empirical evidence.

54. Stuart Kauffman, *At Home in the Universe: The Search for the Laws of Self-Organization and Complexity* (Oxford: Oxford University Press), 1995. For a critique, see Nancy Pearcey, "The Molecule Is the Message," *First Things* (June/July 1996): 13-14.

55. Richard Dawkins, *River Out of Eden: A Darwinian View of Life* (New York: HarperCollins, 1995), 17.

56. See Nancy Pearcey, "Nature and Nature's God: What Information Theory Tells Us," *Bible-Science Newsletter,* July 1986; Nancy Pearcey, "Who Wrote the DNA Code? A Report on an Interdisciplinary Conference," *Bible-Science Newsletter,* March 1991. For a briefer treatment, see "Life in a Test Tube," chapter 8 in *How Now?*

57. George Williams, interview by John Brockman, "George C. Williams: 'A Package of Information,'" in John Brockman, *The Third Culture: Beyond the Scientific Revolution* (New York: Simon & Schuster, 1995), 43. The distinction between the medium and the message may have become clearer since the dawn of the computer age, Williams says: "The constant process of transferring information from one physical medium to another and then being able to recover the same information in the original medium brings home the separability of information and matter. In biology, when you're talking about things like genes and genotypes and gene pools, you're talking about information, not physical objective reality" (43).

58. Paul Davies, "How We Could Create Life: The Key to Existence Will Be Found Not in Primordial Sludge, but in the Nanotechnology of the Living Cell," *The Guardian,* December 11, 2002, emphasis added.

59. Both Dean Kenyon and Charles Thaxton were influenced by the works of Wilder-Smith. Thaxton in turn encouraged young scholars like Steve Meyer, Bill Dembski, and Paul Nelson. See A. E. Wilder-Smith, *The Creation of Life: A Cybernetic Approach to Evolution* (Costa Mesa, Calif.: The Word for Today, 1970); *Man's Origin, Man's Destiny: A Critical Survey of the Principles of Evolution and Christianity* (Minneapolis: Bethany, 1968); *The Natural Sciences Know Nothing of Evolution* (Costa Mesa, Calif.: The Word for Today, 1981); *The Scientific Alternative to Neo-Darwinian Evolutionary Theory: Information Sources and Structures* (Costa Mesa, Calif.: The Word For Today, 1987).

60. In *The Blind Watchmaker,* Richard Dawkins refers to complex systems that are independently specified—or "specified in advance" (7-8). In *The Fifth Miracle* (New York: Simon and Schuster, 1999), Paul Davies claims that life is not mysterious because of its complexity per se but because of its "tightly specified complexity" (112). For an accessible explanation of the

concept of specified complexity, see my treatment in *Soul of Science* (chapter 10, "A Chemical Code: Resolving Historical Controversies").

61. The term *specified complexity* appears to have been first used by Leslie Orgel in his 1973 book *The Origins of Life* (New York: John Wiley). The concept was developed in detail by Thaxton, Bradley, and Olsen in *Mystery of Life's Origin*. Thaxton also organized a historic conference in 1988 in Tacoma, Washington, named "Information Content of DNA." For more recent treatments, see Walter Bradley and Charles Thaxton, "Information and the Origin of Life," in *The Creation Hypothesis: Scientific Evidence for an Intelligent Designer,* ed. J. P. Moreland (Downers Grove, Ill.: InterVarsity: 1994); Stephen Meyer, "DNA and Other Designs," *First Things* 102 (April 2000): 30-38; at http://www.firstthings.com/ftissues/ft0004/articles/meyer.html; and Stephen Meyer, "DNA and the Origins of Life: Information, Specification, and Explanation," in *Darwinism, Design, and Public Education,* ed. John Angus Campbell and Stephen C. Meyer (Lansing: Michigan State University Press, 2003).

62. Pearcey, "Molecule Is the Message."

63. Daniel Dennett, *Darwin's Dangerous Idea* (New York: Simon & Schuster, 1995), 50.

64. In Darwin, ed., *Life and Letters of Charles Darwin,* vol. 2, 6-7, 28. For a more detailed discussion, see Nancy Pearcey, "You Guys Lost: Is Design a Closed Issue?" in *Mere Creation,* 73-92.

65. Douglas Futuyma, *Evolutionary Biology,* 3rd ed. (Sunderland, Mass.: Sinauer, 1998), 5.

66. David L. Hull, *Darwin and His Critics: The Reception of Darwin's Theory of Evolution by the Scientific Community* (Cambridge, Mass.: Harvard University Press, 1973), 54. For centuries, scholars have sought to draw a firm black line that would define what qualifies as genuine science. Various tests have been proposed for verifiability (and falsifiability). But every time a standard is set up, some scientific theory is found that knocks it down. This is called the "demarcation problem," and the consensus today is that there *is* no way to determine ahead of time what does or does not qualify for scientific status. The only recourse is to test each theory and see how well it explains the data. See Stephen Meyer, "The Methodological Equivalence of Design and Descent: Can There Be a Scientific 'Theory of Creation'?" in *The Creation Hypothesis;* Stephen Meyer, "The Demarcation of Science and Religion," in *The History of Science and Religion in the Western Tradition: An Encyclopedia* (New York: Garland, 2000).

67. Design theorists do not attribute *all* events to the direct activity of a Creator, as they are sometimes accused of doing. They recognize a role for chance and law acting through the history of the universe—what the early scientists called "secondary causes." Design theorists merely want to include an *additional* kind of cause, "primary causes," as an acceptable category within science. As Dembski writes, "All the tried and true tools of science will remain intact. But design adds a new tool to the scientist's explanatory tool chest" ("Science and Design," *First Things,* 86 [October 1998]: 21-27).

68. Phillip E. Johnson, *The Right Questions: Truth, Meaning, and Public Debate* (Downers Grove, Ill.: InterVarsity Press, 2002), 18.

69. His House was operated by Denis and Margie Haack, who became wonderful friends and graciously allowed me to stay with them for two summers when I was a young believer. Later the Haacks joined the staff of InterVarsity, and then founded Ransom Fellowship, a "Schaeffer-esque ministry" (their term) in Rochester, Minnesota. They also produce a monthly publication called *Critique,* designed "to help Christians develop skills in discernment."

70. Phillip E. Johnson, *The Wedge of Truth: Splitting the Foundations of Naturalism* (Downers Grove, Ill.: InterVarsity Press, 2000), 166.

71. Nancey Murphy, "Phillip Johnson on Trial: A Critique of His Critique of Darwin," *Perspectives on Science and Christian Faith* 45, no. 1 (1993): 33. See Johnson's response in *Reason in the Balance* (97-101). The tactic of separating *methodological* from *metaphysical* naturalism is ultimately incoherent: Methodological naturalism is thought to be sound precisely because it is deemed to reflect reality.

72. Ellen T. Charry, *By the Renewing of Your Minds: The Pastoral Function of Christian Doctrine* (New York: Oxford University Press, 1977), 6.

73. John Maddox, "Churchman Preaching to the Unconvertible," review of *God Outside the Box: Why Spiritual People Object to Christianity,* by Richard Harries, *The Times Higher Education Supplement,* February 7, 2003.

74. Francis Schaeffer, *Death in the City,* in *The Complete Works of Francis A. Schaeffer,* vol. 4 (Wheaton, Ill.: Crossway, 1982), see 288-299.

CHAPTER 7: TODAY BIOLOGY, TOMORROW THE WORLD

1. Robert Wright, *The Moral Animal: Why We Are the Way We Are* (New York: Vintage, 1994), 325.
2. John Calvert, in discussion with the author. Calvert has made similar statements in several contexts, many of which are available at http://www.intelligentdesignnetwork.org.
3. See Nancy Pearcey, "Design and the Discriminating Public: Gaining a Hearing from Ordinary People" (*Touchstone,* July/August, 1999); reprinted in *Signs of Intelligence: Understanding Intelligent Design,* ed. William A. Dembski and James M. Kushiner (Grand Rapids, Mich.: Baker, 2001). For a briefer treatment of many of the themes found in chapters 7 and 8, see Nancy Pearcey, "Darwin Meets the Berenstain Bears: How Evolution Changed American Thought," Veritas Forum at Ohio State University, November 6, 2002. The material is adapted and expanded in Nancy Pearcey, "Darwin Meets the Berenstain Bears: The Cultural Impact of Evolution," in *Uncommon Dissent: Intellectuals Who Find Darwinism Unconvincing,* ed. William A. Dembski (Wilmington, Del.: Intercollegiate Studies Institute, 2004).
4. Francis Schaeffer, *A Christian Manifesto,* in *The Complete Works of Francis A. Schaeffer,* vol. 5 (Wheaton, Ill.: Crossway, 1982), 423.
5. Richard Dawkins, *The Selfish Gene* (New York: Oxford University Press, 1976); Robert Wright, *The Moral Animal: Evolutionary Psychology in Everyday Life* (New York: Vintage, 1994); Leonard D. Katz, ed., *Evolutionary Origins of Morality* (New York: Norton, 1998).
6. E. O. Wilson and Michael Ruse, "The Evolution of Ethics," in *Religion and the Natural Sciences: The Range of Engagement,* ed. J. E. Hutchingson (Orlando: Harcourt & Brace, 1991), 310; E. O. Wilson and Michael Ruse, "Moral Philosophy as an Applied Science," *Philosophy* 61 (1986): 179.
7. Richard Wrangham and Dale Peterson, *Demonic Males: Apes and the Origins of Human Violence* (New York: Houghton Mifflin, 1996).
8. Scott Atran, *In Gods We Trust: The Evolutionary Landscape of Religion* (New York: Oxford University Press, 2002); and Pascal Boyer, *Religion Explained: The Evolutionary Origins of Religious Thought* (New York: Basic Books, 2001).
9. Paul H. Rubin, *Darwinian Politics: The Evolutionary Origin of Freedom* (New Brunswick, N.J.: Rutgers University Press, 2002); Arthur E. Gandolfi, Anna S. Gandolfi, and David P. Barash, *Economics as an Evolutionary Science: From Utility to Fitness* (New Brunswick, N.J.: Transaction, 2002); John H. Beckstrom, *Evolutionary Jurisprudence: Prospects and Limitations on the Use of Modern Darwinism Throughout the Legal Process* (Champaign, Ill.: University of Illinois Press, 1989); there is also the more recent book by Suri Ratnapala and Jason Soon, *Evolutionary Jurisprudence* (Aldershot, Hampshire, UK: Ashgate, 2003); Margaret Gruter and Paul Bohannan, eds., *Law, Biology, and Culture: The Evolution of Law* (Portola Valley, Calif.: Ross Erikson, 1983).
10. Dean Keith Simonton, *Origins of Genius: Darwinian Perspectives on Creativity* (New York: Oxford University Press, 1999); Joseph Carroll, *Evolution and Literary Theory* (Columbia: University of Missouri Press, 1994). See also Robert Storey, *Mimesis and the Human Animal: On the Biogenetic Foundations of Literary Representation* (Evanston, Ill.: Northwestern University Press, 1996).
11. Wenda Trevathan, James J. McKenna, and Euclid O. Smith, eds., *Evolutionary Medicine* (New York: Oxford University Press, 1999); Randolph M. Nesse and George C. Williams, *Why We Get Sick: The New Science of Darwinian Medicine* (New York: Vintage, 1996); Anthony Stevens and John Price, *Darwinian Psychiatry* (New York: Routledge, 2000); Paul Gilbert and Kent G. Bailey, eds., *Genes on the Couch: Explorations in Evolutionary Psychology* (London: Brunner-Routledge, 2000).
12. Kingsley Browne, *Divided Labours: An Evolutionary View of Women at Work* (New Haven, Conn.: Yale University Press, 1999); Martin Daly and Margo Wilson, *The Truth About Cinderella: A Darwinian View of Parental Love* (New Haven, Conn.: Yale University Press, 1999); Nigel Nicholson, *Executive Instinct: Managing the Human Animal in the Information Age* (New York: Crown, 2000).
13. David M. Buss, *Evolution of Desire: Strategies of Human Mating* (New York: Basic Books,

1995); Malcolm Potts and Roger Short, *Ever Since Adam and Eve: The Evolution of Human Sexuality* (New York: Cambridge University Press, 1999).

14. Geoffrey Miller, *The Mating Mind: How Sexual Choice Shaped the Evolution of Human Nature* (New York: Doubleday, 2000).

15. Natalie Angier, "Of Altruism, Heroism and Nature's Gifts in the Face of Terror," *New York Times,* September 18, 2001.

16. Cited in Hillary Rose and Steven Rose, ed., *Alas, Poor Darwin: Arguments Against Evolutionary Psychology* (London: Jonathan Cape, 2000), 249.

17. Nancy Pearcey, "Real Heroism," Salem radio editorial. See Jeffrey Schloss, "Evolutionary Accounts of Altruism and the Problem of Goodness by Design," *Mere Creation* (Downers Grove, Ill.: InterVarsity Press, 1998), 236-261. Many biologists "concede that the moral and sacrificial aspects of human behavior most needing explanation cannot be understood in terms of biological causation at all" (252).

18. Stephen Jay Gould seems to have coined the phrase. See Gould, "More Things in Heaven and Earth," in *Alas, Poor Darwin; Arguments Against Evolutionary Psychology,* ed. Hilary Rose and Steven Rose (London: Jonathan Cape, 2000), 94.

19. H. Allen Orr, "Dennett's Strange Idea: Natural Selection: Science of Everything, Universal Acid, Cure for the Common Cold . . . ," in the *Boston Review,* Summer 1996, at http://bostonreview.mit.edu/br21.3/Orr.html.

20. Randy Thornhill and Craig Palmer, "Why Men Rape," *The Sciences* (January/February 2000): 20-28; see also *The Natural History of Rape: Biological Bases of Sexual Coercion* (Cambridge, Mass.: MIT Press, 2000). The same theme is echoed in a recent book by Steven Pinker, *The Blank Slate: The Modern Denial of Human Nature* (New York: Viking, 2002), where he writes that rape is likely an adaptive strategy pursued by low-status males who are "alienated from a community" and "unable to win the consent of women" (364). Hence a gene that predisposes such males to rape will spread.

21. Nancy Pearcey, "Darwin's Dirty Secret," *World,* March 13, 2000.

22. Randy Thornhill, "Controversial New Theory of Rape in Terms of Evolution and Nature," National Public Radio, January 26, 2000, emphasis added.

23. Jerry Coyne and Andrew Berry, "Rape as an Adaptation," *Nature* 404 (March 9, 2000): 121-122.

24. Tom Bethell, "Against Sociobiology," *First Things* 109 (January 2001): 18-24.

25. Steven Pinker, "Why They Kill Their Newborns," *The New York Times,* November 2, 1997.

26. The *Newsweek* article appeared only a few months after a well-publicized infanticide case in Indiana ("Baby Doe"). See Nancy Pearcey, "Evolution and Murder," editorial, *Bible-Science Newsletter,* December 1982. For a longer treatment of the topic, see Nancy Pearcey, "Why People Kill Babies: Are Scientists Becoming Apologists for a New Ethic?" *Bible-Science Newsletter,* August 1986.

27. H. Allen Orr, "Darwinian Storytelling," *The New York Review of Books,* February 27, 2003. Orr describes Pinker's *New York Times* piece as "a nearly data-free account that comes perilously close to parody."

28. Cited in Ben Wiker, "Darwin and the Descent of Morality," *First Things* 117 (November 2001): 10-13; chapter 4 of Darwin's *Descent of Man,* where this quote occurs, may be viewed at http://www.literature.org/authors/darwin-charles/the-descent-of-man/chapter-04.html.

29. Provine's argument can be heard on the video, "Darwinism: Science or Naturalistic Philosophy?" a debate with Phillip Johnson at Stanford University, April 30, 1994. A transcript is available at http://www.arn.org/docs/orpages/or161/161main.htm.

30. Peter Singer, "Heavy Petting," review of *Dearest Pet: On Bestiality,* by Midas Dekkers, at http://www.nerve.com/Opinions/Singer/heavyPetting/main.asp.

31. The play is by Pulitzer Prize–winner Edward Albee, and it won four major awards for best new play (Tony, New York Drama Critics Circle, Drama Desk, and Outer Critics Circle).

32. Nancy Pearcey, "The Birds and the Bees: Pop Culture's Evolutionary Message," *World,* April 22, 2000.

33. For a discussion of Kinsey's thought, see Nancy Pearcey, "Creating the 'New Man': The Hidden Agenda in Sex Education," *Bible-Science Newsletter,* May 1990. For a later treatment, see "Salvation Through Sex?" chapter 25 in *How Now?*

34. For example, geneticist Theodosius Dobzhansky wrote that, in producing the genetic basis of

culture, "biological evolution has transcended itself," surrendering the primary role in human evolution to something that is non-biological (*Mankind Evolving: The Evolution of the Human Species* [New Haven, Conn.: Yale University Press, 1962], 20).

35. Cited in Nancy Pearcey, "Singer in the Rain," *First Things* 106 (October 2000): 57-63.

36. Peter Singer, *A Darwinian Left: Politics, Evolution, and Cooperation* (New Haven, Conn.: Yale University Press, 2000), 6.

37. Robin Dunbar, Chris Knight, and Camilla Power, eds., *The Evolution of Culture: An Interdisciplinary View* (New Brunswick, N.J.: Rutgers University Press, 1999); and Robert Aunger, ed., *Darwinizing Culture* (Oxford and New York: Oxford University Press, 2001).

38. Howard Kaye, *The Social Meaning of Modern Biology: From Darwinism to Sociobiology* (1986; reprint, New Brunswick, N.J.: Transaction, 1997). See also my review of Kaye's book in *First Things* 83 (May 1998): 59-62.

39. See Mary Midgely, "Why Memes?" in *Alas, Poor Darwin*, 72-73.

40. Robert Wright, *The Moral Animal: Why We Are the Way We Are* (New York: Vintage, 1994), 336, 351, 324-325, 350, 355, 325.

41. Ibid., 376, 336ff.

42. Dawkins, *Selfish Gene*, 215.

43. Steven Pinker, *How the Mind Works* (New York: Norton, 1997), 52.

44. Richard Dawkins, "The Evolution of Bill Clinton: Sex and Power," *The Observer* (London), Sunday, March 22, 1998.

45. See Francis Schaeffer, *The God Who Is There*, in *Complete Works*, vol. 1, 69, 133.

46. Singer, *Darwinian Left*, 62. See my review, "Singer in the Rain."

47. Singer, *Darwinian Left*, 63. In the last sentence, he is quoting Richard Dawkins.

48. Ibid.

49. C. S. Lewis, *God in the Dock: Essays on Theology and Ethics*, ed. Walter Hooper (Grand Rapids, Mich.: Eerdmans, 1970), part 1, chapter 12.

50. Ernst Mayr, "Evolution and God," *Nature* 248 (March 22, 1974): 285, emphasis added.

51. Richard Dawkins, *A Devil's Chaplain*, ed. Latha Menon (London: Weidenfeld & Nicolson, 2003). See also Richard Dawkins, "Viruses of the Mind," *Free Inquiry* 13 no. 3 (Summer 1993): 34-41.

52. Leo Strauss, *Natural Right and History* (Chicago: University of Chicago Press, 1950, 1953), 7-8. See also 166.

53. Dean E. Murphy, "Scout Not Prepared for Group's Ultimatum: Get Right with God," *The New York Times*, November 9, 2002.

54. Michael Shermer, *How We Believe: The Search for God in an Age of Science* (New York: W. H. Freeman, 2000), 2-3.

55. Michael Shermer, "How We Believe: The Search for God in an Age of Science," Michael Shermer's E-Skeptic of October 2, 1999, Skeptics Society, Altadena, Calif., at http://www.e-skeptic.de/021099.htm.

56. E. O. Wilson, "Toward a Humanistic Biology," *The Humanist* 42 (September/October 1982): 40.

57. E. O. Wilson, *Consilience: The Unity of Knowledge* (New York: Knopf, 1998), 4.

58. E. O. Wilson, *Naturalist* (Washington, D.C.: Island, 1994), 45. For additional detail on how Wilson turned evolution itself into a religion, see "The Drama of Despair," chapter 27 in *How Now?*

59. Abraham Kuyper, *Lectures on Calvinism* (Grand Rapids, Mich.: Eerdmans, 1931), 11.

60. Bill Overn (who later became executive director of the Bible-Science Association), in discussion with the author. One day when Bill was a student at the University of Minnesota, he found himself running late to class, and stuck out his thumb to hitchhike. When a car stopped, he was picked up by an engaging young man who introduced himself as Henry Morris, a graduate student in hydraulic engineering. Morris was later to become the founder of the Institute for Creation Research, and already he had written a book defending the scientific reliability of the Bible. By the time Bill got out of the car, he had become excited about the cause, and ever since he has been a tireless promoter of the scientific case for creation.

CHAPTER 8: DARWINS OF THE MIND

1. Robert Frost, "Accidentally on Purpose," in *Robert Frost; Collected Poems, Prose and Plays* (New York: Library of America, 1995), 438.

2. The story was originally told in E. Yaroslavsky, *Landmarks in the Life of Stalin* (Moscow: Foreign Languages Publishing House, 1940), 8-9.

3. Stow Persons, ed., *Evolutionary Thought in America* (New York: George Braziller, 1956).

4. John Dewey was heavily influenced by psychologist G. Stanley Hall, who was proud at having earned the nickname "Darwin of the mind," a moniker I've adapted for the title of this chapter. For a more general discussion on the impact of evolution on the social sciences, see Nancy Pearcey, "Where Is Evolution Taking Us? Sociology and the New World Order," *Bible-Science Newsletter*, February 1988.

5. Paul Conkin, *When All the Gods Trembled: Darwinism, Scopes, and American Intellectuals* (Lanham, Md.: Rowman & Littlefield, 1998), see especially 39-40, 143-144. Conkin gives greater detail in *Puritans and Pragmatists: Eight Eminent American Thinkers* (Bloomington: Indiana University Press, 1976).

6. See Albert W. Alschuler, *Law Without Values: The Life, Work, and Legacy of Justice Holmes* (Chicago: University of Chicago Press, 2000), 41.

7. Holmes recorded his thoughts a few years afterward in a notebook. Cited in Louis Menand, *The Metaphysical Club: A Story of Ideas in America* (New York: Farrar, Straus, & Giroux, 2001), 37.

8. Menand, *Metaphysical Club*, 4.

9. Oliver Wendell Holmes Jr., "Law in Science and Science in Law," *Harvard Law Review* 12:443 (1899), in *The Essential Holmes*, edited with an introduction by Richard A. Posner (Chicago: University of Chicago Press, 1996), 188-190. See also E. Donald Elliott, "The Evolutionary Tradition in Jurisprudence," *Columbia Law Review* 85, no. 38 (1985): 52-53. This article provides a good overview of legal theories that draw explicit metaphors to evolution.

10. Conkin, *When All the Gods Trembled*, 42.

11. John Dewey, "The Influence of Darwin on Philosophy," in *The Influence of Darwin on Philosophy and Other Essays in Contemporary Thought* (New York: Henry Holt, 1910), 9.

12. See Menand, *Metaphysical Club*, 361.

13. Ibid., 357-358, 369.

14. Ibid., 355, 358.

15. James Miller, "Holmes, Peirce, and Legal Pragmatism," *Yale Law Journal* 84 (1975): 1123, 1132.

16. As Christopher Kaiser explains, among the early modern scientists, the natural world was considered comprehensible because "the same Logos that is responsible for its ordering is also reflected in human reason" (*Creation and the History of Science* [Grand Rapids, Mich.: Eerdmans, 1991], 10). Likewise, historian Richard Cohen notes that the rise of science required a belief in a "rational creator of all things," with its corollary that "we lesser rational beings might, by virtue of that Godlike rationality, be able to decipher the laws of nature" ("Alternative Interpretations of the History of Science," in *The Validation of Scientific Theories*, ed. Philip Frank [Boston: Beacon, 1956], 227). On how the idea of the image of God persisted even among thinkers who were not Christian (where God was replaced by the Absolute, for example), see Edward Craig, *The Image of God and the Works of Man* (Oxford: Clarendon, 1987).

17. Cited in Menand, *Metaphysical Club*, 353.

18. Cited in ibid., 355-356. Elsewhere he wrote, "If theological ideas prove to have a value for concrete life, they will be true, for pragmatism, in the sense of being good for so much" ("What Pragmatism Means," in *Pragmatism: A New Name for Old Ways of Thinking* [New York: Longman, Green, 1907]). See also William James, *Varieties of Religious Experience* (New York: Touchstone, 1997).

19. Cited in Paul F. Boller, Jr., *American Thought in Transition: The Impact of Evolutionary Naturalism, 1865–1900* (Chicago: Rand McNally, 1969), 142, emphasis in original.

20. Bertrand Russell, *A History of Western Philosophy* (Forage Village, Mass.: Simon & Schuster, 1945), 818.

21. Jon Roberts and James Turner, *The Sacred and the Secular University* (Princeton, N.J.:

Princeton University Press, 2000). Part 1 of this book deals with the sciences, part 2 with the humanities.

22. As Conkin explains, the two-realm theory of truth seemed to divide the human person himself: The lower story exalted empirically verifiable facts, but it led to a determinism that denied "the validity of his ideals and his feelings of worth and purpose." Meanwhile the upper story affirmed the reality of moral and spiritual ideals, but "at the expense of logic [and] fact." It seemed one had to choose either a naturalism that cared about nothing but scientific facts, or else an airy idealism that offered sweeping visions of Purpose and Right (*Puritans and Pragmatists*, 275).

23. Morton White, *Science and Sentiment in America: Philosophical Thought from Jonathan Edwards to John Dewey* (New York: Oxford University Press, 1972). White even titles one chapter in his book "John Dewey: Rebel Against Dualism" (chapter 11).

24. James Kloppenberg, *Uncertain Victory: Social Democracy and Progressivism in European and American Thought, 1870–1920* (Oxford: Oxford University Press, 1986), 26. Dewey used the phrase "via media" specifically in describing the thought of William James, but Kloppenberg uses it as a rubric for all the pragmatists as well as others who sought to reconcile the rival traditions of empiricism and idealism.

25. Kloppenberg says James suffered the nineteenth century's "philosophical friction" between naturalism and idealism "as an acutely personal affliction" (*Uncertain Victory*, 37).

26. Conkin says James "saw science, as sponsored and popularized in America, as a new church, rich in prestige, imperialistic in its claims, and intolerable in its intellectual pretensions" (*Puritans and Pragmatists*, 276-277).

27. Henry Steele Commager says the two-realm division of truth seemed to confront people with a choice "between a 'brute,' tough-minded philosophy which banished idealism and mysticism in the name of science" (the lower story), and a "tender-minded philosophy which banished science in the name of mysticism and idealism" (the upper story) (*The American Mind: An Interpretation of American Thought and Character Since the 1880s* [New Haven, Conn.: Yale University Press, 1950], 93).

28. William James, "The Present Dilemma in Philosophy," in *Pragmatism* (New York: Longman, Green, 1907), at http://www.4literature.net/William_James/Pragmatism. Conkin says: "The noble goal of pragmatism, in James's own terms, was the bridging of fact and value, science and religion" (*Puritans and Pragmatists*, 324).

29. Bruce Kuklick, *Churchmen and Philosophers: From Jonathan Edwards to John Dewey* (New Haven, Conn.: Yale University Press, 1985), 223.

30. This was, in fact, *the* central concept that William James took from evolution. The "elusive but genuine character of individual spontaneity in both the external world and in man is in James's view of evolution epitomized by 'saltatory' mutations, original, spontaneous, irreducible phases of experience" (Philip P. Wiener, *Evolution and the Founders of Pragmatism* [Gloucester, Mass.: Peter Smith, 1969; orig., Cambridge, Mass.: Harvard University Press, 1949], 101). Peirce thought that even the laws of nature had evolved by chance—a view he said derived from Darwin: "My opinion is only Darwinism analyzed, generalized, and brought into the realm of Ontology" (cited in Menand, *Metaphysical Club*, 277).

31. James Ward Smith, "Religion and Science in American Philosophy," in *The Shaping of American Religion*, ed. James Ward Smith and A. Leland Jamison (Princeton, N.J.: Princeton University Press, 1961), 421 and passim. This is a tendency Smith himself supports, while deriding all other responses to evolution as "superficial." See also Stow Persons, "Religion and Modernity, 1865–1914," in the same volume.

32. See Wiener, *Evolution and the Founders of Pragmatism*, chapter 4. William James likewise taught a finite god, who is neither omnipotent nor omniscient. "His finiteness evaded all problems of evil and foreknowledge," says Conkin (*Puritans and Pragmatists*, 339). By the end of his life, James had come to see God as a cosmic consciousness, a pooling or weaving together of all individual consciousness.

33. "Hartshorne later claimed that Peirce and Whitehead were the two philosophers who influenced him most" (G. Douglas Browning, Robert Kane, Donald Viney, Stephen Phillips, "Hartshorne Tribute," *Proceedings and Addresses of the American Philosophical Association* [May 2001], at http://www.hyattcarter.com/hartshorne_tribute.htm. See also John B. Cobb, "Charles Hartshorne: The Einstein of Religious Thought, 1897–2000," Courtesy of the Center for Process Studies, Claremont, Calif., at http://www.ctr4process.org).

34. If you have read appendix 2, you will recognize this as a form of neo-Platonism—the world as an emanation of God's own essence.

35. See Boller, "William James and the Open Universe," in *American Thought in Transition,* especially 134-138. See also Allen C. Guelzo, "The Return of the Will," in *Edwards in Our Time: Jonathan Edwards and the Shaping of American Religion,* ed. Sang Hyun Lee and Allen C. Guelzo (Grand Rapids, Mich.: Eerdmans, 1999), 100-102. Some proponents of Open Theism acknowledge the influence of Peirce and Whitehead, while others insist that they are simply trying to explain how God can interact with a temporal and changing world (for example, responding to prayer) if He really is eternal, unchanging, immutable, and impassible. Philosopher John Passmore (who is not a professing Christian) shows that many conceptions of divine perfection were adopted from Greek philosophy and are incompatible with biblical theology (see *The Perfectibility of Man,* 3rd ed. [Indianapolis: Liberty Fund, 2000; orig., New York: Scribner's, 1970]).

36. The underlying problem for Christian thinkers is the rise of historical consciousness. In the Middle Ages, the church developed an essentially static or cyclical worldview. As a result, it had difficulty responding to the new sense of historical development that began in the Renaissance and came to full flower in the Romantic movement. See Nancy Pearcey, "Recent Developments in the History of Science and Christianity" and "Reply," *Pro Rege* 30, no. 4 (June 2002), 22.

The two great challenges to the faith that arose at the end of the nineteenth century were German higher criticism and Darwinism, both representing the new historicist mindset—the first in theology, the second in science. Higher criticism insisted that Christianity itself had to be explained as a product of evolving religious ideas and customs. It did not regard Scripture as divine revelation but merely as the expression of evolving conceptions of God within human culture. Thus it imposed an evolutionary schema onto the Bible itself—a sequence from animism to totemism, to polytheism, and finally to monotheism. Where the biblical account did not fit that preconceived schema, the critics simply pronounced it unreliable and riddled with errors. See Nancy Pearcey, "Interpreting Genesis: A Reply to the Critics," *Bible-Science Newsletter,* August 1984; Nancy Pearcey, "Real People in a Real World: The Lessons of Archaeology," *Bible-Science Newsletter,* June 1985.

The problem with historicism is that, like every "ism," it selects one aspect of the created world and elevates it into the single, unifying principle of interpretation for all reality. As Herman Dooyeweerd put it, historicism "absolutizes" the historical aspect of created reality. (Whenever God is rejected as the absolute reality, some part of creation will be elevated into an absolute, and everything else will be reduced to its categories.) Dooyeweerd also offered a Christian conceptualization of history as the "unfolding" of the inbuilt potentials of creation. For an accessible introduction to Dooyeweerd's philosophy, see L. Kalsbeek, *Contours of a Christian Philosophy,* ed. Bernard and Josina Zylstra (Toronto: Wedge, 1975), 111-113. See also C. T. McIntire, "Dooyeweerd's Philosophy of History," in *The Legacy of Herman Dooyeweerd* (Lanham, Md.: University Press of America, 1985).

37. The pragmatists adopted the Darwinian notion that law is merely "a human instrument for adjusting conflicting desires in the struggle for existence" (Wiener, *Evolution and the Founders of Pragmatism,* 153). For more on the impact of evolution on legal philosophy, see Nancy Pearcey, "Law and Democracy: Creation—A Complete Worldview," *Bible-Science Newsletter,* October 1983.

38. For more on the philosophical background of legal pragmatism, see Nancy R. Pearcey, "Darwin's New Bulldogs," *Regent University Law Review* 13, no. 2 (2000–2001): 483-511. An adapted version appeared as "Why Judges Make Law: The Roots and Remedies of Judicial Imperialism," *Human Events,* December 1, 2000, at http://arn.org/pearcey/nphome.htm.

39. Holmes, "Law in Science," 191.

40. Ibid., 92.

41. Holmes, "The Path of the Law," *Essential Holmes,* 170.

42. Holmes, "Law in Science," *Essential Holmes,* 198. The goal of studying law, Holmes said, is merely "the prediction of the incidence of the public force through the instrumentality of the courts." Phillip Johnson comments that for Holmes, law is "the science of state coercion"— the empirical study of how the state in fact uses its coercive power to enforce policies (*Reason in the Balance: The Case Against Naturalism in Science, Law, and Education* [Downers Grove,

Ill.: InterVarsity, 1995], 140). For a review see Nancy Pearcey, "Naturalism on Trial," *First Things* 60 (February 1996): 62-65.

43. As I was writing this chapter, I clipped an article from the *New York Times* announcing with great excitement that in the state's highest court, nineteen law professors had filed a brief arguing that judges should be free to make up their own minds about the acceptability of capital punishment, regardless of what the law says. The *Times* called this "a novel theory" but it was really just an application of Holmes's legal pragmatism. See "Law Professors Give State Court a Novel Theory on Executions," *New York Times*, May 6, 2002. See also the commentary by John Leo, "Stealth Strategy to Subvert Democracy," May 13, 2002, at http://www.townhall.com.columnists/johnleo/jl20020513.shtml.

44. Darwinism has influenced abortion even more directly by fostering the eugenics movement. See Richard Weikart, "Progress Through Racial Extermination: Social Darwinism, Eugenics, and Pacifism in Germany, 1860–1918," *German Studies Review* 26 (2003): 273-294; and "Darwinism and Death: Devaluing Human Life in Germany, 1860–1920," *Journal of the History of Ideas* 63 (2002): 323-344. See also Weikart's recent book, *From Darwin to Hitler: Evolutionary Ethics, Eugenics, and Devaluing Human Life in Germany* (New York: Palgrave Macmillan, 2004).

45. Kuklick, *Churchmen and Philosophers*, 230-231.

46. Cited in Menand, *Metaphysical Club*, 369. See Kuklick, *Churchmen and Philosophers*, 232-235, 219, 243.

47. Kuklick, *Churchmen and Philosophers*, 241. Conkin says, "Dewey remained a nominal Christian until his thirties" (*Puritans and Pragmatists*, 346).

48. Conkin, *Puritans and Pragmatists*, 354. Dewey's naturalistic faith permeated his highly influential educational philosophy—see Dewey's "Education as a Religion," *The New Republic,* August, 1922, 64ff.

49. See Nancy Pearcey, "The Evolving Child: John Dewey's Impact on Modern Education," parts 1 and 2, *Bible-Science Newsletter,* January and February 1991; and Nancy Pearcey, "What Is Evolution Doing to Education?" *Bible-Science Newsletter,* January 1986. For a later treatment, see "Still at Risk," chapter 34 in *How Now?*

50. Merrill Harmin, Howard Kirschenbaum, and Sidney Simon, *Clarifying Values Through Subject Matter: Applications for the Classroom* (Minneapolis: Hart, 1973), 31.

51. Thomas Lickona, *Educating for Character* (New York: Bantam, 1992), 237.

52. William Kilpatrick, *Why Johnny Can't Tell Right from Wrong: Moral Illiteracy and the Case for Character Education* (New York: Simon & Schuster, 1992), 93-94.

53. Catherine Fosnot, "Constructivism: A Psychological Theory of Learning," in *Constructivism: Theory, Perspectives, and Practice,* ed. Catherine Fosnot (New York: Teachers College Press, 1996), 8-33, emphasis added.

54. J. F. Osborne, "Beyond Constructivism," *Science Education* 80 (1996): 63.

55. Cited in Allen Quist, *FedEd: The Federal Curriculum and How It's Enforced* (St. Paul, Minn.: Maple River Education Coalition, 2002), 118.

56. "After looking at instructional methods textbooks, one could quickly conclude that constructivism is an instructional methodology," writes one educator. But "this conclusion would be incorrect. Constructivism is an epistemology, a philosophical explanation about the nature of knowledge. . . . In fact, according to constructivism, laws of nature do not exist; rather all knowledge is subjective and personal and is a product of our own cognitive acts" (Terry Simpson, "Dare I Oppose Constructivist Theory?" in *The Educational Forum* [Kappa Delta Pi] 66 [Summer 2002]: 347-354).

57. Ernst von Glasersfeld, "A Constructivist Approach to Teaching," in *Constructivism in Education,* ed. L. P. Steffe and J. Gale (Hillsdale, N.J.: Lawrence Erlbaum Associates, 1995), 3-15; also available online at http://platon.ee.duth.gr/~soeist7t/Lessons/lesson7.htm.

58. The school superintendent was from Brazil, which means this radical epistemology has already spread beyond the industrialized nations. Christian teachers often interpret constructivism in a strictly practical sense to mean that they should encourage students to actively figure out answers on their own, or that they should temporarily ignore students' mistakes for limited purposes (e.g., to encourage creative writing without the constant fear of being marked wrong). These are sound educational practices that good teachers have always adopted, especially in the early elementary grades. But Christian teachers need to be aware of the worldview implications of constructivism as well, understanding that in the secular world it is not merely

a pedagogical method but a relativistic epistemology based on the idea that truth is a social construction.

A balanced discussion of constructivism can be found in *Mathematics in a Postmodern Age: A Christian Perspective*, ed. Russell W. Howell and W. James Bradley (Grand Rapids, Mich.: Eerdmans, 2001). See especially chapter 12, "Teaching and Learning Mathematics: The Influence of Constructivism." For more on the impact of philosophical pragmatism on education, see Nancy Pearcey, "Darwin Meets the Berenstain Bears: The Cultural Impact of Evolution," in *Uncommon Dissent: Intellectuals Who Find Darwinism Unconvincing*, ed. William A. Dembski (Wilmington, Del.: Intercollegiate Studies Institute, 2004).

59. Though not all postmodernists are pragmatists, they hold many intellectual roots in common. See the first two sections of Eugene F. Miller, "Positivism, Historicism, and Political Inquiry," *American Political Science Review* 66, no. 3 (September 1972): 796-817; also available online at http://members.shaw.ca/compilerpress1/Anno%20Miller.htm.

60. Richard Rorty, *Contingency, Irony, and Solidarity* (Cambridge and New York: Cambridge University Press, 1989), chapter 1, passim. Interestingly, Rorty is echoed by educators who say that constructivism, too, hinges on the question, "Is knowledge made or discovered?" See D. C. Phillips, "The Good, the Bad, and the Ugly: The Many Faces of Constructivism," *Educational Researcher* 24, no. 7 (October 1995): 5-12.

61. Richard Rorty, "Untruth and Consequences," a review of *Killing Time* by Paul Feyerabend, in *The New Republic*, July 31, 1995, 32-36.

62. Rorty, *Contingency, Irony, and Solidarity*, 17.

63. Rorty, "Untruth and Consequences."

64. Rorty, *Contingency, Irony, and Solidarity*, 15.

65. In Francis Darwin, ed., *Life and Letters of Charles Darwin*, vol. 1 (New York: D. Appleton, 1898), 285. For several additional quotations from Darwin on this conundrum, see Nancy Pearcey, "The Influence of Evolution on Philosophy and Ethics," in *Science at the Crossroads: Observation or Speculation? Papers of the 1983 National Creation Conference* (Richfield, Minn.: Onesimus, 1985), 166-171.

66. Alvin Plantinga, *Warrant and Proper Function* (New York: Oxford University Press, 1993), 218.

67. Roger Trigg, *Philosophy Matters* (Oxford: Blackwell, 2002), 83.

68. If one begins with naturalistic evolution, explains historian George Marsden, then "the most consistent conclusion" is "postmodern skepticism" (*The Soul of the American University: From Protestant Establishment to Established Nonbelief* [New York: Oxford University Press, 1994], 440. See also 430-431).

69. Francis Schaeffer, *The God Who Is There*, in *The Complete Works of Francis A. Schaeffer*, vol. 1 (Wheaton, Ill.: Crossway, 1982), 140-142.

70. Phillip E. Johnson, "The Limits of Pragmatism," *First Things* 59 (June/July 1996): 52, 54.

71. "Lewis Mumford, Waldo Frank, and some years earlier Randolph Bourne, denounced what Mumford called 'the pragmatic acquiescence,' a phrase that caught their common conviction that pragmatism was a philosophy of means rather than ends, and that it took an unexamined conception of its ends, such as they were, from the surrounding culture" (Alan Ryan, in "Pragmatism, Social Identity, Patriotism, and Self-Criticism," a paper delivered at a conference titled "Conference on Identity: Personal, Cultural, and National," sponsored by the National Humanities Center, June 2–June 4, 1994; at http://www.nhc.rtp.nc.us:8080/publications/hongkong/ryan.htm).

72. Cited in Alschuler, *Law Without Values*, 59. This was a recurring theme in Holmes's writings. The law should be shaped "in accordance with the will of the de facto supreme power in the community," he wrote (cited in Alschuler, 58). And: "The ultimate question is what do the dominant forces of the community want and do they want it hard enough to disregard whatever inhibitions may stand in the way" (letter to John C. H. Wu, 1926, cited in Thomas C. Grey, "Holmes and Legal Pragmatism," *Stanford Law Review* 41 [1989]: 823). As Alschuler comments, Holmes's view means that "every government is good until it is ousted" (60).

73. Holmes, "Natural Law," in *Essential Holmes*, 180.

74. Bertrand Russell, "Pragmatism" (1909), in *Philosophical Essays* (London: Longmans, Green, 1910), 109.

75. Rorty, *Contingency, Irony, and Solidarity*, 5.

76. Jacob D. Bekenstein, "Information in the Holographic Universe," Scientific American.com,

July 14, 2003, at http://www.sciam.com/article.cfm?articleID=000AF072-4891-1F0A-97AE80A84189EEDF

77. Rorty, *Contingency, Irony, and Solidarity*, 21, emphasis added.
78. Schaeffer, *He Is There and He Is Not Silent*, in *Complete Works*, vol. 1.
79. Roberts and Turner, *The Sacred and the Secular University*, 90, emphasis added.

CHAPTER 9: WHAT'S SO GOOD ABOUT EVANGELICALISM?

1. James McGready, *Short Narrative of the Revival of Religion in Logan County, in the State of Kentucky, and the Adjacent Settlements in the State of Tennessee, from May 1797, Until September 1800,* cited in Iain Murray, *Revival and Revivalism: The Making and Marring of American Evangelicalism 1750–1858* (Edinburgh: Banner of Truth, 1994), 150.
2. "Denzel," in discussion with the author. The name has been changed to protect his privacy, but otherwise the story is completely true and accurate.
3. From John Wesley's journal for May 14, 1738, in *The Journal of the Rev. John Wesley,* ed. Nehemiah Curnock, 8 vols. (London: Epworth, 1938), 1:475-476.
4. Evangelicalism's "distinctive feature is not so much a theology as a devotional ethos" (Alister McGrath, *Evangelicalism and the Future of Christianity* [Downers Grove, Ill.: InterVarsity Press, 1995], 132; see also 57-59).
5. Ibid., chapter 6.
6. James Turner, *Without God, Without Creed: The Origins of Unbelief in America* (Baltimore: Johns Hopkins University Press, 1985), 75-76. Mark Noll calls the two wings "formalist" and "anti-formalist" (*America's God: From Jonathan Edwards to Abraham Lincoln* [Oxford: Oxford University Press, 2002], 175-176). Within contemporary American evangelicalism, James Davison Hunter identifies four major traditions: (1) Baptist, (2) Holiness-Pentecostal, (3) Anabaptist, (4) Reformational-Confessional (*American Evangelicalism: Conservative Religion and the Quandary of Modernity* [New Brunswick, N.J.: Rutgers University Press, 1983], 7-9). The first three of these would fall roughly within the populist wing, while the last would fall within the scholarly wing. For a helpful taxonomy by the Polis Center at Purdue University showing where individual denominations fit under broader categories, see http://www.polis.iupui.edu/RUC/Research/Glenmary_by_Polis_Types_as_table.htm.
7. The term itself has a longer history: "The term *evangelical* dates from the sixteenth century, and it was first used to refer to Catholic writers who wished to revert to more biblical beliefs and practices than those associated with the late medieval church." It was later applied to the Reformers (McGrath, *Evangelicalism and the Future of Christianity*, 19).
8. D. G. Hart, *That Old-Time Religion in Modern America: Evangelical Protestantism in the Twentieth Century* (Chicago: Ivan R. Dee, 2002), 9. For a list of the defining distinctives of evangelicalism, see David Bebbington, *Evangelicalism in Modern Britain: A History from the 1730s to the 1980s* (Grand Rapids, Mich.: Baker, 1992), 2-17.
9. For a discussion of the differences between confessional and evangelical churches, see the Introduction to D. G. Hart, *The Lost Soul of American Protestantism* (Lanham, Md.: Rowman & Littlefield, 2002). Presbyterians split during the first Awakening in 1741 (New Side versus Old Side), then reunited, then split again during the second Awakening in 1837 (New School versus Old School), only to reunite again in 1869. Thus the Presbyterians probably succeeded more than most groups in straddling both the populist and the scholarly strands of evangelicalism. Through the nineteenth century, they exercised strong intellectual leadership in the religious world and in American society generally, while also nurturing a warm and vibrant piety.
10. Mark Noll, *The Scandal of the Evangelical Mind* (Grand Rapids, Mich.: Eerdmans, 1994), 9.
11. Philip Jenkins, *The Next Christendom: The Coming of Global Christianity* (Oxford: Oxford University Press, 2002). An excellent introduction to Jenkins's book can be found in his article, "The Next Christianity," *The Atlantic Monthly,* October 2002, at http://www.the atlantic.com/issues/2002/10/jenkins.htm.
12. Roger Finke and Rodney Stark, *The Churching of America 1776–1990: Winners and Losers in Our Religious Economy* (New Brunswick, N.J.: Rutgers University Press, 1992).
13. This does not necessarily mean that people in early America were irreligious. The low rates are partly explained by the fact that the requirements for church membership were very rigorous, so that many attended church without becoming members. In addition, in frontier

areas there were often no churches to attend. Even taking these factors into account, however, the numbers are low compared to the common stereotype.

14. The percentages of religious adherents add up to less than 100 percent because the numbers do not include smaller groups, such as Lutheran, Dutch Reformed, Quaker, Mennonite, Huguenot, Moravian, Jewish, and so on.

15. Jon Butler, *Awash in a Sea of Faith: Christianizing the American People* (Cambridge, Mass.: Harvard University Press, 1990), see especially chapter 4. Butler offers a relatively positive view of the established churches, arguing that they served their constituents well. On suppression of dissenters, Nathan Hatch notes, "As late as the 1770s, Baptist preachers in Virginia were still being thrown in jail" (*The Democratization of American Christianity* [New Haven, Conn.: Yale University Press, 1989], 59).

16. Cited in Bebbington, *Evangelicalism in Modern Britain,* 11.

17. Cited in Finke and Stark, *Churching of America,* 19, emphasis added. For more detail, see chapter 2, "The Colonial Era Revisited."

18. The exceptions are places like Ireland and Quebec, where the Catholic church has also served as the primary vehicle for political resistance to external domination.

19. Finke and Stark, *Churching of America,* 238, 212.

20. "As the people moved westward after the Revolution, they were forever outrunning the institutions of settled society. . . . Organizations dissolved; restraints disappeared. Churches, social bonds, and cultural institutions often broke down, and they could not be reconstituted before the frontier families made yet another leap into the wilderness or the prairie" (Richard Hofstadter, *Anti-Intellectualism in American Life* [New York: Random House, 1966], 76).

21. Cited in Mark A. Noll, Nathan O. Hatch, and George M. Marsden, *The Search for Christian America* (Westchester, Ill.: Crossway, 1983), 111, emphasis added.

22. Finke and Stark, *Churching of America,* 33, emphasis added. This model applies even to the colonial period, when "the West" meant western Pennsylvania or Kentucky. Frontier conditions tend to be pretty much the same anywhere.

23. Hart, *That Old-Time Religion,* 7.

24. Hatch (*Democratization of American Christianity,* 87) cites a study finding that of the first 650 Methodist circuit riders, nearly half died before the age of thirty, almost 200 of them within their first five years of service. See also Finke and Stark, *Churching of America,* 153. The phrase God's "light artillery" is from Horace Bushnell, cited in Hatch, ibid., 67. The saying about "crows and Methodist preachers" is from Hofstadter, *Anti-Intellectualism in American Life,* 96.

25. Critics often accuse the revivalists of being anti-cultural and anti-intellectual, but to be fair many were simply responding to the condition of the frontier itself. Even Richard Hofstadter, generally critical of evangelical Christianity, wrote, "It must be said that they were not lowering the level of a high culture but trying to bring the ordinary restraints and institutions of a civilized society into an area which had hardly any culture at all" (*Anti-Intellectualism in American Life,* 79).

26. Cited in Hatch, *Democratization of American Christianity,* 127.

27. Hatch, *Democratization of American Christianity,* 102.

28. Cited in ibid., 104.

29. Among non-evangelical denominations, the ones that did best were those willing to adopt a similar approach. For example, Catholics began holding revival meetings using vernacular language and emotional appeals that were virtually identical to their Baptist and Methodist counterparts. In the early twentieth century, Catholics even built special vans and train cars outfitted with altars and religious symbols inside, which functioned as portable sanctuaries to take priests into unchurched areas. The vans, called "motor chapels," had wide doors on the side that opened outward, revealing an altar that could then be used to hold open-air masses in rural areas (see Finke and Stark, *Churching of America,* chapter 4).

30. Dean Kelley, *Why Conservative Churches Are Growing* (New York: Harper & Row, 1972). Of course the decline of the mainline churches has been slow and gradual, and their institutional power remained strong even as they lost numbers. For a good history, see Robert Handy, *A Christian America: Protestant Hopes and Historical Realities* (Oxford: Oxford University Press, 1984).

31. The achievement of the American evangelical movement stands out even more strongly when highlighted against the British experience. In England, John Wesley's Methodist movement was

eventually taken over by leaders more interested in maintaining rules and respectability than in reaching the poor and ragged masses—and they didn't care if that meant a loss in numbers. They banned camp meetings and expelled those who protested, until nearly one-third of their members had either left or been expelled. Eventually, the Methodist church in Britain lost contact with the working classes, with the result that today they are highly secularized. By contrast, in America the working classes remain *more* religious than the rest of the population. See Hatch, *Democratization of American Christianity*, 92-93. Here too, however, eventually the Methodist church followed the lure of respectability. Finke and Stark include a fascinating chapter on how the Methodist church became wealthy and went mainstream, and then began to decline almost as rapidly as it had once grown. See *Churching of America*, chapter 5.

32. Noll, *Scandal of the Evangelical Mind*, 63.

33. Stout, *The Divine Dramatist: George Whitefield and the Rise of Modern Evangelicalism* (Grand Rapids, Mich.: Eerdmans, 1991), xix. See also Harry Stout, "George Whitefield in Three Countries," in *Evangelicalism: Comparative Studies of Popular Protestantism in North America, the British Isles, and Beyond, 1700–1990*, ed. Mark Noll, David Bebbington, George Rawlyk (New York: Oxford University Press, 1994). Stephen Marini writes: "The Whitefieldian gospel . . . was Calvinist, but it neither dilated on theological problems nor spoke the language of doctrine and hermeneutic. It was more a matter of style and emphasis, drama and rhetoric designed to move emotions and change hearts" (*Radical Sects of Revolutionary New England* [Cambridge, Mass.: Harvard University Press, 1982], 12). For an inspiring account of Whitefield's life, see Arnold Dallimore, *George Whitefield: God's Anointed Servant in the Great Revival of the Eighteenth Century* (Wheaton, Ill.: Crossway, 1990).

34. Hart, *Lost Soul of American Protestantism*, 11. Whitefield relied so heavily on marketing techniques borrowed from the commercial world that one book calls him a "pedlar in divinity" (Frank Lambert, *"Pedlar in Divinity": George Whitefield and the Transatlantic Revivals, 1737–1770* [Princeton, N.J.: Princeton University Press, 2002]).

35. Stout, *Divine Dramatist*, xiii. Stout writes that Whitefield "was the first in a long line of public figures whose claim to influence would rest on celebrity and popularity rather than birth, breeding, or institutional fiat" (xiv).

36. Cited in Alan Heimert, *Religion and the American Mind: From the Great Awakening to the Revolution* (Cambridge, Mass.: Harvard University Press, 1966), 44.

37. Cited in ibid., 208.

38. Cited in ibid.

39. William H. Foote, *Sketches of North Carolina*, 396, cited in Murray, *Revival and Revivalism*, 149-150.

40. McGready, *Short Narrative*, cited in Murray, *Revival and Revivalism*, 150, emphasis added.

41. Heimert, *Religion and the American Mind*, 43. References to the joys of conversion are found throughout chapter 1, "The Nature and Necessity of the New Birth."

42. Heimert writes that defenders and opponents of the Awakening "each marked the independent fulfillment of one of the strains that in Puritanism had been held in precarious balance: 'piety' and 'reason'" (*Religion and the American Mind*, 3).

43. Patricia Bonomi, *Under the Cope of Heaven: Religion, Society, and Politics in Colonial America* (New York: Oxford University Press, 1986), 147.

44. Donald M. Scott, *From Office to Profession: The New England Ministry, 1750–1850* (Philadelphia: University of Pennsylvania Press, 1978). For a description of "Protestant communalism," see Barry Alan Shain, *The Myth of American Individualism: The Protestant Origins of American Political Thought* (Princeton, N.J.: Princeton University Press, 1994).

45. Harry Stout, *Divine Dramatist*, xx.

46. Cited in Bonomi, *Under the Cope of Heaven*, 158, 154, emphasis in original.

47. Bonomi, ibid., 158.

48. George Marsden, *The Soul of the American University: From Protestant Establishment to Established Nonbelief* (New York: Oxford University Press, 1994), 54.

49. Cited in Heimert, *Religion and the American Mind*, 119.

50. What the first Awakening did "was to plant seeds of individualism and immediatism that would eventually exert a profound effect on Christian thinking" (Noll, *Scandal of the Evangelical Mind*, 61). "The revivals led by Edwards and Whitefield planted seeds that would

challenge this older version of Protestantism and eventually yield the basic ingredients of evangelicalism" (Hart, *That Old-Time Religion,* 7).

CHAPTER 10: WHEN AMERICA MET CHRISTIANITY—GUESS WHO WON?

1. Thomas Paine, *Common Sense,* at www.pagebypagebooks.com/Thomas_Paine/Common_ Sense/Appendix_p4.html.
2. Interestingly, camp meetings had roots in sacramental gatherings in Scotland. Since communion was observed infrequently, only two to four times a year, thousands of people would gather from miles around and camp out for several days to hear sermons and receive the Lord's Supper. See Leigh Eric Schmidt, *Holy Fairs: Scotland and the Making of American Revivalism,* 2nd ed. (Grand Rapids, Mich.: Eerdmans, 1989).
3. Gordon S. Wood, *The Radicalism of the American Revolution: How a Revolution Transformed a Monarchial Society into a Democratic One Unlike Any That Had Ever Existed* (New York: Knopf, 1992), 361-362, emphasis added.
4. Cited in Nathan Hatch, *The Democratization of American Christianity* (New Haven, Conn.: Yale University Press, 1991), 36-38, see also 186. Similar themes are found in Mark Noll, *The Scandal of the Evangelical Mind* (Grand Rapids, Mich.: Eerdmans, 1994), especially chapter 3. A more popular treatment of anti-intellectualism in American evangelicalism is found in Os Guinness, *Fit Bodies, Fat Minds: Why Evangelicals Don't Think and What to Do About It* (Grand Rapids, Mich.: Baker, 1994).
5. The identification of religion with politics began in the First Great Awakening and is treated in detail in Nathan O. Hatch, *The Sacred Cause of Liberty: Republican Thought and the Millennium in Revolutionary New England* (New Haven, Conn.: Yale University Press, 1977). Hatch opens the book with a telling anecdote contrasting Jonathan Edwards who prayed in 1747 for a revival, with a group of ministers who prayed in 1787 for "the spirit of true republican government" (1-2). Clearly there had been a shift in spiritual concern from holiness to liberty.
6. Alexis de Tocqueville, *Democracy in America,* vol. 1 (New York: Knopf, 1980), 306-307.
7. John Leland, "The Connecticut Dissenters' Strong Box: No. 1, New London, 1802," at http://www.uark.edu/depts/comminfo/cambridge/strongbox1.html.
8. Cited in Hatch, *Democratization of American Christianity,* 98.
9. D. G. Hart, *The Lost Soul of American Protestantism* (Lanham, Md.: Rowman & Littlefield, 2002), 18.
10. Cited in Hatch, *Democratization of American Christianity,* 69-70, emphasis in original.
11. Cited in ibid., 71.
12. Cited in Richard T. Hughes and C. Leonard Allen, *Illusions of Innocence: Protestant Primitivism in America, 1630–1875* (Chicago: University of Chicago Press, 1988), 105.
13. Evangelicals "appropriated the rhetoric of civil and religious liberty that the respectable clergy had made popular during the Revolution and marshaled it for an entirely new purpose: to topple its architects." The enemy was no longer the British but "elites of all kinds, particularly the clergy" (Hatch, *Democratization of American Christianity,* 76).
14. Cited in ibid.
15. Patricia Bonomi, *Under the Cope of Heaven: Religion, Society, and Politics in Colonial America* (New York: Oxford University Press, 1986), 158-159. Bonomi describes the new theology of conversion in connection with the First Great Awakening, but since its development was a gradual process, her description is, if anything, even more applicable to the Second Great Awakening.
16. The Puritans "elaborated a 'morphology of conversion,' successive states of consciousness through which the hopeful saint could evaluate the evidence of divine election. Every step in this lifelong process of growth in grace was carefully defined by appropriate attitudes and behavior. *In principle, the Puritans never knew they were saved;* they could only trust that their minds were enabled by grace to penetrate beyond the veil and dimly discern the hand of God leading them to glory" (Stephen Marini, *Radical Sects of Revolutionary New England* [Cambridge, Mass.: Harvard University Press, 1982], 12, emphasis added).
17. Hughes and Allen, *Illusions of Innocence,* 113, 115. John Walsh writes, "Evangelical preaching of an immediate, personal assurance came to some as a welcome surprise," especially to those "who had found it difficult to reach the experience of regeneration that their

Puritan culture expected of them" ("'Methodism' and the Origins of English-Speaking Evangelicalism," in *Evangelicalism: Comparative Studies of Popular Protestantism in North America, the British Isles, and Beyond, 1700–1990,* ed. Mark Noll, David Bebbington, George Rawlyk [New York: Oxford University Press, 1994], 29-31). David Bebbington writes, "Whereas the Puritans had held that assurance is rare, late, and the fruit of struggle in the experience of believers, the Evangelicals believed it to be general, normally given at conversion, and the result of simple acceptance of the gift of God" (*Evangelicalism in Modern Britain: A History from the 1730s to the 1980s* [Grand Rapids, Mich.: Baker, 1989], 43).

18. Gordon S. Wood, *The Creation of the American Republic, 1776–1787* (Chapel Hill: University of North Carolina Press, 1969), 599.

19. Cited in Henry May, *The Enlightenment in America* (New York: Oxford University Press, 1976), 163. Thomas Paine's book *Common Sense* is available online at www.pagebypage books.com/Thomas_Paine/Common_Sense/index.html, Appendix, 4.

20. Wood, *Creation of the American Republic,* 590, 601, 612, 607.

21. Richard Hofstadter, *Anti-Intellectualism in American Life* (New York: Random House, 1966), 82-83.

22. Sidney Mead, *The Lively Experiment: The Shaping of Christianity in America* (New York: Harper & Row, 1963), 108-111.

23. Charles Malik, *The Two Tasks* (Westchester, Ill.: Cornerstone, 1980), 33.

24. "So distinctive and so separated was the aristocracy from ordinary folk that many still thought the two groups represented two orders of being. Indeed, we will never appreciate the radicalism of the eighteenth-century revolutionary idea that all men were created equal unless we see it within this age-old tradition of difference. Gentlemen and commoners had different psyches, different emotional makeups, different natures. Ordinary people were made only 'to be born and eat and sleep and die, and be forgotten'" (Wood, *Radicalism of the American Revolution,* 27).

25. Wood, *Creation of the American Republic,* 418. See also Barry Alan Shain, *The Myth of American Individualism: The Protestant Origins of American Political Thought* (Princeton, N.J.: Princeton University Press, 1994); and Joyce Appleby, *Capitalism and a New Social Order: The Republican Vision of the 1790s* (New York: New York University Press, 1984), 8-9, 81. Appleby writes, "Classical republicanism taught that a carefully constructed constitution balancing the forces in society alone held out hope for checking the lust for power and selfish drives of human beings" (95). Noll describes the parallels between classical republicanism and Puritan theology in *Scandal of the Evangelical Mind,* 70-71.

26. Appleby, *Capitalism and a New Social Order,* 82, 36-37.

27. Since populist evangelicals privatized virtue by locating it in the individual heart and conscience, they tended to agree with liberals that the state was not the locus of any inherent virtue (Justice or Right). Thus they accepted the liberal view of a purely instrumental state—with a functional or procedural definition of the nature of government as a facilitator of economic progress. See Michael Gauvreau, "The Empire of Evangelicalism: Varieties of Common Sense in Scotland, Canada, and the United States," in *Evangelicalism,* ed. Noll, Bebbington, and Rawlyk, 225-233. By "privatized" I don't mean they retreated from the public square, for evangelicals initiated many social reforms. I mean they believed that the locus of virtue was not in external social structures but in the individual human heart, and that social reform itself had to start with personal transformation.

28. Cited in May, *Enlightenment in America,* 339, 304, see also 273, 274. The terminology can be confusing, because *republican* was sometimes used by liberals as well. (Recall the quotation from Elias Smith complaining that many are "but half republicans.") What's more, churchmen who were theologically *liberal* tended to be quite *conservative* politically and socially. Unitarians and other rationalists were mostly Federalists, striving to maintain the old elitism of classical republicanism (since they themselves were among the elites). See 350ff.; as well as Alan Heimert, *Religion and the American Mind: From the Great Awakening to the Revolution* (Cambridge, Mass.: Harvard University Press, 1966), viii, 15ff, 23, and passim.

29. Noll, *Scandal of the Evangelical Mind,* 75.

30. Appleby, *Capitalism and a New Social Order,* 27. In 1820 in America, the percentage of the labor force in agriculture still stood at nearly 80 percent (Wood, *Radicalism of the American Revolution,* 312).

31. Roger Finke and Rodney Stark, *The Churching of America 1776–1990: Winners and Losers in Our Religious Economy* (New Brunswick, N.J.: Rutgers University Press, 1992), 44.

32. Wood, *Radicalism of the American Revolution*, 359.

33. See Martin Marty, "The Revival of Evangelicalism and Southern Religion," in *Varieties of Southern Evangelicalism*, ed. David E. Jarrell, Jr. (Macon, Ga.: Mercer University Press, 1981), 14.

34. Gary Thomas, *Revivalism and Cultural Change: Christianity, Nation Building, and the Market in the Nineteenth-Century United States* (Chicago: University of Chicago Press, 1989), 8, 18, 83, 88-89. Carroll Smith-Rosenberg likewise draws parallels between the economic and the religious visions of society: During the Second Great Awakening, she writes, "The last vestiges of orthodox eighteenth-century Congregationalism—an insistence on an all-powerful Father-God, upon the passivity and powerlessness of man, upon an eternity patterned after agrarian patriarchy, and upon a spiritual economy of scarcity represented theologically by predestination—all were challenged and ultimately abandoned." Evangelicalism assumed a new freedom and self-assertion: "Renouncing a spiritual economy of scarcity, Finney preached a loving God who rewarded with limitless grace those who sought salvation. Anyone, rich or poor, who with her free will would assert her belief in God and her determination to do good could now achieve salvation" ("The Cross and the Pedestal: Women, Anti-Ritualism, and the Emergence of the American Bourgeoisie," in *Disorderly Conduct: Visions of Gender in Victorian America* [New York: Oxford University Press, 1985], 142, 153).

35. Wood, *Radicalism of the American Revolution*, 145.

36. Gauvreau, "Empire of Evangelicalism," 223. Gauvreau is speaking of Canadian evangelicalism, and his comment reminds us that evangelicalism was a phenomenon in Canada and Britain as well as in the United States. He writes, "Evangelical groups in both the United States and English Canada played a leading role in the democratization of politics and culture and reshaped social relationships according to the tenets of voluntarism" (220). In the same volume, another Canadian historian, George Rawlyk, writes: "Although British North America had rejected the American Revolution and all that American republicanism represented, . . . in Canada . . . evangelicalism was *more* radical, more anarchistic, more democratic and more popular than its American counterpart" ("'A Total Revolution in Religious and Civil Government': The Maritimes, New England, and the Evolving Evangelical Ethos, 1776–1812," in *Evangelicalism*, ed. Noll, Bebbington, and Rawlyk, 146). On Britain, see David Bebbington, *Evangelicalism in Modern Britain: A History from the 1730s to the 1980s* (Grand Rapids, Mich.: Baker, 1989).

37. In many ways, American evangelicals were echoing themes from the Radical Reformation. The Reformation consisted of three streams—Luther and his followers, Calvin and his followers, and a third group of separatists called Anabaptists and spiritualists, often termed the Radical Reformers. Luther and Calvin retained a territorial model of the church: Everyone living within a certain territory belonged to the same church as the ruler; they were baptized as infants; becoming a Christian was a matter of gradual growth and catechesis; the Christian life was defined primarily in terms of participating in the corporate, sacramental worship of the church. By contrast, the Radical Reformers promoted a "gathered church" or "believers' church" or "free church," which included only those who could claim a conscious conversion experience; thus subjective experience became more important than objective church membership. Only adults who had made a conscious choice were baptized (not infants). The sacraments were demoted from means of grace (something *God* does) to merely external symbols enacted out of obedience (something *we* do). The church was democratic and egalitarian, with the difference between clergy and laity being merely functional. As Ernst Troeltsch first noted in the late nineteenth century, the Anabaptists with their democratic conception of the church were actually quite "modern." See discussion in Steven Ozment, *The Age of Reform 1250–1550: An Intellectual and Religious History of Late Medieval and Reformation Europe* (New Haven, Conn.: Yale University Press, 1980), chapter 10.

It's interesting that the evangelical movement in America came to reflect the views of the Radical Reformers more closely than those of the major Reformers. Roland Bainton says of the Radical Reformers that "they anticipated all other religious bodies in the proclamation and exemplification of three principles which, on the North American continent, are among those truths which we hold to be self-evident: the voluntary Church, the separation of Church and state, and religious liberty" (*Studies on the Reformation* [Boston: Beacon, 1963], 199).

38. Cited in Hofstadter, *Anti-Intellectualism in American Life*, 85.

39. Ibid., 86.

40. Donald M. Scott, *From Office to Profession: The New England Ministry, 1750–1850* (Philadelphia: University of Pennsylvania Press, 1978), 128, 153.

41. Cited in ibid., 143-147.

42. Hatch, *Democratization of American Christianity*, 134.

43. Hofstadter, *Anti-Intellectualism in American Life*, 86.

44. Hatch, *Democratization of American Christianity*, 133.

45. Hofstadter, *Anti-Intellectualism in American Life*, 86.

46. Jonathan Edwards, *A Faithful Narrative of the Surprising Work of God* (1790; reprint, Grand Rapids, Mich.: Baker, 1979).

47. Hofstadter, *Anti-Intellectualism in American Life*, 92.

48. Cited in Hatch, *Democratization of American Christianity*, 135.

49. Cited in Finke and Stark, *Churching of America*, 89-92; and Noll, *Scandal of the Evangelical Mind*, 96. See Charles Finney, "A Revival of Religion Is Not a Miracle," in *A Documentary History of Religion in America to the Civil War*, ed. Edwin Gaustad (Grand Rapids, Mich.: Eerdmans, 1982), 337.

50. Cited in Joel Carpenter, *Revive Us Again: The Reawakening of American Fundamentalism* (Oxford: Oxford University Press, 1997), 126.

51. Cited in Hatch, *Democratization of American Christianity*, 183.

52. Daniel Calhoun, *The Intelligence of a People* (Princeton, N.J.: Princeton University Press, 1973), 282; the Beecher citation is from 281.

53. Hatch, *Democratization of American Christianity*, 136.

54. Ronald Knox, *Enthusiasm: A Chapter in the History of Religion* (Notre Dame, Ind.: Notre Dame University Press, 1950).

55. Joel Carpenter, *Revive Us Again: The Reawakening of American Fundamentalism* (New York: Oxford University Press, 1997), 244.

56. A good one-chapter description of evangelicalism's transition from cultural dominance in the nineteenth century, through fundamentalism in the early twentieth century, to neo-evangelicalism in our own day can be found in Christian Smith, with Michael Emerson, Sally Gallagher, Paul Kennedy, and David Sikkink, *American Evangelicalism: Embattled and Thriving* (Chicago: University of Chicago Press, 1998), chapter 1, "Resurrecting Engaged Orthodoxy."

57. Richard Quebedeaux, *By What Authority? The Rise of Personality Cults in American Christianity* (New York: Harper & Row, 1982). See especially chapter 2, "Celebrity Leaders in the History of American Christianity: 1865–1960"; and chapter 3, "Celebrity Leaders in the History of American Christianity: 1960–present."

58. Carpenter, *Revive Us Again*, 237.

59. Alan Wolfe, *The Transformation of American Religion: How We Actually Live Our Faith* (New York: Free Press, 2003), 35, 3.

60. Another provocative book that makes a similar point is Harold Bloom's *The American Religion: The Emergence of the Post-Christian Nation* (New York: Simon & Schuster, 1992). Bloom argues that there is a distinctively American form of spirituality, which has taken over most Christian denominations. It is highly emotional, individualistic, and "gnostic," by which he means it focuses on the individual soul in immediate relationship to God, apart from our bodily existence as members of families and historically rooted churches. External expressions of religion, such as churches, creeds, and liturgy are regarded at best as unnecessary, and at worst as barriers to genuine worship.

61. Wade Clark Roof, *Spiritual Marketplace: Baby Boomers and the Remaking of American Religion* (Princeton, N.J.: Princeton University Press, 1999), 84-85, 130, emphasis added.

62. Wolfe, *Transformation of American Religion*, 80. See also Udo Middelmann, *The Market Driven Church: The Worldly Influence of Modern Culture on the Church in America* (Wheaton, Ill.: Crossway, 2004). Writing from a European perspective, Middelmann is well situated to discern both the positive and negative aspects of contemporary evangelicalism. While appreciating the way American Christians speak openly about their faith, he also warns that they often treat it as merely a matter of personal growth and private interpretation, having lost the sense that it is also public truth.

CHAPTER 11: EVANGELICALS' TWO-STORY TRUTH

1. Martin Marty, *The Modern Schism: Three Paths to the Secular* (New York: Harper & Row, 1969), 98.

2. See Donald Dayton, "'The Search for the Historical Evangelicalism': George Marsden's History of Fuller Seminary as a Case Study," in *Christian Scholar's Review*, September 1993, with responses by Marsden, Joel Carpenter, and others.

3. James Turner, *Without God, Without Creed: The Origins of Unbelief in America* (Baltimore: Johns Hopkins University Press, 1985), 75-76.

4. Theodore Dwight Bozeman, *Protestants in the Age of Science: The Baconian Ideal and Antebellum American Religious Thought* (Chapel Hill: University of North Carolina Press, 1977), 51, 132.

5. Herbert W. Schneider, cited in Daniel Walker Howe, *The Unitarian Conscience: Harvard Moral Philosophy, 1805–1861* (Cambridge, Mass.: Harvard University Press, 1970), 31.

6. Henry May, *The Enlightenment in America* (New York: Oxford University Press, 1976), 121.

7. Thomas Reid, the founder of Common Sense realism, "has almost disappeared from the canon used for teaching modern philosophy in the universities of the West. Yet from the last decade or two of the eighteenth century, on through most of the nineteenth, he was probably the most popular of all philosophers in Great Britain and North America and enjoyed considerable popularity on the continent of Europe as well" (Nicholas Wolterstorff, *Thomas Reid and the Story of Epistemology* [Cambridge: Cambridge University Press, 2001], ix).

8. Herbert Hovenkamp, *Science and Religion in America, 1800–1860* (Philadelphia: University of Pennsylvania Press, 1978), 5, 10, emphasis added.

9. Hume recognized that philosophy can never undermine what he calls "common life" (the equivalent of Reid's Common Sense). He wrote that "nature" will always assert its rights over any philosophical conclusions that contradict "common life" (David Hume, *An Inquiry Concerning Human Understanding*, ed. Charles W. Hendel [Indianapolis: Bobbs-Merrill, 1955 (1748)], 5.1, page 55). As he explains more fully: "The great subverter of *Pyrrhonism* or the excessive principles of scepticism is action, and employment, and the occupation of common life. These principles may flourish and triumph in the schools; where it is, indeed, difficult, if not impossible, to refute them. But as soon as they leave the shade, and by the presence of the real objects, which actuate our passions and sentiments, are put in opposition to the more powerful principles of our nature, they vanish like smoke, and leave the most determined sceptic in the same condition as other mortals" (12.2, page 167).

10. Thomas Reid, *Essays on the Intellectual Powers of Man*, 2.20.

11. British empiricists (starting with John Locke) tended to champion the inductive method of their fellow countryman Francis Bacon, over against Continental rationalists (starting with René Descartes), who championed the deductive method.

12. Thomas Reid, *Essays on the Intellectual Powers of Man*, 2.8.

13. "Reid's words [were] embalmed in the 'self-evident truths' of the Declaration of Independence" (Turner, *Without God, Without Creed*, 62). See also Garry Wills, *Inventing America: Jefferson's Declaration of Independence* (New York: Doubleday, 1978), chapter 12, "Self-Evident."

14. Cited in Charles Whitney, *Francis Bacon and Modernity* (New Haven, Conn.: Yale University Press, 1986), 11, 40. The momentous implications of the shift from a deductive model of knowledge (producing absolute certainty) to an inductive model of knowledge (producing only probability) is discussed in Jeffrey Stout, *The Flight from Authority: Religion, Morality, and the Quest for Autonomy* (Notre Dame, Ind.: University of Notre Dame Press, 1981).

15. Cited in Bozeman, *Protestants in the Age of Science*, 151.

16. Charles Hodge, *Introduction to Systematic Theology* (1872), excerpted in *The Princeton Theology 1812–1921: Scripture, Science, and Theological Method from Archibald Alexander to Benjamin Warfield*, ed. Mark Noll (Grand Rapids, Mich.: Baker, 2001), 119. See also George Marsden, "Everyone One's Own Interpreter? The Bible, Science, and Authority in Mid-Nineteenth-Century America," in *The Bible in America: Essays in Cultural History*, ed. Nathan Hatch and Mark Noll (New York: Oxford University Press, 1982), 84.

17. The Baconian method appealed to Protestants for other reasons as well—in particular, because its rejection of tradition and church authority was useful in their ongoing polemic against Roman Catholicism. By the same token, Catholics *rejected* the Baconian method because it supported the right of private interpretation apart from church authority. Catholics tended to

be more critical of Baconianism as a scientific method as well. They argued that its empiricism led to materialism (only what we know by the senses is real) and to hedonism (*good* and *evil* are just names we give to whatever causes sensations of pain and pleasure). (See George H. Daniels, *American Science in the Age of Jackson* [New York: Columbia University Press, 1968], 68, 79, 83, 84.) Catholics may have been more sensitized to the tendency of empiricism to lead to materialism because in France, that is precisely where it *did* lead. As Henry May explains, in Catholic France, Newtonian physics was interpreted to imply "a self-sufficient world machine of matter and motion"—thus supporting materialism. By contrast, in Protestant England, the Newtonian system led to an image of the universe as a cosmic machine requiring a Maker—thus supporting religion (May, *Enlightenment in America*, 108, 110).

18. Cited in Robert Richardson, *Memoirs of Alexander Campbell*, vol. 1 (1868), at http://www.mun.ca/rels/restmov/texts/rrichardson/mac/MAC103.HTM, emphasis in original.

19. Cited in Nathan Hatch, *The Democratization of American Christianity* (New Haven, Conn.: Yale University Press, 1991), 169, 176, 177.

20. Cited in Michael Casey, "The Origins of the Hermeneutics of the Churches of Christ. Part Two: The Philosophical Background," *Restoration Quarterly* 31, no. 4 (1989): 193-206.

21. Cited in Hatch, *Democratization of American Christianity*, 163.

22. Cited in Stephen E. Broyles, "James Sanford Lamar and the Substructure of Biblical Interpretation in the Restoration Movement," *Restoration Quarterly* 29, no. 3 (1987), 143-151, emphasis added; also available online at http://www.stephenbroyles.com/J.%20S.%20 Lamar.htm.

23. In fact, Campbell added, he didn't trust his *own* judgments of a week ago, or even a day ago, but remained "on my guard" against *any* outside influence as he approached the Scripture completely fresh each day (cited in Hatch, *Democratization of American Christianity*, 179).

24. Walter H. Conser, Jr., *God and the Natural World: Religion and Science in Antebellum America* (Columbia: University of South Carolina Press, 1993), 72.

25. For historians of science, I want to clarify that I am not discussing Bacon himself but only the way his thought was interpreted and applied by eighteenth- and nineteenth-century American evangelicals.

26. When one reads the Bible as a random collection of data to be mined, "one does not so much read it consecutively for its own sake as ransack it for data bearing on a particular question" (Broyles, "James Sanford Lamar and the Substructure of Biblical Interpretation in the Restoration Movement").

27. C. S. Lewis, "On the Reading of Old Books," in *God in the Dock: Essays on Theology and Ethics,* ed. Walter Hooper (Grand Rapids, Mich.: Eerdmans, 1970).

28. Among nineteenth-century evangelicals, there were some who tried to stand against the anti-creedal implications of Baconianism—for example, the Old School Presbyterians. They abhorred the attempt by Campbell's "Christian" movement to do away with all systematic treatises, because they adamantly wished to retain their *own* existing confessions and statements of faith. But having adopted the Baconian model themselves, how could they avoid its implications?

Some tried to have their cake and eat it too by drawing a parallel to science: Just as a scientist equips himself by studying precedents, they said, so the theologian should study preexisting systems and creeds simply as background information. Thus James Alexander wrote that a theological system is "a simple *hypothesis,* an approximation to the truth, and a directory for future inquiries" (cited in Bozeman, *Protestants in the Age of Science*, 152-153). Yet this strategy reduced existing theological statements to mere hypotheses for generating new discoveries. In this way, the logic of induction served to undercut doctrinal authority even among champions of orthodoxy.

29. "Not taking any chances, however, most sixteenth- and seventeenth-century Protestant groups doubly fortified their positions by drawing up creeds that effectively precluded private interpretations" (Marsden, "Everyone One's Own Interpreter?" 80).

30. Cited in Hatch, *Democratization of American Christianity*, 180.

31. Ibid., 81. For example, sentiment against creeds was so strong in 1845 that the Baptists who founded the Southern Baptist Convention refused to write a statement of beliefs, saying they would follow "no creed but the Bible."

32. Of course, the hypothetico-deductive method itself has been subject to critique and modifications, and there have been ongoing debates over how to define the scientific method:

Percy Bridgman's operationalism, Michael Polanyi's personal knowledge, Karl Popper's falsificationism, Imre Lakatos's research programs, Thomas Kuhn's paradigm shifts. These are reviewed in any basic text on the philosophy of science. A good one from a Christian perspective is Del Ratzsch, *Science and Its Limits: The Natural Sciences in Christian Perspective* (Downers Grove, Ill.: InterVarsity Press, 2000; originally published as *Philosophy of Science*).

33. Richard T. Hughes and C. Leonard Allen, *Illusions of Innocence: Protestant Primitivism in America, 1630–1875* (Chicago: University of Chicago Press, 1988), 130; see also 119.

34. Ibid., 168, 169. Similarly, E. Brooks Holifield discusses the embrace of Common Sense realism on the part of Southern theologians, and concludes, "Southern religious conservatives often claimed to be devotees purely and simply of Scripture, but their self-perception was inaccurate. . . . Religious conservatism in the Old South was always as much a matter of philosophical as of Biblical considerations" (*The Gentlemen Theologians: American Theology in Southern Culture 1795–1860* [Durham, N.C.: Duke University Press, 1978], 125).

35. Sidney Mead, *The Lively Experiment: The Shaping of Christianity in America* (New York: Harper & Row, 1963), 108.

36. Anthony Trollope, *Barchester Towers* (London: J. M. Dent, 1906), 96.

37. Mark Noll, *America's God: From Jonathan Edwards to Abraham Lincoln* (Oxford: Oxford University Press, 2002), 94.

38. Cited in Holifield, *Gentlemen Theologians*, 136-137.

39. Cited in Mark Noll, *The Scandal of the Evangelical Mind* (Grand Rapids, Mich.: Eerdmans, 1994), 89.

40. Cited in George Marsden, "The Collapse of American Evangelical Academia," in *Faith and Rationality*, ed. Alvin Plantinga and Nicholas Wolterstorff (Notre Dame, Ind.: University of Notre Dame Press, 1984), 231.

41. Allen Guelzo, "'The Science of Duty': Moral Philosophy and the Epistemology of Science in Nineteenth-Century America," in *Evangelicals and Science in Historical Perspective*, ed. David Livingstone, D. G. Hart, and Mark Noll (New York: Oxford University Press, 1999), 273.

42. John Witherspoon, "Lectures on Moral Philosophy," cited in Mark Noll, Nathan Hatch, and George Marsden, *The Search for Christian America*, expanded edition (Colorado Springs: Helmers & Howard, 1989), 90. See also Douglas Sloan, *The Scottish Enlightenment and the American College Ideal* (New York: Teachers College Press, Columbia University, 1971), 123.

43. Stow Persons, *American Minds: A History of Ideas* (New York: Henry Holt, 1958), 191. Another historian describes moral science as an "effort to offer moral theory independently of theological dogmatics" (D. H. Meyer, *The Instructed Conscience: The Shaping of the American National Ethic* [Philadelphia: University of Pennsylvania Press, 1972], 136). Holifield writes, "Morality was not dependent on Biblical revelation, which merely validated and enforced the conclusions of a sound moral philosophy" (*Gentlemen Theologians*, 127).

44. C. S. Lewis, *The Abolition of Man*.

45. Elizabeth Flower and Murray G. Murphey, *A History of Philosophy in America* (New York: Putnam, 1977), 1:234, emphasis added. Flower and Murphey are referring to Witherspoon's thought in particular, but their description applies to other forms of nineteenth-century moral science as well.

46. Turner, *Without God, Without Creed*, 59, 60.

47. George Marsden, *Understanding Fundamentalism and Evangelicalism* (Grand Rapids, Mich.: Eerdmans, 1991), 131.

48. Cited in Neal Gillespie, *Charles Darwin and the Problem of Creation* (Chicago: University of Chicago Press, 1979), 14.

49. George Marsden, *The Soul of the American University* (New York: Oxford University Press, 1994), 129, 199. For a discussion of evangelicals' embrace of Baconian ideals of "free inquiry," how they treated the disciplines as essentially autonomous, and how these same tactics were turned against them to introduce anti-Christian philosophies, see especially pages 85, 120, 154-155, and chapter 7.

50. "Darwin's rejection of special creation was part of the transformation of biology into a positive [positivistic] science, one committed to thoroughly naturalistic explanations based on material causes and the uniformity of nature" (Gillespie, *Charles Darwin and the Problem of Creation*, 19). Many historians treat the conflict as though it centered on the Baconian rejection of speculative hypotheses (e.g., Bozeman, *Protestants in the Age of Science*, 166-169), and that

was a genuine factor as well. Historian John Hedley Brooke explains, "These hypothetico-deductive structures were very effective, but they transgressed a popular perception of Baconian science. It meant that Darwin's theory would be attacked, and not just by clergymen, for its philosophical license. . . . In his *Origin of Species,* Darwin repeatedly wrote that natural selection 'could explain', 'might explain' phenomena previously inscrutable. This laid him open to the objection that he was launching a speculative programme rather than providing rigorous science. . . . Huxley himself once conceded that if there were a weak point in Darwin's armour it was that the transformation of one species into another could not be directly observed. . . . Darwin had introduced his assertions with statements like 'I do not doubt', 'it is not incredible', 'it is conceivable'. 'What new words are these', [Samuel] Wilberforce asked, 'for a loyal disciple of the true Baconian philosophy?'" (from a lecture delivered in the Queen's Lecture Theatre, Emmanuel College, Cambridge, on Monday, February 26, 2001 [no title given], at http://www.st-edmunds.cam.ac.uk/cis/brooke/lecture0.html).

51. Edward A. Purcell, Jr., *The Crisis of Democratic Theory: Scientific Naturalism and the Problem of Value* (Lexington: University of Kentucky Press, 1973), 8-9. For a good half century after Darwin, the majority of those who considered themselves Darwinians actually placed the theory within a philosophical context of purpose and progress. See Nancy Pearcey, "You Guys Lost: Is Design a Closed Issue?" in *Mere Creation,* ed. William A. Dembski (Downers Grove, Ill.: InterVarsity Press), 73-92.

52. Mark Noll and David Livingstone, eds., *B. B. Warfield—Evolution, Science, and Scripture: Selected Writings* (Grand Rapids, Mich.: Baker, 2000), 29.

53. McCosh regarded even natural evolutionary processes as merely the unfolding of a design that God had front-loaded into the creation. Marsden, *Soul of the American University,* 203-204.

54. This is Gillespie's interpretation of Gray. See *Charles Darwin and the Problem of Creation,* 111-114. A good discussion of Darwinism as a worldview can be found in John Greene, *Science, Ideology, and Worldview: Essays in the History of Evolutionary Ideas* (Los Angeles: University of California Press, 1981).

55. Charles Hodge, *What Is Darwinism? And Other Writings on Science and Religion,* ed. Mark Noll and David Livingstone (Grand Rapids, Mich.: Baker, 1994), 92, 155.

56. Phillip E. Johnson, *The Right Questions* (Downers Grove, Ill.: InterVarsity Press, 2002), 61-62. On a similar note, J. P. Moreland and William Lane Craig write that the debate "is not merely one about scientific fact. It never has been, because beginning with Darwin himself, the creation-evolution controversy has significantly been a debate about philosophy of science: Should theology directly interact and enter into the very fabric of science or should science adopt methodological naturalism?" Moreland and Craig then list various ways in which religious or theological concepts may function as control beliefs guiding the formation of testable hypotheses in science (J. P. Moreland and William Lane Craig, *Philosophical Foundations for a Christian Worldview* [Downers Grove, Ill.: InterVarsity Press, 2003], 354-356).

57. Gilman, *The Launching of a University* (1906), cited in Jon Roberts and James Turner, *The Sacred and the Secular University* (Princeton, N.J.: Princeton University Press, 2000), 105-106.

58. Friedrich Heinrich Jacobi, cited in Marty, *Modern Schism,* 41.

59. Douglas Sloan, *Faith and Knowledge: Mainline Protestantism and American Higher Education* (Louisville: Westminster John Knox, 1994), 23.

60. Marsden, *Understanding Fundamentalism and Evangelicalism,* 145, emphasis added.

61. The British theologian John Henry Newman enumerated some of those undeniable items of experience: "Of course we all believe, without any doubt, that we exist; that we have an individuality and identity all our own, that we think, feel, and act." We are also sure that "we have a present sense of good and evil, of a right and a wrong, of a true and a false." Finally, "We are sure beyond all hazard of a mistake that our own self is not the only being existing; that there is an external world." Newman concludes: "On all these truths we have an immediate and an unhesitating hold" (John Henry Newman, *An Essay in Aid of a Grammar of Assent* [1870; reprint Garden City, N.Y.: Doubleday, 1955], 148-150).

62. "Common Sense had a special appeal in America because it purported to be an anti-philosophy" (Marsden, "Everyone One's Own Interpreter?" 82).

63. Reid, *Inquiry,* 1.4.

64. Ibid., 7.4.

65. Cited in Bozeman, *Protestants in the Age of Science,* 58-59.

66. Noll, *Scandal of the Evangelical Mind,* 88, emphasis added.

67. Marsden, *Understanding Fundamentalism and Evangelicalism,* 151; see also chapter 5. Marsden designates the two groups the "Warfieldians" and the "Kuyperians."

68. Schaeffer studied at Westminster Theological Seminary under J. Gresham Machen, from whom he learned the Old Princeton tradition of Common Sense realism. He also studied under Cornelius Van Til, from whom he learned the Dutch neo-Calvinism of Kuyper and Dooyeweerd. In addition, after he moved to Europe, he was influenced by the Dutch art professor Hans Rookmaaker, who had come to faith in a Nazi prison camp, where he was tutored by a fellow prisoner, J. P. A. Mekkes, a student of Dooyeweerd. Schaeffer explains how he resolves these two approaches, not so much in theory as in practice, in "A Review of a Review," *The Bible Today,* May 1948, at http://www.pcanet.org/history/documents/schaefferreview.html. See also Francis Schaeffer, *The God Who Is There,* in *The Complete Works of Francis A. Schaeffer,* vol. 1 (Wheaton, Ill.: Crossway, 1982), 137-138. Analyses of Schaeffer's apologetic method can be found in Gordon Lewis, "Schaeffer's Apologetic Method," in *Reflections on Francis Schaeffer,* ed. Ronald Ruegsegger (Grand Rapids, Mich.: Zondervan, 1986); and Kenneth Boa and Robert Bowman, *Faith Has Its Reasons: An Apologetics Handbook* (Colorado Springs: NavPress, 2001).

69. Roy Clouser, *The Myth of Religious Neutrality: An Essay on the Hidden Role of Religious Belief in Theories* (Notre Dame, Ind.: University of Notre Dame Press, 1991), 69, emphasis added.

70. Herman Dooyeweerd, *In the Twilight of Western Thought: Studies in the Pretended Autonomy of Philosophical Thought* (Nutley, N.J.: Craig, 1972), 18.

71. Alvin Plantinga, *Warrant and Proper Function* (New York: Oxford University Press, 1993), especially chapter 5, "Perception." Thomas Reid wrote, "Our senses, our memory and our reason, are all limited and imperfect—this is the lot of humanity: but they are such as the Author of our being saw to be best fitted for us in our present state" (*Essays on the Intellectual Powers of Man,* 2.22).

72. Udo Middelmann, *Proexistence: The Place of Man in the Circle of Reality* (Downers Grove, Ill.: InterVarsity Press, 1974), 62.

73. Paul Davies, "Was Einstein Wrong?" *Prospect,* April 2003, at http://www.prospect-magazine.co.uk/ArticleView.asp?accessible=yes&P_Article=11889.

74. David Hume, *An Inquiry Concerning Human Understanding* (1748; reprint, LaSalle, Ill.: Open Court, 1956), 4.2, page 34.

75. Eugene Wigner, "The Unreasonable Effectiveness of Mathematics in the Natural Sciences," in *Mathematics: People, Problems, Results,* ed. Douglas M. Campbell and John C. Higgins, vol. 3 (Belmont, Calif.: Wadsworth, 1984), 117. See also Nancy Pearcey, "Mind Your Mathematics: A Two-Part Series on the Role of Mathematics in Science," *Bible-Science Newsletter,* March and April 1990; for a later treatment, see *Soul of Science,* chapters 6 and 7.

76. Morris Kline, *Mathematics: The Loss of Certainty* (New York: Oxford University Press, 1980), 35.

77. Plantinga, *Warrant and Proper Function,* 136.

78. Cited in Plantinga, *Warrant and Proper Function,* 50.

79. Hume, *A Treatise of Human Nature,* ed. L. A. Selby-Bigge (Oxford: Oxford University Press, 1978), 1.4.6, page 252.

80. See appendix 2 for more detail on Eastern and New Age thought.

81. Daniel Dennett, in *Freedom Evolves* (New York: Viking, 2003), concedes that genuine or pure altruism—doing good for another without any expectation of good for oneself—may be unattainable through natural selection. Evolution can give rise only to what he calls "pseudo-altruism"—a kind of far-sighted self-interest that recognizes the long-term benefits of cooperation and even of (temporary) self-sacrifice (196, 217).

82. Whether the nonbeliever is a brilliant professor or an uneducated dockworker, Schaeffer wrote, "you are facing a man in tension; and it is this tension which works on your behalf as you speak to him" (*The God Who Is There,* in *Complete Works,* vol. 1, 133). "If the man before you were logical to his non-Christian presuppositions, you would have no point of communication with him. . . . But in reality no one can live logically according to his own non-Christian presuppositions, and consequently, because he is faced with the real world and himself, in *practice* you will find a place where you can talk. . . . The nearer he is to the real world, the more illogical he is to his presuppositions" (ibid., 137, emphasis in original).

83. John Gray, review of *Freedom Evolves*, by Daniel Dennett, *The Independent* online, February 8, 2003, at http://enjoyment.independent.co.uk/books/reviews/story.jsp?story=376373.

84. John Gray, "Exposing the Myth of Secularism," *Australian Financial Review*, January 3, 2003, at http://afr.com/review/2003/01/03/FFX9CQAJFAD.html.

85. Plantinga's books include *Warrant: The Current Debate; Warrant and Proper Function;* and *Warranted Christian Belief* (New York: Oxford University Press, 1993, 1993, and 2002, respectively). The phrase cited is from *Warrant and Proper Function,* 13.

86. James Turner, "The Evangelical Mind Awakens," *Commonweal,* January 15, 1999.

87. The Yale historian was Jon Butler. See Darryl Hart, "What's So Special About the University, Anyway?" in *Religious Advocacy and American History,* ed. Bruce Kuklick and D. G. Hart (Grand Rapids, Mich.: Eerdmans, 1997), 137.

88. Marty, *Modern Schism,* 98, 135, 140.

89. Ibid., 98.

90. Cited in ibid., 129-130.

91. Richard Hofstadter, *Anti-Intellectualism in American Life* (New York: Random House, 1966), 87, emphasis added.

CHAPTER 12: HOW WOMEN STARTED THE CULTURE WAR

1. Peter Berger, *Facing Up to Modernity: Excursions in Society, Politics, and Religion* (New York: Basic Books, 1977), 133.

2. The article was by Sarah Grimké, cited in Carroll Smith-Rosenberg, "Beauty, the Beast, and the Militant Woman," in *Disorderly Conduct: Visions of Gender in Victorian America* (New York: Oxford University Press, 1985), 125.

3. Sarah Grimké, "Letters on the Equality of the Sexes, Addressed to Mary S. Parker, President of the Boston Female Anti-Slavery Society, 1837; Letter I: The Original Equality of Woman," at http://www.pinn.net/~sunshine/book-sum/grimke3.html.

4. Leon Podles, *The Church Impotent: The Feminization of Christianity* (Dallas: Spence, 1999), ix, emphasis added. On sex ratios in early America, see Roger Finke and Rodney Stark, *The Churching of America 1776–1990: Winners and Losers in Our Religious Economy* (New Brunswick, N.J.: Rutgers University Press, 1992), 33-35, 66-67. On sex ratios in contemporary America, see Christian Smith, with Michael Emerson, Sally Gallagher, Paul Kennedy, and David Sikkink, *American Evangelicalism: Embattled and Thriving* (Chicago: University of Chicago Press, 1998), 80, which contains the following findings from a 1996 survey on the percentage of men versus women in various branches of the American church:

	Male	Female
Evangelicals	43	57
Fundamentalists	35	65
Mainline Protestant	34	66
Liberal Protestant	33	67
Catholic	30	70

Exactly *when* women began to predominate in Christianity has been much debated. In *The Rise of Christianity* (Princeton, N.J.: Princeton University Press, 1996), Rodney Stark claims that Christianity attracted more women than men right from the first century. He writes that "Christianity was unusually appealing to pagan women" because in the Christian subculture women enjoyed far higher status than in the Greco-Roman world at large: Christianity recognized women as equal to men, children of God with the same supernatural destiny. Moreover, he says, the Christian moral code prohibiting polygamy, divorce, birth control, abortion, infanticide, etc., enhanced the dignity and well-being of women.

In contrast, Podles claims that "before the year 1200, men and women played an equal role in the life of the church. . . . Not until the High Middle Ages did something happen to the gender balance of the Church" (*Church Impotent,* 101). Finally, in America, Jon Butler sees a change in the years leading up to the First Great Awakening: "Between 1680 and 1740 a new spiritual couple emerged in New England, the member wife and the nonmember, or delayed-member, husband. Women made up the majority of members in most New England established churches in the 1680s. By the 1720s women dominated membership in virtually all known New England churches" (*Awash in a Sea of Faith: Christianizing the American People* [Cambridge, Mass.: Harvard University Press, 1990], 170).

5. Podles, *Church Impotent,* ix.

6. This chapter draws heavily on two journal articles: Nancy Pearcey, "Is Love Enough? Recreating the Economic Base of the Family," *The Family in America* 4, no. 1 (January 1990); and Nancy Pearcey, "Rediscovering Parenthood in the Information Age," *The Family in America* 8, no. 3 (March 1994). A combined and updated version of that material was delivered as a keynote address at "Gender and Faith: An Examination of Women's Roles in Society," a conference sponsored by the Francis Schaeffer Institute at Covenant Theological Seminary, February 2001.

7. Carl N. Degler, *At Odds: Women and the Family in America from the Revolution to the Present* (New York: Oxford University Press, 1980), 5.

8. Ferdinand Lundberg and Marynia F. Farnham, *Modern Woman, the Lost Sex* (New York: Grosset & Dunlap, 1947), 97.

9. Alice S. Rossi, "Social Roots of the Woman's Movement," in *The Feminist Papers,* ed. Alice S. Rossi (New York: Columbia University Press, 1973), 250. See also Lundberg and Farnham, *Modern Woman, the Lost Sex,* 130-131.

10. Degler, *At Odds,* 365. Degler notes that women were also "quite capable of taking over the business temporarily when their husbands traveled out of town." See also Ann Douglas, *The Feminization of American Culture* (New York: Knopf, 1977), 51. "Since a widow is by definition a woman suddenly deprived of male support, the opportunities her culture affords her, the attitude it adopts toward her, are especially revealing of its stance toward women more generally."

11. Dorothy Sayers, *Are Women Human?* (Grand Rapids, Mich.: Eerdmans, 1971), 43. Anthropologists sometimes dismiss the importance of women's work in traditional societies, classifying it as "household management." What they fail to understand is that when productive work is carried out in the home, household management *is* the management of the public economy. There is no dichotomy between public and private (Ruth Bleier, *Science and Gender: A Critique of Biology and Its Theories on Women* [New York: Pergamon Press, 1984], 148).

12. Gordon S. Wood, *The Creation of the American Republic, 1776–1787* (Chapel Hill: University of North Carolina Press, 1969). "The sacrifice of individual interests to the greater good of the whole formed the essence of republicanism" (53). "The representatives of the people would not act as spokesmen for private and partial interests, but all would be 'disinterested men, who could have no interest of their own to seek,' and 'would employ their whole time for the public good; then there would be but one interest, the good of the people at large'" (59, citing the Boston *Independent Chronicle,* July 10, 1777).

13. E. Anthony Rotundo, *American Manhood: Transformations in Masculinity from the Revolution to the Modern Era* (New York: Basic Books, 1993), 2, 12-14.

14. John Demos, *Past, Present, and Personal: The Family and the Life Course in American History* (New York: Oxford University Press, 1986), 44-47.

15. Maxine L. Margolis, *Mothers and Such: Views of American Women and Why They Changed* (Berkeley: University of California Press, 1984), 12-13, 18-22, 60.

16. John R. Gillis, *A World of Their Own Making: Myth, Ritual, and the Quest for Family Values* (New York: HarperCollins, 1996), 183.

17. Cited in ibid., 186.

18. See Robert Young, *Darwin's Metaphor: Nature's Place in Victorian Culture* (Cambridge: Cambridge University Press, 1981).

19. See Christopher Lasch, *Haven in a Heartless World: The Family Besieged* (New York: Basic Books, 1979). It should be noted that these changes happened gradually, and occurred in certain geographical areas and demographic groups earlier than in others. The Industrial Revolution took root first in the Northeast, which means that the social effects described in this chapter appeared there first. In the South, because of the plantation system with its separate slave culture, industrialization took place much later. Finally, through the end of the nineteenth century America always had a frontier moving steadily westward, so that a large segment of the nation remained in frontier conditions, with trappers, hunters, and small farmers. As we saw in chapter 9, in 1850 less than half the continent was even settled, while the eastern states already had a highly developed, two-hundred-year-old culture. In short, the dominant culture was focused in the Northeast and spread to other areas and groups only as they in turn became industrialized, entered the middle class, and absorbed its ethos. That

assimilation may not have been complete for some groups. For example, the loss of women's economic function was never as complete in fact as it was in rhetoric. But the dominant ethos and its rhetoric are still important, because they set the *ideals* to which people aspire.

20. Margolis, *Mothers and Such*, 6, 33.

21. Gillis, *World of Their Own Making*, 190.

22. For a history of the effects of the Industrial Revolution on families, see Allan Carlson, *From Cottage to Work Station: The Family's Search for Harmony in the Industrial Age* (San Francisco: Ignatius, 1993).

23. Douglas, *Feminization of American Culture*, 51.

24. Ibid.

25. See Wood, *Creation of the American Republic*.

26. Rotundo, *American Manhood*, 11-26, 227, 245-246. "Our current notion of a competitive person is a recent historical development. The word *competitive* did not even enter the English language until the early nineteenth century. When it did, it applied to situations ('competitive examination') or institutions ('competitive societies'), not to individuals. Nineteenth-century men and women did not have a language to describe in positive (or even neutral) terms a person who relished contest."

27. Lesslie Newbigin, *Foolishness to the Greeks: The Gospel and Western Culture* (Grand Rapids, Mich.: Eerdmans, 1986), 109.

28. Cited in Glenna Matthews, *"Just a Housewife": The Rise and Fall of Domesticity in America* (New York: Oxford University Press, 1987), 22. Peter Berger notes that both family and church were employed in a strategy for "'containing' the disruptive effects of modernization." These two institutions offered "shelter to the individual from the alienating forces of modernization." It is significant, Berger goes on, that in our own times, "it is precisely these two institutions that have been the major targets of the 'adversary culture' of the intellectuals" (*Facing Up to Modernity*, 65).

29. Kenneth Keniston and the Carnegie Council on Children, *All Our Children: The American Family Under Pressure* (New York: Harcourt Brace, 1977), 10.

30. Cited in Degler, *At Odds*, 31. See also Barbara Welter, "The Cult of True Womanhood: 1820–1860," in *The American Family in Social-Historical Perspective*, ed. Michael Gordon (New York: St. Martin's Press, 1973).

31. Rotundo, *American Manhood*, 18.

32. Cited in Michael Kimmel, *Manhood in America: A Cultural History* (New York: The Free Press, 1996), 176.

33. Douglas, *Feminization of American Culture*, 18. When churchmen wished to portray the Christian graces, they frequently used feminine examples, says Donald M. Scott: "Christian love was warm and caring, best exemplified by the selfless and sometimes suffering, but always receiving and forgiving, mother" (Donald M. Scott, *From Office to Profession: The New England Ministry, 1750–1850* [Philadelphia: University of Pennsylvania Press, 1978], 142).

34. Cited in Douglas, *Feminization of American Culture*, 17.

35. Joel Hawes, quoted in ibid., 113.

36. Cited in Nancy F. Cott, *The Bonds of Womanhood: "Woman's Sphere" in New England, 1780–1835* (New Haven, Conn.: Yale University Press, 1977), 129-130.

37. Ibid., 86, emphasis added.

38. Douglas, *Feminization of American Culture*, 75.

39. Cited in James Turner, *Without God, Without Creed: The Origins of Unbelief in America* (Baltimore: Johns Hopkins University Press, 1985), 203.

40. Frances Willard, cited in Matthews, *"Just a Housewife,"* 86.

41. Cited in Christopher Lasch, *Women and the Common Life: Love, Marriage, and Feminism*, ed. Elisabeth Lasch-Quinn (New York: Norton, 1997), 97.

42. Cited in Robert Smuts, *Women and Work in America* (New York: Columbia University Press, 1959), 129-130. Moreover, they argued, homemaking gives women skill in the management of practical affairs, and isn't the work of government merely homemaking on a larger scale? In the 1850s Theodore Parker defined the political economy as "national housekeeping" and asked, "Does any respectable woman keep house so badly as the United States?" (cited in Matthews, *"Just a Housewife,"* 88).

43. Cited in Cott, *Bonds of Womanhood*, 148.

44. Mary Ryan, *Womanhood in America: From Colonial Times to the Present,* 3rd ed. (New York: Franklin Watts, 1983), 150.

45. "The most vivid result of slavery (to which abolitionists turned again and again) was a system of lust, of unleashed, illicit sexuality. Slavery made the female slave the helpless victim of the master's insatiable sexual desires" (Scott, *From Office to Profession,* 90). For example, Sarah Grimké wrote with horror and indignation of a young slave woman, "remarkable for her beauty and intelligence," sold to an "ugly-looking bachelor" for a sum of $7,000 ("Letters on the Equality of the Sexes, Addressed to Mary S. Parker, President of the Boston Female Anti-Slavery Society, 1837; Letter VIII: On the Condition of Women in the United States," at http://www.pinn.net/~sunshine/book-sum/grimke3.html).

46. Ryan, *Womanhood in America,* 130.

47. Degler, *At Odds,* 287, 282, 283.

48. Rotundo, *American Manhood,* 25.

49. Cited in Degler, *At Odds,* 377.

50. Cited in ibid., 378-379.

51. The classic treatment of the change in the meaning of virtue is Ruth H. Bloch, "The Gendered Meanings of Virtue in Revolutionary America," *Signs* 13 (1987): 37-58.

52. Cited in Rotundo, *American Manhood,* 172.

53. Ibid., 25ff.

54. Cited in Kimmel, *Manhood in America,* 169.

55. Steven Mintz and Susan Kellogg, *Domestic Revolutions: A Social History of American Family Life* (New York: The Free Press, 1988), 117.

56. Matthews, *"Just a Housewife,"* 80-81. Twain himself married a woman who was determined to "sivilize" him: "Livy Clemens undertook to refine her rough-hewn husband as best she could, curbing his penchant for colorful profanity, his habit of eating, writing, and smoking in bed, his heavy drinking, and his spendthrift ways. Like the women in Huck Finn's life, Livy Langdon Clemens had set out to 'sivilize' him against his will. To keep domestic peace, Clemens endured his wife's insistence that he adapt to the niceties of middle-class morality; but he resented in himself the resulting hypocrisy he found blatant in the culture around him" (D. Bruce Lockerbie, *Dismissing God: Modern Writers' Struggle Against Religion* [Grand Rapids, Mich.: Baker, 1998], 114).

57. Cited in Rotundo, *American Manhood,* 229.

58. Rotundo, ibid., 229, 254.

59. Thomas Wentworth Higginson, "Saints and Their Bodies," cited in Kimmel, *Manhood in America,* 177.

60. Cited in ibid., 179.

61. The quotation is from Fred Smith, founder of the Men and Religion Forward Movement, cited in ibid., 180. See also Podles, *Church Impotent,* 158.

62. Cited in Lasch, *Women and the Common Life,* 100.

63. See Matthews, *"Just a Housewife,"* 207ff.

64. Cited in Barbara Ehrenreich, *The Hearts of Men: American Dreams and the Flight from Commitment* (New York: Doubleday, 1983), 47.

65. Robert Griswold, *Fatherhood in America: A History* (New York: Basic Books, 1993), 99.

66. Mintz and Kellogg, *Domestic Revolutions,* 117, 195-196. See also Demos, *Past, Present, and Personal,* 61.

67. David Eggebeen and Peter Uhlenberg, cited in Griswold, *Fatherhood in America,* 229.

68. Cited in Christopher Lasch, *The New Radicalism in America, 1889–1963: The Intellectual as a Social Type* (New York: Vintage, 1965), 58.

69. Nancy Pearcey, "War on the Family: How Social Darwinism Weakened the Home," *Bible-Science Newsletter,* January 1990. Notice the contempt that Social Darwinists expressed for both women's character and women's environment (i.e., the home). Home life was denounced as a drag on evolutionary development. As Matthews puts it, Herbert Spencer's theory of social Darwinism made the home "utterly irrelevant to human progress. Male struggle outside the home is the engine of change" (*"Just a Housewife,"* 121). Darwin's explanation of male superiority was slightly different. He proposed that from their savage beginnings males became strong by fighting over females (sexual selection instead of natural selection). While modern man did not literally fight for a mate, he did continue to struggle to maintain himself

and his family, which increases his mental powers. (It should be remembered that no one in the 1800s understood the mechanism of inheritance, and most assumed that males passed on more of their acquired traits to their sons, and females to their daughters.)

70. See Matthews, *"Just a Housewife,"* 131.

71. Charlotte Perkins Gilman, *The Home: Its Work and Influence,* introduction by William O'Neill (1903; reprint, Chicago: University of Illinois Press, 1972).

72. "Just as women were preceived as separated from 'real life,' so on an unarticulated level religion came to be felt as disjoined from the tangible realities of everyday life" (Turner, *Without God, Without Creed,* 81).

73. William Raspberry, "Women Taming Men," *The Washington Post,* November 24, 1993. Raspberry cites George Gilder (*Men and Marriage* [Gretna, La.: Pelican, 1986]), who defines the male nature as inherently brutish, barbarian, and war-like. By contrast, Gilder says, the female nature is shaped by the broader rhythms of her sexual functions: by the long-term commitments imposed on her through pregnancy, lactation, and infant care. The future of civilization, in Gilder's biological reductionism, depends on females accepting the task of taming men, persuading them to submit to the long-term horizons of female sexuality.

74. Dorothy Sayers, "The Human-Not-Quite-Human," in *Unpopular Opinions* (London: Victor Gollancz, 1946). For a response to abortion that takes into account historical forces affecting the family, see Nancy Pearcey, "A Plea for Changes in the Workplace," in *Pro-Life Feminism: Different Voices,* ed. Gail Grenier Sweet (Toronto: Life Cycle Books, 1985), 203-207.

75. For a discussion of the "ideal-worker" standard, see Joan Williams, *Unbending Gender: Why Family and Work Conflict and What to Do About It* (Oxford: Oxford University Press, 2002). The book includes a nice summary of the historical process described in this chapter (though the solutions offered are radical and not recommended).

76. See Nancy Pearcey, "The American Mother: Balancing Career and Family," *The World & I,* July 1990; Nancy Pearcey, "Rediscovering Motherhood," *The World & I,* May 1991; and Nancy Pearcey, "The Family that Works Together," *The World & I,* March 1989. Many Christians have also suggested measures to make the tax structure more family friendly—for example, increasing the child exemption or giving a tax credit, which would make it more financially feasible in many families for one parent to earn less and spend more time with children. Some have even proposed a "parental GI bill": Just as American men were given the GI bill to help make up for lost career time after serving in the armed forces during World War II, so parents who take time out to raise children would be given a bill to compensate for their contribution to society and to give them a boost in reentering the job market. See Don S. Browning, Bonnie J. Miller-McLemore, Pamela D. Couture, K. Brynolf Lyon, and Robert M. Franklin, *From Culture Wars to Common Ground: Religion and the American Family Debate* (Louisville: Westminster John Knox, 1997), 331.

77. Importance of Job Characteristics, By Age Group:

% Very Important	21-29	30-39	40-49	50-59
Schedule which allows family time	82	82	67	68
Relations with co-workers	72	75	74	82
Doing challenging work	76	78	80	76
Job security	56	59	64	53
Work which helps society or my community	40	50	35	40
A high salary	46	45	46	33
High prestige or status	27	26	24	22

Source: 2000 Life's Work Survey by Radcliffe Public Policy Center. See Mark Baumgartner, "On the Daddy Track: Fathers Opt for More Time with Families," ABCNews.com, June 15, 2001.

Several additional surveys are cited in James Levine and Todd Pittinsky, *Working Fathers: New Strategies for Balancing Work and Family* (New York: Harcourt Brace, 1997). Surveys show that fathers experience significantly higher work/family tensions than is generally acknowledged.

78. See Nancy Pearcey, "Unlikely Entrepreneurs," *The World & I,* December 1990.

79. Scott, *From Office to Profession,* 150-151.

80. Newbigin, *Foolishness to the Greeks,* 19, 31.

81. Rachel Cusk, *A Life's Work: On Becoming a Mother* (New York: Picadore, 2001).

82. Cusk, *Life's Work,* 3.

83. The story of how my own attitudes changed profoundly through having my first child is told in Nancy Pearcey,"Why I Am Not a Feminist (Any More)," *The Human Life Review,* Summer 1987.

CHAPTER 13: TRUE SPIRITUALITY AND CHRISTIAN WORLDVIEW

1. Cited in Henry Chadwick, *Augustine: A Very Short Introduction* (Oxford: Oxford University Press, 2001), 54.
2. "Tony," in discussion with the author. The name has been changed to protect his privacy, but otherwise the story is completely true and accurate.
3. Wurmbrand later founded Voice of the Martyrs to minister to believers around the globe who are persecuted for their faith. See www.persecution.com. His best-known books are *Tortured for Christ* (Middlebury, Ind.: Living Sacrifice, 1969), and *In God's Underground* (London: W. H. Allen, 1968), which describe his years in captivity. His testimony before the Senate is at http://www.christianmonitor.org/Testimony/Wurmbrand.html.
4. I don't have the space here to treat the problem of evil, or what theologians call "theodicy" (how can a good God allow evil and suffering?), but readers may wish to see how I dealt with that question in "Does Suffering Make Sense?" chapter 21 in *How Now?* The related question of the origin of sin and evil is discussed in "A Snake in the Garden," chapter 20 in *How Now?*
5. Francis Schaeffer, *True Spirituality,* in *The Complete Works of Francis A. Schaeffer,* vol. 3 (Wheaton, Ill.: Crossway, 1982), 196.
6. "The order—*rejected, slain, raised*—is also the order of the Christian life of true spirituality: there is no other" (Schaeffer, ibid., 221).
7. See Gene Edward Veith, *The Spirituality of the Cross: The Way of the First Evangelicals* (St. Louis: Concordia, 1999).
8. Henry F. Lyte, "Jesus, I My Cross Have Taken," in *The Trinity Hymnal* (Atlanta: Great Commission Publications, 1998), 707.
9. Francis Schaeffer, *The Finished Work of Christ: The Truth of Romans 1–8* (Wheaton, Ill.: Crossway, 1998), 162, 161. "Sadly, it is all too possible for a Christian to give himself to the devil and become a weapon in the devil's battle against God" (171).
10. Schaeffer writes, "The Lord's work done in human energy is not the Lord's work any longer. It is something, but it is not the Lord's work" (*True Spirituality,* in *Complete Works,* vol. 3), 260.
11. Schaeffer, *No Little People,* in *Complete Works,* vol. 3, 47.
12. Douglas Sloan, *Faith and Knowledge: Mainline Protestantism and American Higher Education* (Louisville: Westminster John Knox, 1994), 23.
13. Franklin Hamline Littell, *From State Church to Pluralism: A Protestant Interpretation of Religion in American History* (Chicago: Aldine, 1962), 107-108.
14. Sloan, *Faith and Knowledge,* 241.
15. The stories told throughout this chapter were related to me by individuals from a variety of different ministries—local, statewide, national, and international.
16. Francis Schaeffer, *No Little People,* in *Complete Works,* vol. 3, 44ff.
17. H. Richard Niebuhr, *Radical Monotheism and Western Culture* (New York: Harper & Row, 1960), 140.
18. Joel Carpenter, "Contemporary Evangelicalism and Mammon: Some Thoughts," in *More Money, More Ministry: Money and Evangelicals in Recent North American History,* ed. Larry Eskridge and Mark Noll (Grand Rapids, Mich.: Eerdmans, 2000), 401.
19. Thomas Berg, "'Too Good to Be True': The New Era Foundation Scandal and Its Implications," in *More Money, More Ministry,* 383.
20. Ken Blue, *Healing Spiritual Abuse: How to Break Free from Bad Church Experiences* (Downers Grove, Ill.: InterVarsity, 1993), 70-71.
21. Schaeffer, *True Spirituality,* in *Complete Works,* vol. 3, 363.
22. David Johnson and Jeff VanVonderen, *The Subtle Power of Spiritual Abuse: Recognizing and Escaping Spiritual Manipulation and False Spiritual Authority Within the Church* (Minneapolis: Bethany, 1991); Blue, *Healing Spiritual Abuse.* Another title is George Bloomer, *Authority Abusers: Breaking Free from Spiritual Abuse* (New Kensington, Pa.: Whitaker, 1995).
    Mistreatment of employees in the workplace has spawned a new genre of secular books on workplace abuse, including Gary Namie and Ruth Namie, *The Bully at Work: What You*

Can Do to Stop the Hurt and Reclaim Your Dignity On the Job (Naperville, Ill.: Sourcebooks, 2000); and Harvey Hornstein, *Brutal Bosses and their Prey* (New York: Riverhead, 1996). Despite the sensationalized titles, many of these books offer a sober assessment of the way supervisors can and do abuse the power they hold over a worker's career and livelihood.

23. The website for the Best Christian Workplaces Institute is http://www.bcwinstitute.com.

24. Quoted in Helen Lee, "The Forty Best Christian Places to Work," *Christianity Today*, April 2003.

25. Quoted in Lee, "Forty Best Christian Places to Work." See John D. Beckett's *Loving Monday* (Downers Grove, Ill.: InterVarsity Press, 2001) for additional ideas on how businesses can enact policies that express genuine respect for workers as made in the image of God.

26. Organizations like CBMC ("Connecting Business Men to Christ") and the Christian Labour Association of Canada bring a biblical worldview perspective to the world of business and industry, demonstrating that biblical principles actually work in guiding day-by-day decisions and procedures. Other groups include Marketplace Leaders (www.marketplaceleaders.org) and the International Coalition of Workplace Ministries (www.icwm.net). For additional groups and links, see http://www.elevate2004.com/main/marketplace_ministries_links.html.

27. Jim Collins, interview (on the website for the National Association of Convenience Stores), at www.nacsonline.com/NACS/Resource/ Corporate/cm_010901a_ir.htm - 36k. See also Jim Collins, *Good to Great* (New York: HarperCollins, 2001).

28. David Aikman, "A Christian Publishing Scandal," *Charisma*, July 2002.

29. Schaeffer, *No Little People*, in *Complete Works*, vol. 3, 5.

30. Of course, there can be morally acceptable forms of collaboration that are not deceptive. For example, if an expert genuinely contributes his own ideas, he might team up with a writer to give them literary form—as long as the writer has an equal byline, so that the public is not misled into thinking the expert has suddenly acquired the writer's talents. The moral principle at stake is telling the truth and avoiding deception.

31. Jerram Barrs, personal correspondence, March 18, 2003.

32. Rick Santorum, "The Necessity of Truth," Heritage Lecture #643. August 6, 1999, at http://www.heritage.org/Research/Religion/HL643.cfm.

33. Kurt Senske, *Executive Values: A Christian Approach to Organizational Leadership* (Minneapolis: Augsburg, 2003), 11, 22, 24-26. A website promoting the book says, "Senske is president and CEO of Lutheran Social Services of the South, Inc., a multi-faceted social service agency with an annual operating budget of more than $70 million. During his tenure at LSS, he has been responsible for more than doubling the size of the agency and steering the once-troubled agency back to financial stability."

34. Lesslie Newbigin writes: "We ought not to ask each Christian in solitude to bear the burden of the real front-line warfare. . . . the Church must find ways of expressing its solidarity with those who stand in these frontier situations, who have to make decisions that may cost not only their own livelihood but also that of their families" (Newbigin, "Basic Issues in Church Union," in *We Were Brought Together*, ed. David M. Taylor [Sydney: Australian Council for World Council of Churches], 155-169; address given at the National Conference of Australian Churches, Melbourne, February 1960). Newbigin is talking about the church's imperative to support Christians who suffer for confronting secular organizations, but the principle certainly applies equally well to those who confront unethical practices within Christian organizations.

35. Many of the letters were later gathered into a book (Edith Schaeffer, *Dear Family: The L'Abri Family Letters, 1961–1986* [San Francisco: HarperCollins, 1989]).

36. John Vander Stelt, professor emeritus of philosophy at Dordt College, personal communication, May 28, 2003.

37. "What Is 'True'? The ASAP Poll," *Forbes ASAP*, October 2, 2000. Margie Haack brought this article to my attention in her presentation, "Postmodern Credo: Authenticity Rules, Hypocrisy Rots," sponsored by the Francis Schaeffer Institute at Covenant Theological Seminary, January 24, 2002.

38. Lesslie Newbigin, *The Gospel in a Pluralist Society* (Grand Rapids, Mich.: Eerdmans, 1989), 229.

39. Ibid., 188, 227.

Appendix 1: How American Politics Became Secularized

1. See E. Harris Harbison, *The Age of Reformation* (Ithaca, N.Y.: Cornell University Press, 1955), chapter 3, "The Struggle for Power."
2. Jeffrey Stout, *The Flight from Authority: Religion, Morality, and the Quest for Autonomy* (Notre Dame, Ind.: University of Notre Dame Press, 1981), 175 (emphasis added). As Quentin Skinner explains, the Reformers, as much as the Catholics, believed that "one of the main aims of government must be to maintain 'true religion' and the Church of Christ." But "as soon as the protagonists of the rival creeds showed that they were willing to fight each other to the death, it began to seem obvious to a number of *politique* theorists that, if there were to be any prospect of achieving civic peace, the powers of the State would have to be divorced from the duty to uphold any particular faith" (*The Foundations of Modern Political Thought*, 2 vols. [Cambridge: Cambridge University Press, 1978], 2:352). Thus was born the idea that to be secular was to be religiously "neutral." Such an idea was plausible back in an age when religious institutions were powerful, while the secular arena was small. Today, when secularism itself is a powerful force, we more easily recognize that it is not "neutral" at all, but a definite philosophical stance in itself.
3. The following discussion relies heavily on Nancy Pearcey, "The Creation Myth of Modern Political Philosophy," presented at the sixth annual Kuyper Lecture, the Center for Public Justice, 2000. My interpretation in turn owes much to Pierre Manent, *An Intellectual History of Liberalism* (Princeton, N. J.: Princeton University Press, 1994).
4. Paul Marshall, in discussion with the author, December 2001. Marshall is author of *Thine Is the Kingdom: A Biblical Perspective on the Nature of Government and Politics Today* (Grand Rapids, Mich: Eerdmans, 1986), and *God and the Constitution: Christianity and American Politics* (Lanham, Md.: Rowman & Littlefield, 2002).
5. Cited in Joyce Appleby, *Capitalism and a New Social Order: The Republican Vision of the 1790s* (New York: New York University Press, 1984), 36; see also 20.
6. Christian social theory accounts much better for the social dimension of human nature, based on the doctrine of the interdependent unity of the three Persons in the Trinity. This starting premise provides the metaphysical grounds for a political order that supports both the dignity of the individual *and* the authority of the social institutions necessary for a humane existence. (Refer back to chapter 4 for a discussion of the social implications of the doctrine of the Trinity.)
7. George Marsden, *Understanding Fundamentalism and Evangelicalism* (Grand Rapids, Mich.: Eerdmans, 1991), 131-132.
8. Stanley Kurtz, "The Future of 'History'," *Policy Review* 113 (June/July 2002), at //www.policy review.org/JUN02/kurtz.html.

Appendix 2: Modern Islam and the New Age Movement

1. Neo-Platonism was founded by Ammonius Saccas, who explicitly acknowledged his debt to the religion of India. Plotinus was his student, and he was so enthralled with his teacher's ideas that he determined to travel to Persia and India to study Eastern philosophies firsthand, though historians are uncertain how far he actually got in his travels.
2. Swami Krishnananda, "Plotinus," in *Studies in Comparative Philosophy,* the Divine Life Society, at http://www.swami-krishnananda.org/com/com_plot.html.
3. Paulos Gregorios, ed., *Neo-Platonism and Indian Philosophy* (New York: SUNY Press, 2001). The quotation is from the back cover. The Bahá'í faith, which became trendy in the 1970s, likewise developed from neo-Platonism. Juan R. Cole points out that "the mystical theology of Plotinus (203–269/70 A.D.), the founder of Neoplatonism, particularly influenced the cultural context of the Bahá'í writings" (*The Concept of the Manifestation in the Bahá'í Writings,* originally published as *Bahá'í Studies* monograph 9 [1982]: 1-38, by the Association for Bahá'í Studies, Ottawa, Ontario; also available online at http://www-personal.umich.edu/~jrcole/bhmanif.htm).
4. I have discussed neo-Platonism's influence on the early modern scientists extensively in *Soul of Science*. A major theme in the book is that, since the scientific revolution, scientific theories have been shaped by three basic worldviews—Aristotelian, neo-Platonic, and mechanistic. Though the mechanistic worldview has become dominant, the other two remain as minority positions within science even today.
5. For recent treatments, see Parviz Morewedge, ed., *Neoplatonism and Islamic Thought,* Studies in Neoplatonism: Ancient and Modern, vol. 5 (New York: SUNY Press, 1992); Majid Fakhry,

Al-Farabi, Founder of Islamic Neoplatonism: His Life, Works and Influence (Rockport, Mass.: Oneworld, 2002); Ian Richard Netton, *Muslim Neoplatonists: An Introduction to the Thought of the Brethren of Purity (Ikhwan Al-Safa')* (New York: Routledge/Curzon, 2003). A helpful summary by Netton can be found under "Neoplatonism in Islamic Philosophy," at http://www.muslimphilosophy.com/ip/rep/H003.htm.

6. Prominent European proponents of perennial philosophy who converted to Islam include René Guenon, Fritjof Schuon, and Martin Lings. Today the best-known Muslim proponent of perennial philosophy is Sayyed Hossien Nasr.

7. Sachiko Murata and William C. Chittik, "The Koran," at http://www.quran.org.uk/ieb_quran_chittik. htm.

8. Rodney Stark, "Why Gods Should Matter in Social Science," *Chronicle of Higher Education* 49, no. 39 (June 6, 2003): B7; also available online at http://chronicle.com/free/v49/i39/39b00701.htm. The article was adapted from Stark's book *For the Glory of God: How Monotheism Led to Reformations, Science, Witch-Hunts, and the End of Slavery* (Princeton, N.J.: Princeton University Press, 2003).

9. C. S. Lewis, *Miracles: A Preliminary Study* (1947; reprint, New York: Macmillan, 1960), 81, 82, 83, emphasis added.

APPENDIX 3: THE LONG WAR BETWEEN MATERIALISM AND CHRISTIANITY

1. See the discussion of Peirce in Paul Conkin, *Puritans and Pragmatists: Eight Eminent American Thinkers* (New York: Dodd, Mead, 1968), 244ff. Epicurus accounted for an element of chance in the physical world by assuming that atoms sometimes "swerve" in unpredictable ways, which he presented as the physical basis for a belief in free will.

2. Lucretius, *On the Nature of the Universe,* book 2, line 98.

3. Elsewhere I have written, "In the 1970s Max Delbrück delivered an address titled 'How Aristotle Discovered DNA,' in which he half playfully suggested that, if Nobel Prizes were ever awarded posthumously, Aristotle ought to receive one. The Aristotelian concept of Form, Delbrück argued, is remarkably similar to the modern concept of a genetic program—a 'preimposed plan' according to which the embryo develops into an adult" (*Soul of Science,* 236).

4. On the importance of teleological concepts of morality in contemporary philosophy, see the brief discussion of Leo Strauss in chapter 4.

5. Attacks against Epicurus were included in Tatian's *Address to the Greeks,* Justin Martyr's *Hortatory Address to the Greeks* and *On the Resurrection,* Irenaeus's *Against the Heretics,* Tertullian's *The Prescription Against Heretics,* Hippolytus's *Refutation of All Heresies,* Origen's *Contra Celsum,* Lactantius's *The Divine Institutes,* Athanasius's *On the Incarnation,* Jerome's *Against Jovinian,* and many of Augustine's writings.

6. See Margaret Osler, *Divine Will and the Mechanical Philosophy: Gassendi and Descartes on Contingency and Necessity in the Created World* (Cambridge: Cambridge University Press, 1994).

7. See Nancy Pearcey, "What's in a Name? Taxonomy and the Genesis 'Kinds'," in *Bible-Science Newsletter,* September 1985.

8. Benjamin Wiker makes a strong case that Darwinism represents the revival of Epicurean metaphysics and ethics in *Moral Darwinism* (Downers Grove, Ill.: InterVarsity Press, 2002).

9. John Dewey, *The Influence of Darwin on Philosophy and Other Essays* (New York: Henry Holt, 1910), 9. See also John Dewey, *The Quest for Certainty* (1929; reprint, New York: Putnam, 1960).

10. Cited in Nancy Pearcey, "Creating the 'New Man': The Hidden Agenda in Sex Education," *Bible-Science Newsletter,* May 1990.

11. Cited in Nancy Pearcey, "Phillip Johnson Was Right: The Unhappy Evolution of Darwinism," *World* (February 24, 2001).

12. Scientists were not the only ones to resurrect ancient Epicurean philosophy. Think of the social contract theory of Hobbes, Locke, and Rousseau (appendix 2), which begins with the premise of atomistic individualism in a "state of nature." That was an application of Epicurean atomism to society. Likewise, moral philosophers (like the utilitarians Jeremy Bentham and John Stuart Mill) began to define morality in terms of pain and pleasure, just as Epicurus had done. Utilitarianism defined morality as the greatest happiness for the greatest number, and was essentially an attempt to formulate an ethical system compatible with an atomistic view of society, in which each person's interest carries the same weight,

and the good of all is arrived at by merely tabulating the pain/pleasure ratio of the sum of autonomous individuals.

APPENDIX 4: ISMS ON THE RUN: PRACTICAL APOLOGETICS AT L'ABRI

1. N. R. Hanson, *Patterns of Discovery* (London: Cambridge University Press, 1958), 90.
2. Melvin Konner, "The Buck Stops Here," *Nature* 423 (May 8, 2003): 17-18.
3. Thomas W. Clark, review of *The Illusion of Conscious Will*, by Daniel Wegner, in *Science and Consciousness Review* (May 2002), at http://psych.pomona.edu/scr/reviews/20020508.html.
4. This is the theme of Dennett's *Consciousness Explained* (Cambridge: MIT Press, 1992). For a critique from a Christian perspective, see Angus Menuge, *Agents Under Fire: Materialism and the Rationality of Science* (Lanham, Md.: Rowman & Littlefield, 2004).
5. Galen Strawson, "'Freedom Evolves': Evolution Explains It All for You," a review of "Freedom Evolves," by Daniel C. Dennett, *The New York Times*, March 2, 2003.
6. John Searle, interview by Jeffrey Mishlove, *Thinking Allowed: Conversations on the Leading Edge of Knowledge and Discovery*, PBS, at http://www.williamjames.com/transcripts/searle.htm.
7. C. S. Lewis, *Mere Christianity* (New York: Macmillan, 1952), 20.

RECOMMENDED READING

In the following list I have not sought to give a comprehensive listing of resources (for additional titles, see the footnotes). Instead I have focused on works that are particularly helpful in giving a worldview perspective on topics addressed throughout the book. Nor have I given a complete summary of each resource, instead highlighting only the themes that contribute to a better understanding of Christian worldview.

PART I: CRAFTING A CHRISTIAN WORLDVIEW

Albert M. Wolters, *Creation Regained: Biblical Basics for a Reformational Worldview* (Grand Rapids, Mich.: Eerdmans, 1985).

> A great place to begin in understanding worldview concepts such as the structural elements of Creation, Fall, and Redemption.

C. S. Lewis, *Miracles, Mere Christianity,* and *The Abolition of Man* (all published most recently by HarperSanFrancisco, 2001); and *God in the Dock: Essays on Theology and Ethics,* ed. Walter Hooper (Grand Rapids, Mich.: Eerdmans, 1970).

> Lewis's books are indispensable for anyone who aspires to develop a Christian mind. His apologetics arguments are presented in such a lucid style that they can be understood by those with no philosophical background.

Paul Marshall with Lela Gilbert, *Heaven Is Not My Home: Living in the Now of God's Creation* (Nashville: Word, 1998).

> A delightful, colorful introduction to Christian worldview thinking. Marshall explains the framework of Creation-Fall-Redemption (he adds a fourth category: Consummation), and then explores what those categories mean for topics such as work, politics, the arts, and technology. The provocative title is meant to press home the theme that God's creation is good, even though fallen, and that our final destiny is not to live in a disembodied state but to inhabit a new earth.

James Sire, *The Universe Next Door: A Basic World View Catalog,* 3rd ed. (Downers Grove, Ill.: InterVarsity Press, 1997).

> Sire lines up various philosophies side by side, from theism to naturalism to New Age pantheism to postmodernism, comparing their answers to basic worldview questions such as: What is ultimate reality? What is human nature? Where is human history going? Working through Sire's comparisons provides a good lesson in how to do worldview analysis. He promotes similar themes in more recent titles such as *Habits of the Mind, Discipleship of the Mind,* and *Naming the Elephant.*

Arthur Holmes, *All Truth Is God's Truth* (Grand Rapids, Mich.: Eerdmans, 1977).

> A classic discussion of worldview that remains a useful introduction.

John Stott, *Your Mind Matters* (Downers Grove, Ill.: InterVarsity, 1973).
A small classic that I read myself as a recent convert to Christianity, and which has remained popular for three decades. Gives a forceful defense of the importance of the mind in Christian discipleship.

J. P. Moreland, *Love Your God with All Your Mind: The Role of Reason in the Life of the Soul* (Colorado Springs: NavPress, 1997).
Moreland makes a powerful case for the role of the mind in spiritual growth.

Gene Edward Veith, *Loving God with All Your Mind: Thinking as a Christian in the Postmodern World,* rev. ed. (Wheaton, Ill.: Crossway, 2003).
Veith urges Christians to affirm what is good about modernity, while exposing what is false and harmful. He has written several other books with a strong worldview perspective: a book on literature (*Reading Between the Lines*), one on the arts (*State of the Arts*), and another on postmodernism (*Postmodern Times*) (published by Crossway, 1990, 1991, and 1994, respectively). All are recommended as informative and accessible treatments of the impact of worldviews.

David Naugle, *Worldview: The History of a Concept* (Grand Rapids, Mich.: Eerdmans, 2002).
Naugle has done great service in tracing the source and development of the concept of "worldview" from the time the word was coined back in 1790 by Immanuel Kant ("Weltanschauung"). The term later was used by thinkers from Abraham Kuyper to Carl F. H. Henry to Francis Schaeffer to urge that Christianity must be understood as a comprehensive, holistic philosophy of life.

Abraham Kuyper, *Lectures on Calvinism* (Grand Rapids, Mich.: Eerdmans, 1931).
A good primer on Dutch neo-Calvinism. Kuyper argues that secularism is a comprehensive worldview, and that Christians will not be able to counter it unless they develop an equally comprehensive biblical worldview. He bases the call to worldview thinking on the Calvinist emphasis on God's sovereignty, which implies that the Lordship of Christ is meant to extend over all aspects of society—politics, science, the arts, and so on. This is not a theocratic vision, for the task is not to be accomplished by ecclesiastical control (that was the mistake of the Middle Ages) but rather by persuasion.

Roy Clouser, *The Myth of Religious Neutrality: An Essay on the Hidden Role of Religious Belief in Theories* (Notre Dame, Ind.: University of Notre Dame Press, 1991).
Clouser is a neo-Calvinist philosopher who shows that every theory (whether in physics, mathematics, or psychology) must make fundamental assumptions about what is ultimately real. Whatever a theory treats as ultimate, self-existent reality is essentially what plays the role of the divine. In this sense, every philosophy is religious: It takes some part of creation and absolutizes it into an ultimate principle that defines the parameters of what counts as genuine knowledge. This is the source of all forms of reductionism.

Etienne Gilson, *The Unity of Philosophical Experience: The Medieval Experiment, the Cartesian Experiment, the Modern Experiment* (San Francisco: Ignatius, 1937).
As a Thomist, Gilson writes from a very different perspective from Clouser, yet his theme is similar. The reason various philosophies fail, he shows, is that they fasten upon some aspect of creation and elevate it into an ultimate principle—and then reduce everything else to that single principle.

The Two-Realm Theory of Truth

H. Evan Runner, *The Relation of the Bible to Learning* (Toronto: Wedge, 1970).
  Runner was a powerful teacher whose influence ran primarily through his students. He taught them to be Christians *in* their work but also to develop a Christian perspective *on* the work itself, in every field. Runner opposed any form of dualism that would compartmentalize Christianity or treat any area of learning as autonomous from God's truth.

Herman Dooyeweerd, *Roots of Western Culture: Pagan, Secular, and Christian Options* (Toronto: Wedge, 1979; originally published by J. B. van den Brink, 1959); and *In the Twilight of Western Thought* (Nutley, N.J.: Craig, 1972; originally published by Presbyterian & Reformed, 1960).
  As a neo-Calvinist, Dooyeweerd offered what is arguably the most substantial systematic philosophy produced within Protestantism, and his work is worth getting to know for that reason alone. His treatment of intellectual history emphasized the two-story division of knowledge that Schaeffer later simplified and made accessible to a wider readership.

Francis Schaeffer, *Escape from Reason* (Downers Grove, Ill.: InterVarsity Press, 1977); and *The God Who Is There* (Downers Grove, Ill.: InterVarsity Press, 1998); both also available in *The Complete Works of Francis A. Schaeffer*, vol. 1 (Wheaton, Ill.: Crossway, 1982).
  In these books, Schaeffer explains the history of the two-story division of knowledge, often referred to today as the fact/value split. He also describes his highly effective apologetics method, which combined elements of both evidentialism and presuppositionalism.

Lesslie Newbigin, *Truth to Tell: The Gospel as Public Truth* (Grand Rapids, Mich.: Eerdmans, 1991); and *Foolishness to the Greeks: The Gospel and Western Culture* (Grand Rapids, Mich.: Eerdmans, 1986).
  When Newbigin returned to the West after forty years as a missionary in India, he was struck by the way the fact/value split locks Western Christianity into the private sphere of personal values. He writes persuasively on the need to present the gospel as "public truth."

Jon Roberts and James Turner, *The Sacred and the Secular University* (Princeton, N.J.: Princeton University Press, 2000).
  An informative account of how the two-story division of knowledge was expressed in a division within the university curriculum between the sciences and the humanities. Part 1 deals with the sciences, and how they were taken over by philosophical naturalism. Part 2 with the humanities, and how they adopted relativism and historicism, giving birth in our own day to postmodernism.

Douglas Sloan, *Faith and Knowledge: Mainline Protestantism and American Higher Education* (Louisville: Westminster John Knox, 1994).
  An outstanding treatment of the two-realm theory of truth. Sloan argues that believers will not be effective in introducing the *content* of a Christian worldview into the public arena (like the university) unless they first challenge the *epistemology* that defines knowledge in terms of philosophical naturalism.

Martin Marty, *The Modern Schism: Three Paths to the Secular* (New York: Harper & Row, 1969).

A good historical account of how Christian churches throughout the West gave in to a "division of labor," in which they were no longer permitted to speak to the public arena but only to private life.

Christian Smith, with Michael Emerson, Sally Gallagher, Paul Kennedy, and David Sikkink, *American Evangelicalism: Embattled and Thriving* (Chicago: University of Chicago Press, 1998).

This is a report of a massive, three-year survey of self-identified evangelicals. It found that though evangelicals are more likely than ever to be highly educated, they still largely compartmentalize their faith in the private realm of emotion and experience. The book also offers a theoretical explanation of why evangelicalism continues to thrive in modern culture, confounding sociologists who had predicted that it would die out.

David L. Schindler, ed., *Catholicism and Secularization in America: Essays on Nature, Grace, and Culture* (Huntington, Ind.: Our Sunday Visitor, Communio Books, 1990).

This collection of essays includes helpful critiques of the grace/nature division by several contemporary Catholic theologians.

Applications of Worldview

Gene Edward Veith, *God at Work: Your Christian Vocation in All of Life* (Wheaton, Ill.: Crossway, 2002).

Veith offers a good discussion of the Reformation theme of Christian vocation, which rejected the secular/sacred dualism while giving spiritual meaning to every kind of work.

Angus Menuge, ed., *Reading God's World: The Vocation of Scientist*, forthcoming from the Cranach Institute, Concordia University in Milwaukee.

A book of essays, produced by a Lutheran think tank, on the topic of why science is a valid calling for Christians.

Pierre Manent, *An Intellectual History of Liberalism* (Princeton, N.J.: Princeton University Press, 1994).

A former Marxist who converted to Christianity, Manent gives a penetrating analysis of the way early modern political philosophy was framed in terms that were specifically intended to eliminate religiously derived moral ideals as the foundation for civil society. Manent traces the development of the concept of the individual who has no goals outside the confines of the self, and of a state that has no purpose except to prevent individuals from dominating one another.

Alasdair MacIntyre, *After Virtue: A Study in Moral Theology* (Notre Dame, Ind.: University of Notre Dame Press, 1997).

An influential book that diagnoses the collapse of Enlightenment moral philosophy, while arguing for a traditional morality based on natural teleology. The only alternative today is a postmodern approach, derived from Nietzsche, that reduces morality to a mask for irrational power.

John D. Beckett, *Loving Monday: Succeeding in Business Without Selling Your Soul* (Downers Grove, Ill.: InterVarsity Press, 1998).

Influenced by Schaeffer, Beckett does a nice job of introducing worldview principles to men and women involved in business.

Udo Middelmann, *Pro-Existence: The Place of Man in the Circle of Reality* (Downers Grove, Ill.: InterVarsity Press, 1974).

Middelmann gives a Christian worldview approach to topics such as work, creativity, and private property.

Glenn Stanton, *Why Marriage Matters: Reasons to Believe in Marriage in Postmodern Society* (Colorado Springs: Pinon, 1997); Patrick Glynn, *God, The Evidence: The Reconciliation of Faith and Reason in a Postsecular World* (Rocklin, Calif.: Prima, 1997); Guenther Lewy, *Why America Needs Religion: Secular Modernity and Its Discontents* (Grand Rapids, Mich.: Eerdmans, 1996); Linda Waite and Maggie Gallagher, *The Case for Marriage: Why Married People Are Happier, Healthier, and Better Off Financially* (New York: Doubleday, 2001).

When Christian worldview principles are applied in the practical arena, they create a powerful witness to the truth of God's Word. Empirical research is accumulating to show that Christian principles work better in the real world—that they make people happier and healthier.

PART 2: DARWINISM AND INTELLIGENT DESIGN

Denyse O'Leary, *By Design or By Chance? The Growing Controversy over the Origin of Life in the Universe* (Oakville, Ontario, Canada: Castle Quay, 2004).

Written in clear, punchy prose, this book takes an objective approach aimed at the undecided, so it is a good book to hand to friends who are not Christian. A former textbook writer, O'Leary maintains an informative tone and includes lots of little text boxes with interesting tidbits.

Jacques Barzun, *Darwin, Marx, Wagner: Critique of a Heritage* (Chicago: University of Chicago Press, 1941).

Barzun's classic treatment of the philosophical issues at stake in Darwinism remains instructive. "By substituting Natural Selection for Providence, the new science . . . had to become a religion."

Jonathan Wells, *Icons of Evolution* (Washington, D.C.: Regnery, 2000).

This is a great place to begin if you are new to the topic of Intelligent Design. Wells dissects what's wrong with the images employed most frequently to support Darwinism in textbooks and museums—the images that were no doubt implanted in your mind as a child, and that your own children will encounter as well.

Phillip E. Johnson, *Reason in the Balance: The Case Against Naturalism in Science, Law, and Education* (Downers Grove, Ill.: InterVarsity Press, 1995); and *The Wedge of Truth: Splitting the Foundations of Naturalism* (Downers Grove, Ill.: InterVarsity Press, 2000).

As a lawyer, Johnson has led the way in framing the logic of the case for Intelligent Design. He is also adept at describing the broader cultural implications of Darwinian naturalism. In these two books, he highlights the way Darwinism cements the fact/value split, keeping Christianity marginalized in the private sphere.

Michael Behe, *Darwin's Black Box: The Biochemical Challenge to Evolution* (New York: Touchstone, 1996).

Behe teaches science writing as well as biochemistry, which explains why his book is written in such a clear and readable style, sprinkled with illustrations and analogies to bring it to life for the ordinary reader. Behe explicates the concept of "irreducible complexity," arguing that it cannot be accounted for by any gradualist, Darwinian process.

Neal Gillespie, *Charles Darwin and the Problem of Creation* (Chicago: University of Chicago Press, 1979).
A collection of substantial, sometimes technical essays given at the conference that
Gillespie focuses the debate over Darwinism on the question of what constitutes genuine knowledge. Darwin's goal, he shows, was to change the very definition of scientific knowledge to permit only unguided natural causes.

William A. Dembski, *The Design Inference* (Cambridge: Cambridge University Press, 1998); *Intelligent Design: The Bridge Between Science and Theology* (Downers Grove, Ill.: InterVarsity Press, 1999); *No Free Lunch: Why Specified Complexity Cannot Be Purchased Without Intelligence* (Lanham, Md.: Rowman & Littlefield, 2002).
Dembski is a prolific theorist for the Intelligent Design movement. He has developed a three-stage Explanatory Filter to formalize the criteria we employ in determining whether an event is the product of chance, law, or design.

Mere Creation, ed. William A. Dembski (Downers Grove, Ill.: InterVarsity Press, 1998).
A collection of substantial, sometimes technical essays given at the conference that officially started the Intelligent Design movement. The range of essays gives a sense of the breadth of issues involved in the debate.

Signs of Intelligence: Understanding Intelligent Design, ed. William A. Dembski and James M. Kushiner (Grand Rapids, Mich.: Baker, 2001).
A less technical collection of essays on Intelligent Design theory, suitable for a general audience.

Darwinism, Design, and Public Education, ed. John Angus Campbell and Stephen C. Meyer (Lansing: Michigan State University Press, 2003).
What makes this book significant is, first, that it was peer-reviewed and published by a mainstream university press. Second, it contains essays by both proponents and critics of Intelligent Design theory, engaging in genuine dialogue (though the pros outnumber the cons). Third, it contains some of the most recent, cutting-edge arguments.

Uncommon Dissent: Intellectuals Who Find Darwinism Unconvincing, ed. William A. Dembski (Wilmington, Del.: Intercollegiate Studies Institute, 2004).
A fascinating collection of essays by public intellectuals from various theological perspectives who explain their reasons for questioning Darwinism.

Francis Beckwith, *Law, Darwinism, and Public Education: The Establishment Clause and the Challenge of Intelligent Design* (Lanham, Md.: Rowman & Littlefield, 2003).
A brilliantly argued defense of the constitutionality of teaching Intelligent Design theory in the public schools. A thorough and comprehensive treatment of the legal issues.

Charles Thaxton, Walter Bradley, and Roger Olsen, *The Mystery of Life's Origin* (Dallas: Lewis and Stanley, 1992; originally published by Philosophical Library, 1984).
Though somewhat dated, this book still gives an excellent critique of standard origin of life theories. It also gives a clear exposition of the concept of "specified complexity" as the defining characteristic of information.

A. E. Wilder-Smith, *The Creation of Life: A Cybernetic Approach to Evolution* (Costa Mesa, Calif.: The Word for Today, 1970); *Man's Origin, Man's Destiny: A Critical Survey of the Principles of Evolution and Christianity* (Minneapolis: Bethany, 1968); *The Natural Sciences Know Nothing of Evolution* (Costa Mesa, Calif.: The Word for Today, 1981).

> With his creative and wide-ranging intellect, Wilder-Smith was the first to develop the argument for design based on information in DNA.

Guillermo Gonzalez and Jay Richards, *The Privileged Planet: How Our Place in the Cosmos Is Designed for Discovery* (Washington D.C.: Regnery, 2004).

> The argument from design used to focus on examples from the world of living things, but today there is evidence for design in the physical universe itself.

Philosophical Implications of Darwin

Hillary Rose and Steven Rose, eds., *Alas, Poor Darwin: Arguments Against Evolutionary Psychology* (London: Jonathan Cape, 2000).

> A collection of essays making the case against evolutionary psychology as nothing but pseudoscience.

Tom Bethell, "Against Sociobiology," *First Things* 109 (January 2001): 18-24.

> In his trademark elegant style, Bethell identifies the weaknesses of sociobiology and of its offshoot, evolutionary psychology.

Philip P. Wiener, *Evolution and the Founders of Pragmatism* (Gloucester, Mass.: Peter Smith, 1969; originally published by Harvard University Press, 1949).

> An older book giving a solid introduction to the way the founders of philosophical pragmatism sought to apply Darwinism to the human sciences.

Paul Conkin, *Puritans and Pragmatists: Eight Eminent American Thinkers* (New York: Dodd, Mead, 1968).

> Conkin gives a clear, thorough history of the philosophical pragmatists. Also recommended is his book on the intellectual impact of the Scopes trial, *When All the Gods Trembled: Darwinism, Scopes, and American Intellectuals* (Lanham, Md.: Rowman & Littlefield, 1998).

Louis Menand, *The Metaphysical Club: A Story of Ideas in America* (New York: Farrar, Straus, & Giroux, 2001).

> A readable and engaging account of the pragmatists' life and thought.

Nancy R. Pearcey, "Darwin's New Bulldogs," *Regent University Law Review* 13, no. 2 (2000–2001): 483-511.

> A comprehensive philosophical treatment of legal pragmatism, from Oliver Wendell Holmes to Richard Posner, explaining the central role played by Darwinian concepts.

Albert W. Alschuler, *Law Without Values: The Life, Work, and Legacy of Justice Holmes* (Chicago: University of Chicago Press, 2000).

> A critical evaluation of Oliver Wendell Holmes's legal philosophy, emphasizing his adoption of Social Darwinism.

Paul F. Boller, Jr., *American Thought in Transition: The Impact of Evolutionary Naturalism, 1865–1900* (Chicago: Rand McNally, 1969).

> This book does exactly what the title says: It describes the rise and spread of the

philosophy of evolutionary naturalism after Darwin, focusing on its broader cultural impact.

Edward A. Purcell, Jr., *The Crisis of Democratic Theory: Scientific Naturalism and the Problem of Value* (Lexington: University Press of Kentucky, 1973).
> A legal historian, Purcell shows how Darwinism led to a new naturalistic view of knowledge, in which the concept of "value" was stripped of objective content. He then traces the difficulties this caused in providing a moral basis for American democracy.

Benjamin Wiker, *Moral Darwinism* (Downers Grove, Ill.: InterVarsity Press, 2002).
> Wiker makes a strong case that Darwinism represents a revival of Epicurean metaphysics and ethics.

Richard Rorty, *Contingency, Irony, and Solidarity* (Cambridge: Cambridge University Press, 1989).
> Rejecting the Enlightenment assumption that humans are capable of a "God's-eye" view, Rorty reduces all thought to historically contingent cultural conventions. He labels his own version of postmodernism "neo-pragmatism," claiming that it merely draws out the implications in Dewey's classic pragmatism—rooted ultimately in a Darwinian view of knowledge.

PART 3: EVANGELICALISM AND ITS HISTORY

Roger Finke and Rodney Stark, *The Churching of America 1776–1990: Winners and Losers in Our Religious Economy* (New Brunswick, N.J.: Rutgers University Press, 1992).
> Written in readable, even sprightly prose, this book by two sociologists shows why evangelicalism has been such a powerful and vibrant force on the American religious scene. The authors explain why, historically, the evangelical denominations outstripped the established churches, and why evangelical groups continue to thrive and grow today.

Mark Noll, *The Scandal of the Evangelical Mind* (Grand Rapids, Mich.: Eerdmans, 1994).
> A good place to start in seeking to understand why evangelicalism has historically had a weak intellectual tradition. "The scandal of the evangelical mind is that there is not much of an evangelical mind," Noll writes, adapting the most famous line from Harry Blamires's classic book *The Christian Mind*. Focusing on fundamentalism, Pentecostalism, and dispensationalism, Noll diagnoses the negative effect these movements have had on Christian intellectual life.

Os Guinness, *Fit Bodies, Fat Minds: Why Evangelicals Don't Think and What to Do About It* (Grand Rapids, Mich.: Baker, 1994).
> A semi-popular treatment of anti-intellectualism in American evangelicalism. Guinness argues that "the real damage to evangelicals was self-inflicted," through internal trends such as pietism, primitivism, and populism.

The Bible in America: Essays in Cultural History, ed. Nathan O. Hatch and Mark A. Noll (New York: Oxford University Press, 1982); *Amazing Grace: Evangelicalism in Australia, Britain, Canada, and the United States,* ed. George A. Rawlyk and Mark A. Noll (Grand Rapids, Mich.: Baker, 1993); *Evangelicalism: Comparative Studies of Popular Protestantism in North America, the British Isles, and Beyond, 1700–1990,* ed.

Mark A. Noll, David Bebbington, and George Rawlyk (New York: Oxford University Press, 1994); *Reckoning with the Past: Historical Essays on American Evangelicalism from the Institute for the Study of American Evangelicals,* ed. D. G. Hart (Grand Rapids, Mich.: Baker, 1995); *Evangelicals and Science in Historical Perspective,* ed. David Livingstone, D. G. Hart, and Mark A. Noll (New York: Oxford University Press, 1999).

> The scholarly study of evangelicalism has exploded in recent years, and much of the best and most current work is found in collections of essays like the titles above. In recent years, a cadre of evangelical historians (Marsden, Noll, Stout, Hart, Hatch, Wacker) has grown so prolific that some have warned of a "new evangelical thesis" taking over the study of American religious history.

Mark A. Noll, *America's God: From Jonathan Edwards to Abraham Lincoln* (Oxford: Oxford University Press, 2002).

> Noll's latest and most comprehensive history of American religion. Its underlying thesis is that a specifically American evangelicalism, different from European forms of Christianity, was forged during and after the American Revolution through a unique synthesis of republicanism and Common Sense philosophy.

Iain Murray, *Revival and Revivalism: The Making and Marring of American Evangelicalism 1750–1858* (Edinburgh: Banner of Truth, 1994).

> Murray cites frequently from original sources, conveying a good firsthand sense of the revivalists' warm piety and earnest efforts to bring people to salvation. He also explains why some supporters of the revival movement later broke away, objecting to new high-pressure techniques touted as the means to guarantee sure-fire, near-mechanical results.

Richard Hofstadter, *Anti-Intellectualism in American Life* (New York: Random House, 1966).

> This older treatment still contains large elements of truth, especially in its critique of the anti-intellectual elements within evangelicalism.

David Bebbington, *Evangelicalism in Modern Britain: A History from the 1730s to the 1980s* (Grand Rapids, Mich.: Baker, 1989).

> To put American evangelicalism within a wider context, it is good to understand evangelicalism in Britain as well.

The First Great Awakening

Allen C. Guelzo, "God's Designs: The Literature of the Colonial Revivals of Religion, 1735–1760," in *New Directions in American Religious History,* ed. Harry Stout and D. G. Hart (New York: Oxford University Press, 1997).

> Guelzo surveys the literature on the First Great Awakening, explaining the interpretative slant taken by various historians. A good way to get oriented before digging into the literature itself.

Ronald Knox, *Enthusiasm: A Chapter in the History of Religion* (Notre Dame, Ind.: Notre Dame University Press, 1950).

> As a Catholic, Knox started out as a critic of pietism and evangelicalism. But after spending a decade studying figures like Wesley and Whitefield, he ended up with a profound appreciation for the evangelicals' sincere and dedicated commitment to the gospel.

Alan Heimert, *Religion and the American Mind: From the Great Awakening to the Revolution* (Cambridge, Mass.: Harvard University Press, 1966).

Heimert gives a good account of the emerging conflict between "head" and "heart" in the First Great Awakening, though his interpretation of the relationship between the awakening and the American Revolution remains controversial.

Patricia Bonomi, *Under the Cope of Heaven: Religion, Society, and Politics in Colonial America* (New York: Oxford University Press, 1986).

Bonomi stresses how the revivalists "rehearsed" themes of autonomy and popular sovereignty that contributed to the revolutionary mentality in America's drive for independence from Britain.

Nathan O. Hatch, *The Sacred Cause of Liberty: Republican Thought and the Millennium in Revolutionary New England* (New Haven, Conn.: Yale University Press, 1977).

Hatch emphasizes the identification of religion with revolutionary politics that was characteristic of the First Great Awakening. Whereas religion had traditionally concerned itself with *holiness,* religious leaders in pre-Revolutionary America became concerned with *liberty.* Whereas the enemy of religion had traditionally been identified as *heresy,* it was now identified as *tyranny.*

Harry Stout, *The Divine Dramatist: George Whitefield and the Rise of Modern Evangelicalism* (Grand Rapids, Mich.: Eerdmans, 1991); Stephen Marini, *Radical Sects of Revolutionary New England* (Cambridge, Mass.: Harvard University Press, 1982).

Both books give a somewhat critical perspective on Whitefield as the initiator of many of the trends that have become problematic in evangelicalism today—the emotionalism, the focus on celebrities, the use of commercial marketing techniques, and so on. Balance this interpretation with the more positive account given by Arnold Dallimore in *George Whitefield: God's Anointed Servant in the Great Revival of the Eighteenth Century* (Wheaton, Ill.: Crossway, 1990).

Second Great Awakening

Nathan O. Hatch, *The Democratization of American Christianity* (New Haven, Conn.: Yale University Press, 1989).

If you want to understand the history of American evangelicalism, this is the place to begin. It focuses on the Methodists, Baptists, Disciples, and other groups once dismissed as "upstarts" by the established churches, but whose form of spirituality has become in many ways the most widespread in America today.

Richard T. Hughes and C. Leonard Allen, *Illusions of Innocence: Protestant Primitivism in America, 1630–1875* (Chicago: University of Chicago Press, 1988).

An excellent description of the tendency toward "primitivism" in American evangelicalism—the idea that it is possible and desirable to throw aside centuries of church history and recover the original New Testament church.

Donald M. Scott, *From Office to Profession: The New England Ministry, 1750–1850* (Philadelphia: University of Pennsylvania Press, 1978).

A fascinating account of changes in the concept of the ministry from colonial times, when parishes were localized, communal, stable, hierarchical, and integrated into the whole of society—to the modern conception of the church as merely one marginalized segment of a society, competing for power and influence, and offering a career track for aspiring religious professionals.

Gordon S. Wood, *The Creation of the American Republic, 1776–1787* (Chapel Hill: University of North Carolina Press, 1969); and *The Radicalism of the American Revolution: How a Revolution Transformed a Monarchial Society into a Democratic One Unlike Any that Had Ever Existed* (New York: Knopf, 1992).

> An outstanding historian, Wood explains how American concepts of social order changed from the classical republicanism of the colonial period, embracing hierarchy and deference, to a post-revolutionary embrace of democratic individualism. These social and political trends influenced the church, feeding into the "democratization" of Christianity described by Hatch. For a short introduction to Wood's thought, see his essay, "Religion and the American Revolution," in *New Directions in American Religious History,* ed. Harry Stout and D. G. Hart (New York: Oxford University Press, 1997).

Joyce Appleby, *Capitalism and a New Social Order: The Republican Vision of the 1790s* (New York: New York University Press, 1984).

> In this short, readable book, Appleby describes the same trend treated by Gordon Wood—the rise of democratic individualism—while focusing more narrowly on the economic sphere.

Michael Gauvreau, "The Empire of Evangelicalism: Varieties of Common Sense in Scotland, Canada, and the United States," in Mark Noll, David Bebbington, and George Rawlyk, eds., *Evangelicalism: Comparative Studies of Popular Protestantism in North America, the British Isles, and Beyond, 1700–1990* (New York: Oxford University Press, 1994).

> This Canadian historian is particularly attuned to how evangelicalism, despite its premodern message of sin and salvation, actually contributed to the ethos of modernity.

Gary Thomas, *Revivalism and Cultural Change: Christianity, Nation Building, and the Market in the Nineteenth-Century United States* (Chicago: University of Chicago Press, 1989).

> As a sociologist, Thomas is interested in the "plausibility structures"—the social and economic changes—that rendered the evangelical theology of the revivalists more attractive to Americans than the older Calvinist theology.

Joel Carpenter, *Revive Us Again: The Reawakening of American Fundamentalism* (Oxford: Oxford University Press, 1997).

> Carpenter gives an excellent history of what happened *after* the awakenings, during the fundamentalist era. He details both the humiliating defeat of fundamentalism during the Scopes trial, and its resilience and strength in building a vibrant subculture of churches, Bible schools, summer camps, and radio programs.

Richard Quebedeaux, *By What Authority? The Rise of Personality Cults in American Christianity* (New York: Harper & Row, 1982).

> Quebedeaux offers a good discussion of the rise of celebrityism in American evangelicalism.

Alan Wolfe, *The Transformation of American Religion: How We Actually Live Our Faith* (New York: Free Press, 2003).

> A sociologist examines religion in America and concludes that "we are all evan-

gelicals now"—by which he means that the evangelical style of worship has become dominant even in non-evangelical denominations and religions. The characteristics of evangelicalism include an emphasis on emotional response, individual choice, and experiential engagement—along with a *de*-emphasis on doctrine and theology.

D. G. Hart, *That Old-Time Religion in Modern America: Evangelical Protestantism in the Twentieth Century* (Chicago: Ivan R. Dee, 2002); *The Lost Soul of American Protestantism* (Lanham, Md.: Rowman & Littlefield, 2002); *Recovering Mother Kirk: The Case for Liturgy in the Reformed Tradition* (Grand Rapids, Mich.: Baker, 2003).

　　Hart is a Presbyterian historian who gives a helpful description of the differences between confessional and evangelical churches, while arguing for the ongoing validity of the confessional church.

Evangelical Intellectual Traditions

Henry May, *The Enlightenment in America* (New York: Oxford University Press, 1976).

　　Because America started as a colony, it remained for a long time on the outskirts of intellectual life, importing most of its ideas from Europe. May gives a helpful analysis of *which* ideas successfully crossed the Atlantic and put down deep roots in the soil of the New World. Those that proved most popular in America were the ideas of the Scottish Enlightenment—which were in some ways actually *anti*-Enlightenment because they were proposed in order to defend against radical skepticism and atheism.

Norman Fiering, *Moral Philosophy at Seventeenth-Century Harvard: A Discipline in Transition* (Chapel Hill: University of North Carolina Press, 1981); D. H. Meyer, *The Instructed Conscience: The Shaping of the American National Ethic* (Philadelphia: University of Pennsylvania Press, 1972); Allen Guelzo, "'The Science of Duty': Moral Philosophy and the Epistemology of Science in Nineteenth-Century America," in *Evangelicals and Science in Historical Perspective,* ed. David Livingstone, D. G. Hart, and Mark A. Noll (New York: Oxford University Press, 1999).

　　When we hear the word *Enlightenment,* we typically think of the rise of modern science and the mechanistic worldview. But equally significant historically was the rise of a new moral philosophy (or "moral science"), which proposed a more naturalistic approach to understanding human nature. Courses on moral philosophy took the place once given to theology as the capstone of the university curriculum.

Jeffrey Stout, *The Flight from Authority: Religion, Morality, and the Quest for Autonomy* (Notre Dame, Ind.: University of Notre Dame Press, 1981).

　　Stout shows how the concept of "the secular" arose as a reaction against a century of religious warfare, which drove early modern thinkers to seek a "neutral" arena between clashing religious factions. Thus Christians themselves, by being willing to spill one another's blood, were partly the cause of the rise of secularism.

George Marsden, *Understanding Fundamentalism and Evangelicalism* (Grand Rapids, Mich.: Eerdmans, 1991); *Fundamentalism and American Culture: The Shaping of Twentieth-Century Evangelicalism, 1870–1925* (New York: Oxford University Press, 1980).

　　The doyen of evangelical historians, in these books Marsden offers an intellectual history of evangelicalism.

George Marsden, *The Soul of the American University: From Protestant Establishment to Established Nonbelief* (New York: Oxford University Press, 1994).

A comprehensive account of how American universities, most of which were founded as Christian institutions, eventually gave way to secularism. Marsden goes on to argue that today's secularized universities, which pride themselves on their diversity, have no reason to practice the deliberate exclusion of religiously based thinking.

The Secular Revolution: Power, Interest, and Conflict in the Secularization of American Public Life, ed. Christian Smith (Los Angeles: University of California Press, 2003).

Essays by sociologists who reject the old adage that when societies modernize, secularization is inevitable. Instead, these essays identify specific historical forces that were responsible for the secularization process in fields such as education, law, and science—forces that were historically contingent, and therefore potentially reversible.

Men, Women, and the Family

Nancy Pearcey, "Is Love Enough? Recreating the Economic Base of the Family," *The Family in America* 4, no. 1 (January 1990); and "Rediscovering Parenthood in the Information Age," *The Family in America* 8, no. 3 (March 1994).

The first journal article deals primarily with the effects of the Industrial Revolution on the status of women and their work in the home. The second describes the effects on men and the changing definitions of masculinity. (A taped lecture combining highlights of both articles can be obtained from the Francis Schaeffer Institute at Covenant Theological Seminary, delivered at a conference on "Gender and Faith," February 2001.)

Peter Berger, *Facing Up to Modernity: Excursions in Society, Politics, and Religion* (New York: Basic Books, 1977).

Berger describes the rise of the dichotomy between public and private spheres in modern society, explaining how both the church and the family have been privatized and marginalized.

Barbara Welter, "The Cult of True Womanhood: 1820–1860," in *The American Family in Social-Historical Perspective,* ed. Michael Gordon (New York: St. Martin's Press, 1973).

A seminal treatment of the emergence of the doctrine of "separate spheres" after the Industrial Revolution—a private sphere for women, home, and the gentler virtues, over against a public sphere of competitive individualism where men labored during the day.

Nancy F. Cott, *The Bonds of Womanhood: "Woman's Sphere" in New England, 1780–1835* (New Haven, Conn.: Yale University Press, 1977).

An excellent historical account of the doctrine of "separate spheres," sometimes called "the cult of domesticity," and its impact on women—including the rise of a new concept of femininity and a drastic constriction of the scope of women's work.

Mary Ryan, *Womanhood in America: From Colonial Times to the Present,* 3rd ed. (New York: Franklin Watts, 1983).

A good overall history of the changes in family structure brought about by the

Industrial Revolution—the reduction of women's role from producer to consumer, and at the same time the reduction of men's role from primary to secondary parent.

E. Anthony Rotundo, *American Manhood: Transformations in Masculinity from the Revolution to the Modern Era* (New York: HarperCollins, 1993); and Michael Kimmel, *Manhood in America: A Cultural History* (New York: Free Press, 1996).

Read together, these two books paint a clear picture of changing concepts of masculinity throughout American history. The Puritan concept of "communal manhood," which placed men within an organic, hierarchical community, was supplanted by the modern concept of "individual manhood," autonomous selves who create their own place and status.

Robert Griswold, *Fatherhood in America: A History* (New York: Basic Books, 1993).

As the Industrial Revolution took fathers out of the home, fatherhood was steadily devalued. Instead of passing on essential skills to prepare their children for adulthood, men were reduced to mere breadwinners, invisible throughout most of the day. With the rise of fields like child development and child psychology, a class of professionals began to take over the role of fathers in decreeing how children should be raised.

Christopher Lasch, *Haven in a Heartless World: The Family Besieged* (New York: Basic Books, 1979).

In this classic book on the history of the family, Lasch explains how it has been marginalized, privatized, and devalued in modern society. The home has been stripped of its historic functions and reduced to a place of merely emotional succor.

Allan Carlson, *From Cottage to Work Station: The Family's Search for Harmony in the Industrial Age* (San Francisco: Ignatius, 1993).

An economist, Carlson gives a good history of the effects of the Industrial Revolution on the family.

Glenna Matthews, *"Just a Housewife": The Rise and Fall of Domesticity in America* (New York: Oxford University Press, 1987).

Matthews gives a sympathetic account of the history of women's household work, focusing on the way it was devalued after the Industrial Revolution, when much of the skilled work was removed to factories.

Carl N. Degler, *At Odds: Women and the Family in America from the Revolution to the Present* (New York: Oxford University Press, 1980).

Degler gives a particularly clear account of the emergence of the double standard, whereby women were held responsible for controlling the unruly passions of men.

PART 4: APPLIED WORLDVIEW

Francis Schaeffer, *True Spirituality* (Wheaton, Ill.: Tyndale, 1979); also available in *The Complete Works of Francis A. Schaeffer,* vol. 3 (Wheaton, Ill.: Crossway, 1982).

Schaeffer speaks to the crucial need to apply Christian worldview in the personal and practical domains, so that it does not become merely an abstract set of ideas. Those who aspire to develop a Christian mind must follow Christ to the cross—accepting suffering as a means of dying to old sinful patterns of behavior, in order to be resurrected with the mind of Christ.

Francis Schaeffer, *The Finished Work of Christ: The Truth of Romans 1–8* (Wheaton, Ill.: Crossway, 1998).

In these Bible studies, Schaeffer works out in detail the message of dying to personal zeal and ambition, in order to live in Christ's resurrection power, so that we may become "life-producing machines." "We produce either life or death as people around us either accept or reject God because of what we say to them and how we live before them."

Francis Schaeffer, *No Little People: Sixteen Sermons for the Twentieth Century* (Downers Grove, Ill.: InterVarsity Press, 1974); also available in *The Complete Works of Francis A. Schaeffer*, vol. 3 (Wheaton, Ill.: Crossway, 1982).

The sermon "The Lord's Work, the Lord's Way" is particularly relevant, warning that God will not honor those who try to do His work in their own strength. Christians must demonstrate something more than sheer activism, which the world can duplicate.

Gene Edward Veith, *The Spirituality of the Cross: The Way of the First Evangelicals* (St. Louis: Concordia, 1999).

Luther said Christian spirituality is focused not on glory (that comes later, with Christ's return) but rather on the cross—on identification and participation with the sufferings of Christ, finding renewal through an inversion of the world's values.

Ken Blue, *Healing Spiritual Abuse: How to Break Free from Bad Church Experiences* (Downers Grove, Ill.: InterVarsity Press, 1993); David Johnson and Jeff VanVonderen, *The Subtle Power of Spiritual Abuse: Recognizing and Escaping Spiritual Manipulation and False Spiritual Authority Within the Church* (Minneapolis: Bethany, 1991).

The suffering that Christians encounter in this life may come through relationships. Unhealthy relationships with a spiritual dimension—e.g., in a church or parachurch ministry—have dynamics that are unique enough that some have coined the phrase "spiritual abuse." These books describe situations where leaders use their spiritual authority to control and dominate others instead of serving them—using people to meet their own needs for importance, power, and image.

Henry Cloud and John Townsend, *Boundaries: When to Say Yes, When to Say No, to Take Control of Your Life* (Grand Rapids, Mich.: Zondervan, 1992).

This book and its many sequels and tapes offer helpful guidelines from Scripture and psychology on how to create healthy relationships, in the family as well as in churches and other Christian organizations.

INDEX

STUDY GUIDE

This study guide will help you master the major worldview themes in *Total Truth*. Through additional stories, examples, and illustrations, you will gain practical experience in applying what you have learned. You will also join a "conversation" with earlier readers whose questions and comments helped to shape the material. Each chapter begins with several discussion questions to clarify and expand its central themes, then ends with a short list of review questions ("Test Yourself"), followed by suggestions for open-ended learning activities ("Continuing the Conversation"), which are especially valuable for small group study.

I am thankful to all who have contributed to the ongoing conversation about *Total Truth* since it was published, especially John Haynes, owner of Cornerstone Christian Store in Atlanta, Georgia, where I gave a presentation broadcast by C-SPAN's Book TV; the Heritage Foundation; campus groups at Stanford University, Texas A&M, and the University of Georgia; Probe Ministries; the Portico; and several public policy groups, Christian colleges, and homeschooling organizations. Online reviews have sparked a lively discussion in the blog world, thanks especially to Al Mohler, Tim Challies, and the reviewers for Stacy Harp's Mind & Media. Finally, I have been honored to receive a wealth of correspondence from readers, and though unable to respond to each personally, I am grateful to all of you who continue to keep the conversation going.

NOTE: *Questions are thematic rather than strictly sequential. Page numbers are given so you can cross reference broad themes throughout the book.*

Introduction

The Introduction lays out the unifying themes that run like so many silver threads through the tapestry of the book. Let's work through several new examples to make sure you have those threads firmly in hand before moving on. Since underlying worldview themes often bubble to the surface during times of cultural upheaval, we will begin with illustrations from the 2004 presidential election that help us to identify long-standing worldview conflicts.

The election was nothing less than "a conflict between two worldviews," pitting "faith against reason," said Jonathan Freedland in the *Guardian* (Oct. 20, 2004). In the *New York Times* (Nov. 7, 2004) Maureen Dowd fumed that moral conservatives would replace "science with religion, facts with faith." The cover of *Stanford Medicine* (Fall 2004) featured a dramatic illustration of a clergyman holding up a Bible, facing off against a white-coated scientist holding up a test tube, with the ground cracking open between them. The message? That America is becoming divided between those who believe the Bible, and those who believe in science.

1. Our worldview detectors ought to buzz loudly whenever we hear phrases like "faith against reason." How do the examples above express the fact/value split? (20-22)

The defining feature of the 2004 election was a "morality gap," said Thomas Byrne Edsall in the *Atlantic Monthly* (Jan./Feb. 2003). In the past, the left/right division in American politics was over economic issues. It was an accepted axiom that people vote their pocketbooks. But today the cutting-edge issues have to do with sex and reproduction: abortion, homosexual marriage, embryonic stem cell research, and so on. "Whereas elections once pitted the party of the working class against the party of Wall Street," the article concludes, "they now pit voters who believe in a *fixed and universal morality* against those who see moral issues, especially sexual ones, as *elastic and subject to personal choice.*"

Notice that the issue is not the *content* of morality (i.e., which actions are right or wrong) so much as the *truth status* of moral claims. Is morality a universal normative standard? Or merely a matter of subjective preference? This question lies at the heart of the cultural conflict that will continue long past the election.

2. The morality gap pits those who hold an objective view of morality against those who reduce morality to subjective "values." Explain the difference. (20)

At the Democratic National Convention, Ron Reagan, son of the former president, made a widely publicized remark about opponents of embryonic stem cell research. "Their belief is just that—an article of faith—and they are entitled to it," he said. "But it does not follow that the theology of a few should be allowed to forestall the health and well-being of the many."

What's the worldview here? Notice that people are invited to believe whatever they want—they're even "entitled to it"—so long as they are willing to hold it as a subjective "article of faith," *not* something objectively true that should be allowed to guide scientific research.

3. Which side of the morality gap is Reagan on? How can you tell? (20-21)

To be cultural missionaries, we must understand the language of the people we want to reach. A college economics textbook explains the modernist definition of *fact* and *value*:

> "Facts are objective, that is, they can be measured, and their truth tested. . . . Value judgments, on the other hand, are subjective, being matters of personal preference. . . . Such preferences are based on personal likes and feelings, rather than on facts and reasons" (*Economics for Decision Making* [D.C. Heath, 1988]).

4. How does the definition of values in this quotation differ from the way Christians typically use the term? How does this explain why we often have difficulty communicating in the public arena? (22, 176-178)

What we see in these examples is that the challenge to Christianity is much more radical than it was in the past. Secularists used to argue that religion is *false*—which meant at least we could engage them in discussions about reasons, evidence, logic, and arguments. But today secularists are much more likely to argue that religion does not have the status of a testable truth claim at all.

To get a handle on this, imagine you present your position on some subject and the other person responds, "Oh, that's just science, that's just facts, don't impose it on me." Of course, no one says that. But they *do* say, "That's just your religion, don't impose it on me." Why the difference? Because science is regarded as public truth, binding on everyone, while religion has been reduced to private feelings relevant only to those who believe it.

5. Explain how the fact/value grid functions as a gatekeeper to keep Christian perspectives out of the public square. (21-22)

"Science is a predictive discipline based on empirically falsifiable facts," says physicist Lawrence Krauss. "Religion is a hopeful discipline based on inner faith." In other words, religion is no longer even considered in the category of true or false. There's a story about a famous physicist, Wolfgang Pauli, who once told a colleague, Your theory is so bad, *it's not even wrong*. It's not even in the ballpark of possible answers. That's how religious claims are regarded today: They are not even candidates for truth.

6. *Why is the fact/value split the main reason for the "cultural captivity" of the gospel? (22)*

TEST YOURSELF:

7. *What is the difference between fundamentalism and evangelicalism? Which more closely describes your own background? (18)*

8. *In your view, are Christians today too quick to reach for political solutions? (18-19)*

9. *Explain what a worldview is. What are the biblical roots of the idea that everyone has a worldview? (23-24)*

10. *The concept of worldview "remains largely a buzzword used in the context of political discussions and fundraising for Christian parachurch organizations," writes Ray Bohlin of Probe Ministries (http://www.probe.org/ content/view/1130/169/). Describe other common misinterpretations of the concept. (24-25, 26, 50-51)*

CONTINUING THE CONVERSATION:

Collect examples of the fact/value dichotomy from books, movies, conversations with friends. How can we get past the gatekeeper, making it clear that Christianity is not a private "value" but a claim to cosmic truth?

PART 1

Chapter 1

While setting up for a television interview, the host explained to me that the program aimed at being biblical in both message *and* methods. "For example," she said, "we don't exaggerate the number of our listeners."

"Of course not," I responded. Not fudging the numbers seemed a pretty obvious moral principle.

"Most people in the industry do," the host replied, explaining that certain statistical tricks are commonly used to inflate audience numbers. "When we told another Christian television producer that we don't use those tricks, he said, '*What?* You don't inflate your numbers? Then how do you stay in business?'"

Sadly, it is possible to be Christian in our beliefs, yet secular in the way we live. Chapter 1 opens with the story of "Sarah" who was a sincere believer, but who had absorbed moral relativism as part of the professional ethos of her field.

1. How do stories like these illustrate the danger of the sacred/secular split? (31-33)

The vast majority of Christian colleges and universities perpetuate the sacred/secular divide, according to a study by Robert Benne (*Quality with Soul* [Eerdmans, 2001]). He calls it the "add-on" approach because it treats Christianity as something *added on* to the curriculum—through chapel, Bible studies, and prayer groups—while the course content is essentially the same as in any secular university. These colleges define themselves as Christian primarily because of their ethos and atmosphere, not because they teach a distinctive vision of the world.

The upshot is that many of our churches and schools are turning out young people who are Christian in their *religious* life, but secular in their *mental* life. As a result, it is all too easy to absorb secular worldviews from the surrounding culture.

2. How would you show that an "add-on" approach is unbiblical? (36-39, 44)

The Enlightenment treated reason as a neutral source of truths, independent of any philosophical or religious commitment. But the Augustinian view is much more holistic, teaching that when we turn away from God, our minds rationalize our sinful choices and become "darkened" (Romans 1:21). As a result, claims made in the name of reason often reflect hidden religious and philosophical motivations.

3. What does it mean to say there is no neutral knowledge? (38-46, 93-94, 98-99)

Labels like "science" or "reason" are often used to mask a hidden agenda. During the 2004 campaign, Eleanor Clift criticized President Bush in *Newsweek* (Aug. 13, 2004) for allowing religion to inform public policy in matters like abortion, while she praised John Kerry for keeping faith out of politics. "Voters have a choice," she concluded, "between a president who governs by *belief* and a challenger who puts his faith in *rational decision-making.*"

What's the implication here? Obviously, that Christianity is *not* rational. But notice that Clift is also presenting the liberal position as though it were not any particular ideology, but only a rational weighing of the facts. The article was titled "Faith Versus Reason," as though liberal views were purely a product of reason.

In reality, the liberal position on abortion and bioethics is an expression of utilitarianism and pragmatism, based on a cost-benefit analysis. The lesson is that worldviews do not come neatly labeled. No one says the conflict is a *utilitarian, pragmatic* standard of ethics versus a *normative, transcendent* standard. No, they say it's science versus religion, facts versus faith. Whenever we hear that kind of language, we should aim our worldview detectors beneath the surface to uncover the implicit worldview assumptions.

4. What does materialism propose as ultimate reality? Naturalism? Empiricism? Pantheism? (41-46, 135, 147, 389)

Critics often debunk Christianity as irrational and biased, based on faith—while presenting secular beliefs as unbiased and objective, based on reason. But this is sheer bluff. All systems of thought are structurally the same: Each starts by proposing *something* as ultimate reality, then seeks to explain the world on that basis—spinning out the implications, garnering empirical support, and so on. By uncovering these hidden assumptions, we can level the playing the field among competing worldviews.

5. After I converted to Christianity, a college classmate said, "You can't be objective, like I am." How would you respond to this kind of dismissal? How is the concept of neutral reason often used to discredit Christianity? (38-46, 93-94)

TEST YOURSELF:

6. The text says "Sarah" held Christianity as a collection of truths but not as Truth about all of reality. Explain the difference. (32-33, 34-35, 398 note 3)

7. The idea that the secular realm is unbiased and neutral arose during Europe's religious wars. Explain how it developed. (381-382, 448 note 2)

8. How do Christians explain the wide range of practical agreement among people holding divergent worldviews? (43)

9. Many readers of Total Truth say the discussion on mathematics was especially powerful in opening their eyes to the impact of worldviews. (43-44) Of course, some fields are more "worldview sensitive" than others. Explain why. (399 note 25)

10. *According to the doctrine of Creation, God is the source of all cosmic order—not just the moral order but also the physical order, social order, political order, aesthetic order, etc. How does this provide a basis for a Christian worldview? (34-35, 45-46, 84)*

11. *How does a biblical doctrine of "vocation" inform our understanding of worldview? (47-51)*

CONTINUING THE CONVERSATION:

The stories that conclude chapter 1 illustrate how a Christian may recognize data that others miss because they are blinded by secular presuppositions. Collect other instances where a biblical perspective directs our attention to facts that others overlook due to worldview blinders. (58-62)

Chapter 2

When financial scandals erupted a few years ago across the corporate world, Christians were shocked to learn that some of the top executives were regular churchgoers, even deacons and Sunday School leaders. They attended church on Sunday, but during the rest of the week they were cooking the books for their own self-enrichment. "Top managers of firms such as Enron, Global Crossing, and, it now appears, Xerox systematically lied about the condition of their enterprises to rationalize granting themselves huge sums diverted from equity," writes columnist Gregg Easterbrook in an article appropriately titled "Greed Isn't Good" (The New Republic Online, July 1, 2002). "If this isn't common theft—lying in order to abscond with someone else's money—what is?"

Why are Christians sometimes susceptible to corruption? The answer has much to do with the sacred/secular split. As Dan Edelen writes (www.dedelen.com), "Their tragedy—and ours—is their disjointed worldview that kept their faith from influencing their real-life work situations." Believers who live in a two-story mental universe do not sense any obligation to apply a biblical perspective to their work—which means that some *other* worldview seeps in to fill the vacuum. Many Christians in business have absorbed the legally enshrined "finance model," which portrays corporations as amoral entities existing solely to maximize profit and shareholder value—a worldview that makes it far too easy to rationalize immoral practices.

1. *Using Os Guinness's image of a "toolbox," explain why failing to develop **biblical** tools of analysis makes us susceptible to picking up **non-biblical** tools. (44)*

Those who act as "enablers" for the misdeeds of others are likewise responsible. When scandals broke at Tyco, the corporate attorney turned out to be a devout Catholic (see Steve Fishman, *New York* magazine, Aug. 9, 2004). Though not found legally guilty of criminal wrongdoing, jury members still said, "He was morally guilty." Why? Because he had failed to follow up on clear indications of corruption, while allowing his own impeccable reputation to shore up the company's image.

Recently a well-known minister and speaker was forced to step down because of alcohol abuse and other moral failings, which prompted a fellow pastor to write an article apologizing to the public. Why? Because he had continued to invite the minister to speak at his own church even after seeing signs of the problems. By letting his own name be associated with the speaker, he had helped prop up the man's credibility and shield him from accountability.

2. How do these scandals remind us that the topic of worldview is not merely academic, but has a profoundly practical impact? How can we hold Christians in leadership positions accountable?

If asked to apply a biblical perspective to their work, many believers wouldn't know how to do much more than quote Bible verses—which is rarely effective in a secular setting. To engage with modern culture, we need to construct a general account of the world that "translates" biblical truth into the language of the various disciplines: a Christian *philosophy of* business and economics, a Christian *philosophy of* science, a Christian *philosophy of* politics, and so on. A worldview functions as a bridge that takes us from Scripture to the issues of our time.

3. Since the Bible does not explicitly address many aspects of modern society, how do we make the case that Christianity applies to every area of life? (47-49, 50, 81)

The sacred/secular split is a hangover from Greek dualism, and we recognize it today in a tendency to rate professional religious work as more valuable than other forms of work. A high-ranking government official who attended Harvard told me, "In my campus group, the message was clear: If you really wanted to live for the Lord, your options were The Three M's. You could be a minister, a missionary, . . . or a Mrs. (the *wife* of a minister or missionary)."

Another reader says that until reading *Total Truth,* "I had never even considered that the secular/sacred dichotomy was *not* part of the Christian worldview. I'd always been brought to see 'true' Christian work as the ministry, while the rest of us were to do the best we could in our 'regular' work so as to be able to give more to 'ministry' work."

4. Do these stories describe attitudes you have encountered? (66-67, 74-77, 80-83) How would you explain that all valid callings are forms of obedience to the Cultural Mandate? (36-37, 47-49, 86-87)

An especially clear example of the medieval nature/grace dualism comes from the writings of Dante—yes, the same Dante whose *Divine Comedy* you read in English class. "Man's goal is twofold," he writes in *Monarchy,* "happiness in this life" and "happiness in the eternal life." The earthly goal we can reach by "the exercise of our own powers" of reason. But the heavenly goal requires "spiritual teachings which transcend human reason," that is, "revealed truth."

The most familiar critique of this nature/grace dualism was by Francis Schaeffer, but it has been criticized on a more scholarly level by Catholic thinkers (80, 94, 404 note 58, 405 note 7). The most penetrating analysis was by the French Jesuit Henri de Lubac in *Augustinianism and Modern Theology.* The problem with the idea of "parallel, duplicate orders," he explained, is that the dimension of grace came to be viewed as a mere addition to nature, "a sort of second story carefully placed on top of a lower nature" ([Herder & Herder, 2000, 1965], 234). Lubac found seeds of this false dichotomy in Thomas Aquinas (though not yet in a pernicious form). Eventually it led to the idea of a natural order functioning independently of God in the lower story, which was responsible for a drift toward naturalism that has continued to our own day.

5. If nature operates independently of God, then it can be understood solely by reason and science—and theology will be regarded as irrelevant, even an intrusion. How would a teacher react if you suggested a serious consideration of a Christian view of history, economics, psychology, or any other subject in the classroom today?

TEST YOURSELF:

6. Why have many churches succumbed to a therapeutic form of religion? (68-69)

7. Did you find the survey by Christian Smith helpful in giving a firsthand glimpse into the ways we often privatize religion? (69-73)

8. Total Truth is not written as a history of philosophy but as a history of ideas. That means it does not give a full, comprehensive account of various philosophers, but asks only how each one contributed to the development of a spe-

cific idea—namely, the two-story divide. Explain how Platonism and Aristotelianism influenced Christian forms of dualism. (74-82, 92-94, 99-101, Appendix 2)

9. Explain "structure" versus "direction." (85)

CONTINUING THE CONVERSATION:

Many readers say the discussion of Creation, Fall, and Redemption was the most helpful part of the entire book. Apply the three-part grid to better understand your own theological background. (83-95)

Chapter 3

A person is merely an automaton—"a big bag of skin full of biomolecules" interacting by the laws of physics and chemistry, says Rodney Brooks of MIT (*Flesh and Machines* [Pantheon, 2002], 174). It is not easy to think this way, he admits. But "when I look at my children, I can, when I force myself, . . . see that they are machines."

And yet, and yet. "That is not how I treat them. . . . They have my unconditional love, the furthest one might be able to get from rational analysis." If this sounds incoherent, Brooks admits as much: "I maintain two sets of inconsistent beliefs."

This is a secular form of dualism, and chapter 3 traces its emergence through Descartes, Kant, and several contemporary thinkers. Let's tune up our worldview detectors for a closer look.

Steven Pinker's worldview could be called scientific naturalism—nature is all there is. Our minds are nothing but computers, complex data-processing machines. This is Pinker's professional ideology, the one he adopts in the laboratory. Yet when he goes home to his family and friends, he realizes that his scientific naturalism doesn't work. You can't treat your wife like a complex data processing machine. You can't treat your children like little computers, as Brooks admits in the quotation above. So in real life, these scientists admit that they have to switch to a completely contradictory paradigm—one that has no basis within their own intellectual system. As Marvin Minsky puts it, we are "forced" to believe in freedom of will, "*even though we know it's false.*" False, that is, according to scientific naturalism.

1. Explain what a secular leap of faith is, and why the text calls this "the tragedy of the postmodern age." (105-112, 217-221)

Christians who adopt the label *postmodern* say the church must leave the modernist age behind and move forward into postmodernism, or risk becoming irrelevant. But this is based on the mistaken idea that modernism and postmodernism are sequential stages in history. In reality, they coexist within the same two-track divide that has been endemic in Western thought since the ancient Greeks. Modernism remains firmly entrenched in the lower level—in the hard sciences and the world of politics, finance, and industry. (No one designs an airplane by postmodern principles.) Postmodernism is simply the current form of the upper level.

2. How would you use this insight to respond to Christians who embrace postmodernism? (21, 113-115)

This is not to deny that something new is taking place in our day. But a more accurate way to picture the change is that the two stories are moving farther apart from one another. In the downstairs, modernism is growing increasingly materialistic and reductionistic. Today there even is a school of thought called eliminative materialism that denies the reality of consciousness, reducing humans to "zombies" (111-112, 394). At the same time in the upstairs, postmodernism is growing ever more subjective and relativistic, celebrating the non-rational as a form of liberation (113-115).

You might picture the lower story angling downward while the upper story angles upward, with the gap *between* them growing ever wider.

3. An analytical person—a scientist or engineer—is likely to be sympathetic to modernism (lower level). A creative person—an artist or writer—typically leans toward romanticism and postmodernism (upper level). How can we present the claims of Christianity in a credible way to both types?

Many readers of *Total Truth* have asked, Does liberating Christianity from its cultural captivity in the upper story mean simply moving it to the lower story? Absolutely not! As chapter 3 shows, the lower story has been taken over by radical reductionism and positivism, with no room for any religious perspective. Our goal is to reject the dichotomy altogether, replacing it with a multifaceted concept of knowledge that recognizes many types of truth.

We still find relics in our culture of an older, holistic view of truth. A few years ago, a teachers association stated, "People have many ways of knowing about their world, including scientific knowledge, societal knowledge, religious knowledge and cultural knowledge" (415 note 74). That's close to the biblical view, and we could add more categories as well, like mathematical, moral, and aesthetic knowledge. A multidimensional conception of truth acknowledges many "ways of knowing" about the richly diverse world God has created.

4. Explain why Christians reject the contemporary definition of both "fact" and "value." (119)

TEST YOURSELF:

5. Secularists typically equate "reason" with materialism or naturalism— which renders Christianity "unreasonable" by definition. How would you show that they are cheating by assimilating a set of worldview premises into their very definition of reason? (101)

6. How does the upper/lower story analysis make sense of both theological liberalism and postmodern spirituality? (115-118)

7. What is the difference between the biblical concept of faith and the modernist leap of faith? (111, 116, 119-122, Appendix 4)

CONTINUING THE CONVERSATION:

How would you make the case that Christianity gives a unified, logically consistent basis for exactly those things that are so problematic for scientific naturalism, like human dignity and moral freedom? (110-111, 217-221, 314-321, Appendix 4)

Chapter 4

As I was writing this study guide, Terri Schiavo died after her feeding tube was removed by a court order. Now, Christian ethicists agree that there is no moral obligation to prolong the dying process, but Terri was not dying. So the heart of the issue is a theory of "personhood" that says just being part of the human race is not enough to accord any intrinsic moral worth. You have to meet a set of *additional* criteria—a certain level of autonomy, the ability to make choices, and so on. Anyone who lacks full cognitive abilities is considered a "non-person," a category that includes the fetus, the newborn, and the mentally impaired. Many ethicists have begun to argue that "non-persons" can be used for research and experimentation, or harvesting organs, or other utilitarian purposes. So let's aim our worldview detectors at the ideas driving the culture of death.

It was René Descartes who applied the two-story divide to the human person. In his philosophy, the physical body is a glorified machine, while the mind is an autonomous power that in a sense *uses* the body in an instrumental way— almost the way you use a car to take you where you want to go (103).

In the 1970s, ethicist Paul Ramsey noticed that this Cartesian dualism had become the underlying worldview in abortion, euthanasia, genetic engineering, and the other life issues (*The Patient as Person* [Yale University Press, 1970]). For a long time, pro-life groups have thought the battle was over getting people to agree that the fetus is human life. Today, however, abortion advocates are perfectly willing to say the fetus is *physiologically* human—but that fact is regarded as irrelevant to its moral status, and does not warrant legal protection. The deciding factor is "personhood," typically defined in terms of autonomy or the power of choice.

The two-story approach to life issues:

PERSONHOOD
Warrants Legal Protection

PHYSIOLOGICALLY HUMAN
Irrelevant to Moral Status

For example, during the 2004 presidential campaign, John Kerry surprised everyone by agreeing that "life begins at conception." How, then, could he support abortion? Because, as he explained, the fetus is "not the form of life that takes [on] *personhood*" as we have defined it (ABC News, July 22, 2004).

This is the logic being applied to euthanasia. In a television debate, bioethicist Bill Allen was asked point blank, "Do you think Terri is a person?" He replied, "No, I do not. I think having awareness is an essential criterion of personhood" (Court TV Online, Mar. 25, 2004). Those who favored letting Terri die included some, like Dr. Ronald Cranford, who have openly defended denying food and water even to disabled people who are conscious and partly mobile, like the case of a Washington man who could operate an electric wheelchair (see Robert Johansen, National Review Online, Mar. 16, 2005).

1. Critics say the pro-life position is based on mere faith that life begins at conception—yet the beginning of life is a biological fact. By contrast, arguments for abortion rest on the concept of "personhood," a non-empirical, non-scientific philosophical concept. Does this suggest a way for pro-lifers to turn the tables on their critics?

A similar dualism underlies the liberal approach to sexuality. The body is treated as simply an instrument that can be used by the autonomous self for giving and receiving pleasure. In a widely used sex education video, sex is defined as merely "something done by two adults to give each other pleasure"

("What Kids Want to Know about Sex and Growing Up," Children's Television Workshop, 1998).

In fact, the cutting edge today is the postmodern idea that gender is a social construction, and therefore it can be *de*constructed. People "don't want to fit into any boxes—not gay, straight, lesbian, or bisexual ones. . . . they want to be free to change their minds," says a magazine for homosexuals (Bret Johnson, *In the Family,* July 1998). "It's as if we're seeing a challenge to the old modernist way of thinking 'This is who I am, period,' and a movement toward a postmodern version, 'This is who I am right now'." All forms of sexual identity are treated as matters of choice.

"This is seen as liberating, a way to take control of one's own identity, rather than accepting the one that has been culturally 'assigned'," writes Gene Edward Veith (*World,* Mar. 27, 2004). "At some colleges, students no longer have to check 'M' or 'F' on their health forms. Instead they are asked to 'describe your gender identity history'."

The body has become an instrumental tool that can be used by the autonomous self any way it chooses, in a pragmatic calculus of pain and pleasure:

AUTONOMOUS SELF
Uses the body any way it chooses

PHYSICAL BODY
Morally neutral mechanism for pain or pleasure

*2. Christianity used to be criticized for having a low view of bodily life. But today it has a much **higher** view than secularism's utilitarian, pragmatic view. The Bible teaches that our bodies are temples of the Holy Spirit, and will be resurrected at the end of time. How can we turn the tables to show that it is Christianity that gives a basis for a high view of embodied existence?*

The idolizing of choice lies at the heart of the crisis in marriage as well. In Rousseau's social contract theory, the original human condition is a "state of nature" in which there are no relationships—no marriage, no family, no civil society. In this primal state, we are atomistic, disconnected, autonomous individuals (137-141).

But if this our natural state—if we are originally and inherently autonomous individuals—then where do social relationships like marriage come from? Answer: They are created by choice. And if we *create* marriage by choice, then clearly we can also *recreate* it by choice. We can redefine it any way we want.

Vice President Dick Cheney has defended homosexuality by saying: "People ought to be free to enter into any kind of relationship they want to" (CBSNews.com, Aug. 25, 2004).

3. Explain how Rousseau's ideas have filtered down to ordinary people, until today many regard any normative standards for marriage as discriminatory and oppressive.

TEST YOURSELF:

4. Explain why the Trinity is the Rosetta stone for Christian social theory. (130-134, 138)

5. The text says Greek philosophy defined the human dilemma as metaphysical instead of moral (76). What does that mean? Explain how the worldviews analyzed in this chapter likewise define the problem with human nature (the Fall) in metaphysical rather than moral terms. (127-149)

6. Practice applying the grid of Creation-Fall-Redemption to various worldviews you encounter, especially in your field of work.

CONTINUING THE CONVERSATION:

Using the categories of Creation, Fall, and Redemption, construct the basic elements of a Christian worldview on politics and the state, business and economics, and other subjects.

PART 2

Chapter 5

America's public schools are growing more dogmatic in their teaching of evolution, but many teenagers aren't buying it. In a 2005 Gallup poll of teenagers, 38 percent affirm that "God created human beings pretty much in their present form." Another 43 percent hold that humans developed from less advanced life forms, "but God guided" the process. All told, 81 percent believe that God was somehow involved.

"You have to be educated into *not* seeing the design around you in the natural world," comments Mark Hartwig (*Baptist Press News,* Mar. 9, 2005). "You have to be either bullied or . . . socialized out of it."

Part 2 will equip you to protect yourself and your children from being bullied or socialized out of recognizing the design in nature. As you read about the standard evidence for Darwinism, make it your goal to grasp the underlying logic. You may encounter a wide diversity of examples in books, museums, and television programs, but all rely on the same logic—namely, that minute, nearly imperceptible changes add up over time to create new structures (limbs and organs), until finally a new species appears.

Because the process takes too long to be observed, the theory rests on an extrapolation—a projection into the past supposedly based on changes observed today. In reality, however, it *contradicts* the pattern of change we actually observe. Small-scale changes simply do not add up the way the theory requires.

1. State in your own words why the logic of Darwinian theory is faulty. (158-161, 165-168)

The reason the public is concerned about Darwinism is that it puts Christianity in the upper story, on the level of fantasy and fairy tales. In the *New York Times* (July 12, 2003), the Darwinist philosopher Daniel Dennett said bluntly, "We don't believe in ghosts or elves or the Easter Bunny—or God."

In a *Times* interview (Nov. 28, 2004), Richard Dawkins was once asked whether he would be so hard-hearted as to persuade a religious person "that his life was based on a falsehood," if that person "had always harmlessly derived comfort and consolation from his faith." Dawkins magnanimously replied that if the person "was really deriving consolation, perhaps in bereavement, from something I thought was nonsense, I wouldn't wish to shatter that person's dream."

2. Should Christians really seek this kind of concession—a grudging tolerance of religion so long as it is a harmless "dream"? (106, 153-154, 174, 176-178, 202-203)

If the impact of Darwinism was to push religion off into the realm of wish fulfillment, then Creation gives the basis for recovering a unified truth (154-155, 247). Readers of *Total Truth* often ask what it means to talk about the unity of truth. It does not mean ignoring ordinary disciplinary boundaries: Science remains distinct from theology, mathematics from music, etc., and each discipline has its own appropriate methodology. The metaphor of two stories is picture language for the *truth status* of an idea. To put Christianity in the upper story is a way of saying it is grounded *not* in truth but in things like emotional need, myths and symbols, the will to believe, or cultural tradition.

Think of the rules of a game like baseball. "Three strikes, you're out"—is that true or false? Neither, of course. It's just a rule for playing the game. Similarly, theology is no longer regarded as a matter of true or false, but merely cultural convention or personal preference.

3. Before we can argue that Christianity is true, we must often first make the case that it is even in the category of things that can be true or false. How would you make that case?

Tragically, many Christians have capitulated to the fact/value split (177-178, 201-204). How can you test whether *you* have slipped into two-level thinking? Ask yourself two questions. First, if Christianity were decisively shown to be false, would you stop believing it? No doubt, you would take several years to think about it before taking such a significant step. But in the end, can you honestly say that if Christianity were persuasively shown to be false, you would stop believing it?

The idea that Christianity could potentially be falsified may seem contrary to the biblical admonition to have faith. But it is the attitude of Elijah on Mt. Carmel, subjecting God's existence to a highly public empirical test. It is the attitude of Paul telling his audiences to consult the 500 people who were eye-witnesses of Jesus' resurrection (116, 121).

4. Think of similar examples given throughout Scripture.

The second diagnostic question is whether religion has any consequences for other areas of knowledge. In the academic world, theology is expected to accommodate to the findings of science, but never the other way around. If you suggest that science should take into account the truths of theology—well, you have violated the canons of scholarship! Theology is allowed to give a spiritual spin on the story told by naturalistic science, but it is not allowed to change the story itself. It has to take *that* as a given.

5. Is there two-way traffic between your faith and the way you think about work, social issues, politics, and family life? Or does the traffic go only one way? (115-116, 203-204)

TEST YOURSELF:

6. What is the difference between classic Darwinism and punctuated equilibrium? (165-168)

7. Define philosophical naturalism. What role does it play in the evolution debate? (156-158, 168-175, 202-205)

8. To what degree is a commitment to evolution driven by anti-religious motivations? (171-173)

9. How does the Intelligent Design paradigm represent a new approach to faith-and-science issues? (173-175)

10. "Every school child knows that values are relative," Allan Bloom writes (177). He goes on: "They are not based on facts but are mere individual subjective preferences." What do Christians communicate to the world when they use the term "values"?

CONTINUING THE CONVERSATION:

Do you use mostly emotive language when talking about Christianity? The faith we hold dear? The beliefs we cherish? Comfort and consolation? That is like waving a white flag telling secularists not to take us seriously. How can we speak so that non-Christians will listen?

Chapter 6

Shortly after *Total Truth* was published, the academic world was rocked by the news that a prominent atheist had changed his mind. For the past half century, the name of philosopher Antony Flew was virtually synonymous with atheism. But now he has decided there is a God after all.

What brought such an entrenched atheist to change his mind? The scientific case for Intelligent Design (ID). Investigation of DNA "has shown, by the almost unbelievable complexity of the arrangements which are needed to produce (life), that intelligence must have been involved," Flew says in a video ("Has Science Discovered God?" The Institute for Metascientific Research, 2004). Though atheist colleagues were outraged by his change of mind, Flew replied calmly, "My whole life has been guided by the principle of Plato's Socrates: Follow the evidence, wherever it leads."

1. Critics often dismiss ID theory as religion dressed up in scientific garb. But Flew's turnabout shows that the evidence for ID can be weighed on its own merits. Are you convinced that Christianity is capable of standing up to the test of "following the evidence wherever it leads"?

The media consistently distorts the goal of the ID movement, claiming that it wants to ban the teaching of evolution. Not so. Proponents of ID want *more* taught in schools, not less. They want to open the classroom to criticism of scientific naturalism and discussion of dissenting positions. Their slogan is *teach the controversy.*

This approach can serve as a model in other fields as well. To be well educated, students should be taught to think critically about *all* the worldviews they are likely to encounter in our pluralistic society—religious worldviews as well as secular worldviews. Teaching subjects from an exclusively secular viewpoint "actively discourages critical thinking by failing to provide students any critical distance on the secular ways of thinking and living," says philosopher Warren Nord (*Darwinism, Design, and Public Education* [Michigan State University Press, 2003], 47).

2. How can we make a case for teaching critical thinking in public schools by including the study of all major worldviews?

It is all too easy for Christians to fall into the old stereotype of simply banning ideas they disagree with. A prominent Christian radio commentator recently urged his audience to take a controversial book and "throw it away!" But putting on blinders is not the way to become critical thinkers. Nor does it show respect for our opponents, who are made in the image of God. Christians should lead the way in modeling what it means to take ideas seriously, "giving honest answers to honest questions," as Schaeffer put it.

Back in the age of state churches, it was Christian dissenters who framed the case for pluralism and religious liberty. Today, in the age of state schools, Christians ought to be framing the case for pluralism and freedom in education as well.

3. Pluralism is often misunderstood to mean relativism. What would genuine pluralism look like in the classroom?

TEST YOURSELF:

4. What is the defining claim of Intelligent Design theory? (180-182)

5. What is irreducible complexity and how does it pose a challenge to Darwinism? (184-188)

6. Explain the logic of the explanatory filter—chance, law, design—and how it applies to the origin of life and of the universe. (188-201)

7. What distinguishes ID from theistic evolution? (203-204)

8. What distinguishes ID from classic creationism? (415 note 70)

9. Critics say ID breaks the rules because science, by definition, may consider only natural causes. How would you respond? (169, 203)

CONTINUING THE CONVERSATION:

Select a few contested issues in public education and think through how to apply a "teach the controversy" approach.

Chapter 7

Religion itself "is a product of evolution," claims a recent book. Because religion "enables groups to function as adaptive units," a tendency to believe was selected for in our evolutionary history (David Sloan-Wilson, *Darwin's Cathedral* [University of Chicago Press, 2003], 6). The fast-growing field of evolutionary psychology aims to expand naturalistic evolution into an all-encompassing worldview explaining every aspect of human experience.

Yet virtually every proponent of the theory ends up making a secular leap of faith. Chapter 7 walks you through several examples (you might also want to review chapter 3), so that you can make this an indispensable tool in your apologetics toolbox. In evangelism our goal is to bring people to recognize their need for God, including their intellectual need. How? By showing them that no worldview except Christianity adequately accounts for the world as we actually experience it (217-221, 396).

The fundamental principle is this: *Every worldview not based on biblical truth ends up with some form of reductionism.* After all, if you do not begin with God, then you must begin with something *less* than God. And whatever you propose as ultimate reality provides the categories for explaining everything else. Materialism reduces everything to particles in motion. Scientific naturalism reduces everything to complex mechanisms, operating by inexorable laws of nature. Pantheism reduces all individual existence to an underlying spiritual unity. Every worldview reduces the richly diverse, multileveled world that God created to a limited paradigm that absolutizes one *part* of creation (41-42).

Recognizing this dynamic will give you a powerful tool for apologetics. You can be utterly confident that any worldview that is not biblical will be "too small" to account for all of reality. For example, the biblical teaching that humans are made in the image of God leads to a richer concept of human nature than any other worldview—because every alternative reduces humans to the image of some aspect of creation.

1. Explain what Schaeffer meant by saying that, in every nonbiblical worldview, some part of human nature will always "stick out" of the paradigm. (110-111)

Since every nonbiblical worldview is too narrow to account for the full range of reality as God created it, adherents will not be able live within the confines of their own belief systems. We are not merely data processing machines, no matter what scientific materialism says. We are not merely products of natural selection maximizing our chances of survival, no matter what naturalistic evolution says. At some point people are compelled to tell their genes to "go jump in the lake" (to use Pinker's phrase [218]), while they take a leap of faith to affirm things that are *not* accounted for within their own worldview.

That point of inconsistency is your opening. Gently and prayerfully direct people to the testimony of their own lives—to the fact that they cannot live consistently on the basis of their own professed worldview. They may then be open, by God's grace, to hearing about the only worldview that *does* account for the full range of human experience—because it does not begin with any part of creation but with the transcendent Creator.

2. *When speaking with nonbelievers we cannot simply quote the Bible. But what we **can** do is show that their own worldview fails to account for the world as **they themselves experience it**. How would you make the case that Christianity alone gives a complete and consistent account of reality? (217-221, 314-321, Appendix 4)*

TEST YOURSELF:

3. *Explain "kin selection" and "tit for tat." Do these theories provide an adequate account of altruism? (208-212, 317-318)*

4. *Do you agree that evolution and evolutionary psychology are a package deal—that if you accept the premise, then you must accept the conclusion? (210-216)*

5. *Is it fair to say that evolution often functions as a religion? (172-173, 223-224)*

CONTINUING THE CONVERSATION:

Practice identifying examples of the secular leap of faith in movies, articles, politicians' speeches, etc.

Chapter 8

At the start of each class, a high school history teacher begins with a short warm-up exercise—but the exercise has nothing to do with history. Instead the teacher posts moral dilemmas on the blackboard (like the well-known "lifeboat" problem), which prod students to question the moral standards learned at home and church in order to work out their own personal values.

When the same teacher gets around to teaching history, he presents that subject from a relativistic framework as well. At a Back-to-School night, when asked what perspective he employs in teaching history, he replied, "There's really no way to know what's true and false, what's right or wrong. History is open to individual interpretation." (See Pam Glass, *ChristianBookPreviews.com.*)

The label for this view is social constructivism—that knowledge is not *discovered* but *created* (241-242). When the pragmatist philosophers applied evolution to the realm of ideas, they concluded that there are no transcendent, unchanging truths. All ideas are social constructions, subject to evolutionary development.

1. A theory of knowledge is called an epistemology. Explain why an evolutionary epistemology leads to relativism across the curriculum. (229-232)

In moral theory, John Dewey realized that an evolutionary approach must begin with whatever the individual happens to value. Thus moral education should teach students to clarify what they value, then weigh alternatives to decide which course of action has consequences that match their values.

2. Explain how this naturalistic approach is the basis for moral education in the public schools today. (238-241)

In his hugely successful *Conversations with God for Teens* (Hampton Roads, 2001), Neale Donald Walsch answers teenagers' questions as if he were God.

> Question: But how can I ever erase the bad things I've done from your judgment book? (Ayla, age 13)
>
> GOD: There *is* no "judgment book." . . . It may be a surprise for most humans to learn that there is no such thing as right and wrong. There is only what works and what doesn't work. . . . Absolute Right and Absolute Wrong do not exist.
>
> Question: So "right" and "wrong" are a changing thing?
>
> GOD: Yes, changing and shifting from time to time and place to place.

3. How does Walsch express an evolutionary epistemology in this passage?

When Christian students are not taught a critical worldview grid, they easily absorb the same relativistic, pragmatic view of morality. Christopher Hall at Eastern University says most of his students "are rampantly promiscuous"

(*Philadelphia Inquirer*, Mar. 13, 2005). The journals they write for class, he said, jump wildly from their experiences in praise and worship to their sexual activity: "There is a significant gap between what the young profess to believe and how they live."

4. Morality is always derivative—it stems from a person's worldview. How would you give a worldview context and rationale for biblical ethics?

TEST YOURSELF:

5. Process theology is widespread in mainline seminaries today. Identify both its appeal and its flaws. (235-236)

6. Give examples of the ongoing impact of legal pragmatism. (237-238)

7. How do Christian teachers often inject their own interpretation into the term "constructivism," failing to recognize its evolutionary origin? (427 note 58)

*8. Explain this irony: Postmodernism denies all objective truths **except** the truth of Darwinism. (242-243)*

9. What fatal flaw in evolutionary epistemology did Darwin himself recognize? (243-244)

CONTINUING THE CONVERSATION:

In chapters 7 and 8 we learned how philosophical naturalism has permeated all subject areas. Collect examples to show how naturalistic assumptions underlie the ideas you encounter at work, at school, or in politics.

PART 3

Chapters 9 and 10

Members of an Eastern European missionary organization invited me to dinner to discuss translating *Total Truth* into Slovakian. Though honored, I was also a little curious. "Some material in the book focuses closely on the American experience," I said (thinking especially of Part 3). "Would it really be relevant to other parts of the world?"

The head of the organization threw back his head and laughed. *"Where do you think all our missionaries come from?"* he asked. "Since so many missions groups originate in the States, American definitions of the spiritual life have an impact all around the globe."

Chapters 9 and 10 describe the rise of a distinctively American form of spirituality and church life. Many readers say this section provided categories for understanding features of their own church experience that have troubled them—the emotionalism, the anti-intellectualism, the celebrity-style leadership. Because these chapters together tell a continuous story, the study questions are combined into a single unit.

1. How do scholars define the term "evangelical"? (256-257) What characteristics of evangelicalism do you recognize in your own background?

Ronald Knox, who wrote a history of the early evangelicals (290-291), also said that a healthy church is one that maintains a balance between *inspiration* and *institution*. Most reform movements are driven by people who are hungry for a deeper spiritual reality, who castigate the institutional church for its empty ritualism and dead orthodoxy. But eventually every beneficial reform, in order to have lasting effects, must itself give rise to institutions. It must be developed into a systematic teaching (theology), proclaimed in corporate statements of faith (creeds and confessions), expressed in worship ceremonies (rituals and hymns), taught and transmitted to the next generation (churches, schools, seminaries). The institutional aspect of the church is like a pipeline, protecting and channeling the precious water of life within.

As long as evangelicalism remained a reform movement within existing churches, it could focus on *inspiration* while taking the benefits of the *institution* for granted. As evangelical groups began to break away and become independent, however, inspiration alone was not enough. That's when they began to exhibit the traits described in these chapters, becoming anti-intellectual, anti-historical, individualistic, and celebrity-driven (253).

2. Today there is a small but significant movement out of evangelical churches into churches with a greater "institutional" component—Episcopal, Orthodox, Catholic. How would you explain the appeal of these liturgical, sacramental, communal, historically rooted churches?

Many readers of *Total Truth* have asked about the "Emergent Church." Certainly it fits the pattern of movements that focus on inspiration while protesting the failings of the institutional church, and a good model for our response would be Francis Schaeffer's balanced approach to the counterculture of his day. Though aware of the dangers of the youth culture (e.g., drugs), he nevertheless commended it for protesting against a materialistic, market-driven bourgeois society. "The hippies of the 1960s . . . were right in fighting the plastic culture, and the church should have been fighting it too" (*Pollution and the Death of Man* [Hodder & Stoughton, 1970], 19). Schaeffer affirmed the hunger for hope and meaning that underlay even some of the counterculture's excesses (407 note 4).

The Emergent movement likewise has its excesses—in many cases a weak view of Scripture, an embrace of postmodern relativism, and an eclecticism that can look a lot like religious consumerism. Yet we should also affirm its underlying hunger for transcendence and authentic community. The movement is right to protest so much of mainstream evangelicalism that is slickly packaged and commercialized. Cliché-ridden praise choruses that are virtually content-free. Church growth programs that are impersonal, relying on manipulative formulas and techniques of mass marketing. Publicity and management techniques borrowed from the corporate world (286-290, 292, 364-376).

"Why do so many pastors use principles designed to lead an organization to maximize profit rather than to shepherd and lead people into knowing God?" asks Jay Bauman on an Emergent Church website (www.theooze.com, Feb. 2, 2005). "Modern management theory has little to do with the well being or spiritual growth of the individuals involved; usually the opposite, seeing them as a means to an end—growing a larger organization (in this case, church)." Big Business and Big Government have been joined by Big Ministry—churches and parachurch groups that value large budgets and extensive programs. We forget that spiritual authority is not given to the savvy businessman or the powerful political operative, but to those who weep before the Lord over the brokenness of the world and the spiritual bankruptcy of the church.

TEST YOURSELF:

3. Finke and Stark found that religious groups grow most rapidly when they are at odds with the surrounding culture. Why is that the case? (261-262)

4. The First Great Awakening largely succeeded in balancing heart and head. Explain how it nevertheless sowed the seeds of anti-intellectualism. (266-272)

5. Why did social contract theory become a widely accepted assumption among Americans? (279-284) Today ontological individualism is so far advanced (see definition on 131, 141-142) that even our most intimate relationships have become fragile and easily fragmented. How has this given rise to a hunger for genuine community within the church?

6. Why did C. S. Lewis urge Christians to read "old books"? (282, 302, 305)

7. What changes in the political and economic realms made the evangelical message seem plausible? (282-286)

8. Describe the new model of leadership that emerged. Do you recognize elements of this pattern today? (286-290)

CONTINUING THE CONVERSATION:

What can your own church do to maintain a healthy balance between inspiration and institution?

Chapter 11

A Christian journalist once told me point-blank, "When you enter the newsroom, you have to leave your faith behind. You can't bring a Christian perspective into your reporting." An economist teaching at a church college used almost identical words: "There is no Christian approach to economics. It's just a science based on facts." A science student at a Christian university said, "I believe there's a Creator, but there's no *scientific* evidence for it. You have to accept it strictly by faith." In chapter 11, we dip into history to understand the source of this all-too-typical compartmentalized thinking.

Through most of Western history, the world was interpreted as a rich web of moral and spiritual meanings. Historians were expected to draw moral lessons from historical events. Scientists praised the Creator for His ingenious "contrivances" in nature. Artists sought to inspire virtue and character. Economists did not talk about competition among self-interested individuals, but about stewardship of the earth and the just use of resources. In colonial America, school primers taught religious lessons alongside the ABCs: "In *Adam's* fall, we sinned all."

In the nineteenth century, however, evangelical scholars accepted a definition of knowledge that would contribute to the unraveling of this moral universe. They adopted a two-story framework that treated the lower story as religiously neutral. This approach had its roots in Common Sense realism, which presumed that scholarship functions without any philosophical framework—that "simple induction from empirical observation would merit universal rational assent" (James D. Bratt, in *Models for Christian Higher Education* [Eerdmans, 1997], 135-136).

1. Explain Scottish Common Sense realism and how it arose to counter skepticism. (296-298)

Because they embraced the ideal of neutral knowledge, evangelicals did not think it was necessary to craft an explicitly Christian worldview to guide scholarly research in the lower story. Instead they were confident that whatever reason discovers by free inquiry would ultimately support biblical teachings. Historians call this the *convergence* model of faith and scholarship, because it holds that reason, when it is working properly, will *converge* with the scriptural teachings.

What's the key phrase here? *When it is working properly.* But what happens when reason and faith do *not* converge? When the deliverances of science, history, or psychology contradict Scripture? Hidden under the banner of "science" and "free inquiry" is often some *ism* skewing the results.

2. When scholarship does not converge with scriptural teachings, either our interpretation of Scripture is faulty, or the scholarly research was driven by implicit worldview assumptions. Think of examples of each to show how this can happen.

Today most universities do not teach anything resembling neutral scholarship. Take economics: Throughout Western history, Christian thinkers have produced a rich body of literature on economics (traditionally as part of moral theology). Yet a survey of college textbooks found that economics texts do not acquaint students with a wide range of religious and philosophical views. Instead they teach one view exclusively—namely, neo-classical economic theory, which defines people as self-interested utility-maximizers, and the economic realm as the scene of competition by atomistic individuals for scarce resources.

The same survey found that home economics textbooks, in their treatment of morally sensitive subjects like marriage and sexuality, have dropped the traditional moral language of duty, obligation, and principle. Instead they uncritically employ the language of self-esteem, telling students again and again that they must choose their own values:

> Only you can choose the best alternative in making your own decisions. . . . Ask yourself what benefits or advantages will result from [your] choice. . . . Then choose the alternative that does the best job for you with the fewest disadvantages (*The Business of Living,* South-Western, 1986*).*

Moral decisions are treated as a matter of cost-benefit analysis, weighing the effects of various actions and calculating which works best. (The survey is described in Warren Nord, *Religion and American Education* [University of North Carolina Press, 1995], chapter 4.)

3. How did the ideal of neutral knowledge open the way for university courses to teach completely secularized views? How were evangelicals blinded to what was happening? Give examples from moral philosophy and natural science. (305-311)

Beginning in the nineteenth century, evangelicals themselves began to accept a largely utilitarian, pragmatic approach in areas like business, management, finance, and marketing. We witness the effects today when churches and parachurch ministries promote a biblical *message*, while relying on questionable *methods* informed by secular definitions of success.

For example, a pastor recently told me about a Christian ministry that funded a scientific study to prove the effectiveness of its programs. Experts in the field published critiques demonstrating that the study was badly flawed. Yet the ministry continued to use the invalid numbers in its PR and fundraising efforts.

4. In Christian circles, cutting ethical corners is often justified by saying, "It's for the ministry." Explain how two-story thinking can cause Christians to be blinded by a spiritualized utilitarianism (the end justifies the means). (85, 97-99, 311, 364-376)

TEST YOURSELF:

5. Describe "Baconian" hermeneutics. What are its strengths and weaknesses? (299-305)

6. In what ways does American evangelicalism differ from classic Reformation theology? (302-303, 434 note 37)

*7. How does the embrace of **methodological** naturalism open the door to **metaphysical** naturalism? (307, 311)*

8. Explain how Schaeffer combined elements of evidentialism and presuppositionalism into an effective apologetics method. (313-321, Appendix 4)

9. What is philosophical "cheating"? Give examples of ways people engage in it to avoid the logical conclusions of the premises they hold. (319-321)

CONTINUING THE CONVERSATION:

Collect examples from your textbooks (or your children's) to demonstrate that public schools are not neutral but teach from an exclusively secular point of view.

Chapter 12

While attending a conference, I noticed a young man reading *Total Truth* so eagerly that he was ignoring the speaker at the podium. When the lecture ended, he rushed into the hallway and spoke excitedly into a cell phone. Later the young man introduced himself as Kirk Martin and explained that he had been so inspired by chapter 12 that, right then and there, he had called his wife and they had decided to change their lifestyle.

Martin posted his comments on the Amazon website for *Total Truth*: "In the Colonial Period, men were integral as actively engaged fathers and leaders of virtue. The family worked together daily in a family industry," he writes. "During the Industrial Age, this dynamic changed. Women became responsible for 'civilizing' men (which led to the destructive mindset that excused and perhaps expected crude behavior from men). . . . The family dynamic became disjointed and lost its force."

Martin has decided to foment a quiet reformation, starting with his own family: "Our family's personal goal now is to recapture that family dynamic in which we can run a business together from home, and in which both my wife and I are responsible for educating and raising my son."

We often hear feminists complain that women are squeezed into narrow, constricting definitions of femininity. But we hear much less about the way men have been constrained by stunted definitions of masculinity. My students and other young adults frequently find this chapter the most personally relevant. "I'm urging all my friends to read your book," a brilliant young woman who graduated from MIT said enthusiastically. "I'm telling them it explains why Christian men are so lame!" Not exactly the way I would have phrased it, but it does capture the loss of traditional moral and spiritual standards for men.

TEST YOURSELF:

1. After the Industrial Revolution, how did accepted definitions of masculinity grow narrower, excusing men from many of their traditional responsibilities?

2. How did the Industrial Revolution change women's work?

3. What is the origin of the double standard? Does it still exist today? (333-338, 343, 344)

4. How can churches support families seeking to integrate work and home life? (344-346)

CONTINUING THE CONVERSATION:

What surprised you most about this chapter? Does it affect your plans on how to organize the family/work relationship in your own life?

PART 4

Chapter 13

Your life is a story. Do you believe that? Do you believe that the events of your life fit into an overarching story that invests them with eternal significance? The reason we are captivated as children by adventures and fairy tales is that they portray spiritual truths in picture language. A well-told story stirs a longing to be caught up in an exciting drama ourselves. We have a God-given hunger to live for a great and noble cause, and the reason is that our lives really *are* part of a larger story—one that God Himself is telling.

Yet we are often blind and deaf to this spiritual drama. Because we are immersed in a secular culture, which hammers out the relentless message that the material realm is all that exists, we find it extraordinarily difficult *not* to focus solely on the horizon of the visible realm—to function in our day-to-day lives as though events occur by a kind of mechanical necessity, a chain of natural causes and effects, instead of being shaped by God to fulfill a larger purpose.

I gained a fresh appreciation of the Christian story when someone handed me a copy of Hollywood's most popular guidebook for writing screenplays, *The Writer's Journey* by Christopher Vogler (Michael Wiese Productions, 1998). Every good story is a variation on the same basic narrative pattern, just as every symphony builds on a fundamental musical structure. And what is that universal pattern? I was stunned by the biblical overtones in Vogler's answer: It is a sequence of events that takes the hero through death to resurrection.

In the classic hero story, the protagonist is called out of ordinary life into a grand adventure. In *The Wizard of Oz,* Dorothy is literally lifted out of Kansas and dropped into the enchanted Land of Oz. In *The Hobbit,* Bilbo Baggins is jolted out of his tranquil life to fight the dragon Smaug. The hero is then taken through a series of trials and tests, until the story climaxes in a symbolic death—some immense crisis that requires the hero to die to the old self, sacrificing old patterns and ways of life, in order to be transformed into a new self. Broken but healed, the hero returns to home and family to offer them the benefits of his new-found wisdom.

Does this story line sound familiar? Besides being the underlying structure for virtually all adventure stories, it also has a profound spiritual resonance—for it is the shape of Christ's life. The epic saga begins when Christ laid aside His divine prerogatives, His heavenly glory, and emptied himself (Philippians 2) to enter human history. "He left his father's home above," says a hymn, and "emptied Himself of all but love."

During His life on earth, Jesus endured tempting and trials from Satan, mockery and misunderstanding from those around him. He "learned obedience through what He suffered" (Hebrews 5:8), living the life we should have lived. And then, in the momentous climax of human history, He died the death we should have died, suffering the darkest loss and tragedy the cosmos has ever known. "My God, my God, why have you forsaken me?"

Yet death could not hold down the Author of life. In a burst of radiant energy, Jesus broke open the grave, shattering the power of death. Through His sacrifice He is now the faithful High Priest interceding for His people. It is a breathtaking story if we can strip away the mental dullness from constant retelling in Sunday School classes, in order to hear it with fresh ears.

And yet, it is more than a story of what Jesus did *for* us. It is also what Jesus promises to do *in* us. Our own lives are likewise meant to unfold as a saga of death and resurrection. Sanctification is a process of dying to our old personality patterns, our ingrained coping mechanisms, our worldly definitions of success, our driven attempts to prove ourselves. The process often climaxes in a life-shattering crisis of loss, remorse, or injustice that jolts us out of our predictable patterns and casts us spiritually into the valley of the shadow of death. Only when we share in Christ's suffering is there a promise of sharing in His resurrection power.

TEST YOURSELF:

1. What are some of the most common idols that prevent you from applying a Christian worldview?

2. Are you tempted by fear of being ridiculed by your peers, of losing professional opportunities, of missing out on career advancement if you were to openly apply a biblical perspective to your field?

3. Are there personal ambitions for image and influence, for success and acclaim, to which you need to "die" in order to be truly free to follow Christ?

CONTINUING THE CONVERSATION:

A Christian worldview is not merely about ideas and arguments. It really begins with dying to the idols in our hearts that keep us from being led by God in everything we do—including our intellectual work. Ask God to conduct a searching examination of your own hidden motivations, to reveal the idols in your heart and then set you free to serve Him alone.

ABOUT THE AUTHOR

NANCY RANDOLPH PEARCEY is Scholar for Worldview Studies at Philadelphia Biblical University and editor at large of the Pearcey Report (www.pearceyreport.com). In 2005 *Total Truth* received the Award of Merit in Christianity Today's book awards, and the ECPA Gold Medallion Award for best book of the year in the Christianity & Society category.

A former agnostic, Pearcey studied violin in Heidelberg, Germany, in the early 1970s and then traveled to Switzerland to study Christian worldview under Francis Schaeffer at L'Abri Fellowship. After graduating from Iowa State University with a Distributed Studies degree (philosophy, German, music), she earned a master's degree in Biblical Studies from Covenant Theological Seminary in St. Louis, then pursued further graduate work in the history of philosophy at the Institute for Christian Studies in Toronto (with emphases on ancient and Reformational philosophy).

Formerly the Francis A. Schaeffer Scholar at the World Journalism Institute, Pearcey is currently a senior fellow at the Discovery Institute, where the focus of her work is on the cultural and philosophical implications of the evolution controversy. A frequent public lecturer, Pearcey has spoken to actors and screenwriters in Hollywood; students and faculty at universities such as Dartmouth, Stanford, USC, and Princeton; scientists at national labs such as Sandia and Los Alamos; staffers at Congress and the White House; and various activist and church groups around the country, including the Heritage Foundation in Washington, D.C. She has appeared on NPR, and a lecture based on *Total Truth* was broadcast by C-SPAN.

Pearcey began writing in 1977 for the nationally distributed *Bible-Science Newsletter,* where for thirteen years she wrote pioneering in-depth monthly articles on issues related to science and Christian worldview. In 1991 she became the founding editor of "BreakPoint," a national daily radio commentary program, and continued as the program's executive editor for nearly nine years, heading up a team of writers. Under her leadership, the program grew into an influential organ for teaching a Christian worldview perspective on current events, with an estimated weekly audience of 5 million. She was also policy director and senior fellow of the Wilberforce Forum, and for five years coauthored a monthly column in *Christianity Today.*

Pearcey has served as a visiting scholar at Biola University's Torrey Honors Institute, managing editor of the science journal *Origins and Design,* an editorial board member for Salem Communications Network, and a commentator on Public Square Radio. Her articles have appeared in numerous journals and magazines, including the *Washington Times, Human Events, First Things, Books and Culture, World, Pro Rege, Human Life Review, American Enterprise, The World and I, Homeschool Enrichment, Christianity Today,* and the *Regent University Law Review.*

Pearcey has authored or contributed to several works, including *The Soul of Science,* which treats the history of science and Christianity, and the bestselling, award-winning *How Now Shall We Live?* She was invited to contribute the Foreword in *The Right Questions,* as well as chapters in *Mere Creation, Of Pandas and People, Pro-Life Feminism, Genetic Ethics, Signs of Intelligence, Reading God's World, Uncommon Dissent,* and a Phillip Johnson Festschrift titled *Darwin's Nemesis.*

Pearcey resides in Northern Virginia, where she and her husband are homeschooling the second of their two sons. She can be contacted at npearcey@pobox.com.